I0825398

GHOST WALK

KAY SOLO

Ghost Walk
Kay Solo

ISBN-13: 9781549938221

Cover Art by CL Smith.

Character Art (Print Only) by Pinxiedust.

PART I

1

THE GHOST HUNTERS

A SINGLE BRIGHT red apple floated down the busy streets of Sark. It ducked and wove through crowds of cloaked people who were picking up fruits and baked goods from the many boxes and carts lining what made up Sark's market district. Vendors sold pies, loaves of bread, fruits, and vegetables to anyone who had the money—or whoever could provide something worth their while. Not many people noticed the apple as it glided along, and those who did simply attributed it to a few too many drinks the night before.

The apple changed direction a few times before it seemed to focus on a young woman with dark brown skin leaning against a wall in one of the nearby alleys, almost completely hidden from view. She was seventeen, but her face bore a hint of maturity and experience that was supposed to come in years not yet passed. Long black hair fell to her waist while bangs partially covered her dark brown eyes. She was shorter than most girls her age, standing barely above five feet tall, but she was slender and clearly fit, a result of many years on the move. Speed and agility were a must; she didn't have the build to risk getting into fights, and it was always better to escape any pursuers than to get injured doing something stupid.

The apple hesitated next to her, then dropped itself in her pocket. Rather than looking surprised, the young woman nodded, then stood up and walked out from the alley into the street.

"Thanks," she murmured.

The mood in the street seemed to change almost instantly at her arrival. The community in Sark might have looked friendly enough to those unfamiliar with it, but most people here gave the young woman a wide berth.

Whispers of "thief" and "magician" reached her ears, and she ignored them with a blank expression. This was something she had gotten used to over the years ever since her stroke of luck—if she could call it that.

"You stay away from my shop, you hear?" one of the vendors said from the safety of her cart. "Got enough trouble feeding my family without you taking all my goods."

"If you're looking for a fool, you won't find one here, Ghost!" another called out to her. "My eyes are too sharp for your tricks."

Maaya Sahni smiled lightly with just a trace of bitterness, but otherwise ignored them all. *Ghost.* That was her nickname. The people of Sark said that she had the ability to steal something from you even as she stood right in front of you, that she could rob just about any place without ever being seen or even entering. She could see how they had come up with such a nickname, but it also amused her at least a little. They had no idea how close they were to being right.

She left the street and started down a narrow alley before making a hard left, then a right, and then another left. Then she took three more turns and looped back on the path she had already taken. It wasn't common for people to actually follow her—most of them knew rumor and suspicion weren't enough to stalk someone—but it had happened before. Because of that, it was important to either confuse or exhaust anyone trying to pursue her, especially when she made her way home.

Finally, fifteen minutes later, she turned down a dark and narrow street and stepped silently into a nearby building, a tiny two-story cottage that looked long abandoned. However, when she opened the door, she was greeted by the cheers of many voices, and three children jumped down the stairs to meet her. One was a girl just a year younger than Maaya, and the other two were boys just barely into their teen years.

"Food's 'ere!" The older boy cried, and the three of them crowded around Maaya with expectant expressions.

"Slow down or you'll crush the pastries," Maaya said easily, taking out a variety of goods from her pockets and distributing them evenly.

"You're the best, Maaya. My stomach has been growling all morning," the girl exclaimed.

"Hey now, you know I don't do most of the work; I just do the delivery," Maaya laughed. "Give some credit where it's due."

After the food was handed out, she took the apple from her pocket and tossed it casually into the air—but it never came down.

To most people it would appear as though the apple had once again taken on a mind of its own. But to everyone in this home, the source of the illusion was no secret.

A third girl stood with her hand in the air, grasping the apple firmly and fixating her sharp blue eyes on Maaya. She looked very different from everyone else in the town, dressed in flowing robes that fell past her light wood sandals, and her long white hair adorned with a number of colorful ribbons. A scarf of the same material was draped around her shoulders and around one arm, and a silver circlet with a single bright red crystal sat clasped around her forehead. However, the most interesting of her physical qualities was the fact that she was floating a few inches off the floor.

"What's that look for?" Maaya asked.

"You really ought to consider letting one of the kids do this soon. If just earlier is anything to go by, you've got too many eyes on you to do this safely for a while," she said agitatedly.

"I know. I hope not to make this a habit," Maaya replied with a small smile. "We'll figure something out like we always do. Now let me have my apple. I'm hungry."

Saber sighed and tossed the apple back to her, looking away.

"I also wasn't kidding when I said I was impatient. I guess I figured that in a group called the Ghost Hunters we'd be doing a bit more *hunting ghosts* and less nicking food from random shop owners."

"Well, we've got to keep up our strength if we want to hunt properly, don't we? If the ghosts we're hunting are anything like you, we've got our work cut out for us."

Maaya winked at her as she took a bite of her apple, then ducked away with a laugh as Saber threw a chair cushion in her direction.

Maaya was the leader of her small group—though this hadn't entirely been by choice—and so it had fallen to her to do her best to provide for them. Most of the people in town weren't rich, but they were certainly far better off than Maaya and her friends were. In between their theft and secrecy, they were also often between homes, keeping out of sight of law enforcement and victims with longstanding grudges. It wasn't an easy life, but they dealt with it as best they could.

However, this was not a group of ordinary children. Maaya had come to meet them because all four of them shared in a very unusual life experience: they all had connections to the supernatural world, letting them see things that most people swore never existed. In Sark, the ability to see things others couldn't usually led to abandonment—or death. Eager to save these children from an ill fate, one she had almost met herself, she had taken them with her, and they soon became inseparable. It soon came to be that they called themselves the Ghost Hunters, as much of what they did involved running around town looking for spirits of the long departed and sending them to the afterworld. The group was diverse in many ways, but even more humorously so by the presence of Saber: the group's resident ghost.

It had been four years since Maaya found her. During a dangerous solo raid on a recently abandoned mansion, she had found a silver circlet lying in a dark corner of the basement next to an old rusty sword. She wondered why such a pretty thing had been tossed so haphazardly away. She took both items with her, but while she placed the sword aside to sell for a pittance, she felt an odd desire to keep the circlet. At the time, she hadn't been able to explain why. Raiding a recently abandoned house was dangerous, if only because every other thief in the area had the same idea, and nothing was stolen to keep for looks. It was all to sell, and people were often willing to kill for whatever they could find.

When Maaya found a safe place to sleep that night and pulled out the circlet, she ran her fingers over it, impressed with its craftsmanship. When her finger brushed the crystal embedded in the circlet, the ghost had suddenly appeared as if from nowhere, wearing the circlet Maaya had just picked up—and she looked incredibly grateful.

"You can see me? You can hear me?" she had asked, moving her face right up close to Maaya's. At Maaya's shocked nod of affirmation, the ghost had let out a cry of glee and taken her into a powerful hug. "Finally! I felt like I would be lost in that in-between forever. It's been… oh, it must have been a hundred years at least!"

Ever since then the ghost had been her constant companion. She had little memory of who she used to be; her name, her history, her family, and anything else she might have been when she was alive was forever lost. Sometimes Maaya could tell it made her feel bitter, but there was nothing Maaya could do. While attempting to think of an appropriate name for such a strange girl, Maaya's eyes had fallen upon the sword, and so she gave her the nickname Saber. To her surprise, the name stuck. Saber was with her every moment of every day, helping her find places to sleep and taking food for her to eat. It was help Saber felt was more than warranted in exchange for the gift of companionship after a century of being completely and utterly alone.

Maaya looked fondly over at the girl who now sat peering out the window with a bored expression as she watched the people on the streets go by. The ghost caught her looking at her and raised an eyebrow.

"What?"

"Oh, nothing. Just remembering how we met, is all," she replied with a smile, and Saber rolled her eyes, but had to look away to hide her grin.

For Maaya and the others, daytime was best spent resting. Ghosts were easier to find and typically more active during the night, and the remnants of summer heat that persisted into fall exhausted them far more quickly during the day. There was some danger to letting their guard down while the people of Sark went about their business during the day, so while the rest of them slept, Saber kept an eye out. Being invisible was nice, but the fact that she never had to sleep was even more helpful.

Once the sun began to set, however, the children became restless. They dressed in their dark clothes and lightweight shoes to help them keep quiet and out of sight. Ghost hunting was partly looking for ghosts and partly keeping out of sight from the townsfolk. Running around in the dark was not easy to explain, and it was easier to simply avoid having to explain altogether. The people were paranoid enough without giving them any help.

Maaya watched them as they got ready. She was feeling particularly sentimental tonight, though she often did. After so many years spent alone and on the run, it was nice to have a place she could call home. It was also nice to have people around her she could call a family. She had never had one by blood to call her own; she certainly didn't count anyone at the orphanages among them.

Kim, the only other living girl, was the one Maaya was closest to apart from Saber. They were the closest in age and in interests, and she had also been the first person Maaya had found to take along with her. She stood a few inches taller than Maaya, with short wavy hair and amber eyes. She was typically soft-spoken, but around her friends there was another side to her—one full of energy and excitement. She was also a strategic thinker, and Maaya often relied on her for alternative perspectives and brainstorming.

Kalil and Sovaan might well have been brothers for how close they were despite being so different. Kalil, older by roughly a year and a half, was bold to the point of foolishness on occasion, though he was driven by a desire to do good for others and to protect his own. Tall and strong, with piercing dark eyes, black hair, and an ever-determined countenance, he was the one who would throw himself into danger willingly if it meant he could keep his friends from being hurt. He was ambitious and headstrong, always desiring to better himself, and though it sometimes meant he would jump to action a little too quickly, there was no matching his heart.

Sovaan, on the other hand, was a smaller boy, and well aware of his limitations in that regard. The youngest of the group, he could be swift, but also tired easily. Like Kim, he was a strategic thinker, but while Kim had a gift for seeing a situation from all its angles, he had a fascinating memory, and knew just about every street, shop, and intersection in the entire town. When they needed an efficient route to get somewhere or a safe escape from danger, Sovaan was the one they consulted.

At the moment, they were all busy writing symbols on small slips of paper. These cards could later be used by whoever carried them as a kind of supernatural magic that Maaya still hadn't entirely figured out. Depending on the symbols, the cards served different purposes; some made the wearer stronger or faster, while others provided the temporary ability to control elements like fire and water. A different card still was able to heal wounds. There was a last class of card, one more unique and powerful than any of the others, and these the Ghost Hunters used to get rid of ghosts wherever they decided to cause trouble.

Saber was currently away, looking through the nearby streets to make sure they wouldn't encounter any surprises. On more than one occasion, Maaya and the others had been met with people driven to fury by fear of the rumors surrounding them. Unlike the town police, these people tended to try to dole out justice with fists and weapons instead of handcuffs and locked rooms.

As the sun vanished behind the distant hills, Saber nonchalantly floated through the door, surveying the room to see if everyone was ready before giving them all a cheerful wave.

"Looks like we should be clear. It's the middle of the week, so everyone is more concerned about getting sleep than anything else. We'll be fine until we hit the outer roads; I didn't check that far. Can we hurry up already?"

Maaya smiled. If there was one thing Saber loved, it was ghost hunting. It always put her in a good mood, which was always contagious. The others leapt to their feet, put out all the candles in the house, and then snuck quietly out into the night.

There was another reason Saber was so impatient. Tonight they had decided to go far beyond their usual hunting grounds. They typically moved around Sark, looking through old buildings and unoccupied homes, but now they were venturing into the abandoned and empty lands outside the town's borders. Long ago they had been farmlands, but the economic failure of the country had caused a drop in demand, which subsequently caused many farmers to move away to seek more reliable trades. With no other use for the land, it had fallen into ruin, and the areas outside town were almost never traversed anymore. Because of the lack of any people, spirits tended to be much more plentiful out there… and often much more dangerous.

They reached the borders of Sark without incident, hopping stealthily over the town wall and moving into the countryside. They spent the first leg of their journey walking down an old path lined with mostly dead trees that crossed overhead. In decades past they had been well-kept and trimmed, but they were now left to nature's whims, long ignored; as a result, the party had to constantly duck to avoid low-hanging branches and webs.

Saber would occasionally float ahead to check their route, but this was mostly a result of her boredom, not any concern for safety. Hardly anyone took this path anymore, and even fewer traveled on it at night. It was far more likely they would meet a ghost than another living human.

Despite this, Maaya was still startled when she heard a voice right next to her.

"You're not going out on adventures as often as you used to. I've been lonely out here."

Maaya jumped, then turned to see a girl her own age keeping pace beside her, nonchalantly moving along as though she had been traveling with them the whole time. Her long straight hair was a deep purple to match the silk pajamas that were a few sizes too large on her, and her skin was pale as the moon. A crow with one eye sat perched on her shoulder, gazing at them inquisitively. However, like Saber, the girl's most distinguishing trait was the fact that she wasn't actually touching the ground as she moved.

"Holy hell, Sylvia, you scared me," Maaya sighed as she resumed her walk.

"I know," the girl replied simply.

Sovaan ran over excitedly and held out his arm. As though this was an everyday routine, the crow hopped down from Sylvia's shoulder and landed on the boy's arm, hardly moving as he pet its head.

"I see your bird is still there," Maaya said quietly, eyeing the dark creature warily.

"As I expect he always will be, though he's become more restless lately. I don't know why. Perhaps he can sense something I cannot, but then, he can't exactly tell me. Still, I feel like he'll stay with me until I'm gone completely."

Maaya shivered uncomfortably. Sylvia herself was a strange one. She was a ghost, but at the same time, she wasn't. She seemed to be caught between worlds, existing and not existing at the same time. They had first met when Maaya and her group tried to banish her, an attempt which had been completely unsuccessful. Upon discovering her strange predicament, they had then tried to figure out how she had come to be. They soon theorized that she had a body alive in the real world somewhere, perhaps very sick or comatose, but as the girl had no memory or recollection of such a thing, they were quickly forced to give up. Sovaan had hypothesized that if Sylvia was alive in the real world somewhere, she would cease to exist even as a ghost once she took her last breath. This was not something they liked to think about, and so they never spoke of it again.

Sylvia often joined them when they walked down the path along with her crow. It rarely made a sound and it never left the girl's side. It had no name and no past. It was simply there.

"I take it you're looking for more spirits in the countryside," Sylvia guessed.

"Yeah. We're going to look in some of the old abandoned farmhouses and other things. I feel sorry for the ones out there."

"Someday you'll leave those poor spirits alone, perhaps," Sylvia replied, but smiled. "I know where you could look. I've been there. I've seen them. The walkers. You should find them."

"The what? Where?" Maaya asked, suddenly interested.

"I don't know what to call them. They were on the hill past the river, last I saw them. But they were strange. They didn't move as ghosts do. Ghosts are always there. But these came from nowhere, and then disappeared again. That shouldn't be possible... should it?" she asked, more to herself than anyone else.

There was a shout from up ahead, and Maaya turned to see Saber waving from far down the path.

"Ah, your friend is with you again," Sylvia said, hanging back. "I should go now."

"Did I hear we're going to cross the river? Does that mean what I think it means?" Kalil asked excitedly as the crow fluttered back to Sylvia's shoulder.

Sylvia smiled.

"I believe it does. You'll have to talk to Styx."

2

STYX

Not much was known about the world by those who lived in Sark. All most people knew were war and survival. The history that was commonly accepted told of a massive earthquake some millennia ago that drastically changed the face of the world, leaving two continents on opposite sides of the planet. The continents were named Krethus and Selenthia, and a powerful lord ruled over each one long ago, their kingdoms reaching from shore to shore. They were said to be equal in power and had been fighting for centuries. The world had changed in some ways since then, and if asked, most people couldn't even answer why the war was going on anymore. All that mattered was that the war was won.

The war, while not being particularly disastrous in terms of lives lost—at least, not during Maaya's lifetime—had caused a global economic stagnation. Maaya had heard rumors that the larger cities still engaged in trade and business, even managing to do well for themselves, but the outlying towns like Sark seemed almost forgotten. Smaller towns rarely traded with each other because they had few excess goods to trade, and so they became isolated, the roads between them falling into ruin. Technological advancement had slowed. The world today, at least for the impoverished, was almost exactly the same as it had been for decades. Maaya had heard stories that, in better times, people had traveled between cities for *fun*, and that there was much more wealth for everyone.

She wasn't sure she believed it. For her part, any money she got was spent almost immediately simply in order to survive—and she never had much of it at once. The currency of the world was the *rial*, and supposedly came in five different denominations, all coins of increasing size. Maaya had only ever seen two, though she was sure the pockets of Sark's wealthy were full of them all.

Maaya lived in Selenthia, and despite all the hardships she faced, she had come to like it. Or perhaps it was more accurate to say she had forced herself to become comfortable there as she slowly accepted she would never go anywhere else. She couldn't speak to the country outside Sark; the town of about ten thousand people was the only place she'd ever lived. She dreamed of someday moving elsewhere and starting a new life free of the necessity of theft and deceit, but she knew her troubles would follow her. Her reputation as a thief was one thing, but the constant presence of ghosts only she could see made life difficult in a society that was paranoid and superstitious.

Though she struggled with this ability to see the dead for many years, she had gradually come to accept it, and in the years that followed, the Ghost Hunters were born. New ghosts always appeared in the world from time to time, but not quite as fast as Maaya and her friends got rid of them. As ghosts often had a real impact on the world—often a negative one—she believed she was doing the world and its living people a service.

Gradually, the Ghost Hunters began pursuing only troublesome spirits; they'd learned that forming relationships with friendly ghosts was not only strategically advantageous, but plenty of fun. Perhaps if she tried hard enough, Maaya thought, people would gradually stop acting so suspicious and frightened. People were still occasionally put to death for practicing "magic," which left Maaya disgusted and often afraid. What she knew of her countrymen was that they were slow to learn, easy to fool, and stupid in numbers.

Saber floated lazily back down the path toward them and took her usual place at Maaya's side, though Maaya noticed that the ghost was very determinedly not looking at her. The differences in her moods were as easy to discern as the difference between night and day, and she was also incredibly impatient. All Maaya had to do was wait.

"I suppose that answers my question as to whether she's still around or not. Figures that of all the ghosts we can't banish, she's the one," Saber said dully.

"She always joins us when we leave the town, you know that."

"But you don't have to talk to her. She's not even a real ghost!"

"I think that makes her more interesting."

"Interesting?" Saber asked hotly. "It does not! I can do so many more things than her. All she has is that stupid bird. And she talks funny. You're just encouraging this behavior. I'm just saying she could stand to go *anywhere else* from time to time."

Maaya laughed. This conversation had happened many times before. Saber had her reasons for disliking Sylvia, and Maaya was just grateful that Saber waited until Sylvia was out of earshot to vocalize her irritation.

This time, however, Maaya was preoccupied by Sylvia's words. *The walkers* she had called them. Maaya admittedly didn't know too much about ghosts, but she did know that they had to come from somewhere. Each and every ghost had been alive as a person at some point, and with the apparent exception of Sylvia, all ghosts were most certainly completely dead. And while they were invisible to everyone who could not see them, they certainly could not appear and disappear at will. She had to see for himself. Sylvia had always been strange, but never dishonest, or even one to exaggerate.

It didn't take long for them to approach the river, and as they walked out of the line of trees and closer to the shore they felt the familiar chilly breeze reach out to them from over the still water. The "river" was more like a large lake, moving so slowly that most would assume it simply didn't at all. The water was almost always close to freezing, and most people avoided it carefully due to superstition, believing that ghosts of old prisoners and victims of assassinations resided beneath the surface. Maaya thought this highly amusing, given that this would be the one time their superstitions were correct.

An old wooden dock, decayed and broken with age, rose halfway out of the water, splinters and rusted steel saluting its only visitors. Loosely tied to the dock was an old wooden boat with an ancient gas-powered motor on the back. It had no benches inside and it seemed as though the slightest touch would sink it, but it was a surprisingly steady craft. That would be their ride.

Sitting at the edge of what was left of the dock that still remained above water was a large and lopsided shape that appeared to be nothing more than a load of long-forgotten cargo covered in tarp. But as they approached, it moved.

It shifted slowly, then rose. It continued rising until it stood at least twice as tall as Maaya, dwarfing the entire company in height and sheer mass. There was a groaning creaking metallic sound, and then the massive shape turned.

"Maaya! And you brought Saber and the kids, too! It's about time you came back to visit. I haven't seen you in… ah… damn, my internal chronometer is broken again. But it must have been months. Come here you lot."

The young ones immediately ran forward and gave him a hug, or at least their best attempt. The figure standing before them was so massive that they struggled to wrap their arms around more than a small portion of his coat.

Styx was a large being indeed, by now more machine than he was man. He stood roughly ten feet tall with the help of his mechanical augments, and was as wide as all the others put together and then some. Most of his body was covered by a large coat that was obviously custom made, but one could see a mostly human arm up one sleeve, and a mechanical pincer-like claw up the other. His head was covered in shaggy black hair, and one mechanical red eye glinted from behind it. A broad smile contrasted his intimidating figure, and he took extra care when returning their hugs so as not to crush the children.

Saber had a smile on her face too. It was no secret that she loved Styx, but few who knew him didn't. Anyone who got to meet him quickly came to find that he was a cheerful man, as peaceful as they came. However, his company was rare; he lived alone on the dock where few living creatures ever traveled, and those who heard stories of his existence tended to give the area a wide berth if they passed through. Rumors said he was an immortal being of great strength, one who did not need to eat or sleep, and that he attacked any traveler who dared pass through his domain.

To be fair to the ignorant believers of said rumors, two of the three points were correct. Since his body was mostly machine by now, he did not need any form of sustenance, though over the years he started to lose functionality if he didn't perform any maintenance. He also still very much enjoyed eating, and Maaya and the others obliged him whenever they could afford to. His mechanical augments were also the reason for his incredible strength; Maaya had seen him lift the boat they occasionally traveled in as if it were nothing.

Maaya wasn't entirely sure where the rumor about the attacks came from, though she suspected it had originated back when Styx had attempted to seek out travelers for a friendly chat. His motives were purely friendly, but as it happened, seeing a ten-foot tall figure with the build of a bear charging at you through the trees was not the best way to start a conversation, and Styx had since resigned himself to sitting at the end of the dock, shutting down his internal systems to remain in a constant state of near hibernation when he was without company. For the first few months after she had met him, Maaya had begged him to live in Sark where conditions were more favorable, but he had eventually convinced her that the people of Sark were not open-minded enough to let him live in peace. She had to admit he had a point.

Saber flew over to him, using her ability to fly as an advantage to tightly hug his upper arm.

"It hasn't been *that* long. It's been a few weeks at most! It just seems that way because you've missed us so much. We've been planning on stopping by and bringing some food, but the living ones have hardly had enough for themselves lately. And yes, I've missed you too."

"Are we here for a visit or a ride?" Styx asked, looking hopefully at his trusty ancient boat.

"Both, actually," Maaya answered, and as she thought about Sylvia's words, she began to feel slightly anxious. "We'd like to head across the river to the old hill. I heard there were some strange types of ghosts there."

"Ah, you've been talking to Sylvia, then," Styx replied with a nod. He rubbed his chin thoughtfully, looking out across the silent misty river at the silhouette of a small hill in the distance. "Normally I'd say that stupid bird of hers was getting to her head, but she's right on this one. I've definitely noticed these ones around, and they're different from anything I've ever seen. But before we chat too much, let's get going! I'm impatient for another trip."

Styx stepped into the boat, which looked as though it might snap in half under his weight, but it stubbornly held together. He held out his arm to help the others in, watching with amusement as Saber flitted back and forth in excitement. She easily became frustrated while waiting for the others to keep up.

After everyone had taken a seat, Styx sent the boat off from the broken dock with a powerful thrust of the oars. He had fashioned his own oars from fallen trees, finally getting tired of breaking those meant for smaller hands. The boat sped out across the river, its wake disturbing the surface of the otherwise eerily calm water.

"Why can't we use the engine?" Kalil asked. "It goes a lot faster."

"Makes too much noise," Styx replied, the boat rushing forward with another powerful stroke. "Not really safe to draw so much attention to yourself out here anymore. Especially at night."

They slowed down as they reached the middle of the river. The mist was thicker here, and the distant hill and dock had both vanished from sight. All they could see around them was the still water. Even Saber had returned, sitting next to Maaya and peering around as they went. On more than one occasion they had met some of the ghosts of those drowned in the river long ago, and while most were friendly, others got quite grumpy upon being disturbed. Maaya couldn't imagine living forever at the bottom of a freezing dark river, much less choosing to do so voluntarily. She shivered at the thought.

"So why'sit you want to go looking after these ghosts Sylvia told you about, eh?" Styx asked quietly as they continued on their way. "I know you've met all sorts, but these just give me a bad feeling. You know, one of 'em looked at me, I swear it did, and it was like it was staring right into my soul."

"We didn't mean to do that when we started out, but now she mentioned it, I figured we'd better take a look," Maya explained. "If these ghosts are weird enough to give other ghosts the creeps, I think we should try to find out what's going on."

"They give *her* the creeps; I'm not scared," Saber said indignantly from her side.

"You also haven't seen 'em yet," Styx grunted pointedly. "They was all the same, like people dressed in sheets, moving all quiet like in a big line. Nearly as tall as me, they were. They didn't look around at all, but if you ask me it seems they was looking for something, or they had a purpose there. Then they just disappeared, right quick as they had come."

"That is a little strange," Maaya said thoughtfully. Styx was able to see ghosts because of his ocular implant—the mechanical device that had replaced one of his eyes—but that shouldn't have made a difference; ghosts weren't supposed to disappear. If there was a new kind of ghost out here that could, the Ghost Hunters were definitely in for a challenge.

"All I'm sayin' is, be careful. You know some dead folks just don't like being disturbed, and with how many of them there were… just be careful."

"We'll be fine!" Sovaan said, patting Styx' massive arm. "We're always careful."

"I know. I'd just hate for anything to happen to you kids, all of ye. Seems you're getting more and more adventurous. I don't mind—means I get to see you more often—but there are some really dangerous… oi!"

Styx started suddenly, causing the entire boat to tilt dangerously, but it stubbornly kept its balance. Maaya whirled around to see what had frightened the massive man so much only to see a slightly translucent green head poking up out of the water near the starboard oar. The face of a young man stared back at them, covered with unkempt hair. His most discerning feature was the large metal spike that penetrated his left eye, sinking deep into his skull. This particular ghost had also been a thief back in his day, but punishments had evidently been much harsher then.

"Evenin', ladies and gents!" the head said, and a ghostly hand soon followed to give a polite wave.

"Milo, for the love of… you can't keep sneaking up on me like that, I've got delicate instruments running what organs I got left in 'ere," Styx protested, smacking the oar at the floating head. The oar went right through him, and Milo only grinned.

"Fair's fair, I've been watching you sit on the dock for weeks not moving an inch, an' I've gotten quite bored down here. Anyway, couldn't help but hear you're thinking about heading to the hill. By the old mill and barn, right?"

Maaya nodded, and Milo shook his head.

"I wouldn't recommend it, kid. You're a bright one, and as much as we'd have a jolly good time in the afterlife together, I want you to have a *living* life first."

"We don't plan on dying out there, Milo, they're just ghosts. The most they can do to us is be a nuisance."

"These aren't normal ghosts!" Milo said. "These ones, they kill people. I saw it with my own… uh, eye."

"What did you see?" Maaya asked, suddenly much more curious.

"I was closer than the big guy here. They weren't just walking, they were killing. Didn't move a muscle 'cept floating over the ground, as we do, but every living thing in their path just vanished. Gone. Poof! Everything from the bugs to the dogs and cats. And then there were two vagrants there, camped out in the barn for safety. They vanished too."

"Did you see them actually die?" Maaya pressed, feeling a chill down her spine.

"Didn't have to. Only needed to see their ghosts as proof. Now, here's the spooky part. The ghosts of the two guys? They were only there a few moments, and then it was like some force just up and sucked them away into thin air. Took 'em both, kicking and screaming, then they and all the others vanished. I'm telling you, they aren't normals like us. By all accounts I know of ghosts—and let me tell you, I'm speaking from experience here—they shouldn't exist."

The boat went quiet. Nobody spoke. Styx had stopped rowing, and he looked extremely uncomfortable.

"But… ghosts can't disappear," Kim said quietly, and Milo shook his head again.

"These ones can. They appear out of nowhere without warning, take every living creature with 'em, then vanish like they weren't never there. So, if I were you I'd turn right around and get back home. They can probably get you there, too, but at least you'd be nice and warm at home when it happened, eh?"

Maaya turned to the others. Styx looked like he agreed completely with Milo's suggestion, but she wanted to hear what the others had to say. They had always gone through with these things together, and they had heard scary stories before.

"I think we should take a look. We haven't ever run from a challenge before," Sovaan said finally, and the others nodded.

"Well then, it sounds like we're in agreement," Maaya replied confidently, though she didn't feel as sure of herself as she sounded. If Milo's stories were true, they'd have to be extra careful. Ghosts always talked about each other with either affection or irritation—never fear. If these new ghosts had managed to scare the dead so badly, there must be a good reason for it.

Styx sighed, looking torn, then nodded.

"All right, fine. But make it quick. If you kids go more than fifteen minutes up there and I don't hear from you, I'm going to come find you, and it ain't gonna be pleasant."

"My hero," Saber said warmly, taking a seat comfortably on his shoulder.

From the side of the boat, Milo clicked his tongue.

"Do what you want. You know, if you die, the river down here ain't so bad. Like living inside your own aquarium, and—oh blast, Alfred's awake. I'll stall him if you hurry outta here."

Milo's head vanished instantly beneath the water and out of sight.

"Yes, let's hurry, I don't want to calm Alfred down again," Maaya said, and Styx needed no convincing. With another powerful push the boat shot forward again, moving again in the direction of the dark, quiet hill beyond the mist.

3

INVESTIGATIONS

Styx took them to the edge of the slow-moving river and pulled the boat quietly onto the shore. Maaya and the others stepped out carefully, looking around nervously as they did so. Maaya felt distinctly uneasy. No matter where they went she could usually feel… something. Anything. But here the land was as lifeless as it was cold and empty, and she felt nothing. Dry brush swayed slightly in the breeze that pierced their clothes, but apart from the light rustling of long-dead plants, it was utterly still and quiet.

"I'll stay here with the boat; I'm not any use against ghosts, even if I can see 'em," Styx said in a low voice. "All the same, if you run into any trouble, give a holler."

Maaya nodded, then led the way slowly up the hill up to where two ancient buildings sat in ruin. The typically calm weather had helped preserve them through the years, but the wood of the mill and barn abandoned nearly a hundred years ago could only last so long. The mill was almost entirely inaccessible; the roof had caved in just a few years ago, taking most of the walls with it. The barn, however, was still mostly intact. There were a few holes in the roof, and the interior was completely empty, but it served often as a home for the poor and for travelers, providing shelter from the wind and from prying eyes, even if most of those eyes belonged to the dead.

As they approached, the four living friends each pulled a card out from their pockets, looking around cautiously. These cards were red, painted with their own blood—the only cards capable of banishing a ghost from the realm of the living.

But there was nothing. The total desolation pervaded Maaya's heart, and it made her anxious. She wasn't used to this. There was *always* something, some animal or insect, but here it was as though the earth had been wiped clean, as though she stood helplessly within the history of the world, staring at the framework of what used to be before the last breath on earth was taken and then lost in the wind.

She shook her head resolutely, trying to look at the positive side of things. If she couldn't sense anything nearby, that must mean there *wasn't* anything nearby, which meant they weren't in danger.

The others seemed to feel it, too. Even Saber hovered closer to the group than usual, staying by Maaya's side rather than flitting excitedly about as she usually did. Maaya thought she knew what troubled her. She was used to being immune from danger as a ghost; the few people or creatures that could even see her at all couldn't do anything to harm her. But if Milo's story had told them anything, even ghosts weren't safe from… whatever these were.

"All right, everyone. Let's split up in two," Maaya instructed the group quietly. "Keep your eyes and ears open. If you run into any trouble, run away, don't engage. Meet up with the rest of us. We'll stand a better chance if we work together."

Kim, Kalil, and Sovaan headed off toward the mill, leaving Maaya and Saber to explore the barn. Maaya shivered. She was hoping it wouldn't be her task to look inside the old building, but as the oldest of the group, she usually ended up doing the scariest jobs whether she wanted to or not.

Saber floated nervously behind her, but upon seeing that the barn was very much empty, she started to explore on her own. What they were looking for, they weren't entirely sure. Maaya hoped to find some evidence of what happened here, though if what Milo said was true, they wouldn't find much.

She ran his story over and over again in her mind. Everything he described went against everything she knew about ghosts. Not only could ghosts not vanish at will, every ghost took on the appearance of the person they had been in life, so Milo's description of a group of identical faceless ghosts made no sense to her either.

Maaya was beginning to entertain the thought that Milo was playing a trick on them—it wouldn't have been the first time—when Saber called to her from the other side of the barn.

"Maaya, come look! I think I found where the men were sleeping. And it… it…"

Maaya rushed over, stopping at Saber's side next to a pile of blankets, clothes, bags, old food containers, and magazines. In one of the boxes rested a half-eaten sandwich, sitting politely at the bottom as though expecting its consumer to pick it back up any moment.

But Maaya wasn't looking too hard at the pile of belongings. Instead, she stared at Saber, who had a frightened expression on her face.

"What is it?" Maaya asked concernedly.

"This is where they disappeared, right?" Saber asked softly.

"That's what Milo said."

"And what do you see here?"

Maaya took a closer look, but she didn't see anything out of the ordinary, apart from the fact that it looked like this little camp had been abandoned in an instant, as though whoever had been staying here had suddenly needed to escape.

"I'm not sure what—"

"Their bodies, Maaya!" Saber almost cried. "When someone dies, even if they become a ghost, their body is still there. But these two, their bodies aren't here anymore. That can't happen! That *shouldn't* happen… right?"

Maaya stared. She hadn't thought about that. As the thought passed through her mind, she suppressed a shudder of fear.

"Wait," Maaya said. "There could be many reasons for that. They didn't just die, so someone else could have come and taken their bodies, or some animals could have—"

"And left no bones or any trace of them? And left all their supplies, including their food?" Saber interrupted.

She was visibly upset, and looked almost frightened. Maaya couldn't think of anything to say, because she was starting to understand the magnitude of the problem. If these strange ghosts did take away every trace of these humans—and everything else nearby—they were dealing with something they'd never even considered before. Ghosts didn't have much power over the living, which is why most people were hesitant to believe in their existence in the first place. They didn't have much power over each other, either; they were consciously tied to this world and had a very minimal presence, but that was about it. Saber, as a ghost herself, was typically fearless when dealing with other ghosts, and even some people—she simply couldn't be touched. But this was far different.

Maaya put a comforting hand on Saber's shoulder as she struggled for words.

"Let's not worry just yet. We haven't even seen them, and there's no solid proof of anything right now. Besides, this is what we do, and we're good at it. We'll figure this out, okay?"

It took a few moments, but Saber finally nodded. She still looked scared, but said nothing more on the subject.

"I guess we won't find anything else here. Let's go find the kids," Saber suggested, and Maaya agreed.

They left the barn and stepped carefully through the fields on their way to the mill. The others stood talking outside, evidently waiting for Maaya and Saber to finish up. Maaya guessed that the others had no luck whatsoever, and tonight this calmed her. Usually she came away disappointed from a search with no results, but at the moment she only felt a strong desire to get home to safety. Saber clearly felt the same, and she hovered slightly behind Maaya as though she were trying to use Maaya's body as a shield against whatever dangers they had yet to see.

As the five friends met up, they heard a call from the bottom of the hill.

"You kids all right up there?" boomed Styx' voice.

"We're coming!" Maaya called, then turned to the others. "Anything?"

"Nope," Kalil said. "If there was anything here, it was gone a long time before we started poking around."

The others nodded, and Maaya sighed with relief. The longer this went on, and the more Maaya heard about them, the more she feared she and her friends weren't ready to deal with this after all—especially if there were as many of them as Styx and Milo had claimed.

They headed back down the hill in silence, and Maaya tried to keep her expression neutral. She didn't want the others to see that she was worried just yet. As they walked, Saber glanced fervently around as though expecting something to leap out from behind them and snatch them all away, but the hill was silent and dead just as before.

Styx greeted them as they arrived at the bottom of the hill near the edge of the river, beckoning them toward the boat in a manner that suggested he was quite frustrated.

"It's not you, you're fine," he said, heading off Maaya's question before she could ask. "Absolutely no peace on the river these days. Soon as Milo got around to saying you lot were back, the whole group pestered me to fetch ye so they could say hello. No respect for important business, those jokers. Then again, half of 'ems missing eyes, the other half missing hands, and the whole lot is missing brains. Luckily, they're impatient, so when you didn't get down here this instant, most of 'em left. Anyhow, what did you see up there? You don't look too excited."

"Nothing," Maaya answered quickly, so much that Styx looked at her suspiciously. "We saw where the men had been camping out, but didn't see anything else. There's no trace of anything left, just like Milo said."

"All right," grunted Styx. "That's what I was hoping for anyway. Not that I don't appreciate your visits, but I'd rather we do something less dangerous. Aren't there enough ghosts for you to take care of in the town itself?"

"Not too much anymore, thanks to us," Saber said proudly as she followed the others into the boat. It appeared she had already gotten over her fear now they were heading home. "It's also harder for us to move around since we have a reputation, though. People have started watching out for the kids, so we need to be careful."

"Yeah… come to think of it, it might be safer for you out here. I'll say this about the living people, they're just about as obnoxious as the dead ones, and definitely more dangerous," Styx mused.

The giant man gave the boat a mighty push, then quickly hopped in as it glided over the waters. The boat rocked as he took his seat and then took the oars into his hands.

As the younger children talked, Maaya remained silent. By now the night had gotten much colder, and she shivered. Saber put her arms around her, and though it did nothing, Maaya appreciated the gesture.

"You know, it's probably nothing," Saber murmured, so quietly that only Maaya could hear. "We don't know if they were there to begin with, those two. They could have been out taking a walk and died somewhere we didn't see. It's not safe out there; who knows what happened to them?"

"What about their ghosts?" Maaya asked quietly.

"Not everyone becomes ghosts," Saber reminded her. "The more I think about it, the more I'm sure Milo was just trying to play tricks on us."

"But Styx…" Maaya started, but broke off as Saber put a finger to Maaya's lips.

"I'm sure he saw what he saw, but that doesn't mean it's connected to anything else. You were right: we shouldn't worry, so don't you start. You're talking to a ghost; you're the last person who should let your imagination run away with you."

Saber's tone was reassuring and confident, even though Maaya knew the ghost was trying to convince herself, too. Despite that, Maaya started to feel a little better. Besides, even if there was some type of ghost they had never encountered before, the odds of them being in any danger in the town was very small. For all they knew, these types of ghosts were common out here and no one knew about them because no living human ever dared venture beyond the gates in this direction anymore.

And then, Maaya made a mistake. She turned in her seat to look back at the old hill as it shrunk in the distance, and she saw something she hadn't seen before. A faint light could be seen at the top of the hill, and for a split second she felt a glimmer of hope in her heart. Someone was up there with a lantern—could the men have returned? Had they just been away, or perhaps fled when they saw other humans coming?

But then the light began to grow stronger as it moved down the hill toward the side of the river, and she felt her heart drop. The light didn't bob and weave as though carried by someone fighting their way through the dead weeds. It floated smoothly, and as it came, it grew larger. Maaya felt a chill as though she had fallen into the nearly-frozen river; there before them was one of the ghosts Styx had described: tall and silent, with nothing to distinguish its face except for two gaping empty sockets that might once have been eyes.

It was nearly seven feet tall with no visible limbs. It might have even looked comical, like a sheet draped over a tall man as a costume on a budget, but there was something different about this one. Its very existence seemed to exude an aura of dread and hopelessness. Maaya found that she couldn't look away, as though its empty eyes were trying to pull her in, and she felt almost powerless to resist.

No one else in the boat said anything, and Maaya soon realized that this was because the others hadn't seen it yet. Styx, though facing the hill, was preoccupied in a conversation with Sovaan and Kim, who delighted in catching him up with everything they had done between now and the last time they had seen him.

Maaya looked back, and a fear she had never felt before pushed its way from her heart into her throat. To her horror, she realized the ghost was moving straight for them – and it was catching up quickly. There was no doubt in her mind what it was after, and her terror grew as she tried to speak but couldn't utter a sound.

"Hey, what's up?" Saber asked from her side. "You look like you've just seen a gho–"

The rest of her joke never made it past her lips as she looked over to see what Maaya was staring at. At Saber's silence, the others looked up, and for a moment, all was quiet. And then Kim gasped.

"It's one of them!"

"Go, Styx, go!" Maaya cried finally, her voice cracking.

Styx' eyes were wide, but his reaction was instantaneous. He pulled at the oars with all his strength and the tiny boat shot forward; if not for Styx' weight in the front, it surely would have overturned at the sudden burst of speed. And yet, as the shore came speedily closer and closer, the ghost seemed to close the distance between them just as easily as before.

"Seals out!" Maaya continued, and her voice became stronger as she fell back into protocol. In a single swift motion, the four of them pulled their cards made with blood out from their clothes. Maaya stood up, facing the ghost, holding her card between two fingers. Saber, though clearly terrified, floated up next to her, ready and waiting to do her part.

The faceless ghost seemed completely unperturbed. It didn't even slow down as it reached the water's edge, and the very ripples in the river seemed to quell in its wake, as though even the life of the water was being snuffed out by its presence.

Maaya gulped. She had been hoping the ghost might break off once it realized everyone was staring at it. Still, she didn't take her eyes off the ghost as it approached. She refused to let her fear paralyze her; her friends were here, she refused to let anything happen to them. She knew how to deal with ghosts, and she had never met a ghost immune to the power of a blood card.

So long as she still stood, she would keep the other safe no matter what danger she faced.

However, it appeared that standing wasn't something Maaya would be able to do much longer. As the ghost drew still closer despite Styx' best efforts, she felt suddenly weak. Her blood card fluttered from her hand into the water and her legs buckled beneath her, and if not for Saber's quick reaction she would have fallen into the frigid river. Saber caught her deftly, then lay her down against the inside of the boat, floating protectively over her. The other three took her place at the front of the boat, and without a moment's hesitation, flung their cards out across the river at the ghost.

The cards shot out over the water as straight and fast as arrows, but what happened next, Maaya wasn't sure. She saw a bright flash of red sparks as the cards struck the ghost, but her vision was fading quickly. She heard someone cry out, but she didn't know who, nor why. She fought the oncoming darkness, desperate to get back up and defend herself, but before she had even finished the thought, she fell unconscious.

The next thing she remembered, she felt someone gently shaking her awake. She was disoriented and distinctly uncomfortable. Wherever she was lying, it wasn't her home. All the same, there was a great warm weight on her, and in her current state she might have liked to stay.

She opened her eyes to five pairs of worried eyes above her. As soon as they saw she was awake, relief broke over their faces and they smiled. Maaya recognized them as her friends, but was still unsure of where she was. When she attempted to sit up, however, Saber put a hand on her shoulder.

"Hey, not yet, stay still," Saber said. "Don't make yourself dizzy and then faint again."

"Where am I?" Maaya asked quietly.

"Jus' on the dock, you haven't gone far," Styx said warmly. "You've been out only five minutes, but you gave us a good scare."

"Is everyone all right?" Maaya asked. "What happened?"

"We all threw our cards, and the ghost disappeared," Kalil explained. "It felt different from sealing a normal ghost somehow, but it's gone anyway."

"Thank goodness," Maaya sighed, then struggled to sit up. This time, Saber didn't try to stop her. The weight of Styx' coat made it difficult, but Saber helped her to her feet where she remained unsteadily for a moment. Styx looked at her with concern, but she gave him a reassuring smile.

"I told you kids you don't want to mess with stuff like this," he grumbled. "What about you, Maaya? Never seen you react that way before; what happened?"

"I… I don't know," Maaya said, and it was true. Now that she had time to think about it, it surprised her as much as anyone else. "I was staring at it, and it felt like… it felt like it was sucking the life out of me or something. I couldn't look away. It was like it had a hold over me."

Saber looked troubled, but then patted her living friend on the shoulder.

"Well, that's easy, then! Don't look them in the eyes and we'll be just fine. We've had ghosts give us more trouble than that."

"Did you feel anything?" Maaya asked, and Saber hesitated.

"I felt something I never felt before, that's for sure. If I could never feel it again that would be great. But I guess being in the Ghost Hunters isn't always supposed to be a comfortable job."

"All right, you lot, you should get home," Styx interrupted. "The ghost is gone, but that was just one of 'em, and I don't want to chance they decide to come back again. Besides, Maaya could use some rest."

"I'm fine, we don't have to—" Maaya started, but Styx shook his head resolutely.

"You know this is dangerous business, Maaya. Messin' with ghosts and the like. Considering this has never happened to you before, you want to take it easy for a bit, make sure there's no lasting effects. If not for you, do it for them. You can't provide for your group if you're fallin' unconscious."

Maaya couldn't argue with that, and as she accepted his words, she accepted the weakness she still felt in her body. Every moment she was awake she felt better, but the experience had unnerved her. And it wasn't just her. She noticed that everyone seemed subdued, as though they had all been affected and didn't know how to react just yet.

She put on a comforting smile and nodded.

"Let's get back home. We'll feel more comfortable in a safe house by the fire with something to eat."

The others agreed instantly, and after many hugs and promises to visit Styx again soon, they departed back down the road, walking faster this time. As they approached the town walls, Maaya glanced around for Sylvia, hoping to talk to her about what she had just experienced, but the girl and her bird were nowhere in sight. Slightly disappointed, she hopped swiftly back over the town gates and moved silently into the back roads toward their house.

As they filed inside, Maaya took one last glance around the dark and empty streets, then closed and locked the door. Then, and only then, did she breathe easily.

4

BACK TO THE GRIND

Maaya awoke to the sounds and smells of a delicious breakfast. She opened her eyes slowly. The room was bright with sunlight and pleasantly warm, and she rested comfortably on her favorite old overstuffed couch. For a moment she was tempted to go back to sleep, so content was she in the warmth and safety of her house, but then she recalled what had happened the night before. Fear gripped her for a moment before she remembered that she was safe and back at home and that everything was okay.

This thought fresh in her mind, she stretched and yawned, then sat up and rubbed her eyes, suddenly more interested in the smell of food than anything else. She got unsteadily to her feet, then jumped in shock as she felt a pair of hands hold her at the shoulders.

"Sorry! Just wanted to make sure you wouldn't fall over and knock yourself out," came Saber's voice from behind her. "How do you feel? You slept like a rock, hardly moved all night."

"I feel fine," Maaya assured her. "Were you watching me sleep?"

"Someone had to make sure you were all right," Saber replied bluntly, and Maaya grinned. "Anyway, you should get something to eat. If you haven't noticed, we've got plenty."

"Yeah… what's all this?" Maaya asked in surprise as she looked over at the stovetop.

Rice, benne dose, matar paratha, and biscuits rested on plates by the stove as multiple meats sizzled in pans on every burner. Chopped vegetables, sauces, and seasonings sat nearby, as well as a dish piled high with pakora. The smell was so delicious she almost couldn't bear it, and she would have dived right in if not for two things: her concern over where this abundance of food had suddenly come from and the absence of the others.

"Ah, well..." Saber started, and she suddenly looked uncomfortable. "Rahu came by. He has another job for us."

"I see."

Hearing the man's name caused a sudden dip in her mood. She'd been afraid of that. Rahu was a local wealthy man, but unlike most other citizens, he was more understanding of the things most humans couldn't see even though he didn't have any gifts of his own. Despite his lack of any particular supernatural talent, he had found a way make good money under the guise of a holy man; whenever strange events happened around town that couldn't be explained by anyone else, the people called Rahu, who in turn contracted out the jobs to those most capable: in this case, as with every other, the Ghost Hunters.

In exchange for their work, Rahu provided them with food, but she had no love for him. He provided no other protection and he insisted on taking a generous portion of the profits from his misled customers—that being *all* the profits. The Ghost Hunters had never seen a cent of the impressive amount of coin he had earned from their work, and there was nothing they could do about it. Rahu hid his outsourcing, claiming to do all the work himself, and had in the past made it clear to Maaya what he would do if she were to protest any part of their situation. Perhaps even worse than this, if a job wasn't done exactly right, Rahu would simply withhold food, happily taking his pay while leaving Maaya and her friends with nothing. She was convinced he sometimes did this for no other reason than to prevent them from getting too comfortable or independent.

This particular fact irritated Maaya the most. They were dependent on him to survive so long as they lived in Sark, and they didn't have the resources to flee. He made sure of that. Rahu provided only as much as it took to keep the people necessary for his income alive and nothing more.

"Is he still here?" Maaya asked quietly, looking around as though expecting him to pop out from under the stairwell, but Saber shook her head.

"No, he left about half an hour ago. He took the kids with him, though."

"He what?!"

"Wait, don't panic just yet," Saber soothed her hastily. "He just wanted them to see the, uh... job site. So they could plan ahead, you know. They won't be gone long. He won't do anything to them, you know that."

"He'd better not," Maaya growled, though she knew Saber was right. The children were too young to understand the conflict between Maaya and Rahu, and they loved him. In turn, he treated them well. She held her tongue for that reason only, knowing that they'd be much worse off without his help. He'd told her never to speak ill of him to them, though she hadn't needed his guidance. She was uncomfortable by her friends' appreciation of him, but it was better than them knowing the reality of their situation. "Did he not let them eat before they left?"

"He did! He gave us so much this time that this is just what's left over—and even *that's* only what they made for breakfast. You should see what's in storage."

"If he's given us this much he must be asking a lot," Maaya sighed, then shook her head. "It doesn't matter. The supplies are here, so the job's as good as done. Where did they go? I'll see if I can catch up."

Saber hesitated.

"What?"

"Well… okay, now don't be mad. But Kim accidentally let slip what happened to you last night, and he said… well, he said he wants the kids to do the job on their own. He wants you to rest."

"He wants me to…?" She trailed off, anger already growing within her. "We have a big job and he wants them to go by themselves because I fainted once? I'm perfectly capable of doing this and he knows it! He just wants to get under my skin, and–"

"And it's *working*," Saber said emphatically. "Look, we don't even know what the job is yet, and there's no way for him to enforce this; you know he won't show up at the job site himself. Plus, as much as I hate him, he has a point, just like Styx did. This has never happened before, so you need to be careful, at least for a little."

Maaya looked like she wanted to retort, but after a few moments she sighed, and her shoulders dropped.

"I guess. I just hate that they're alone with him. I guess I knew this would start happening, but I didn't want to think about it."

"I know what you mean," Saber agreed darkly, then gently pulled Maaya over to the table. "Here, eat. I know you need it. Frankly, by the looks of these dishes, I wish I did too."

Maaya let herself smile, and she started to feel better. Rahu wasn't a new evil; she had been dealing with him for years. They only saw him every once in a while, and his visits were short, even if they were unpleasant for Maaya. But they had always adapted and always survived, and they would get through this, too.

"So, here's what you do when they get back," Saber explained as Maaya ate. "Thank him for his concern and say you will do your best to get back in good health as soon as possible. Act like he's doing you a favor by letting you stay home and rest. Express your full confidence in the rest of the team to get the job done and done well. Then, thank him *graciously* for what he has given us and explain you will make sure it is used responsibly so that you and the team are ready whenever he needs us. Just convince him his team is self-sustained and ready when he needs them; the less he has to worry about your health and safety, the better your job security."

Maaya raised her eyebrows.

"You *must* have been some sort of politician when you were alive," she said.

Saber glanced down at her flowing robes and colorful hair ribbons.

"I think by now I'm convinced I was part of a court. I've seen frilly outfits like these in portraits before. Anyway, I obviously died young, so I doubt anyone would know who I was even if they saw me. Not like anyone around here is any sort of historian anyway."

Saber's voice was calm, but Maaya sensed the familiar hint of bitterness that usually came about whenever they discussed Saber's past. Though she eventually resigned herself to the fact that they would likely never find out who she was, it still ate at her constantly.

"Well, you are quite a princess sometimes," Maaya continued, amused.

Saber narrowed her eyes.

"I'm choosing to take that as a compliment. Now finish your food, peasant."

Maaya laughed, nearly choking on the pakora she had just taken a bite of, and Saber laughed too.

Maaya was just finishing up her third plate of breakfast when Saber, who had gone outside to keep watch, floated quickly back through the door.

"They're coming down the block; they'll be here in a minute. Stay seated and look like you're trying to relax. Remember what I said: be nice and be *grateful.* I know it will hurt, but it's for everyone's benefit. Play along and you'll make sure the kids get to eat like this more often."

Maaya didn't have time to reply before the cottage door opened and the children filed happily inside, followed by the man whose mere presence instantly made Maaya's blood run hot.

He was tall and dressed in a fine black suit clearly made for a man of wealth and business. He held a cane that was more for appearance than assistance in one gloved hand, and his other hand fiddled with the gold chain of a pocket watch worth more than everything the Ghost Hunters had ever collected and stolen combined. A set of thin spectacles sat on his straight nose, and he pushed them up with his finger as he walked in and took off his long coat. Maaya felt a surge of irritation. Even his mannerisms were condescending.

"Ah, Maaya, good to see you're awake. I was quite concerned after I heard what happened to you last night," Rahu said with exaggerated warmth in his voice.

Maaya already wanted to hit him, but Saber cleared her throat from her side. Rahu couldn't see ghosts, which meant he also couldn't hear them; anyone who lacked one sense of them lacked them all, and Saber often used this to her advantage to offer counsel to Maaya whenever she needed to talk herself out of a tough situation.

"I appreciate your concern, and I'm feeling much better now. The rest and food has done me well," she replied pleasantly.

"Wonderful! As glad as I am to hear you feel better, I'd still like you to take the next day or two off. We've just landed a big job, and you need to make sure you're in top shape before you get back to business. Not to worry, though; I took the young ones to survey the job site and they believe they are well prepared."

When Maaya only nodded in understanding, Saber hissed into her ear, "You didn't know where they were."

"Oh! Is that where they were?" Maaya asked quickly, feigning relief. "I was so worried. I woke up and the house was empty."

"Yes, they were taken good care of," Rahu answered. "Did you like your breakfast?"

"Very much," Maaya said, thinking that this was the only honest answer she could give him. "Thank you so much for all of this; I'm so grateful for your help. I'm sure we all are."

The others nodded earnestly, having returned to their plates to eat still more food. Rahu smiled.

"Of course. Anything for my most talented team. Now remember: the poor woman wants this case resolved tonight, so be swift. There is no room for error."

"Who's the client?" Maaya asked.

"Some wealthy woman," Rahu said dismissively, but this didn't surprise Maaya. All of his clients were wealthy. That was how he made a living, after all. "Her husband and daughter died in an accident a year ago, and now her son is acting strangely. He talks when no one is there, and strange things keep happening around the house. Recently he got in trouble for fighting a schoolyard bully, and witnesses said the victim was beaten to a pulp without the boy even touching him. Needless to say, I knew immediately who to call."

Suddenly Maaya understood why the project was so important. Normally when the Ghost Hunters went after troublesome spirits, they were alone—but if Rahu's story was true, then this was a case where a ghost was working with another human, and this made them much more dangerous to deal with. Ghosts that did the bidding of humans were much more mischievous, if not outright malicious. On top of that, trying to deal with a living person at the same time presented a rare challenge, one that Maaya was not fond of.

"At any rate, I feel like this will be a good opportunity for the others to show what they're made of. I know you've been training them well. Besides, if they can't handle something like this without your aid, you might as well be working on your own, no?"

"You're going to be going with them anyway. Just say what you need to say to get him out of here," Saber muttered.

"I know," Maaya hissed.

"What?" Rahu asked.

"Sorry, I meant, I agree," Maaya answered, looking quickly back at him. "I'm sure they'll be able to do a great job. They were able to handle the ghost from last night by themselves, anyway."

"So I heard." Rahu took one last look around the room, his eyes stopping just above Maaya's shoulder where Saber currently floated, and for a moment Maaya was afraid he might suspect something, but then he turned to grab his coat. "I must be going. Make sure you rest up, Maaya. I don't want my star out of commission should something more dangerous come up."

"I'll make sure I'm ready," she assured him. Rahu smiled, then left, closing the door smoothly behind him.

Maaya sighed. This had been a shorter visit than usual, and it still left her feeling sick to her stomach. As time went on she felt her patience and her temper growing shorter, and she didn't know how long she would be able to keep up her act. She told herself she was doing it for her friends, but could she really say that anymore? They had been between several homes, constantly in danger, and regularly hungry, and there was no end in sight. On top of that, Rahu was now apparently asking the younger members to go off and do dangerous jobs by themselves. How could she say she was doing her best to keep them safe when she allowed things like that to happen?

What's more, she knew exactly why he was doing it. He wanted to remind her of his power over them. He didn't want any of their success to make them feel as though they were in any way capable of being independent. What was worse, he only seemed truly concerned about Maaya; whether the others lived or died was of no concern to him, Maaya knew that much. He could afford to risk their lives for his own profit, and Maaya, the one who had taken charge of training them and keeping them safe, was powerless to stop it. She would be forced to continue working with him if she wanted to live, even as he toyed with their safety.

It was a good thing Maaya had eaten her fill before Rahu came, she thought, because she had now lost her appetite. As the other three crowded around the table, eating happily and talking excitedly about the job to come, she walked upstairs and sat down on the floor in the hall outside one of the rooms where her friends slept. She leaned her back against the wall and put her face in her hands.

"Hey, what's wrong? You did a good job!" Saber said encouragingly. "I mean it, he was awfully pleasant all things considered, and..."

But then Maaya was crying. Saber looked taken aback, then concerned, but was momentarily at a loss for words.

"I can't keep doing this!" Maaya breathed so the others downstairs wouldn't hear.

"What are you talking about? It wasn't so bad! He got what he wanted and left, and we got all this—"

"That's not what I meant. I mean *this.*" Maaya gestured vaguely around her. "I mean all of this. I wanted to make a place where we were all safe and didn't have to steal food or live in danger anymore. I wanted them to be free of him, to not be forced to work for him like I've been. Now Rahu's sending them off to go do jobs by themselves. Even if I can sneak out with them this time, I don't know if I can't do that every time. I wanted a better life for us, and I... I can't keep subjecting everyone to this life. There has to be something better, but I feel so helpless."

Saber put her arms around Maaya's shoulders and hugged her tightly.

"Listen, you've done the best you could, and you *have* made things better. Where would the kids be today without you? You've managed to take care of three other people and taught them how to take care of themselves, too. Most of the people out there who look down on you can't even do that. Things are tough sometimes, but so what? You always come out on top. As for Rahu, well, he's temporary. He'll be out of the picture someday. It's a big world out there. When the time comes we'll be out of here without a trace."

"Where can we go?" Maaya asked hopelessly. "Even if we wanted to leave, we have no resources to do it with. I don't know where the next town is, if we could make it there, how they would treat us even if we made it… what if the problem isn't the place, but me?"

"You're underestimating yourself because he's made you think he's got power over you. You don't have your reputation because of him, you have it because of *you.* Remember who you are, Ghost." She nudged Maaya playfully in the shoulder. "We'll be out of here someday. I'll always be here, and so will your friends. We'll worry about that when the time comes."

Maaya sighed. She wanted to believe her, but the weight of the world felt so heavy today. Loving the world and loving life was for those at the top of the ladder, but for those at the bottom, those left staring at what used to be the way up with all its rungs broken, life wasn't beautiful at all. And for Maaya, there was no escape. She'd known people who had left before, and she'd never heard from them again. While she was here, she had responsibilities and people to take care of, and days like today reminded her what an incredible task that was.

"Maybe you're right," Maaya relented. They'd had this talk before, and there was little purpose to drawing it out again.

Saber smiled happily.

"Of course I am. Here, I'll get you something to drink, and then you should get some more rest. We've got a big job tonight! Then after that's over we can talk about our plans for the future in more detail, what do you think?"

Maaya nodded. Saber helped her to her feet, and then they headed back downstairs. Maaya wiped her face before they reached the bottom, but the others hadn't noticed anything. They were still excited about the job to come.

As Maaya watched them talk, she began to feel a little more optimistic. They were a little younger than her, but their training had definitely paid off. Combined, the three of them were a force to be reckoned with whether their opponent was living or dead, and she felt a surge of pride. For a split second she even considered the idea of letting them go off and do the job themselves, taking advantage of her time to rest. She didn't want to admit it, but she was still feeling a little weak and dizzy from the night before. But she shook the idea out of her head immediately. That day might come eventually, but it wasn't here yet.

"Hey, Maaya, did you hear?" Kalil called over to her. She walked over to the table and sat down, and they eagerly made room for her. "If we do this one well and impress Rahu, he says we'll eat like this for the rest of our lives."

"I didn't hear that part, but I'm not surprised he'd say something like that. He speaks well of you to me," Maaya said, and after a moment of hesitation, continued, "I'm still coming with you, you know."

All at once, three voices cried out in protest.

"But you're not well!" Kim exclaimed, and though Maaya knew this came from a place of concern, it only made her feel more irritable.

"Did Rahu tell you that?" Maaya asked sharply, and Kim nodded meekly. "Well, he's wrong. He wants you to go alone because he knows it will bother me, but I'm coming along anyway. We're just not going to tell him."

"Why would ol' Rahu do a thing like that?" Kalil asked.

"He and I have our disagreements, but that's nothing we need to talk about right now," Maaya sighed. "Plus… would it really bother you guys that much if I came with you?"

"It's not that!" Sovaan interjected. "We were just really excited to show him what we can do! You're *Ghost*, everyone knows you're smooth and can always get a job done, but we've never had a chance to prove that too. Impressing Rahu is a bit of it, but…"

"We were hoping to impress *you*," Kim finished. "We wanted to show you all our training paid off. If we can do this by ourselves, you might worry about us less, and you could stay here and get better without having to push yourself. You look so tired sometimes and we haven't been able to help."

Maaya was momentarily speechless. She hadn't expected this. Sure, she knew her friends had wanted to do their own jobs eventually, much as students eventually want to graduate, but she hadn't imagined that they thought anything like this.

She suddenly reached over and pulled Kim into a tight hug. Kim squirmed, but Maaya held on, laughing.

"I didn't know you were so concerned! Trying to impress me… you guys are so cute." Deciding Kim had suffered enough, she let the girl go, and Kim blushed furiously. "Look, I understand where you guys are coming from, and you'll have that chance, okay? But this job seems really dangerous, so I at least want to come with you one more time. Is that all right?"

The others nodded slowly, looking disappointed, but they didn't protest any longer. Saber floated nearer to the table and stared at each of them in turn.

"You made the right choice. It's been a while since I've gone on a proper hunt, and if you didn't allow us to come along tonight, I was going to be very… upset."

Maaya patted her on the shoulder as the others grinned.

"All right, everyone. Finish eating, prep your supplies, then get some rest. We want to make sure we're prepared for everything."

5

A COMPLICATION

THE FOUR LIVING friends dozed throughout the day. When Maaya was conscious she listened to the sounds of the streets outside, full of people selling their wares and making their way home from work. Carriages pulled by horses passed by, and as evening drew near, a small fight broke out a few blocks down outside one of the bars. Maaya hardly payed any attention. Most people avoided the back streets where the little building they called home was located.

The next thing she knew she was gently being shaken awake. The windows were dark, and their source of light now came from several oil lamps placed around the room. Maaya opened her eyes to see Kim looking down at her, and the girl smiled.

"We're going to be leaving in about half an hour. All your stuff is ready. Saber is out scouting now, but we think the route should be clear."

Maaya sat up, rubbing her eyes, and Kim walked over to join Sovaan who was again painting symbols onto cards. Maaya noticed that the designs on these were a little more intricate; these were more powerful cards, and Maaya was glad they had thought to bring them.

In terms of what these cards did, there was little variety. Maaya only knew of the two elemental cards, the two physical augment cards, healing cards, and blood cards. But there were varying levels of power to them. The stronger and more skilled a person was, the more powerful cards they could use.

While almost every card worked the same, however, the blood card was the exception as far as she knew. The other cards offered marvelous abilities to the people who knew how to use them, but only the blood card could truly affect a ghost. The catch was, as the name implied, that the sigil on the card had to be painted with the blood of a living human.

Maaya had learned all this from a book she had stolen years and years ago while she and Saber had been on their own. She had originally taken it because it was elaborately designed and ancient looking, and she guessed it would fetch a fair price, but while searching its pages to see how to advertise such a product she realized that the book contained information about ghosts. At the time, Maaya didn't know anyone else could see them, so she hung tightly onto the book for no other reason than it signified a connection to someone else in the world, probably long dead, who was just like her. At a time when she had never felt more alone, she needed that comfort.

As time went on she began to peruse the pages more seriously. It had been difficult, given her limited ability to read, but she had managed to glean the basics of how the cards worked. The entire system, from the creation of cards to the mysterious power behind it, was called *libris*, and it involved tapping into the power of the user and the second world they were connected to, channeling that energy into whatever the symbols on the card dictated. Maaya hadn't been a believer in magic at the time. Magic came from storybooks with wizards and dragons, which was an entirely different kind of magic than being able to see the dead. But even still, she had to admit there was something curious and alluring about it.

All the same, she'd initially felt as though it were a book of tricks, perhaps a compilation of lore for a cult that was a little too full of itself. And so one day she created a crude representation of a first-level fire card and moved her arms as the book directed to control the path of the flame. She laughed to herself as she did so, thinking that she looked utterly ridiculous, and that she couldn't believe the fake things that people came up with to feel special.

Maaya had lost her home in the ensuing fire, but she managed to escape mostly unscathed. From that time on she treated the book with great care, and for many weeks she refused to create another card… but any and all doubt she felt had gone up in flames with the building she had called home.

Now, years down the road, she had attempted to master and subsequently teach the art of *libris* with great care, and though her friends came from such poverty that they could not read a word, they learned it quickly and efficiently under her guidance.

It appeared that not just anyone could master *libris*, however; from what Maaya could understand, creating the cards was just one aspect. In the hands of someone who had no ties to the other world, they would simply be pieces of paper that symbolized a waste of time. This connection was necessary to make use of the cards. At the moment, Maaya was capable of using almost any second-level card, whereas her friends—with the exception of Kim—were limited to first-level cards. Anything higher in their hands was unusable, despite their best efforts.

The other interesting thing about *libris* cards was that, since they relied on a user's connection to the other world to use their power, ghosts could also use them. It was rare that ghosts managed to do so—few knew of the existence of *libris*, and even fewer what to do with it—but when they did, it usually resulted in a very dangerous situation. Ghosts were already troublesome enough since they could only truly be dealt with using blood cards, but on more than one occasion Maaya had run into a particularly angry ghost that flung fire at them or moved almost too fast to track.

As night drew on, the town outside fell still and silent. The lamps that lined the streets started to flicker and die as their supplies of oil were used up, and the last of the drunks found way home, whatever that meant for them. It must have been an early hour of the morning, Maaya deduced, as the oddest sorts of people were usually up until at least midnight.

She grew anxious as she waited for Saber to return and as she thought about her plan to join the others on their hunt. She knew there was no reason why Rahu should find out considering he never joined their hunts. He was probably asleep anyway. And yet…

What if he did find out? a voice nagged in the back of her head.

She jumped as a small stack of cards suddenly appeared before her. Sovaan stood in front of her, his arm outstretched.

"All done! Here's yours for the night. Hurry and get dressed, Saber will be mad if you aren't ready."

He trotted off, and Maaya realized she hadn't done anything to get ready at all. She stood up quickly, then headed upstairs to change, picking up her pile of supplies that the others had kindly prepared for her. First she put on a pair of black skin-tight leggings and a matching long-sleeved shirt; they served as protection against the cold without restricting her movement. Over this she put on a looser pair of pants that fell halfway below the knee. Then she put on a loose top with no left sleeve. She strapped a small rectangular pouch to her left arm above the elbow, then slipped the small stack of cards into it. Finally, she put on the shoes she used for hunting: lightweight and with plenty of grip.

She tied her long hair back as she walked back downstairs. Her heart was starting to pound heavily in her chest as it always did when the hunt was about to begin. She didn't know as much as she wanted to about their opponent, and that also made her a little nervous. Some ghosts went quietly, almost gratefully, but some were vicious, and injuries were common after a difficult job.

Saber still hadn't returned, so Maaya walked over to the others and sat down. Kalil was wrapping a bandage around Kim's finger, and Maaya guessed who had been responsible for their blood cards that night.

"We were just talking about what we're up against tonight," Sovaan explained. "We think this kid's sister is still around and beating up anyone who gives him trouble. Only problem is he kind of let the power get to his head and now no one wants to be around him because they think he makes bad things happen."

"How old is he?"

"Eleven, I think? They were twins, too. Apparently they were really close, so it's no wonder she's doing this for him."

"We don't know if that's the case for sure. It could be the dad or even a total stranger," Kim replied, wincing as Kalil taped the bandage tightly. "In the end, it doesn't matter who it is. They have to go. Then maybe that family can have some peace."

"You'd think he'd just tell his sister to stop after he got a reputation like that," Kalil mused.

"Not really. Think about it," Sovaan interjected. "You're eleven, you've been bullied all your life, then you lose half your family on top of that. Then suddenly you get a magic ticket to make it all go away. When all you've known is hurt, then you can make all that hurt go away, who cares what your reputation is?"

"It's not right!" Kim exclaimed. "His hurt isn't gone; he's just delaying it. We all know this can't last. How is he supposed to grow up like this?"

"Kim's right. Whatever's going on, it needs to stop, and that's what we're here for. Or, should I say, what Rahu is here for," Maaya said, unable to keep the bitterness from her voice. "We don't need to get into the moral issues of the discussion; we just need to do our job and get out."

"Don't you think we ever should, though?" Sovaan asked.

"Not really," Maaya said airily. At everyone's inquiring looks, she continued, "Well, if we start asking questions, we'll eventually have to ask ourselves why one of the best members of the Ghost Hunters is a *ghost*."

"Fair's fair," Kalil answered quickly. "We all know our policy."

"*Don't ask questions*," echoed four voices from around the table.

It was lighthearted enough, Maaya thought, but it came from a place of emotional necessity. Asking questions meant getting involved, and getting involved meant getting hurt. They couldn't afford to become attached, because in any issue where they dealt with the dead, there were no satisfying resolutions, no happy endings. There was only one answer to the problem of ghosts, and it was something none of them liked to think about.

"I have to break policy for a moment, though; where is Saber?" Maaya asked impatiently.

"She only went out a few minutes before you woke up, she's not late yet," Kim answered.

"She'd better not be having all the fun without us. You know how she misses her solo trips," Sovaan continued.

Maaya opened her mouth to reply, but before she could do so, Saber flew quickly in through the door, a mixture of irritation and worry on her face.

"What's up?" Maaya asked concernedly.

"We've got problems. You, get upstairs and change into normal clothes, quick," she directed at Maaya.

"What? Why?"

"Rahu's here. He's come to take the others. If he sees you like that—"

Before she could finish, there came a light knocking at the door. The others looked at each other, suddenly worried.

"Go!" Saber hissed at Maaya. "Act like you were asleep upstairs. I'll handle things down here."

Maaya hesitated for a moment, then ran quietly upstairs and sat on the bed in Kim's room, which happened to be closest to the stairway. Her heart thudded in her chest. What was Rahu doing here? He never came to see them before missions! The idea that he suspected her plan to go with them crossed her mind, and she felt a wave of relief rush over her at Saber's advanced warning. She thought to change as Saber had directed, but she was too nervous to move.

The door opened downstairs, and Kim answered it. She heard voices, though she couldn't make out what they were discussing. Whatever it was, it seemed Rahu wasn't in the mood to stick around, because within a minute, the door had closed again, and the house was silent.

Maaya peeked downstairs to verify that the house was empty, and upon seeing that everyone had indeed left, she ran to the window that faced the street. Making sure all the nearby lights were out, she looked through a small sliver in the curtains to look down the street. Sure enough, Rahu stood there talking to the three others while Saber hovered nearby. After a few moments, Rahu gestured to the street ahead, and they all walked away.

Maaya watched until they were out of sight, then sat on the couch, fighting the urge to cry. So it had happened after all. Rahu must have suspected something; there was no other reason he'd come to the poorest area of the town alone in the middle of the night. It wasn't like he could protect them. With no abilities of his own, he was practically useless in a fight. No, he had guessed somehow, and the fact that he had won in the end made her furious to tears. He had gotten what he wanted.

A few minutes later Saber flew back in, kneeling in front of Maaya.

"You okay?" she asked quietly. Maaya didn't have to say anything. "I know. That dirty snake. I don't know why tonight of all nights he decided to show up, but I have a feeling he guessed what you might try to do on their first mission with you."

"That's what I thought," Maaya said glumly, then sighed. "I know they'll be all right. They're going to be stronger than me someday, and they're close to it now. I just hate him so much. What if this ends up being really dangerous? What if—?"

"No, don't do that," Saber interrupted gently. "We don't do what ifs. Plus, I'll be looking after them. If anything happens, you'll be the first to know. But it won't, because I'll be there, and this will go nice and smooth. Instead of worrying, think about how Rahu will reward us for a job well done."

Maaya smiled. Every time she took a bite of food Rahu had paid for, she thought of it as her own form of personal revenge. Every bite she took was money out of Rahu's pocket, money that should have been theirs.

"Well, go on, then. Go make sure they're safe," Maaya said, and Saber's face lit up. "Yeah, I know you've been waiting for a fight. Don't worry about me. You can fill me in when you guys get back."

"Whatever you say, cap'n," Saber grinned, and after a playful salute, she was back out the door.

As Maaya watched her go, she started to relax. What she had said before had been true: she knew the others would do well. She would have liked to be there all the same, but after some thought she realized that most of her frustration was directed at Rahu for getting in the way again. He had a habit of doing that at crucial moments in their lives, always seeming to be there to remind them that they were under his control, reminding them that there was no escape.

After some thought, she realized that what bothered her was how he was putting his own success over the lives of her friends. That was something he had always done, of course, but he had never split them up before. She knew that he wanted her to feel better so she could get back to work, but she also knew that this was a power play on his part, reminding Maaya specifically that she and her friends couldn't even be together if he didn't want them to be.

As the hours passed, Maaya's confidence began to falter. She paced back and forth, looking impatiently through the window down the still-dark streets of Sark. They weren't taking any longer than usual, and Saber hadn't come back to report anything out of the ordinary, but she couldn't think of anything else. She almost laughed at herself, thinking that she seemed like a mother anxiously awaiting her children's return from their first day at school.

Despite how much rest she had gotten earlier, the hours started to take their toll on her. As the eastern sky started to lighten ever so much, she surrendered to her tiredness and lay on the couch, thinking that the sooner she fell asleep the sooner she would know the answer to how this night's mission had gone.

6

WHISPERS OF WAR

For the second time that week, Maaya awoke to the sounds of food sizzling in pans on the stovetop. The smells hit her a moment later, and she smiled, stretching comfortably on the couch. The room was pleasantly warm and quiet, and she soon became aware that her blanket had been draped over her during the night. If every morning could be like this, maybe it wouldn't be so bad to stay under Rahu's control, her sleepy mind thought. But then it snapped to attention.

Rahu.

She sat up quickly, looking around for any signs of her friends. She heard no voices, but as she glanced near the front door she saw that the others' coats were hung on the rack nearby and that the door itself was unlocked.

Before she could get up to investigate, Saber flitted down from upstairs. Apparently not noticing that Maaya was awake, she darted over to the stove, checking on each pan in turn and using a wooden spoon to stir and turn ingredients as necessary. She looked at a larger pot, then turned her head toward the door irritably.

"The water pump isn't *that* far away," she muttered to herself. "If they don't get back soon—"

"Morning, Saber," Maaya greeted her pleasantly. Saber jumped—or whatever the equivalent was for someone who wasn't affected by gravity—and whirled around to look at Maaya.

"You're up!" she said. "Did I wake you? I tried to keep things quiet; I wasn't sure when you'd gone to sleep last night."

"It's fine. I waited as long as I could, but I fell asleep before sunrise. And anyway, I'd be fine with less sleep if it meant waking up to this more often," Maaya yawned.

"Easy for you to say. You're a right grump when you're tired, and I'm always the one stuck taking care of you," Saber teased.

Maaya laughed, then looked out the window. The streets were bustling as usual, though she also noticed a few groups of people huddled here and there in small groups. This wasn't unusual—it often happened when there was some new subject of gossip—but it made her uneasy. Sometimes the subject of said gossip was the Ghost Hunters themselves, and that never resulted in anything good.

"Where are the others?" Maaya asked.

"Out getting water for breakfast. Or at least that's what they *should* be doing. They were so excited after last night's mission I don't doubt they've gotten distracted. If their breakfast gets burned it's not my fault."

"Do you want me to go look for them?" Maaya asked, amused. "I want to hear all about how it went last night, anyway."

"No need; sit down and rest, they'll probably be back soon," Saber answered, but Maaya scoffed.

"I'm not helpless, Saber," she protested, quickly getting dressed and tying her shoes. Within a minute, she was out the door.

She immediately turned down the side street nearest to their house. Water pumps could be found on many streets in the poorer districts of Sark, designed for those not wealthy enough to have running water in their own homes. It was an inconvenience, but luckily nothing more; the supply of water at each fountain was usually clean and consistent, and there had never been any shortage as far as Maaya could remember. Not with the amount of rain Sark saw on a regular basis.

As she walked down the street she noticed something was different, though it took her a few moments to figure out what it was. There were plenty of people around, talking and browsing goods as usual… but for once, they were completely ignoring her. A few looked at her as she passed, but then they turned away as though she were nothing more than a stranger. Usually people's stares and whispers followed her, and so this lack of attention—this feeling that she was just a normal person like anyone else—was initially more unnerving than it was comforting. She couldn't hear what any of them were saying, but she wasn't sure she cared. As long as something else was taking their attention away from her she didn't really care what it was.

However, as she continued on in search of her friends, she noticed that the nearby gossipers' expressions weren't those of mild interest, not the inquisitive looks of people hoping to figure out the latest dirty secret of a local politician or wealthy man. Instead, they looked worried, even scared, and they spoke in hushed tones as though afraid that speaking too loudly would make their fears, whatever they were, manifest right before their eyes.

Maaya slowed down and walked a little closer to a group of three women huddled nearby. As expected, they took no notice of her, and simply continued whispering urgently.

"...entire street of people gone. Belongings and everything still there, even their little clothes laid out like they was about to go to school that morning, but everything else..."

"Couldn't have been a chemical, you think? Like poison?"

"Poison would leave them dead sure enough, but then where did their bodies go? No, it's not right, it's something worse than..."

Maaya had walked too far to hear any more, and she wasn't yet brave enough to stand still and eavesdrop, but she had heard enough to make her uncomfortable. People disappearing was never good. The people who did had usually gotten on the wrong side of local criminals—or even worse, the state. The latter didn't happen often here, as Sark wasn't important enough to be on the central government's radar, but she had heard stories. Regardless, criminals and state organizations did have one thing in common: they made no effort to hide when they made someone disappear. There wouldn't be a point otherwise.

Her uneasiness quickly faded as she kept moving. If anything, being a petty thief like Maaya made her safer than most. She never incurred the wrath of organized crime—in fact, she was on decent terms with some of their members—and also wasn't important enough to attract the attention of more than the occasional beat officer who chased her only until he became winded, which was usually quickly. Simply put, Maaya wasn't worth the trouble.

When she got to the pump she looked through the line of people patiently waiting with buckets and tubs, but didn't see her friends. She sighed, looking up and down the intersecting streets. If they weren't here and weren't at home, there was little chance of finding them until they decided to make their way back.

She had just turned around to head back home when she nearly ran into a person who had been standing right behind her.

"Sorry! Oh, Roshan, it's you."

The boy she almost ran into took an easy step back to avoid their collision, then smiled.

"Morning! You look a little distracted. Is everything all right?"

He had a kind face, tidy dark brown hair, and startling grey-blue eyes. He stood at least half a head taller than Maaya and was dressed neatly in a workman's smock already dirty from the morning's labor. He held a bucket in his hands, fiddling idly with the handle as he glanced over at the ever-growing line. This was Roshan Kulkarni, son of one of the town's blacksmiths, and he had been a friend of Maaya's for years.

"Everything's fine. I'm just looking for the others. They were supposed to get water for breakfast, but it'll burn if they don't get back soon."

Roshan looked down the street thoughtfully.

"I wish I could say I saw them on my way over, but I was more concerned with trying to get here before the line got too long. I never seem to be able to skip the crowd."

"What do you need water from here for?" Maaya asked.

In an effort to try to increase productivity and help combat the economic stall that had overtaken the rest of the country, Sark's council had managed to obtain funding to provide all local artisans with water supplies of their own. This had the added benefit of drastically shortening the lines at the pumps, as artisans needed a constant supply of water throughout the day.

"Oh, this?" Roshan asked, lifting the bucket as though Maaya could have been talking about anything else. "I finished my chores early this morning, so dad sent me off to collect water for the nearby kitchen. They don't have enough hands to send someone off for water, and the council won't give them water of their own, so I volunteered."

"You're so sweet, Roshan," Maaya said warmly. "I should let you hurry on, then."

"Wait, before you go…" Roshan shifted to hold the empty bucket at his side, then stepped closer to Maaya, lowering his voice. "Did you hear what happened?"

"What do you mean? That thing everyone's talking about?" Maaya replied.

"Yeah. The people that disappeared. They say it happened sometime last night, but no one saw or heard anything."

"People disappear all the time, Roshan, this isn't anything to—"

"A whole street full? They were women and children, Maaya; this isn't normal. There are no signs of a fight, and everything looks like everyone just stepped out to the market for a minute, but everyone is gone."

Maaya opened her mouth to argue, but she stopped. That *wasn't* normal. Organized criminals rarely touched women and children, and the government wouldn't do something like that either. They were even less popular than the criminals.

"Wait, so… so what happened?" Maaya asked quietly, suddenly feeling distinctly worried.

"People are saying it's the Krethans," Roshan almost whispered. "Some type of new weapon. No idea what it is or how it works, but everyone's denying any involvement, and if the Krethans can make people disappear without a trace…"

"That makes no sense. Why would the Krethans want anything to do with Sark? We're about as unimportant as it's possible to be."

"That's exactly the reason. The perfect place to test a weapon like that is in a place no one cares about, where no one will notice."

Maaya shook her head.

"I can't believe… this doesn't make sense. Even if it was them, what kind of weapon could they suddenly have come up with that has that kind of power? We've been evenly matched for centuries. Why now?"

"Who knows. From what I heard, we aren't doing as well as our government says we are. The Krethans have the resources to come up with new weapons and technology. Some are saying this is a kind of poison or invisible gas, something that dissolves all living matter but leaves the rest. That would explain why everyone's gone without a trace."

Maaya shuddered.

"This is really not what I wanted to think about over breakfast," she murmured.

In response, Roshan put his bucket down and gave her a tight hug. She accepted it gratefully.

"I'm sorry. I didn't mean to scare you. It's just that everyone's discussing it and I don't really have anyone I can talk honestly to. Dad thinks everyone is just being foolish, and I don't trust anyone else enough to open my mouth around them." He let her go, looking at her concernedly. "Are you sure everything's all right? Have you been getting enough to eat? Maybe I can sneak—"

"I'm fine, Roshan, really," Maaya said, her smile back on her face. "Actually, better than usual. Rahu 'paid' us again, so we've plenty to eat."

"Did he manage to find a way to do that without showing his ugly mug in your house?" Roshan asked with a grin.

"No, but he didn't stay long, so I don't think we need to worry about contamination."

"Good. Honestly, if the Krethans ever wanted a deadly weapon they could just take a mold of his face."

The two laughed, attracting stares from a few people in line, but they didn't care.

Before they could continue, Maaya noticed movement out of the corner of her eye as a figure came up to them. She turned to look, and her surprise, saw Saber floating there, a look of mild irritation on her face.

Saber looked around to make sure no one was watching Maaya, then spoke.

"It is so hard keeping track of the four of you. The others came back, so I thought you'd be close behind, but then you didn't come back either. Let's hurry back before they figure out another excuse to escape before we get back."

"Sorry," Maaya said quietly, her smile still on her face. Roshan looked slightly confused for a moment, then relaxed.

"Hey, Saber," he said in her general direction, and she waved, fully aware he couldn't see.

Roshan couldn't see ghosts, but Maaya had come to trust him enough to tell him about her existence. Saber approved of him as well, so whenever they found the time, they communicated as directly as they could. The first time they "spoke" with each other, Saber used a box of small metal letters to spell out words for him to read. She soon became impatient and used a pen and paper instead.

Maaya liked how the two got along. Maaya still wasn't a good reader, and so she couldn't keep up with how quickly Saber wrote, but Roshan would read her messages aloud. In this way, when the three of them ever had free time together, Maaya found herself improving all the time.

"She says hello, but we really need to get going," Maaya explained. "We actually have enough food for breakfast now, and I want to get back before it's cold."

Roshan grinned, then picked up his bucket again.

"I'd best get this filled and back to the kitchens or there will be a riot. Have a good one, ladies." Lowering his voice again, he continued, "Be careful."

"What did he mean?" Saber asked concernedly as they walked back down the narrow street toward their house.

Maaya shook her head. She was finally getting comfortable with the fact that people weren't paying attention to her, but if she started talking to herself in the street that would change very quickly. Saber nodded in understanding and waited patiently until they got home. But the instant they stepped inside and the door was closed and locked, Saber whirled around, her face inches from Maaya's.

"What did he mean, 'be careful'? Is someone threatening you? Do I need to make an example of—?"

"No, no!" Maaya protested hurriedly. "It's not like that. Something apparently happened in Sark last night and it's got people on edge. Did you notice everyone huddled up and talking?"

"I did, but the living are easily spooked and the ones in Sark are especially stupid anyway so I didn't pay it any mind. Why?"

"Not here," Maaya said, glancing over at the table.

She led Saber upstairs where Maaya sat on the edge of Kim's bed and Saber joined her. As soon as Maaya made sure none of the others were eavesdropping, she repeated to Saber what Roshan had told her on the street. Saber's expression was hard to decipher, but she didn't look frightened, and this alone helped soothe Maaya's nerves.

"So basically that whole street full of people is gone, and no one has any idea what happened to them," Maaya finished.

"That's definitely unusual. With so many eyes in that area you'd think someone would have seen what happened," Saber mused.

"This feels wrong. If it is a Krethan weapon, and if they are using it on small towns like this, we're not safe anywhere."

"Before you work yourself into a panic, consider that we don't even know the real story yet," Saber said calmly. "All you have is a story from someone who heard it from someone else, who probably heard it from someone else. For all we know it's been blown entirely out of proportion."

"But what if it's true? What if something did kill all those people? What if they're really all dead?" Maaya protested.

In response, Saber raised an eyebrow.

"Then let's go ask them what happened."

7

MAYBERRY STREET

Breakfast that morning was delicious. Or at least it would have been if she were capable of tasting it. Since her conversation with Saber just a few minutes before, her heart had been pounding in her chest with anticipation. She had given herself about two minutes to scold herself mentally for not thinking of it. Despite how large a part ghosts played in her life, she still hadn't reached the point where her first thought after some type of disaster was interviewing everyone who had died in it.

But the anticipation she felt was not fear. Not this time. She wasn't sure if she would call it excitement—though that definitely applied to her four friends—but she had a certain eagerness about this trip all the same. For Maaya, searching through the now-vacant street meant a chance to discover what could have possibly happened that had the entire town talking. For Saber and the others it was a chance to meet new friends—or to put a stop to the troublesome dead before they went very far. And, as was often the case in situations like these, it was a chance for all of them to meet the newest ghosts in the world and help them settle or move on, whatever they wished.

Since they wouldn't be able to leave until nightfall, Maaya immersed herself in conversation. This was the first time she had seen her friends since the night before, and already there was much to share. Now that Maaya and Saber had agreed to visit the site of the mass disappearance, Maaya decided it was time everyone else knew what happened. To their credit, none of them seemed scared. If anything, they only seemed excited at the prospect of seeing and meeting new ghosts, not to mention investigating a mystery. Their reactions might have seemed callous to the uninitiated, but that was one thing constantly being around ghosts did to a person: death became much less frightening and all but completely lost its sense of permanence.

However, nothing could hold back their excitement from the events of the night before, and they quickly lost interest in their upcoming expedition in favor of filling Maaya in on everything that had happened.

"Well, we were right. The boy's sister was still around terrorizing anyone who got too close to him or even looked at him funny. That included us, by the way," Sovaan said proudly.

"It was worse than we thought," Kim added. "It turns out the client's husband was still there, too. He didn't like what his daughter was doing, and apparently their fights were starting to destroy the house. The poor woman was so scared she hadn't slept in nearly a week."

"What happened? How did you guys finish it?" Maaya asked intently.

"Oh, it was intense," Sovaan continued, clearly excited to tell the story. "The woman kept her son locked in his room, right? We walked in and the whole room was dark except for the moonlight from the window, and the boy was just sitting right there staring down at his feet. He didn't even move or respond when we talked to him. But then the door slammed shut behind us, and he looked up, and just… *screamed.* It was like a bunch of voices all at once!"

"Did you see his sister?" Maaya asked, horrified.

"No, but we had forgotten about her for the moment," Saber said dismissively. "We were more worried about the kid, because he was starting to rise up in the air, and he looked angry."

"Wait, he *flew*?"

"It really threw us off," Kim explained. "We'd never seen anything like it. So while he started flying after us and screaming, we were completely out of sorts. We could feel the ghost's presence there, but we couldn't see her, and that confused us even more."

"We were scared out of our minds until we realized the kid wasn't actually doing anything to us, and that since he was still alive we could just hit him. So I gave him a nice kick to the stomach and he fell down and didn't move," Kalil continued.

"That's when we realized what was happening. The ghost of his sister had been *inside* him using him like a puppet almost. I say *almost* because he was clearly in on it," Saber said.

"I… I didn't think that was possible," Maaya said slowly.

"It isn't usually. A ghost can't take over the body of a person without their explicit willingness. We aren't completely tied to this world, so we can't take over something that *is* if there's anything less than total consent. Even unawareness isn't enough. But it's a different story if the person lets them in.

It's still hard on the ghost, since they have the weight of a whole person on them, but they can do it."

"Why would she do that? And why would he agree to it?" Maaya pressed. "Neither of them can do much harm at all that way."

"That was the point. For anyone else, the sight of a child floating and screaming like that would have been enough to make them run for the hills. It's a good way to get rid of people without having to hurt them."

"But that clearly didn't work on us, and we'd just hurt her brother, so she was absolutely furious," Kalil went on. "She was on us before we knew what was happening. Saber stalled her long enough for us to get our cards out, but once she saw what we were holding she left through the door before we could seal the room. When we tried to follow her, we found the old lady locked us in, so we had to break the door down."

Maaya listened with growing surprise as they told the story of how they broke down the door, cracking half the wall in the process, and proceeded to chase the ghost through the massive dark house. The ghost knew the house better than they did and had taken advantage of that fact to split them up. She had managed to injure Kim and Sovaan before coming face to face with Saber, who had gotten quite irritated at the chase. Saber held the girl firmly in place while Kalil prepared to seal her away.

"...and just when we thought things couldn't get any more chaotic, that's when her dad showed up," Sovaan laughed.

"What happened?" Maaya asked, her eyes wide.

"Well, we thought we were in for a big fight. Two of us were down, and this girl's dad walks in on us right as we're attacking his daughter. But then..."

"The girl's father proceeded to give her a stern lecture in front of everyone in the room," Saber finished, laughing. "Told her off for causing trouble for strangers and ruining his nice house, not to mention being such a brat to his wife. The daughter tried to argue, but he shut her down said she should be ashamed of herself, then said he wanted us to seal them both."

"That's when it got a little sad," Sovaan continued. "The girl's brother burst into the room just then and begged her not to go, and his mum was right behind him even though she had no idea what was going on. But suddenly she seemed to understand, and they had kind of this... moment, you know? They all kind of hugged it out, and the mum was at wit's end, you know, since she could feel it but couldn't see it. But then they were all crying, and then we were, too."

"I didn't cry," Saber replied indignantly.

"Well, yeah, your tear ducts are as dead as you are," Sovaan chuckled. "But you would've."

As Sovaan and Saber argued, Kim scooted a little closer to Maaya to finish the story.

"While that was going on, we kind of stood around awkwardly, and once they were done, the dad asked us again to seal them, and so we did. Then it was quiet, and the mother and her son were crying still, but it felt peaceful, too. They didn't seem like they could talk, so Kalil and Saber made sure we were all right, then we left."

"Where was Rahu during all this?" Maaya asked.

"Oh, just standing outside waiting for us. I guess if anyone passed by, he would wave around some holy water and say some gibberish, but mostly he just waited."

"Wouldn't people think it weird that he wouldn't go inside the house to clear the ghosts out?" Maaya pressed.

"I doubt it. No one knew enough details to be suspicious. They're afraid, so they blindly trust him. Besides, if he'd gone inside no one would see him, and that's the most important thing. He had to make a big public deal of it."

"While you guys did all the work," Maaya said crossly. "I'm curious, though. Why didn't the father tell off his daughter like this before?"

"He tried. She'd just run away from him, I guess. Since they were both dead he had no control over her. She broke stuff, scared people… basically did whatever she wanted and just stayed away from him. The threat of us being there finally forced her to listen to him, and she must have known it was over."

"Well, good job you guys," Maaya said proudly. Saber and Sovaan stopped quarreling long enough to look pleased with themselves, then got right back to it. Maaya rolled her eyes, then turned back to Kim. "How are you two healing up?"

"I'm doing okay. The girl hit me in the head with a curtain rod, so I was too dizzy to do anything for a while. Sovaan got a little scraped up, but he recovered pretty fast. Oh, but I feel better now!" Kim finished hastily, as though worried she might be told to stay home and rest. Sovaan simply nodded beside her, his mouth full of food between retorts to the ghost.

"Good. We'll need everyone tonight; there's no telling how many ghosts will be there after something like that," Maaya continued. "You know the drill. Eat, drink, and rest up. I'll do our bloods tonight since I didn't have to go last night."

"Eat more meat, then, we're going to need more cards than usual," Saber commented, shoving a hot bowl of kormaa at her.

Maaya ate happily until she was sure she might be sick. It was a bad habit they all shared. When Rahu didn't have jobs for a while, their food supplies dwindled until they were forced to live off stolen food, which often wasn't enough. When new supplies came in, they ate like they might never eat again.

Time passed more quickly on a full stomach, Maaya found. When she went without food there was no escaping the ache in her belly. Every passing second would constantly remind her how hungry she was, her organs oblivious to the fact that desire alone could not procure edible goods. When she was hungry, it was all she could think about. But when she didn't have to worry about where her next meal was coming from, her mind was allowed to wander.

She dozed on the sofa in the warmth of the sunlight trickling through the window, daydreaming of other worlds and better places. She imagined what life could be like when they were all free of Rahu. She would have a grand house for herself and Saber and all the others. Everyone would have their own room, their own bed. Rent would always be paid, food would always be on the table, and they would never have to worry about anything again.

The last remnants of the day's sun clung to the deep red clouds that dotted the sky, and for once, Saber remained behind. She sat silently on the edge of the sofa, gazing out the window as if it were her first time seeing the sunset.

"Weird to see it from inside, isn't it?" Maaya said, and Saber gave her a half smile, but didn't reply. Maaya sat up, leaning closer to the ghost. "Hey, you okay?"

"I'm fine," Saber replied unconvincingly.

"Your voice is shaking."

Saber opened her mouth to retort, then seemed to realize it wouldn't do any good. She closed it tightly again, looking directly away from Maaya. Maaya grinned.

"You're nervous, aren't you?"

"Nervous about what? I'm a ghost; they can't do anything to hurt me."

"Saber…"

"Fine. Yes, I'm nervous. We've never done anything like this before. Do you remember the last time there was a disaster that wiped out a large group of people? The number of ghosts in the area increased tenfold, and we well near had an undead riot on our hands. They were all so… malicious. The four of you almost died!"

"Well, it was a maximum-security prison that burned down. I don't think they're representative of the general population," Maaya countered.

"We've already established that you are far more optimistic about humanity than I am," Saber replied. "Regardless, it's not me I'm worried about. The whole world could be burnt to ash and I wouldn't be bothered, but… there are some people I'd prefer to stay alive, you know."

Saber got up before Maaya could answer, then floated quickly through the wall and out of sight.

Maaya's smile didn't leave her face as she started getting dressed for the evening. It wasn't easy for Saber to talk about her feelings; she could take charge of any situation with ease, and she even excelled at offering emotional advice to those in need of it, but being sentimental herself was something she struggled with. For Maaya, Saber suddenly leaving the room in a fit of embarrassment was just one of the ways she attempted to show her affection.

Saber came floating back in an hour after sunset, and it seemed her "walk" had done her some good. She looked excited, and she floated quickly over to where Kim was carefully bandaging Maaya's hand.

"The coast is clear, probably because it's so cold out there. Dress warm. Oh, and hurry up. We have company."

Maaya's heart leapt into her throat. There was only one person who offered company for something like this, and he was the last person she wanted to see.

Before she could dash upstairs and pretend to be asleep, however, Roshan stepped into the room, closing the door quickly behind him. He sighed with relief, rubbing his hands together.

"It is absolutely freezing out there. Do you mind if I sit by the fire? I just want to warm my toes so they don't fall off."

"Roshan!" Maaya breathed.

Roshan smiled at Maaya, then laughed.

"You should see the look on your face. Did I scare you?"

"Saber mentioned we had company; she just didn't say *who*," Maaya replied, glaring at Saber. The ghost twiddled her thumbs innocently. "Anyway, what are you doing here? Isn't it a little late for you to be out?"

"It is, but I figured you'd be going out tonight, so I thought I'd give you some company."

Maaya paused. He knew her well enough that sometimes he still surprised her.

"I… not that I don't appreciate that, but given what we just heard about earlier…"

"That's exactly why I want to come with you. No, not to keep you safe. Let's not kid ourselves; you'd be the one protecting me." He laughed again, then his expression turned serious. "But I do want to know what happened out there. I know you usually do your thing in secret, but there's a chance this might not just be about you anymore. A whole street full of living people just disappeared, and that means everyone could be in danger."

"We could always tell you as soon as we find out, Roshan," Maaya said, folding her arms. "You should stay at home where it's safe."

"If the Krethans have a weapon that can kill whole blocks of people in their own homes, nowhere is safe," Roshan pressed. "Besides, I wouldn't be able to wait."

"What if we do find out what happened? Then what?" Maaya asked.

"Then I'll tell my father. He has the ear of the people. Lots of them trust him and listen to what he has to say. I don't even know if we'll find out what happened, or that if we do there will be a solution, but if we do, I want to be able to tell someone who can actually do something."

"But this is dangerous! We don't know anything about them or how they might react to us being there. One ghost by itself can be dangerous, and we're talking about maybe hundreds."

"They also have the answers we need. You are literally the only people in the town who can talk to them, and I really feel like I need to be there."

"Oh, Roshan…"

Maaya walked over to him and put her hands on his shoulders, looking intently up at him with an expression of admiration and fear.

"What?"

"I just… I want you to know what you're getting yourself into tonight," Maaya sighed, finally caving. "Ghosts who are new to the world are sometimes very difficult to deal with. They're confused; some of them still don't know they're dead. Sometimes that confusion turns to violence, and it can be a little hard to defend yourself. Have you ever tried hitting a ghost?"

"What, they can hit me and I can't hit back? That's a little unfair." Roshan smiled. "Believe me, I didn't come here thinking it'd be sunshine and roses. I came here hoping to talk to a bunch of ghosts, so I'm already prepared to accept some weird stuff."

Maaya sighed, and then after a moment, grabbed her coat.

"Let's go."

Half an hour later, Maaya and the others stood at the entrance of a narrow street on the eastern edge of Sark. Saber stood watch out of sight from a few streets away; as Maaya explained, ghosts who didn't know they were dead yet found the sight of another ghost to be quite discomfiting.

A few lanterns burned a dull orange near the crooked street sign declaring "Mayberry Street," below which another sign had been added by the town police, proclaiming that anyone caught trespassing would be duly punished. Of course, no officer was willing to stand at the end of an empty street during the night—not because they were afraid, but because they were easily bored. It was likely the neighbors had gotten to all the dead's possessions before the police had, so there wasn't even a reason for most people to want to trespass in the first place.

Behind them stood a dark and empty warehouse, and in front of them, tall buildings rose up on either side of the street, nearly touching each other to form a solid wall of small apartments five stories high, reaching down to the back of the cul de sac and around to the other side like an old rusty horseshoe. Some of the buildings leaned dangerously, and tenants and landlords over the years had fought back against gravity with beams, rocks, and concrete in a manner that suggested no one with any actual carpentry experience had gotten anywhere near them.

A wilted-looking dog trotted past them, pausing for only a moment to tilt its head at them before continuing its search for scraps. If there had been any other living people on the street that night they might have given the group a similar look for being so fascinated with an empty street after sunset.

To Maaya's eyes, however, the street was bustling as it always had.

She hadn't managed to spot the ghosts before they arrived at the street given how tall the buildings were, but now they could see inside the cul de sac, she saw them—hundreds of them—walking the sidewalk, sticking their heads out of windows, or pacing nervously.

"Okay. We need to do this very cautiously," Maaya instructed, mostly for Roshan's benefit. "We'll walk up slowly on the side so as not to attract attention. If we meet them one by one, it'll be easier on all of—"

"YOU."

Maaya shrieked before she could stop herself. The ghost of a woman somewhere in her thirties had walked straight through the door of the nearby warehouse, and she now stood crossly in the street, looking at Maaya with an expression she might have otherwise shared only with her unruly children. Roshan stepped quickly to her side, but Maaya quickly regained her bearings enough to shoot Roshan a glance that told him it was time to play along. Roshan quickly stepped back, then tried to look in the general direction of where Maaya's gaze fell.

"Y-yes?" Maaya answered meekly.

"You *can* see me, right?"

"Yes."

"I thought so. Thank you. I have been stressed about this all afternoon and into the evening. I knew people in this town were rude, but not so much as to ignore someone crying for help right in front of them. Every one of them, too. None of our neighbors had any luck, either."

"Do you know what happened here earlier?" Maaya asked, calming now that the woman appeared temporarily sated.

"I was hoping someone could tell us that," the woman scoffed. "All I know is I've been trying to get someone's attention the entire day, and no one has so much as looked at us. My kids haven't eaten yet, and my husband muttered something about how we were all dead before he wandered off, and he hasn't been back since. The idiot. Oh—yes, here! They're talking to me!"

Maaya turned to see who she could be talking to, and her heart dropped. No fewer than fifty ghosts were making their way casually over to where they stood. Some appeared perturbed, while others seemed only mildly confused. A few even appeared relieved. None of them looked angry, though, which Maaya took to be an excellent sign.

"And what's your names, then?" an old man asked as the ghosts made a circle around Maaya and the others. Trying to suppress the claustrophobia suddenly clawing at her insides, she gave them their names in turn. "Well, I don't recognize you, and I ain't 'eard of you before, but you're talking to us, so that's already better than everyone else in this area."

The other ghosts murmured and shook their heads disapprovingly.

"Ah, yes, well… no big deal, of course, it's only polite," Maaya replied with a nervous laugh.

"What are you doing wandering around at this time of night? It's not safe for kids your age," another woman scolded gently from the side.

"We heard something happened here yesterday and we came here hoping to find out what," Maaya answered, regaining control of her vocal cords.

A few of the ghosts' expressions turned to disappointment.

"Ah, we was hoping you could tell us. Everyone's acting like we don't exist, all of us, and of course the only ones who answer us don't know what's going on, either," the old man grumbled.

Maaya paused. There was definitely something unusual about this. It wasn't uncommon for the newly dead to have some trouble accepting the fact that they were, in fact, dead, but an entire street full of people? When the prison had burned down, the inmates who remained had figured out they were dead by the time Maaya and the others arrived, and had already started plotting how to take advantage of that.

Maaya looked around at them all just to make sure her eyes were working properly. They all *looked* like ghosts, and yet none of them apparently thought that was suspicious.

She stifled a sigh. This was probably going to make things even more difficult.

"All I know is what I heard. We don't live nearby, so all we have is the word of others, but from what they described… well, they said an entire street full of people disappeared."

"Ah, you've got the wrong street then," the man chuckled without missing a beat. Maaya looked up at him in surprise. "Well, clearly, no disappearing has gone on here, has it? They must've been talking about someplace else. That's a right downer, though, but I suppose news doesn't travel very far 'ere."

The crowd started to disperse, though some looked eager to remain nearby, finally in the company of another person who acknowledged their presence. Maaya, meanwhile, was completely lost for words. She stared after the departing ghosts, her mouth half open, and jumped slightly when Roshan touched her arm.

"So, uh… how's it going?" he asked tentatively.

"I have never seen anything like this before," Maaya breathed. "Something is very wrong here."

"We're not in danger, are we?"

"No, no… this is just the strangest thing I've ever seen."

At her side, Sovaan tugged on her sleeve.

"Can we go talk to them? They seem nice."

A shrug was all Maaya could muster, and Sovaan and the other two spread out in the street, quickly getting swept up in conversation by people who were only too happy to talk to new faces.

"What happened? Who's 'they'?" Roshan asked, looking a little more at ease, though he was unable to hide his fascination at watching only one side of each conversation his young friends were having.

"It looks like almost everyone from the street is still here. I was talking to a small crowd of them just now. But here's the weird thing: none of them know they're dead. They seem slightly inconvenienced at most, and they're all wondering why no one's talking to them," Maaya answered softly.

"Is that unusual?" Roshan continued, looking lost.

"Very. Sometimes ghosts don't know they're dead, but they know *something* is wrong. Others know they're dead and are angry or upset about it; there's almost always some sort of crisis for the newly dead. But all these people are going about like nothing has changed."

Roshan looked around before speaking, before quickly remembering that he couldn't actually see if anyone was eavesdropping.

"Not to be rude, but… have they looked at each other? I've never seen a ghost, but I imagine that would give them some sort of hint."

"That's what I don't get. Ghosts know other ghosts when they see them, but that doesn't seem to be the case here—and the first person I talked to walked through a door."

"Did any of them mention seeing anything? Even if they're a bit slow on the uptake about being dead and all, they must remember seeing something out of the ordinary."

"I… I didn't get a chance to ask about specifics," Maaya said awkwardly. "There were so many of them, and this is just so strange it just kind of took me by surprise."

"We should probably get to it," Roshan said warily, looking around the street. At Maaya's inquisitive glance he continued, "If anyone else comes along, all they're going to see are three kids standing in the street talking to thin air, and you don't need more of a reputation than you already have."

"You're right. I'll try to make this quick."

"What should I do?" Roshan asked, looking slightly intimidated at the thought of being left alone.

"Could you grab the kids and meet up with Saber? Even though this place isn't dangerous I've still got a bad feeling. I don't want to stay here any longer than I have to."

Roshan nodded and walked carefully in Kim's direction, as though worried he might bump into one of their invisible friends. Maaya thought to warn him about how disturbing walking through a ghost could be, but at this rate she didn't think any of them would notice anyway.

One of the nearby ghosts, a young boy of probably not even ten, walked uneasily over to Maaya as soon as Roshan left. He looked nervous, like he'd rather not talk to a stranger at all, but evidently whatever he had to say was important.

"How come you can see us?" he asked quietly.

"Why not? I can see everyone else," Maaya answered, hoping she sounded convincing.

"Yeah, but… we're ghosts," the boy said bluntly.

Maaya froze. She hadn't been expecting that.

"I… uh…"

"Could you always see ghosts? I thought it was just me," the boy continued.

"Yeah, I've been able to see ghosts for as long as I can remember," Maaya said. "Wait, does this mean… you could see ghosts before all this happened?"

"Yes. That's how I know we're ghosts, because I know what ghosts look like."

"So what happened here? What caused this?" Maaya asked urgently, keeping her voice low.

"Ghosts did. I never saw ghosts like them before, but they walked through the street and everyone died. I tried to tell people, but they didn't believe me. They all just stopped moving and then they died."

"What… what did the ghosts look like?" Maaya asked, her blood suddenly running cold.

"Really tall. A lot taller than my dad even. They all looked the same, too. And they had these big, dark eyes. They didn't have arms or legs or faces. There was a bright light around them too, like they were all carrying lights, but they weren't."

Maaya shuddered and fought to stay calm. The good news, she supposed, was that this wasn't the result of a Krethan weapon, even if one such weapon did exist. The bad news was that this was the result of the type of ghost Maaya had seen on the river the night before—and that they were now making their way into Sark.

"I tried to tell everyone we're all dead, but they didn't believe me either," the boy said irritably. "No one listens to me."

"You don't seem very afraid… how do you feel?" Maaya asked. She couldn't forget her second mission here; these were still new ghosts and they deserved to be helped in any way she could.

"I'm all right I guess. I didn't want to die, but I know it's not so bad. It should be fun; I had a few dead friends and they always made fun of me that I couldn't fly and that I had to go to bed. But now I can be with them all the time."

"That's… one way of thinking about it," Maaya nodded, even as she felt her heart break. Not getting emotionally connected was sometimes very difficult. "So, I know people aren't listening to you about this, but I think they'll come around. I've been doing this for years—helping ghosts adjust, I mean. I'd like to help all of you—"

"Excuse me, girl, do you see that over there?" the woman who had initially confronted Maaya said suddenly from nearby. "Look there, coming down the road with your friend."

Maaya turned to look, and to her dismay, she saw Saber and the others coming back down the street toward them. Saber, in the lead, had no doubt decided to come down and see what was taking Maaya so long—which in any other situation would have been fine, except Maaya had only now started getting some answers. If the other ghosts saw Saber for what she was…

"It's probably nothing," Maaya started hastily, trying to distract the woman. "I was wondering if you could tell me more about what the community here is like, if you have a neighborhood watch, and if they saw—"

But it was too late. The woman could not take her eyes from Saber, and as she approached, the woman's eyes widened slightly in fear.

"It's… it's one of them," she said slowly, taking a step back.

"Hey, wait, it's okay, you don't have to—" Maaya pleaded, but the woman didn't seem to hear her at all now.

"You're a ghost!" she cried, pointing at Saber as she approached. A few people nearby glanced over at the commotion, then did a double take as they noticed Saber floating there.

"Well, give the lady a medal," Saber answered dully, oblivious to the stares, then faced Maaya. "You were taking too long so I decided to come see what the holdup was. I see you've met Mayberry Street's resident genius, however, so I'll assume everything is fine."

Now, finally, the woman looked down at Maaya, but her expression told her the damage had been done.

"You can see her? You know her?" he asked accusingly. "What are you, some kind of witch?"

At least twenty people were starting to gather now, coming cautiously closer to Saber despite their obvious fear.

"*You* can see me, too. Does that make you a wizard or a sorcerer?" Saber remarked, but her casual sarcasm was betrayed by the growing expression of concern on her face as the residents of Mayberry Street started to surround them.

"Leave them alone! They're here to help!" the young boy cried, but as expected, no one paid him any mind.

Maaya slowly backed up against the warehouse, tugging Roshan back with her as they moved. Though he couldn't see or hear any of what was going on, he seemed to detect the sudden change in mood.

"What's going on?" he whispered.

"Cards out," Maaya murmured in response. "Roshan, stay behind the others." Kim, Sovaan, and Kalil quietly pulled out their stacks of cards, and Saber tensed, looking ready to fight. Maaya, however, took a careful step forward and raised both hands.

"Listen, please. You all know that something happened to all of you earlier, and I think I can explain—"

"Did you cause this? Did you do something to us?" a woman asked sharply.

"No! But I think I know what did."

"That's awfully suspicious, you think?" the old man from earlier said, stepping to the fore. "You've never even been 'ere, you don't know any of us. As I recall, you came here asking questions. But now suddenly you know what happened? I don't suppose you're responsible for whatever happened, are you? Did you get everyone to ignore us?"

"Have you considered taking up long jumping? You've already demonstrated you're quite good at leaping to conclusions," Saber retorted. "If we were here to harm you, we'd be doing a poor job of it by showing up completely outnumbered and fighting with children."

"Guys, please—" Maaya interjected.

"And haven't you noticed something a little strange about all of you? Something that was wrong long before we ever got here? The reason you all might be able to see me? Maybe I can spell it out for you," Saber continued fiercely.

Maaya's face paled.

"Saber, don't—"

"*You're all dead.*"

The silence that fell pressed against Maaya so hard she thought that if she looked away for even a moment she might forget anyone else was there. So still was the scene that it was like looking at a photograph: the small smile that played over Saber's features as she stared directly at the old man, the expressions of confusion and horror on the other ghosts' faces, and the quiet and empty street behind them.

This, however, was a feeling Maaya recognized, and as frightening as it was, she clung to it, seeking solace in its familiarity. She knew what often happened when ghosts were told they were dead. When any ghost was told they were dead, it was like something clicked inside their brains and they were suddenly able to see the world—and themselves—as they should. What came after was often unpleasant, but this was territory Maaya knew. And that gave her the advantage.

Before any of the ghosts could recover or start vocalizing their anger and denial, Maaya took a step back and glanced quickly at the others, who looked equally prepared.

"Distract them for me; I'm going to get Roshan to safety, then I'll be back," Maaya commanded. Her friends nodded, and in one swift synchronous motion, held their cards up like fans before their eyes.

"Something tells me diplomacy isn't going well," Roshan said nervously, staring as Maaya pulled out a card of her own.

By now the residents of Mayberry Street had started to recover, and it seemed as though their anger was quickly overcoming their fear. They started to move forward hesitantly, unsure of who should lead, but there wasn't much free space between them.

Maaya took a quick breath, then knelt and pressed the card against the skin on her right calf. The green ink on the card glowed brilliantly, and as the paper of the card dissolved into thin air, the designs seemed to imprint themselves in the air an inch above Maaya's skin like a hovering neon tattoo, stretching down to cover her ankle and up to her thigh. A mirror image of the patterns appeared over her left leg as well until both were equal, the intricate green lines pulsating slightly in the dark.

"That… uh…" Roshan started, his eyes wide, and then he yelped as Maaya picked him up in her arms.

"Just hold on," she instructed, and she started to run.

The scene around them became a blur, and the only sound she could hear was that of the air rushing furiously against her ears. Roshan's mouth was open like he wanted to say something, but she wasn't sure if his words got lost somewhere in his throat or on the wind.

Only a few moments later she knelt again, sitting Roshan up against the wall of a building so he could stand up himself. He didn't appear ready or willing to try, however, and he simply gawked at Maaya as she panted.

Despite only running for a few seconds, Maaya had taken them both roughly four blocks down the road.

"How in the… what…?" Roshan started, but that was all he could muster.

"I'll explain later," Maaya said breathlessly. "Find your way back to our house from here. There's about a hundred angry ghosts back there and I have to get back."

"Uh… yeah, will do, but—"

Before he could continue, Maaya was gone.

She reappeared at the entrance to Mayberry Street to find an all-out brawl going on, though it appeared to be pretty one sided. Though initially emboldened by their strength in numbers, the ghosts were now in disarray as her friends demonstrated an impressive display of strength, speed, and elemental control. Kim had attached one of her elemental cards to her wrists, and as she twirled her arms about her in moves that would have otherwise seemed appropriate for a ballet, flames followed like ribbons of red and gold.

Kalil mirrored her moves at her back, though his wrists glowed blue, and streams of water appeared out of thin air. The ghosts seemed less impressed by this display, though they quickly changed their attitude when a roaring tumult of water rushed across the sidewalk at them, taking with it all sorts of debris like the receding pull of a tidal wave. While the fire and water couldn't technically harm ghosts, the supernatural element to them at least made the ghosts uncomfortable, and for ghosts who were only just realizing they were dead, the psychological impact was powerful.

Sovaan, meanwhile, had set himself up on advantageous spot on a nearby rooftop, keeping watch for the two below and providing even more of a distraction. The ghosts evidently had not realized they could fly yet, and so some hurried inside, reaching out the top-floor windows in a futile attempt to catch him.

For all their grand displays, Saber was the only one who appeared to be enjoying herself. She, like Kim, preferred fire—only instead of a dance of distraction, she flung fireballs down at the scattering crowd below. Many of the ghosts were now fleeing in all directions, a situation Maaya could see getting very bad very quickly.

"Kim! Block the street!" she cried. Kim quickly raised her arms high, and a wall of flame erupted behind her, just wide enough to reach across the street and sidewalks without touching the nearby buildings. Those who had been attempting to flee the cul de sac now stopped, crying out in terror.

None of this was going the way Maaya planned. The screaming tore at her heart. She didn't want to frighten anyone, especially like this. This wasn't a dignified sealing of spirits; it was the terrorizing of innocents.

"Enough!" Maaya commanded, and though she spoke to everyone, her eyes locked with Saber's as she spoke. Stubborn as Saber was, she knew well enough not to argue now. "Seals out, now!"

Four hands drew four cards written in blood, holding them firmly between their first and middle fingers, tense with all the preparedness of seasoned archers ready to fire. Maaya knew it was going to take a lot of work, but she was going to see it done. The sooner this was over, the better.

Before she could give the final order, however, a tremendous roar of thunder echoed in the skies above. Maaya was temporarily annoyed at the interruption until she looked up—and a wave of dizziness washed over her.

A deep red tear had opened miles above them, stretching across the entire visible sky like a gaping maw beyond which there was only unending darkness. It was so vast that Maaya's brain didn't seem to know how to process it, and as her depth perception failed, so did her legs. The others seemed equally affected, and their spell cards failed one by one, the lights of all colors flickering and fading away from their limbs. Kim caught Kalil as he staggered, and they both sat down quickly, looking anywhere but up.

The ghosts of Mayberry Street seemed more concerned with their freedom than the troubles of the sky for the moment, and took advantage of this distraction to run. But they soon found another force holding them back.

Though Maaya could not feel it herself, she heard it all around her and saw it in the clothes and hair of the ghosts as they struggled to move; it was as though they pushed against an unrelenting hurricane that was growing steadily stronger. Their screams grew louder, and to Maaya's horror, they started falling *up* into the sky toward the yawning hole. Some grabbed on to whatever nearby anchor they could, but the pull of the invisible wind was inescapable. All of them, every man, woman, and child, dotted the sky as they were sucked into the void.

Somewhere in Maaya's terrified brain, something clicked. Every living being on the street seemed entirely unaffected by the pull of the sky. Saber, however, did not fall into that category. Despite herself, Maaya tore her eyes from the ground and searched the sky frantically, but she caught no glimpse of the ghost in her white flowing robes. Finally, Maaya had to look away as dizziness overtook her again.

After what felt like at least an hour, but was surely only a few minutes, the howling wind quickly faded, and when Maaya chanced a brief glance upward, she saw that the tear was almost gone. It sealed itself completely in a matter of seconds, the crimson scar that remained fading just as fast, the only thing left of it being the image it burned in Maaya's eyes and memory.

All was still and silent once again, and this time, Maaya and the others were truly alone.

Relief washed over her only momentarily before she remembered.

"Saber?" Maaya called, and her voice cracked. There was no response. She called again, louder this time, and her voice echoed pitifully around the street.

"I'm here," came Saber's voice finally. Maaya whirled around to see Saber coming hesitantly out of the warehouse. Her voice was calm, but she looked stricken. "Say, that's a new one. I don't remember you using that card before. Very effective, though."

"That wasn't me," Maaya answered softly, and Saber nodded. The ghost's lower lip trembled as though she might cry, but she steadfastly refused to let even a whimper escape. Instead, she took a deep breath, then came closer to Maaya.

"Yeah, I know. It was worth a shot, though."

Maaya put a reassuring hand on the ghost's shoulder, and they shared a glance in the way that only those united in dread could do. All their questions spilled unspoken in the air between them and were answered just as quickly in the stares of helpless eyes.

Kim was the first to truly regain her bearings, though she looked as haunted and frightened as the rest. As Sovaan leapt down from the rooftop and Kalil got unsteadily to his feet, she murmured urgently to them.

"We should get out of here before anyone sees."

8

THE UNKNOWN SPECTER

MAAYA'S LEGS felt weak as she walked home, and she was struck by the conflicting forces of terror that screamed at her to run and the dread that threatened to freeze her where she should. As they continued in silence, Maaya realized what she was feeling. It wasn't the helplessness she felt when dealing with Rahu or when trying to figure out how to feed the four of them when there was no food left. It was the helplessness one felt when they were suddenly confronted with something that was bigger and enormously more powerful than they were.

Until now, Maaya and the others had been dealing with ghosts. Some were more troublesome than others, but Maaya had never felt particularly uncomfortable when dealing with the supernatural. Now, however, it had revealed itself to contain more mystery and power than she had ever thought possible. For all the experience she had and for all the knowledge she had accumulated over the years, she was back to feeling as though she knew nothing at all. She was a stranger given a mere glimpse into a world other than her own, one so infinite and broad in scope that it likely didn't even realize, or care, that she existed.

Not a word was spoken as they walked slowly home. The only sound came from Kim's quiet frightened sobs and Kalil's hushed attempts at consoling her. Maaya felt terrible. They were bold, they all were, but they were still young. They put on brave faces whenever they could, but sometimes the work and danger got to them. After this, Maaya couldn't blame them.

Finally, after what seemed like hours, they reached the front door of their cottage. Before Maaya could even touch the handle, the door opened, and Roshan stood in the doorway. His expression of relief at seeing them safe turned to concern as he saw their faces.

"What happened? Are you guys okay?" he asked quietly.

"I don't know," Maaya replied softly, stepping past him and taking a seat on the couch. She felt as though she would collapse if she had to stand even a moment more.

The others gathered nearby, sitting close to the fire. Maaya hadn't realized how cold she was; in the midst of everything else, she had attributed her feeling of numbness to dread.

It took a moment for her to realize that Roshan was sitting next to her, and she could tell by his expression that his impatience would quickly take over the front of polite silence he was giving her.

"When you were walking home… did you see anything? Hear anything?" she asked quietly.

Roshan shook his head.

"I heard you yell something, but that was about it. Why? Did something go wrong?"

Maaya sighed, trying to figure out how to explain something she didn't even understand herself.

"I don't know. We were trying to seal the ghosts as usual, but then… then the sky just opened up. There was a great big dark hole in the sky—no, not in the sky, it was like it *was* the sky—and it just sucked all the ghosts into it. It took them all, screaming and crying, and then it disappeared. I… I've never seen anything like that before."

"All the ghosts?" Roshan asked apprehensively. "Saber?"

"No, she's fine. She's here," Maaya assured him quickly. "I don't know why, but it didn't seem to affect her."

"Thank goodness for that," Roshan said, but he still looked uneasy. "How strange. I didn't see anything out of the ordinary at all. So… none of you caused whatever that was?"

"No way," Kim answered from the floor, and the others shook their heads emphatically.

Roshan fell silent, drumming his fingers on the arm of the sofa. Maaya hoped he wouldn't ask any more questions. She had no more answers to give. She only had questions of her own, and she didn't think there was anyone in the world capable of answering them.

"So what should I tell my father? Anything?" Roshan asked finally.

Maaya shrugged.

"Nothing yet. I wouldn't even know where to begin. What happened was definitely out of the ordinary, but if we have no explanation, we would only cause people to be afraid. We need answers, but… I don't know how to get them. I need some time to think. Maybe we can plan something for later, another investigation maybe, but for now…"

Maaya trailed off. The weight of responsibility was crushing her, and she didn't think she was capable of dealing with it now. The room felt small and the heat of the fire invaded her lungs, making it difficult to breathe. It was hard enough trying to manage with her friends, and now she had been dragged into solving the mystery of why hundreds of people had been killed by an unseen force—the same force, perhaps, that dragged the spirits of the newly dead into a vast nothingness. This was too much.

"Hey. Maaya." Roshan reached over and put his hand on hers. She glanced up, trying to keep her expression neutral, but she guessed he had already seen enough. "It's all right. I won't tell him anything. If what you say is true, then I wouldn't blame you if you weren't able to figure this out right away."

Maaya nodded. Somehow he always knew what to say to make her feel better in the moment.

"But what if this happens again?" Kim asked anxiously. Her eyes were still pink from crying, and Kalil remained at her side, his arm protectively around her shoulder.

"We're going to try to stop this before it happens again," Maaya replied firmly. "I have at least an idea as to what caused this. Until then, we're all exhausted and we need to get some rest."

"What was it? Did someone have an answer for you?" Roshan asked intently.

"He did. And it matches another story we heard before," Maaya sighed, then told everyone what the little boy had told her.

"Like the ghost on the river. The one Styx and Sylvia and Milo warned us about," Sovaan said softly.

"Seems like it," Maaya affirmed. "I don't know about what happened after that, but it seems like the ghosts were definitely responsible for everyone dying. Everything seems similar."

"Wait, there are ghosts that can kill people now?" Roshan asked, stunned.

"I think so. But this is the first time they've ever been in Sark. Hopefully it won't happen again, but… if it does, we need to be ready to fight them."

"Wait, hold on. If they're actually killing people, if they can kill a whole street of people, there's no way you should—"

"That's our *job*, Roshan. Besides, they can be hurt by our blood cards just like any other ghost. If they try this again, we'll be here to send them back," Maaya said determinedly, though she was unable to fight off a yawn at the end.

That was one of the caveats to using *libris.* No one was suddenly given extra powers for free. It took a lot of energy to use them, and she was almost always left feeling drained after a fight. Even Saber looked tired, and she looked a little more transparent than usual. Maaya wasn't sure exactly what prolonged use of *libris* would do to a ghost, so they had decided simply not to put it to the test.

"Hey, speaking of your cards… what did you do to me earlier?" Roshan asked, looking unwilling to argue the previous point any further. Despite herself, Maaya smiled.

"I'm sorry about that. I didn't think there was time to tell you. One of the things we can use our cards for is to move faster. We can also use them to make us stronger, or to heal, but I… I just wanted to make sure I got you somewhere safe."

"My hero," Roshan grinned. "Though if I had a preference, I wouldn't do it again."

"That's up to you," Maaya winked. "Now… I'm sorry to have to tell you to go, but I think we all want some sleep."

"It's all right. I suppose I found out what I needed to know, even if the thought is pretty scary. But I guess I can sleep well at night knowing you're watching over Sark."

"Oh, hush," Maaya said, shoving him gently across the couch, and he laughed.

As Kim stood up and ushered the others upstairs to get ready for bed, Maaya walked Roshan to the door. She knew he would have to be up in a matter of hours to help his father work, and she felt guilty for keeping him out this late, even though it was his decision to begin with. Saber hovered slightly behind, though she remained silent.

As cold as the night was, Maaya breathed easier in the frigid air. It felt better to be outside, at least for now. But Roshan was shivering, and he looked as though he might fall asleep at the door if he didn't keep moving.

"I don't suppose I could convince you to stay out of trouble?" Roshan asked. She knew he would return to that eventually, but she couldn't be angry. He was so disarming and so genuine that he could get away with talking about things with her that no one else except perhaps Saber could.

"You could try!" she replied. "But this is important, Roshan. You didn't see what I saw. If you did you'd understand."

"Oh, I understand fine. If anything, that makes me want to try to convince you even more. I'm not into the stuff you are, but I do care about you a lot. Your enemies are the things I can't see, so I can't do anything but hope."

"Oh, Roshan."

She hugged him tightly. She knew how it must have felt, which was part of why she was trying so hard to keep her fear from him. She hated it when her own friends put themselves in danger, and here she was doing the same thing to Roshan. The sooner this was over, the better.

"I assume that still means no, but that you appreciate the thought?" Roshan quipped, and Maaya giggled.

"Go get some sleep; you have to be up soon. I promise I'll be safe, and I'll keep the others safe, too. I'll let you know if I find out anything, ok?"

"I'll tell my dad he's in good hands."

With that, they said goodbye, and Maaya stood at the door until Roshan passed out of sight a few blocks down. She felt a lump in her throat, as she often did when she didn't want a conversation to end but there was nothing left to say. She consoled herself by remembering that they would see each other again soon one way or another, and that for now, all she had to worry about was finding a comfortable position on the sofa.

She closed the door quietly as she re-entered the house. Saber hadn't moved far. The ghost lingered hesitantly near the door, as though there was something she wanted to say but hadn't yet figured out how to do so.

"You okay?" Maaya asked, walking over to the sofa and pulling the worn blanket down from the back.

"Maybe we should stay out of trouble. Just this once," Saber said hesitantly. Maaya paused and looked up at her, and Saber continued, "I mean, there must be *someone* else out there who can see ghosts who can take care of something like this. Why is it always us? Whatever that was, whatever we saw out there, we don't stand a chance against that. Not at all. I think Roshan has the right idea asking us to sit this one out for a while."

Maaya shook her head.

"I can't. I won't ask you to do anything with me, but people are in real danger now. You and me and the others, we have a gift very few people have. If we don't put that to use, this could continue. It was a whole street this time, but it could be worse next time."

"There might not even be a next time!" Saber protested.

"In that case, you have nothing to worry about."

"Look, I'm just saying—"

"Enough, please," Maaya said tiredly. "If you don't want to join me, then don't. But if what happened there can happen again, there's no way we can sit this out. And in case you didn't notice, this thing can hurt ghosts, too. I'm going to look out for my own like I always do, and that includes you."

Saber nodded apologetically, then floated silently upstairs, leaving Maaya with only the company of the dwindling fire. Maaya put a few more logs into the small fireplace, then lay down on the sofa, falling asleep almost instantly.

. . .

Maaya had been looking forward to sleeping until at least the early afternoon, but the sun had hardly risen before she was awakened by a loud pounding at the front door. Momentarily disoriented, she sat bolt upright, looking around for the source of the noise. When she realized there was someone at the door, she leapt from the sofa and grabbed an old broom that sat in a corner on the other side of the room.

The pounding came again, louder and more impatient this time. Maaya's mind raced frantically. Had someone with a grudge found out where they lived? If so, why were they bothering to knock? At the same time, it couldn't be anyone they were familiar with; anyone she knew was typically wise enough to leave her alone during the day while they slept.

Saber appeared at the bottom of the stairs and darted to the door, peeking her head through it. A moment later she turned around, and while Maaya was slightly comforted that Saber's expression was one of confusion and not fear, she wasn't sure she liked that, either.

"It's Rahu. He doesn't look happy. You'd better hurry."

"Oh, wonderful."

Maaya sighed and put the broom back, then strode quickly across the room. She opened the door and squinted as the glaring sunlight attacked her eyes, so she didn't notice Rahu immediately push his way across the threshold. Maaya nearly lost her balance and might have fallen if Saber hadn't been behind her to catch her. Rahu thankfully didn't notice, but Saber had been right—he did not look pleased.

"I'm sorry, were you sleeping?" Rahu asked in a tone that made it clear he genuinely did not care. Maaya was about to answer, but Saber stopped her.

"Don't be tricked. If you say you were going to sleep all day, he'll know you were out last night."

"It's okay, I was about to wake up and start cooking breakfast," Maaya answered, ever thankful for Saber's shrewd input. "Is everything all right? Do you have a new job for us?"

"Not yet, and if you keep acting so foolishly, it may stay that way," Rahu said sharply. Maaya was stunned. She wasn't sure what she possibly could have done, and it wasn't like Rahu to be so openly antagonistic.

"What do you mean? I thought our last client was happy with—"

"This isn't about our *last client.* This is about you and your friends traipsing about in the middle of the night and causing disturbances all over town. Imagine my surprise when I heard rumors of four children wandering the scene of a crime, and causing damage, no less? You think because you occasionally are ordered to take care of my business that the night streets are your playground?"

"No, sir, I—"

"Let's be absolutely clear here. I own you, and I expect at least a *measure* of decorum from those I employ. If any of you get into trouble, there's nothing I can do for you, nor would I if I could. If you want any more assistance from me you will do as you're told, and only as you're told, do you understand? You aren't a free agent anymore. My work may not be fun, but it puts food on your table and keeps you out of trouble. You're the adult here, Maaya. Think of your friends before you selfishly put everything you have in jeopardy."

Maaya's gaze fell to the floor. His words were a mix of condescension, cruelty… and truth. Going out to Mayberry Street had been foolish. She knew that before she went, and her experiences there only solidified that, but she hadn't imagined Rahu would ever find out about it.

At the same time, she thought she detected the tiniest hint of concern in his voice. Sure, most of why he wanted Maaya and the others to stay safe was because they were his tools, and he couldn't profit off broken tools. All the same, she couldn't help but wonder if there was something more to it than that buried under years and years of selfishness, anger, and narcissism.

Suddenly, Saber spoke.

"Tell him you went there for his benefit. You figured he would be best for the job since the circumstances were so mysterious, and that you felt it would greatly help his already growing reputation and help get him more work."

Maaya blinked. She hadn't thought about that. Maybe there was a way out of this after all. She took a deep breath, then dared meet Rahu's eyes.

"Actually, uhm… the only reason we went out there is because we figured there was something supernatural at work. We… we figured that if we could find out what happened, we could tell you about it. Everyone's frightened and everyone wants answers. We thought it might be a good job for us—for you." Rahu's expression didn't change, but he remained silent, which Maaya took as an indication to keep speaking. "You're always the one coming to us with work. We thought we owed it to you to take some initiative."

"That's all very well, but why go out in the middle of the night immediately after the crime occurred? That seems suspicious, you must admit," Rahu answered slowly.

"The sooner the better," Maaya replied, and as she continued, her confidence grew. "If we get on this right away, that makes you the first person to take charge. You would be there before anyone else. If you could solve this mystery before even the police could, that would look really good. We wanted to find the answers for you so all you'd have to do was show up and we'd handle the rest as usual."

"I have a hard time believing that you would be motivated to go to such lengths out of altruism alone. My reputation stands fine as it is," Rahu said, but Maaya detected a faint glimmer of doubt in his eyes.

"To tell the truth, sir, it's for us as well," Maaya replied. "When you get a lot of work, we get enough to eat. That's all we want. You've always provided for us, and I've worked for you for years. I want to show you that I can be more than just an errand girl. And especially after what happened a few nights ago, I… I want to prove myself."

Rahu raised an eyebrow.

"Admirable, but unnecessary. So long as you get the work done, I don't care about your ambition. You have no need to prove anything to me. When work gets done, you get paid. That has always been our deal, as it always will be. That said…" Rahu paced the room, his gloved hand to his chin, and Maaya noticed with some relief that he appeared more relaxed now. "If you decide to take some initiative, I suppose you may. But you are to be far more careful about it than you were last night. This does not change our deal—you are not to be seen, and you will not get credit for any of this. You will, however, continue to be taken care of, and if you are so lucky, you will receive my gratitude."

He spoke the last word as though it was unfamiliar and distasteful to him, but Maaya was more surprised that he had said it at all. There was no gratitude in business, not even reluctantly.

"I understand. I apologize for our sloppy work," Maaya replied, hoping to sate him and get this conversation over quickly. As far as she knew, the others were still asleep upstairs, and she didn't want them to wake up to Rahu's presence.

However, it appeared Rahu wasn't done yet. To Maaya's dismay, he took off his coat and hung it on the rack near the door, then took a seat at the kitchen table.

"Onto business, then," he said, beckoning at Maaya to sit with him. She did so unenthusiastically, not wanting to get any closer to the man than she had to. "Tell me everything you found out about the crime scene last night."

"It was strange. I'm sure you heard the rumors that everyone on the street just disappeared, which is why we went to look. It looks like everyone died at once somehow; their ghosts were all still there, every one of them."

"Every one? That means hundreds of ghosts on that street alone. There's the potential for far more of a disturbance than might be caused by just one or two," Rahu said thoughtfully. Maaya could practically see gold coins dancing in his eyes.

"That's true. They were also very unhappy. That's where some of the damage came from, not from us," Maaya continued. She felt terrible to lie about such a thing, but if Rahu discovered the truth, there was still time for him to ruin everything.

"What did you do, then?" Rahu pressed.

"We… uh…"

"Tell him you sealed them all, but that no one else knows yet. There's still time for Rahu to drop by, work his magic, and then promise that no further disturbances will happen there," Saber instructed from her side.

Maaya passed this message along, and Rahu sighed, but he didn't look upset.

"Ah, so you took care of it already. I wish you would have told me that. You're cutting this very close, you know," Rahu said.

"I'm sorry. There were so many of them, and I thought—"

"Yes, I know what you thought. Fine then. I suppose I'll have to stop by immediately if there's any hope of still taking advantage of this. Now… what caused this? Why did they all die?"

"More angry spirits," Maaya said. It wasn't *technically* a lie. "I've never seen anything like that, but we destroyed them, too. We've been on top of keeping them at bay in Sark."

To Maaya, that was vague enough to sound plausible without actually explaining anything. Rather than looking perturbed or puzzled with this lack of information, however, Rahu looked troubled. But in an instant, his expression was back to its impenetrable apathy.

"I see. How unfortunate. Let's hope this doesn't happen again. If it does, I hope you're able to find out something more definitive." Rahu stood up promptly, then took his coat from the wall and put it on impatiently. "I'm going to go take care of the mess people still think exists down there. You know I've always appreciated your drive, Maaya, but I thought you were smarter than this. Do be more careful next time. Oh, and when you complete a job before I know about it, I expect to be informed more expeditiously. Are we clear?"

"Absolutely."

"Good. I'll let you know if this goes well. In the meantime, rest up. Just because you're finding additional work on your own doesn't mean I'm going to give you any less."

And then he was gone.

Maaya slumped over onto the table, resting her head in her arms. That had been a close one.

"Well, that was certainly interesting," Saber said thoughtfully.

"How do you mean?"

"Something you said frightened that man. I've never seen that look on his face before, but I wouldn't mind seeing it again," Saber continued, a hint of malice in her tone.

"Frightened? By what?" Maaya sat up, fighting the urge to keep her head down and simply fall asleep at the table.

"No idea. It was when you told him how all those people died. It's probably just his mortality kicking in. The living are so very afraid of death, especially the rich ones—with all their money and power, it's the one thing they can't avoid. Anyway, you should get back to sleep. I'll keep an eye on the kids and make sure they don't wake you too early."

"Yeah, good idea."

Maaya stood up and stretched, then made her way wearily back to the sofa. Saber followed hesitantly, then took her usual place on the arm of the sofa next to Maaya's pillow. She opened her mouth like she wanted to say something, then looked away.

"What?" Maaya said.

"Listen, about last night…"

"Don't, please," Maaya said softly. "I shouldn't have been harsh with you. I'm sorry. I know how you feel, and if this were a different situation I would probably listen. I'm just afraid that if we don't figure out what's happening, none of us will be safe, not even in hiding."

Saber fidgeted.

"You're probably right. I just want us all to make it out of this one day. Get that big house you always talk about. Things are starting to get more dangerous and I'm worried."

"I know. I want this to end as much as you do. Let's make sure we're safe, take what last jobs we can get from Rahu, then get out of here. Maybe we can even go to Krethus and start a new life. If nothing else, it can't be worse there than it is here."

"That's the spirit. No pun intended," Saber said, and Maaya snorted. "No hard feelings?"

"Of course not! I always want you to speak your mind. Especially when it's saving me from Rahu…"

The girls laughed, then shared a hug. Maaya hadn't realized how much she needed it.

9

THE STRANGER

Sleep didn't come as easily as Maaya hoped, and instead she spent most of the day drifting in and out of consciousness. She was vaguely aware of her friends waking up and getting quiet bites to eat as Saber shushed them repeatedly, but also aware of the disturbing dreams that flickered in and out of sight, so interspersed with reality that she often had trouble telling the difference. After one particularly frightening dream where she found herself being pulled into the gaping black sky while looking down at her own lifeless body below, her eyes snapped open to make sure she was still safe at home.

As she rested, she tried to think. She knew Saber was right about one thing: surely there had to be other people with the ability to see ghosts out there. The fact that she had picked up three other children in her own town alone was hopefully proof of that. But if any more were out there, she wasn't sure how she would find them. She was too busy now. What's more, even if they were out there, there wasn't any guarantee that they would fare any better solving this mystery—if they were even aware it existed in the first place.

Eventually, Maaya made a decision. Saber probably wasn't going to like it, but she would just have to deal with it.

Finally, as the sun started its descent, Maaya finally sat up and rubbed her eyes. She hadn't slept very well, but it was the best she was going to do. She cursed Rahu under her breath and stood up. The first floor was quiet and empty, but she heard her friends talking quietly upstairs, and so she made her way to the kitchen to see if there were any leftovers.

"There's some bhatura and curry left if you want," Saber's voice came from nearby as the ghost floated lazily over to Maaya. "Sleep well?"

"Not really," Maaya murmured, pulling out a worn plate from the cupboard. "I feel more rested, though."

"That's all right. You guys get to stay in tonight for once, so no pressure. Want me to go nick a board game from somewhere? I was thinking about exploring that new toy shop across town anyway. I'd give it back, promise."

"I, uh…"

Maaya looked determinedly away from Saber and down at her food. Saber raised an eyebrow and put her hands on her hips, and for a moment Maaya feared she was in for another attempted lecture. But then Saber sighed exasperatedly and rolled her eyes.

"Oh, all right then. Where are we going?"

Two hours later Maaya and Saber stood at the end of the dock near the nearly-frozen river. With them was Styx, Sylvia and her crow, and Milo. If Maaya wasn't already used to this, it would probably be one of the strangest gatherings she had ever witnessed, and that would be saying a lot.

"How ye feeling, Maaya? Better?" Styx asked gently.

"Much better, thank you," Maaya answered warmly. "But I wanted to see you all because something happened in the town last night. Something big."

"Oh, don't we know it," Milo replied. "We felt that all the way out here. Then again, I figured the whole world would know about it, seeing as it was the sky itself opening up on us."

"Do you know what happened?" Sylvia asked placidly, as though she were mildly interested in a weather event that happened elsewhere.

"I know a few things, but I was hoping you could give me more. We heard the entire street got wiped out two days ago and that everyone just disappeared, so we went to investigate. They were all dead, and their ghosts were all there. When I asked them what happened that morning, they had no idea. They just thought it was odd that everyone in town was ignoring them."

"Did any of them see anything?" Milo asked.

"Nothing. Only a single one of them even realized they were dead," Maaya said, feeling her heart sink again as she thought of the little boy.

"And their bodies?" Milo pressed.

"Gone. There was no trace of them or any struggle."

Milo shook his head.

"Figured as much. Well, that only tells me one thing, and I'm guessing you've already arrived at the same conclusion, my friend."

"I didn't see it happen, but it sounds like what you told me about the ghosts on the hill that night," Maaya said softly.

"Now hang on, it's not the same," Styx interrupted. He adjusted himself slightly where he sat, causing the whole dock to shake. "Accordin' to Maaya, all those ghosts were still around. But Milo said even the ghosts of the guys livin' up there on the hill disappeared. Got sucked right up, wasn't it?"

Maaya shivered. She had forgotten that part.

"They weren't around for long," Saber said. "We had a brief encounter with them, but then..."

"When the sky opened up like that, when it was like the whole thing was just ripped open... every ghost on the street, hundreds of them, were sucked into the sky. They all disappeared," Maaya finished.

Everyone fell silent. Maaya was starting to fear it was unarguably true. Whatever this new type of ghost was, it was still around, and it was more dangerous than any Maaya had ever encountered. What's more, it was a danger to both the living *and* the dead. Maaya couldn't imagine where such a thing could come from, and this utter lack of any information frightened her.

Saber, sensing Maaya's unease, put a hand on the girl's shoulder, then spoke to the others.

"That answers that, then. Now, do you any of you know any more details that might help? Where these ghosts come from, what their weaknesses are, or any signs of their presence we can watch out for?"

"I got nothing. Then again, I only saw 'em the once. Far as I know they just appear right on top of you, and then it's already too late," Milo mused.

"Much as I can tell, there aren't too many of 'em," Styx grumbled. "I've been out 'ere this entire time for months and not one's approached me 'cept the one chasin' after you, Maaya."

'I noticed something," Sylvia offered quietly, and everyone turned to face her. Looking unaccustomed to so much undivided attention, she shifted her gaze downward. "Ghosts who are already ghosts should be safe from them. Those things, the walkers, they only seem to go after the dead if they're the ones that killed them."

"Now that's interesting..." Saber said thoughtfully, her eyes narrowing. "So their only targets seem to be the living."

"Now you mention it, that seems to be it. But then why would they do that? The living are gonna die anyway; trying to speed up that process is just a waste of time and energy," Milo reasoned.

"Because people aren't just dying. That'd be bad enough, but something is happening once they hit the other side, and it's a power we don't understand at all," Saber answered. "We can reason the intentions of these ghosts all we like, but what happens after is arguably even more important, especially since we have no idea what causes it or where it comes from."

"Some people were talking about it being a Krethan weapon... do you think there's any truth to that?" Maaya asked.

"Nah. The Krethans would never have time and resources to devote to something like this to kill people when they could just use good old-fashioned weapons instead," Milo answered confidently. "At least back when I was alive the Krethans weren't doing so hot. Not that we were either, but being equally terrible at least meant neither one had the advantage."

"I almost wish it were them—at least then we'd have an explanation," Maaya sighed, pinching the bridge of her nose.

"Seems to me there's only one way to keep the good people of Selenthia safe. We just gotta kill everyone before these weird other ghosts do!" Milo continued cheerily.

"Knock it off, Milo," Styx growled.

"What? Could you imagine the looks on their faces? Well, suppose you couldn't, seeing as how they don't have faces, but you get me."

"Hey, Styx..." Maaya started, and Styx looked away from the one-eyed ghost. "Your ocular implants let you see the weird ghosts too, right?"

"Unfortunately," Styx said.

"Do you know who made it? Maybe... maybe we can find out a way to get more, to let everyone see the ghosts. If everyone can see them they'll at least stand more of a chance."

Styx shook his head sadly.

"A fine idea, but as far as I know there isn't a gearworks or steamsmith in the whole town. Not in a place like Sark. No market or money for them. You'd have to convince the governments they'd be necessary to combat a threat no one but you can see, and I'm sure you can guess how well that'd go over. Not to mention most people don't believe in ghosts anyway, so they wouldn't make devices to see 'em with; this 'ere's a special one."

"So what can we do?" Maaya asked despairingly.

"Don't you worry too much yet," Styx said consolingly. "Don't forget, you can hurt 'em with your cards. I know I said to keep safe, but it seems like that isn't much an option anymore, so now I say give 'em hell. Send 'em back to whatever rock they crawled out from under."

Saber crossed her arms and nodded confidently, and Milo pumped his fist, but Maaya didn't feel any better. Just attacking these ghosts the same way they did all the others wasn't going to be enough, she could feel that much. There was some greater power at play here, one whose motivations were irrelevant. Her mind kept replaying the vision of the great red scar in the sky and how utterly helpless she felt under its vast emptiness. Nothing she knew about *libris* or the afterlife had prepared her for this. How naïve she felt, to think that what she knew now was how the rest of the world worked. To think that it was so simple. She thought her gift and her cards gave her power, when in reality they simply let her into a world where she was nothing more than an unimportant guest.

"Right, so we know the big tall ghosts and the sucking away into nothingness are related at this point," Milo posited.

"Fat lot of good that does us," Styx said, but Milo interrupted.

"No, s'great! See, this simplifies things a whole lot. No matter which way you look at it, it all starts with those weird ghosts, right? So all we gotta do is get rid of them and all the other problems will stop. Doesn't matter what powers they've got, they can't use 'em if they don't exist. Easy peasy."

Maaya had to admire his optimism, even if she wasn't sure she agreed with his assessment of its difficulty. Still, it was hard to argue. It seemed, for now at least, that a return to basics would be their best chance of success—at least until they discovered something better.

"I guess that settles it then," Maaya announced. "We'll just have to focus on taking them out just like we've done everything else. I just hope it'll work."

"It should. You've got the best team working with ye, after all. These new ghosts won't know what hit 'em," Styx winked, and then his expression turned more serious. "This'll probably be tough, but if anyone can do it, it's you lot. Just be careful. You know that's all I ask."

"There can't be an infinite number of them, anyway," Sylvia said calmly. "Eventually, you'll win."

With nothing left to discuss, the friends said their goodbyes and headed their separate ways. Sylvia and her crow opted not to walk Maaya and Saber home, a fact which pleased Saber visibly.

"That went well!" Saber commented as they headed down the dark empty road back to town.

"Did it? I feel like we don't know any more than when we started," Maaya replied glumly.

"Sure it did! We might not know too much more about them, but we know that doesn't really matter. All we have to do to them is the same thing we've spent years practicing on every other ghost we've ever met. How convenient is that?"

"I suppose…"

In response, Saber patted her lightly on the shoulder.

"You just need a good night's rest. If you feel up to it after that, we can go chasing some normal ghosts for a while and get your adrenaline pumping. It'll be all right, you'll see."

It wasn't long before they arrived back at the house. Faint candlelight still filtered through the curtains, and as Maaya opened the door, the smell of a freshly made dinner met her nose. If Rahu really did intend to let them work more, this was going to become a more frequent occurrence, and Maaya was quite all right with that.

"Maaya! I'm glad you're back. I was worried you'd be out all night again."

To Maaya's surprise, Roshan stood in the kitchen, deep frying koftas and preparing gravy on the stove as Sovaan stood on a chair nearby, watching their progress eagerly.

"What are you doing here? Have you decided not to sleep anymore?" Maaya asked, a small smile flitting across her face.

"I've told dad I've come down with something. After I fetch the water and get everything prepped for the day, he lets me sleep a little. Anyway, there was something important I wanted to talk to you about."

"What is it?"

"While we eat. Here, help me with this."

They worked together while the others set the table. Saber peeked over their shoulders, looking enviously down at the food they were preparing until finally Maaya shooed her away. She was slightly concerned at Roshan's reappearance so soon, but if it was something that could wait to be talked about over dinner, it must not have been all that troubling.

Soon the table was prepared and everyone sat down to eat. For a few minutes there was only silence, interspersed with the sounds of clinking silverware and glasses. Though Roshan's visit had been a surprise, evidently the others had been planning on a big dinner anyway, and their stomachs had been pining for it all day. Luckily, it turned out Roshan made an excellent malai kofta, and Maaya forced herself to slow down to enjoy the flavor.

As eating slowed, Roshan wiped his mouth with a napkin and cleared his throat.

"Right. I wanted to tell you something interesting my dad learned earlier today. There's a new wealthy guy in town—and he's working with Rahu."

Maaya didn't so much as look up from her plate.

"What, Rahu working with another wealthy man? I'm shocked."

"It's not just that," Roshan scoffed. "First, let's be realistic. Who wants to *come* to Sark? Most people with money try to get out. Secondly… dad thinks he might be a Krethan."

This time, everyone looked up at him.

"What makes you say that?" Maaya asked.

"Dad only got a glimpse of him, but it was pretty clear that they were both trying to avoid being seen as much as possible. Apparently this guy didn't look like any Selenthian he knew, and he guessed they knew that and didn't want to attract any attention. And here's the funny bit: they didn't head off to Rahu's mansion. From what dad said they were walking up east —toward Mayberry Street."

"Oh! There's a reason for that," Maaya explained hastily. "He came by earlier today because he apparently found out we were there last night, and he was furious. Saber managed to get me to convince him we did it to make him look good, so he went off in the morning to go wave his arms around and speak gibberish or whatever he usually does."

"He did, but this was a second time, in the afternoon. I don't know if he actually went there, but they were in a hurry. Dad said Rahu looked a bit nervous."

"Okay, that part is a little weird. But still, Rahu spends a lot of time with rich people. That's his thing. And so what if he knows a Krethan? The war is politics for us bottom feeders to pay attention to, it doesn't actually concern—"

"Don't overestimate him, Maaya," Roshan said quietly. "He's rich by Sark standards, but otherwise he's just another fake holy man profiting off other people's misery. The world is full of those. He's nowhere near important enough to have Krethan contacts; that's banned even to most province-level politicians. A Krethan wandering around here is definitely out of the ordinary, and if Rahu has his ear, that's even worse."

"Why? If Rahu is such a big fish in a small pond, what could…?"

Maaya trailed off. She had been about to ask how Rahu could possibly benefit from any allegiance with a Krethan, but she realized had been thinking too narrowly. A man of Rahu's ambition could certainly stand to make a profit by working with a Krethan—especially if that Krethan had ulterior motives. What those motives might be she had no clue, but she wouldn't put it past Rahu.

"Dad thinks he might be a spy or a scout or something like that. He's a man of money, that's for sure, and there's no reason for a wealthy guy from the other side of the world to come here unless he had a very specific purpose."

"What purpose would that be, though? Sark is nothing to anyone," Maaya argued.

"Yeah, I remember. That's what you said when everyone on Mayberry Street disappeared."

These words hit Maaya like a brick. She thought the idea of a Krethan attack on Sark to be ridiculous, and so far nothing had come along to substantiate those claims—but now there was a Krethan here of all places. This wasn't necessarily proof of anything, but it didn't look good.

"That man… how long has he been here? Do you know?" Maaya asked slowly.

"About a week, if that. Dad asked around and reports varied, but that's his estimate. I was going to bring that up because I wanted to ask if you knew how long these attacks had been going on. Mayberry Street wasn't the first, was it?"

No one at the table was eating now. Even if the others didn't understand the depth of Roshan's implication, they understood well enough to know that whatever was going on in Sark was likely not some mysterious and random event.

"So, if I understand what you're saying…" Maaya said slowly.

"I don't know anything for sure. All I know is that some seriously dangerous and weird stuff started happening ever since that guy arrived," Roshan replied.

"But why would Rahu help that man?" Sovaan asked intently. "Rahu lives here; why would he mess that up on purpose?"

"He's got money. He can leave whenever he wants. Maybe this new guy is offering Rahu more money than Sark is giving him. You think he wouldn't throw this entire town under the bus for some extra coin? If he's got any alliance with the Krethan, he can live anywhere in the world."

"And you think this Krethan is testing a weapon here," Maaya continued. "But why get Rahu's help for that?"

"I'm not sure. The only theory I have isn't something you want to hear," Roshan answered, turning his eyes away from her. As his four living friends raised their voices in protest however, he relented. "All right. Look. This weapon deals with ghosts, right? And Rahu's the guy who deals with ghosts in this town."

"Yeah, but that'd make the Krethan some idiot," Kim said hotly. "Rahu can't even see–"

"Which makes me think that this stranger knows about *you*," Roshan finished.

Maaya felt like she might throw up. This was too much information to take in, especially on a full stomach. There was a chance that a stranger was testing a deadly weapon in her town, and that the stranger knew about her and the others. She didn't know what that meant for them or how much danger it put them in, if any at all, but at the very least, she knew that she and her friends may have been unwillingly pulled into something far, far bigger than they could ever imagine, or want.

"Now, before you panic, let me remind you I don't know anything for certain—" Roshan started, but Maaya cut him off.

"Then why tell us? Why come in here and scare us with this if you don't know? This is terrifying, Roshan! We can't afford to live without Rahu's help and now you're saying there's a chance he could be involved with a plan to wipe Sark off the map! If this new offer of his is so tempting, he'll get rid of us right away. If we're lucky enough to hold on to our lives in whatever comes next, we won't be able to keep them for long," she cried.

"That's not true," Roshan pleaded. "Besides, I thought you might want to know because you have an advantage neither of them have. You can *see* the results of this weapon. You can fight it when no one else can. Besides, no one suspects you of anything."

Maaya's blood ran cold.

"That's not true. He knows we went to Mayberry Street. I told him that we talked to the people there. I didn't explain the details, but he definitely knows we saw something strange there, maybe something he thinks we shouldn't have seen."

"Sure, but he's visited you since you went there, and nothing bad happened, did it? Rahu wouldn't wait around if there was that big of a problem. He still needs you."

Maaya was about to respond when Saber interjected.

"Now, hold on a moment," she said pensively. "Our detective here could very well be wrong, but this is still valuable information. Rahu is dealing with a new man, potentially a foreign enemy, and it's clear that he doesn't want news of this relationship to spread. I think it's worth keeping an eye on these two to see what other juicy tidbits we can find. Maybe there's some other information Rahu doesn't want anyone finding out about... maybe even information he would pay to keep hidden if someone were to threaten its release."

"You're thinking of blackmail at a time like this?" Maaya asked, aghast.

"Why not? If we find that this Krethan is responsible for the weapon, all we have to do is take him out. He's just a single living human," Saber replied simply. "Then, once that problem is taken care of, we take all our proof to the authorities. Rahu goes down, we're heroes, and the government has information on this secret new weapon."

"That sounds bold, even for you," Maaya retorted.

"Now is a time to *be* bold. Let's find out what they're up to. I happen to be invisible, which makes this job infinitely easier, so why not? Worst case scenario, the stranger is just some weirdo, there's no threat at all from him, and we're back to dealing with just the one threat."

Maaya sighed. Roshan already looked confused, and Maaya wasn't sure she had the energy to explain it to him. Luckily, Kim jumped in.

"Saber thinks it's a good idea to spy on Rahu and his friend to find out what they're up to. If there's something fishy going on, we can get proof and use it against him."

Roshan nodded.

"I was thinking that'd be a good start. Since there's the risk that this guy knows about you—and Rahu definitely does—I'll do the spying. I'll ask if any of dad's friends can join me. Neither of them have any idea who I am, so it'll be easy."

"Saber also volunteered, and no one can see her," Maaya said irritably. She appreciated that he was willing to help, but was also upset that he had come over just to drop this news on them. She was already trying to figure out why an entire street full of people disappeared; she didn't need to be involved in any potential relationship with her country's mortal enemies.

"That's a clever thought, but we don't know anything about this stranger yet. Since he might be responsible for these ghosts, he might be able to see them, too," Roshan mused.

"He has a point, and that frustrates me," Saber sighed.

"You would really be okay doing this, Roshan?" Kim asked quietly.

"Absolutely, yeah," Roshan said enthusiastically. "I'll get some friends together and we'll track these guys. They won't have any idea. In the meantime, you guys just sit tight and keep doing what he wants. But since he just had a big job for you I have a feeling you won't see him any time soon. Maybe you can focus on figuring out the ghost part."

"Maybe."

Maaya didn't want to deal with this anymore. She hadn't slept well the night before thanks to Rahu, she had already been out to see Styx and the others to try to deal with the disappearances on Mayberry Street, and now this. There was only so much she could emotionally handle in one day, and she needed to sleep.

"Ah, listen," Roshan said awkwardly. "I'm sorry about this. I know this isn't great news but I figured some heads up would be most useful. Something big is going on, and I just want you to know that you've got some friends helping you try to figure it out."

"Thanks. I appreciate it, I do, this is just… so much to deal with right now," Maaya replied weakly.

"Well hey, when this is over, we can celebrate, yeah?" Roshan suggested, a genuine smile on his face. "When my parents hear we fixed all these problems, I'm sure they'll want to treat you guys."

Maaya forced a smile. She was ready for this conversation to be over.

"I look forward to it. In the meantime, if you're going to be so busy, you should go get some rest."

"Yeah, you're right. I want to be up early to talk to dad about this. I'll send you updates whenever I can, okay?"

Maaya nodded, then guided her friend over to the door somewhat more forcefully than she intended. Roshan seemed to finally understand that it was time to cut things short, and so without another word, he vanished into the night.

Maaya closed the door hard, then bolted it shut. When she turned around to head back to the table, her friends quickly lowered their heads and began eating again. Only Saber glanced at her, raising an amused eyebrow.

The silence didn't last long. It didn't seem like anything could dampen her friends' spirits. After a brief discussion about what they heard from Roshan, which consisted mostly of incredulity that Rahu would be capable of doing anything bad, they turned to other matters. Maaya hardly paid attention as she picked at her food, but she was glad for the distraction. All she wanted to do was finish her food and then sleep.

"Hey, cheer up," Saber said quietly at her side, not wanting to draw the attention of the others. "We've got plenty of time to do our own thing while Rahu's distracted with his new buddy. You can finally get a good night's rest. You need to do that before you think about anything else."

"I hope there's still a town to wake up to tomorrow," Maaya murmured glumly.

"Of course there will be. You're still here." Saber nudged her shoulder playfully. "I'll keep an eye out as usual, and if I see anything you'll be the first to know. Keep your cards out, and by the time anything gets close, you'll be ready to shut them down."

"You really think we can fight them?" Maaya asked.

"We already know the cards affect them, and from what we know they just kind of glide around slowly. Not exactly the picture of a threatening opponent."

"But how do we know if getting rid of them will do anything if we don't know where they're coming from?" Maaya protested.

"Let Roshan and the others work out that stuff. For now, keep doing what you do best, and it'll all work out. Also, get some *sleep*." At this, she raised her voice so that the other could hear. "That goes for all of you, all right? You've got time to catch up, so use it wisely. And if any of you wake up Maaya during the night…"

"We know, Saber, we'll have to deal with you," Kim laughed, thoroughly unintimidated.

After every last bite had been eaten, the dirty dishes were piled up to be dealt with later, and everyone started preparing for bed. At Saber's suggestion, everyone kept their deck of cards near their pillow as a precaution, but she stressed that she doubted it would be necessary.

All the same, as the last candles were being blown out, Kim walked slowly up to Maaya as she folded down her blankets from the top of the sofa. It took a moment for Maaya to notice, and when she did, Kim wouldn't meet her eyes.

"Is everything all right?" Maaya asked concernedly.

"Yeah, everything's fine, I just… uhm, I was wondering… can I sleep down here tonight? With you?" She bit her lip as she finished her sentence as though trying to punish it for letting these words escape.

"Of course," Maaya replied gently. "Did Roshan scare you?"

"All of this scares me," Kim answered simply, finally looking up at her.

Maaya pulled her into a long hug, and she could almost feel the relief wash over her younger friend. She held her close. She didn't say it often enough, but she was grateful to the others for their presence alone. They stuck together no matter what obstacles they faced, and after spending years of her life completely by herself, Maaya relished this company. She wasn't one to realize what she had only after it was gone.

After a minute, Maaya finally let Kim go, then turned to the old couch, her hands on her hips.

"Well, there's not too much extra space here, but if you're willing to squeeze a little we can share the blankets."

"I'd like that."

Darkness fell in the house as Maaya and Kim lay their heads down and Saber left the house to go on one of her nightly prowls. Kim fell asleep within minutes, but Maaya stayed awake as the events of the night played over and over in her mind. The more time that passed since the conversation, the better she felt. Maybe Saber was right. Things were going to be okay somehow.

She repositioned herself slightly, trying not to wake her sleeping friend, and finally closed her eyes. At the very least, she thought, she was thankful for not having to see Rahu again for a long time.

10

THIEVERY

THE TIME MAAYA enjoyed without Rahu's presence lasted from the moment she closed her eyes until the moment she opened them again.

The sun was high in the sky already, and Maaya felt wonderfully rested. She took a moment to stretch, taking a deep breath and then letting it out slowly as her back cracked. These were the moments she lived for.

Kim was still fast asleep, so Maaya got up slowly and stepped over her to head toward the kitchen. Even if no one else was awake, it was definitely time to get something for breakfast. She took a moment to appreciate how she could simply now walk to the cupboard and look for something to eat, much as she was sure most other residents of Sark had done their entire lives. But this was rare for her, and each step closer to the kitchen was something to savor.

She hadn't quite made it when she heard a tapping at the window. She looked over, and at first was unable to tell what was making the noise, so dirty and cloudy was the glass. But as she got closer she recognized what it was, and her mood darkened almost immediately.

Standing on the windowsill was a small mechanical bird made entirely of gold and silver. It was hardly larger than a hummingbird, but was designed to be just as sleek as one. Rather than a solid body, its frame was constructed of thin metal to minimize its weight, and Maaya could see the gears and other mechanisms turning and clicking inside. Only its eyes differed in color; they were two tiny green jewels that peered almost irritably up at Maaya through the glass.

Maaya sighed. While others might have looked at it as a technical marvel, it was only a nuisance to her. This bird belonged to Rahu, and it delivered his messages when he couldn't be bothered to show up at their door.

Immediately after Maaya opened the window, the bird flew in, landing deftly on one of the coat hooks near the door. It waited for Maaya to approach, tilting its head expectantly.

"What is it?" Maaya asked impatiently.

The bird opened its tiny beak, and a tinny and crackly version of Rahu's voice emanated from within.

Maaya. I have another job for you. This one is top secret. I can't be seen in your area right now—important business to attend to—thus, the bird. Listen carefully. You're to go to the following address: Corridor B, Westshire Street, Unit 12. It's an abandoned mansion. You aren't hunting ghosts this time; you're looking for something for me. There's a red gem somewhere in that house, and you have a deadline: tonight. Keep any other things you find for yourself if you'd like. Hang on to the gem until it's safe for me to come see you in a few days. I'll send a bird in advance. Also, you must not be seen under any circumstance. I would do it myself if my absence here wouldn't look suspicious. Now, you have your orders. Do this well and I will see to it that you are very well rewarded, but fail, and… well, I'm sure you're imaginative enough to think of the consequences.

The bird shut its beak as the recording ended, then tilted its head again. Maaya rushed to get something to write with and hastily scrawled down the address. She muttered something bitterly about Rahu not being bothered to repeat it, but she was certain she had gotten it right. After a moment of silence, she seemed to remember the bird was still there, and she glanced up at it, throwing it a withering look.

"Yes, I got it all. Go back home."

The bird immediately opened its well-oiled wings, and without a sound, it disappeared out the open window again.

Still grumbling, Maaya walked over and shut the window behind it. It was bad enough that Rahu himself occasionally came around, but if he kept sending his contraptions here, people would start asking questions. Only the wealthiest people in Sark had any kind of technology like that. This lack of technology didn't bother Maaya, but what did was the possibility of jealous eyes fixating themselves on an old house where this technology sometimes visited.

Kim stirred on the sofa, and Maaya let loose another stream of quiet curses at the bird for waking up her friend. Then she jumped as Saber peeked her head through the wall next to the window.

"Ha! That doesn't get old," the ghost laughed quietly, then pointed backward over her shoulder. "What was that about? Don't tell me Rahu's talking to you again already."

"He is," Maaya glowered. Saber came in and sat innocently on the arm of the sofa, ready for details. "He's got a pretty basic job for us, except there are no ghosts involved this time. He wants us to go search some abandoned house to look for something he wants."

Saber didn't appear surprised.

"I never thought I would look forward to a boring assignment, but here we are. Then again, if Rahu wants something, it must be important. What's he want?"

"Some gemstone, I guess. He just told us to look for it and hang on to it for a few days until he can come get it from us."

"Huh. So he wants us to search through an old house for some jewelry that might've been left behind? How original. Did you tell him half the town already does that?"

"I don't even care," Maaya shrugged. "It's easy, and he said he would reward us really well if we did it right, so we're going to do it right."

"Fair enough! I won't ask questions. This seems almost insultingly easy, but I'll take it over what happened the other night. Speaking of which, let's take tonight off. Let's have a night together where we're *not* witnessing or causing mayhem of some kind."

"We can't. Rahu said the deadline is tonight," Maaya explained as she started back toward the kitchen.

"If he isn't even going to see us for a few days, how's he going to know?" Saber asked pointedly.

"I'd rather not tempt fate, especially not when it seems to hold some kind of grudge against us already," Maaya replied. "And this doesn't mean you can start asking questions now. We've broken our policy too much already."

Saber pouted.

"Well I just think it's weird, that's all. Where are we going? If it's not far, we can be in and out with enough time to relax when we get back."

"I wrote down the address as best I could. I don't recognize it, so I'm going to let Sovaan take a look at it when he gets up," Maaya answered absently as she started making breakfast. If anyone knew this address by memory—and could draw a map with directions to it—it would be him.

Saber floated over the table and frowned down at the scrap of paper.

"Oh, now this is interesting. Corridor B, huh? We're talking some serious money here."

Though much of Sark had been haphazardly thrown together, there was some structure to what constituted the downtown area. There were a number of "corridors," which were essentially districts, going from A to F. The wealthiest district was A, and they grew progressively poorer. Corridor B wasn't the very wealthiest area of Sark, but many less important politicians and successful businessmen lived there in mansions with enough space for several houses of the size Maaya lived in and then some. Thankfully, it was not a gated district like Corridor A was. That would have made things considerably more difficult.

Maaya remained unimpressed.

"That's probably why we're being 'paid' so well to do this. Come help me with breakfast."

"It's never fair that I have to help cook what I can't eat," Saber muttered, but she went to help nonetheless.

It was early afternoon by the time everyone else in the house was awake, and they spent the day doing what they usually did: hardly anything at all. Once their stomachs had been filled, they continued to rest, saving their strength for the night to come. Cards were drawn to replace the ones used on Mayberry Street a few nights prior, but that was about all the effort they were willing to expend.

Maaya was slightly frustrated at their looming deadline. Being forced to completely the job tonight meant they had no time to scope out the premises, which meant they would playing the whole task by ear. Saber could hypothetically scout things out, but the area would not be the same during the day as it was during the night. On top of that, Saber had no way of showing them anything she saw—they would have to rely on her descriptions alone.

Nonetheless, Saber flew off to see what information she could glean before it came time to head out. Maaya almost wished she had stayed; she was feeling reclusive lately, and the only company she really wanted was Saber's, if she had to have company at all.

Still, when Sovaan came over to sit next to her, Maaya didn't protest.

"You look lonely," he said simply. Maaya smiled down at him.

"I'm just thinking a lot lately, that's all. How are you holding up?"

"Good! I'm not afraid," he answered determinedly, fending off an accusation yet to be made. "I'm sad there won't be any ghosts tonight. The ones across town were all so friendly at first. I'm sad we had to fight them."

"Me too. Unfortunately, things don't all go the way we want them too," Maaya sighed, putting her arm around the boy's shoulders.

"They were just scared and it made them act funny. That's why I'm not afraid," Sovaan said thoughtfully.

Maaya laughed.

"That's good! I think if more people could see what we see they wouldn't be so afraid."

"Or mean," Sovaan said bitterly. "It doesn't make sense people would get angry at us for being able to see things they can't. They're probably just jealous."

"What doesn't make sense is they get mad at us for seeing ghosts but they give Rahu money because they think he can, too. What's the difference between him and us?" Kalil grumbled from the kitchen.

"Presentation, probably," Kim answered. "We aren't nice-looking rich people who can make their problems go away, so we're witches instead."

"We're not all girls, though, so we can't all be witches," Sovaan pointed out. "Hey Kalil, let's open a business! We can do like Rahu does!"

"Oh? And what about me and Maaya?" Kim asked, raising an eyebrow.

"You come with us, of course," Sovaan replied like it was the most obvious thing in the world. "We show people girls can do just as much as we can and maybe they'll calm down a bit."

Kim seemed to approve of this answer, because she smiled faintly and turned back to finishing up her cards.

Saber floated in casually an hour after sunset, looking completely bored.

"This job is going to be the worst," she groaned immediately. "No one on the street seems to leave their houses, and the house we're after is completely empty. There's some security, but minimal. We shouldn't have any trouble getting there, searching it, or coming back."

"What took you so long, then?" Maaya teased.

"I went around the neighborhood a bit to see if anything would liven me up. Thought I could get some juicy gossip from the neighbors, but they just sit there in their suits and dresses *harrumphing* over the newspaper or talking about going to some party with other equally dull people. If this was how I spent my days alive we might have to seriously consider my death was a case of suicide," Saber continued, dragging her fingers down her face, and the others laughed.

"Hey, did you go in any of the big houses?" Kalil asked keenly.

"I did! I couldn't resist. Why?" Saber inquired.

"Just curious: what happens when a ghost goes into a living room?"

Saber opened her mouth to give a thoughtful reply, paused, and then rolled her eyes.

"Har de har. I'm genuinely surprised I haven't heard that one yet."

In any case, Saber's presence meant that it was time to go. As everyone pulled on their shoes, Saber disappeared again, scouting out the nearby streets to make sure the coast was clear. Upon her return only minutes later, the five friends started out into the cool empty streets of Sark. Sovaan led the way, and they moved cautiously, but there was not another soul outside. Most sensible people were probably already asleep. It wasn't until they reached downtown some thirty minutes later that they started to slow down.

Downtown was something Maaya wasn't accustomed to, and she wasn't very fond of it. The buildings were tall and tightly clustered, but mostly clean, and the light of the multitude of streetlamps reflected off the glass of storefronts and office windows. The cobblestones were well kept and smooth, and gentlemen in suits and ladies in puffy dresses walked here and there for no discernible reason. Horses and carriages also trundled through, driven by men in long coats and silly hats. It was all very pretty, if a bit ridiculous, but Maaya didn't like it. More light meant a higher chance of being seen. She glanced down at her clothes before she could stop herself. Being seen here was definitely not a good idea.

But Sovaan's knowledge of the streets didn't falter, and they passed only a few blocks to reach one of the many entrances to Corridor B. Unlike Corridor A's gated and highly secured entrance, every street into Corridor B was simply decorated with a wall of stones and neatly trimmed rosebushes. A few guardhouses stood lonely on the corners, but no one was in them now that it was nighttime. *Not when it would make the most sense to have them there,* Maaya thought.

They slowed once again as they made their way down the sidewalk, though this time it wasn't out of fear of being seen. The younger ones gaped in awe at the size of the houses, the cleanliness of the streets, and the fountains of clean water that were placed only for decoration. Even in the dark it was easy to see that there was color here. There were sweeping lawns and flowers and trees, all well trimmed, all very tidy. It was hard to believe that something like this existed less than an hour from where Maaya lived, but people like her had no reason to come here. There was nothing for them here, and anyone who didn't have the presence of mind to sneak would be turned around long before they entered the higher corridors.

As they walked, Maaya had a sudden realization: she had been here before. She hadn't been able to place the feeling of familiarity at first because she had only been here once, but she had definitely been down this specific street four years ago. When she had gotten the news that a rich family had moved out of one of the mansions there, she had endeavored to be one of the first to claim its treasures. Unfortunately for Maaya it had been almost completely emptied when she arrived—with the exception of a single sword and a silver circlet.

If she had been asked to go back to that particular mansion, though, she'd never be able to do it. There were multiple mansions left unoccupied given the state of the economy, and it was also possible that another family had since moved in. At the time, she had been so concerned with getting in and out safely that she had little idea what the home itself even looked like. Still, it was almost a pleasant walk down memory lane despite the circumstances. Saber had never been here before, having been awakened from the gem only after Maaya got home, but for Maaya it was like reliving an old dream.

"We're here," Sovaan announced.

Distracted by her thoughts, Maaya hadn't noticed they had walked almost four blocks into the corridor. She turned to survey the building in front of her. It was huge, much like the others, but completely dark. The neighbors on either side had taken great care to manage the plants on their own sides of the property, but left the rest to grow wild and unchecked. The walkway to the front door wound through tangles of weeds, which had also taken over every dark lamppost on the way. The house itself, however, looked as though it were simply unoccupied. None of the windows were broken or boarded, and there were none of the other signs of abandonment and decay Maaya was so used to. She figured that's when the other residents of the street would finally have enough and ask for it to be taken care of lest their poor eyes have to rest on such a dilapidated sight over breakfast.

She squinted at the front of the house to make out every detail she could, wondering if by some wild coincidence they were looking at the same house she had broken into years before. Logically, however, it made no sense; if it had been all but wiped clean within days of the original family leaving, it was almost a guarantee that nothing would remain. That meant this home had belonged to someone else… the question, of course, was who.

"Now who would go and leave a place like this all abandoned?" Kalil mused, his chin in his palm. "I say The Ghost Hunters deserve a new place to live, seeing as this castle is on the market and all."

"That would never work, and you know it," Kim chastised, but she was having difficulty taking her eyes of it.

"I see why this might be a little more challenging than we originally thought, though. Searching a place like this won't be a quick job," Saber said.

"Let's try to make it quick anyway," Maaya said nervously. At her friends' inquiring glances, she continued, "I don't want to be in a neighborhood like this longer than I have to. The sooner we're out, the sooner we're safe."

They fought their way to the front door, and to Maaya's great surprise, it was unlocked. As they entered, Maaya found out why.

The inside of the mansion was completely empty. The floor, walls, and ceiling were all bare, as were the countertops and windowsills. Not even any carpet, rugs, or curtains remained. It was as though the house had only just finished being built. Only the thick layer of dust that coated everything gave evidence to the contrary.

"Well, that makes things a little easier," Maaya whispered, and even her barely audible voice seemed to echo in the cavernous emptiness. "Split up like usual. You three, top floor. Saber and I will take this one. Stay armed and ready. If there are any surprises here, make sure you're the ones giving them."

With that, the group split up, moving out across the empty mansion without a sound. She wasn't worried about their thoroughness; while Rahu's instructions were vague, it wasn't like red gemstones were all that common, and it wasn't like there would be anything else here. She was sure squatters wouldn't last long here, not in a neighborhood with regular patrols and nosy neighbors. What did instill doubt in her was the thought that any house abandoned for this long would have anything of any value left in it.

She was glad for Saber's presence as the ghost peered around every corner before letting Maaya pass. The ghost briefly left to check for an attic —which houses of this size usually had—but returned minutes later saying the attic was just as devoid of anything at all as everything else.

That left only the possibility of the yard and potentially a basement. Wealthy homeowners often indulged themselves with private wine stores and sitting rooms, neither of which were likely to hold jewelry, but some people came up with creative ways of hiding their riches. Maaya wished she had thought to tell the others to look for hidden passages or compartments, but in retrospect, she guessed they probably already knew that. If nothing else, it was a job for Saber.

Deciding to leave the yard until last, the girls looked around for an entrance to the basement. Luckily, this was much easier to find; a door off one of the kitchens led to a plain wooden staircase that disappeared into total darkness. Maaya could get by with even a little light, but she couldn't properly move around with no light at all, and so she waited while Saber flew off to get a candle from one of the others.

Though by now they had ascertained that no one else was in the house with them, Maaya was now very uncomfortable almost to the point of being frightened. The more she thought about her task, she more she expected something to go wrong; maybe it was a trap, or maybe they would get spotted. She determinedly avoided looking at the staircase, afraid that if she looked down too deep, something would reach up from below and pull her into the void.

She shook her head quickly. She was better than this kind of childish thinking.

Luckily, Saber soon returned, carefully holding a bright candle. Maaya welcomed the light, but glanced around apprehensively. Even if a ghost was holding the candle, anyone could see its light.

"Let's get below quick," she murmured, and Saber agreed.

The staircase was much shorter than Maaya expected, and once she reached the bottom of the stairs she realized the basement wasn't very large, either. It extended maybe twenty feet in both directions and, like the rest of the house, was completely barren. She could see all four corners in the dim light of the candle, and this comforted her a little. However, her persistent feeling of discomfort was even stronger here. Something felt very wrong, and it was centered here in the basement—whatever it was.

"Hey, you all right?" Saber asked, nudging Maaya gently. "You look spooked."

"I'm fine. I just don't like being in a place like this for very long; it was hard enough to get in and out without being seen last time."

"Fair enough. Well, we're almost done. Let's search this basement, and if we don't find anything, we'll get the kids and figure out what to do then."

Saber flitted toward the distant corners of the room, and Maaya chose to look under the stairs. She ducked, but it seemed not even spiders wanted to make their home here.

She squinted. She couldn't tell if the ground was covered in dirt or if the dust was simply that thick, but she peered down at it carefully, looking for anything that might reflect in the candlelight. She moved some of the dirt with her shoe, exposing a bit of rough wooden floor beneath.

The more she stared, the more familiar this all seemed. She fought the idea that she had been here before; it wouldn't make sense that a house abandoned for this long would have anything left of any value, much less what Rahu wanted. A piece of jewelry being left in a place like this for longer than a few hours would be a miracle.

She glanced up at Saber, who was still determinedly searching the corners of the basement. Maaya had to hand it to her; she was undeterred by the thought that other thieves might have gotten there first, and she floated slowly along the wall, peering at the dust below, the candlelight glinting off her circlet and the gem inside it.

The red gem.

Maaya gasped.

Saber was at her side in an instant.

"What's wrong? Are you hurt?"

"No, I… this…" Maaya stammered, looking wildly around. She knew this place. She *had* been here before after all. In this exact spot under the stairs, no less. And so had Saber. "This is where I found you. This basement, right here, it's where… it's where I found…"

The thoughts connected in Maaya's head too fast for her to verbalize them. She should have seen it the instant Rahu's bird had given her the directions. Rahu wanted a red gem. A red gem from an abandoned mansion in a neighborhood she'd been to before. That seemed like an awfully familiar story to Maaya, especially now, as she stared at the circlet on Saber's head.

Saber's mouth dropped open for a moment, and then she whistled.

"Oh stars, that's quite a coincidence. To think Rahu is after *this* old thing. I wonder how he knows about it. Not even I know where it's from, and if it was found down here by a common thief—no offense—it must not have been well known. Or valuable. Hey, you listening?"

Maaya couldn't speak. Her uneasiness had been replaced by dread as the realization of their situation started to sink in. The gem Rahu was after, being worn by a ghost, was quite literally invisible to the rest of the world, and there was no way to change that. Rahu wouldn't be getting his gem, and that meant only that his nebulous *consequences* were sure to come.

It took a moment of prodding, but finally, Saber got Maaya to speak.

"We're doomed. We're completely doomed," Maaya said, too overwhelmed to even focus her eyes on her friend. She fell to her knees on the dusty floor. "Rahu very specifically wanted this one thing, and it's the one thing we can't give! He threatened that there would be consequences if we couldn't get it. We'll be out of a home for sure, we'll be out of food…"

Saber put her hand under Maaya's chin and gently lifted so Maaya was looking into her eyes.

"Now, don't you start that," Saber said sternly. "We are absolutely not doomed, and Rahu will still get his gem."

"How?" Maaya asked desperately. "I couldn't take that from you even if I wanted to! And even if I did, he still couldn't see it!"

"Oh, you sweet, innocent child," Saber smiled. "If our guesses at my age are anywhere near correct, this gem has been missing far longer than Rahu has been alive. Meaning Rahu has no idea what the real thing actually looks like. *Meaning,*" Saber continued with emphasis, "that I can nick any old lookalike gem from some store or rich person in town and he won't know the difference."

"I… but…"

"No, hold on, it gets better," Saber explained, now grinning widely. "See, if Rahu or anyone else comes to check here for the gem on his orders, it won't be here, which means they'll all know we did our job. That also means we're safe in case he's decided to test us. And, as a bonus, if I steal some important person's jewelry, and Rahu is found to have it? Well, he'll be in a spot of trouble, won't he? But either way, he'll get his gem, and we'll all be safe and fine. We *will.* Understand?"

Maaya nodded speechlessly, then before she knew what was happening, burst into tears of relief. Saber, who looked like she had been expecting this, put her arms around Maaya's shoulders.

"There now, you see? We're going to be fine," Saber said soothingly, running her fingers through the girl's hair. "Though I wish you'd remember I was dead more often; it'd save you a lot of stress."

Maaya laughed despite herself. Saber had a point. The ghost had helped Maaya out of more messes than she could count by taking advantage of her invisibility and cunning, including many dealing with Rahu. There was no reason why this had to be any different. There was, of course, the mystery of why Rahu would be looking for this particular gem, but they could work on that later.

"I'm sorry," Maaya said weakly, her nose already stuffy from crying. "I shouldn't get so worried so fast."

"It's all right!" Saber said, wiping the tears from the girl's cheeks. "We haven't got a lot, so the thought of losing it is tough, especially when Rahu's pulling the strings. But we'll be all right, and that's a promise."

Before Maaya could let relief wash over her for much longer, she heard rapid footsteps approach the doorway at the top of the stairs. She glanced up quickly, but saw only Sovaan standing there.

"We gotta go. Someone's coming," he said quickly, then vanished.

Maaya and Saber shared a look of alarm, then hurried upstairs. The others were waiting for her in the kitchen, motioning at her to follow them. Maaya extinguished the candle and rushed after them through a back door to the yard, where they quickly ran to the wall at the edge of the property. From there they made their way slowly toward the street under the cover of bushes and low-hanging trees. Maaya kept her eyes peeled for any signs of movement, and she quickly found it.

A man in a suit and cloak made his way up the walk toward the front door, making absolutely no effort to hide himself. He held a walking stick in one hand and a large bag in the other. At the top of his walking stick was fastened a small lantern, and from the light, she caught the glint of a bronze ocular implant. He opened the front door as though knowing it was unlocked, then stepped inside without pause.

"Who is that?" Kim whispered, watching the light from the man's lantern filter through various windows.

"No idea. We should get out of here," Maaya responded. "Did any of you leave any traces that you were there?"

"Nope, not a one," Kalil answered. "Closed every door we opened and brushed any footprints we left."

"Ah, we weren't quite as careful. I'll go brush away our footsteps in the basement," Saber said quietly. "You guys go on; I'll only be a minute. Or maybe I'll stay and see what this guy is up to?"

"If you do, don't follow him in the open; he's got an implant, so he might be able to see you," Maaya instructed.

Saber saluted, then floated back toward the house and out of sight. Maaya watched anxiously, but the movement of the light didn't change. She would have stayed longer if Kim hadn't tugged at her sleeve.

They made their way swiftly up the street, which was just as empty as it had been on their way down. It was slightly darker now as most of its residents had gone or were going to bed, and only once did they have to hide from a lonely patrol, but that was the only semblance of trouble they encountered.

The group stopped a block away from the entrance to the downtown area, somewhere they were sure Saber would be able to find. Here it was bright enough to be seen, but not an area where four poor children resting against the wall would seem wholly unusual.

Maaya's friends turned to each other, eager to share what they had seen—or not seen, as was the case—but Maaya couldn't focus. She felt emotionally drained, and she was still concerned about Saber. Then there was the issue of the stranger and what he had been doing there, as well as the mystery of Saber's gem and what Rahu wanted with it. There were far too many unanswered questions for her liking, and she didn't know how to find answers for any of them.

It took almost half an hour for Saber to arrive. Maaya searched the ghost's expression for any sign of what happened, but she appeared as bored as usual.

"What happened?" Maaya asked quickly as Saber approached, waving nonchalantly.

"A whole lot of nothing is what," Saber scoffed. "I cleared any traces we left then just watched him dawdle for a bit. It looked like he was searching for something, but he didn't seem very comfortable doing it. He was probably worried about getting dust on those fine shoes of his."

"What do you think he was looking for?" Kim asked curiously.

"I can only assume he was looking for the same thing we were," Saber posited. Maaya looked up in surprise, and Saber shrugged. "It just fits. That's why Rahu wanted us in there tonight. My guess is more than one person knows about this gem and he wanted to make sure he got to it first. And the only people to know about such a thing would already have money, and this stranger most certainly did. But he won't find it, will he?"

"Why not? Did you guys find it?" Kim demanded.

"Yep!" Saber said, then laughed and tapped the crystal in the circlet on her forehead. "Maaya remembered she found this very gem in that basement we were just in. Turns out Rahu is looking for this! How funny is that? To think it's been hovering right in front of his ugly face for years and he had no idea. But like I already told Maaya, I'm just going to grab some similar-looking gem for you guys to give to Rahu and everything will be all right."

The others snickered. It was unlikely they were concerned with the details of any of this; all that mattered to them was that the job was as good as done. Even Maaya, whose brain was working overtime to find her something to panic about, couldn't resist a smile at the thought that they were also pulling one over on Rahu at the same time.

"All right, kiddos, you should get home and rest. While we're here, I'm going to find myself a nice fancy jewelry shop to steal from. Only the best for Rahu, after all," Saber said gleefully.

With that, she dashed off down the street toward the bright lights and men in funny hats. The others, eager to get back to their comfortable darkness, turned and started back home.

"So what do you think Rahu's gonna get us?" Sovaan asked excitedly.

"Probably more food. He'd never give us money," Maaya replied, but she didn't mind. Food was the best possible thing they could get. If they got any lavish gifts or money, they'd just get food with those anyway.

As they approached their house, Maaya saw a familiar face nearby. Once again, Roshan Kulkarni stood at the door. This time, however, he looked quite upset. As he noticed them approaching, she saw relief wash over his face even from a distance, and without waiting for them to arrive, he rushed over to meet them.

"Where on earth have you all *been?*" he asked hurriedly. "I've been waiting for an hour at least!"

"I'm sorry, Roshan. Turns out Rahu had another job for us. It was an easy one this time," Maaya said, hoping to comfort him, but he looked even more nervous at this news.

"What was it? Who was the job for?" he asked forcefully.

"He… he said it was just for himself this time," Maaya said, taken aback. "It was a simple job; he just wanted us to steal something from an abandoned mansion on Corridor B, that's all. No ghosts, no danger, nothing."

Roshan ran his hand anxiously through his hair, then stared directly at Maaya.

"That's what I was afraid of. But you're all safe? Saber, too? Did you see anyone else while you were there?"

"Yes, of course, we're all fine. We saw someone else, but it was just some rich man. He didn't see us. What's wrong, Roshan? You're scaring me," Maaya replied slowly.

"Whatever you were sent to do, the job wasn't for Rahu. I found out something earlier, something I was hoping to tell you before you left to do anything for him." Roshan stepped closer, lowering his voice. "He's interested in an abandoned mansion in Corridor B, probably the one you went to. The only reason I know is because one of dad's friends overheard him talking about it with his client. Or maybe partner, I should say. The person who has business there isn't Rahu, Maaya. It's the Krethan."

11

THE FIRST WALK

THIS TIME, Maaya didn't have the energy to send Roshan away. She hadn't yet mentally recuperated from the stress of his last bad news, and now here he was with more. At least that's what she thought. Roshan's concern was infectious, but if she tried to focus just on what he was telling her at face value, it didn't sound so bad. But then she became concerned at the disparity; if she wasn't very worried but he was, then obviously she must be missing something.

It took a polite nudge from Kim to get Maaya to realize she had gone almost a full minute without speaking, and now Roshan looked like he might panic. Eager to avoid making a scene in the middle of the dark street, she tiredly gestured over at the front door.

"After you."

They entered quietly, the younger ones hurrying to light candles so they wouldn't bump into any furniture, and then they sat down. Maaya took her usual spot on the couch this time; if she was to be bombarded with bad news she was going to do it from a place she felt comfortable and safe.

"So what's the disaster this time?" she asked, and it came out a little more rudely than she intended. "Er, sorry."

Roshan waved it off.

"Whatever you did tonight, it was because the Krethan wanted it. He and Rahu were talking when the subject of the house came up. I don't know anything more than that, but it's no coincidence they were talking about the house just before Rahu sent you over to it. What was it he wanted, anyway?"

"Like I said, it was a simple theft. He claimed there was something in the house that he wanted urgently. Either way, he's not going to get it, because what he wanted wasn't there," Maaya answered tiredly.

Roshan looked only slightly relieved at this news.

"Just a theft? What would he have you steal from that old place?"

"He wants a red gem. I don't know how he knew it was there, but it's not anymore. The place was empty. I'm sorry, Roshan, I just can't be scared by this news. If we were working on some secret Krethan orders, I imagine it'd be something more serious than looting jewelry—that is, unless you think Rahu plans on proposing to him."

Kim, who had been sipping from a glass of water, snorted with laughter and started to cough.

"I don't know. Maybe it's nothing, but this job still has the Krethan's fingers all over this, and since we know they're working together, I don't like it," Roshan said.

"Hey, if you're gonna bring down the town, you might as well look good doing it," Kalil said from the kitchen sink.

"You should take this seriously!" Roshan protested.

"I'm sorry. We've been really busy lately and it's just hard to imagine this being something serious," Maaya said. "Besides, even if this was a job that worked to their ends somehow, we didn't accomplish what he wanted, so what does it matter?"

Before Roshan could reply, the front door opened, then closed again. Saber entered the room, triumphantly carrying a red gem in her hands that looked almost identical to the one on her forehead.

"Eh? Can I pick 'em, or can I pick 'em?" she said proudly, holding it aloft for everyone to see. "Even being invisible, it was a pain getting this one snuck out unseen. The doors were so secure I had to carry it up and out of the chimney, and then I was all sorts of turned around. What's he looking at me like that for?" she asked suddenly, looking at Roshan.

"He can't see you, remember?" Maaya smiled.

"Oh. Hullo, Saber," Roshan said with dawning realization, peering up at the stolen gem before him. "And you, expensive floating jewelry."

"Right. Ah, well. I figure this will do the job nicely. The best part is, it's really pricey. I didn't stop long enough to look, but I did see a lot of zeroes. Where should I keep it?"

"Hide it in the cupboard right upstairs, that should be safe enough until Rahu comes by to grab it," Maaya instructed, and Saber flew off to put it away.

"I, uh… I thought you said you didn't manage to find what he wanted," Roshan said distractedly, following the gem with his eyes. Maaya felt a flicker of amusement at how it must feel to watch expensive jewelry float right before his eyes.

"Long story," Maaya sighed. "It's a fake. It'll get him off our tails, and if we're lucky, get him into trouble. Saber suggesting pinning the thievery on him."

"That'll be the day," Roshan muttered. "Anyway, even if it's a fake and he's not getting what he wants, there are important questions we need to ask here. You of all people should understand how serious this is."

"I know I should probably be worried about this, but I'm not sure where to start. Honestly, I'm still processing what you told us last time. Help me?" Maaya replied.

"Right. Well." Roshan stood and began pacing, counting with his fingers as though he had already prepared an itemized list of discussion topics. "If Rahu and the Krethan are working together, why did they need you guys to get involved? And why this of all things? I can't imagine a gem being part of whatever weapon they're working on—"

"*If* they're building a weapon," Maaya reminded him.

"Or doing whatever has caused these deaths to happen, the semantics don't really matter at this point," Roshan said. "But you guys are involved, like it or not, so that brings us to the next question: are the Ghost Hunters aiding a Krethan? I don't mean that you want to!" he added quickly, seeing the accusatory looks on his friends' faces. "Just that if you're doing jobs for him, well…"

"I don't think so," Kim said immediately, though not unkindly. "We take each job as it comes. If Rahu asks us to do something we know is dangerous, we'd probably… I don't know…"

"And that's another thing you have to consider. If you have to refuse a job, what then? I'm sure my folks would let you guys stay a few nights while you get on your feet, but…"

"No, you're right," Maaya said thoughtfully. She pulled her knees up to her chest and hugged them, taking a deep breath and then letting it out slowly. "I'm not ready to ditch Rahu, if only because we don't know for sure what he's up to yet. We can't get rid of our only source of 'income' like that. But if what you're saying is true, we might have to make a big move."

"Shouldn't be so tough, we've moved before! And there are a ton of empty houses in Sark," Kalil said.

"No, you don't understand. If we stop working for Rahu, we won't be welcome anywhere in the town at all. He'll put out posters and imprison us —or worse," Maaya said darkly.

"That's if Sark still exists at all," Saber added, coming slowly down the stairs. "The way I see it, this can go one of four ways. One, we help Rahu and hope all our guesses about him are wrong, and we keep getting by. Two, we help Rahu, it turns out he is bringing about the apocalypse, and Sark gets wiped off the map. Three, we refuse to help Rahu and get kicked out of the town—if we aren't caught and burned first, that is. Four, we figure out what he's up to and expose him to the town before he has a chance to do anything."

As much as it helped to have it all laid out on the table like that, Maaya was distinctly uncomfortable again. She was quickly feeling overwhelmed these days, and this was a situation they could no longer escape. They were talking about potentially going up against a very powerful and wealthy man, and the odds that it could end well weren't good at all.

Roshan, who had just heard Saber's message relayed through Kim, spoke again.

"I think Saber's right. So options one and two are out; we can't just sit around and wait for something to happen. We need to look into this. If it turns out he's not up to anything suspicious, then things can return to normal, but if not… we need to know before they get even more ghosts to wipe us out."

"There's one thing I don't get. You're saying they're building a weapon together that makes these ghosts come and kill people, but if it's not done yet, how did it already happen twice?" Sovaan asked.

"It could be done already and they're just trying to make it better, or they have a prototype or something," Roshan suggested.

"How do you think they managed to build a weapon that controls ghosts? I didn't think there was anything like that, and I've been able to see ghosts all my life," Kalil wondered.

"Since we can see ghosts, it stands to reason some Krethans can, too. Maybe they thought to weaponize them while people in Selenthia were just shoving the issue of ghosts under the rug," Maaya responded.

"If that's the case, our job is pretty easy," Kim said, and everyone looked at her. "Well, we just need to find the weapon, don't we? Why don't we give Rahu the gem when he comes for it and then Saber can follow him to see where he takes it? I'm assuming they have to be near it to use it, so they'll lead us to it eventually."

"And if not, we can find out whatever other information we might need on the way," Saber added.

The message was passed along again, and Roshan shook his head.

"Easier said than done. They're taking great care to avoid being seen. It's all I can do to get information on the few things dad's friends have overheard."

"We have one advantage. Every attack so far has happened at night, which means that's when they're doing their thing. That's the perfect time for us to tail them. No one's out at night, not in the places that are being hit," Kalil said.

"Well, there was that one guy we saw," Sovaan said, and Roshan glanced over at him quickly.

"What? Who did you see?"

"It was after we were done exploring the mansion. Some rich man with a cane came up to it and went inside. Saber said he was searching the place, too, but she couldn't get too close because he had an implant on his eye like Styx does."

Roshan looked deeply troubled.

"That's almost definitely the Krethan. Rich-looking guy moving around at night with no one to see him, walking stick, implant… that has to be him. From what I've heard it's not the first time he's been there. And it's no coincidence he was there that night."

Despite herself, Maaya felt a shiver run down her spine. Not being involved in politics, she had never felt the hatred many politicians seemed to have for Krethans, but the idea that one had almost found them—and potentially on purpose—was unnerving.

But something about Roshan's words puzzled Maaya. If it was true that he had been to the mansion before, why was it only now they were being asked to retrieve the gem? Wouldn't the Krethan have stumbled across it already? The alternative was that the Krethan wasn't looking for the gem at all—and that meant he was using the mansion for another purpose.

When Maaya brought this up to Roshan, he nodded.

"That's my thought. I haven't heard of Rahu going there, but that might be on purpose. He might know he'd be recognized. People in Corridor B won't ask questions about someone walking the streets at night, not if he looks like he belongs, so he's probably sending the Krethan to do… whatever it is they're doing."

"Well then, this is perfect!" Saber said in that way that suggested anyone who thought this *wasn't* a ludicrously simple endeavor was out of their minds. "If that's their hideout then we don't even have to go looking for them. Let's hang out there again and see if he comes back, and if he does, we can find out what he's up to."

"I'm not comfortable working off that many assumptions. We don't know if that man was the Krethan, and we don't know if they're doing anything there. We searched the entire place top to bottom, remember?" Maaya replied.

"Well, sort of. I remember we were interrupted before we could explore the whole thing. Besides, it's possible he takes any equipment away with him whenever he leaves. He did have that big bag, remember? Anyway, what harm can it do? Either way we'll get more information, and you have to admit we're sorely lacking in that department right now."

The house fell silent as everyone looked at Maaya, and she begrudgingly accepted that, once again, she was going to have to be the one to make the call. She really, truly did not want to do this, but she didn't see any other choice. They had no other leads, and the lead they did have was shaky at best. But since there had been at least two attacks, one of which had wiped out an entire street, time was of the essence.

"Okay, we can do it," Maaya relented, and the others grinned. What joy they found in this job she had no idea. "But we need more than this. Roshan, we need people to follow both of these men on a regular basis. Even if we can't hear what they're saying, we need to know where they hang out, where they sneak off to. We need places we can investigate. I feel like we're winging it right now and that's not good."

Roshan nodded.

"I agree. I'll talk to dad tomorrow and see what he can do. As far as I know, Rahu's kept himself holed up at home when he's not meeting with the Krethan. Still, can't hurt to make sure."

"And if you hear *anything* about what might be a weapon, no matter how insignificant, tell us immediately," Saber instructed forcefully, then faltered, her eyes darting to Kim. "Er, you tell him."

"Hey, I think we should talk to Styx and the others," Kim suggested after she passed the message along. "One of the attacks happened out there, so someone must have seen something."

"They did, they saw that spooky ghost," Kalil said, and Kim glared at him.

"I *mean*, we don't know how this weapon works. Maybe the attacks happen wherever the weapon is. If these ghosts come out of nowhere like Styx said, they have to know where to show up, right? There has to be something that summons them."

"That's not a bad idea," Roshan said. "I guess we'll find out when we start having them followed. Hopefully I can get you some news by the end of the week."

"In the meantime we'll go stake out that old mansion. Tomorrow night should work. But I'll need one of you to stay behind," Maaya said as she turned to face the others.

"What? Why?" Sovaan protested, and the others quickly joined him.

"Because Rahu said he'll be sending a bird before he comes to pick up the gem. Someone needs to be here in case the bird comes by so they can quickly come let us know Rahu is on his way."

"Why couldn't we just give it to him ourselves? And why would he come at night?" Sovaan pressured her.

"Because if he sees only one person home he'll wonder what the rest of us are doing. I don't want him being suspicious of us right now. He would come at night to avoid being seen. And don't you get fussy with me, you're coming along; we need you for directions."

Sovaan looked pleased and sat back without another word.

"I'll do it," Kim said, and everyone glanced at her in surprise. Usually if anyone had to stay home during a mission there was at least twenty minutes of arguing that usually ended in drawing straws. "I, um… I'm feeling tired. I could use the extra rest."

"You just want to see *him* again, don't you?" Sovaan said, but was cut off as Kim quickly covered his mouth with her hand.

Maaya raised an eyebrow, but the expression on Kim's face said she did not want to talk about it, so she let it be.

"All right, then it's settled. We have our job for tomorrow night, so you all should get some rest. Roshan, you're welcome to sleep here, if you'd like," Maaya offered, but Roshan shook his head.

"I appreciate it, but I should get back. I'll tell dad what you told me so he can get started right away tomorrow. Oh, and… next time I'm bringing good news. Promise."

He smiled in that way he always did, and Maaya found herself feeling calmer already. It really was nice to know they weren't alone.

"I'll hold you to that," she said playfully as she got to her feet.

The others looked at her quizzically.

"Are we going somewhere?" Sovaan asked excitedly, having escaped Kim's grasp.

"The three of *you* are going to bed. Saber and I are going to talk to anybody we can find over by the river and see if we can't figure something out." As the others started to complain, Maaya continued, "If any of you come with us, I don't want to see you yawn even *once* tomorrow night or you're all banned from future jobs for a week. Deal?"

The others mumbled their disagreements quietly, but started upstairs to get ready for bed, Kim still glowering in Sovaan's direction.

Smiling, Maaya walked Roshan to the door, and then she and Saber headed off toward the town gates. For them, the night was still young.

THE FOLLOWING EVENING, Maaya was even more annoyed than usual. Their trip to the river the previous night had been almost completely worthless, except for Milo pointing out that he had seen a man walking up to the house on the hill once earlier in the week.

"He was a rich bloke, far as I could tell. Got one of them fancy eye things Styx has got. Figured he was inspecting the property or looking for squatters or something. Anyway, he only spent a few minutes in there before he left again, so I thought he got bored and left. Nothing interesting for people with coin up there," Milo had recalled.

Maaya knew that if she had heard this at any other time, she would have been mildly suspicious, but then immediately ignored it. It wasn't her business, and anyway, he hadn't spent much time there. She probably would have assumed the same and forgotten all about it by the time she got home.

This time, however, was different. If this was the person they thought it was, then it made all the difference in the world. The Krethan had supposedly been to the abandoned house on the hill, and they knew he had gone in the direction of Mayberry Street—both places where the strange ghosts had attacked and left everyone in the area dead.

Unfortunately, since in any other instance this man would have been almost completely unremarkable, no one else had bothered to pay any attention to him or what he might have been doing. They promised to keep a lookout in the future, but that didn't help them very much now.

In the present evening, her friends were more energetic than she had the capacity to deal with. Sovaan and Kalil were a handful on their own, and Saber was in one of her moods where she felt like joining them rather than telling them off. To make matters even more interesting, Sylvia had stopped by for one of her rare visits; while initially Maaya had hoped her presence would keep things calm, the opposite was true.

Kim, only halfway finished with her meal, had abruptly stood up and headed upstairs, informing the others she would write everyone's blood cards since she was staying home that night. On any other night the others might have been concerned at her sudden departure, but this time they took hardly any notice. After nearly half an hour Maaya decided to check on her, grateful for any excuse to get away from the noise.

Kim hardly looked up as Maaya knocked lightly on the door frame, busy with her work. But when Maaya sat down on the bed next to her and Kim still refused to meet her eye, Maaya guessed something else was going on.

"Is something bothering you?" Maaya asked gently. Whatever it was, Kim seemed more embarrassed than upset, which usually meant it would take a little prodding to get her friend to talk.

"Not if it's not bothering anyone else, no," Kim replied bitterly.

"Not if what's bothering anyone else? What's going on?"

"Have any of the others said anything? About me?" Kim asked, still focused intently on her cards. "I can't even stand to be around them right now."

Maaya was taken aback.

"What? Why? What did they do?"

Kim sighed and finally looked away from her cards, though she still wouldn't meet Maaya's gaze.

"Sovaan read my diary a few nights ago, and he found out that… he found out something, and he's been teasing me about it ever since. He brought it up last night. I don't know if anyone noticed, but if anyone else finds out…"

"Well, given that I still don't know what you're talking about, I doubt anyone else does, either," Maaya said soothingly. "The whole time I was down there for dinner no one said anything about you except wondering if you'd had enough to eat or if you'd be bored tonight."

Kim looked slightly comforted, and her expression of frustration gave way to one of embarrassment.

"That's good. So, hey, um… I don't suppose you've ever…" She trailed off, looking around the room as if she might find the words she was looking for lurking in a dusty corner. "How do you tell someone you like them?" she asked finally, staring at Maaya.

Maaya opened her mouth, but was silent. Just when she thought her friends couldn't surprise her anymore.

"I know, it's dumb. I shouldn't have written anything, and I shouldn't have said anything, it's just… I wanted to practice my writing since I was finally getting my letters down, and so I started keeping a diary. I didn't think Sovaan could read that well."

Maaya put a hand on Kim's shoulder, and Kim's cheeks turned pink.

"That's great! It's a really good idea to practice like that. Sovaan is young, but we'll have to teach him about boundaries. He shouldn't have done that. Now, to answer your question… I don't know. I've honestly never been in that kind of situation before. I always thought that if it came to it, I would just tell them. No games, nothing silly. But it's… well, it's definitely easier said than done."

"Really? You've never been in that position at all?" Kim asked, looking genuinely surprised. "I thought maybe you and Roshan—"

"Oh, no," Maaya laughed. "He's a wonderful friend, but he's not my type."

"What *is* your type?" Kim pressed, suddenly looking very interested.

"Women, to start," Maaya replied. "But don't change the subject; we were talking about you."

"Right. So… I know this is silly. I know relationships don't work for people like us. We're always moving, we're usually wanted by the law, and sometimes we don't have a home at all. I've been thinking about how to tell him I like him, but… maybe I just shouldn't say anything at all. I don't want to drag the rest of us down."

"Don't make any rash decisions just yet! Times are changing. Big things are happening. We're going to do everything in our power to make sure they change for the better, but either way, there's a policy I've always dreamed of someday living by." At Kim's curious glance, Maaya continued: "No regrets. Someday I want to be able to look back and say that I never missed a chance, that I never let something slip through my fingers. I haven't always been able to do that so far, but that's what got me thinking about it. I was going to wait until things were more stable, but there's no reason we can't start sooner. Do you want my advice?" Kim nodded. "Tell him. Don't plan, don't make a big deal of it, just pull him aside and tell him."

"But… are you sure? What if he says—?"

"If he says yes, you're on the same page and have a chance to do something about it. If he says no, you tried your best and don't have to worry about it anymore. Nice and simple, right? At least… it sounds that way. Honestly, I don't know if I'd be brave enough to confess my love to someone."

"Come on, you hunt ghosts for a living," Kim teased.

"Yeah, and I've encountered a thousand ghosts before. I've never encountered anything more than a crush before, and I never said anything about it at that," Maaya winked. "What is his name?"

"Anrik," Kim said, staring back at the floor. "I don't think you'd know him. We met at the water pump a few weeks ago and we've tried to see each other a few days a week since."

"That's a nice name. What is he like? What do you like about him?" Maaya asked, lying down on her side and resting the side of her head on her palm. Kim's cheeks burned red.

"Well, he's… he feels safe, I guess. With everyone else I talk to I feel like I need to hide, but it's different with him. He's never judged me for anything. He's always saying I could be anything and he'd still like me. I don't know, he's just… he's someone I feel like I can really trust, and I know I have you guys here, but it feels good to get that from someone else. Someone who met me as a stranger, who doesn't have any reason to pretend to like me, but he still does."

"That's sweet. Does he live nearby?"

"Sort of. A few miles east. He only showed up at our pump because the one in his neighborhood was broken, but now… well, he comes here whenever he can."

"So is he why you're staying behind tonight?" Maaya asked, amused.

"No. I mean, if he somehow showed up, that'd be great, but… I never told him where I lived. I just would rather stay home tonight and spend some time by myself," Kim replied quietly.

Maaya sat up and hugged the girl.

"You do what you need to do, and if there's ever anything I can help you with, you know where to find me," Maaya smiled. "Finish up and meet us downstairs."

"Okay! And… thank you. Really, thank you. It's nice to know I have someone I can talk to about this," Kim said quietly.

"You know I'm always here for you. Even if I don't have an answer, I can always listen," Maaya finished warmly, then walked back downstairs.

"Oh, Maaya, good of you to join us," Saber said as Maaya entered the kitchen for one last bite before their trip. She seemed in a better mood than before, this probably due to the fact that Sylvia was nowhere in sight. "I'm going to be staying here tonight, just so you know."

Maaya paused, her hand halfway to her mouth.

"Why?"

"I don't feel comfortable leaving a single person here alone, even if it is in the comfort of our lovely tiny home. Since Rahu's bird and Roshan have been coming around more lately, I'm worried they might be attracting attention. I'll just keep watch and keep Kim company while you're away. Plus, if any bird does come, I'll get to you much faster than she could."

"That's fair, I suppose. I hadn't thought of that. Aren't you worried you'll miss the action?"

"Don't remind me. Just take a moment to appreciate the sacrifice I'm making for you, that's all I ask."

The others laughed, then scurried to get ready. It was dark already, which meant they had little time to spare. When they had gone out last time the night had only been a few hours young before the alleged Krethan showed up, so they didn't want to risk missing him.

Kim came downstairs and handed everyone their cards, saving a few for herself just in case. Then she and Saber settled on the couch, already engaged in conversation as the others headed for the door, and Maaya found herself slightly envious. One of these nights she was going to stay inside overnight and spend some time relaxing with her friends.

The journey back to Corridor B didn't take as long as Maaya remembered, and twenty minutes later they wove their way expertly through the clean wide streets, avoiding the lights and the stares of passersby as though they had been traveling this area their whole lives.

Still, Maaya felt uncomfortable as they arrived at the abandoned house. This time it wasn't because of the strange familiarity of the area; she had solved that particular mystery. It was the absence of the others that bothered her this time. She was accustomed to traveling in a large group or with Saber alone. This in-between feeling was discomfiting, and she wished the others were here to watch with her.

They found a hiding place in the overgrown trees that gave them a view of most of the walk and the front door. They were doubly obscured by shadows and the low-hanging leaves of a massive willow. Maaya hoped it would be enough.

Minutes turned to hours, and still nobody showed up. Maaya caught herself fending off yawns, and as she looked over at the others, she noticed that while they were doing their best to pay attention, their tiredness and sheer boredom were getting the better of them. Stakeouts weren't their typical line of work. Whatever they usually did, they did on the move.

Maaya stood for a moment to stretch and alleviate the pressure in her aching muscles when she spotted a dark figure walking slowly up the path toward the house. Cursing under her breath, she dropped back down, silently alerting the others.

The figure walked slowly, casually, and didn't seem to have any idea he was being watched. All the same, as he walked up the path, Maaya and the others ducked lower, collectively holding their breaths. As the man passed, Maaya noticed he wore a long coat and carried a walking stick with a lantern in one hand and a large bag in the other.

"That's our guy," Kalil whispered, and Maaya nodded.

The man disappeared into the house as he had done before, and now Maaya really wished Saber were here. She stood a better chance of spying on him than any of the others did.

"Should we follow him?" Kalil asked quietly, and Maaya shook her head.

"It's too dangerous. We can't be seen."

"Well, how will we know what he's doing in there if we can't follow him in?" Kalil murmured.

"I… I don't know. Look, at least we know Roshan was right. For whatever reason he keeps coming back here and leaving no trace after he's gone. Maybe… maybe I can…"

She trailed off. She hated to admit it, but she hadn't thought of what they could do if the man actually came back. No matter what, finding out what was going on inside would take having someone inside the house, and that was simply too risky. If this kept up, however, it might be a risk she would have to take.

Maaya was about to tell the others to stay put while she took a quick look inside when something tapped her on the shoulder. She gasped before she could stop herself, then whirled around to see Saber hovering nearby.

"Sorry!" Saber said quietly, not teasing this time. "Why are we all so quiet? Is the Krethan back?"

"Yeah, he's inside. What are you doing here? Did we get a bird?" Maaya asked, breathing slowly to calm herself.

"Nah. Kim was getting anxious about you guys since it's been hours, so she wanted me to check on you really quick. She said she'd be okay. Anything I can do while I'm here?"

"Well, he's still inside, so I was thinking about going in alone. It's too risky for all of us," Maaya explained. "But now that you're here…"

"Say no more," Saber said delightedly. "I didn't think we'd get a chance to spy on our Krethan guest so soon. I'll go inside in a minute; let's let those people pass by so their light doesn't disturb our hiding spot."

"What people?"

In response, Saber pointed up the road. Far away at the very end of the street were at least a dozen bright white lights. They were so far away that Maaya hadn't noticed them at first, but now that she focused on them, she saw more and more with each passing second.

"What are so many people doing in the street at this hour? Throwing a parade?" Kalil asked.

"That's what I'd do if I had the money these people had," Sovaan chuckled. "There's not some sort of march going on, you think?"

"Nah, those aren't torch lights. But there really are a lot of them, aren't there?"

"Maybe we should…" Maaya started, but her words caught in her throat as dread washed over her like a petrifying wave.

She could barely make them out from this distance, but her excellent eyesight let her see enough. The lights grew brighter and brighter still, covering the entire width of the street. They moved slowly but uniformly, not bobbing side to side or wavering like any flame or lantern. As they came closer, she could just barely make out the outlines of tall white figures. Dozens of them. And they were coming straight for Maaya and the others.

"We… w-we need to…" Maaya stammered, but it was Saber who took charge.

"Oh, stars. They're here. We need to get out of here, now. All of you, come on, quickly now. Back to the road, head for home, and *do not* look back."

"Can't we fight them?" Kalil asked, standing on tiptoe to look at the approaching ghosts, but Saber grabbed him by the shoulders and turned him around.

"Not that many. We aren't all here, and there are way more of them than there are of us. I don't want to take any chances. Get moving. NOW."

The other three hurried out of their cover, staying low and in the shadows as best they could. Maaya expected at any moment to hear a cry from behind them as the man discovered they had been spying on him, but they made it safely off the grounds without incident. They walked swiftly, staring straight ahead under the strict gaze of Saber, but Maaya couldn't help it. She had to see.

She paused and turned around, keeping the ghosts in her peripheral vision. They hadn't caught up very much, as slow as they were, but she could see them washing over everything in their path. She couldn't help but notice that they weren't going directly down the street; as the street curved, they continued in a straight line—straight toward the abandoned mansion.

"Maaya, what are you doing?" Saber hissed.

Maaya didn't answer. She couldn't answer. The ghosts, tall, still, and silent, passed through every enormous house in their way. She watched the plants die and wither away between their floating bodies. A stray cat, sensing danger, made to sprint away, but it keeled over dead in an instant as the ghosts passed over it.

She had never seen anything like this before in her life. One of the ghosts had been bad enough, but now there were dozens of them. They formed an impenetrable wall, their gaping black eyes staring straight ahead, and Maaya suddenly realized why they made her so uncomfortable. Looking into their empty eyes gave her the same feeling as when she stared into the maw of the open black sky. That same desolation was found in every one of these… whatever they were.

Maaya almost couldn't breathe for fear, and she reached instinctively for her cards, but Saber stayed her hand.

"Not yet. They aren't coming for us. Don't attract their attention."

Sure enough, the ghosts continued straight ahead as though the rest of the world didn't exist. They floated slowly right toward the row of houses in which the abandoned mansion stood.

Suddenly, Maaya was struck by a horrifying thought.

"Oh god. Saber, there are people in those houses, all of them. If we don't—"

"There's nothing we can do, Maaya. Not against that many. We don't have time."

"But we can't just—!"

"Maaya, listen to me," Saber said, pulling Maaya's face so that she was staring directly at her. "There is *nothing* we can do. We aren't prepared for this. We–"

She broke off, then quickly grabbed Maaya's wrist and pulled her toward a line of shrubs in a neighboring yard. Maaya nearly cried out in pain, but stopped herself as she noticed the reason for Saber's sudden move.

The Krethan had exited the abandoned mansion just moments before the ghosts washed over it, and he sprinted to the sidewalk across the street, watching the ghosts pass through where he had only just been standing. He stared at them as they passed. Maaya couldn't see his expression from their distance, but it seemed to her that he didn't appear frightened by their presence; if anything, he was observing them. Studying them.

Maaya shuddered.

"Saber, it's… it's true," she uttered softly. "The Krethan, he… he's doing this. He's calling them somehow. He's calling them!"

Saber hovered next to her, her arms wrapped protectively around her friend's shoulders. The other two kept low, watching the ghosts in fascination and terror. They watched as the ghosts completely enveloped at least five mansions, leaving no room untouched.

Then, just as Maaya thought it couldn't get any worse, she heard the screams.

They were faint at first, simple cries of shock and confusion. But then came the shrieks of terror and desperation. Bright flashes of light emanated from the windows, and then the screaming was suddenly cut off. Maaya knew those screams. They weren't from the living who could see the ghosts. They were the screams of the dead. Maaya couldn't see what was going on inside, but she didn't have to. She remembered what Sylvia had said about the ghosts only taking away the spirits of those they had killed, and she thought she might be sick.

The ghosts continued on, unyielding and impervious, and through each building the same thing happened. Every time, the silent wave brought cries of pure horror in its wake, then cut them off as though death visited each victim swiftly a second time.

Then, just when Maaya thought she couldn't take it any longer, the ghosts vanished as suddenly as they had come, fading away in seconds until there was nothing left of any of them.

For a few moments all was still and quiet. Their eyes returned to the Krethan, looking for any reaction, but he too was still until, finally, he muttered something angrily under his breath and threw his hat upon the ground. He paced back and forth for a few moments, then picked up his hat, dusted it off, and stalked down the street in the opposite direction.

Maaya couldn't breathe. She couldn't think. Her brain struggled to process what it had just seen, as well as all the questions this answered. She had so much to tell Roshan. But first she had to make it home, and she didn't have enough energy to blink, much less get up and walk all the way home.

Saber nudged her softly, and Maaya started.

"Hey. You guys stay here. I'm going to check the mansions those things went through. Take some deep breaths and recover. I won't be long."

Maaya only nodded as Saber floated off, disappearing into one of the now-silent houses. She traveled between a few of them, spending only a few minutes in each one, then returned, her expression somber and serious.

"They… gone?" Maaya managed.

"Yeah. All of them. Gone like they weren't ever there," Saber answered, her voice quivering slightly. "Now we have our answer."

"Now we have our answer," Maaya repeated, getting shakily to her feet. "You guys okay?"

"I think so," Sovaan answered. "Is that… is that what happened to Mayberry Street?"

"Yeah. That's what happened," Maaya answered. Her body felt numb. All she wanted to do was to get home and collapse on her couch, the one place in the world where nothing could hurt her and where sleep would take her away from all this.

"What do we do?" Sovaan asked. To his credit, he seemed more inquisitive than afraid.

"We need to destroy them all," Kalil answered angrily, gritting his teeth. "We shouldn't have stood by this time!"

"There were too many of them to deal with by ourselves," Maaya said. "For now we need to get home to tell Kim what happened, and then we need to get a message to Roshan. Would you be able to do that, Saber?" Maaya asked.

"Yeah, I can do that. He's bound to still have paper and an inkwell in his bedroom. I'll make sure he wakes up to our report."

"Good. As for the rest of us, we still have to deal with Rahu when he decides to come around, so let's make sure we're rested for that."

"You don't think Rahu would be responsible for something like this, do you?" Kalil asked quietly, looking back over his shoulder as they started moving on.

"I don't know anymore," Maaya said. "I didn't think so, but… it's hard to argue what we just saw."

The others, mercifully, didn't seem to want to talk about it anymore, and they spent the rest of their trip home in silence. A small voice of hope in the back of Maaya's mind told her that now they had some of the information they desperately needed, but it was quickly shut down. This information came at a price, and it was one she would never be able to justify.

12

TO CATCH A KRETHAN

It only took a few minutes to fill Kim in on what she had missed, but to Maaya it felt like an eternity. When she answered the girl's seemingly endless questions, she made it clear that any further discussion was going to take place *after* they had all gotten some rest, and had gone resolutely to bed.

Though she fell asleep as soon as her head touched the pillow, she awoke early the next morning, bleary eyed, feeling like she hadn't slept at all. Given how tired she was, she struggled for a few moments to figure out why she had woken up at all until she heard a steady *tap tap tap* at the window. She leapt quickly to her feet and walked over to it. Sure enough, one of Rahu's birds sat on the windowsill, looking up at her expectantly.

She let it in begrudgingly, watching as it fluttered over to the kitchen table.

"Go on then, what is it?" Maaya yawned.

Good morning. I'm leaving my house to see you now. I expect to be there shortly. Make sure you have what I asked for ready by the time I get there; I don't want to stay long, especially not with something this valuable. I'm operating under the assumption that you succeeded—don't prove me wrong.

The bird didn't wait for Maaya to acknowledge the message before flying away this time. Even Rahu's mechanical messenger seemed to be in a hurry, and that didn't bode well for Maaya's hopes of getting back to sleep. With any luck Rahu wouldn't have another job for them, and she would be able to take a nap after she handed off the gem.

As she walked quietly upstairs to fetch the gem from its hiding place, she tried to avoid the questions her mind was asking her. What was the gem for?

Why did Rahu want it? Was she aiding a foreign enemy? What did this mean for Sark, or even for Maaya's future?

She shook her head. Despite mounting evidence to the contrary, she didn't want to believe it. It was just a piece of jewelry. That's all it was. Besides, it wasn't even the one he wanted, so she didn't have any reason to worry he could use it for his ill purposes… at least, not yet.

Saber flitted in as Maaya came back downstairs, and glanced up at her in surprise.

"You're awake already? Who did it? I'll box their ears for sure, I warned them not to—"

"Rahu's bird," Maaya answered tiredly. The sun hurt her eyes and she felt a headache coming on. "If you want to box his ears when he gets here, believe me you're more than welcome."

Saber made a rude noise.

"It's unfair that he expects you out and about at nights to do his work, then to also be awake in the early morning to receive him."

"To be fair, we weren't out last night on his orders," Maaya replied, though the idea of being fair to Rahu in any respect left a bad taste in her mouth.

"Well, at least we can say he's punctual," Saber said, rolling her eyes. "He's coming up the road, by the way. Uh, you might want to put some pants on."

Maaya scrambled to get dressed, and opened the door just as Rahu stepped up, his hand raised and ready to knock.

"Ah, good, you're ready. …what happened to you? You look terrible," he said, inviting himself in.

"Just tired. There've been more sightings of those strange ghosts, so I thought we should check them out, but no luck," Maaya explained.

"Ah. Unfortunate," Rahu replied apathetically. "Let's get to it. Do you have what I asked for?"

"Y-yes, I do," Maaya said, pulling it carefully from her pocket. She was suddenly struck with a near paralyzing fear. What if Rahu realized this wasn't the gem he asked for? How would he punish her for lying to him over something so important?

Rahu, however, seemed pleased at the sight of the gem. He took it in his hands, holding it as he might a newborn, inspecting it from every angle and letting the sunlight cast brilliant reflections all around the room. Even in the midst of her fear, Maaya had to admire the craftsmanship that had gone into making it—and again she had to admire Saber's pick.

"Excellent. Most excellent," Rahu breathed, and Maaya could almost see the wave of relief wash over him. Whatever he wanted this for, it was undoubtedly extremely important. "I knew you could find it. You know, word has apparently spread about this gem for nearly a hundred years, but no one has ever been able to locate it. And now… now it's mine."

As though fearful someone else in the room might see despite the fact that they were alone, Rahu pulled a small brown sack out of his pocket, slipped the gem inside, tied it up tight, then put it back into his pocket.

"May I ask… what is this gem for?" Maaya inquired, feeling more comfortable speaking now that she was sure Rahu didn't suspect their ruse.

"As I said, this gemstone has high historical significance. It is widely sought after on both continents of the world. How it arrived here I'm not entirely sure, but rumor spread that the wealthy family who lived in that mansion up until just a few years ago purchased it from someone who came from Krethus. The family didn't do so well after that; they believed it brought bad luck upon them, and so they left town. That they left the gem behind was only a guess, but I imagine they wanted to be rid of it. This rumor only just recently reached my ears, and from a reliable source, too. Thus, your deadline. Half the people in my circles knew about it by the time it got to me, so it was very important that you got there first. But then, I'm surprised some other street urchins didn't find it before now."

"Ah, well, I… I'm glad we were able to help," Maaya replied, unsure of what to say. Rahu was clearly in a good mood, but her main interest now was payment—and, of course, getting back to sleep.

Rahu placed his hand protectively over his pocket, already feeling to make sure the gem was still there.

"I've been thinking, Maaya. You all work hard for me—you especially so—and after this job you've shown me that I can always count on you to do what I need at a moment's notice. This was no small feat, I want you to understand that. But I understand this must be taxing, what with your… living situation." Rahu looked around disdainfully at the house, and so disgusted was his expression that Maaya almost felt like jumping in to defend her home. "Living so far from me, and in such conditions, could potentially result a situation in which you may not be able to do something for me as quickly as I would like. Such a thing would disappoint me, and I don't think any of us want that.

"My proposal is this. I'd like to set you up in a home in Corridor D. I will pay for everything you need to live there and eat well. In exchange, you will fall under my permanent employ. No more wandering the streets at night or having your own adventures. You will work for me full time, and will be at my beck and call every hour of every day. In exchange, your every need will be met. How does that sound?"

"It… I, uh…"

"Agree to it immediately," Saber whispered from her side. "He's saying this with the expectation that you jump at the chance, and let's face it: you don't have a choice."

Rahu raised an eyebrow at Maaya's silence.

"I mean, of course! It sounds wonderful!" Maaya said, trying as hard as she could to sound enthusiastic. "That stability would be nice, and we would all be more than happy to work for you that way."

She bit her tongue before she started talking herself into a hole. Rahu, however, seemed satisfied, a rehearsed smile passing over his face. He knew she couldn't refuse.

"Wonderful, wonderful. I expect I'll be needing you much more often in the coming weeks, so I'll see to it that your accommodations are purchased and set up quickly. Then you can finally say goodbye to this heap of rotted wood."

Maaya only nodded, forcing herself to stay pleasant. But then a thought flickered into her mind, one that made her feel slightly sick again.

"Uh, sir… I don't suppose you've heard about the disappearing of people in Corridor B?" Maaya asked cautiously.

"Explain that you weren't there to witness it; if he thinks you knew before anyone else, he'll wonder why you didn't inform him," Saber hissed.

"I mean, I've just heard rumors going around the streets, I haven't seen anything myself for sure," Maaya clarified quickly, and Saber nodded.

"I haven't. It's probably hearsay; if such a thing did happen in a place like that, I would have heard about it already," Rahu said dismissively, but Maaya noticed that he blinked faster when he spoke. At least for him, this was a sign he was being more dishonest than usual. "Anyway, now that I have what I need, I need to go downtown to look for a new home for my best employees."

Rahu flashed Maaya what she assumed was a smile, and then he swiftly exited the building.

Maaya let out a long breath.

"Thank you again, Saber," she said weakly, and Saber grinned.

"I am ever at your service," she replied, but then her expression turned serious. "There's no doubt he knows about what happened in Corridor B. For whatever reason he wants us ignorant of the fact that he knows, and he really shouldn't care. That he's trying to keep us in the dark has got suspicion written all over it."

"Yeah, but it doesn't matter. We already know he's involved. The question now is what we should do about it," Maaya said.

"Well, we can tail him," Saber suggested.

"What?"

"He thinks he's got the gem he was looking for. Remember what Kim said? If we follow him now, he might take us right to where he plans on using it. We won't get another chance like this."

Maaya couldn't help but gaze longingly back at the couch, and then she moaned in disappointment and went to get her shoes.

Following Rahu was easier than following most people. Unlike most people in Sark, Rahu *wanted* attention, so it was easy to keep track of him. In addition, everyone focusing on Rahu had the added benefit of taking away any attention to Maaya, who normally had to endure suspicious glances and evil looks—and if she were lucky, that's all she got.

Unfortunately for Maaya, Rahu also progressed at an infuriatingly slow pace. She supposed that someone with that much money didn't really need to hurry anywhere. He painted a stark contrast to the tradesmen and other poor workers rushing here and there, trying to get as much accomplished in a working day as they could.

After almost an hour of walking slowly through the streets, which became progressively cleaner and more extravagantly decorated as they traveled, he turned down a gated street Maaya knew she could not possibly enter. She and Saber hung back behind a street vendor's cart, watching as he slowly walked away.

As luck would have it, he walked up the steps of one of the first large homes on the street, pulled a key from his pocket, and disappeared inside.

"That must be where Rahu lives," Maaya said quietly.

"How anticlimactic," Saber muttered. "Not that I expected him to lead us to his secret villain's lair or something, but I figured he'd be in a rush to get that gem somewhere important considering he woke you up so early to grab it. Should I go spy on him?"

Maaya was about to approve this idea when they noticed a cloaked man hurry up the walk, then step up to Rahu's door. He rapped quickly on it, and when it opened, looked around quickly before stepping inside as though he were afraid someone might be watching. Though Maaya caught only a glimpse of his face, she was certain she knew who it was: the Krethan.

"Well, there goes that idea," Saber sighed. "I guess this means we should stick around and see if anything happens. Want me to grab you a snack while we wait?"

"I'd rather buy something so people don't start staring at me for hanging out around the carts," Maaya murmured, and Saber chuckled.

"Say no more."

Saber disappeared into the crowds, leaving Maaya to watch the house. Apart from waiting for someone to come out, however, there was nothing she could do. All the windows were covered by curtains, and there was no way to get any closer. She was probably attracting enough suspicion as it was.

A few minutes later, however, she felt her pocket suddenly get heavier.

She reached into it and felt a number of coins, enough to buy herself lunch at least.

"Where did you get these?" Maaya whispered.

"Probably best you don't ask. But they weren't from anyone who would miss them, if that's your concern," Saber said proudly.

Maaya smiled slightly, then took the coins out of her pocket as she approached one of the vendors. The man behind the cart stood up quickly as soon as he noticed her, and seemed ready to yell, but stopped at the sight of the coins in her hand. He was a large man, and his thick tanned arms were bare beneath his grey-brown tunic. A mop of unruly hair had been pulled back behind his head and a thick mustache and beard almost completely concealed his grim jaw.

"I… uh… you want something?" he asked suspiciously.

"Yes. Just a plate of pav bhaji, please," Maaya said politely, making sure the coins were in full view. The man stared between her and the coins for a few moments, then shrugged and turned to the counters behind him.

"I heard of you. I seen you around before. People says you can rob anyone without touchin' them. Surprised you're coming up paying for your food like everyone else."

"People like to exaggerate," Maaya replied. "If you knew me better you'd know I work for what I've got."

"Why I never see you paying for things at the carts, then?" the man asked, his back still turned to her as he prepared the vegetables.

"Mostly because any time I get near, people start screaming that I'm a thief," Maaya said, a hint of bitterness seeping into her voice. The man paused for a moment.

"That's… fair. Sorry."

An uncomfortable silence hung over them until the man turned around, holding the plate out to her. Maaya eagerly dropped the coins into his expectant hand before taking the plate, and she watched as he held them tightly as though afraid they would disappear if he loosened his grip.

"Uh, enjoy, then," he muttered awkwardly. "Feel free to come back if you like it."

"Thank you," Maaya smiled, then walked across the street, sitting with her back against the wall while she ate. Rahu's house was still in plain sight, but it didn't look like anything had changed.

It had been months since she had eaten hot fresh street food. If Rahu really was going to do for them what he said he was, this was something she could easily get used to. She fought the urge to eat quickly, reminding herself that there was plenty of food at home, but it was almost too delicious to resist. She temporarily forgot all about Rahu and focused on her meal, silently thanking Saber. She did, however, feel slightly guilty—in her attempt to prove that she wasn't a thief to one person, she had ended up stealing from another.

"Hey, look," Saber said, gently nudging Maaya's shoulder and pointing over at Rahu's house.

The front door opened and the Krethan stepped out. Rather than making any attempt to avoid attention, he now looked furious. Maaya couldn't hear what he was saying from this distance, but she saw him look back at the direction of the still-open door, gesturing and pointing angrily. The door closed a moment after, interrupting the Krethan, who stood gazing at the door for a moment. He looked so angry that for a moment Maaya thought he might try to break the door down and go back inside, but he set off down the street instead, looking thoroughly displeased.

"Oh, what's this? Drama between business partners? Now that's interesting," Saber mused. Maaya could almost see the gears in her political mind spinning, trying to think of reasons for why two people engaged in such a deadly project would be angry with each other.

"Well, if they're having trouble, that just means good news for us," Maaya replied wearily. She mopped up the last bit of curry with her bread and ate it, then stood up to find a place to throw her trash.

"Maybe the Krethan doesn't understand Rahu's love of deadlines just yet," Saber continued thoughtfully as they walked back across the street. "Or, now that it's down to the wire, one of them is having second thoughts. Oh, the possibilities this conflict brings! You could—"

"You! Ghost!" came a shrill voice from the side.

Maaya whirled around to see an angry-looking woman and two large men walking quickly up to her, pointing accusatorially at the plate in her hand. "Who did you steal from this time? The nerve you have, stealing from these hard-working folk in broad daylight!"

"I didn't steal this, I—" Maaya started, but broke off in fear as the woman stepped closer, her face only a foot from Maaya's. The woman stood at least a head taller than Maaya, more than enough to intimidate the girl.

"*Lies,*" the woman hissed, and the men took places on both sides of Maaya, preventing her escape. "You're staying right here until we find the police, and then you can explain to them why you—"

"Oi! You get away from that girl, you hear?" came an angry voice from nearby. Maaya turned to look and saw the man she'd bought her breakfast from bearing down on them. He was much larger than he looked from inside his cart, standing well over six feet tall, and his intimidating image was only helped by the knife he still held in his hand.

The trio turned to face him, and the woman raised her nose.

"Do you know who this is? She's a well-known thief, and we just caught her stealing food from—"

"She's no thief, that food there she bought from me," the man growled, and the woman's anger was replaced with genuine surprise. "She paid for it fair and square. You leave her alone, or I'll have the police on *you* for scaring away my paying customers."

"But… but she has a reputation, she always steals—"

"You ever seen her do it? Anyone ever *seen* her do it? Or are you just repeating hearsay because it makes you feel good?" the man returned forcefully, loud enough to make everyone in the area turn their heads to face him.

"Well… no, I've never seen, but I've heard—"

"That's what I thought, then," the man grunted. "Hearsay like the rest of it all. Here's your infamous *Ghost* 'ere, comin' up and paying for her meal like anyone else, and I've got the rial in my pocket to prove it. She might do it more often if she could get a bite to eat without people like you charging up to her in the street. Now, I'll say this one more time: you leave her alone, and keep your trap shut while you're at it. That goes for the rest of you as well. I'll not have my business harmed because you don't know how to control your worthless gossip."

Though done speaking, he stood his ground and stared at the others until, finally, the woman and her accomplices turned away, muttering to themselves and casting dirty looks over their shoulder at Maaya.

Maaya realized she hadn't been breathing, and she sighed heavily. The man walked over to her and put a strong hand on her shoulder.

"You all right?"

"Yes. Yes, thank you. Thank you so much," Maaya said gratefully, and she meant it. She could almost cry. Nearby, other vendors and customers were looking at her, but this time they were stares of confusion, as though the man's words had caused them all to at least question what they thought they knew. She knew it wouldn't change much, not all at once, but it was a start.

"Glad to hear it. I don't claim to know what you do, and maybe what they've said is true, but rumors are dangerous things. I'll trust my eyes, and my eyes say you're an honest customer like the rest. Hard enough to get by here without people frightening off the few people with rial to spare. Say, what's your job, anyway?"

"I'm, uh…"

"You're an independent contractor. You take miscellaneous jobs from anyone willing to hire you," Saber advised.

Maaya relayed this information, and the vendor appeared content.

"That's tough work, but it's no less honest than the rest of us. Anyway, I best get back to it. I've attracted some attention, and some of that attention might be hungry. You like the food?"

"Oh, yes!" Maaya exclaimed. "I'll be back."

The man smiled, and it was a kind smile, Maaya thought.

"You take of yourself now," the man said, then lumbered back to his cart.

Maaya and Saber started up the street back toward home, and again Maaya relished in being free of accusing stares and fingers.

"Hey, you know I would have beat them all up if that guy hadn't come along, right?" Saber said as they approached their front door.

"We both know that would have made things infinitely worse, but I appreciate the thought," Maaya laughed.

"Nonsense. If you get a reputation for beating up people without touching them—"

"Then they'll call Rahu, and we'd have a lot of explaining to do. We've been through this before, remember?"

"All right, all right. So hey, what do you think that was all about back there?" Saber asked eagerly as they re-entered the house. It was still quiet, and Maaya realized it wasn't even yet mid-morning.

"I wish I could say. I assume it has something to do with the gem if it has the Krethan that angry. That's the only thing we really know he wants," Maaya said.

"You know what? I have a theory," Saber said as they sat down on the couch together. Maaya listened intently. "I think Rahu wants to use that gem as a bargaining chip in whatever deal they have going on, and the Krethan only just found out about it."

"Bargaining chip? How?"

"Well, think about it. If this gem is necessary for their plans, they both know about it, right? But Rahu didn't wait around; he made sure *we* got it and that we held on to it for him. And then there's the fact that as we were looking for the gem in the mansion, who should come along but the Krethan? He needs it, Rahu knows it, and now Rahu's holding it over his head."

"That's… actually really interesting," Maaya said thoughtfully, sitting back. She was too tired to piece together what it could mean, but she knew it was important—and so very much like the Rahu she knew. She wouldn't put it past him to take advantage of his own partner if it meant personal gain.

"Isn't it? It does make me wonder all the more what the gem is being used for, since apparently this weapon of his is already complete. Though this does put us at a slight disadvantage; so long as Rahu is keeping that gem from the Krethan, we can't figure out what its use is."

"I know a way we can find out," Maaya said slowly, and Saber glanced at her, her eyes alight. "We'll go back to the mansion tonight and corner the Krethan. We'll take his weapon and figure out what he's up to."

Saber's eyebrows rose in shock, and then she laughed, pushing Maaya playfully.

"Oh, Maaya, that is *bold*. I would never have expected you to suggest something like that!"

"It's like you said: now's a time to be bold," Maaya replied simply, and Saber's grin widened.

"You know, all of this is downright miserable, but I like what it's doing to you. You are easily my favorite living person. Aren't you afraid that he might get the better of us, though?"

"No," Maaya answered shortly. "There are five of us and one of him, and we have our *libris*. We know he travels alone, and the only thing he could use to fight is his walking stick. Besides, I'm tired of chasing after ghosts. We need answers, and we're going to stop him before he can use his weapon again."

"That's all well and good, my brave soldier, but you should get some sleep first; you're having trouble keeping your eyes open," Saber said, amused.

Maaya agreed, and she undressed as Saber spread out her blanket over the couch. Her headache had only gotten worse as the morning went on, and though the food had helped, she was eager to shut her eyes again. She lay down and pulled the blanket over her, letting the warmth embrace her.

"I'll keep our little recruits quiet until you've had enough rest. Should I brief them on tonight's mission while I'm at it?"

"Yes, please," Maaya murmured. She heard Saber snicker, but she was too tired to care. The last thing she remembered as she drifted off to sleep was Saber gently brushing her hair from her face.

By the time Maaya awoke, it was already dark. The house was pleasantly warm and a low fire crackled in the fireplace. A few lit candles in the room told Maaya everyone else was awake, but the house was remarkably quiet. Saber had done a good job keeping the others quiet—almost too good a job. Maaya glanced out the window and saw the moon already high in the sky, and she suddenly wondered if she had been asleep for too long.

As she sat up, however, she noticed her four friends at the kitchen table, whispering quietly amongst themselves. Saber glanced over at Maaya, then flashed her a grin.

"Our valiant captain has awoken! Make her a plate, kids, we've got a dangerous mission ahead."

All at once the house was filled with more light and sound. The others, no longer worried about keeping their voices down, talked over each other about visiting the mansion and cornering the foreign operative. Rather than sounding frightened or intimidated, they sounded eager to track down the

Krethan before he could do any more damage. So vehement was their discussion that Maaya had to jump in.

"We're not going to *kill* him. At least not if we can help it," she instructed. "We need to get information from him first."

"And *then* we kill him, right?" Saber asked hopefully.

"Only if we have no other choice," Maaya replied flatly. "Murder isn't our line of work."

"I thought we made exceptions for Krethans," Saber protested.

"I want to make that judgment for myself. I'm not going to blindly kill someone because the politics I don't care about say I should. Most Krethans are probably like us: only hating the other because that's what we've been told to do."

"That's true, but most Krethans don't have death machines that summon ghosts. Probably."

Maaya simply rolled her eyes and gratefully took the plate of food Sovaan offered her. It was lukewarm, but still delicious.

"Oh, by the way, Roshan stopped by while you were asleep," Saber continued. "He doesn't have much on the news front; he just said that his dad has changed tactics a little. He's trying to put evidence together that will implicate Rahu for conspiring with a foreign enemy. It's not much, but it's something."

"What, not another disaster? I'm disappointed, it's been at least a day since we last got news of one," Maaya said sardonically.

"I know, right? I'm hoping we'll have good news for him tomorrow. If we can stop the Krethan tonight, that's one huge cog out of this doomsday machine. Probably the most important one. Anyway, hurry and get your gear so we can go kill— er, find this guy."

Maaya hurriedly finished her food, then pulled on her nighttime clothing. Her heart began pounding in her chest as she fastened her card pouch to her left arm and tied her shoes tight. This time she also added a strap with a dagger to her left leg. There was no such thing as being too careful in a situation like this. She looked over at Kalil who was currently going through his inventory, selecting what would be appropriate for Kim and Sovaan to arm themselves with based on their individual builds and strengths.

Only a few minutes later they were on their way. Her friends' excitement was palpable; while ordinarily they would travel quietly, this time they could hardly keep their voices down. Evidently hunting ghosts had gotten stale, and the prospect of hunting living prey was adding some much-needed joy to their lives. Maaya just hoped it wouldn't get to their heads. There was an element of fun to danger, but Maaya was no thrill seeker. She also felt a twinge of discomfort at how eagerly they seemed to want to hurt this man. Enemy or not, she found no happiness in inflicting pain on others.

"What should we do when we find this guy? Should we make him explain how the weapon works so we can turn him in? Or should we make him turn it on so he can summon a ghost walk on himself?" Saber asked.

"Ghost walk?" Maaya said.

"I thought we should come up with a name for these occurrences," Saber replied proudly. "They're so uniform and mechanical, these ghosts. It wouldn't make much sense to call them floats."

"What about ghost marches?" Kalil suggested.

"Nah, not enough knee lifting. They probably don't even have knees," Saber said, as though the thought of something without knees was the most ridiculous idea she'd ever heard.

"I think 'walk' fits. It sounds like an event, you know? I heard some cities in the north have celebrations for their dead; a ghost walk sounds like something they'd do," Kim said.

Saber looked highly offended.

"I should hope not. Ghost walks are my idea, and I'm sticking with it."

"Let's just hope we can prevent another one from happening at all," Maaya said testily.

Before long they found themselves once again in Corridor B. She had just started feeling like she was growing comfortable with the place, but now it looked very different than it had only the night before. Most of the mansions on the right side of the street were dark and cordoned off. There weren't currently any officials looking through the buildings, but she knew the area would be under higher scrutiny. She wondered if that would be enough to scare the Krethan away from coming to the mansion.

She tried to keep her eyes on the sidewalk rather than at the silhouettes of the huge buildings as they approached. She could still hear the screams in her mind, and she could still see the wave of faceless ghosts.

"You know, I've been thinking," Kim started, and Maaya glanced over at her, welcoming to the distraction. "Milo said when he saw the ghosts attack those homeless men they were taken right away, but the ghosts at Mayberry Street weren't affected until later that night. Then here, with these people, it was instant again. What's the difference, do you think?"

"I haven't the slightest," Maaya said. "At the least, it's not something we can use to our advantage. I don't think it's something we could stop even if we knew it was coming."

"I think it has to do with the number of people. Two people on a hill isn't much, and there aren't many people in these grand houses so it doesn't take much effort. But hundreds of people on a crowded street is another story," Saber hypothesized.

"Hold," Maaya said suddenly. "We're here."

The mansion loomed in front of them as dark and silent as the rest, but somehow infinitely more ominous. The overgrown brush, which had on previous nights served to shield them from prying eyes, now loomed high ahead of them, threatening to consume them. A shiver ran down Maaya's spine. Her eyes darted back and forth, taking in every inch of the front yard, but there was no sign of the Krethan.

"It doesn't look like he's in there," Saber said, squinting up at the dark house. "He usually has a light with him."

"Can you double check?" Maaya asked, and Saber nodded, gliding off into the house through a second-floor window. "Come on, let's hide," she continued to the others, and they quickly sought the shelter of the massive willow.

"Plan?" Kim asked quietly. All traces of eagerness had vanished from her face, replaced by grim apprehension and a hint of fear.

"We locate him first and wait for him to move somewhere we can get the jump on him. I'll knock him down first. Kalil, I need you to help hold him and prevent him from fighting back or escaping. Sovaan, keep an eye out for this weapon of his and make sure he can't use it. Kim, keep an eye on our surroundings and make sure we aren't the target of an ambush. We'll do this quick and quiet. Once we've got things secured we keep him cornered and question him."

The other three nodded in unison, and Maaya felt slightly relieved. Now that it was time to get down to business, their excitement and jokes had faded away.

Saber returned quickly, hurrying over to them while attempting to stay low to the ground.

"He's there," the ghost whispered. "Down in the basement, I suppose so the light won't show from the outside. He's got his bag with him. You know what that means."

Maaya's heart dropped. If he was already there and already working, they had almost no time.

"All right, everyone. Cards out."

The four friends drew cards in a swift motion, then placed them on their calves. The green lines of speed and purple lines of strength glowed over their limbs, flickering softly in the darkness as the paper burned away into ash. It was taxing on the body to use more than one type of card at once, but they needed every advantage they could get. Maaya hoped none of the neighbors were watching; even from the safety of the tree the glow of the lines on their bodies would make them visible from a block away at least.

"Any updates to the plan?" Kim asked nervously.

"Nope. Let's move. Saber, any help you can offer would be greatly appreciated."

"I'll do my best. And if he hurts any of you I'll break his neck," Saber said menacingly.

It was time to go. Without another word they dashed silently inside the mansion with inhuman speed. They sped through the entrance room and down the hall toward the kitchen where the door to the basement stood. Saber floated through the door and disappeared. Then, after counting to three, Maaya and the others burst through the door and ran downstairs.

At their speed, all Maaya saw was a flash of white hair on top of a cloaked body and a walking stick with a lantern affixed to the top. He was currently facing away from the stairs, looking toward where Saber floated near the ceiling in front of him. She painted an intimidating picture; her hair stood on end, her arms were raised wide, and a dangerous smile played across her lips.

Maaya didn't wait. Before the man could even turn at the sound of the door opening, she slammed into him from behind. Her augmented strength sent the man flying across the basement, hitting the stone wall hard. He crumpled, looking dazed.

The others were upon him in an instant. Kalil searched his pockets and kept a firm grip on one of the man's wrists while Sovaan searched his bag, and Kim stood watch at the top of the stairs. The man looked too shocked to try to get away, and Maaya took advantage of this to get a good look at him. He looked young, in his late twenties at most, and he would have been tall had he been standing. His hair was pure white and neatly combed, and Maaya's gaze was immediately drawn to his brilliant green eyes, one of which was behind an elegant removable ocular implant made of bronze. He was pale, paler than any Selenthian she knew. She had never seen a Krethan before, but she had been told of their fair skin and bright eyes.

After a moment he seemed to regain his bearings.

"Ghost!" he cried, looking at the point slightly behind Maaya's head where Saber hovered menacingly. "Get out of here before it takes you!"

"Well, that's rude," Saber replied, raising an eyebrow.

"You… you can talk?"

"Oh, yes. I can do tricks, too, if you like."

The man paused, clearly muddled, and his eyes flicked between Saber, Maaya, and the others. His mouth hung half open, as if he were too overwhelmed to say any more.

"You… you're using *libris*," he uttered finally, staring Maaya up and down. His searching gaze made her suddenly uncomfortable, but she couldn't deny her surprise. "Does that mean… you can see her?"

"Who? Her?" Maaya asked, pointing up at Saber. The man nodded. "Yeah. She's a friend. Bad luck for you, I guess."

"I… if you're here to rob me, I haven't brought much money with—"

"We're not here to rob you, idiot," Saber said scathingly. Her appearance had returned to normal, and she floated down slowly to stare straight into the man's face. "We're here to stop you from using your doomsday machine. We saw what you did with it last night, and if you thought you were going to get away with—"

"You saw!" the man cried. "You saw them? Then you… you must be the ones working for Rahu."

He said these words despairingly, and Maaya suddenly felt confused.

"That's what we thought until we discovered *you* were working with him," she shot back venomously. "We know you and Rahu been causing these attacks and setting these ghosts on people, and you're going to tell us everything you know."

"You think we… what?" the man asked, perplexed. "I've done no such thing! And Rahu and I are hardly on friendly terms at the moment—"

"*Don't. Lie,*" Maaya hissed, pushing his chest hard against the wall. His confusion was contagious, but as she looked into his eyes she remembered the horrifying sight of hundreds of ghosts being sucked into an endless void in the sky. "You were here last night when it happened, you were at Mayberry Street when that attack happened, and we know you were at the barn across the river when two men up there were killed."

"Yes, I know about the attacks, but I haven't been causing them!" the man coughed. "You must believe me. There have been problems in Krethus—some machine malfunctioned, killing millions—my government has found a way to hopefully fix this machine, but we need something that was rumored to be here. A gem of some sort, but—"

"So it's just a coincidence that these… ghost walks all happened in places you were?" Maaya continued harshly.

"I don't know. Rahu and I were investigating to try to find out why they were happening here suddenly. As far as I know, Sark is one of the only places outside Krethus to be experiencing these attacks. Why, I don't know. My government has limited knowledge of how these ghosts work. All I know is I'm to retrieve this gem and take it back home with me to hopefully put a stop to them. But I have no control over them at all. Please believe me!"

Maaya faltered. She could usually tell when a person was lying, and this man, for all she could see, was not. This complicated things significantly.

After a moment, Maaya stood up, taking her hands off the man. When he moved to stand, however, she held up her hand.

"You, just… stay there. Tell me more. How is the gem connected to the ghost attacks?"

"I haven't a clue," the man admitted. "All I know is apparently it's something that can fix the malfunctioning machine. The ghosts, they're not like others—you can see ghosts, so I'm sure you're aware. The machine kills people, and out come these ghosts. They show up randomly, wiping out streets full of people, then disappear. They're completely uncontrolled. This gem my government seeks is apparently no ordinary jewelry. How it differs, I don't know, but it's supposed to be able to stop this machine from working and prevent these attacks from happening again."

"Why not just destroy the machine with weapons?" Saber asked slowly, as though she were talking to a very young child.

"We can't get near it. Any human being that enters a certain radius is turned into one of those… things. Any machinery is suddenly rendered inoperable, so we can't even drop explosives. The gem hypothetically protects whoever carries it from those effects and allow them to get to the machine and shut it down."

"Who would design such a thing? Did they want to use it against Selenthia?" Maaya continued.

"I don't know. I'm not even sure the government knows; if they do, they haven't told me. I'm not exactly a ranking official. But this has been going on for so long we don't care anymore. We just want to shut it down. Before it consumes the world, you know."

Maaya shuddered involuntarily.

"What do you mean?" she said quietly.

"Well, like I said, anyone who enters a certain radius of the machine is killed almost instantly," the man answered weakly. "And the thing is, that radius is… expanding. It wasn't much when it started a hundred years ago, from what I'm told, but a few years ago, it suddenly started accelerating. We're not sure why, but it's moving fast."

"Wait, you're saying this machine has been calling ghost walks for a *hundred years?*" Saber asked in disbelief.

"Roughly, yes," the man sighed. "Krethus is in a state of disarray. No one is safe since these things can just appear anywhere. We've done what we can, and the government has endorsed the use of *libris* to defend who we can, but there are only so many people who can use it. We've yet to find any permanent solution. All the while millions have died, and as more people die, the more of *them* there are."

"And now they've come to Selenthia…" Kim murmured.

"Yes. You see, this has far-reaching implications. If the machine now has the power to reach across the entire ocean, it will not stop until every living being on this planet is dead."

13

A CHANGE OF PLANS

Maaya stood awkwardly in the silence that fell. She wasn't sure if she was breathing. She felt like she needed to say something, but the words she hadn't yet figured out were caught in her throat. Absolutely nothing so far had gone as expected, and she wasn't yet sure if that was good or bad. On one hand, it didn't seem like the weapon they imagined actually existed, and it didn't appear as though the ghost walks were being purposefully set on anyone. On the other hand, this now meant they no longer had a good explanation for why they occurred—and that the only definitive source was supposedly on the other side of the planet. At least, that was if this man's story was to be believed.

"Uh, so… my name is Svante," the Krethan said nervously. He extended his arm halfway, then pulled it back.

"Maaya," Maaya replied distractedly. "So… hang on, so you and Rahu were trying to *stop* these attacks?"

"Yes. He and I connected in the past because of my limited work with ghosts. I was assigned to search this area of Selenthia for the gem, and since I heard he worked with the supernatural, I quickly got in touch. He said he had contacts here who might be able to help. I assume he meant you. At first I thought he was acting altruistically, but now… now I'm not so sure."

"Yes, we witnessed your little fight earlier," Saber said in a way that indicated she was clearly enjoying herself. "What was that about?"

A look of irritation flickered across Svante's face.

"When I arrived in Sark, I told him the gem I needed might be somewhere in this town. By that time I hadn't yet tracked it to this building. He seemed concerned about the potential for more attacks, and so he said we could look for it together. I eventually figured out its possible location from information my government sent me, and I informed him I would be going to seek it out. Except it turns out he raced to get it before me. Now he is refusing to give it to me unless I give him a substantial amount of money!"

Maaya and Saber shared an amused look. Saber had been right, and this was territory they were familiar with.

"I'm sorry," Maaya said hastily at Svante's affronted look. "It's just that we've been working with Rahu for years now, and we all know him to be an insufferable selfish idiot. I'm not surprised at all that he would do something like this."

"How could you work with a man with such a lack of conscience?" Svante asked angrily. "Lives are at stake! He's holding a precious item hostage so he can make some coin!"

"We don't really have a choice," Maaya protested, feeling a pang of guilt. "He gives us food. If we make him angry he'll starve us at best and kill us at worst. We can't escape the town because we have no money, and he won't give us any. I hate him more than you do, I can guarantee that, but I can't cross him. At least… I couldn't before. I don't know anymore."

"Well, you seem like decent enough people. I would hate to imagine everyone in this town is like him. Say, uh… may I stand up now?" Maaya nodded, and Svante got shakily to his feet. "I feel like I was hit by a carriage. You definitely know your *libris* well."

"It's come in handy," Maaya replied shortly, and the lights flickered from her limbs, then disappeared. Her friends looked at each other warily, and then their lights disappeared as well. "So if you haven't been causing these attacks, what *have* you been doing?"

"At first I was looking for the gem, but now I'm simply investigating. I'm trying to find out if there's any pattern to the attacks or perhaps something that draws them out. They've only just recently arrived in Selenthia at all, so there must be something. I only have a theory at this point, and I was hoping to explore it, but… well, I'm a stranger in a strange land, and the one man I thought was helping me is now working against me."

"Why not just pay him? You look like you've got enough coin," Saber asked, looking Svante up and down.

"You don't know how much he's asking," Svante protested. "He wants a sum worth far more than this whole town is worth, and this is a very purposeful move. He wants my government to be indebted to him."

"He would do something that stupid?" Kim asked incredulously, trotting over to join them. "How can he think making the Krethan government angry will work out well for him?"

"He knows the Krethan state is in shambles. If Selenthia knew, the war would be over in a month. We cannot afford to do anything but bow to his demands. He has the upper hand and he knows it."

Maaya ran her fingers through her hair. Once again, everything bad about this situation came back to Rahu. He wasn't responsible for the attacks, but he wasn't doing anything to stop them, either. In his search for power, he was putting everyone at risk.

"What can we do?" Maaya asked exasperatedly. "Have you talked to your people back home?"

"I have, but the council I answer to will need time to deliberate. In the meantime there's nothing else we can possibly do."

"Are all you Krethans so monumentally narrowminded?" Saber said. Svante looked up at her in surprise. "Rahu is openly bargaining with a foreign government for his own gain. Do you not think that's something he could get into a wee bit of trouble for if that were exposed?"

"Saber, we've talked about this—" Maaya started, but Saber interrupted her.

"Because it's a *good idea,"* she said impatiently. "Don't you understand? We were forced to work for him because we had no dirt on him at all, and now we've got more dirt than we can possibly handle. If we keep trying to take out the ghosts at their source, all we're doing is cleaning up Rahu's messes for him! We need to bring him down already."

"If you think you could present a compelling case against him I would gladly assist you in any way I could. Unfortunately, I fear that may be extremely difficult," Svante shrugged.

"Right. We can keep that option on the table and explore it if anything comes up," Maaya said. "Now, you mentioned having a theory. What is it? Is it something we can work with?"

"Oh, uh… possibly. Though you may not like what I have to say."

"Believe me, we're far past that point already," Maaya retorted.

"Fair enough. Well… my associates and I believe that these ghosts are attracted to beings with connections to the supernatural world. That is, people who can see ghosts. It's been hard to verify, as people with such connections didn't used to make themselves known—"

"Gee, I can't imagine why," Saber quipped.

"—but even now that has changed, there simply aren't that many people who can see the dead, much less command *libris*. There are only a few dozen in Krethus actively fighting the ghosts."

"That doesn't mean anything. Anyone who can see ghosts would stay as far away from your government as possible; that's just the smart thing to do for people who don't want to get killed," Maaya said bitterly.

"Not necessarily so. When millions die and the proof is visible, that changes things," Svante said. "We were forced to face our prejudices long ago if we wanted to survive. But in the past, before the government came to be more accepting, it did occasionally track those individuals through police reports in various cities, and—"

"You tracked people who think they can see ghosts?" Kim asked, narrowing her eyes at Svante.

"Occasionally. And not anymore. It's been decades at least. But they did find a connection between people who made these claims and people who made use of *libris*, and while the former was mostly harmless, the latter could prove dangerous. My government isn't stupid; it recognizes that these arts exist and that they can come in quite handy now we realize where the danger is coming from. But it is unnerving that areas with higher concentrations of *libris* usage suffered more frequent and more severe attacks."

"Does that mean the ghosts being here is our fault?" Sovaan asked quietly.

"No, it doesn't," Maaya answered before Svante could respond. "It's just a theory. And anyway, those ghosts showed up in places we'd never been before."

"Are you the only ones who can see ghosts in this whole town?" Svante asked doubtfully.

Maaya paused. She knew they weren't. At the very least, she had met another one recently: the young boy from Mayberry Street.

"Does your theory say anything else?" Saber asked, noticing the troubled look on Maaya's face.

"This gem, in theory, might produce the opposite effect. That is, it would keep ghosts away. Not over a very large area, of course, as the gem is quite small—but if combined with the machine, it might cancel out the machine's effects, rendering it useless," Svante said.

"So either way, you're saying that the only way we can truly stop this is by getting this gem to Krethus?" Maaya asked hopelessly.

"That… is the theory, yes," Svante said guiltily.

To everyone's surprise, Saber started laughing.

"What?" Maaya asked, furrowing her brows.

"I'm sorry, it's just… we're all worked up over this gem—and the fact that Rahu has it—that we're forgetting the one he has is a fake!" Saber said gleefully.

"I… I'm sorry, what did you say?" Svante gaped.

"You want to know why the gem wasn't here when you came to look for it? It's because Rahu sent us to grab it first. Only trouble is, it wasn't here when we got here, either," Saber laughed. "And you want to know why *that* is?"

Saber pointed to the gem in the circlet on her forehead.

"I… but…"

"And since Rahu threatened the kids that he'd bring down some nebulous *consequences* on them if they didn't get his gem, I just nicked one from a local shop. When it comes to your little machine, he's playing a dangerous game of blackmail with an entire nation's government over a completely ordinary rock."

Svante simply stared at her in stunned silence for a moment, then recovered himself.

"Well, I suppose that all makes sense. I was told the gem originated in Krethus, anyway."

Saber stopped laughing.

"Huh? Hey, what's that supposed to mean?"

"Well, you're Krethan, aren't you?"

All eyes were on Saber now, and Maaya could see where Svante would have gotten the idea. Saber's pale skin and white hair had nothing to do with her being a ghost, and her eyes were as brightly blue as Svante's were green.

"You're a very rude man. I didn't claim to know where *you* were from based on the way you looked," Saber said.

"Isn't that exactly what you did?" Kim asked, but shrank back at the glare Saber threw her way.

"Oh, of course not!" Svante said. "It's your clothing and ribbons. Those robes haven't been used in nearly a hundred years, but I recognize them from my books; you were part of the emperor's high court. I couldn't tell you which position, though..."

Saber's mouth fell open, and Maaya would have laughed at her expression if she weren't equally shocked. For a moment, Maaya forgot all about the machine on the other side of the world. For years, she and Saber had assumed that they would never find any details about Saber's past, and now, out of nowhere, they had done just that.

"Does this mean... could you tell me who I am?" Saber asked softly. "My name? Anything?"

"Unfortunately not. Not off the top of my head, anyway," Svante said apologetically. "Even the high court had thousands of members, most of whom only lasted a few years at a time. But if you were there for even a few months there must be some record of your name somewhere. Do you remember anything at all?"

"Nothing. I feel as though it may be somewhere in my mind, locked away where I can't grasp it. It's not gone completely; I know how to read and write and speak, and I evidently have some talent for negotiation. But I... I don't remember anything specific."

"Well... listen," Svante said slowly. "What if you were to come back with me to Krethus? Once we shut down this machine, I can look that up for you. I have a whole staff who could assist me."

Saber's eyes brightened.

"You would do that?"

"Of course! Research is my forte, and I do love my history. That which hasn't been destroyed, that is. But I'm sure I could get you started."

Saber looked so delighted that Maaya didn't want to interrupt. Despite the fact that she had only known this man for a few minutes, she already felt almost envious of him for being able to offer Saber something that she so desperately wanted—and now that this particular box had been opened, she knew there was no shutting it again. But there were currently more important problems to think about—one of which could directly interfere with Svante's offer.

"I really appreciate what you want to do for my friend, but we have a minor problem," Maaya finally interjected. "If we return with the gem, there's a chance we can stop the machine… but what do we do about the fact that the gem you're after is currently being worn by a ghost?"

Svante stammered, then fell silent, looking troubled. Maaya wasn't surprised. If Svante's theory was correct, this was going to be the hardest part of the problem to solve.

Before they could dwell on this for too long, however, Kim suddenly turned to face the door at the top of the stairs.

"What is it?" Maaya whispered, instinctively putting her hand to her card pouch.

"Can you hear that? It sounds like screaming," Kim answered, closing her eyes to focus.

Everyone stopped moving. Maaya could hear it too, just barely. From the basement it was hard to tell what direction it was coming from, but the fact that they could hear it from here meant it had to be close.

"What do you think that's about?" Kalil asked slowly.

"You don't think the ghosts are back?" Kim asked, horrified.

"Saber, go," Maaya ordered, and without pausing even to acknowledge her words, Saber disappeared up through the ceiling. "Everyone else, let's get out of here. Run!"

They hurried up the stairs, and as they ran through the house Maaya looked frantically through every window they passed, looking for any signs of bright white lights. She saw a few flashes of orange from the windows facing the street, but a second glance revealed that they were only lanterns and torches.

Svante stumbled behind her as he tried to keep up with the agile Ghost Hunters, but Maaya didn't wait for him. The screaming had made her suddenly anxious; screaming meant attention, and attention was the last thing she wanted here.

They rushed out the front door and looked all around. A handful of confused people were in the street or on the front walks of nearby houses, but the noise wasn't coming from them.

Saber soon glided down to meet them just as Svante stumbled out after them, clumsily donning his cloak and pulling its hood over his white hair.

"There's a walk happening right now in Corridor C," Saber said quickly, gesturing somewhere behind the abandoned mansion. "We can catch it if we hurry."

Without waiting for an answer, Saber started up the street.

"How many?" Maaya asked as the others ran after her.

"A dozen or so. I think we can take them," Saber replied.

"Is that a good idea with so many people freaking out?" Sovaan said.

"We can take advantage of the confusion and be out by the time anyone recognizes who we are. But we have to stop them before they take any more people."

"Wait!" Svante cried breathlessly from behind them. "You cannot attack them!"

"Sure we can, we've done it already," Kalil replied, but Svante shook his head violently.

"You don't understand. Remember my theory! They're attracted to the use of *libris*, so whatever you do to take them out will only cause more to come!"

"Let them come," Kalil growled. "We'll take down every one."

Svante's further protests were lost on the wind as they all sprinted down the walk. Even if they hadn't been able to see the ghosts, it wouldn't have been hard to tell where they were. The commotion was growing quickly, and while it may have originated a few streets down, it was quickly spilling over into the adjoining neighborhoods. Those who weren't already panicking didn't take long to start, and it didn't help that no one seemed to understand what was going on. People were afraid because other people were afraid, and so it traveled swiftly.

But Maaya and the others could see them. Tall, silent, and horrifying as they ever were, at least a dozen ghosts made their way slowly down the street. It was easy to see why people were panicking; to any of their eyes it would look as though others were simply disappearing into thin air while shrieking in terror, and because no one could see the ghosts, no one knew where to run. It was complete chaos.

"Seals out!" Maaya called loudly, but no one nearby paid her any mind. No one paid attention as the four living humans pulled out cards streaked with blood, heading in the opposite direction of the rest of the panicked mob.

"Everyone, split out in an arc so we can get some clear shots, there's no way we'll be able to..." Maaya started, then trailed off, feeling suddenly weak. She made the mistake of looking into the eyes of one of the ghosts, and as its hollow gaze met hers, she suddenly felt all her strength leave her body. She tried to look away, but its stare seemed to lock her in place. Her peripheral vision started to fade, and she could only see the ghost.

"Oh no you don't," Saber cried. She quickly pressed an orange card to her wrist, and in an instant she was surrounded by fire. She sent a wave of flames toward the ghosts, bright and powerful enough to startle any creature, living or dead.

But the ghosts did not even pause.

"Seals! Now!" Saber called to the others, and three cards soared through the air.

A moment later, three small blasts echoed around the street from where the cards had met their targets. Several ghosts disappeared, but the rest moved ever onward as though nothing had happened.

"Again!" Saber ordered sharply.

This was the last Maaya heard. Once more, though she fought as hard as she could against it, she fell into the clutches of unconsciousness.

Maaya was vaguely aware of being nudged gently awake. She was vaguely aware that this had happened before, but she couldn't immediately place where from. This time, however, it all came flooding back much more quickly.

She sat up with a start, breathing heavily and looking wildly around her.

"Where are they? Where's...?"

"It's all right, it's all right," Saber said, placing her hands comfortingly on Maaya's shoulders. "The ghosts are all gone. It seems like our blood cards worked again."

"Everyone okay?" Maaya continued anxiously.

"Yep. We're all still here and in one piece. If nothing else, it seems our tried and true methods of ghost hunting are still effective," Saber said reassuringly.

Maaya took some deep breaths and looked around. They weren't home, but they weren't where they had been when she fainted. From what she could gather through the haze of her still-waking mind, they were at least half a dozen blocks away. It was darker here, and while some people were in the street talking concernedly with each other, there was no hysteria or panic.

"Why... does this keep happening to me?" Maaya asked.

"That's one reason the ghosts are so dangerous," came a voice from Maaya's left. She turned quickly to see Svante leaning against the cold wall next to her. "When you meet its eyes, it's like it starts to take the life out of you, and it paralyzes you. It affects even those who can't see them. Did you notice it with the ones they took tonight?"

Maaya shook her head.

"I saw it. It was scary," Kim said, hugging her knees to her chest. "People were running, and then suddenly they would just… stop. They would just stare straight ahead, like they wanted to run but couldn't control their bodies anymore."

"Did it happen to any of you?" Maaya asked, and the others shook their heads.

"You were at the head of the group. It's only natural it would get you first. Luckily, your friends were quick on the draw," Svante said gently. "Do you feel well enough to stand?"

"I think so," Maaya said, and Saber helped her to her feet. "We should head home. And you… I guess you should come with us."

Svante nodded, as though he had already considered this his plan, and they started off in the direction of home.

"I wonder why it happened there," Svante mused as they walked. "I don't know Sark all too well, but from my time in Corridor C, it didn't seem like there was any *libris* activity there."

"Ah, well, I may know the reason for that," Saber said remorsefully, and everyone looked at her. "When I flew over to look, I saw where it started. Do you remember Rahu's client, the woman who lost her daughter and husband and thought her son was possessed? It… it was her house."

"Oh… oh no…" Kim gasped softly.

"But we weren't there tonight!" Kalil protested, his voice hard. "It's been days!"

"It's possible there is some delay between when *libris* is used and when the ghosts appear. I haven't been able to tell," Svante admitted. "Did you know the woman well?"

"No, we were just helping her," Kim said softly, and she looked like she might cry. "Her daughter and husband died, but their ghosts were still there. The girl's ghost was helping her brother fight off bullies, but everyone thought he was crazy. We visited them and spent all night there trying to fix it, and we did. They… they were happy, all of them, in the end. I thought everything would be okay. I can't believe…"

"We can't have done this," Kalil said angrily. "We do good for people, we *don't* hurt them."

"Perhaps you're right," Svante conceded, looking thoroughly troubled at the children's reactions. "Probably just a horrible coincidence. These things are often random, as I said."

They walked the rest of the way in silence. Maaya wasn't sure she could talk any more even if she wanted to. She felt weak, much more so than she had before, and it was all she could do to stay on her feet. Along with the weakness that spread through her entire body, the dizziness wasn't going away, either. She guessed it was because she had retained eye contact with the ghost for longer this time, and had been much closer. She couldn't get the image of its eyes out of her head, thinking that if she had ever felt true terror in her life, it had been when she was trapped in the ghosts' empty stare.

When they arrived, Sovaan jogged ahead to unlock the door for everyone, and they headed quickly inside. Maaya didn't even bother to look around to make sure no one was watching. She was sure the presence of the Krethan would be suspicious if anyone saw, but right now she didn't care.

Svante removed his hood and looked around as the candles were lit, then glanced over at Maaya almost sympathetically.

"This is where you all live?"

"Home sweet home," Maaya replied tiredly. Saber helped her to the couch. Just sitting down was bliss, and she fought hard to avoid falling asleep right then and there.

"It's not so bad. We've lived here for a while now. There's room for all of us and there's no trouble in this neighborhood. Not with us, anyway," Sovaan elaborated helpfully.

"So what do we do now?" Kalil asked reservedly. He looked angry still; Maaya knew that the deaths of the woman and her son, and the mere possibility that he and the others might have caused them, must be eating at him.

"I'm not sure," Svante sighed. "With your *libris* you stand at least some chance of defending Sark, but I feel that by making things better in the short term, things may get worse in the long term. We must find a way to deal with this machine."

"How will you do that without the gem?" Kalil pressed.

"Oh, don't be ridiculous," Saber scolded him, then tapped her forehead. "The gem still exists, and luckily, we have it in our possession. Honestly, this problem is not a difficult one to solve."

Maaya looked up at her, realizing what she was suggesting.

"Saber… you realize you're talking about leaving Sark," she said slowly.

"Yes, I am. And a hard choice it was, too, considering how absolutely lovely Sark is," Saber returned, but grinned. "This is great for all of us, don't you see? We escape Rahu and this dead-end town, we travel across the world, and we're in the company of this rich guy so eating won't exactly be a problem. Oh, and I get to find out who I am! What's not to like about this plan?"

"Do you think the gem would work in its current state? Like Maaya mentioned, it's… well…" Svante started hesitantly.

In response, Saber reached out and flicked Svante on the nose, causing him to yelp. Despite herself, Maaya laughed.

"It might be invisible, but it's still very real," Saber said proudly. "Besides, the fact that I'm dead makes me more valuable of an asset than you realize. Those ghosts only attack the living, and since I'm already dead, they don't look at me twice. Not to mention I'm invisible to the vast majority of people in the world. I'm basically invulnerable. How cool is that for you?"

Svante didn't look entirely convinced, but he appeared to realize it was in his best interest to agree with her.

"So, um… we're taking a trip, then?" Kim asked, and the others cheered as though this was already the affirmation they needed.

"I, uh, I suppose that would be the best course of action," Svante said uncertainly. "But you must realize this is a heavy undertaking. My government expects me to come back alone, you see, and I hadn't expected to make accommodations for three extra people—"

"I'm sure your government would be much more willing to give funding for a few extra people than they would to give Rahu as much money as he wants for a gem that isn't even real," Saber said lazily, floating on her back and peering at him upside down.

"Yeah! Not only are you bringing back the gem, but you'll be escorted by an elite ghost-fighting force!" Sovaan said exultantly.

Maaya smiled. Her friends' optimism was infectious. She had to admit, as nervous as she was at the prospect of leaving Sark, she was becoming more comfortable with it by the minute already. They would all be together, which was the most important part, and they would be traveling in the company of someone whose government had sanctioned his mission. There was also the fact that he seemed like a kind enough person, even if he was a little strange. *And a Krethan,* she almost caught herself thinking, but she glanced at Saber. It turned out she already knew one, and she wouldn't have traded that friendship for anything.

Suddenly, there was a knock at the door. The house immediately fell quiet, and Saber flipped right side up, then floated cautiously to the door to see who it was. She stuck her head through the door and then immediately came back inside, visibly relieved.

"It's just Roshan," she said. "Serious question, have we considered getting him a bed yet? He comes here so often he might as well—"

"Just let him in," Maaya said faintly, nodding at the door.

Saber obliged, and Roshan walked in comfortably, not looking at all perturbed that the door had just opened on its own, or that it shut itself behind him. He did, however, look concerned—and that concern quickly turned to anger as he saw Svante standing in the middle of the room.

"What are you doing here?" he demanded furiously, and started toward the Krethan, but paused when all three children hastened to stop him.

"Wait! He's all right," Kim said quickly. "He's on our side."

"Yeah, he's not causing the attacks. He's trying to stop them," Kalil added.

"I… he what? Maaya? Is this true?" Roshan asked uncertainly, and Maaya nodded.

"Long story. No energy. Just don't kill him, please, he's our ride."

"He's your… oi." Roshan's expression changed multiple times in the span of a moment before finally settling on acceptance, and he made his way over the couch, sitting next to Maaya. "I've only been gone a day and you've gone from tracking this guy down as a dangerous criminal to going with him somewhere, is that it? I can't keep up with you lot."

"Honestly, Roshan, you should be used to this by now," Kim teased.

For the moment, the tension dissipated from the room. Roshan stared uncertainly at Svante but didn't say a word. Luckily, Kim came over to catch him up on everything that had happened. Maaya, struggling to keep her eyes open, only half paid attention. It was hard enough to think about the future when the past was being rehashed every time a new person arrived on the scene.

"I can't believe I'm hearing this correctly," Roshan said ten minutes later, shaking his head. "You're all going to Krethus? Just like that?"

"We could always stay and just let everyone die," Saber offered, and Maaya glared up at her, thankful Roshan couldn't hear her.

"We have to. Saber's got the gem they need and we stand a better chance of making it to that machine if we're all together," Kim said. "But we'll come back when we're done!"

"I just… this is so sudden. And do you know how far away Krethus is? It'll take you weeks to get there by the fastest ship, and you won't get the fastest ship. Not even with his money," Roshan continued, gracing Svante with temporary eye contact. "Plus, even when you make it back, Rahu won't let you anywhere near the town. You even thinking about leaving him like this will be a total betrayal in his eyes. He'll be furious."

"Let him be angry. His gem is a fake, he won't get any money from the Krethans, and he won't get any money from anyone else once we're gone," Maaya said.

Roshan opened and closed his mouth repeatedly, and his discomfort started to make Maaya uncomfortable. Ever the relentless optimist, ever the one with something uplifting to say, it was unusual for him to be this constantly at a loss for words or a silver lining.

"So, that's really the only way, is it?" he asked finally.

"That we know of, unfortunately," Svante replied. "If I knew any other way, I wouldn't have traveled this far."

"I see."

The silence that followed was almost too painful to bear. Maaya felt awful. She couldn't imagine how Roshan must feel, coming to visit his friends only to find out that they were thinking about traveling across the world with someone he was still realizing was not their mortal enemy—not to mention having to find out like this. She knew it wasn't their fault. They had only just started discussing the idea before Roshan had arrived. Still, the thought bothered her. They had been friends for a long time, and he deserved better than this.

"I… Roshan, I'm… sorry," Maaya said ashamedly. She wasn't able to meet his eyes no matter how hard she tried. "This is all happening very quickly, and to be honest, we still haven't decided anything for certain. And I promise, if we had known any sooner, I would've—"

"Hey, don't worry," Roshan interrupted, forcing a smile. "This isn't exactly a situation we're familiar with. I… I guess I just didn't picture you having to leave to fix all this. I thought you'd always be here."

"But we'll come back. I promise we'll come back. We'll find somewhere to stay nearby and everything will work out, I promise," Maaya said eagerly. She couldn't bear to see him like this, much less to be the one to cause it. "All we need to do is stop this machine of theirs and then we'll come right back, and it'll be like we never left. You wanted us to solve this, and now I finally feel like getting there."

"It'll be that much better when we get back, too," Kim said. "No more ghosts! And maybe Rahu will have gone out of business by then."

"Not to mention you can still get him for fraternizing with the enemy," Saber said pointedly. "Svante's a good one, but no one else has to know that."

"Thanks, I think?" Svante mumbled.

Roshan sighed heavily, then stood up with a smile.

"I won't pretend to be a fan of this, but you have to do what you have to do. This is what we set out to do, after all. I'll keep the town in good shape while you're gone. In the meantime, how about I make you guys some food? You all look exhausted."

The others agreed emphatically, and Roshan got right to it, looking glad for something to do to help. Maaya still felt terribly guilty, but she was glad he understood. Somehow he always did.

"Hey, what did you come by for, anyway? Do you have more news?" Kim asked as she helped Roshan set out the pots and utensils.

"I just wanted to make sure you guys were okay. There was a huge commotion down near Corridor C—I'm guessing another attack happened, and I wanted to see if you were safe."

"Oh, yes. We were there for that, actually. These children, they put a stop to it quickly. It was very impressive," Svante said encouragingly.

Roshan looked conflicted between relief at the good news and irritation at who was delivering it, but settled with a nod of understanding.

"I figured. I can't imagine what else you guys must've done tonight that'd leave you looking this exhausted. Especially you, Maaya; you look like you're about to pass out right there."

"That's because—" Kim started, but Maaya silenced her with a glare.

"I had to use some cards, that's why," she explained. As Roshan went back to cooking, she continued in a much quieter voice to Kim, "He's worried enough already. I don't want him to know about… about that."

Half an hour later it was time to eat. Roshan even set a place for Svante, who looked absolutely delighted at being invited to eat with them. As was tradition, the first few minutes of their meal was silent as everyone scarfed down their food. Then, as things settled and their eating slowed, Roshan again was the one to break the silence.

"So… when do you have to leave, anyway?"

Everyone at the table turned to look at Svante. They hadn't figured that part out yet.

"Well, uh… I don't exactly have a set departure date, but obviously the sooner the better. I need to resolve some things with Rahu and prepare my belongings and then send a final message to my government updating them on our situation. So, when all is said and done, I believe we should be prepared to leave Sark in… two days."

"Won't Rahu suspect something's up?" Kalil asked through a mouthful of food.

"I doubt it. I'll simply say that the council has requested my presence that I might receive his money for him. So long as I continue to feign Rahu's allegiance, Sark's government won't have any reason to suspect me, either. The man holds an uncomfortable amount of sway here. As for you, he has no idea we've even met, so you'll be in no trouble. By the time he is able to put everything together we'll be safely out of his reach."

"And dad and I will keep working on getting him into some deep legal trouble from our end," Roshan said enthusiastically. "With any luck Rahu will be so mad he'll slip up and give us something big to work with."

Despite the excitement of the night, dinner ended quickly; everyone at the table was simply too exhausted to talk anymore. Svante, who seemed eager to continue discussing details, nevertheless seemed to get the hint when Sovaan fell asleep at the table.

Svante pulled on his cloak as Roshan cleared the table, ignoring Maaya's requests for him to leave it alone for them to take care of in the morning. Svante didn't seem to want to leave just yet, but didn't look confident enough to help Roshan cleared the table, and so instead he stood awkwardly by the door fiddling with the clasp on his cloak.

"Do you need something?" Saber asked finally, raising an amused eyebrow.

"Oh, I just, I wanted to say… thank you for having me for dinner. And for listening to me and for being willing to do this with me. You're all wonderful people."

"Us? 'Wonderful?' My dear man, please raise your standards at least a little," Saber replied with a grin.

"I'll be in touch when I have more specifics about our, uh, departure," Svante continued with a nervous glance in Roshan's direction. "I may not see you until right before we need to leave so we aren't spotted together. Suspicion, you know. So, just… be ready, if you will."

"I'll make sure the kids are ready to go the instant you arrive," Saber agreed. "Now, in the meantime, go home so they can get some shuteye. They're quite fatigued from trying to beat the life out of you earlier."

Kim repeated what she said to Roshan, who smirked, but said nothing. Svante nodded, and then, evidently unsure of how to properly say goodbye, simply opened the door and vanished into the night.

"All right, get some sleep everyone," Maaya said sleepily, and the others looked only too happy to oblige. They filed quietly upstairs, and not another sound was heard.

Roshan finished cleaning the dishes a few minutes later, then blew out most of the candles in the room, leaving only the ones over the fireplace. Saber, sensing his departure was near, retrieved Maaya's pillow and blanket for her.

"Hey, so… are we okay?" Maaya asked guiltily. Roshan peered over at her inquisitively. "I mean, us. Are we okay? Sorry, I know that's awkward, it's just… you've been working so hard and I feel like I'm suddenly abandoning you, and I want to make sure…"

"Everything's fine, I promise," Roshan interrupted gently, hugging her tightly. "None of this is going how I thought, but I guess I should have expected this wouldn't be nice and easy to fix. But I'd rather you do this than stay home because you feel bad for leaving me for a little while."

"I'm so glad. Still, I'm sorry. I'll make this up to you, I promise."

"You want to make this up to me? Get a good night's sleep for once," Roshan said, and Maaya giggled.

"I'll try my best. The town can manage without me for that long, I'm sure."

"Don't jinx it," Roshan laughed.

They said their goodnights quickly, as Maaya was only barely conscious by this point, and Roshan left quietly after blowing out the last candles. Saber made sure her friend was comfortable, locked the door behind Roshan, and then for the first time in a long while, lay down near Maaya to spend the night inside.

14

THE GREATEST LOSS

Even as Maaya drifted off to sleep she wondered if she was going to be awoken early the next morning by Rahu or his bird. With everything that was going on in the town recently, she was sure he wouldn't give them a moment's peace.

However, when she awoke the next day, the light of early afternoon sun filtered through the grimy windows of their small house. The town outside bustled as usual, and for the first time in a while, Maaya realized she had nothing to do that day. She had a feeling they wouldn't be seeing Rahu today. If he ever came, it was bright and early in the morning.

Unfortunately, it seemed like everyone else in the house was still asleep; Maaya had quite enjoyed waking up to the smell of a delicious breakfast.

She got up slowly and stretched, making sure any remnants of the previous night's dizziness had faded. She still felt slightly weak, but she knew that was mostly the effects of the cards she had used and not her encounter with the ghosts. That, at least, was comforting.

When she had first started using *libris* it had taken some getting used to, and at first she thought the powers behind them had been making her sick. After her first real attempt at using the magic, which had caused her to pass out from the worst pain she'd ever felt in her life, she started to understand the way they really worked. *Libris* didn't grant any *additional* power the user didn't already have. It simply let the wielder of the card use as much power as they wanted in bursts, only to make up for that effort later. If she used a card that let her run three blocks in a matter of seconds, her body still reacted as though she had run three blocks regardless of how fast she got there. Cards that improved her strength let her lift greater weights, but her muscles were still put under the same amount of strain, and she felt every bit of it as soon as she let the magic fade.

Even with healing cards the effect was the same, so she had to be careful. If she used a card to heal a cut in seconds, her body still used the same amount of energy and nutrients it would have taken to heal in a normal period of time—just all at once. Healing serious wounds left her feeling drained, and plenty of rest and food was required to make up for the loss.

It was still a more comforting feeling than what she experienced in both encounters with the ghosts, however. Both times she had experienced a total loss of control of her own body, which terrified her. Her ability to move was what kept her alive. She had had a few experiences with sleep paralysis, and they were among the most frightening moments in her life.

Her mind drifted back to the ghosts. Beyond this power of theirs to completely shut her down if they made eye contact, there didn't seem to be anything particularly special about them. Their ability to kill was reliant on their ability to make contact with people, and they could only do that because people couldn't see them; otherwise they moved slowly in straight lines and only lasted for the duration of a few blocks.

But still they killed. And from what Svante had explained, that was only going to get worse. The vast majority of the world had no defense at all against them.

Maaya shifted uncomfortably. The weight of responsibility hung heavily over her, and she wasn't even thinking about her planned expedition to Krethus. The world was having problems with ghosts, and as was usually the case, Maaya and her friends appeared to be some of the only people who could do anything about it. She knew the ghosts had to be stopped, but she wasn't sure she could handle just how big this was. She fought with ghosts over control of a building or a street—not the entire world.

Saber floated lazily downstairs and grinned as she made eye contact with Maaya, coming over quickly to sit with her.

"Thank goodness. I thought everyone in this house was going to sleep until nightfall," Saber said.

"That'd be nice," Maaya sighed, resting her face in her hands. "I think we're pushing ourselves too hard lately."

"Well, yeah," Saber said as though this was the most obvious thing in the world. "But that'll change soon. No more jobs for Rahu and an all-expenses-paid trip to Krethus coming up soon. Provided there aren't any ghosts out in the middle of the ocean, you should be able to rest as much as you want. You won't have anything else to do."

"Yeah, about that… do you think we're jumping into this too quickly?" Maaya asked slowly.

"Absolutely," Saber answered without missing a beat. "But the apocalypse never happens according to schedule. Besides, it's not so bad. All we're doing is taking a trip. We won't have to fight anybody or do anything too crazy. I just need to escort you to this machine with my forehead, you blow it up, and we're good to go. Not much worth hanging around here for anyway."

"What about life after that? What will we do? Where will we go?" Maaya pressed.

"We do what we want. We'll be free of Rahu and our ghost problem will be gone. Maybe you guys can even take up some, uh… what's the word I'm looking for… oh yes, *honest* work. Besides, I don't think Svante would leave us out in the cold. Not after doing that kind of job for him."

"I suppose. This just all seems very sudden. I hope we can trust him."

"Hey, he's a Krethan. I know Krethans to be very honest and genuine individuals."

Maaya raised her eyebrow.

"You're taking the news about your identity very well."

"What am I supposed to do, be ashamed? I have no allegiance to Selenthia. Besides, I was part of a high court! How amazing is that? I wonder if I knew any princesses. Or *was* a princess," Saber chuckled.

"I can't wait to find out with you," Maaya smiled. "Now, Your Majesty, help me make some breakfast."

"So what do you think we should do about Rahu?" asked Saber as they got up off the couch and headed to the kitchen.

"In what way?"

"Well, we're going to be ditching him soon, but we're not out of the woods yet. Do we confront him about what we know? If Roshan and his father add what information we've got to what they already have, we could make a hell of a departure by making sure he's safely and miserably in prison first."

"I figured we'd have as little to do with him as possible. If he gets used to not seeing us every day again it'll take that much longer for him to notice we've skipped town. I want us to have as much of a head start as possible."

"That's smart thinking right there," Saber said, tapping her finger to her temple. "I can't help but wonder if we should let him know we know what's going on, though. If anything comes crashing down while we're still here, I want him to see us as a valuable asset to hold on to, not something he can quickly discard. It'd be our way of protecting ourselves."

"Do you think we should find a temporary place to stay before we leave with Svante?" Maaya asked. Saber put her chin in her palm thoughtfully, then shook her head.

"If we're trying to avoid suspicion, that'd be too dangerous. If he comes looking for us and we aren't here he'll immediately know something is up. If we're in his sight we can at least hope to talk our way out of trouble if it comes. Oh, and speaking of trouble..."

Maaya looked out one of the cloudy windows facing the nearby street and blinked in disbelief. As though on cue, Rahu was making his way toward their house.

"Why in the world... in the middle of the day!" Maaya cursed. "He'll draw the whole block here!"

Rahu, however, didn't seem intent on parading himself about as usual. He seemed to be keeping a low profile, and if anyone waved his way, he completely ignored them. He disappeared from the view of the window, and a moment later there came a quiet knock at the door.

"Stay with me?" Maaya pleaded as she walked over to the door.

"As always," Saber assured her.

As soon as Maaya opened the door, Rahu came in quickly and shut the door behind him. This alone was already enough to surprise Maaya; usually he wouldn't deign to open or close a door for himself when someone like Maaya was nearby to do it for him.

"Afternoon," he said abruptly. "We need to speak."

"Is everything all right?" Maaya asked, but paused when Saber shook her head.

"Don't play too dumb. He'll expect you to know about last night's attacks; ask him if this is about that."

Maaya passed her message along, and Rahu nodded.

"I knew you would have heard about it by now. There's something going on in this town and it's getting worse. In the short term this is wonderful news for me, but this is a mystery I have not solved. If it continues to get worse, people will start to lose their faith in me. *Why* aren't you taking care of this problem?" he finished almost angrily.

"You've been working on it but it's proving difficult to figure out given the strange nature of the ghosts you're facing. Perhaps it would be useful if he could provide any additional information he may have," Saber suggested.

Again, Maaya repeated the message.

"Information *I* have? Have you forgotten how our relationship works? The information I give you is only as much as you need to find your way to a client's house."

"You saw him working with someone new recently and you thought perhaps you had called him in to discuss the problem; he's too smart to have all his eggs in one basket," Saber continued.

Maaya suppressed a shudder of fear. Telling Rahu that they knew about the Krethan was a dangerous gamble. There was a fine line between being helpful and being nosy, and like Rahu had said, he wasn't interested in Maaya's initiative.

"Oh, it's just that I saw you working with someone I haven't seen before recently. I thought you might have called in someone else to help work on the problem at the same time as us. I know you're a man of business and you have to make smart choices, so I just assumed that was it. And I thought it might be effective if we worked together." Maaya bit her tongue hard, both to prevent herself from continuing to talk and also because complimenting Rahu was extremely difficult.

"Ah. I was hoping that my interactions with that man would have been a little more discreet. I don't want him ruining my reputation. If you see him again, stay clear of him. He is as manipulative and dishonest as they come."

"And that, my dear fellow, is called speaking from experience," Saber said loudly.

Not helping, Maaya mouthed angrily when Rahu looked away for a moment. The ghost simply winked.

"You're right, however," Rahu continued. "I *was* working with him in the beginning. He claimed to have some knowledge about this new type of ghost and wanted to combine it with something I have in my possession. A tool of some sort, I'm not entirely certain. But he revealed himself to be completely devoid of morals; he wanted my tool, I gave him a price, and he would not pay it. His money is evidently more important than the lives of innocents."

"You lying vermin. You're the one holding it over his head for a price!" Saber hissed, immediately incensed.

"That's awful," Maaya said. "Can we do anything to help? Is there something we can steal from him for you, perhaps?"

"No, he—" Rahu started dismissively, then paused as though he had been struck by a revelation. "Actually, it would be very helpful if you could track him for me. He doesn't know you, so he wouldn't realize he's being followed. Don't take anything; just keep track of where he goes, at what times, and who else he talks to. I doubt he will have given up his mission just because one man presented a slight obstacle."

"Mission?"

"I have a suspicion that he is an enemy of the state and that he is actually the source of these attacks. I have no proof, of course; that's where you come in. Gather information for me—something compelling that I can provide to the police."

"Don't the police have professionals for that kind of work?" Maaya asked hesitantly.

"You are professionals. Your current job title simply doesn't reflect that. Anyway, get one of your ghost friends to do the job with you. They're bound to be more effective than any police spy."

"I... all right," Maaya relented. Rahu clearly had a story he wanted to convince them of, and the sooner she acted like she had fallen for it the sooner he would leave. "Do you have a name? Address?"

"No, and no," Rahu answered. "But you can't miss him. He spends a lot of time near the government corridor, no doubt because he expects to gain something there. He's got pale skin and hair white as snow; not exactly a local."

"Right... if he sticks out that much, won't the police be after him first?"

"We aren't barbarians, Maaya; what talk is this? They wouldn't pursue him because of his appearance. Right now the assumption is he's working with me, so he's free to roam. For now."

"Understood," Maaya said. "Was... there anything else?"

"Actually, yes," Rahu said. "You and the others clearly aren't working hard enough at getting rid of, or even slowing down, these attacks. You're on a mission for me tonight. I want you to split up and take positions around the town during the night. I want you to track possible attacks and then put them down before they have a chance to progress. Perhaps once we show them they mean business they'll think twice before striking again. But you need to be more aggressive."

"Where should we go?" Maaya asked, fully intent on not cooperating with these instructions.

"I don't care, that's for you to figure out," Rahu snapped. "If I have to spell out street corners for you to walk to I might as well do the job myself."

"Right, sorry. We'll strategize tonight and then get out there," Maaya affirmed hastily. "As soon as one shows up we'll be right on top of it."

"Good. Though... if you want to let it build ever so slightly--just enough to cause a scene—I wouldn't mind. People need to know that there's a threat and that I'm the one protecting them from it."

Saber made a gagging sound from right behind him.

"Should we tell you the instant one happens, then?" Maaya asked.

"Yes. Don't bother finding me; that would take too long. I brought my bird with me. When an attack occurs, tell the bird its location and tell it to go straight home. I'll be ready."

He took his metal bird out of his pocket, holding it like one might hold a small ball. With its wings folded and head tucked down it was small enough even to fit into one of Maaya's small pockets.

"Sir, if I may... if you want us to stop attacks at night and spy on that man during the day, how are we supposed to get any rest?"

"I told you you'd be busy. There are four of you. Work in shifts," Rahu answered shortly. "There's a lot to do right now for people with your skills. We need to stop these ghosts and figure out the true purpose behind this man's visit here, and we need to do so quickly. If there aren't any people left in town, there's no one left to pay for my services. Also, before I forget..." Rahu had started toward the door, then paused and turned to stare directly at Maaya. "There are a lot of politics involved in a situation like this. Politics are not for you. Do what you're told and nothing more. If you get nosy, you may find yourself on the receiving end of the law just like my white-haired friend."

Maaya nodded. She had to admit he was a perceptive man. He covered his bases, and this would be effective for people who actually followed his instructions. Under most circumstances Maaya would have done her best to keep her friends safe but otherwise do exactly as Rahu said. Now, however, with their imminent departure from Sark, she had no plans on following any more of Rahu's instructions. Especially not if they involved seeking out the strange ghosts.

At least, that's what she had in mind before Rahu spoke again.

"I'll be sending birds to check up on you throughout the night. Since you already have one of mine, they'll be able to find you easily."

"But... we're already going to send you a message the instant anything happens, you don't need to..." Maaya attempted feebly.

"I do, though," Rahu replied dryly. "I need to make sure you're doing as you're told. I know you usually do, but this is more important than anything you've done before. Maybe you fail to grasp the severity of a weapon no one can see or hear wiping out streets full of people, but I don't, and frankly, I don't want to be next. They *must* be stopped. If you don't find any ghosts this evening, maybe you'll at least find a sense of perspective."

With that, Rahu departed, closing the door firmly behind him.

Maaya fumed in the ensuing silence. She should have known Rahu would find a way to mess things up one last time. Along with the fact that they would be forced to scout the town at night, his implication that she didn't understand how serious this was made her blood boil. The knowledge that he was faking everything didn't help. He had always had the ability to get under her skin like no one else ever could.

"There are so many things wrong with what just happened I don't even know where to begin," Saber commented as she watched Rahu walk swiftly back down the street.

"Don't begin at all, please," Maaya sighed. "There's no point. We have one last job to do and we'll have to do it whether or not we point out all the flaws in his lies."

"He was honest enough about wanting the attacks to stop. The man is legitimately terrified," Saber pointed out. "Sure, he might be lying about Svante and just about everything else, but Rahu doesn't gain anything from this in the long run. He's just putting on airs so you don't see his fear, that's all."

"I hope he's next," Maaya said bitterly. "If there's any attack tonight, let it get him and no one else. At least then we wouldn't have to worry about having to see him in the afterlife, either."

"Oh, Rahu existing for eternity is not something I want to imagine. Apart from my suspicions that he has contingency plans that could put you in danger, that's been the only thing stopping me from killing him in his sleep, you know. He's angry and evil enough to come back."

Lunch was soon made, and at the smell of food, the others in the house quickly came downstairs, still rubbing the sleep from their eyes. Maaya was thankful Rahu's intrusion hadn't woken them. It would have undoubtedly frightened them.

When everyone's eating had slowed, Maaya spoke.

"Rahu came by earlier. He has a job for me tonight."

"For you? By yourself?" Kim asked, confused. In the chair beside her, Saber raised her eyebrows, awaiting an explanation.

"Well, technically, he wants us all to do it. But I want you guys to rest tonight. You haven't had a night off in a long time."

At once, the table erupted in protests.

"You haven't even told us what the job is!"

"We always go together, you know that."

"Relaxing isn't even fun if you aren't here!"

"If you go, Saber's gonna go with you, so it'll be lonely here."

"We *like* taking jobs, you know."

Maaya raised her hands to plead for silence, and gradually, the protests subsided.

"I know, I know, but hear me out. Rahu wants us to split up around town and actively hunt these ghosts. I don't like either part of that idea. The ghosts are dangerous enough when we're a full group, and splitting up makes that even worse. I just don't want you guys in any danger. All we have to do is hold out for one or two more nights and then we're out of here anyway; I don't want you to have to do any more of Rahu's work before we leave."

"How come you're going, then?" Sovaan asked.

"Rahu gave me one of his birds. I'm supposed to use it to notify him if there's an attack, but he can also use it to track me," Maaya sighed. "But he only gave me one, which means only one of us has to go."

"Why shouldn't we do it? Seems like a fair enough request, even if it's dangerous," Kalil jumped in. "We want these ghosts gone as much as anyone, why not do our part?"

"We *are* doing our part, that's why we're traveling to Krethus," Maaya rebutted.

"And what, we're supposed to spend the whole time until then packing for the trip? I dunno if you've noticed, but we don't own a whole lot—"

"Stop it!" Maaya cried suddenly, and the table quieted in surprise. "We've been lucky enough to fight them off so far, but that's just it: luck. They've been coming in larger numbers every time. Combine that with splitting up and we're just asking for trouble. Besides, you haven't felt what they can do to you. I *can't* let that happen to you."

"What about you?" Kim asked quietly. "It's only happened to you so far. Wouldn't it be better if someone took your place? Just for tonight?"

Though she knew Kim didn't mean it negatively, the implication stung.

"It's just a coincidence. I've been closest to them both times," Maaya said. "Besides, I'll have Saber with me. I don't intend on doing anything dangerous, and with any luck there won't even be any attacks tonight. The only reason I'm doing this is because if Rahu sees we've stayed home we'll be in deep trouble."

"We'll have to go somewhere else for the night, then," Kalil said. "He's bound to stop by the house."

"Where else can we go, really?" Kim asked.

"We could always hang out with Styx and the others. Bet they love seeing so much of us lately," Sovaan suggested.

"Maybe you should let everyone come along," Saber suggested, and Maaya glanced at her in surprise. "Kalil's right; we all have to be out of the house anyway. Besides, we'd only be splitting up for the sake of keeping an eye on things. As soon as anything happens, we group up and tackle them, Rahu gets his credit, and he might leave us alone until we're out of here."

"Yeah, it'll be fine," Kalil said, jumping quickly on this opportunity. "We wouldn't just jump in without letting everyone else know first. We'd play it safe as always."

"We do work best when we're a team," Saber added.

"I know, I just… we're so close to making it out of here safely. I want to take as few risks as possible."

"Well, how do you think we feel?" Kim asked, looking hurt. "You tell us there's a dangerous job but that you're going to do it by yourself. We care about you just like you care about us, you know. If something happened to you I'd never forgive myself for just sitting at home avoiding danger."

"I… that's fair, but…" Maaya said, feeling utterly deflated.

"When you first met me and asked me to join you, you told me to make sure I knew what I was getting into," Kim pressed. "Well, I did then, and I do now. You're stuck with us, just like you always wanted."

"And hey, these kids have been doing this for a long time now. They know their stuff," Saber said, and the others nodded proudly. "We'll be fine. There's safety in numbers, and we'll do this by the book. We'll be fine."

"I don't think there's a book on stuff like this, Saber," Kalil grinned.

"We'll write it, then," Saber said determinedly.

"Yeah, for all the dozen people in the world who can read," Sovaan joked.

The others laughed, but Maaya felt sick to her stomach. It was a feeling she was becoming uncomfortably familiar with recently. She soothed herself by remembering that their trip was only a day or so away. She was sure that would have dangers of its own, but they would be away from Rahu and Sark, at least. In addition, they would be with Svante, who if nothing else could provide some kind of financial stability.

The others by now were already acting as though the decision had been made and that they were joining Maaya during the coming night, and Maaya decided not to press the issue. She knew they would listen to her if she absolutely forced them to stay put, but she didn't want to deal with the aftermath. The look on Kim's face had been all Maaya needed to see.

The evening dragged on, and after the candles and fireplace were lit, Maaya found herself sitting on the floor in a circle with the others as they made new cards. Everyone was contributing to the blood cards tonight; there was no telling how many ghosts would show up. Upon Maaya's instruction, each person was to have no fewer than two dozen blood cards.

"Until we all get together in a group, bloods are to be used for defensive purposes only, and only if necessary," Maaya told them. "Otherwise, burn your greens and purples to keep out of range and sight. Once we're all together we can coordinate an attack."

"Oh, and don't look them in the eyes, whatever you do," Saber advised.

"If one of you is disabled in any way, the others need to take them and retreat. Under no circumstance will you stay and fight. Understand?" Maaya continued.

The others nodded in unison. It was all they could do to hide their anticipation, but they knew Maaya's serious tone was not one to respond to with jest.

As Maaya was tying the laces on her shoes, there came a knock at the door. For once, Maaya wasn't very concerned. She knew it wasn't Rahu; he had already come to see them once that day, and if he wanted to get in touch with them again, he had access to multiple birds. That left only Roshan, and she was greatly looking forward to seeing him again.

When she opened the door, however, she saw Svante standing on the step.

"What are you doing here? Come in, quick, before anyone sees," Maaya said hurriedly. Svante obliged, and Maaya closed and locked the door behind him.

"I, uh, I just wanted to tell you that I've managed to secure passage out of town tomorrow afternoon," Svante said, rubbing his hands together from the cold. "The carriage will take us to Anorath, and from there we'll just be one ride away from the port city of Levien, where I entered the country. I already have someone who can take us to Krethus from there; we just need to get to them. But, ah… am I interrupting something?"

"We're going ghost hunting!" Sovaan announced gleefully from his spot by the fireplace.

"You're not going after those horrid things, surely," Svante said.

"Unfortunately, we have no choice. Rahu gave us orders, complete with a tracking device," Maaya explained, holding out the mechanical bird. "We're just going to do this one last thing for him to get him off our backs. He could still ruin our lives before tomorrow afternoon if he really put his mind to it."

"I see…" Svante said, looking troubled. "Most unfortunate timing. I don't suppose there's anything I could do to help?"

"Got anything to eat?" Sovaan asked immediately, grinning as Kim shushed him.

"Actually, I wouldn't mind if you joined us," Maaya answered. "Your implant lets you see ghosts, so you could help us look."

"Are you going to fight them? I'm no use fighting them," Svante said nervously.

"Not unless we have to. If we do, we're going in as a group. Mostly we're just hoping none of them show up tonight."

"Also, you can help by not making yourself obvious," Saber said. "If Rahu checks up on us and notices that you're with us, well, you're all in deep, deep trouble."

"Ah, right, of course," Svante said. "Has he, uh, mentioned our little disagreement?"

"He gave us his version, yeah. And then he asked us to get dirt on you," Maaya said, and couldn't help but smile at the look on Svante's face. "That's not going to happen, obviously. But it means he doesn't know we've communicated at all."

"It means he doesn't know a *lot* of things," Saber sniffed. "He thinks he's so very clever."

"Any semblance of power does give that illusion," Svante mused. "Don't you worry. I'll stay out of sight and trouble. Where are we all headed, anyway?"

"Kalil, Sovaan, and Kim are headed down to patrol between the government corridor and the area around Mayberry Street, and Saber and I are going to be scouting other parts near downtown," Maaya decided. "We figure it's better to be closer to where more people are. If the ghosts show up in a crowded area, we'll need to get to them right away or they'll… well, you know."

"Sounds wonderful. How long will we be doing this?"

"Until we think we can get back home without getting in trouble."

"Say, this is all very dangerous, don't you think? Why not come stay with me until we can leave tomorrow afternoon? I doubt Rahu would be able to search the entire town by then," Svante suggested timidly.

"No, but he could always have the police block all the exits and get everyone to be on the lookout for you. You stand out just a little," Saber said. "Besides, if an attack happens, we'd probably find ourselves there anyway because we're not fond of letting people die."

Svante opened his mouth to protest, then closed it again without saying a word. Unfortunately, Maaya thought, Saber was right. Rahu was only one man, but he had the power of many. The town seemed awfully big until half its population was on the lookout for someone; it was still small enough where most people in a community knew each other and where news spread fast.

"We'll be off, then," Kalil said, and with a wave and a grin, he stepped out the door and into the night.

"I guess we'll get going as well," Kim added nervously, gesturing at Sovaan.

"Maybe we'll meet your *boyfriend* out there," Sovaan said slyly, and Kim glared at him. "What? You've told him by now, right?"

"N-not… we've been busy," Kim stammered, her face turning pink. "But I will do it before we leave. Tomorrow. I'll do it tomorrow."

She glanced at Maaya as she said these words, and Maaya gave her an encouraging smile.

"Good luck, you two. And Sovaan, be nice."

"Yes'm," Sovaan chuckled, and then he and Kim walked out of the house, jogging to catch up to Kalil.

The house seemed oddly empty now. For a split second, as the loneliness swept in, Maaya wanted to take it all back. They could spend some time with Styx or go exploring together like they had always done. But she resisted the urge. It was just one more night, just a few more hours until the next phase of their journey began.

"I guess that means we're next," Svante said. "I'll follow your lead; I assume you know the town much better than I do."

Saber locked the door from the inside after they left, then glided through the wall to join them as they started toward downtown. Svante stared at her in fascination, but said nothing.

"You've never actually talked to a ghost before, have you?" Saber said finally, a smile playing across the corners of her lips.

"Ah, no, actually," Svante said awkwardly. "I've seen a few since getting this implant, but I've been too afraid to approach them. I'm afraid that's why I mistook you for one of the other ghosts at first."

"How very *living* of you," Saber replied with amusement. "But I can't say

I blame you. Many ghosts are just plain out of their minds. The longer they've been dead the worse it gets. Honestly, you're safer if you can't see them."

"But you seem so… so…"

"Pleasant? Warm? Kindhearted? Well, as you know, I've lost my memories. I know nothing about who I was while I was alive so I've none of the scars of life to ruin my death. Besides, I'm somewhat indebted to the living, as it was a living person who brought me out of my in-between state, as it were."

"What do you mean?" Svante asked, already fascinated.

"There was a time when I was not alive, but not in this form, either. I have very limited memory of that time, too; it's like I was in a dream. I was vaguely aware of the passage of time, but only so much that when I finally took this form you see now, I knew it had been a very, very long time."

"May I ask what form you were in before, if any?"

In response, Saber tapped the gem on her forehead.

"Maaya found this circlet in the basement of that abandoned mansion. Something about her touch brought me out of it, and I became completely aware of the world. She and I have been together ever since, causing mischief and all that. You know, you intrigue me, Krethan," she continued before he could speak. "The only humans I've met so far who could see ghosts didn't have a choice, and claiming to be able to do so gets you burned alive. Why would you seek something like that on purpose?"

"The Krethan government has known about the ghosts for quite a while now. Longer than I've been alive. This machine really forced us to change our view on things; before that, it wasn't too much different there than it is here," Svante said. "There are few with natural abilities, and those among them who can use *libris* are recruited to defend the country. The elites, they're called. I have no powers myself, but I've always been a man of science, so I wanted to join the fight in whatever way I could. Besides, I must admit, after knowing ghosts have been among us all this time, I… very much wanted to see them. To talk to them."

"So what's it like in Krethus now for people who can see ghosts?" Maaya asked. "Now that everyone knows they really exist, I mean."

"It's quite a different world. Not perfect, but better. Those who practice *libris* do so openly, and are even admired. Some people still hold on to the old fears, but necessity begets change. I for one am optimistic about our country's future."

"Maybe a few more disasters here wouldn't hurt. We could change some minds here as well," Saber said acidly.

They walked the rest of the way in silence until they reached downtown. The streets became brighter and cleaner, and despite the lateness of the hour, many of Sark's wealthier citizens still roamed the streets. Svante pulled up his cloak to cover his hair, and they continued on.

After their third time awkwardly turning to face each other in conversation when people passed closely by, Maaya decided to look for a higher vantage point. Glancing around, she found a rooftop balcony on one of the apartment buildings nearby which had a convenient fire escape ladder leading up to it and every level below. With Svante blustering some excuse to passersby about how they had locked themselves out of their rooms, he and Maaya climbed quickly to the top, where they sat down out of sight of those below.

Despite how much she disliked the light, Maaya had to admit it was a beautiful view. The lights stretched onward for many blocks, and the longer she looked, the more it appeared warm, friendly, and inviting. She suddenly found herself longing for a day where she could walk freely in that light, no longer afraid to show herself. That day would come, she knew that much. The world was an unfair place, but she was strong. She and her friends would get to enjoy that one day.

A cool breeze blew gently by, and Svante rubbed his hands together again. Maaya smiled slightly. He wasn't at all what she had expected him to be. He was an intelligent man, smart in the way of books but not of the streets, and even a little awkward in an endearing sort of way, nothing like the sly and villainous criminal she had been expecting. But clearly this was of no detriment to him; he worked for the Krethan government, after all.

"So what's it like? Krethus?" Maaya asked after a long period of silence. "What's it look like?"

"I'm probably biased, but I think it's a beautiful place. Much of it has been ravaged, but what remains… well, it's something else," Svante said reminiscently. "We still have gleaming cities full of light and friendly people. We have wonderful landscapes, too. The mountains and oceans and rivers are a painter's dream. Still… it's just not the same as it used to be. There is still much beauty there, but the undercurrent of fear that has persisted there for so long has somewhat tarnished it."

"Until we change that," Maaya said softly.

"Yes. We can. We must. It's hard to believe, you know. Everyone grows up studying the 'fall' of Krethus at the start of these attacks, and everyone is trained to be vigilant, to be creative, to look for solutions. We're also taught to expect disappointment. This is what life is now, we've all known that our entire lives. And yet, here I sit, with one possible means, perhaps *the* means, of ending this forever sitting right beside me. It's… quite a feeling."

"Imagine the fanfare you'll return home to," Saber said, raising her arm in a sweeping gesture before her. "The hero of Krethus returns! Savior of the century!"

Svante chuckled, shaking his head.

"Oh, never. Not that. Save me the fanfare and let me return home to my wife and daughter. All I want is a comfortable job that doesn't have me traveling the world, a good book to read in the evenings, and tea on Wednesday afternoons. That's all I ask."

"Why Wednesday?" Maaya laughed.

"To celebrate the middle of the week! It's a nice break, you know. You work hard, but then you take a moment every now and then to sit back and enjoy the world before your eyes before getting back to it. It's nice to ground yourself every once in a while. Go adventuring, work hard, get caught up in gossip or what have you, but always keep one foot back home. That way you can pull yourself out of anything if ever you need to."

"That sounds perfect," Maaya said contentedly, leaning back with her palms on the ground behind her. "That's all I want for me and my friends. We've talked about it for years. Someday we're going to have a big house in the countryside where everyone gets a room all to themselves, and we'll just live peacefully there forever."

"An admirable goal. I'm glad you understand. For me, life is so much about the small comforts. When you get too far, you start to lose sight of them. If you can find joy in the little things you'll truly be content. At least that's how I view it. When I return home when this is all over, I'll already have everything I could ever need."

"You two are saps, ugh," Saber said from behind them, and the three of them laughed.

The more Svante talked, however, the more Maaya grew to like him, and subsequently, to trust him. He spoke from the heart, and his words connected with her in a way she was sure many of his colleagues couldn't relate to. His words were too genuine to be dishonest.

Hours passed, and there was still no sign of any ghost walk or any word from Rahu or the others. Maaya, Svante, and Saber passed the time by talking about themselves, asking questions of each other, or playing trivia games. Maaya and Saber weren't very good at those, but they enjoyed hearing questions about things they had never imagined before and then hearing the answers to them, which were even more interesting than the questions.

In the midst of Svante telling an entertaining story about how a prank in the office had quickly gotten out of hand when one of his superiors' hair caught fire, a mechanical bird fluttered down to meet them, its metal feet clinking lightly against the metal of the railing.

"Stay quiet," Saber hissed at Svante.

"Can it see me?" Svante asked nervously, staring at the bird's vivid eyes.

"I don't think so, but keep your hood up and look away."

The bird's tiny mouth opened, and Rahu's voice played to them. Maaya felt a twinge of irritation despite how distorted and tinny it was.

No news is good news, I take it. It's getting early into the morning and we've never seen an attack this late. With any luck that means we're safe for the night. Still, I expect you to remain vigilant until at least sunrise, and I still expect a report when you're done. Tell me where you went, what you saw, and how you divided yourselves up. I want to be confident that you have a system in place for when we really need it. Also, don't think I've forgotten about your payment for delivering the gem to me. I've been in talks to purchase a house that should be finalized by the end of the week. I hope I was not too hasty in doing such a thing.

The bird closed its mouth and cocked its head slightly, and Maaya nodded impatiently.

"Yes, I got it. Go home."

The bird obliged, immediately taking flight and disappearing into the darkness.

Svante glanced cautiously at the railing to make sure the bird was gone, then lowered his hood again.

"Honestly, if that's how closely he monitors you, I don't blame you for trying so hard not to displease him. Also… did he say he's buying a house?"

"He was so pleased we got him the gem that he decided to *hire* us full time," Maaya said sardonically. "He's getting us a house closer to him. It sounds nice in theory, but he still wouldn't be paying us. He just wants us on an even tighter leash."

"Well, good thing we're cutting that off entirely, isn't it?" Svante grinned. "It is a horridly boring thing to sit out here in the cold all night, though."

"Have you always gotten cold so easily?" Saber asked in amusement as the Krethan bundled his cloak more tightly about himself.

"Oh, yes. I'm used to a warmer climate; it's almost always sunny and warm where I live. Some would call it boring, and we've had our struggles with drought, but I quite like it. How do you endure it?"

"More layers. That and our lovely fireplace. Say what you want about our tiny house, but it doesn't take much to heat it up," Maaya answered. "I can't stand the heat of summer. At least when I'm cold I can put more on, but if it's hot there's only so much I—"

She broke off as Saber made a gesture at her side. The ghost had suddenly perked up, and now she looked off into the distance. Her eyes searched the dark horizon, but when Maaya followed her gaze, she could see nothing.

"What is it?" Svante whispered.

"I thought I heard something," Saber murmured. "Someone screaming."

The trio fell completely silent. Svante stood slowly, squinting into the distance. Maaya heard a tiny motor whir and click within his ocular implant, and she was temporarily distracted, fascinated by the way the lens moved in and out.

"I'm trying to get a closer look," Svante explained when he caught Maaya's expression. "It's no expensive telescope, but it's useful. Still, I'm not seeing anything. They'd be hard to miss, wouldn't they? What with how bright they are."

"That's my thought," Saber said slowly, finally turning back to the others. "And I suppose screams aren't all that uncommon at night in Sark. Would that it was just a normal murder this time."

Svante gaped.

"I apologize if I sound rude, but are the dead usually so uncouth?"

Saber threw him a withering look.

Before she could reply, however, there came a cry from much closer. It echoed through the bright streets, and before it had faded, another came. Then another.

"Where are they coming from?" Maaya asked quickly.

Saber floated a few feet into the air to get a better view, then pointed off into the distance.

"There! Northeast of us. Can you see the light?"

It took her a moment, but then she saw it. It was faint at first, but growing quickly. It was pure white, unlike the light that any lantern or fire could provide. Her stomach dropped.

"That's up toward Mayberry Street. The others could be there. Come on!"

Maaya started for the ladder, but Saber quickly stopped her.

"No time for conventional means of transport. We'll get there faster over the rooftops."

"Right."

Maaya immediately pulled one each of a green and purple card from her pouch, then paused and glanced over at Svante.

"I'm sorry, Svante. If you can't keep up we'll need to leave you behind."

"Not to worry; I have a trick or two up my sleeve. Or trousers, I suppose," Svante replied. He lifted his trouser leg slightly; where Maaya expected to see more pale skin, she saw the gleam of a bronze limb augment.

Saber, despite her rush, did a double take.

"You keep impressing me, Krethan. Now let's move."

Maaya burned her cards, and soon they were leaping across the rooftops over the streets below. Since this was a wealthier area the buildings were situated farther apart, and it took significantly more effort to make each jump. Maaya knew that when she lay down to rest when this was all over, she was definitely going to feel it.

To his credit, Svante was managing to keep up somewhat. It was clear that while his augments granted him some extra speed and mobility, they were no match for the power of *libris*, but despite quickly running out of breath he made every effort to stay at least a few buildings behind.

The town passed in a blur as Maaya and Saber continued on. As they got closer to their destination, the streets again became more cramped, giving Maaya more footholds and places to launch herself to and from. The bright light was only a dozen streets away now, brighter than the full moon. She frantically scanned the adjacent rooftops and scanned the streets quickly when she could, looking for any sign of her friends, but she saw nothing. Trying desperately not to think the worst, she pressed on toward the light and the screams that were now so painfully clear.

Moments before she arrived, however, the light suddenly vanished.

Maaya dodged around the last few chimneys, then came to a stop on a rooftop overlooking the street where the light had just been. The scene below was chaos. People ran in and out of buildings and in all directions, crying out in fear. As the noise spread, so too did the confusion; already the people in the next block were starting to wake and panic. It didn't matter that the ghosts were already gone.

"Do you see them?" Maaya cried. Saber stared down at the mass of people below, but then shook her head.

"They probably got out of here like we told them to," Saber said, and Maaya nodded, though she didn't feel any better. She had to be sure.

Svante arrived only a few moments later, panting heavily.

"Stars," he murmured as he looked down at the swirling mass of frightened people below. "What should we do? Should we try to calm them? The ghosts are already gone!"

"No, we should try to avoid being seen; the problem will sort itself out," Maaya replied. "We should probably get back and try to meet up with—"

"Maaya, look," Saber gasped. "Another one."

Maaya glanced up in shock. Sure enough, another mass of white light had appeared—this time toward the government corridor."

Maaya and Saber were on their way immediately, and though Svante tried valiantly to keep up, this time he fell behind. Maaya ignored him. She couldn't think about anything but her friends right now.

Again, however, just moments before Maaya and Saber arrived, the light suddenly disappeared, leaving screams and panic in its wake. Maaya looked around in growing despair. There was no sign of her friends. She glanced around the rooftops, hoping for a flash of purple or green that might indicate their fleeing presence, but there was nothing.

"Maaya, don't," Saber said firmly, reading Maaya's expression. "They're not here because we specifically told them not to be."

"Where should we go?" Maaya asked, trying to keep her voice level.

"Well, the ghosts are already gone. There's nothing we can do here. Our best bet is to get somewhere near the center of town so we can retain our advantageous position. We can keep a lookout for more walks and our friends while we're there. The others will probably be thinking the same thing."

Without a word, Maaya took off again, heading as fast as she could back toward their original position. Her heart pounded in her chest and it was all she could do to keep her breathing under control. Surely it was no coincidence that the ghosts had appeared only where her friends had been patrolling so far. But why were they disappearing so fast? Was it because they had killed the people they were after? Or perhaps because the victims they sought had instead defeated them?

Maaya berated herself furiously for not assigning a meetup point in the event of an emergency; she had assumed the town was so small that finding each other would be easy, but Sark had never seemed bigger. With every passing second, her brain fought to convince her of the worst.

As the girls approached the rooftop they had perched on earlier, Maaya saw a figure standing there. She felt a glimmer of hope, but that was quickly stifled as she realized it was only Svante. He looked up as he approached, relief washing over his face.

"I was hoping you'd come back here," he said tiredly. "What news?"

"They keep disappearing before we can catch them, and there's no sign of our friends," Maaya said. "Have you seen them?"

"I'm afraid not, but I've been keeping an eye out while you were away. There haven't been any more, ah, ghost walks anywhere else in town so far. I hope it stays that way."

"Likewise," Saber said, then cast a sideways glance at Maaya. "You can't keep those running for much longer or you'll be out of commission for days."

"We'll worry about that later," Maaya replied flatly. "Where do you think they've gone? Back to the house maybe?"

"I can go check if you'd like. It looks like the sun is going to be coming up soon anyway," Saber said. "With any luck the ghosts will be gone for the day and we'll find everyone home safe and sound."

Maaya breathed a low sigh of relief at the slowly brightening sky. In the midst of her frantic running and searching, she hadn't even noticed. Rahu had only specified sunrise. Soon enough she could send him his bird and then find the others. Svante's implant would come in handy there.

"Hey, Svante," Saber continued. "Why do the ghosts never come out during the day?"

Svante didn't answer. He stared east toward the growing light, watching it as though he had never seen it before.

"Hey, are you listening?" Saber asked crossly. "I know sunrise is beautiful, but you—"

Svante tore his gaze away from the light, and in his eyes Maaya saw only horror.

"That's not the sun."

There was a brief pause as the impact of these words hit them.

"Oh… oh stars, that's…" Saber stammered, slowly looking back toward the light.

It was near impossible to tell from this distance, but now that Svante had pointed it out, Maaya knew. The sun didn't rise that fast. Already the light was bright enough to fall upon the building they stood on, and her careful eye detected small flickers and changes in what should have been steady.

"How… how many can there be…?" Maaya whimpered.

"Hundreds," Svante answered quietly. "They've formed a line wide enough to wipe out multiple blocks at once, and they're converging on the town center."

"What's in the town center?" Saber asked urgently.

"I have no idea, but we will be soon," Maaya said determinedly.

"What? We can't go there! Not against that many, and we don't have the others with us!" Saber argued.

"Maybe they'll be there. Even if they aren't, we need to stop this. They'll wipe out all of Sark at this rate!"

"Hopefully they'll dissipate quickly like the others," Svante said, still staring intently over toward the light.

"Shouldn't you know how they work by now?" Saber asked harshly.

"No. That's why they've been so difficult to deal with," Svante answered without meeting her eyes. "Only the machine knows."

"Well, I'm going. You can come with me or stay behind, but I'm going," Maaya said, preparing to leap from the rails.

"There's no point to foolish heroism!" Saber said desperately. "We've already got a plan in motion to do something about this, but you need to stay alive in order—"

"The gem's on your head, Saber, not mine," Maaya snarled, and Saber looked taken aback. "I'm not going to do anything stupid, but I can't just stand by and do nothing."

"I… but… fine," Saber said, clearly flustered. "But before you do, at *least* send Rahu his bird. If there are this many, he needs to know. And heaven knows he's useless when it comes to things like this, but there's a tiny chance he might be able to do something."

Maaya paused, unable to take her eyes off the light. At a time like this, taking a break to send Rahu a message seemed like the stupidest and most pointless thing imaginable. She didn't have even the tiny amount of faith in

Rahu that Saber seemed to, but she did realize that if he didn't receive a message soon, he would probably be very unhappy.

She pulled the bird out of her pocket, and in that moment, she realized she had no idea how it was supposed to work.

"I… how do I make it go?" she asked helplessly. Svante immediately stepped to her side.

"If it works like all the others I've used, tap it twice on its head to turn it on. Then say 'record,' and speak. Say 'message complete' when you're done, and it will ask you who the recipient is; since this is Rahu's bird, just say his name."

Maaya nodded gratefully, then tapped the bird. It unfolded itself until it stood still in her palm, staring up at her expectantly.

"Record," Maaya said, and the bird's eyes glowed. "Rahu, there's a huge number of ghosts going toward the town center right now. I'm on my way there to deal with them. Thought you might want to know. Uh, message complete."

The light in the bird's eyes flickered off, and then a mechanical voice spoke.

"Recipient?"

"Rahu," Maaya said. The bird spread its wings without hesitation and flew off quickly into the night.

"Handy, that," Saber commented. "We should get going. This one doesn't look like it's going to stop any time soon."

Maaya immediately launched herself over the rails. With the power of her *libris* cards she didn't feel the least bit tired or out of breath despite everything she had done so far. She knew she was going to regret it later, but if she could make sure the town was safe for the night and find her friends, it would be worth it.

Svante, though he had caught his breath, didn't look as though he could keep up with them again so soon. He tried his best, but quickly faded from view behind them.

The light was almost blinding. Maaya's eyes adjusted the closer she got, and she had to remind herself to keep breathing. It stretched for blocks and blocks, and as she got closer she heard the deafening screams of terror from every direction. They rang in her ears just as they had done that night in Corridor B and during the night they had investigated Mayberry Street. They shook her to her core like no encounter with the dead ever had, and it took every ounce of willpower she had in her to avoid turning and running away.

The center of town was as populous as it was wealthy. Full of marble columns, etched stone, and statues, it was where trade with other towns once occurred, where laws were argued about and passed, and where visiting politicians stayed and dined. It was usually an impressive sight to behold; at least that's what Maaya had heard. She had never been there before. There was no disguise or excuse that could make someone like her look like she belonged, and there was no such thing as darkness there.

Ironically, that was even more the case than usual at the moment. Maaya slowed down as she arrived at the top of the immense capitol building, taking in the square at a glance to search for any good positions or hiding spots—but then she saw them.

She had never seen so many of them. The entire street was alight with the glowing figures, and even from her vantage point this high up she was uncomfortably aware of just how tall and menacing they were. There were no people here; there was simply no room for them. The ghosts below were like a blanket, slowly moving forward in an unstoppable march, so many in number that Maaya could not see the ground at all. The ghosts spread from one side of the square to the other, and as she looked on, more and more kept appearing out of thin air. Others materialized through the walls of nearby buildings they had evidently just been inside.

"Careful not to look in their eyes," Saber reminded, though she appeared too stunned to say anymore.

"This… this is impossible," Maaya breathed. "What do we do? They aren't stopping!"

"We need to stay safe. There's no way we can possibly fight this many."

Screams echoed from below, cutting off as quickly as they started as the wave swept through the square, and then the screams began farther away. Maaya look all around her in despair. All the blood cards they had ever made combined wouldn't have been enough to deal with this.

She knew, based on what Svante had said, that there may be more attacks, perhaps larger or more frequent. But she hadn't expected anything like this. At the rate this was progressing she feared it might soon sweep over the entire corridor—if not the town itself.

Suddenly, she glanced up in alarm.

"Roshan! Do you think—?"

"He should be safe. They're moving away from where he lives," Saber said, though she didn't look entirely convinced. "Let's find our own first, then we can worry about Roshan. Whatever we do, we need to get away from here."

"But they aren't stopping! How can we—?"

"There's an *army* down there, Maaya! We stand no chance. We need to run," Saber cried.

Maaya glanced helplessly down at the ghosts below, then back at Saber. She knew the ghost was right, but the screams pierced her skull, every interrupted cry of terror the mark of one less person who would be waking up that morning.

Still, as she looked on, she knew there was no fight to be made here. More and more ghosts were appearing by the minute. Hundreds upon hundreds of the tall white specters glided slowly toward a destination only they knew, moving in straight quiet lines as though they were not aware at all of the town around them or the people they were passing through.

Out of the corner of her eye Maaya saw a family from an adjacent street run, panicked, out of their home. A mother, father, and three children dashed out onto the street. Maaya couldn't hear what they were saying, but it was evident they were looking to flee whatever disaster was happening. The husband pointed, and they started to run—right into the wave of oncoming ghosts.

Maaya tried to cry out, to warn them, to stop them, but her voice caught in her throat. It was too late. Almost immediately, all five of them stopped in the middle of the street, standing completely still as though they had forgotten how to walk. They stared straight ahead with blank expressions, then fell to their knees. What happened after, Maaya couldn't know; the ghostly wave overtook them, and they vanished from sight.

"Stars… this is bad," Saber said quietly, putting a hand to her mouth. "We should get out of here before all our escape routes are closed off. Let's head back to the house; the others should be on their way if they saw this."

Maaya finally managed to tear her gaze from the spectacle below and dashed off across the rooftops before she could think twice. She used all her strength to push herself as far as she could go, desperate to get away. She was half afraid that the ghosts would find a way to reach her even at this height, and half afraid that she would double back and try to fight if she continued to watch. So she pressed on, leaping swiftly over streets and houses, with Saber right behind her.

And then, chancing a glance down at one of the grand entrances to the town square, she saw the thing she dreaded the most.

Kim, Sovaan, and Kalil stood backed against a massive building, defiantly facing the oncoming wave. Even with their *libris* activated the building was too tall to scale, and the oncoming ghosts were too close and too numerous to allow any method of escape.

"Oh, no. Oh gods, no!"

In an instant, Maaya changed course, speeding down toward her friends. She saw repeated bursts of light as blood cards connected with the oncoming wave, and though some of the ghosts disappeared, they were replaced in an instant. Maaya's heart filled with dread. There was no way they could escape—and there were only seconds left before the wave hit them.

"Maaya! Wait!" Saber cried from behind her. "If you join them you'll be trapped, too. Let me lift them out!"

"Hurry then!" Maaya demanded. "I'll do what I can from here."

Maaya stopped on a nearby rooftop, drawing blood cards from her pack. As Saber soared past her toward her three living friends, she hurled her cards with the accuracy of a military archer, striking ghost after ghost. Each ghost she struck vanished into nothingness. Still more came, but with enough cards she knew she might be able to delay them just long enough for an escape.

Luckily for her, the ghosts didn't even seem to notice Maaya or their disappearing companions. They didn't so much as shift their gaze or speed, still moving slowly and resolutely ahead. Free of their numbing power at least for now, Maaya continued to attack. So long as the four of them continued their sustained assault they should have enough combined power to delay the ghosts' progress.

Maaya forced herself to breathe, to keep attacking. She tried not to look at her friends below, their frightened faces, or the endless wave of faceless phantoms. This was the moment she had always feared, but it was fine. She was here. She wouldn't let anything happen to them while she was here. She wasn't too late.

From below, her friends cried out in joy as they saw Saber flying swiftly toward them.

"About time you made it," Kalil said distractedly as he vaporized three nearby ghosts in one strike.

"Help us out of here!" Kim shouted in a state of near panic.

And then, their attention momentarily diverted by the sight of their imminent rescue, they stared straight into the gaping dark eyes of the ghosts.

In an instant their arms fell limp at their sides, and their expressions became blank. Their cards fluttered from their fingers, and all three of them fell to their knees.

"No! Saber!" Maaya screamed.

The ghosts converged on them. Saber, cursing audibly from below, took Kim and Sovaan by the wrists and attempted to pull them up, but it was too late. Unable to lift them quickly enough, Saber was forced to flee as the ghosts passed through them, disappearing through the wall behind them.

Maaya flung herself down from the rooftop, blood cards in both hands, desperately letting them fly at any ghost she could reach, but it was not enough.

She hit the ground nearby just in time to see her friends fall lifeless to the ground.

Maaya couldn't move. She could only watch as the ghosts continued their silent march over her friends' bodies as though they weren't even there. Her friends weren't moving. Their vacant eyes stared at nothing, and even through the blinding white, Maaya could see they did not breathe.

She tried to push the thought from her mind, as though she could change what was about to happen if she refused to believe it. She was still here. It wasn't too late. *It can't be too late. I can still change this.*

And then, from the three lifeless bodies rose three pale silhouettes, shapeless at first, but then they quickly became recognizable. As they took form, Maaya choked on a sob.

The ghosts of Kim, Kalil, and Sovaan rose, confused and frightened, glancing about as if they didn't know who or where they were. In the midst of the faceless wave they looked helpless and lost. Despite the despair that overwhelmed and numbed Maaya's mind, she felt almost comforted at the sight. A relentless voice inside her screamed that there was still time, still time, for there they were before her.

"Maaya?" Kim asked, her voice high and unsteady with fear. For the first time since Maaya saw them from the rooftops, their eyes met, and in Kim's eyes was a terror she had never seen before. "Maaya, I… I'm dead?"

They stared at each other with the eyes of those who feared they would never see each other again, afraid even to blink lest the other vanish in that instant. Maaya begged herself to speak, to form words of comfort or direction, but none came. Her lips moved in a feeble attempt to say what her mind hadn't yet figured out.

Then she remembered what came next.

"Kim," she gasped hoarsely, finally finding some semblance of her voice. "All of you, get out! Get away from them!"

But whether because they did not hear or could not move, her friends remained motionless in the sea of ghosts. Maaya cried out again, but the others only stared back at her, pleading silently for her to do something that was beyond her control.

Time seemed almost to stop, and for a tiny moment Maaya felt a flicker of hope. *Surely it would have happened by now.*

But then it began.

The sky ripped open above them as the void appeared, every star in the universe snuffed out behind the dark. The ghosts of her friends began to move toward it, pulled as if by some tremendous wind only they could feel. They struggled desperately against it, but in vain, their transparent hands scratching helplessly at the cobblestones.

Maaya felt a sudden rush of energy and leapt forward, but was just as quickly stopped by a strong pair of arms that encircled her waist and arms.

"No! If you so much as touch one of those things, you're dead too," Saber said sharply.

"They're still there! I can get them out!" Maaya cried, fighting against

Saber's grip, but the ghost held her fast. Maaya, frustrated at not being able to break free despite her increased strength, noticed that Saber was now using a strength augment of her own, one she must have pulled from Maaya's deck when she wasn't looking.

"Maaya!" Kim's ghost shrieked, and the terror in her voice sent shivers down Maaya's spine. "Please, don't let them–!"

Her voice was lost in the panicked screams of the others as they were pulled upward toward the void. From across the town she saw other ghosts being pulled upward as well, their screams so loud and many they might well have been coming from inside her own head.

Her friends reached for her, arms swinging wildly against the invisible current. Maaya could only watch as they were pulled backward. Through it all, they did not tear their horrified stares from Maaya.

And then, just like before, the void disappeared. The screams suddenly ceased, and all was silent.

15

EXILE

SILENCE.

Maaya was vaguely aware that the ghosts still marched on, and that she still breathed, somehow, but beyond that she perceived nothing.

Too late.

These two words played over and over in her mind. It had become increasingly difficult for her to process the events of the past week, especially as they became steadily worse, but this, it seemed, was the catalyst for her understanding. A block of strangers here and there was a tragedy, but not enough to undo the foundation of civil society. Not for her. Somehow she had believed herself and her friends above it all, their gifts giving them immunity from the troubles of the world. They could see and fight the enemies no one else could. And with their gifts they would have soon been bound for Krethus, free of the fear and heartbreak that plagued Sark in their absence.

And now, of the four there were just minutes ago, Maaya was the only one left. These same creatures who would take any blind living being that stumbled directly into their path had taken the ones tasked with exterminating them. Children. Her friends.

The vision of their frightened and pleading faces would not leave her. As she kneeled helplessly in the street she was forced to witness it over and over again. Their last moments, both in life and death, had been terror, and Maaya had been unable to do anything but watch. For as long as she had known them she told herself that she would protect them, that she would never feel the regret that came with not appreciating something until it was gone.

And now she felt that regret, though in its current state it manifested as heart-wrenching pain, one that would not even let her utter a sound or take a breath without sharply reminding her of its presence. She seemed simultaneously overwhelmed and empty, filled with dread and drained of any will to live.

Sovaan, so young and clever and optimistic. Kalil, ambitious and brave, a source of stability and strength. And Kim, compassionate and cunning, the one Maaya expected to overtake her in due time. Dead. Dead and gone without a trace to show they had ever existed at all, without even bodies to lay to rest.

Maaya wasn't sure if it was the heavy weight of grief or the forced and compartmentalized pragmatism she had been made to adopt over the years to survive, but something in her mind told her it was time to go. Before they got her, too.

The past is the past, it said. *Grieve later. Survive now. You can't control what happened then, but you can control what happens now.*

Maaya fought her way to her feet, the world a blur around her. She didn't even feel Saber's steadying hands take her arm as she rose.

Now that she was on her feet, she realized she wasn't sure what to do next. Shock had prevented her from planning that far ahead. She knew she had to deal with Rahu, that she should probably check on Roshan and Svante, and even that she had to prepare for her upcoming trip, but everything seemed so unimportant now, unworthy of even a second thought. There was no purpose to any of it now.

Saber gently touched her shoulder, and this time, Maaya felt it.

"We can't stay here. This might get worse," the ghost murmured.

Maaya didn't acknowledge her, but started to turn away, every ounce of willpower she possessed necessary for a task as simple as moving her own two feet. Her gaze passed over the impenetrable wall of ghosts before her, marching onward unperturbed.

She wondered how they could do it—how they could kill so effortlessly and show nothing for it. There was no emotion, no reaction whatsoever. It was inhuman, and it disturbed her. They wandered through the world as if they were completely unaware of it; this was not malice that drove them, and that made them harder to fight. They were a force of nature, wild and dangerous as an ocean storm, and to fight them was as fruitless as fighting a current.

But the sight of them now instilled something in Maaya that no tempest ever had. She paused, unable to take her eyes away from them, but this time it was not because she was under their control.

Maaya turned away from Saber, ignoring the ghost's audible surprise and fear. The glowing marks hovering over her limbs flickered, then suddenly burned brighter. She unconsciously reached to the pack on her arm, pulling from it every blood card she had left in her possession. She paused only feet away from where the ghostly lines filed on.

Their silence and indifference, which previously frightened her, now enraged her. How could they be so apathetic? Were they simply so used to killing that each life they took now meant nothing? She would make them feel *something* for what they had done, even if it took all the life she had left in her.

"Maaya, what are you doing?" Saber cried. "There's no fighting those things!"

"I'm ending this now," Maaya said quietly, her voice trembling with anger. "No more running."

Saber started to say something else, but Maaya was already gone.

Pushing herself high in the air above the ghosts below, Maaya flung blood cards from both hands. Before they even connected, causing the phantoms to vanish in bursts of red sparks, she had thrown more, her aim only as accurate as necessary to hit whatever was nearest to her. Each card hit its mark with the deadly precision of years of practice, and the wave made an easy target. As a result of Maaya's furious attacks, small pockets soon appeared in the ghosts' ranks.

Still they moved slowly, silently, not responding at all.

This only further provoked Maaya's ire. She leapt nimbly from building to building, throwing her cards in wide arcs with all the strength she had in her. In any other situation she might have been proud of her own skill, but right now she knew it was only because she no longer felt the fear of death. She was going to fight on until she succumbed to her enemy or exhaustion—whichever came first.

Dozens of the ghosts fell before her, and soon she ran out of blood cards. She replaced them with a card of fire and immediately began raining flames down upon the ghosts. This had less of an effect, and in fact seemed to do nothing at all to them, but Maaya continued relentlessly, blinded by fury. By some miracle she missed the nearby buildings, and the flames burned out harmlessly on the cobblestones.

Suddenly, the ghosts began to fade. Unperturbed, they marched on, but became less visible with every passing second. The walk was finally ending.

"NO!" Maaya shouted.

She leapt from her vantage point on a nearby roof directly toward the ground, right toward the middle of the fading ghosts, but by the time she landed, they had completely disappeared. She stared around her in disbelief. The street was completely empty and still, and now it was dark. Only a small portion of the sky was lit in the distance from the morning sun, which had now begun to rise.

"I'm not done with you!" Maaya screamed at the empty street. Her voice echoed harmlessly off the high walls of the nearby buildings, mocking her.

If anyone was left in the town, living or dead, she could not see or hear them. She had been able to hear the screams before, but they had all faded; she wasn't sure if the people of Sark had escaped or been killed. A shudder of fear swept over her at the thought of being the only one left in Sark.

She was alone.

This realization overtook her in an instant, and whatever she had intended to say next came out as sobs instead. She knelt in the street, leaning down until her forehead touched the cold ground, and her bright *libris* lines finally flickered and died. Her body shook with the force of her cries. With no adversary left to bear the brunt of her anger, she was forced to confront reality, and it struck her ruthlessly.

Saber hovered slowly over to her and put a comforting hand on her shoulder, but said nothing, and Maaya didn't react.

Maaya wasn't sure how long she knelt in the street, but by the time she looked up, the sun was now peeking over the horizon. On a normal day the artisans and tradesmen would soon be waking up to prepare their day's work, and the market would be bustling only an hour later. In the light of the sun, Sark seemed almost a different world. The deadly walk already seemed like it had happened a long time ago.

Too exhausted to cry anymore, Maaya wiped her eyes on her sleeve and took a deep breath. It was unlikely the ghosts would return during the day—at least, they hadn't in the past. If there were still people left alive, it was Maaya's job to find them. If for any reason news of the disaster hadn't already spread to every person within the town's walls, it would soon. There was simply no hiding something this big.

What's more, they only had the coming day to prepare for what might come next. Maaya couldn't imagine anyone staying in town after they found out what happened, so evacuating would be necessary. That would be an arduous process all on its own, and Maaya's energy was already spent. It would have to be something she thought about later, perhaps after she had an hour or two to sleep.

Maaya couldn't remember the last time she felt so tired. She tried to stand, but with almost no strength left in her, she collapsed to the ground. She lay on her side, making only a small effort to keep her eyes from fluttering shut. She did not fear anyone coming across her in the street. Even if anyone was left, they would be too preoccupied to care.

Saber, however, seemed worried. She knelt next to Maaya, bending low so that Maaya did not have to lift her head to look at her.

"Let's get back to the house at least," she suggested, looking up and down the empty street. Maaya only sighed, but made no attempt to move.

Suddenly, there came a metallic *thump* from behind them, and Maaya started, sitting up quickly and looking around.

Svante stood nearby, his breathing deep and ragged, and he limped his way over to them, sitting down heavily next to her. He was too out of breath to speak, and Maaya said nothing. She was oddly comforted by his presence. Of all the people to still be alive, she was glad he was one of them. She hadn't even thought of him earlier, but now she realized it was a very good thing he was here—he was their way out of Sark.

After a few minutes, he finally appeared well enough to speak, even if only in short bursts.

"You two all right?" he panted.

"I don't know how to answer that," Saber answered monotonously. "What happened to you?"

"Keeping up with you was more than these limbs could handle. They've suffered some damage, but it's nothing I can't fix. I do so look forward to finding a bed, though. I haven't had this kind of exercise since my early school days. I saw the ghosts disappear; was that you?"

"We got rid of a few dozen of them, but I think they disappeared on their own this time. There were just too many," Saber said quietly.

"Either way, I'm glad they're gone," Svante continued tiredly. "From what I can tell there aren't any more in the town. It seems daylight still works as a deterrent here. It won't be so in Krethus, at least not close to the machine. They're somehow less scary in sunlight, I will say that much."

"Did you see any people?" Maaya asked. "Anyone left alive?"

"Oh, plenty," Svante answered with a smile. "Most of them got right out of the way. They're afraid, but they're still there. I expect they'll start filtering back in soon enough. But I think we should make use of the disturbance to get out of here."

Maaya nodded. So most of them had lived. There was that little bit of good news at least. She had no particular love for anyone here, but none of them deserved this—except, perhaps, for one, and Maaya had a feeling that he was still perfectly fine.

"At any rate, I should go get my belongings," Svante said, getting to his feet with difficulty. "We can all sleep on the road. You should go as well and make sure the others are ready."

A sharp pain struck Maaya's heart, and she involuntarily let out a shaky gasp. When she looked hastily away, Svante stared attentively at her.

"Is everything all right? Are you hurt?" he asked concernedly.

"There's something you should know," Saber said, and though Maaya was afraid to hear the truth spoken aloud, she was glad the ghost was saying it for her. "Our friends… they're all dead. They were trapped, then taken away by those monsters. We tried to fight off the ghosts, but there were just too many."

Svante gaped, horrified.

"Oh… my word, I… I'm so terribly sorry. Curses upon these things! May they someday endure even half the suffering they've inflicted." He hesitated, then glanced down at Maaya. "Will you be well enough to travel?"

"We have no choice," Maaya said blankly. "I can't stand to be here a minute longer anyway. I just need a little rest and then I'll go get what little I have. Where should we meet?"

"A mile or so outside the north gate. Most survivors fled west, so it should be no trouble avoiding prying eyes, but it'd still be best to meet where there's little chance anyone else will be around."

"Understood. We'll be there in an hour at most."

Svante gave her his best attempt at an encouraging smile, then turned and limped off.

"Can you stand?" Saber asked, holding out her hand. Maaya took it gratefully and struggled to her feet. Her legs were still very weak, but with Saber's help she managed to stay upright. "Good. Now let's get back to the house, easy now."

They started back toward home, and Maaya was glad for the lack of people. She was sure she looked very odd to anyone who couldn't see Saber, but she wasn't sure she would be able to make it without her help. Even with Saber's strength, every step was laborious and painful.

They walked slowly up the street and into the square. Its size made Maaya uncomfortable, and she felt her instinct to hide returning, but this was the fastest way home.

Before they had gone too far, Maaya started hearing voices. She motioned to Saber to let her rest on the steps leading up to the town's capitol so no one would see her walking with invisible support. No sooner had she sat down than a small group of people emerged from a nearby street. When they looked over at Maaya, her body tensed, but they waved at her eagerly and started in her direction.

"I'm so glad there's someone here. It's been total chaos all morning. Do you know what happened here?" one of the women asked her.

"I don't know, but I think everyone is safe now," Maaya answered wearily.

"Thank heavens. So much screaming and panicking. Still, I fear it will happen again. Someone *must* call for Rahu before this goes any further; he'll know what to do."

Maaya shuddered involuntarily upon hearing his name, and she felt a pang of fear. This ghost walk had gotten out of hand; he would surely be furious with her for not being able to contain it.

As the minutes passed, more and more people filtered into the square. By their attire she guessed most of them usually had no place here, but this appeared to be the location everyone had decided to congregate. It was large enough to hold a large crowd, and based on what Maaya could overhear, they were expecting some sort of announcement.

"The police will tell us what happened. They really ought to! No sense a disturbance this big can happen and they'll be silent," one man said gruffly, and everyone in the vicinity muttered and grumbled with approval. Maaya could tell that as everyone got over their relief, tension was taking its place. Demands for answers became more passionate, and there came more and more calls for the police and for Rahu.

Though Maaya sat alone on the steps, no one paid her any attention save for a few kind people who walked over to check on her. Temporarily united by tragedy, the people of Sark seemed concerned for one another regardless of their social status.

As yet more people came to the square, Saber scanned the crowds continuously. What she was looking for Maaya wasn't sure until the ghost glanced down at her and caught her eye.

"No sign yet of Roshan," she said quietly. "I'll let you know if I see him."

Maaya felt a jolt in her stomach. In the turmoil of the night, she had almost forgotten about him as well. She consoled herself by remembering that the ghosts hadn't struck his part of town and that there were far more survivors than Maaya originally thought, but until she saw him again she wouldn't be able to put her mind at ease.

Still more people filtered tiredly in, and many of them cried out as they were reunited with family and friends. Less fortunate people called out the names of their loved ones in vain, frantically asking everyone within reach if they had seen them. Children without parents huddled frightened in corners or behind pillars, and parents without children tearfully called for them, standing on walls and benches to scan the crowd for people they would never see again.

Soon, however, there came a growing cry from the edge of the square. Maaya got unsteadily to her feet, standing on tiptoe, but she was still too small to see over the heads of the now immense crowd.

"What's going on?" she asked quietly.

"Rahu's coming," Saber replied shortly.

"How… how does he look?" Maaya asked fearfully.

"Not angry," Saber said, sensing Maaya's concern. "My guess is he'll be happy to see you."

"How?"

"He's being asked to answer the entire town's questions, and to do that, he needs information. You'll be able to provide exactly that."

"What do I tell him?" Maaya asked despairingly.

"That it's under control. He can do a show to comfort everyone now, and we'll take care of the rest," Saber instructed.

"Will he believe that?"

"He has no choice."

Rahu pushed his way through the crowds and over toward the steps, evidently looking for a platform on which to extricate himself from the masses. Maaya couldn't help but notice his expression as he came closer, and it surprised her. For the first time she could remember, he looked afraid. Tired and pale, he walked swiftly through the crowd, ignoring everyone's attention and pleas for answers and help.

Then he noticed Maaya, and a wave of relief passed over his face. He strode directly up to her, apparently unconcerned with how his association with her might influence his reputation as he usually was.

He put his arm around Maaya's shoulder, pulling her with him to look away from the crowd.

"Maaya, there you are. I looked all over the square for you. What on earth happened here? I got your message, but it feels like some major disaster just occurred. Where are the others?"

"It was more of those ghosts. More than I've ever seen. We got rid of many of them, and they disappeared. We managed to stop them before they got too far, but it was difficult," Maaya lied at Saber's encouraging nod.

"So you stopped them. They're all gone, all of them?" Rahu pressed urgently, and Maaya nodded. Rahu sighed audibly. "That's good. Now tell me more. Where did it originate? How many were taken? I need to know what to tell these people. Is everything under control?"

"It mostly hit the square and surrounding neighborhoods. There were smaller walks in two other areas, but they didn't do very much. It hit the strongest here and we were already here already to fight them off. By then most people had escaped. I... Rahu, they're gone for now, but every time they come back there are more. We need to get everyone out of Sark."

Rahu did a double take, then shook his head.

"Absolutely not. You've fought them off already and you'll continue to do so. There can't be an unlimited number of them; sooner or later you'll get rid of this infestation. In the meantime I'll calm the crowds and tell them we're all safe. Where are the other children, by the way? Don't tell me they were sleeping on the job."

"They're dead, Rahu. They all died fighting off the ghosts like you ordered them to," Maaya said icily, staring him straight in the eye. In any other situation he surely would have struck her, but now she detected a flicker of hurt in his face.

"I… I see. I'm sorry to hear that," he said. Maaya was as surprised by his words as she was by the fact that they appeared to be genuine; he spoke in the way men usually spoke when they struggled to convey emotions they weren't used to sharing. "Give me a few moments to speak, and then you can return home. Your work is done for now."

He stepped away from her, turning back to face the crowd. It was lucky he did, Maaya thought; by now they appeared near mad with desperation, and it was all Rahu could do to silence them so he could speak.

Maaya didn't bother to listen. She knew what he would say. There had been some kind of supernatural disaster, but never fear, Rahu had come in to save the day. He would go into detail about fake battles and fake hardships, but would explain that his holy powers had overcome in the end, and that he, ever their vigilant public servant, would continue to work himself to exhaustion until all the evils that plagued Sark were defeated and sent scurrying back to the unearthly pits from whence they came. The usual.

"If I have to listen to that man talk himself up any longer I'm certain I might just die again," Saber said, floating over and sitting next to Maaya on the steps. Despite herself, Maaya smiled. "Anyhow, let's talk logistics. We need to pack light, so think about which of your many outfits you want to bring."

"Oh, I'm not sure how I could ever choose," Maaya whispered sardonically, and Saber winked.

"Hey, I just thought of something. Traveling with a rich guy should have its benefits. He can buy us plenty of stuff, plus suitcases to put it all in. I'll make him buy you a party gown, how's that? We can get you all decked out in jewels and face powder."

"Can you imagine a man like Svante shopping for that kind of thing?" Maaya asked, amused.

"Oh yes. That's partially why I'll encourage him to do that. Oh, and then we can get him to buy you some fancy underthings—"

"*Saber*," Maaya protested, hiding her burning face in her hands, and the ghost laughed.

"Fine, fine. But think about it. We can go to all the best restaurants and sleep in all the best hotels. Well, you can, I suppose. And I can enjoy them vicariously through you. Say, maybe Svante's research can give me back my sense of taste, if nothing else. I would eat absolutely *everything*."

"That doesn't seem fitting behavior for royalty," Maaya chuckled.

"Hey, we don't know if I was yet. And even if I were, it's not bad table manners if no one can see. All I'm saying is traveling with money is going to be wonderful. Hey, do you think you can walk on your own? It looks like our lord and savior is wrapping up his heroic monologue."

"I think so," Maaya said. She pulled herself shakily to her feet, noticing she felt slightly stronger already. This minimal amount of rest had done her some good.

Sure enough, Rahu seemed to be wrapping up. To his credit, the people of Sark seemed at least temporarily sated. They still looked nervous, but in the way that a child felt comfortable showing fear once they were already safely in their parents' arms.

"I'm quite tired, as I'm sure all of you are as well, so I cannot answer any more questions. Just be assured that I am working my hardest for you and will use every tool at my disposal to keep you all safe."

"Hey, he's talking about you," Saber said, raising an eyebrow.

Maaya rolled her eyes and made to start walking away, but Rahu stopped her. He stood between her and the crowd, keeping their eyes off her, and took her gently by the arm. She looked up at him, startled.

"I want you to go home and get plenty of rest. Do what you must to keep these evil things away from the people, but beyond that… well, you've earned some rest. I'm sure you need some time after what's happened. Take a few days for yourself, and then I'll contact you again to—"

"Rahu! Let go of that girl!" a voice called.

Maaya's heart sank. Svante pushed his way toward the steps, an angry look on his face. In his hands he held his walking stick and his bag, and another traveling bag was slung over his shoulder. At once, Maaya wished she could tell him to leave, to hide, but she could not speak.

Svante walked up to Rahu, who stepped back, looking thoroughly taken aback. The Krethan stepped between them, then glanced concernedly at Maaya.

"Are you all right? Did he hurt you?" he asked. Maaya shook her head wordlessly, hoping desperately that the look in her eyes would convince Svante to run while he still could. "Good. I was passing the square and saw that Rahu had you in his grasp."

Rahu was quick to recover, and his surprise gave way to suspicion… and then anger.

"Now this I never would have guessed," he said in a low voice, staring at Svante with contempt. "My star working with the Krethan."

"You're behind the times, my friend. When you made me an enemy, did you expect me to run back to Krethus with my tail between my legs? We're a hardier sort than that. You can't intimidate me as easily as you think."

"No… I suppose I can't," Rahu said slowly, then looked at Maaya. Any semblance of the sympathy he had felt just moments before was gone, and she shrank back under his intense stare. "I asked you to follow this man for me, and instead you start to work with him. May I ask for how long you expected this to go unnoticed?"

"Rahu, it's not like that. Please, we've only been trying to figure out where the ghosts are coming from, and—"

"Oh, I understand. We're all trying to figure out where they come from. But you, I fear, are much closer to the answer than I think you want to be." Before Maaya could speak again, Rahu pointed at Svante, then raised his voice to the crowd. "This man here! Look here, all of you! He is responsible for the attacks on our town!"

The crowd turned its confused eyes on Svante, who stared defiantly at Rahu.

"The people of Sark are better than that, Rahu," he said loudly in response. "You think they—?"

"Svante, get out of here, please," Maaya begged him quietly. "You don't understand—"

"The beings which attack us are Krethan in origin!" Rahu continued shouting, gesturing angrily at Svante as though he had not heard. "And look! A Krethan agent! He has been working against us from within! He is the one who has directed these forces to terrorize your families, to take your husbands and wives and children!"

The muttering started, followed by cries of fear—and anger.

"How do you know this, Rahu?" a man nearby asked, aghast.

"I can feel the evil he exudes. Look at him! He's not one of us. He has come here to make us the subjects of his foul experiments… and he has not been working alone." Maaya knew what was coming, and her blood ran cold. "Look here at this one they call *Ghost.* Who better for him to employ than one who calls upon the spirits themselves? She attracts them with her mere existence!"

At the sound of this familiar and unfortunate nickname, a number of people called out furiously, jeering in her direction.

"Wait!" Maaya cried. "He's wrong! We've been trying to stop them, not to help them—"

"Is that so? You admit to being able to see this evil, but how can you prove you have been fighting it if no one else can see? Is there anyone who will speak on your behalf?" Rahu demanded.

"I will," Svante replied adamantly, but Rahu only laughed.

"Of course the *Krethan* would defend his ally," Rahu said, and the jeering grew louder. "Do not grow complacent, my good people! We have caught them in their deception but they are still dangerous. This man is an enemy of the entire nation of Selenthia, and thus, our Ghost is as well!"

"You *need* me, Rahu," Maaya said venomously. This betrayal was not altogether surprising from a man like him, but it still stung. "How are you going to get rid of the ghosts without me?"

"Oh, Maaya, you flatter yourself. Just because I used you doesn't mean I needed you. I was very up front about that for our entire working relationship. You were convenient, but that was all. If you think you're the only person in Sark who can see ghosts, you are even more delusional than I thought. But as of now, you are more threatening to me than you are useful."

A number of officers had since arrived, standing behind Rahu while waiting for him to explain the situation. A handful of them kept the jeering crowd at bay, and Svante was starting to look worried, but he still remained. He seemed genuinely unaware of the danger he was in.

"Leave!" Maaya cried frantically. "Please, go!"

"Nonsense. I'm not going anywhere without you."

"That much you have correct," Rahu said smoothly, and all at once two officers grabbed Svante's arms, holding them behind his back. "Our law dictates one simple punishment for enemies of our nation—and those who conspire with them."

"No!" Maaya screamed, and she tried to push her way toward Svante, but Rahu blocked her path. He wrapped an arm around her, pinning her arms to her side with ease.

"You can't be serious!" Svante protested. "Listen to me! Rahu has been communicating with the Krethan government. Look for his communications with them, they are there! He seeks money over all your lives!"

"Krethan lies from Krethan spies," Rahu said cheerily. "I have always been, and will ever be, a humble servant of the people. And there are more than enough of them here who will attest to my successes."

"Because I did the work for you!" Maaya shouted angrily.

"Ah, the poor child has gone mad now that her web of deceit is falling apart around her. Gentlemen, let us get started. I fear there is no time for the bureaucratic legal process with dangerous individuals like these; they will find a way to escape if we let them languish in your cells. We must do this quickly."

The police glanced at each other uncertainly, but Rahu's smooth words and the screaming of the crowd behind them made them hesitant to object.

"If you don't kill 'em, we will!" someone shouted, and a deafening roar of approval followed.

"That's enough! Get back, get back!" an officer ordered, and he and his men formed a strong line separating the crowd from Maaya and the others on the steps. Maaya knew it wouldn't last long.

"You see? The people are afraid. We know these two are guilty; they have already admitted as much. Justice must be swift, no?" Rahu continued, holding onto Maaya more tightly as she struggled desperately. If she weren't so exhausted she might have been able to fight him off, but she was in no state to do that now.

Saber's gaze flicked nervously between Svante and Maaya, unsure of what to do. It was possible Saber could create a distraction or free Svante, but dead as she was, she only had the strength of one human being. That wasn't enough to escape the angry mob, and with Maaya's exhaustion and Svante's damaged limbs, getting even halfway down the street would be a miracle.

The policemen holding Svante jerked him roughly forward, then forced him to his knees. A higher-ranking officer stepped up to him, holding a shiny brass pistol in his hand. Maaya screamed something in protest, but it was lost in the noise of the crowd. Svante himself fought angrily now, but the policemen held him still.

"Rahu, please! Stop this! Don't kill him, please—" Maaya cried, but stopped short as a loud crack rang through the air.

Svante immediately stopped struggling, and his body fell limp to the pavement, blood pooling slowly around his head. The crowd cheered wildly.

Maaya stopped fighting as shock overtook her. The roar of the crowd and the sight in front of her overloaded her senses. It was over. Her old friends were dead, her new friend and only means of escape was dead, and she was too weak to fight or run. She had broken too many of her rules, the rules that kept her alive, and now she was paying for it.

Saber flew down directly in front of her, fumbling in the pack of cards on Maaya's arm.

"What are you…?" Maaya whispered, but trailed off as Saber held up one green and one purple card, then an orange elemental card for herself.

"You're going to regret this later, but if you want to survive, you'll do this. I'll help you, but we have to go *now*. You're next if we don't."

Maaya hesitated, then nodded quickly. The other officers seemed preoccupied with moving Svante's body and evidently did not consider the small girl in Rahu's arms to be much of a threat, so they didn't notice.

Saber slipped the cards into Maaya's fingers. Maaya and the ghost looked at each other, and the moment seemed to last an hour. This was their last chance.

In one swift movement Maaya reached down and burned one card on her lower leg, then crossed her arms and burned the second card on her forearm. Rahu, thinking she had resumed struggling, held her tighter—but now it did him no good.

With renewed strength and speed, Maaya easily pushed Rahu away from her, sending him crashing against the steps. The crowd gasped as they noticed the bright lines hovering just above her skin, and the officers whirled about to confront her.

Maaya felt well again, but she knew it wouldn't last long this time. She also knew that, as powerful as these cards made her feel, they would not protect her against bullets. They had to leave.

"Go, Maaya! Go!" Saber shouted, and Maaya fled.

Behind her, she felt a wave of heat as Saber used the card she had taken for herself to create a wall of flame behind them. It wouldn't last long, but it would hopefully be enough. She heard new screams of fear and anger, and a few cracks of gunfire, but she felt nothing.

She was nebulously aware of the danger she was in, but the rest was automatic. She knew the streets. She knew where she had to go. With all her previous plans now in ruins, her only option now was to leave Sark. She knew that she somehow still needed to get to Krethus, but she'd worry about that later. She would worry about everything later. It was time to return to doing things her way.

They passed empty block after empty block, and it felt almost like she was in another place entirely. She had never seen this part of town from up here, nor did she frequent it at this hour of the morning. Even then, there had always been people. But now it was a ghost town, and Maaya thought grimly that it fit that description in more ways than one.

She had no idea what the future of Sark would entail. With Maaya gone and her friends dead, she doubted there was anyone else in town who could even see the ghosts much less fight them off. And at the rate they were increasing, Sark itself would likely be entirely overrun within days. What then, she didn't know, but she could only assume that the walks would start to occur elsewhere in Selenthia. If Svante had been right in everything he had said, the ghosts would start to appear in more and more places—likely wherever Maaya was. She promised herself that she would use her cards only if absolutely necessary. She hoped that would be enough.

Rahu's accusation echoed in her head as she fled. She knew he had been attempting to rile up the crowd, to play on their fears… but had he been right about the ghosts being attracted to her? That had been Svante's theory, and he had confided that in good faith. Maybe that had even been something they had collaborated on before Rahu had betrayed Svante.

A few blocks from the north gate, the lights on Maaya's limbs flickered, then vanished, and Maaya collapsed. Her strength finally gone, she fell hard into a pile of crates near an abandoned building. She struggled to get up, but was too weak to move. The last of her energy had been spent.

Saber was at her side in an instant. She lifted the girl gingerly out of the damaged crates and lay her gently onto the cold ground.

Maaya's breathing was shallow and ragged. Saber had been right: she regretted using those cards to escape, but at the moment it was because they were still within Sark's walls. They hadn't escaped yet.

"How… we get out now?" Maaya breathed.

"I'll carry you. At least until we're safely hidden from the town," Saber answered, glancing quickly over her shoulder. The streets behind them were still empty, but they both knew they wouldn't remain that way for long. "I assume we're going to see Styx."

Maaya nodded, too exhausted to reply.

"All right. Now relax, and don't try to move or talk. I've got you."

Maaya took this advice to heart. She didn't think she had fallen asleep, but it only seemed like a few minutes later when she heard another familiar voice.

"Maaya! Oh, hell, Saber, what 'appened? Is she alive?"

Before Saber answered, Maaya felt herself swept into a much larger and stronger pair of arms. She forced herself to open her eyes, if only so Styx could see that she was, in fact, alive. He let out a heavy sigh of relief, his eyes asking so many questions his mouth couldn't possibly keep up with, but mercifully, he let her be.

"She's exhausted. All her energy was spent on *libris* during the night and she hasn't slept a wink or had anything to eat," Saber explained. "*I'm* exhausted, and I'm not even sure how that works. Anyway, we need to get out of here. Sark isn't safe for us anymore."

"What? Why not?" Styx asked, his eyes wide with concern.

"Long story," Maaya murmured. "We… we have to get to—"

"You, hush. I'll tell the story," Saber reprimanded her gently. "I think we should be safe, but have the boat ready just in case. I'm going to run back to town for a quick moment."

"Wha? Saber?" Maaya gasped, her voice cracking with the effort, but the ghost was already gone.

"Don't you worry, she said she won't be long," Styx said consolingly, though it was clear he could only wait so long to get answers.

While they waited, he prepared his boat so that, if necessary, they would only need to quickly untie the rope holding it to the dock to make a quick getaway. Maaya lay on the dock, Styx' massive coat serving as a pillow, and dozed. There was something quite comfortable about the warmth of the morning sun and the sound of the slow water lapping against the dark stones of the shore. This was the only sound that reached her save for the occasional impatient grunt from Styx as he worked.

Styx soon looked up hopefully, then his shoulders fell slightly. Maaya strained to look down the road and saw Sylvia coming up to meet them, crow on her shoulder as he always was.

"Oh dear. You look like you've taken ill," Sylvia said, raising her eyebrows slightly in a display of emotion that was rare for her. "Why are you lying out here in the middle of the morning? Your bed must be more comfortable."

"That's what we're waitin' to find out. Saber should be back soon," Styx replied gruffly.

"Oh. Well, I suppose she must always be around, mustn't she?" Sylvia said, averting her eyes.

When Saber came back, however, she didn't appear at all bothered by Sylvia's presence. In fact, she greeted the girl with a small smile, something that clearly disturbed Sylvia.

"Now I definitely know something's amiss," she commented quietly, but Saber's smile soon vanished, and it was apparent that something else was on her mind.

"Everything all right?" Styx asked warily.

"Well, our home is in flames, so that's slightly upsetting. Other than that… well, no, apart from that, everything else is terrible, too. I'll start at the beginning," Saber added quickly at the expression on Styx' face.

Maaya tuned her out as Saber started to explain everything to the others. She didn't have the heart to listen to it all. Not yet. These issues were not for a tired mind. Besides, there was no point in rehashing the past when there was still the future to think about. She knew what was going to happen. Styx and maybe even Sylvia were going to react with horror, ask dozens of questions, and then offer them sympathy and comfort. She couldn't bear it. All Maaya wanted at the moment was to be alone.

As she gazed in the direction of the far-off town she saw a small plume of smoke start to rise above the dead trees, and she turned away so the others wouldn't see her cry. It hadn't been much, but it had been home. All her belongings, and the belongings of her friends, were in that rundown old building. Now it was no more. Any last traces of her friends' mere being was currently burning. She realized that she was probably the only person left alive who even knew they even existed—save, perhaps, for the boy Kim had mentioned.

She shook her head. She was *not* going to think about that.

It took some time for Saber to finish her explanation, and when she did, there was silence. Styx and Sylvia both looked too stunned to speak. Maaya felt guilty even though she hadn't said a word; the look of hurt on the kind man's face was almost too much for her to take. Sylvia put her hand to her mouth in dismay.

"How is the world so cruel?" Sylvia murmured. "You were all just trying to help."

"And I would say we learned our lesson, but we're not done yet," Saber replied in a hard tone. "There are a lot of really stupid, angry, and mean people out there who need saving."

"Why bother?" Sylvia asked, tilting her head, but then floated back slightly under Saber's sharp glare.

"Don't even get me started, because I don't know the answer to that myself. If it were up to me, I would say none of them deserve to keep the miserable lives they have for even a day longer. But I do have one unique responsibility. I don't particularly care for the living, and my disdain has only been proven correct every day I've spent in this world, but for particular people, well… that changes things."

"You've got more a heart than I do," Styx said angrily. "This isn't right, none of it. No one in that town deserves people fighting for their right to survive, not anymore."

"That's not fair," Maaya said, sitting up with effort. "Most of them were misled. This is Rahu's fault. He lied and he played them all. There are still plenty of people in there who are on our side."

"Where were they then, eh?" Styx growled. "Where were they when you needed them?"

"I don't even know if they're still alive. I didn't have time to find out," Maaya said, averting her eyes.

Styx opened his mouth to reply, paused, and then closed it again.

"What will you do now?" Sylvia asked quietly.

Maaya sighed.

"We'll move on. Saber and I are going to Krethus. Styx… could you give us a ride to the nearest city?"

"Can you not at least rest a bit?" Styx asked hopelessly. "Look at you, you're too exhausted to even—"

"We don't have that luxury," Maaya interrupted. "The ghosts are hitting Sark every night now, and there are more of them each time. Every night this machine isn't destroyed is a night more people will die."

"What about your ride? How will you find him?" Sylvia continued.

"I don't know. Svante never mentioned who he was—only where we'd meet him," Saber sighed. "And I suppose we can't just traipse around town asking who's setting sail for Krethus."

"We'll figure it out when we get there," Maaya said tiredly. "In the meantime, we should probably get going. I don't want to stay here anymore, and I don't want anyone happening across us here."

"Agreed. For now, Styx, just take us east. You know these rivers well; just take us where we need to go," Saber directed.

Styx looked hesitant.

"What is it?" the ghost pressed.

"I just… this is all happening so fast, y'know?" the giant man said slowly. "All this news, all at once, and now you're leavin'. Across the sea, no less. I, uh… I never expected our goodbye to be like this."

"Oh, no no," Saber said quickly, floating up and attempting to wrap her arms around his massive shoulders. "Goodbye, nonsense. This is a 'see you soon' at most. We're coming back, obviously."

"Providin' there's anything here left to come back to," Styx said morosely, then straightened up. "But I'll make sure you get well on your way at least. I'd take you to Krethus myself if this old thing would survive the waves. That n' I'm afraid this would do poor Maaya no favors in respect to gettin' seasick."

Maaya gave him a small smile. If there was any positive aspect to her exhaustion, it was that she was too tired to feel the full brunt of grief. She knew it would hit later, but for now, it was time to focus on escaping.

"Do you want to come with us?" Saber asked Sylvia, to Maaya's great surprise.

Sylvia's eyes widened ever so slightly, but she shook her head.

"I'm not one for adventures. I would be more of a hindrance than a help. Besides, you need someone to look out for Sark for you while you're gone. Styx and I, we'll take care of everything."

Saber raised an eyebrow.

"Really?"

"Really. I know Roshan knows of us, so perhaps I can talk to him and see about moving the people somewhere safe. And Styx knows the land like few others do."

"Always thought it was stupid of people to isolate themselves like this," Styx grumbled. "No point or purpose. But ah, speak of the devil." He stood up tall, glancing down the long brick path leading to Sark. "Looks like some of 'em are brave enough to leave, and I have a feeling they're not takin' a walk for fun."

"Let's go," Saber commanded, and at once she was at Maaya's side, helping her stand.

Maaya got shakily into the boat, and if not for the ghost's aid, would have immediately fallen at the boat's unstable movements. She lay against the inside of the boat, her head raised high enough to see over the top. She didn't feel afraid anymore. She was too tired to feel afraid, and she felt safe in the presence of her giant friend. She was sure that even a small crowd of people would turn away in fear if Styx decided to try to intimidate them.

But before she could think about any confrontation for too long, Styx heaved himself into the boat after Maaya, then unwound the rope from the dock. Taking his oars easily in his hands, he pushed off quickly, the boat tilting dangerously as it always did.

"Sylvia! Be safe!" Maaya called weakly, and Sylvia gave a small bow.

"I look forward to your return."

The dock was soon out of sight, the boat's wake fading quickly behind them. If any of their pursuers were brave enough to make their way to the shore, Maaya would already be too far gone to see.

Maaya fought hard to stay awake and watch where they were going, but the steady rocking of the boat quickly lulled her almost to sleep. For the first few minutes Saber hovered near Styx' shoulder, looking behind them to make sure they would not be followed over the water, but then she floated slowly down to join Maaya.

"You have time to sleep, you know. We probably won't be making land for a long while."

"I know," Maaya sighed sleepily. "I… I'm afraid to sleep. I'm afraid my dreams will just remind me of reality rather than letting me escape it."

Saber ran her fingers softly through Maaya's hair.

"If it looks like you're having a nightmare, I'll wake you. But sleep, and get some of your strength back. Styx won't be able to come into town with us, and I won't be able to carry you if there are people around, so you'll need to be able to at least make it to an inn."

"How will we afford to… oh, never mind," Maaya rolled her eyes as Saber grinned widely. "Hey… what did you go back for, anyway? Just there on the dock?"

Saber's smile faltered, and she looked away from Maaya. Then, after a moment's pause, she pulled something out from behind her back. Maaya gasped.

"It isn't much, but I thought you might want something. Anything. You know… as a reminder," Saber said softly.

Maaya took it wordlessly. She held the plain black notebook in her hands, holding it gingerly as though afraid it might turn to dust if she gripped it too hard. But then a flood of emotions swept through her, and she held Kim's diary to her chest, closing her eyes to hide the tears that were already flowing.

"Thank you," Maaya managed to whisper. "Thank you."

She couldn't say any more, and Saber understood.

And so they fled, away from Sark, and away from the only life Maaya had ever known. Away from her enemies and away from the few friends she had left, if they were even still alive. Away from the memories that healed, and the ones that hurt.

Despite Saber's determination that they were coming back, Maaya couldn't imagine a future that involved doing so. Regardless of what she accomplished or who she became, Sark would still always be the same town, full of its own prejudices, aided by its isolation. It knew not and cared not for the rest of the world. It was a world all its own, and so if Maaya were ever to return, it would remember her just as it did when she left.

Meanwhile, Maaya had only Saber. Her friends were gone, her possessions were gone, and her home was gone. Surviving in just one town had been challenging enough; she didn't know how they could possibly make it across the world. Saber's talents could only amount to so much.

As Maaya drifted off to sleep, she ran her fingers over the diary again and again. It was the only thing left she had of her friends, and while it reminded her of the aching in her heart that would surely worsen in the coming days, it comforted her. The world could not remember those it didn't know existed, but Maaya could. She always would. When this was all over, she would tell their stories so that everyone could know them as she had. They deserved at least that much.

PART II

16

WANTED

Maaya wasn't sure if minutes, hours, or days passed. They all went by in a silent blur. During her fleeting moments of consciousness she was faintly aware that she was still in Styx' boat and that they were still moving. Sometimes it was light, and sometimes it was dark—at least that's what she thought. She wasn't sure she could trust her vision at the moment, as exhausted and disoriented as she was. At times she was sure she could hear Saber's voice, but when she worked up the strength to look up, the ghost was nowhere to be seen.

But sleep seemed to do her well, and as time went on she became more acutely aware of her surroundings and her feelings. Prominent among those were a relentless hunger like she had not felt in months and a distinct soreness throughout her entire body. She wasn't sure how much of that was due to her "battle" with the ghosts and how much came from sleeping in a rickety old boat.

When Maaya finally opened her eyes, feeling better than she had since their escape from Sark, she heard the low voices of Saber and Styx nearby.

"I'm tellin' ye, it'd be better for both of you to get all the way to Levien. It's no skin off my bones to take you all the way there in one sitting. You'll stay farther ahead of the law that way."

"Maybe it's not a problem for you, but she's *human,* Styx. Completely human, that is. And one who's been through a lot in the past week or two. This has all taken its toll on her, and as much as I agree with you about the logistics, she needs some food in her and a decent place to sleep, at least for a night. Otherwise I'm honestly worried her body will give out completely."

"Why can't we stop for a few just so you can grab somethin' for her? And me as well, come to think of it. She's been asleep the whole time anyway."

"At the bottom of your boat, yes. Poor thing probably has a side full of splinters. I'll get you whatever you want, but we need to stop for a night for her sake. She's been pushed to the limit, so at the very least a proper bed will do her well. You don't run yourself ragged from *libris* and then get up and about the next day like nothing happened. What will we do if we get to Levien and she's still too out of sorts to even stand?"

"I jus' don't want a repeat of last night. I can't defend you in town, and if you two come chargin' out with an angry mob behind you, I can't guarantee we can escape."

"It'll only be for a night. Even if word has reached the next city by the time we get there, we'll be able to elude them for that long."

"Really? I imagine the reward's big for catching someone accused of conspiring with a Krethan, and I also imagine it's not too hard to find you if you're booked up in an inn somewhere."

"People keep secrets for a price, you know that. Especially if you find the right ones. Besides, keeping out of sight is what we do best. I'll look after her and then we can be on our way again."

"Right, if ye say so. What am I supposed to do then?"

"You should rest, too. You're not *completely* mechanical. Get some rest and tell me what you want to eat. Anything you like."

"Well, ye couldn't go wrong to bring me a few bowls of churumuri. A few dozen if you can carry it all. Then my mouth will be too full to express any displeasure, see?"

The two laughed quietly, and then after a brief silence, Saber spoke again.

"What's next on our route, anyway?"

"Anorath. Decent enough town I suppose, in that I've not heard too much of murder or people disappearing. Smaller than Sark, even. Mostly keeps to itself. Not sure if that makes it a smaller or bigger target for anyone lookin' for you, but I can vouch for it well enough."

"Sounds good. I'll do some scouting as we get closer. How far is it?"

"About half an hour at this speed. I can get you there quicker if you want, but it'd make more noise."

"No need. Get us there after nightfall and we'll be safer."

Maaya thought about letting the others know she was awake as their conversation drifted to more unimportant subjects, but then realized she didn't feel like socializing. Now that her mind was clearer it was more readily reminding her of what had just happened, and she closed her eyes again, hoping that sleep would at least temporarily fend off her horrible memories.

After what seemed like only a few moments, she was being gently shaken awake. She rubbed her eyes blearily and sat up slowly, wary of dizziness, but it never came.

"How do you feel?" came Saber's soft voice from beside her.

"Mm, okay," Maaya replied, stifling a yawn. "Where are we?"

"Anorath. We're going to be staying here tonight; I thought you might be a little sore from sleeping here so long, as luxurious as this craft is."

Styx grumbled something from the back of the boat, but Maaya couldn't hear. Saber only snickered.

Maaya looked around. She had never been very far down the river before and the unfamiliarity was almost frightening. The boat was currently hidden behind a tangle of dead trees that had fallen over into the river. Nearby was what remained of an old wood and steel dock that had fallen into an even greater state of disrepair than the one near Sark. What was visible of Anorath seemed innocent enough; much of it stretched right up to the river's edge, and the streets were well lit and cozy. Not many people were out at this hour, and those who were seemed to have some business to attend to unlike many of the less friendly residents of Sark who took advantage of the dark for their own schemes.

"I'm going to go investigate a little just to make sure it's safe," Saber explained. "With any luck we'll be in tonight and out tomorrow morning without most people even realizing we were ever here."

"Then what?" Maaya asked quietly.

"Then it's on to Levien. But one thing at a time. Can you walk?"

Maaya nodded uncertainly.

"All right. I'll be back soon. Do some stretches and try to straighten up your clothes. We'll have an easier time blending in if you aren't limping and wearing clothes that have more wrinkles than Rahu's mother."

Maaya snorted and coughed. Saber grinned, then floated off toward the city.

The girl got shakily to her feet, using one of the oars to assist her. Styx stepped over one of the benches to help her, but his movement sent the boat rocking hard, and Maaya almost fell again.

"I got it," she said hastily.

Styx chuckled apologetically, then stepped more carefully out onto the dock. Offering his hand, he pulled her effortlessly to shore.

"You all righ'? Steady on your feet and all?" he asked, and Maaya nodded. "Good. You slept the whole trip; it's a wonder Saber thinks you can get any more."

"I absolutely can," Maaya affirmed tiredly. "And you're one to talk, you sleep for weeks at a time."

"Yeah, well, you should visit more often," Styx grumbled, not unkindly.

"Anyway, listen… it's all terrible, what happened back there, but I hope ye aren't thinking of blaming yourself for any of—"

"Not now, Styx, please," Maaya interrupted softly. "I don't know what to think yet. I haven't had time to figure it out. It still doesn't even feel real. I just… need some time."

Styx nodded silently, and his expression suddenly sent a wave of guilt sweeping over her even though she knew there was no reason for it. He had always been there for them when they needed him, but for the most part they remained in Sark, confiding in each other while he remained alone on the dock. And now when it was likely they had only a few days left in each other's company, she was shutting him out of what had easily been the worst thing she'd ever lived through.

She shook her head to clear her mind. That wasn't being fair to either of them. There was no rushing something like this and it wouldn't do either of them any good to try. Besides, she reasoned, they would have all the time in the world to spend with each other when she and Saber returned from Krethus.

Maaya sat upon a sturdy part of the dock, straightening and bending her legs carefully, then doing the same with her arms. She ached everywhere, and stretching only seemed to exacerbate the pain, but she felt her range of movement slowly coming back to her. When she felt more comfortable she stood up again, attempting to smooth her clothes out.

Saber floated back to them a few minutes later, and to Maaya's relief, she looked mostly bored.

"There is absolutely nothing of note in this city—at least not in the parts I was able to see. There are plenty of inns and not many people in any of them. Oh, and I'm pretty sure no one in this city can see ghosts, either."

"Why do you say that?" Maaya asked curiously.

"Because there are ghosts *everywhere*," Saber replied. "Even worse than Sark was before we stepped in. But they seem just about as boring as everything else, so even that's not going to be any problem."

"You seem disappointed," Maaya said, amused.

"On the contrary, I've had more than enough excitement for a while. But there is such a thing as *too* dull. If a city can bore the dead, we must seriously question the need for its existence. On the plus side, that likely means no ghost walks have happened here. Anyway, my point is this will be a safe place for us for the night."

"Are ye off then?" Styx asked. Maaya felt another pang of guilt at the thought of leaving him even temporarily, but she nodded. "All righ'. I'll keep things safe and sound 'ere until you're back tomorrow. Saber, you remember what I like?"

"As much as I can carry," Saber grinned, and Styx chuckled.

"All right, get on with you then. Oh, 'ang on, what's this book here? You want to take this with you?"

Maaya turned quickly to see Styx holding Kim's diary. She hesitated, then took it from him. There was no point in taking it with her, but she couldn't bear to let it out of her sight even for a moment.

"Thank you. Will you be all right out here?" Maaya asked.

"As always. 'sides, it won't be dull. I know a few people 'ere. It's been a few years, but I'm sure they're still around. I'd say we have some catching up to do, but that'd imply anything happens here worth catching up on. Now go on, get some rest. I'll see you kids soon."

Evidently sensing Maaya's reluctance, Saber took Maaya by the arm and gently pulled her away. Maaya looked over her shoulder. Styx was already busying himself making sure his boat was fastened securely to the dock, as well as looking it over for anything that might need repair.

"Who would Styx know around here?" Maaya whispered.

Saber shrugged.

"I'm assuming some of his dead buddies. He did spend all those years traveling up and down this river. It's to be expected a good-natured man like him would make some friends, especially if he's the only one who can see a lot of them."

Maaya was initially skeptical, but as they walked through the dense trees on the long-abandoned path toward town, Maaya saw the flickers of other ghosts occasionally floating here and there. Some held animated conversations, though they were too far away to be heard, while others simply wandered.

It was the wanderers Maaya pitied. They were the ones who had been dead for so long that they had lost almost all their humanity. Death had ever so slowly driven them mad, trapping them in the in-between they could exist in but not interact with, the place where they could see and hear all that couldn't see or hear them. Many spoke in languages long dead, if they remembered how to speak at all. In a world full of people they were utterly alone, and over the centuries and millennia they became numb to it all.

As they walked cautiously into Anorath, Maaya noticed it was unremarkable in just about every sense of the word. Even Sark had some charm to it or some aspect of its architecture that made it unique—even if it was often haphazard and dangerous. Everything in Anorath, however, looked almost the same. Every building was of the same construction, style, and materials, all of dull browns and greys, with only signs and size to differentiate between most of the shops and inns. In some ways this meant it was cleaner and more organized than Sark, but something about it made her feel uneasy. She didn't like its uniformity even if there was also a comfort to it.

"We're in luck. Many of the inns are close to the shore so we won't have to travel far. I assume this is because when people actually traveled the river they'd want somewhere to—"

"Well! My goodness gracious, what have we here? A sight for sore eyes is what," came a cheery voice suddenly from nearby.

Saber turned quickly, ready to defend Maaya if necessary, but she dropped her guard as another ghost walked up to them, smiling brightly.

He was tall and well dressed, though by the look of his garb he couldn't have been very wealthy. Tangles of unruly black hair stuck out stubbornly from beneath a sleek black bowler hat, and his beard and mustache were trimmed close and neat to his face. He was a thin man, in his mid-twenties if Maaya was to guess, and he was made to look even taller by the bottoms of his pants, which fell short a full inch above his socks. He reminded Maaya of the tall lanky ringmasters in coattails that directed the circuses she always wanted to see.

"I would be offended, but you look like you're not nearly as boring as the rest of this town. Go on, amuse me," Saber replied, folding her arms.

The man laughed delightedly, then swept his arm across his chest as he took a deep bow.

"Nothing would please me more. It isn't often we get travelers, you know! Especially none so lovely as yourself. I say, who *were* you? You have a most remarkable getup, and you carry yourself like the wealthy and educated do. I say that as a man of some education myself."

"My name is Saber, and this is Maaya," Saber answered, gesturing to her friend. The man didn't give Maaya a second glance until she waved in his direction, at which point he nearly leapt back in shock.

"You! You can… see me?" he asked curiously, stepping closer to her. Maaya nodded. "Fascinating! My goodness, you are full of surprises, my dear lady! Or, should I say, dear ladies. A ghost of the likes I've never seen before, and with a living companion; oh, no wonder this place bores you! My name is Emil, by the way. I am most pleased to make your bizarre acquaintance."

"Same to you. I think," Maaya said tiredly.

"What's someone like you doing in a place like this? Aren't you a little eccentric for this heap of nothing?" Saber asked, raising an eyebrow.

Emil tapped his chin with a finger, his eyes widening in thought.

"Eccentric? I suppose you could say that. But too much for dear old Anorath? Never, my good lady Saber. You mustn't have been here long; once you've been here a while you'll begin to see all the secrets and surprises that lay hidden in plain sight."

"Somehow I doubt it. But we'll explore later. We need somewhere to sleep for the night. I don't suppose you have any recommendations?" Saber asked firmly.

"Oh, I do! For the greatest comfort and the most privacy, you can never go wrong with the Shallow Squid. Three blocks north and two east, then look for the locked staircase in the alleyway. Knock four times quick to be let in. It sounds absolutely suspicious, but it's also hard to spot if you aren't looking for it."

Saber narrowed her eyes.

"You're right. That does sound suspicious. Why would we go there?"

"Because it's hard to find, of course. Let's be honest: the ghost of a wealthy girl traveling with a poor girl who can see the dead, sneaking into town after sundown? You're the type who doesn't want to be seen—perhaps even because someone may be pursuing you."

Maaya looked at Saber in surprise. Emil was evidently more perceptive than she initially thought. Whether that was a good thing or a bad thing only time would tell. For now, Maaya decided to go along with it.

"How much is it?" Maaya asked. Emil turned to her, looking absolutely delighted to speak to her.

"Fair, and that's all I can say, but if you say Emil sent you, you're likely to get a nice discount. You won't find a safer, more secluded spot in town. Oh, and the rooms are quite comfortable as well. I just hope you don't need sunlight."

"Does the innkeeper see ghosts too?" Saber pressed.

"In a manner of speaking," Emil said dismissively. "Now, you two look absolutely beat, so I insist you go and make use of all the hospitality our wonderful town has to offer. We can speak again tomorrow when you've recovered—especially you, Maaya. You… fascinate me," Emil said, staring intently at her.

"Be fascinated at a distance," Saber warned, and Emil smiled.

"Of course! No harm, no harm. But you see, I am at my best when I have all the answers, and with you two… oh, I have so many questions instead. Humor me, won't you? My wealth of information about this town and everything surrounding it is yours, and my price is information in return. You won't find a better deal."

"Right. So… tomorrow, then?" Maaya asked quickly, eager to get away from this man. Emil nodded.

"Don't worry about where to find me. I'll find you."

Before either of the girls could say a word, Emil bowed deeply again, then turned on his heel and walked swiftly away into the night.

"Let's go before he comes back," Maaya murmured, and Saber nodded.

As they walked, Saber looked repeatedly over her shoulder, but there was no sign of Emil or anyone else. The only signs of people they encountered were the silhouettes of people through the windows of homes and taverns and occasional outbursts of laughter. Maaya felt herself growing more comfortable with her situation; even in unfamiliar territory, empty streets in the dark were what she knew. She had no fear of anyone else who might be prowling; she gave them no competition and certainly had nothing to give them if held at knifepoint. Saber also provided an effective distraction and means of intimidation if necessary.

Soon enough they arrived at the alley Emil mentioned. It was almost completely devoid of light; the buildings on either side were dark, and the street as a whole seemed as though it didn't get much traffic at all. Maaya stepped slowly into the alley, taking care not to trip; she could barely make out the shapes of boxes and abandoned furniture, but it was hard to tell where one ended and another began.

It was so dark that Maaya and Saber both almost missed the staircase. It was even more inconspicuous than Maaya had imagined; it looked to be nothing more than the entrance to a cellar. Two heavy wooden doors, slightly angled, lay nearly hidden behind a stack of boxes covered in cloth.

"This can't be what he was talking about, can it?" she asked dubiously.

"This is the only thing remotely resembling an entrance to anything I can see," Saber replied quietly, scanning the alleyway as best she could. "This doesn't seem like a trap, but still. Be ready for anything. I'll knock—you stand back."

Maaya took a step away from the doors as Saber moved uneasily toward it. Then the ghost rapped upon them four times in quick succession.

The sound of her knocking echoed around the street. For a minute after the noise faded there was no other sound to be heard. Maaya was just about to suggest knocking again when both doors suddenly opened, clanging heavily against the building's wall. The girls both jumped back instinctively, but nothing came from within.

Maaya cautiously stepped closer, peering down the long stairway. There appeared to be some kind of light at the bottom of the stairs, but it was too dim to let her make anything out. She did, however, notice that there didn't appear to be anyone there. Either whoever opened the doors had turned and run back down as soon as they had done so, or the doors had opened of their own accord. Maaya wasn't sure which sounded worse.

She moved to start down the stairs, but Saber stopped her.

"I'll go first," she said quietly. "Stay here until I say it's okay."

Maaya obeyed and crouched near the opening as Saber floated slowly downward. She watched the ghost anxiously, but Saber appeared more inquisitive than concerned. Once Saber reached the bottom of the stairs, she peered around her, and then disappeared.

After only a few moments, Saber came back into view. She glanced up at Maaya with an uncertain expression, but beckoned to her. Taking one last look around the alleyway to make sure no one was watching, Maaya stepped quietly down into the dark hallway, closing the doors softly behind her.

Without waiting, Saber left again. As Maaya tread uneasily down the stairs, she could hear Saber's voice—and to her surprise, multiple other voices.

When Maaya reached the bottom, however, all the voices faded. Maaya herself was too surprised to break the silence.

She was standing in what looked like a secret underground pub, and it was full of patrons—all of whom were dead. Some sat at tables, evidently having been in deep conversation, while others stood around billiards tables and dart boards. Branching off from the room were two hallways; what they led to Maaya could not see, but like the main room, they were dimly lit. The room itself was wide, but the ceiling was low, making Maaya feel a little claustrophobic. Beneath her, stretching from wall to wall, was an ancient dark green carpet which clashed almost comfortingly with the deep red wood of the bar and furniture. It might have been a cozy place under better circumstances.

Right now, however, Maaya felt distinctly uncomfortable. Every single ghost in the room was staring right at her, and they did not appear pleased to see her.

"Looks like you let in a living one, new girl," one of the patrons drawled in Saber's direction. "Didn't anyone tell you to keep an eye out before coming down 'ere?"

"No, because I've never *been* here before," Saber replied sharply. "Besides, I told you I was bringing a friend. This is her."

"Ah, you're off your rocker, then," another man said in a thick accent.

"Don't be daft. She must be lonely, is all," the woman next to him chastised. "Not easy to make friends when you're newly dead, you know that s'well as anyone. When you're new, you spend most of your time around the living even as they can't see you."

Saber turned to Maaya exasperatedly.

"Can you talk to them? They think you're my… oh, what's a ghost's equivalent to an imaginary friend?"

Maaya cleared her throat nervously.

"Uh, hello… I'm Maaya. We're just looking for a place to rest tonight and someone recommended this place. At least, I think he did. I don't suppose this is the Shallow Squid?"

Silence fell again, and a few of them looked at her with renewed interest. Maaya expected she was going to have to get used to this. Evidently there was not a single other person in Anorath who could see ghosts. At least in Sark the dead were somewhat used to interacting with the living.

They recovered remarkably quickly, however. To her surprise, rather than asking any questions, they all simply returned to what they had been doing before.

From behind the counter, the ghost of a young woman walked over to Maaya. She was short, with short black hair, gentle brown eyes, and light brown skin. Her linen smock swished about her as she walked up to them.

"Who was it that told you about this place, then?" she asked kindly.

"Someone named Emil," Maaya replied, and to her surprise a number of the ghosts around the room groaned and muttered amongst themselves. "What? Is something wrong?"

"Emil hasn't quite gotten the hang of settling down. He still enjoys being the puppet master of town," said the first man. "Also enjoys playing tour guide, informant… whenever someone new shows up here it's usually because of him."

The woman scoffed.

"Emil is perfectly pleasant, just a little strange. Now then, don't you mind this lot here. They've become accustomed to routine in their old age, and Emil is… the opposite of routine. They aren't upset with you, I promise."

"Seems odd Emil would recommend a place so unlike himself in atmosphere," Saber said, not caring to lower her voice.

"And he's well aware of it, to be sure, but you won't find a safer place to rest, and that's what he cares about. Maaya, dear, you look exhausted, poor thing. Let's get you a room to rest, and I'll send someone by with food once you're comfortable."

Maaya followed the woman wordlessly, taken aback by her warm and pleasant attitude. Ghosts weren't inherently mean, but many were standoffish. Many ghosts, after a certain length of time, became used to routine. They stayed in the same places in the same company and generally had no reason or desire to leave. Beyond that, they were peaceful until disturbed. This was what people didn't understand about ghosts. Most of them didn't harbor any ill will toward the living or have some unexplainable animosity toward inanimate objects—they were just stubborn and didn't like change.

The other ghosts in the room didn't so much as give Maaya a second glance as she and Saber followed the woman down the hallway farthest from the staircase. Maybe meeting a person who could see ghosts really wasn't that big of a surprise in the grand scheme of things. At the very least she hoped this meant they wouldn't cause her any trouble.

The hallway was surprisingly long, with at least a dozen doors on each side. They were led down to the very end of the hallway where the woman disappeared through the last door on the left. There was a clicking sound from within, and then the door opened.

"There you are, dears," the woman said. "It's not much, but it's safe and comfortable. Should be clean, too. I just did the laundry and dusted a fortnight ago." At the girls' surprised looks, she continued with a smile, "I don't have much else to do, and I take pride in a well-run establishment. Besides, I never know when Emil might send more guests here. Better to be prepared, I always say. Oh, by the way! My name is Nadya. If you need anything, don't hesitate to let me know. I'm always here, after all. Food will be by shortly."

"Th-thank you," Maaya said, feeling slightly overwhelmed by Nadya's kindness. She almost didn't want her to go. "How, uh… how much is it? To stay, I mean?"

"For a friend of Emil's? Not a single rial. If you feel like helping out with the chores in exchange for your stay I won't complain, but for now the only thing you need to worry about is getting some rest."

Nadya smiled warmly, gave a small bow, then left the room, closing the door quietly behind her.

Maaya glanced around. The only light came from two oil lamps on either side of the single bed's headboard, but it was enough. The same dark green carpet lined the room, and the wallpaper was an ancient peeling pinstriped pattern of beige and white. Apart from the bed, which was draped in a thick off-white comforter, there was only a small chest of drawers, a bedside cabinet, and a cushioned chair in the corner. A mirror hung over the chest of drawers, and on either side of the mirror were two candlesticks, though there were no candles in them.

Maaya set Kim's diary down on the bedside cabinet, which, to her surprise, was completely free of dust. She made to hop onto the bed, then yelped slightly as she sank down much farther than she had expected.

Saber grinned down at her.

"Comfy?"

"Honestly, I could fall asleep in the boat again if I had to," Maaya yawned, already feeling the weight of her fatigue bearing down upon her again. She struggled up to a sitting position, dangling her legs over the side of the bed. "But I'm sure a night here will be good for us. How are you feeling?"

"I… don't know. I think I'm still caught up in how surreal all of this feels," Saber said, floating gently down to sit beside Maaya. "I'm still questioning whether this is all real, you know? Everything's going too fast for me to actually sit down and process it all. I look around and I'm in an underground hotel run by ghosts in another city because we got driven out of Sark, and it's just… too much right now. Though I think I prefer this confusion to the insufferable emotional nonsense that's sure to come."

Maaya chuckled. She knew the coming days would be hard, but there was no one she trusted more. She only hoped she could offer the same amount of support.

As they sat in silence, however, her thoughts began to overwhelm her.

She heard Rahu's voice in her head, proclaiming to the entire city that it had been she who brought this mysterious wrath down upon them, and she remembered Svante telling them that the ghost walks, as far as he knew, were attracted to the magic of *libris*. She remembered the mother and son, whose family they had help put to rest, being some of the first to fall under the ghosts' aggressive incursions into Sark.

"Hey… do you think Rahu was right?" she asked tentatively, her eyes on the floor. "Do you think the ghosts are pulled to me somehow?"

"What? No, absolutely not," Saber said firmly. She placed her hands on Maaya's shoulders and looked Maaya straight in the eye. "That's not the kind of talk you need to be listening to. While we might not know exactly what causes these things, I'm pretty sure you've never been to Krethus, so unless you took a big overseas trip you're not telling me about, this isn't your fault. Yeah?"

Maaya nodded wordlessly. The ghost's words provided only a little comfort. She couldn't help but think that there were too many coincidences to completely rule out Rahu's claim, even if Rahu had no idea what he had actually been talking about.

"Listen," Saber said, more gently this time, "we've been through some hard times. You're hungry, you haven't slept well, and you have a lot you need to process. Both of us do. It's unfair to start blaming yourself for anything right now; we don't even know what's going on yet. Okay?"

"I suppose," Maaya replied, at least partially convinced. Saber was probably right, but Maaya didn't think she could accept it all yet. "Anyway, at the very least I think we need to stop using *libris*. If there's any chance these ghosts are attracted to it we need to stop using it completely."

"We don't know that for sure," Saber said.

"Svante thought it was true and it was his job to study them," Maaya argued.

"Yes, but he didn't pass all his knowledge on to us. We shouldn't take what little he said and act like we know enough to make that big a claim. *Besides,*" she pressed, as Maaya opened her mouth, "I'm not saying you're wrong. But we should be prepared all the same. *Libris* comes in handy, especially if we have to face more of those things."

"That's true," Maaya sighed, putting her face in her palms. "This is important to me, though. I don't want to do it unless it's absolutely necessary."

"That's fine! Only as a last resort, then," Saber agreed. "I can't imagine we'll need them that often. For some daring escapes, maybe, or to… what? What's wrong?"

I just… they're gone, Saber," Maaya said helplessly, and even as she fought the urge to break down, she could feel it coming. "Our friends are dead because of those things and I couldn't save them. I promised, I *promised* them I would keep them all safe, that's why I took them off the street to begin with, and I… I tried so hard, but I couldn't even…"

"I know, I know. It's all a big awful mess. Come here."

The ghost pulled Maaya into a hug as the girl began to sob. What had begun with Rahu's taunting words was now a torrent of memories, the full impact of what they had been through crashing down on her all at once. Her friends were dead, her home was destroyed, Svante had been killed in front of her, she had no idea if Roshan was still alive, she didn't know what would happen to Sark without her protection, and she was likely wanted by the police. They needed to get to Krethus but they had no money, no transport, no contacts, and no way to prove to the Krethans that they were there to help even if they did make it across the sea. It seemed cruel that for all the emotional turmoil they had been through, the only thing left to speak of the years of history and life they had endured in Sark rested in a small diary Maaya had never read.

They remained there for what seemed like hours, but midnight had not yet arrived when a soft knock came at the door announcing the arrival of their dinner—and by then Maaya was already asleep.

When Maaya woke, she sighed contentedly. She didn't open her eyes just yet. She was lying on a comfortable bed, and with as sore as she still felt she didn't feel like getting up and facing the day. From behind her eyelids it was still dark, so the morning sun likely hadn't risen much just yet. It was quiet, but she occasionally heard calm muffled voices from a distance broken occasionally with laughter. The smell of delicious food wafted from somewhere nearby. For a moment, Maaya was back home, Saber would be coming back from her rounds soon, and one of her friends was making breakfast for everyone.

As her mind cleared, however, she realized she didn't recognize the voices. Her bed was different. And the room was decidedly and unfamiliarly quiet. Her heart sank as she opened her eyes and slowly sat up. Waking up to this realization every morning was going to hurt for a long time.

She glanced around, hoping to see Saber waiting nearby, but the ghost was gone. Maaya felt a twinge of anxiety, fearing the worst, but she quickly stopped herself. She was not going to let herself succumb to paranoia over every little thing. Saber often went on nighttime walks, and in a new town she was probably especially eager to explore. It wasn't like Maaya provided fantastic company while she was asleep anyway.

There was, however, something in the room that had not been there the night before. An old metal cart sat near the foot of the bed. A white cloth was draped over the top, and on top of the cloth was a covered silver platter.

Her stomach growled at the sight. She wasn't sure what was under it, but she wasn't sure if she cared right now. It had been days since she last ate a proper meal. She flung off the covers and sat at the edge of the bed, eagerly taking the lid off the plate.

On the plate was a bowl of curry, a bowl of vegetables, and a smaller plate with rice and some kind of meat Maaya wasn't immediately able to identify. She wasn't sure when it arrived or who had brought it in, but she was still able to feel some heat coming from the food, and the underside of the platter's lid was coated in moisture.

To the right of the platter was a cloth napkin and a few utensils that were clean but clearly very, very old. Maaya might have admired them under different circumstances, but for now she dug in gratefully. It was only slightly warm, and it wasn't a high-quality meal, but right now it was the best food she had ever eaten.

As she ate she thought about the strange ghost they had met the night before. He was definitely the most interesting aspect of Anorath so far—this underground hotel full of dead people notwithstanding—but something about him made her distinctly uncomfortable. Maaya didn't like complex people with obvious secrets. They were harder to figure out, and in many cases that made them dangerous. Emil seemed to feel the same way about Maaya and Saber, so in that respect they were on equal footing, but this was Emil's home turf.

As if on cue, when she sat back for a moment to swallow a particularly large mouthful of vegetables, she noticed a figure in her peripheral vision. Sitting right next to her on the bed was Emil.

Maaya started, then choked. Emil, who had been sitting placidly with his legs crossed and a smile on his face, laughed and patted her firmly on the back.

"Oh, now that won't do. This would be a most anticlimactic death for you. There now, how do you feel?"

Maaya dabbed at her eyes with her napkin to clear her tears, still coughing. Temporarily unable to speak, she threw Emil a dirty look. His grin only widened.

"Now, I may like to play the occasional joke or two, but I am nothing but a gentleman. I wouldn't disturb a lady unless I was sure she was awake first! I was hoping to see your friend as well, but she's so very intrigued by this city; I saw her leave hours ago and she hasn't come back since."

"Were you watching us all night?" Maaya asked suspiciously.

"Oh, heavens no. I'm far too busy a person to do something like that. I was merely on my rounds when I saw her go by. She was so interested in whatever she was doing that I'm afraid she didn't notice me. I expect she'll be back soon to check up on you, so let's make this quick."

"Huh? Make wha—?" Maaya started, then gasped as Emil took her hand and pulled her gently from the bed, holding her waist so that she didn't fall. "Don't do that! You could explain yourself first, you know," she demanded.

"I need to speak with you about something that is most concerning, and I'd like to be somewhere private to do it. This is a wonderful place, but there's never any guarantee that some nosy person won't be listening in. They're a friendly sort, really, but always thirsty for gossip no matter how dull. And this, well, if gossip were a drink, this would poison them. Come now, get your shoes, and let's take a walk. I know the perfect place."

Maaya crossed her arms and stared at him for a moment, then rolled her eyes.

"Fine. But this *will* be quick."

Emil beamed as she reluctantly slipped on her shoes, and they walked out of the room together. A few of the doors in the hallway were open, and as Maaya peered inside each room as they passed, she could see a few men and women in each, fluffing pillows, straightening bedsheets, and moving furniture back to where it was supposed to be.

Her curiosity getting the better of her, Maaya asked, "Do other living guests come here often?"

"Sometimes, yes," Emil said thoughtfully, tapping his chin. "It's generally the same crowd, though. This place attracts a certain type of people, you know, but they come often enough, so we make sure to keep this place clean for them."

"Does that mean… there are other people here who can see ghosts?" Maaya continued. Emil nodded. "Wait, so… is Saber—?"

"Saber is perfectly safe. Those who can see ghosts in this town are a welcoming lot. Perhaps you will meet them! In any case, I've already warned them to leave your friend alone."

Maaya stopped in the middle of the hallway.

"Who *are* you?" she asked intently.

"I am no more and no less than a somewhat charismatic gentleman with an affinity for information. When I was alive that got me into trouble, but now I am free to do as I please."

"And what do you do with that information?"

Emil winked.

"Later. Let's keep moving."

The front room was much emptier than it had been when Maaya arrived the night before. There were only a handful of patrons in the room, and the others busied themselves straightening tables and tidying up. No one gave

Maaya a second glance, but when they noticed Emil, some waved cheerfully while others tried harder not to make eye contact. Emil waved back but did not pause to chat. He led Maaya up the stairs, and then after a quick peek out into the alley, gestured for her to follow.

It was bright and pleasantly warm outside, and Maaya realized it was late into the morning. She felt clearheaded and well rested, but her whole body still ached. She looked forward to resting while Styx took them to Levien.

As they turned onto the main street, Maaya saw the people of Anorath going about their daily business. None of them so much as glanced in her direction, but Maaya instinctively drew back, afraid of being seen. Being entirely in the company of ghosts, she had almost forgotten about other people, but now that she was here all she wanted to do was hide. They would recognize her for sure, point her out, call for the police, or try to capture her.

But Emil put a steady hand at her back and gently guided her forward.

"It's all right. No one's going to pay you any mind. Wherever you came from and whatever happened, remember: you have no reputation here. In your case, that's a good thing."

Slightly comforted, she continued walking, trying her hardest to look normal. Emil would occasionally speak, pointing out interesting people or stores, but Maaya was too afraid to reply. Her whole body was tense, and she was certain that trouble would come somehow. Emil seemed amused, but to his credit, didn't say a word about it.

Before long they arrived at the base of a tall stone clocktower near what Maaya guessed was the center of town. Anorath's town center was quite different from Sark's; there was nothing to immediately distinguish it as being of any importance, and there were few people here. Rather than being lined with large imposing buildings, there were a few shops on one side and a line of small houses on the other. No one seemed to notice the disheveled girl standing by herself next to the clock tower, and if they did, they didn't seem to care.

"Do you feel well enough for some stairs?" Emil asked.

"Not really, no," Maaya said, and Emil chuckled.

"That's fine! Some exercise will do you well. Here, follow me. I'll unlock the door from the inside."

Emil disappeared through the door, and Maaya heard the click of a lock from the other side. Just as she made to pull on the handle she heard a second click, and the door made a loud metallic *clang* as the deadbolt rattled in its frame.

"Emil!" Maaya hissed irritably, and she heard giggling from the other side of the door. Maaya heard a third click, and she opened the door quickly before he could lock it again.

When she stepped into the tower, Emil was gone, but Maaya guessed where he had gone. There was nothing in the tower save for a set of narrow spiral stairs made entirely of the same stone as the outside of the tower. The center of the stairs were worn smooth from hundreds of years of use, and narrow windows placed every dozen steps made sure there was ample lighting.

Maaya took a deep breath, then started to climb. The first few steps were agony, but she soon found a rhythm that caused her less pain. Still, the unevenness of the steps and lack of any sort of railing made it an arduous task. She cursed the ghost under her breath, sure that he was very much enjoying this even if he wasn't watching.

The top of the stairs opened into a wider room filled with old wooden scaffolding and clockwork mechanisms. Maaya had never seen the inside of a clock or watch before, and despite being in pain and out of breath, she had to admire its complexity. She wasn't sure if she could figure out how something like this worked if she studied it her whole life.

Despite there being four sides to the tower, the clock itself only had two faces: one pointed north, the other south. The east and west sides instead had large floor-to-ceiling windows that were kept remarkably clean. Apart from the scaffolding, there was only a single chair in the room. Maaya sat down immediately, grateful to take the weight off her trembling legs.

"You're not much of an athlete, are you?" came Emil's voice from above her. Maaya looked up to see him sitting casually on the minute hand of the clock.

"I hurt," Maaya growled, looking pointedly away from him. A moment later she saw him leap down from the clock and land gracefully next to her.

"Well, you know what they say: no pain, no gain," he said cheerfully.

"If that were true, I'd have a lot more than I do now."

"Mm, yes. Sometimes there is a bit of a delay. Few are aware fate is quite a convoluted bureaucracy. And understaffed, too, from what I understand."

"You must have a reason for bringing me here beyond making me uncomfortable," Maaya sighed. She had agreed to come with him because Saber hadn't come back yet and because she didn't really have anything else to do, but she would very much have preferred to stay in her comfortable bed than climb stairs. Saber would probably tell her off for it later.

"As amusing as that all has been, yes, I do have a reason. In fact, I have more than one, but we'll start somewhere simple. Is it true, Maaya Sahni, that you are responsible for the hundreds of deaths in the nearby town of Sark?"

Maaya's blood ran cold. Of all the things she had been expecting, it hadn't been that.

"How…? How do you know–?"

"Like I told you, my dear, I deal in information," Emil said blankly, but then a wide grin broke over his face. "Don't be alarmed; I only tease. I know what really happened there, which is why I know it wasn't your fault. You tried to save them, even, didn't you?"

"I… something strange was happening, people were dying, I couldn't just—"

"Easy now, Maaya, you aren't in trouble. Actually, I came to see you because you happen to possess talents that make you very valuable to this town. You and Saber together make a formidable team, from what I understand."

"What are you talking about? What talents?" Maaya asked, narrowing her eyes.

"You don't just *see* ghosts; you get *rid* of them. Using a certain card system, as I understand."

Maaya raised her eyebrows.

"And that's something *you* want from me? You do know you're dead, right?"

Emil dramatically put his right hand to his heart.

"What? Say it isn't so!" He smiled, and then his expression became more serious. He gazed out the south clock face at the town below. "There have been strange things happening here. Things I've never seen before. Things that started before your arrival, but which I feel are not entirely a coincidence at your coming. I think you know what I'm talking about."

"Ghost walks," Maaya said in a near whisper, and she suddenly felt weak with dread.

"If that's what you call them. They have been few, but they're occurring more often now. And there are more of them. The other ghosts and I don't know what to make of them, and the living, well… those who remain are terrified of them."

"What do you mean, those who are left? You can't mean some people were already killed?" Maaya gasped.

"Only a few. When those strange ghosts first started appearing, the living who could see ghosts would go out to meet them, as they do. Only this time was different. They didn't come back, dead or alive. Some who saw what happened were too terrified to stay, so they fled Anorath. Where they went I don't know. A few of the others remained, determined to get rid of the hellish things, but they were either taken or frightened off as well. The rest know to keep clear of them, and they think they'll be safe so long as they can stay out of the ghosts' path, but I know differently. From what I hear, you do too."

Maaya's gaze fell to the floor. She had been stupid to think that they would be safe here. There was no logical reason to assume that the ghost walks would occur only in Sark or that they wouldn't spread quickly.

And then her mind was back home again with Roshan and the others. Two nights had passed since she had fled. There was no telling how much worse things had gotten in that short time; she wondered if anyone was left alive at all.

"If you're concerned about your home, worry not," Emil said, his tone softening slightly. "The strange ghosts still visit there, but not nearly as many as there were only nights before. I still believe the best course of action would be for everyone who lives there to flee, but it has not been overrun. Not yet."

"So… you want me to get rid of these ghosts for you?" Maaya asked quietly.

"I'm not entirely sure. I was hoping you might be able to offer some advice. See, while it is quite fortuitous that you possess the power to get rid of troublesome spirits—and I thank you for not using that power on *this* troublesome spirit, by the way—I am also conflicted by the thought that these things may, for whatever reason, be attracted to this power."

Maaya started, and looked up at him in shock.

"You can't believe that," she said, almost desperately. "It's not me. We thought they might be attracted to *libris* but I haven't used any at all since I left. There'd be nothing for them to follow."

"Oh, you misunderstand," Emil said consolingly. "I don't mean to imply you've brought them to Anorath; after all, they arrived here before you did. I simply mean that if I ask you to help in the short term, I may unwittingly be making things worse in the long run. It sounds as though you have some ideas as to how they work, which is what I was hoping would be the case. Perhaps you have some other goal in mind to rid us of them?"

He posed his question innocently, but his knowing expression made Maaya realize he already knew the answer.

"We're trying to get to Krethus," Maaya said, lowering her voice despite there being no one else around. "There's some type of machine there that's creating these things. No living person can get close to it, but we found a way to get close enough to… well, stop it, I guess."

"How very intriguing! The poor girl and her dead friend have a special method that even the governments and greatest minds of the world have not yet been able to devise. Well, go on, tell me what it is."

Maaya, who had been expecting this, shook her head immediately.

"I can't. I've lost enough already by people finding out too much. If we're to have any chance at stopping this thing I need to make sure as few people know about it as possible."

"You offend me," Emil sniffed. "I told you, information is my business. You can't expect me not to try to pry it out of you."

"What do you *do* with that information, anyway?" Maaya asked.

"Oh, it depends. Sometimes it can be sold. Other times it can be withheld. Sometimes it keeps me ahead of those trying to do me or my friends harm, and in some extra special cases it can be used to inflict some harm of my own making. The occasional blackmail, the occasional angry mob. The usual."

"What do you gain from it, though?" Maaya continued. "I mean, it's not like money does you any good in your, ah… current state."

"Ambition doesn't die with the body, my dear, it dies with the mind. Now, let's not get distracted; I understand the need to keep certain things private for your own safety, but I'm still ever so curious. How is it you plan to get all the way across the world by yourself?"

"We… made a friend back in Sark," Maaya explained cautiously. "He was from Krethus. His job was to study these ghosts and he thought he figured out what to do about it. But he couldn't get near the machine; that was our job. He said he would secure passage across the sea and then we'd take it from there."

"That's a surprisingly solid plan. Where is this mysterious friend of yours now?"

"Dead," Maaya said monotonously. "Just after a ghost walk killed three of my friends, he was shot in the head just a few feet in front of me. A man there framed the attacks on us, which is why we're on the run."

For the first time Maaya could remember, Emil looked surprised. He opened his mouth to reply, then closed it and stared out the window again instead. After a minute's pause, he spoke.

"I'm truly sorry for your loss. For what it's worth, I think it's admirable for you to continue to pursue this task despite what it has already cost you. I'm not unfamiliar with the man who has given you so much grief, and I assure you he has no ally in me." He turned and strode back over to Maaya, a hopeful expression on his face. "You've said enough for now. In return, I will make good on my promise: my resources are yours, and I will help you however I am able."

"And what are those resources, exactly?" Maaya asked, narrowing her eyes.

"To start, I can give you safe passage to Levien. Second, I can give you something that will allow you to find friends wherever you go. Friends who can help you."

"What friends?" Maaya continued suspiciously.

"More on that later," Emil grinned, waving his hand with a flourish. "What do you think? Safe and free passage, as well as contacts—seems a mighty deal to me."

"It sounds almost too good to be true, so I don't know why I shouldn't think you're just teasing me or lying to me to get something from me. But I still want to know more. And I'd *also* like to know why you had to drag me all the way up here to have this conversation."

"Ah, now we're getting somewhere!" Emil said delightedly, and he held out his hand to help Maaya to her feet. They walked to one of the wide windows, and Emil made a grand sweeping gesture to the city below. "I wanted you to become acquainted with our lovely little town, and not just on an emotional level. I figured you might find a tour from a high vantage point preferable to a tour by foot."

"Thanks, but I'm not going to be here long, so I don't really need to—" Maaya started, but Emil interrupted.

"Oh, but you do. The ghosts come to visit nearly every night… and you wouldn't want to find yourself in a dead end once they come creeping out."

Maaya sighed. She was too tired to argue and looked forward to getting back to the underground inn. She especially wanted to talk to Saber, both to figure out where she had gone and to tell her about her conversation with Emil.

"Did your information tell you we planned on leaving Anorath today?" Maaya finally said.

"It did, but it also told me your current method of transport is in a rickety old boat on a very exposed river."

"My friend can get us to Levien just fine."

"But what about once you get there? I have no doubt about your ability to traverse a calm river for a short distance, but what about the open ocean? I don't suppose your friend's offer of passage to Krethus is still in effect now he's dead, is it?"

"He… has a contact in Levien," Maaya faltered, and Emil jumped on her uncertainty.

"Who is this contact? What's their name? Do you know where to find them? Do they know you're coming? How will you pay them?"

"Okay, fine, I get it," Maaya snapped irritably. "And your plan is so much better."

"I'm quite certain it is. Now, what do you think about getting rid of these ghosts, then? I have a little something in mind."

"What can I do? You said you were concerned using *libris* might attract more of the ghosts."

"True, but that's only a possibility. On the other hand, my associates and contacts are getting demoralized. Many are leaving the city. The longer this goes on and the worse it gets, the fewer will remain. And that's just bad business. I rely on a constant stream of people coming and going; if people avoid Anorath like the plague, this city will become as boring as you think it is. So what I want from you is… give them a demonstration before you go. Wait for one of these ghost walks to appear, then put it down. Show everyone they can be beaten before you go off to do just that on the other side of the world. You *can* do that, can't you?"

Maaya pinched the bridge of her nose.

"You want me to put on a *show* for you."

"Absolutely," Emil said without missing a beat. "Don't be so dismissive of morale. It's that which has kept you going when all else has failed, no?"

"More like I want to save the people I haven't already lost," Maaya replied bitterly.

"Ah, but you still think it's possible! And that, my dear, is the power of hope. So yes, I'd like you to put on a show. Destroy a few ghosts, save a few lives, and keep me in business. Not to mention, you can help yourself as well."

"How could this possibly help me? If you don't think the risk is that great and you can help me in return, I'll consider it, but I'd only be making things worse for myself by being out in public like that."

"Consider it a chance to show the world the good you do. If they think you're a killer or a criminal, prove them wrong. This could be a way to fight the narrative being set by that delightful holy man from Sark. That said, I do understand you're in pain and I am always empathetic, but you may want to see this done as soon as possible."

"Why the rush?"

In response, Emil gestured down to the street below. A single officer with a stack of papers in his hands had paused at one of the town's many news boards. With some difficulty he attached one of the papers to the board, made sure it was firmly affixed, and then walked away. She couldn't tell exactly what it said from such a distance, but she didn't have to; it shared the same format as every other poster proclaiming a reward for a fugitive being found and brought to justice.

"While it would seem you arrived in Anorath before news about your alleged crimes, it has caught up with you," Emil said seriously. "Relish the time you go unnoticed in this town. It's about to end."

17

SHOWTIME

Emil spent the next half an hour discussing the layout of Anorath with Maaya, pointing out important landmarks and streets as well as places where friendly people and ghosts congregated—and where law enforcement tended to patrol. At first Maaya was entirely uninterested, but as Emil went on it became clear he knew the town as well as it was possible to know, and he was able to share that information in a way that actually sounded interesting. Before long Maaya felt much more comfortable than she had previously—and this was a good thing, because as Emil helpfully pointed out, she would get no chance to explore the streets in-person without risking a run-in with the authorities who were now being familiarized with all the details about her Rahu wanted them to know.

Once Emil was reasonably satisfied with what Maaya had learned he insisted on walking her back to the inn. This time he took care to walk her through narrow back streets and past the sides of buildings that had no windows. Maaya didn't argue. She doubted many people would have seen the posters by now, but she didn't feel like taking any risks, especially in her current state.

They made it back to the Shallow Squid without incident. Emil saw her to the hidden door and opened it for her before explaining that he had errands to run. Maaya decided it was time to reenact her policy of not asking questions; the sooner they did what he wanted the sooner they could get out of Anorath and continue on their journey. She hadn't yet been able to ask Emil for more specifics about his alleged assistance, but asking would entail further conversation, and the only person she cared to speak to right now was Saber—preferably from the comfort of their room.

As she crossed the main room to the hall, she noticed Nadya standing at the counter. Nadya looked up and smiled warmly as Maaya walked in.

"Your friend came back not too long ago. She was asking about you."

Maaya thanked her and headed down the hall straightaway. Saber would likely be upset at being made to wait.

Sure enough, before Maaya had even completely opened the door to their room, Saber was inches from her face, her expression a mixture of relief and irritation.

"Maaya, where have you *been?*" the ghost demanded. "It's not like you to wander off by yourself, and none of the people up front seemed to have any idea where you went. You had me worried!"

"Sorry. Emil came by and wanted to talk. He took me to the top of a clocktower so he could show me the town, and I'm worn out all over again. On that note, get out of my way."

Maaya nudged Saber gently aside and plopped comfortably down onto the bed. She didn't have to look up to know Saber was rolling her eyes.

"Oh, good. He waits until I'm gone to swoop in on you. What did he want? I *know* it wasn't just for a friendly tour. You didn't even finish your breakfast."

"It's… complicated. I want your advice on this. Here…"

Saber's expression changed from irritation to mild interest and then into outright anger as Maaya finished her explanation.

"He wants us to do *what?* Absolutely not. I'm not going to put this town—and especially you—at risk because this man is afraid of losing his makeshift empire. He seems to think highly of his own brain; maybe he can actually put that to use instead of dragging in innocent bystanders."

"Yeah, I'm not sure about this," Maaya said. "But he said he could help us and he seemed genuine about it."

"What could he possibly do for us?" Saber scoffed.

"He said he could provide safe passage to Levien and that he could help us find friends who could help us from there. He was a little vague," Maaya admitted. "But maybe what he can provide is better than nothing at all."

"If he didn't offer any solid details to reel you in that means the details aren't worth mentioning," Saber said scathingly. "We've got what we need. We already have a ride to Levien, and from there we just need to find Svante's contact or another way to Krethus. Spending time finding friends would slow us down and pose a risk."

"Levien is what worries me, though. What will we do once we get there? Even if the police there don't know about us yet, how are we supposed to find one person in the whole city without knowing their name or what they look like? Maybe that's something Emil could—"

"Emil looks out for Emil, and that's that," Saber interrupted. "I'm sorry, I don't like him, and I don't like this. He saw the officer putting up a wanted poster with your face on it and he still asked you to do something like this as publicly as possible. That will make our escape even harder, and I doubt Styx will appreciate us running shortly ahead of an angry mob like he specifically warned us about. *And* you haven't fully recovered yet. Whatever he has to offer can't possibly be worth the risk, and I say that as the one between us who's more inclined to take them."

Maaya sighed. Saber was right and she knew it. She had let herself build up hope that Emil would have some trick up his sleeve, some contact or information that would set them up with a straight ticket to Krethus, but now she was plagued by doubts. If Emil was powerful enough to accomplish any of that, he wouldn't need to ask Maaya for what he had.

"Anyway, now that I've made sure you're safe, I need to go see Styx. It's almost noon and I still haven't brought him the food I promised. He's sure to be worried about you. You should stay here and get some rest."

"Have you figured out how you're going to bring it all to him?" Maaya asked amusedly.

"I have! I met a few of the people who can see me—and of course they all know Emil, so that was almost a deal breaker—but they're friendly enough. I managed to convince one to buy and carry the food for me. I'd like to think it was just as much his good nature as it was my irresistible charm."

"Right," Maaya snorted. "Be careful, okay?"

"You got it. There isn't much to worry about. I don't think they have any idea what *libris* is, and most of the ghosts here aren't troublemakers so no one has ever had a reason to figure it out."

"That's probably because of him, you know," Maaya said teasingly, and Saber mimed gagging.

"He could save the world himself and I still wouldn't like him. Now, enough talk; get some rest. Oh, and don't you worry. I've made some friends among the living, but you'll always hold the most special place in my heart."

Maaya flung a pillow at Saber as the ghost blew a kiss in her direction. Saber ducked quickly through the door, letting the pillow *thud* quietly and harmlessly against it.

Maaya was about to lay back to rest when, to her surprise, the pillow she had just thrown plopped down on the bed next to her. She looked up quickly and saw Nadya standing just inside the door, an apologetic smile on her face.

"I apologize for intruding, but I wanted to make sure you were all right. You looked uncomfortable when you came back."

"Oh, I'm fine, thank you," Maaya said hastily, embarrassed at the thought that Nadya might have seen her playful banter with Saber. "I'm just sore, that's all. It's been a rough week and I haven't had a chance to recover."

"Ah, that's one thing about being alive I don't miss," Nadya said brightly. "May I join you?"

Maaya invited her to sit on the bed with her. Nadya bowed slightly, then came into the room, sitting carefully on the edge of the bed. She looked slightly uncomfortable, like she was unused to sitting and talking with guests in their own rooms, but she said nothing about it. Instead, she gazed inquisitively at Maaya.

"I was going to suggest that you stay here and get some rest for a few more nights, but something tells me you aren't planning on being around that long. Is that right?"

Maaya glanced over at her in surprise.

"Did you overhear us talking? It's not exactly set in stone, but—"

"Oh, no, not at all. I would never eavesdrop," Nadya said quickly. "But you have that look about you. People who don't intend to stay long don't let themselves become acquainted with much. They stick to polite formalities and keep mostly to themselves until it's time to go. It's a shame, but I suppose not everyone is free to stay as long as they wish. Someone as interesting as you, well, I'm sure you've got plenty of obligations in places more interesting than this."

"I was told if I stay long enough I'll get to see how interesting Anorath can really get," Maaya said.

"A sales pitch as old as time. It could just be my perspective, but there isn't really much beneath the surface here. There used to be, but not as much anymore. People are afraid to leave the safety of the town's walls, and those who do don't often come back anymore. It's a strange world we live in now, and some are determined to hold on to glory that no longer exists."

"Do you think that's why Emil wants me to stay? Because things got too boring here?"

Nadya chuckled and turned her gaze reminiscently to the ceiling.

"That's part of it, I'm sure. Above all, he's always loved this place. Even when it killed him. He puts on a show, but much as he's loath to admit it, he has an altruistic streak. Though I will say I haven't seen him so intrigued by a newcomer in quite some time. There's something about you that has him particularly entranced."

Maaya suppressed a shudder at these last words. She didn't want to think about Emil thinking about *her* that way.

"Actually… there is something. He told me this morning that he wants me to do something for him, and that in return he'd help me." At Nadya's inquiring glance she continued, "He's upset that people are getting frightened off. He wants me to make a big public display about getting rid of some of those weird ghosts. He thinks that if his friends see they can be defeated they'll be brave enough to stick around."

"I see. That is a heavy request," Nadya replied slowly. "I understand why you don't want to take him up on that."

"I haven't decided, is the thing," Maaya said uncertainly. "Saber hates the idea and wants us to leave right away, but… I don't know how I feel about that yet."

"You're a very pragmatic person, but you also have an altruistic streak—one that is sometimes too loud to ignore, am I right?" Nadya said.

Maaya nodded.

"I don't know what to do. He makes it sound like it would be such a good thing for everyone. Even me, if you can believe it. And even if I were just thinking about myself, Emil's help could be valuable. Saber and I are all alone otherwise."

"You know what this sounds like to me? It sounds like you've already made up your mind and are asking me for validation," Nadya said gently, and she smiled as Maaya stammered in protest. "I'm not pushing you one way or the other. But if it helps, I think there is no wrong choice. Every decision you need to make contains some element of risk. The way I see it, it's just a matter of deciding which risks you feel comfortable taking, and for what purpose."

Maaya said nothing. Though Nadya claimed not to be pushing her in any particular direction, she was now full of doubt. She had been prepared to leave, albeit reluctantly, but now she felt almost ready to confront Saber when she returned and tell her there had been a change of plans.

Nadya stood up to leave, gave Maaya a polite bow, and then disappeared through the closed door, leaving the girl alone with her thoughts.

Maaya sighed, resting her face in her palms as the ghost's words ran themselves ragged through her mind. *Had* Maaya already made up her mind and she just didn't know it yet? It wouldn't have been the first time, but she had difficulty believing she could still be so indecisive despite everything that had just happened.

Unable to stop herself, she looked over at the bedside table where Kim's diary lay untouched and unopened. She felt a throbbing pain in her chest as she gazed at it. She didn't even have to guess what Kim would have suggested. Kim would have stayed. She would have helped. She would have seen a person in need and done whatever she could. As much as Maaya believed herself to be a cynical and overly cautious person, she had always admired the optimistic side of Kim, and promised herself to someday emulate that mentality. But was she ready to start now?

Maaya didn't remember falling asleep, but the next thing she knew, Saber was shaking her gently awake.

"Finally. I've been trying to wake you up for a good half a minute now. I was about to break out the pots and pans. How do you feel?"

"Tired. The usual," Maaya yawned, sitting up slowly and rubbing her eyes. She didn't know how long she had been asleep, but she felt even worse than before. "What time is it?"

"An hour or so until sunfall. You can sleep in the boat and then hopefully you'll be back to a normal schedule. We should be ready to go as soon as it gets dark; there are signs up all over the place with your face on them. The good news is they're all black and white so they didn't even get your hair color right—"

"We're not leaving just yet," Maaya interrupted. She felt a flicker of fear as she said these words, knowing full well what Saber's reaction would be, but she forced herself to look the ghost in the eye. "Or at least, I'm not leaving."

Saber's expression of shock was almost comical.

"You… you're going to do that favor for Emil, aren't you?" she said finally. Maaya nodded. "Maaya, don't be ridiculous! I hate those ghosts as much as you do but we can't let ourselves be sidetracked every time they show up. They're going to be everywhere soon; if we stop to help every time they bother someone we'll never even make it to Levien."

"I know. But this is different. We can get something in return," Maaya protested.

"Yeah? His vague rewards?" Saber asked sternly.

"Is it so bad to have a way to find help? I don't know about you but I don't want to be alone where we're going."

"Yes, well, I'm skeptical at best about his *friends*. Honestly, Maaya, you shouldn't be so easily fooled; he's a salesman and nothing more. And judging by his clothes, he wasn't even a good one—"

"It's more than that," Maaya said, and the desperation in her own voice annoyed her. "Emil has a point, as much as I don't like him personally. This isn't about just fighting the ghosts. We know that's pointless in the long run. But right now it can give people hope, something to believe in, you know? Isn't a storm so much less scary when you know it will eventually end?"

Saber sighed and looked away, visibly agitated as she struggled to answer.

"You have a point, and I understand that," the ghost said slowly, "but I also know that if we don't hurry there may not be people left alive to feel that hope. Not to mention, you're mortal. You can get hurt, you can get exhausted, you can… well, other things could happen. Right now we need to get to Krethus, and every risk you take before we get there puts that task in jeopardy."

It was Maaya's turn to fall silent. Saber was right again, and Maaya hated it. She knew there was no solid logical argument for doing what she wanted to do. If she had to be completely honest with herself, even she didn't completely understand why she was so intent on doing this. Part of it was for this mysterious help that Emil had promised, part of it was to help inspire others like Emil hoped, and part of it was to help herself—she felt as hopeless as the others.

She shook her head, then spoke before Saber had a chance to protest.

"You have a point too, but we need all the help we can get. Besides, I think he might have a point. I can show people what I really do—that I get rid of the ghosts, not hurt people. If I want any chance of ever coming home, people have to know that. And… I guess I feel like this is important. I feel like I have the chance to do something that actually makes a difference here. I was completely useless back in Sark; if anything, I made things worse. But it could be different here. It won't take long! I'll just draw a few blood cards and destroy a few ghosts, and then we can be on our way just like we planned. I know enough about the city to escape from—"

"So this is for you, then?" Saber asked in a tone Maaya couldn't quite decipher.

"Part of it is, yes," Maaya admitted bluntly. "Isn't that important, too?"

Saber ran her fingers through her hair, and every second the silence hung over them made Maaya more nervous. Finally, however, Saber's shoulders fell, and she looked begrudgingly back at her living friend.

"Fine, fine. I'd be a bad friend if I wasn't there for you when you made stupid decisions. But he'd better follow through or so help me…"

Maaya smiled.

"Thank you, Saber. This means a lot. I'll make it up to you."

Saber raised an eyebrow.

"What could you possibly give me?"

"One free stupid decision free of criticism."

"Please, I'd never get to use it. I'm the pinnacle of logic and reason."

There was a short pause, and then both girls laughed. Maaya felt a wave of relief wash over her. She knew she was asking a lot. She often did, and Saber had stuck with her through it all. But Saber was not one of the dead known for her limitless patience, and Maaya felt that Saber put up with much more than was fair to her. Maaya had been serious about making it up to her, even if she wasn't sure how she was going to do that yet.

"So as admirable as your goal is, how do you plan to fight them when you can't get out of bed without whimpering in pain?" Saber teased.

"I'll make do. Besides, it's not like I have to do anything crazy. There aren't many ghosts here, so I won't even really have to move. As long as I can throw the cards, I'll be fine. Speaking of which, get me a knife."

An hour later, Maaya strode down the hall of the Shallow Squid. As evening fell the usual crowd of ghosts came back from wherever they had been during the day, and the front hall was starting to get crowded. This time, to Maaya's surprise, she saw a few other living people there too, talking amicably with the ghosts like they were all longtime friends. For all Maaya knew, they were.

As she entered the room, everyone looked up at her and followed her with their eyes, though they didn't stop their conversations. Their stares made her distinctly uncomfortable. Surely she couldn't be that unusual.

Saber was currently off telling Styx that they would be slightly delayed. She had offered to be the one to deliver the message, both because it was easier for her to get to him and because she wanted to spare Maaya his sure-to-be disappointed monologue. Maaya had gratefully agreed. While she never even considered being afraid of him, she dreaded ever disappointing him; the very thought sent a pang of guilt through her heart.

In the meantime, Maaya needed to seek out Emil and find out what he needed her to do. She didn't expect this to be difficult. She was, however, prepared for Emil's request to be unnecessarily complex; he had a flair for the dramatic, and from the sounds of it he wanted Maaya's display to be as public as possible.

"Maaya! Wait just a minute, dear."

Nadya waved to her from behind the counter, and Maaya paused near the stairs up to the alley. Everyone's eyes were still upon her, and she wanted nothing more than to leave as quickly as she could. Luckily, Nadya soon made her way over to her, holding something dark in her hands.

"Take this," Nadya said, and Maaya could see she was holding a hooded cloak. "I thought it might be useful for you to have while you're out tonight. It should make it that much harder for anyone to see your face, and I'd like to think it's fairly comfortable, too."

"I… thank you," Maaya said in surprise, taking the cloak and wrapping it around her. It fit well, and while it was light enough that it wouldn't hinder her movements, it was thick enough to keep her plenty warm even at this time of year. It was made of a material as dark as midnight, and the smoothness of the cloth told Maaya this was not an inexpensive garb. "This is beautiful. But I don't think I can borrow this. I have to escape tonight and I'm not sure I could bring it back if I'm being chased."

"I didn't expect you to return it," Nadya laughed. "This is for you to keep! It's a gift."

"Oh! Oh no, I couldn't, you've already given us a room and food and--"

"The least I could do for the person who's off to try to save the world. Sometimes we're allowed to do nice things for others without asking for anything in return. How does it feel?"

"It's wonderful," Maaya said softly, rubbing the smooth material between her fingers. She fastened the single silver clasp in front, then couldn't help but do a twirl, immediately feeling incredibly embarrassed. Nadya laughed quietly, holding her hand delicately in front of her mouth.

"Take good care of it, won't you? It will do the same for you. It was my favorite when I was alive, so I can't bear to see it sitting uselessly in an abandoned closet for any longer."

"I will," Maaya promised. "Even if I can't come back to say goodbye tonight, I'll come back when this is all over."

"Really? To a place like this? Oh, child, you must have better places to go. But I suppose when the world is saved you can go anywhere you like. It means a lot that you'd come back to see us again. You can get to know us properly, and maybe even Emil will behave himself once things are back to the way he likes."

"I would come back just to see that, honestly," Maaya chuckled, then paused. She didn't want to go. She wasn't used to this kindness; it seemed almost in abundance here in Anorath, and now that she had gotten a taste of it she didn't want to leave it behind.

"Don't you worry," Nadya said warmly as though she had read Maaya's thoughts. "We'll still be here when you get back. We're quite frustratingly resistant to change, you know."

"I know," Maaya smiled. "Listen… thank you so much. For everything. You've been so kind to me and you've had no reason to."

"If there's one favor I can ask of you, it's to believe that there never needs to be a reason. It should be the way of things. Maybe when enough of us think that way, it will be. The world is a better place than you think, Maaya. I know part of you believes that. That's why you're doing what you're doing, no?"

Maaya nodded.

"Thank you," Maaya said again with all the feeling she could muster. "I'll remember."

"You'll do well, I know you will. Make us proud out there, all right?"

"I will."

They shared a hug, and Maaya fought the urge to not let go. Nadya was one of the friendliest people she had met in a long time and somehow it was already time to say goodbye. It wasn't fair.

All the same, however, she turned and walked up the steps with renewed purpose. This was a feeling she was unaccustomed to: wherever she went and whatever she did, people were counting on her and believing in her. This was such an unfamiliar feeling that she almost rejected it out of principle, seeking as she so often did that which she already knew, but she forced herself to embrace it. Having these kinds of people in her life was a strength, not a weakness, despite what those darker parts of her mind attempted to make her believe.

When she stepped out carefully into the alley, all was dark and quiet. Saber still hadn't returned, and she realized that she wasn't sure how Saber would find her; even Maaya wasn't sure where she was going or where they would be able to meet if they remained separated. She assumed Emil had some sort of idea in mind; this was all his idea, after all. However, as she stood in the cold dark alley, she also realized that she had no idea where to find him, either.

Evidently Emil had planned for that as well, for no sooner had Maaya taken a step toward the street than he appeared right next to her, walking through the wall of the old building adjacent to the underground inn. She attempted to hide her jump of surprise, but the grin on his face told her she hadn't been remotely successful.

"Lovely night, lovely night," he said casually, falling into stride next to her. "Oh, and lovely cloak. I'm glad Nadya's taken a liking to you so quickly. I like it when my friends become mutual friends; there's something so lovely about that process."

"Yes, wonderful," Maaya replied dryly. She was already irritated. "I'm ready to do what you want. Do you have a plan?"

"No, I thought we would wing it every step of the way. What harm could come from that? I'm joking, by the way," he said as Maaya opened her mouth to reply angrily. "Do I have a plan… what a silly question."

"What is it, then?" she asked shortly.

"Aren't you ever the impatient one? I thought that was your friend's role, but I do suppose bad habits are picked up by exposure. Now then, our first plan is incredibly simple: we wait."

"For the ghosts?"

"Well, them too, of course. But we're waiting for something much more important, something I hope will arrive before our deadly friends."

"And what's that?"

"Our audience, of course."

Emil gestured behind him toward the alley they had just existed, and to Maaya's utter surprise, she saw nearly everyone from the entrance hall, living and dead, filing out of the hidden doorway. To her greater surprise, they appeared to be following her.

"It wouldn't do you much good to go through all the effort of getting rid of those ghosts for the purpose of boosting morale if there was no one around to watch, don't you agree?" Emil said. Maaya was too surprised to answer. She had expected her battle to be seen by whoever might be nearby, but she hadn't expected Emil to gather spectators in advance. "All right, everyone, let's get a move on. Maaya, do you have everything you need? Are you prepared?"

Maaya nodded, feeling for the card pouch on her left arm. It was much lighter than usual, and while this had originally been Maaya's intent, now that she was falling back into her familiar routine she felt exposed. If a serious attack happened, her paltry number of cards wouldn't be enough.

"Won't all these people attract attention?" Maaya asked quietly.

"Not at all. In the relative absence of night life in Anorath, it's not uncommon for people to congregate on the streets in the evening. Besides, even if it weren't, no one of any importance is paid enough to look too closely. Just act like you don't care, and they won't either."

And then they were on the move, living and dead walking casually side by side down the street as though they were on their way to go see a performance in the town square. But then, that's essentially what was happening, Maaya thought crossly. And Maaya was the star of the show.

As they walked, small groups of people and ghosts filtered in from nearby streets to join them. While Maaya hadn't been paying attention, at least three dozen others had joined their already sizeable group, at least half of them alive.

"How many people in this city can see ghosts, exactly?" Maaya asked in a low whisper.

"Quite a few! It probably only amounts to a small percentage of the population, but even given the low number of people who live here anymore, it's sizeable enough that a ghost can't walk through town without being seen at least a few times. That said, despite the fact that it's all peaceful enough, it's still very much something that we keep secret. It's almost like there are two entirely different towns within the borders here."

"Is this what you were talking about when you said Anorath got more interesting if you spent enough time here?" Maaya asked, and she couldn't deny that she was a little fascinated.

"To some extent. This is what I might call the gateway; having access to this community is only the first step in seeing all we have to offer."

"What was it like before? When there were more people here, I mean."

"So much grander than it is now, but still just as secret. If you couldn't see us you might think we were just a small port town, a mind-numbingly dull exporter of grains with a few eateries and hotels, but if you *could* see us, oh, there was so much more. That was the real Anorath, I tell you. People coming and going all hours of the night! You couldn't walk the roads between towns without meeting interesting people. Get-togethers on every corner, underground games and inns and performances. There was a sense of community, of belonging, and you felt connected to the world. There was always someone new coming around with tales from far-off places, and if you felt so inclined, you could up and leave to go see the world with them right then and there. Then you could come home again to tell the tale. It was like a whole different world set right on top of this one, so that you existed in both at once if you were lucky."

"That sounds wonderful. I can understand why you want so badly for it to be like that again," Maaya said, her tone softening.

"With your help, it will be. These new ghosts… sure they're dangerous, but they didn't kill off enough people to drive Anorath into the ground. So many of us could see them anyway and just move slightly to the left. No, it was the fear they induced in everyone. There was no stopping them. Once people knew we had killers in our midst we couldn't fight against, they decided it just wasn't worth it. But now… now things will change."

"Why haven't you tried using *libris* on them?" Maaya asked. "With as many people who can see ghosts here I can't be the only one who can do this."

"It's more difficult than you think," Emil explained. "Just being able to see ghosts doesn't guarantee using *libris* will do anything. Only ever met a select few who could, and those were memorable enough meetings that I remember them all. What's more, even if someone wanted to learn, knowledge of *libris* is so scarce it's hard to find. Lots of these men and women, bless their souls, wouldn't be able to read a book on the subject even if we had a library full, which we definitely do not. Actually, how did you learn? You don't seem like the educated sort. No offense."

"By accident," Maaya admitted. "I stole an important-looking book from some wealthy person's house, and I was going to sell it, but then I noticed it had pictures of ghosts in it. This was before I knew anyone else could see ghosts—I just thought I was crazy—so I taught myself to read a little with Saber's help so I could understand what it was talking about, and it happened to be about *libris*."

"Most interesting," Emil said thoughtfully, putting his chin in his palm. "You were so dedicated as to teach yourself to read just because you saw pictures of ghosts? And you mastered *libris* on top of that? You have a rare gift indeed."

"I absolutely do not," Maaya said firmly. "I forced myself to read because I was desperate to know that I wasn't crazy. I was alone and I had to know why I was this way. Also, I hardly mastered *libris*. My friends were almost as good as I was, and they had much less time to learn than I did. Oh, and the first time I tried to use a card I set my whole house on fire."

Emil burst into laughter, and Maaya couldn't help but laugh with him. As terrifying as it had been at the time, it made for a good story. Still, however, she maintained that she was no prodigy. She felt like she had reached her limit, and had watched with some anticipation as her younger friends quickly rose to become almost as adept as she was. They had all had the potential to become more proficient than her in almost every way; she had only been the leader because of her age.

"All right, friends, this is where we stop," Emil announced loudly, though this seemed to be mostly for effect; the large group of marchers was already slowing down and spreading out. As they moved, Maaya realized they had made it to the clocktower. It looked very different in the dark; there were no lights of any kind nearby, so the flickering firelight from the braziers and lampposts in the square cast eerie moving shadows across the dark silhouette of the tower.

When she glanced back at Emil, she noticed that quite a few of the others were staring expectantly in her direction.

"Have you already told everyone what you want me to do tonight?" Maaya asked uncertainly.

"I have. I knew you would accept so I thought I would spread the word. It wouldn't have been an efficient use of time otherwise. Not to worry; I didn't give them any details, so you can do whatever you think is best. All I ask is that you make it look good."

"How were you so sure I'd agree? Saber was completely against it, and for a little while, so was I."

"I'm usually a good judge of character," Emil winked. "And I was right, wasn't I?"

"Luck," Maaya replied irritably. She didn't have any second thoughts about what she was doing now, but the fact that she had somehow proved Emil right about anything almost made her want to change her mind out of spite. "Anyway, how do you know the ghosts are showing up *here*?"

"I don't. But I've made an educated guess," Emil said. "This is usually where they lurk. Besides, if they show up anywhere else in town, we're central enough that we can make it anywhere we need to be in time."

"Will Saber know where to find us?" Maaya pressed. Surely there had been *something* Emil hadn't thought of.

"I have some of my friends around town to keep an eye out for the ghosts. If they see Saber, they know to send her here."

Maaya bit her lip. She was curious about so much more, but she didn't want to listen to Emil talk anymore. He was so confident, and it was so *annoying*. She couldn't pinpoint exactly why. It was probably his attitude; she reveled in seeing people like him get taken down a notch. Or three.

Her irritation faded slowly as the night went on and was replaced with discomfort. While a few side conversations had broken out here and there amongst the crowd, it was still mostly silent. There wasn't even a breeze to distract her. What's more, despite no sign whatsoever of the mysterious ghosts, nearly everyone in the vicinity kept glancing in her direction—and they were anything but subtle. *Are they expecting me to summon them, too?* Maaya thought agitatedly.

What's more, every moment that Saber didn't return made her more nervous. Surely it couldn't take *that* long to update Styx on their situation and then return. Bringing him food hadn't even taken this long, and then she had relied on the help of someone who couldn't fly.

Despite the crowd around her, Maaya felt isolated. Out here in the open without a trusted friend to watch her back, she was vulnerable. She knew she would be hard to spot in a crowd and that she would easily have time to hide if any of the officers expressed any interest in their group, but she couldn't help but think of all the ways this could possibly go wrong. Surely the police must at least suspect that she was somewhere in town, and with a reward on her head there was an incentive for them to seek her out.

Suddenly she was struck by the horrible familiarity of her situation. It hadn't been all that long ago when she found herself waiting for ghosts with no indication as to when or where they might appear—or in what numbers. If this was anything like last time…

She shook her head quickly to clear her mind. This wasn't going to be like that. Back in Sark it had been she and her few friends against an army in a town otherwise completely clueless. Here, everyone knew. At least, all the people who could really do anything about it.

But where is Saber?

She sought distraction in the conversations of the nearby groups of people. No longer a crowd, everyone had found their groups of friends and were talking casually about everything from food to gossip to how they had slept the previous night and which neighbor's dog had kept them awake. The only thing they didn't appear to mention, Maaya noticed, was the thing they were all here to witness. Nearly everyone appeared completely uninterested and entirely unconcerned about what may have been to come.

Whenever an officer would stroll by, staring suspiciously at the large gathering of people in the dark square, the people standing nearest to Maaya would shift slightly closer, blocking her from their view. She kept her hood up and looked away, pretending to be engaged in animated conversation with someone else. She must have thought it looked awfully strange; there were dozens of people here standing in the dark, and there were so many ghosts among them that it must have looked like at least half of the people were talking to themselves. To the officers' credit, they did little more than shake their heads and continue on their way. Emil had been right about that, too.

As time went on, it seemed to Maaya as though there were more officers nearby, or at the very least that they were walking by more frequently. At first she was concerned, thinking they must have been suspicious, but they continued on their way. She scolded herself silently; of course they would pay closer attention to the square. A large group of people had just convened here for absolutely no reason.

Maaya fought the urge to look up at the clocktower to see how much time had passed. She knew she would end up checking every few minutes, which would just make this already agonizing wait that much more arduous.

Finally, when she was unable to resist the urge no longer, she saw that they had been out in the square for no less than two hours. This came as a pleasant shock to her—maybe the night would pass more quickly than she thought.

Suddenly, Maaya felt a tap on her shoulder. She started and whirled about to see Saber behind her, a grim expression on her face.

"We have a problem," she said urgently.

"What—?" Maaya began, but was interrupted by a cry of surprise from one of the ghosts nearby. Saber and Maaya turned to look in unison, and though Maaya was not tall enough to see over the heads of everyone gathered nearby, she could guess what was happening.

Maaya didn't even need to move. Everyone nearby began to move away from the main street that led up to the river, and as they moved, Maaya was able to see what they were fleeing.

A single group of ghosts, four wide and about half a dozen long, floated slowly down the street in their general direction. They moved ever so slightly off center with the road, which caused them to pass through buildings and light posts as they got closer.

After the army of ghosts she had faced a few nights previous, the first thing Maaya felt was relief. She didn't have as many blood cards as there were ghosts, but that didn't matter. She could dispatch a few easily, and everyone else could move out of the way and let the rest float harmlessly by. She knew the walks dissipated after some time; the smaller the group of ghosts, the faster they seemed to disappear. This small group would likely vanish before they even reached the opposite end of the square.

Still, she reached instinctively for her card pouch, making doubly sure that it was still there and that her paper arsenal was still inside.

"Is this our problem?" Maaya asked. "Really, you could have just said they were here instead of scaring—"

"No, that's not it," Saber hissed. "The police know you're here."

"What?! How do you—?"

Before they could converse any more, Emil took Maaya's arm. Though his voice was level, she could tell he was nervous.

"I hope you're ready. It's showtime."

"Did you hear Saber? The police—"

"I already planned for that eventuality. Right now, you just focus on getting rid of those things. You can do that, right?"

"Yes. It's easy."

"Well, make it look easy if you like, but don't just stand there. Make it look grand and heroic or something. Remember, you're inspiring these people. And me too, for that matter."

"If any part of your ridiculous plan results in Maaya getting hurt, I am going to make you wish you passed on properly a long time ago, are we clear?" Saber said menacingly.

Emil nodded, looking unimpressed.

"Don't worry. You take care of the ghosts, I'll handle the rest."

Without another word, he walked away to take care of the others.

Saber and Maaya glanced at each other, and in that moment, Maaya had a realization: she wasn't afraid. Sure, the ghosts were dangerous, but there weren't very many of them this time. Not for her, anyway. And she knew them to be slow, devoid of any intelligence, and almost completely harmless if they couldn't touch anyone.

This must have been the feeling Emil was after, what he wanted everyone else to feel. She couldn't help but see his wisdom there. When Maaya had first encountered the ghosts, they had terrified her. She had seen what they could do to other people and she had felt what they could do to her. They had seemed untouchable. And then there was the matter of what she had seen in the sky that night. Such power was unthinkable, but looking back, it was a power she could deprive them of by preventing them from taking any victims.

Now she thought of them like she thought of any other ghost she was assigned with getting rid of. She knew their tactics and what they were capable of, and as was often the case, knowledge of a mystery made the fear of it disappear. This would be easy enough.

Maaya pulled her blood cards calmly from her pouch, taking care not to look any of the ghosts in the eyes. Emil, for his part, was doing a decent job helping guide the people in the square away from the ghosts and out of their path. Still, despite being prepared to see the ghosts, the people were frightened and moved erratically, clearly not far from panic.

"Everyone! Watch!" Maaya called, and for the moment, she had their attention. If she was going to put on a show, she might as well start strong.

She held three of her cards between her fingers, then flung them straight at the oncoming line of ghosts. The cards streaked across the square and collided with their targets with three loud bangs that echoed all around them. Red sparks flew from where the cards met their marks, and the ghosts they had struck flickered, then vanished.

Maaya didn't have even a moment to feel proud of herself before the situation descended into complete chaos.

At least a dozen onlookers who hadn't yet moved out of the way, watching the path of Maaya's cards, met the eyes of the ghosts and immediately froze in place, their expressions blank. Those around them cried out in alarm, which caused a sudden surge in activity from everyone else, fear rippling outward until everyone was shouting, disorganized and confused.

In the same instant there came a yell from up the street, and Maaya glanced over to see no fewer than two dozen armed officers running in their direction.

"There she is! She's using her magic on the people!"

"Emil! Get those people out of the way of the ghosts and tell everyone not to look them in the eyes!" Maaya cried, pulling more blood cards from her pouch.

"Understood," Emil called back over the din. "Maaya, get yourself to higher ground. Blackfins! We need a distraction!"

Maaya had absolutely no idea what Blackfins were, but if it was a distraction for her benefit she didn't care where it came from. She rushed toward the clocktower with Saber close behind, tugging on the door handle only to find that it was locked again. Saber, not needing any direction, immediately flew through the door to unlock it. After closing the door tight behind them, they raced to the top of the stairs to get a better view of what was going on down below. Maaya's muscles ached in protest, and she almost collapsed with the pain, but she held on.

To Maaya's surprise, a wall of men and women had formed between the officers and the tower, preventing them from getting through. While they did not fight the officers, they linked arms and stood fast, refusing to move. On the other side, Emil was directing whoever he could to move everyone to safety. It appeared everyone would make it out of the ghosts' way safely, but she knew they wouldn't be able to hold the officers off forever at the same time.

"What are you going to do now?" Saber asked hurriedly.

"I'm just going to get rid of a few more of these ghosts, and I need to make sure everyone sees," Maaya said. "Then we can get out of here. I think they can hold off the police just long enough for us to hide and make it to Styx."

"That's the problem: getting to Styx is no longer an option."

"What? Why?" Maaya asked breathlessly.

"When I went to go see him tonight, I thought it would be prudent to check our escape route to make sure it was clear. But evidently reports from Sark explained that we escaped down the river, and there's now a blockade just outside Anorath. We can't move downriver; we'll have to find another way out."

"But… but where? How?" Maaya asked, trying not to panic. "And what about Styx?"

"I sent him back up to Sark. The blockade isn't moving, but if anyone decides to patrol up the river they might find him, and I don't want to risk him getting in trouble. Plus, I figure that if he goes back to Sark he can tell Sylvia and anyone else what's going on."

"What does he think we're going to do if we can't escape with him?"

"Find another way to Levien, of course. We'll figure something out. Or wasn't that Emil's job?"

A pounding sound from below interrupted their conversation. A quick glance down at the ground far below told Maaya that at least some of the officers had broken their way through the human wall and were now attempting to break into the clocktower.

"Here," Saber said quickly, flying over to one of the massive clock faces and with some effort pushed the glass face open, giving Maaya an opportunity to squeeze through the large brass mechanisms.

Maaya stepped carefully through the clock face and out onto the narrow ledge that made its way around all four walls of the tower. It was a solid foothold, but didn't offer much mobility; one wrong step would send Maaya plummeting to the ground below.

"If you're going to do anything else, now's your chance," Saber reminded her urgently, and Maaya nodded.

As if on cue, a spotlight from below washed over her, temporarily blinding her. She suppressed the panic that welled inside her; being in a spotlight was the worst possible situation for her to be in. This time, however, it had its uses. With all eyes on her, Maaya could put on the show Emil so desperately wanted.

"Everyone look at me!" she shouted, falling back into her role as leader. "Watch them fall!"

With that, three blood cards in each hand, she flung them outward with as much force as she could muster. The officers on the ground ducked, but the cards darted harmlessly overhead, crashing into the still-moving line of ghosts in another shower of sparks. The ghosts instantly disappeared, and now there was a significant hole in their ranks.

Cheers erupted from Emil's companions, and the police looked torn between anger at this disruption and confusion over what they could possibly be cheering about. Maaya briefly wondered if there were any officers who could see ghosts—and if they would tell anyone if they could.

Maaya took out the remaining four cards in her pouch, then hesitated. These were her last blood cards; she would have to make sure they were used strategically.

A crashing sound from behind them made Maaya and Saber whirl about in surprise, Maaya almost losing her balance. The officers who had made it into the tower had made it to the top of the stairs and spotted her, and were now trying to figure out a way to get to her safely.

"Make sure you take her alive!" one of them called to the others.

"Oh Maaya, dear, we're out of time," Saber said, straining against the glass clock face to push it closed again. That would buy them time, but not much.

Maaya took a deep breath.

"Have you got my back?"

"Like you even need to ask."

Maaya looked back down at the chaos below, held her cards tightly in her hand… and then leapt off the edge of the tower.

She heard a few shouts of surprise from the onlookers, including some of the officers, but Maaya didn't pay them any attention. She had to figure out where she was going to go once she landed.

She fell faster and faster, the ground rising up toward her, threatening to break her body inside and out. She felt a wave of dizziness at the sight and closed her eyes to keep herself conscious.

Moments before she hit the ground, Saber grabbed her underneath her arms, slowing her fall and helping her land on her feet with enough momentum to start running immediately. She had only seconds to figure out their next move.

In one direction was the line of officers and Emil's men and women, one group fighting to pass and the other to keep the first group at bay. On the far side was Emil and the others he had led to safety out of harm's way, and in the center was the line of ghosts slowly moving ever closer. If they were going to make an escape, they would need to do so with the help of a distraction.

"Saber, how do you feel about throwing some fire around?" Maaya asked as they ran, and for the first time that night, Saber grinned.

Maaya quickly reached into her pouch with her free hand and handed Saber one of her only elemental cards.

"On my signal," she said. Saber looked slightly disappointed at not being able to start wreaking havoc right away, but she nodded.

At once, Maaya stopped running and turned to face the ghosts. All eyes were on her now. Even the officers had momentarily stopped fighting their way over to her, so surprised were they at Maaya leaping willingly off the tower only to glide safely to the ground.

"This one's for you, Emil," Maaya called, then flung her last four cards at the ghosts. The cards seemed to travel in slow motion. Just as they were about to strike their targets, Maaya cried, "Saber, now!"

A tremendous burst of flame ignited near the tower at the precise moment the cards hit the ghosts. As the ghosts disappeared in a flurry of red sparks, a wave of flame traveled from where Saber had positioned herself near the tower, right in front of Maaya and over to the opposite side of the square, putting a wall of flame between the officers and Emil's group. Saber flew swiftly with her glowing hand barely skimming the ground, fire following her touch as quickly as if she were pouring gasoline in a line.

By some miraculous coincidence, the rest of the ghosts also vanished after their four companions disappeared. Maaya couldn't have asked for better timing. The crowds of living and dead broke into tumultuous cheers once again at the sight of Maaya supposedly destroying the entire line of ghosts, and Saber's impressive display certainly didn't hurt.

Saber quickly flew back to Maaya, taking her arm and urging her forward.

"Let's go, quickly. The fire won't last long; we need to be hidden by the time this all calms down. Excellent idea, by the way. You should let me do that more often."

They sprinted toward one of the dark side streets, quickly taking solace in its cover. There were only businesses here, so at this late hour there was no one to poke their heads out to see what was going on. As they ran, Maaya heard shouting from the officers; she couldn't decipher all of what they said, but among what she could make out "witch," "magic," and "murderer."

Once in the cover of darkness they slowed their pace, but only slightly. Maaya knew vaguely in which direction they needed to go; if the river was now off limits, they needed to go in the opposite direction and take a land route to Levien. She wasn't entirely sure which direction Levien was in, but that was another bridge they would try to cross when they reached it.

As the noise from behind them faded away into nearly nothing, Maaya paused to breathe. Saber looked back at her concernedly, but said nothing. Instead, she floated up higher for a better vantage point to keep watch while Maaya regained her bearing.

In the silence, Maaya was forced to recall how this was the second time in just a few days that she and Saber had fled for their lives—at least, Maaya's life—from a town with pursuers hot on their heels. The police had wanted to take her alive, but she'd heard the furious and frightened accusations of witchcraft and magic. Even if they managed to take her alive, she wouldn't remain that way for long.

This time, at least, she was not fleeing after watching any of her friends be killed in front of her, but this was of little comfort. There were many people who had put themselves in danger to keep her safe, and it was unlikely that she would ever be able to return to Anorath—if indeed she would ever be able to return to Selenthia at all. There were no trials for witches. Unless by some miracle she was able to clear her name, she would no longer be welcome here.

She cursed herself for her own stupidity. While her demonstration had definitely been a success, she had only made things worse for herself in the end. If she still had any benefit of the doubt before her little stunt tonight, it was without a doubt gone now that she had made a show of her *libris* powers right in front of a group of police officers. They couldn't see the ghosts she fought, so from their perspective she was simply using her magic to terrorize the people of Anorath, which was no doubt what they had already heard from Sark. And if these ghost walks continued and anyone died, she would likely be blamed for that as well even if she was no longer in the city when they happened.

Maaya sighed resolutely. There was absolutely no giving up now. They would have to play it safer in the future, but now that she had essentially solidified that they had no home in Selenthia, their next step was to do everything in their power to reach Krethus. This was no longer just about the ghosts. It was necessary if Maaya wanted to stay alive. She wouldn't falter now. Not after all she had lost to make it even this far.

Suddenly, Maaya gasped.

"Saber!"

"What's wrong?" Saber asked attentively, floating down to meet her in an instant.

"The diary," Maaya said almost despairingly. "I left it at the inn, I didn't realize… I didn't think we would…"

"Say no more," Saber said soothingly. "You stay hidden, and I'll be right back."

Without another word, she vanished into the night.

Maaya breathed deeply to calm her pounding heart. If she hadn't remembered before they left town…

"There you are. You move awfully fast for a living one, you know."

Maaya turned to see Emil standing nearby. He had a smile on his face as usual, but his mood seemed tempered now, as though he no longer felt the need to put on airs for anyone now the show was over. He also made no effort to stand too close to her, which for the moment she appreciated greatly.

"You did a great job back there, both of you," he continued. "To be honest, I don't know what exactly I had been expecting, but I'm pretty sure you went above and beyond anyway."

"It's all a disaster," Maaya moaned. "I got rid of the ghosts, but for what? Now the police are even more sure that I'm a witch and that I'm causing these deaths. And your people put themselves in danger to keep me safe, and now they'll be in trouble. Because of me. Now I still have to go to Levien, and I don't even know the way, and…"

"You underestimate yourself still. If you can do something like this when you don't believe in yourself, just imagine what you could do if you did? I'm no doctor, but it seems to me you let yourself get overwhelmed and then you shut down. Things aren't nearly as bad as your brain is trying to convince you they are."

"Well, Nadya was right, anyway," Maaya said. "She said it was a risk no matter what I did and that I needed to decide whether the risk was worth it. I… I don't know if it was."

"Sure it was," Emil said instantly, and Maaya glanced up at him in surprise. "So you bothered a bunch of officers, so what? They were already after you to begin with, so nothing has changed. You lost nothing. But you did gain the support and admiration of half the town in the process, and many of them will share what they saw with everyone they meet here and beyond. You ran away too quickly to see just what you did for them. Considering I'm the only one here, it falls on me to express my genuine and profound gratitude. This doesn't solve everything, but I haven't seen them feeling this confident in a long time."

"Not that I'm not glad I was able to do something, but what does all this good will do for me if I can never come back? They all think I'm responsible for this. They think I'm a witch and a murderer."

"Who's 'they?' A small enough group of people."

"Who happen to be the police! It doesn't matter that there aren't many of them."

Emil nodded placidly.

"Which is why it's important that people be allowed to see the other side of you. If all you do is hide because you're already in trouble, the words of your detractors will be heard far and wide without opposition. But now the people of Anorath are on your side. You'll always have friends here."

"If they can protect me from getting killed then I'm glad for it," Maaya sighed. This was all too much for her to think about even if it was somewhat positive news. "Right now I can't think about anything past getting out of here alive and getting to Levien."

"Ah, yes. It's time for you to go. In that case, follow me," Emil said, beaming. He beckoned to her to follow him, and she did so with trepidation.

Maaya wasn't very keen on any more of Emil's ideas at the moment, even if they were allegedly for her benefit this time and not his. She sincerely hoped this wouldn't involve any more demonstrations. Even if she wanted to do something like that again—and she most certainly did not—her body was just about taxed to its limit. One night of rest was not enough for her to properly recover, at least not if her schedule would consist of this kind of physical exertion on a regular basis.

But Emil led her quietly down a few more side streets where the buildings began to spread out, and all remained dark and calm.

Only about ten minutes later they reached what Maaya assumed was the town limits. Unlike Sark, which was surrounded on most sides by tall sturdy walls, the borders of this side of Anorath simply faded into the wilderness. It was strangely pleasant, and Maaya liked how open and unrestrictive it was, even if this lack of protection made her feel slightly uncomfortable.

The leaves on the trees swayed slowly in the soft breeze, and the moon, unobstructed by the overhanging skeleton of long-dead forests, cast an enchanting glow on everything about them. It was simultaneously lonely and comforting, exuding the air of an as-yet undiscovered piece of the world untouched by man. Maaya took a deep breath as her heart calmed. The air was cool and fresh, and here she could almost forget where she was.

"You would have loved this place back in its prime," Emil said softly. "Unfortunately, you don't have too much time to admire it now. Your ride is here."

"My what? My… oh."

Maaya had been so fascinated by her surroundings that she hadn't noticed the ancient contraption in front of her.

An elegant sleek black coach stood before them. It reminded Maaya of the horse-drawn carriages she would see princesses in storybooks ride in, except this one had no horses. Instead of reigns, the driver's bench had a large golden steering wheel and numerous long levers in front of it. A portly ghost in a top hat and coattails sat atop the red velvet bench, peering down at them expectantly. The coach itself was painted all in black and was decorated with golden trim and four golden lamps, one on each corner. Maaya couldn't see inside, but she imagined it was just as nicely furnished there, too. She started feeling sleepy just at the thought of sitting back on a comfortable cushion.

"This is Apostol, and he'll be taking you to Levien. He's been shuttling this route for… how long would you say, Apos'? Seventy years?"

"Give or take a decade, indeed, sir," Apostol replied in a gravelly voice. Wild tufts of white hair protruded from under his hat, and the brim cast a dark shadow over his eyes that made him look almost intimidating. "Couldn't get enough of it. This must be my first assignment in at least six months."

"Well, let's hope you haven't lost your touch. My passengers need to be transported safely and expeditiously."

"Passengers? Well I know my eyes aren't failing, sir, but I only see one."

"Oh, the second is coming. You'll like her. She's dead," Emil explained happily. "You all right there, Maaya?"

"How does this work?" Maaya asked in fascination. She reached out her hand to touch the coach, but drew her hand back, afraid that it might do something unexpected if she made contact.

"Horseless carriage," Apostol said happily. "One of the best inventions in the world, still today as it was decades ago. That's what the stagnation of technology will do for you. Have you ever been in a motorcar?" When Maaya shook her head in bewilderment, Apostol beamed widely. "Back in the day they were an absolute must for the wealthy. People were equally captivated with and terrified of them, but if you wanted to be anybody, you'd ride in one of these. Own one, if you were lucky. Nowadays I'm not sure most people in these backwoods towns know they exist anymore, but we've kept this one safe. It might be a little scary at first, but you'll get used to it quick enough. Anything I can help you pack, miss?"

"Ah, n-no, thank you," Maaya said slowly. The thought of a carriage that could move all by itself was almost too much for her to comprehend.

"Will Saber be long?" Emil asked, glancing casually back at the street behind them.

"She shouldn't. At least not if she can guess where you've taken me," Maaya answered somewhat passive aggressively. "Do you see something? Are we in danger?"

"Not at all. As far as the officers are concerned you've escaped again, and they don't have the manpower to search the town. They'll just try to make it more difficult for you to escape, and then try to catch you again when you show yourself."

"Except I won't be here," Maaya said.

"Except you won't be here," Emil affirmed. "Our brave men and women in law enforcement certainly do command a lot of respect, but I've found it comes at the expense of their intellect. That's probably why they blockaded the river. They must have thought you'd be silly enough to try to keep traveling the same way you had before."

"Wait, you knew the river was blocked?" Maaya asked in surprise.

"Of course. That's why I had the coach prepared."

"Were you going to *tell* me this?" Maaya continued, narrowing her eyes.

"I didn't think it was necessary; you'd agreed to take my path, and I didn't want to scare or distract you. It was important that you had your head in the game."

Maaya rolled her eyes and looked away. She was starting to figure out just why Emil bothered her so much, even if she was starting to trust him. He may have had their best interests at heart, but she wasn't used to handing over so much control to someone else, much less someone who went to great effort to conceal how much he actually knew. She liked being in the know. Otherwise she felt like a puppet, and that was a feeling she hated—and was uncomfortably familiar with.

Luckily, she didn't have to wait long in the silence before Saber soared down to meet her, the diary safely in her hand. Maaya took it gratefully and hugged it close with relief, then slipped it inside one of her coat's large pockets. Once Saber made sure Maaya was all right, she shot a dark look at Emil.

"Sorry I'm late. I needed to search the area since *someone* evidently changed our meeting spot."

Emil only shrugged.

Apostol cleared his throat politely.

"Now then, the night's getting on and we've a long trip ahead of us. Shall we be going?"

"Yes, you'd better get going. I assume you'll be taking the long way to avoid detection," Emil said, and Apostol nodded. "At least the—oh, hold on now! I almost forgot the most important part."

He rummaged in his pockets and pulled out what appeared to be a small brooch. It was about half the size of Maaya's palm and shaped like a fish's fin. It was entirely black except for a thin gold border and gold lines to denote the fin's rays. The back was silver, and there was a simple clasp there, but nothing to show who might have made it or what its purpose was.

Maaya stared at it for a moment in silence, curious why Emil would give her such a strange gift, then made to fasten it to the cloak Nadya had given her—but Emil stopped her.

"Oh, no. You wouldn't want to be seen in public wearing that. Keep it safe, and keep it *hidden.* It may come in useful."

"How? What is it?" Maaya asked.

"This is how you'll meet your contacts. It's the insignia of the Blackfins. It's vital that you keep this quiet; such a symbol does not gain favor among the law-abiding folk of the world."

"What exactly do I do with it?"

"Keep your eyes and ears open. Wherever you see this symbol, you'll be among friends. Now, get a move on; Levien is far and you should take this chance to rest. Things are only going to get harder from here."

Apostol leapt lightly down from the bench and opened the coach door for the girls. Saber, looking eager to leave Anorath, got in immediately, but Maaya hesitated. She didn't think she had been here long enough to develop any sort of connection to the town, but she felt almost like she would stay if she had the chance.

Emil, noticing her expression, smiled warmly.

"This will all be here when you get back, as will all of us," he said. "Consider that motivation for your journey."

"Promise?" Maaya asked, and even as she said it she felt stupid; she sounded like a child asking her parents if they really would go out to play if she got her chores done. But Emil, for his part, only nodded.

"I promise. Safe journey, ladies. And try not to be too long, Apostol; I feel like there will be an increase in traffic to and from Anorath once the story of Maaya's heroics spreads."

"About bloody time," Apostol grunted. When Maaya made her way into the coach, he shut the door securely behind her, then floated back to the top of the bench.

For a moment all was silent, and then the entire coach rumbled. Maaya, never having heard or felt an engine before, yelped in shock before she realized what was happening. Saber, despite being taken by surprise herself, snorted with laughter.

The coach began to move, and soon they were trundling along at a steady pace. For a few minutes Maaya held tight to the hand rail near the door, every muscle in her body tense, but she soon relaxed as she realized it was safe. Then, finally, she looked around at the inside of the coach.

There were two comfortable benches inside perpendicular to the door, and they faced each other from opposite ends of the coach. In the middle was a simple table that folded back when unlatched, leaving ample room on the floor for two people to sleep and for Maaya to lie down with her legs fully outstretched. There was one window covered by a velvety curtain in the door and another on the adjacent wall, and on the floor beneath the window was a small cabinet; when Maaya opened it, she found a pillow, a blanket, and a box of medical supplies. Two dim lamps lit the interior and a small bell hung in the corner on the door's side. Maaya guessed this was to be used when they wanted to get the coachman's attention. The inside walls were made of dark redwood and the floor was a deep purple carpet kept almost clinically clean despite the coach's age. Every detail about this coach told Maaya that it had once been used by the very, very rich.

By the time she chanced a glance out the window, Anorath was already just a line of lights on the horizon. From what Maaya could tell, they were headed away from the river. She could just barely make out the still dark water in the distance. A moment later she noticed the silhouettes of no fewer than a dozen small ships and boats on the water. They blocked the entirety of the wide river, and bright lights emanated from the boats, scanning over the water. Searching.

Maaya felt her heart skip a beat, and she closed the curtain immediately, afraid that someone might see her and recognize her despite the distance.

"The blockade," Saber said grimly as Maaya pulled back and sat back on the bench. "That's what we would have run into had I not scouted ahead when going to see Styx."

"Apparently Emil already knew, which is why he had this prepared," Maaya sighed, closing her eyes. Even though they were safe, she felt a surge of dread at the thought of having run into those ships during their escape.

Saber scowled.

"Of course he did. And while this is certainly some marvel of technology —and easy on your legs, I'm sure—I don't think what we got in return was worth your little show. A coach ride and jewelry you aren't allowed to wear or talk about. I suppose we could always sell it."

"I couldn't do that. Not if it helps us find people who can help us. Besides, if it's not something I can talk about, it's probably not something I can sell without looking just as suspicious."

"Ah, good point. So it's even *more* useless," Saber mumbled. "How are you feeling, anyway?"

"Exhausted. The usual," Maaya sighed, leaning back. It really was very comfortable, and she fought sleep pulling at her. "It might sound stupid, but I almost didn't want to leave. I haven't made any new friends, or any decent people for that matter, in years. And for the first time in my life I felt like the people who lived there actually liked me."

"I understand. As much as I don't like Emil, everyone else seemed friendly enough. It was actually pretty nice being in a town where living people and ghosts got along so well. I could get used to that."

"Soon," Maaya smiled. "Once this is all over. We're still getting that house, you know. And we can have all our friends there, and it will be just like that."

"You know it. Now lay down and get some sleep before you pass out and hurt yourself," Saber said, moving over to fetch the pillow and blanket for her.

Maaya smiled faintly, then unlatched the table in the middle of the floor and folded it into the side wall. Saber helped her set up her makeshift bed, and then made to fly up toward where Apostol sat outside, but then hesitated. She pursed her lips like she wanted to say something but was too embarrassed to do so.

"What's on your mind?" Maaya asked, hoping she could coax whatever it was from her friend before she decided against it and departed.

Saber sighed.

"I'm still having trouble dealing with what happened in Sark. I can't get it out of my head. Not just because it was so horrific, but because I… I feel like I'm partly to blame for what happened to them. Our friends."

"What? How could you be?" Maaya asked in astonishment.

"They were still fighting when we reached them. Maybe we could have figured something else out. I know what I tried to do was right in the moment, but… the only reason they looked up and met eyes with the ghosts was because of me. I ran to help them, and by doing that I made things worse."

"No! No, no, no," Maaya said quickly, pulling Saber gently down to sit next to her. "You didn't lead the ghosts to them, and you didn't trap them there. They couldn't get out, and you tried your best. I know you did. There was no time for you to have done anything else."

Saber didn't appear convinced.

"I've no doubt of my motives. I just wonder what we might have been able to do had they still remained in control of their bodies. Maybe we could have made a pocket for them, or—"

"Saber, no what-ifs, remember?" Maaya interjected. Her own heart stung with the reminder, but she forced herself to speak for Saber's sake. She found a strange solace in helping relieve others of their burdens, a solace that grew only more powerful the worse she herself was feeling. "We don't know what would have happened and there's no reason to assume that because we might have done something different that we would have been successful."

"Logically, that's right. I know that. I guess I'm struggling with feeling this much hurt. I'm not used to this, being dead and all. And the very thought that I could have had a hand in the deaths of the people I loved the most, well… even if it's not true, it won't leave me alone. I can't get it out of my head."

"I wish I could make it go away. I really do," Maaya said quietly, clasping the ghost's hands in her own. "We're both going to get through this together, and I will be here always to tell you that this wasn't your fault. Not even a little. You didn't even hesitate to try to save them, and that's why we all loved you, and why I'm so glad you're with me. I know it hurts, but try not to think about what could have been. It's not fair to you. Okay?"

Saber stared at the floor, then nodded slowly.

"I'll… try. Like I said, it logically makes sense. I just need to find a way to make logic prevail over these ridiculous emotions." She let out a short breath, then smiled. "Thank you. I'll likely need you again in the future, but thanks for being here for me. I love you a whole lot, you know that?"

"I love you, too." Maaya hugged the ghost tightly, and then let her go, sitting back onto the blankets of her small bed. "If you want to go, please, feel free; I won't be conscious for much more than a minute."

"Yeah, I think I'll spend some time with Apostol and see if I can't figure out how long this will take us. But I'll be back soon enough in case you need me. Sweetest of dreams to you!"

With that, she departed, disappearing up through the roof of the carriage and out of sight.

Maaya moved over to the window and peeked through it one last time, partly to see with her own eyes if they were being pursued. It was almost completely dark outside now, with all light from Anorath far gone. Still, what little she could see of the branches of trees flickering past in the moonlight fascinated her, and from what she could tell they were completely alone out here in the forgotten lands behind the small isolated towns. The path was surprisingly smooth given how rarely it must have been traveled in recent decades, and the hum of the coach's motor made her drowsy.

When she could keep her eyes open no longer, she slid down on the floor to settle underneath the blanket. Her knee hit something hard, and as she reached down, she felt Kim's diary on the floor. She must have knocked it down when she was moving about the cabin.

She felt the familiar pang of heartache return almost immediately, so she placed it on the far side of the bench she had been sitting on and turned her back to it. She didn't want to think about it right now. She had no time or energy to deal with this part of the grieving process yet.

Still, it remained in her thoughts like a persistent fly buzzing in her ear. Keeping it was important for her, but to what end? She hadn't decided if she was ever going to read it yet. She wanted so much to see her friend's words, to see the thoughts she had put to paper. These, unlike her memories, would be new to her, and she would only get to experience that once. But that would come at the expense of the privacy Kim had desired when writing something so secret, privacy that Kim no longer had the power to protect or ask for.

When Saber entered the coach again an hour later to inform Maaya their trip would take them over a full day, she found Maaya already fast asleep, her blanket wrapped tightly around her, the paths of drying tears on her cheeks.

18

LEVIEN

Maaya woke up shivering. Already curled into a tiny ball on the floor, she pulled her blanket closer to her, hoping as so many in the early morning hours did that the cold would simply change its mind and leave once it saw her determination. So resolute was Maaya to take advantage of the prospect of even five minutes more sleep that she didn't even open her eyes until she heard Saber's voice and felt the ghost gently shake her shoulder a moment after.

"Hey, get up already. Breakfast won't be hot forever."

Maaya sat up blearily, reaching for her cloak before she realized she was still wearing it. She grumbled. There were few things that irritated her more than a cold morning she couldn't escape from.

"Why is it so cold suddenly?" she said, stifling a yawn. "And where's that awful breeze coming from?"

"The ocean, probably," Saber replied. At Maaya's surprised glance, she continued, "Yep! Welcome to Levien. Or the outskirts, anyway."

Maaya hurriedly got up and looked outside, but it was still completely dark.

"Sunrise is in less than an hour, but we thought it'd be safest to stop here while it was still dark so we could find a way into the city that isn't a coach driven by a dead guy. Also, *breakfast.* You're making the man wait, come on now."

"The wha? Oh!" Maaya exclaimed. Only now did she realize the door to the coach was open, which explained the cold and the breeze. Just outside the door stood the ghost of a tall bespectacled man wearing an artisan's smock, carrying a wide tray of what appeared to be fresh rolls.

"Sorry to interrupt your sleep, miss, but I was told—quite intently, for that matter—that you'd be hungry." He cast a sideways glance at Saber as he said this, and she smiled brightly.

"And I'm ever so grateful that you agreed to bring all this food all the way out here on such short notice."

"I didn't think I had a choice," the man mumbled. Maaya stared back and forth between the two, but nothing further was said. "Anyway, these are all yours. Do enjoy. And please let her know if you do so she doesn't come after me or somethin'."

He placed the tray of baked goods down on the floor of the coach, then turned and walked swiftly away, evidently eager to escape before Saber could say anything else. For her part, now that food was here, Saber seemed to have already forgotten he existed. She shut the door quickly, shutting out the frigid breeze.

"What did you do to that poor man?" Maaya asked, narrowing her eyes at the ghost.

"I didn't *do* anything, I just asked him to make some food for you. He told me he was a baker, anyway. He was just a little resistant at first, is all."

"As he should be! What does he need to make food for anymore? He's dead."

"You never know. Maybe it's like the Shallow Squid where everyone co-exists with each other. But he ended up doing it, didn't he? We had to steal some ingredients, but he did well enough. Anyway, don't you complain. You have fresh bread to eat and I suggest you get on that before it gets cold."

"How long were you out there? And when did we get here? How long did it take for—?" Maaya broke off with muffled irritation as Saber pushed a roll into her mouth.

"So many questions, child! You eat, I'll explain," she said, grinning at Maaya's cross expression. "We arrived about two hours ago, but you were still fast asleep and it was barely an hour or three into the day, so I went to scope things out and see if I could find you something to eat. Levien is absolutely massive, by the way. I was going to nick something for you, but it was so early that the bakers hadn't started making anything yet, so I found that guy, and… well. There you are. Are they good?"

"Delicious," Maaya groused, but despite her tone, she had to admit they were genuinely very tasty. "Where's Apostol?"

"Going to look for fuel. This engine can apparently get from Anorath to Levien and not a mile further."

"How long was the trip?"

"I don't know the distance we traveled, but it took just over a day. You were asleep the entire time. How do you feel?"

"Still tired somehow, but much better, actually," Maaya said. She hadn't realized how hungry she was, and the food was definitely helping. "Do we have a plan?"

"Not really," Saber admitted with a sigh, shrugging her shoulders. "I figured we would find somewhere to stay and then hunt for Svante's contact."

Before she could stop herself, the image of Svante falling lifeless to the street in a pool of his own blood replayed itself in her mind. She shuddered, pushing it quickly out of her head with as much force as she could muster.

"That sounds about as solid as any other plan we've had so far. We'll have to see if we can come up with something something more specific while we're here. I assume we're ahead of the police, but I can't imagine they'll be far behind."

"They might be if they don't find out we left Anorath," Saber said. "On the bright side, we got here quickly and safely, so that's one big problem out of the way. And hey! We also have Emil's completely useless pin that we can't show to anybody or talk about or sell for money, so we're totally set."

"Don't remind me," Maaya said darkly. "I can't mention it because it's not something I want to be seen talking about, but I'm also supposed to keep my ears open in case someone *else* is talking about it. I didn't think making friends would be this hard."

"We'll forget it for now and figure out our next move. Let's think: if I were the contact of someone who was in Selenthia in secret, and I also owned a boat, where would I be?"

"You're the Krethan, you tell me," Maaya replied amusedly.

"Ah, true. Clearly, I'm the only one with the intellect necessary to piece together this mystery," Saber said grandiloquently. "If I were waiting for someone to get back to me so that I could provide them passage via ship, I would probably be… ah! By the ships! I don't blame you for not being able to figure that one out."

Saber laughed as Maaya shoved her playfully.

"That's a good start, though," Maaya said once she had settled back on the floor, another roll already in hand. "I think we should try to find out information about the owners of each boat. They might be in some public records somewhere, and you'd have no trouble getting to them. We don't know this guy's name, but I assume we'd know it if we saw it."

"Assuming he didn't change his name to something that sounded more Selenthian, or if his contact isn't even a Selenthian anyway," Saber pointed out. "But that's a good start. I'll also narrow my search by looking at what ships take what routes. That way, even if we don't find our guy, we'll know what ship we need to be on to get where we need to be."

"I can't imagine there are any ships that are allowed to travel to Krethus, though, are there?"

"Possibly. Or there may be an indirect route. It's something I'll have to figure out. I'll also see if there are any records of previously purchased tickets. It's possible Svante's ride didn't own a ship but just had money enough to buy a few tickets for one."

"Great ideas," Maaya said approvingly. "What can I do?"

"Well, you need to stay somewhat hidden, given your status as a wanted criminal and everything," Saber answered nonchalantly. "I figure it couldn't hurt if you talked to some of the locals, though. There might be gossip we could make use of. If word about Svante was able to spread in Sark, surely someone will have heard of him here."

"This will be fun if the city is as big as you say it is," Maaya moaned, and Saber giggled. "But I can do that. I'll start with the people who work at the docks, I guess. If anyone would have noticed a Krethan coming to shore, it'd be them."

"Sounds good! Now all we have to do is wait until Apostol comes back so we can ensure no one runs off with his coach, and then we'll be good to go."

"Where exactly are we?" Maaya asked, straining her eyes to see through the darkness outside. The absence of any lights confused her; surely in a city as big as the one Saber was talking about there would be *some* visible light even at a time when most people were sleeping.

"We're hidden behind a hill right now; this was apparently the drop-off point for most of Apostol's passengers, as he was the one who shuttled, uh, less-than-reputable clientele. So we can't be seen, and we're right by an easy access into the city."

"I shouldn't be surprised," Maaya said. "Now what about you? You've made sure I ate and slept and everything, how are you feeling?"

Saber paused.

"I think… I think I'm okay. Physically, at least, I'm doing well. I've recovered from Sark, anyway. Emotionally… well, you and I are on the same page there. But I'm good to keep going if you are. Might help keep our mind off things, anyway."

"Should we be keeping our minds off this?" Maaya asked tentatively. "I mean, it can't be healthy to—"

"Probably not, but we can deal with that when we're safely on a ship heading across the ocean," Saber interrupted softly. "Don't forget, we're still being chased. Our time is limited, so we should make the most of it."

"Right. You're right," Maaya said, sitting up straighter. "Let's head in together at first so we can figure out a place to meet up. Then we can go from there."

Saber put a thoughtful finger to her chin.

"If I may make a slight alteration?"

"Go ahead."

"You haven't seen Levien. When I say it's huge, I mean it's *huge.* We should stick together for the first day until we get the hang of things. Then, while you sleep, I can go look through the paperwork."

"Are you sure? I don't want you to spend literally all twenty-four hours working. Even for you that can't be good."

Saber grinned.

"You know that feeling when you've slept well, had a good meal, and aren't sick at all? That's being dead: just that feeling, all the time. It's great! Sure, I might still get bored, but we're on an adventure now, so it's okay. Just know that when we get on the ship I'm going to do a whole lot of absolutely nothing."

Just then, there was a knock at the coach door. Saber peeked around the curtain cautiously, then smiled and opened the door wide to reveal Apostol hovering before them, holding a large can of fuel. He tipped his hat to them.

"Glad to see you're awake, miss. I'm sure Saber has filled you in already."

"As much as she could, anyway," Maaya replied, extending her hand to the ghost. Her hand was small in his, and his grip was strong, yet gentle. "I'm sorry I didn't get to speak with you more during the trip; I didn't think I was going to sleep the whole way."

"Quite all right, miss, quite all right. It was all I could ask for to be back on the road again. Just promise me when you get back to Levien you'll take my way back to Anorath rather than the easy way up the river, deal?"

"Deal," Maaya smiled.

"Great. By that time hopefully we'll be back in business," Apostol said, setting the fuel can down with a loud *thud.* "Now, if you want to get in before sunrise you'd best get a move on. The sky's starting to turn."

"Is it hard to get in?" Maaya asked.

"Not necessarily, but we figure it's best if you're seen as little as possible. This is the biggest port and trade city in the west, so there's constant security —and not your small-town guards who can't be paid to give a damn, either. Don't worry, though. Saber knows the way."

Maaya and Saber gave their hasty goodbyes to Apostol, who watched them from their place hidden behind the hill until they passed out of sight. Thankfully, he agreed to wait half an hour before starting the coach's engine so as to give them ample time to enter the city without the possibility of the sound attracting unwanted attention.

They climbed the hill with little difficulty, but when they reached the top, Maaya had to pause.

Even in the dark, Maaya could tell Saber had been right—Levien *was* enormous, and not just in the way Maaya pictured. Most of the city sprawled about below them much like Sark almost as far as Maaya could look in either direction along the coast. The great black shadow of the ocean lay beyond, vast and seemingly unending. It reminded her of the great black void that had opened in the sky in Sark, and she shuddered.

There were two exceptions to the flat expanse of buildings below. First was a cluster of several dozen buildings that were much taller than the others. From the looks of them, they served as either business buildings or accommodations for wealthier people who wanted shorefront property. Maaya had never seen buildings so tall in her life, and she would have stared at them for a full minute had something even more impressive not caught her attention.

This second exception was so large and so impressive that Maaya didn't have a word in her vocabulary to properly describe it. It was a superstructure that stretched a quarter mile wide and at least two miles long, starting within the center of the city and moving out into the ocean itself where countless wooden beams kept it just above the water. Where it reached out over the water it split into dozens of parallel structures that were all interconnected. It was tall, almost as tall as the buildings in the cluster, but Maaya couldn't see what was inside.

"What… is that?" Maaya asked breathlessly.

"I didn't get enough time to really get a good look, but it seems to be how Levien handles its imports and exports. I would assume the other major port cities have structures similar to this. That's how they manage to move so much cargo to and from so many ships every day. How they do that I haven't a clue, but I definitely want to take a look."

"But it's so *big*," Maaya continued.

"You're telling me. We're not in Sark anymore, that's for sure. Let's try to act like we belong, at least. Come on, let's hurry."

Maaya followed Saber as the ghost led through toward one of Levien's great outer gates, but rather than passing through it, Saber headed toward a small door nearby. There was no guard posted here, so Saber disappeared through the door, unlocked it from the inside, then silently let Maaya through.

HOURS LATER, just as the sun started its slow descent into early afternoon, the girls arrived at the main port area of Levien. They had spent the previous hours of the morning navigating the city, figuring out where its main landmarks were, and scouting out safe places to get food and sleep. They had also tried to figure out whether the guards would recognize Maaya, and there was no easy way about that. She wore a different cloak and had wrapped her hair up tight beneath her hood, but she guessed that would only do so much. They finally decided to throw caution to the winds and just go, making sure that Maaya had cards to burn to aid in her escape if necessary.

Luckily, it seemed like news of her hadn't yet reached Levien, and so after a few cautious forays into public, they finally realized that they could walk around with relative freedom. This made things easier, but only slightly. Even with the freedom to move about as they pleased, the sheer size of the city made it difficult to locate anything. Maaya had the idea of locating the superstructure and then following it to where it ended, because where there were ships there was sure to be information about them, but the structure was even bigger than it had seemed from a distance. It rose high overhead seemingly no matter where they went, providing shade to a huge swath of the city for hours at a time.

The truly amazing part of the structure was what hung over the water. A vast number of steam-powered machines that looked like giant arms moved in unison, picking up large metal containers from ships that had just arrived in port and placing containers on ships that were preparing to leave. There was one parallel section of the structure for every ship's berth, and one giant machine per section. The metal containers were raised above the ship into the structure, where they disappeared.

Earlier, Maaya and Saber had seen where the containers ended up. The structure acted as a conveyor belt that took the containers to a low but very wide circular building in the center of the city. The building was comprised almost completely of doors, and many of the doors were open at all times, some dispensing goods to large waiting carts and some taking in goods from full carts. Maaya had been fascinated by it, though she couldn't see inside; she couldn't imagine what kind of large-scale efficient system was necessary to handle this much material on a daily basis.

Maaya was equally impressed by the port, if not more so. She had seen boats before, but not any that were nearly this large—or so many. Beyond the ships in their berths there were dozens of both cargo and pleasure ships floating lazily in the sea beyond. She caught glimpses of white sails and wood and metal hulls between the massive clouds of steam that passed over the harbor.

The activity in the port surprised her. She guessed the economy hadn't been so badly hurt here. There were still signs that things were slow, from the few shuttered shops here and there to the beggars she had seen when entering, but beyond that the city was leaps and bounds better off than Sark and

Anorath. She remembered the rumors that the stagnation had mostly affected the poor towns outside major cities, and from the looks of things, those rumors were true. The difference between Levien and the other towns she had seen was staggering, almost enough to make her bitter; how was it fair that anyone lived in a place like this when places like Sark and Anorath were in such poor states that they may well have been forgotten? Sure, each town had their wealthy, but there was also an incredible divide between them and everyone else.

Maaya cleared her head of these thoughts with effort. She had made it here and would try to take advantage of all Levien had to offer. Besides, she couldn't deny everything about the city was mesmerizing—it was like she had stepped into another world entirely.

And then there was the sea itself. Maaya had never seen it before, and she was just as much amazed as she was afraid. She squinted, looking as far into the distant horizon as she could, hoping to see where it ended, but there was only an endless expanse of water.

"Do you want to get a closer look?" Saber asked, watching her with clear amusement.

"I'm not sure…" Maaya said hesitantly, but Saber took her by the arm and gently pulled her along. Maaya, hoping nobody was watching, quickly started walking in a way she hoped looked natural.

Maaya had expected the area around the ships to be off limits to anyone not working the docks, but to her surprise—and somewhat to her dismay—she was allowed nearly anywhere except on the ships themselves, save for areas cordoned off for safety reasons and those dedicated to the moving of goods. Guards stood watch at the boarding ramps to each ship while others patrolled the walkways, but they left her completely alone even as Saber nudged her up to the edge of one of the docks.

The air was clearer here, leaving Maaya with an unobstructed view of the sea. She stepped tentatively forward, close enough to the edge to peer over it, but she saw only darkness. This in itself she was not unused to, but the way the water moved all on its own made her nervous. Here she could see that even the largest of ships rose and fell slightly with the waves, and she was suddenly acutely aware of how the dock beneath her feet moved as well.

Saber snorted.

"What?" Maaya demanded.

"You look like you're learning to walk for the first time," Saber laughed.

"If you had to walk, this would be weird for you, too," Maaya grumbled.

But she couldn't be annoyed for long. The ocean, vast and almost overwhelming as it was, fascinated her, and she couldn't take her eyes away from it. The smell of the salty air and the breeze on her face was refreshing and invigorating, and she couldn't help but smile. In the distance she heard the faint bells of buoys, the creaking of wood and rope, and the cries of birds. The men and women working the docks occasionally called to each other as they moved cargo or directed smaller boats in and out. It had a certain comforting quality to it. Compared to the stifling and cramped world of Sark she was familiar with, she was already taking an immense liking to Levien. Here everything seemed more open and free.

She heard laughter and greetings and caught the scents of delicious foods, both familiar and foreign, drifted on the breeze. She saw little shops open right on the edge of the water, selling hot soup that had been poured *inside* loaves of bread shaped like bowls. Patrons carried plates of sizzling fish and vegetables and meats and curries.

Maaya caught herself staring more than once at passersby. There were many things that set the people here apart from the ones she was familiar with in Sark—the fact that they appeared to have brains notwithstanding—but the first thing she noticed was the abundance of technology. Everywhere she looked she could see people with pocket watches, music boxes, and even small devices that played music for everyone around them to hear. A few clearly wealthier people had ocular implants, and some people who worked on the docks had limb augments, some much like the ones Svante had used.

A short way away, a group of people stood huddled together facing a man holding a box in his hands. They stood completely still, and for a moment, Maaya wondered what they could possibly be doing. But then there was a bright flash of light and a puff of smoke that made Maaya jump, and the group of people cheered, then gathered quickly around the man with the box, all eagerly looking at something she couldn't see.

As she looked skyward, she noticed that some of the birds flying about were mechanical. In Sark she had been used to seeing only one, but here she saw dozens. No one paid them any mind, and this was almost as strange to Maaya as the sheer number of birds was. Were they really so common here that everyone accepted them as a fact of life?

Another wave of delicious scents reached Maaya's nose, and her stomach growled. She hadn't realized just how long ago the early morning had been, and even if it had been recent she would have found a way to make room. If she had money, anyway.

"Right. You go look around at the shops to see what you want and I'll get us some coin," Saber said without prompting.

"This is the second time you've decided to steal money recently. Deciding to be more efficient?" Maaya asked, smiling slightly.

"Oh, don't worry. I'm not going to take money from people who actually need it. From the looks of things I could take enough money for a month's worth of food and nobody would even notice. Besides, I'm not exactly fond of the wealthy recently. I can't fathom why."

"They can't all be like Rahu," Maaya protested.

"Best not take the chance. When you grow up with money you grow up in a whole different world from the rest of us. But that point is moot. Enough coin to get you something to eat won't hurt them, and you buying food out in the open will be good for your reputation."

"I don't hope to be here long enough to get one," Maaya said quietly, gazing out at the ocean. There was no going back now.

"After you've eaten we'll get to work," Saber said. "Now, stay put. I won't be long."

The ghost disappeared quickly into the crowd. Maaya couldn't help but scan their faces, wondering who would be the unfortunate victim of Saber's task. She felt guilty at the thought even if she understood Saber's point of view, but another whiff of the many scents of fresh hot food made this guilt dissipate easily.

As she stared around at Levien she thought about how much she might like to stay here as well. It was completely foreign to her, and she was still so unfamiliar with the layout of the city that she was sure to get lost if she only walked a few feet in any direction, but it was charming in its own way. The abundance of technology was fascinating, both in the likes of the magnificent superstructure and all the little oddities so many people possessed, but the fresh air seemed to do her well. She was still sore, albeit less so than a few nights previous, but she hoped to stay long enough to do some exploring before they left.

She immediately admonished herself. She had an important task to undertake, one that couldn't be delayed by such trifling desires as leisure time in the city. Besides, she reasoned, if the police had made it to Anorath, it wouldn't be long before they decided to push their search onward. No matter how she thought about it, her time was limited.

Any further thoughts were interrupted as the dock she stood upon suddenly shifted under a powerful swell. Maaya gasped and lost her balance, though she had enough presence of mind to direct her body backward as she fell so she would not tumble headfirst into the ocean. She landed painfully, placing her hands solidly onto the dock to steady herself against the dizziness that overcame her as she waited for the dock to stop moving.

"You all right, there?" came a voice from nearby.

Maaya glanced up. A young woman who looked only a year or two older than her walked up to her, dressed in a dark knee-length coat with gold collar pins that Maaya had learned denoted the rank of ship's captain. One arm of the coat was cut at the shoulder, revealing a complex bronze augment on her bare left arm that stretched from her shoulder to her fingertips. Maaya had seen some dock workers use similar devices to enhance their strength, but they were bulky and crude; the girl's, on the other hand, was light and stylish, appearing to be designed more for form than function. She completed the ensemble with a pair of black boots.

What Maaya noticed above all, however, was the girl herself. She had long amber hair that was pulled back into a half ponytail. The rest fell nearly to her waist in delicate waves. Her skin was pale and faint freckles dotted her nose and cheeks under her bright jade-green eyes. She was tall, too; even from where Maaya sat, she could tell she stood nearly a head taller than Maaya.

At first, Maaya didn't answer, so taken aback was she by the girl's appearance and her commanding presence. The red-haired girl didn't seem to mind, and offered her hand with a smile.

"I can always tell when someone's never seen the ocean before. You'll find your sea legs soon enough. Are you here for business or pleasure?"

"Business, I suppose," Maaya replied, forcing the words out with difficulty. She took the girl's hand and was pulled effortlessly to her feet.

"You don't much look like a woman of business, but it's not my place to judge. All I know is you're new here, you look hopelessly lost, and ah, you're hungry," she smiled as Maaya's stomach growled. "Let's get you something to eat, what do you say? A proper welcome to Levien is in order."

"Oh, that's all right, my…" Maaya said, then broke off suddenly. She couldn't exactly tell this stranger about Saber. "That is… I wouldn't want to trouble you. I don't have any money yet."

"Well that's why I'm treating you, isn't it?" the girl replied without missing a beat. "Even if you had money, I wouldn't let you pay. Levien hospitality and all that. Oh, before I forget: my name's Adelaide."

Maaya shook her hand wordlessly before remembering she should probably reply.

"I, er, Maaya," she said. She would have been frustrated that her mouth wasn't cooperating with her mind, but in this case her mind wasn't working properly, either. She assumed it was because she was intimidated by someone of such high rank speaking to her directly—she was trying to avoid authorities, not have lunch with them—but she also couldn't deny that this girl, Adelaide, was *very* good looking.

She felt her face threatening to turn pink at the thought. *No. No time for that. Stop it.*

"Pleasure. Now, what are you feeling?"

"Uh, a little cold, actually," Maaya admitted. As pleasant as it felt, the breeze was starting to get to her. But to her surprise, Adelaide laughed.

"I meant what would you like to eat?"

This time Maaya's face flushed visibly.

"I don't actually know what's around here. I only just arrived this morning, and where I come from, well… selection is limited."

Adelaide clapped her hands delightedly.

"Wonderful! Newcomers really are my favorite people. Now let's get out of the wind and find some hot food."

Adelaide started walking, and Maaya quickly fell into step beside her. The more Adelaide talked, the more Maaya was certain she wasn't a native Selenthian. She hadn't seen many Krethans with red hair—though to be fair, she hadn't seen many Krethans at all—but the captain didn't look like anyone she had ever seen before. Even here in Levien Maaya saw mostly people who looked like her. Those few who looked very different were noticeably more reserved, as though they were trying to be invisible. It wasn't hard to imagine why. It wasn't a good idea to look like a Krethan right now, even if there was very little people could do about some aspects of their appearance.

Maaya suddenly found herself wondering if there were many Krethans who lived in Selenthia who simply didn't say anything about it. Surely there had been travel between the nations before the war, and it wouldn't have been easy for every family to just pick up and go back home once the war started. If anything, she imagined more Krethans would want to come *here*, especially with the ghost situation that had apparently been going on for almost a hundred years now. If any Krethans wanted to come to Selenthia to seek a better life, Maaya couldn't really blame them.

But Adelaide walked boldly through town, attracting plenty of attention, and she seemed not to mind. If anything, she seemed to enjoy it. At first Maaya felt anxious under the stares of so many people, but then she realized that people were smiling and waving in the captain's direction. In fact, no one seemed to be paying any attention to Maaya at all.

"Let's see, what do we want, what do we want…" Adelaide murmured to herself, tapping her chin. "Warm, filling, and tasty. Aha! Here, this is perfect. You can eat seafood, right? Of course you can, you're here in Levien. After you!"

They had arrived at one of the small beach-side shops Maaya had seen earlier. It was larger inside than she thought, with at least a dozen small tables for two, and despite the fact that the line at the counter stretched out the door, most of the tables were open.

The smell of food almost overwhelmed Maaya as she walked in, and her stomach growled again. She saw loaves upon loaves of bread and enormous pots filled with bubbling soup. Cooks pulled platters of sizzling fish, squid, and mussels from within their ovens, diced them neatly, then poured them into the pots of soup. One man near the end of the line took a loaf of bread in one hand and carved the insides out of it faster than Maaya thought possible. The other took the bowls of bread and poured soup into them until they were nearly overflowing.

"Here, take a seat. I'll get us something to eat. I'm absolutely starving."

Maaya took a seat near one of the clear windows that overlooked the ocean while Adelaide stepped up to the front of the line. Contrary to looking annoyed, the man taking orders looked nothing short of delighted to see her.

"Hey, cap'n! Been at least a week since you've been in here. How was the trip?"

"Perfect as always, but too short. I can't stand these local assignments. But that'll be fixed soon."

"Oh yeah? Where you headed?"

"That I can't say," Adelaide winked. "Very important stuff, see. But as you can imagine, I was so very honored to be selected for this task."

"Right, like this isn't the dozenth time you've got a long-term assignment," the man teased. "At least tell me I'll see you again before you head out."

"Absolutely. No point leaving berth on an empty stomach. Oh, that reminds me. Double my usual order; I've got a friend with me."

"You could just tell me their name, you know. I know all your crew by now," the man said, waving behind him at the line of cooks.

"Oh, this one's not part of my crew. She's new! Just arrived here this morning, in fact, from… from, uh… well, somewhere very boring, as I recall. She's never been here before so I decided she needed to start out with something great."

"You're too kind, cap'n," the man said. "I'd come say hello, but you've come during the lunch rush. At the very least, what's their name? I need to know them next time they come in."

"Maaya," Adelaide said warmly, and Maaya thought she had never heard her own name spoken in such a pleasant voice.

"Maaya, excellent. Well you tell Maaya she's not paying for her meal today. You, however, still have to pay, because I've got a business to run."

"Don't be ridiculous. I'm paying for both of us and that's that. I'm paid well and I don't take charity."

The man didn't argue and happily took the coins Adelaide grabbed from her deep coat pocket. Only a few moments later a tray with two enormous bread bowls filled to the brim with soup appeared on the counter in front of Adelaide, who smiled widely, took the tray, then stepped away from the counter.

"Now come back soon, hear?" the man called as he turned his attention to the other customers.

Adelaide set the tray down on the table between them, set a spoon out for Maaya, then immediately dug in.

"Oh, stars. This is wonderful. I'm absolutely starving," Adelaide said delightedly, then narrowed her eyes at Maaya, who had only just slowly picked up her spoon. "No need to be so delicate. If you think you have to impress me with proper table manners you've clearly never seen me eat."

Maaya averted her eyes in embarrassment. She hadn't been eating slowly because she wanted to impress the captain, but because, for the moment, she couldn't take her eyes off her. Sure, part of it was because Maaya felt hopeful at the prospect of perhaps meeting another Krethan—and a seafaring one, at that—but the rest was for reasons she was definitely not about to disclose.

Suddenly, a thought struck her. *What if this is Svante's contact?*

"You like it?" Adelaide said, interrupting her train of thought. She held out her arm for Maaya to see; Maaya was momentarily confused before she realized she had been staring at the captain's augment.

"I do! What… what does it do?" Maaya asked curiously.

Now that Maaya could see it up close, she could see it was even more beautiful than she had first thought. Thin curves of golden metal spidered their way from her shoulder down to her wrist, where smaller metal rods connected by tiny gears at the knuckles spread out over the back of her hand and down to her fingertips. They moved noiselessly and smoothly with every motion she made, as naturally as if it were a limb all on its own. A few tinier gears were placed at the wrist and elbow, allowing her total freedom of movement.

Adelaide smiled and pulled open the collar of her coat, revealing that the shoulder of the device was connected to two sturdy leather straps that wrapped around her torso for support.

"This is an adaptation of the mech augments dockhands use. I wanted something that would give me more strength if I needed it, but I also wanted it to look pretty. Did it work?"

"It's gorgeous," Maaya replied in amazement. "How does it work?"

"It's a mix of pressure distribution and swing phase hydraulics. Something like that, anyway. Honestly, the steamsmith who made it for me tried explaining about half a dozen times, and all I learned is that I'm not cut out to be a steamsmith. Either way, it's great!"

"I love it. Was it expensive?" Maaya asked eagerly.

"You could say that. But then, this was the first of its kind. Most people here are after performance, not looks, so it was tricky to get this one in order. But apparently the smith has gotten a lot of orders for things like this since then, so I might have started a trend. How cool is that?"

Maaya laughed. She could never see herself wearing one—she liked the freedom *libris* cards gave her for the same effects—but there was a definite appeal to this version. Then again, she thought with amusement, maybe that was all because of who was wearing it.

"Say, where you from, anyway?" Adelaide asked.

"Sark. You don't have to tell me you haven't heard of it; I just kind of assume that's the case with everyone who doesn't live there. And half the people who do, probably."

Adelaide burst out laughing.

"So much love for your hometown! But you're right, I haven't heard of it. Is it far?"

"Honestly? I have no idea. I know vaguely how long it took us to get here, but not the distance we traveled."

"Who's 'we?' Are you with family?" Adelaide asked, munching on the lid of her bread bowl.

"Oh, er… I'm alone, actually. I just got used to saying 'we' if I ever had to talk to anyone while traveling by myself. It seemed safer." She couldn't help but feel proud of herself for coming up with that excuse on the fly, and almost wished Saber had been there to overhear it.

"Good idea, good idea," Adelaide said approvingly. "And I will say Levien is a safe city, even for a girl on her own, but you still probably shouldn't tell anyone you're alone. Do you know where you're staying?"

"Not yet," Maaya admitted, and Adelaide smiled.

"Yeah, you probably shouldn't tell anyone that, either. And when you do find a place to stay, you shouldn't tell anyone where that is. Actually… maybe just don't tell anyone anything. And while I'm flattered you think I'm an exception, just be careful."

Maaya nodded.

"Actually, I was wondering if—"

"*There* you are! Good grief. I leave for five minutes and you make friends with a captain and get a free lunch."

Maaya jumped. Saber floated through the window, then gazed irritably up and down at Adelaide before turning to Maaya.

"Don't worry, pretend I'm not here. Just finish up. We've got a lot of work to do, and now you mention it, we should find a place to sleep tonight."

Adelaide looked concernedly at Maaya.

"Everything okay?"

"Yeah, sorry, I just… almost choked," Maaya said lamely. "Anyway, I was wondering if you had any recommendations for places to stay?"

"Definitely. What's your budget?"

"As low as possible," Maaya answered almost guiltily, but Adelaide didn't seem to mind.

"I know a place. Nice and safe and with beautiful views. Free breakfast, too, I think. How long are you staying?"

"Only a night or two, I think," Maaya said, and to her surprise, Adelaide looked disappointed.

"Business calls, I suppose. I know how it goes. I'm setting out tomorrow afternoon for a two-week trip. Two weeks! I'm so excited. I actually get to go out into the open ocean rather than just hugging the shore. Anyway, here. So you have a safe place to sleep." Adelaide again reached into her pocket and pulled out a few coins, placing them on the table in front of Maaya.

Maaya stared.

"You… I can't take—"

"Sure you can! It just wouldn't be right if I let someone go hungry and without a place to lay their head at night. Anyway, the place you want… oh, you'll probably need a map, right." Adelaide pulled a small map of the city from her coat and placed it onto the table, tapping her finger on a street not too far away. "Big blue building, you can't miss it. It's no grand suite, but it's comfortable and warm."

"Why are you being so nice?" Maaya asked. "You're giving me so much already."

"Because you're cute, and I like you," Adelaide replied bluntly. "That aside, I really wouldn't feel right leaving someone stranded if I had the option to help them otherwise. Just promise me you'll come back and visit me, yeah?"

"Of course!" Maaya replied, and she meant it.

Adelaide grinned, and Maaya suddenly noticed that she had already finished her entire bowl of soup. The captain stood, beckoning Maaya to join her. Maaya held out her hand, but her eyes widened in surprise as Adelaide took her into a tight hug.

"I'm sorry to leave you so soon, but I really need to get going. I still have a lot of preparation to do before we set out and my crew probably won't do things the way I like. But I'll see you around, yes?"

"Definitely. Oh, what should I call you? Do I need to call you 'captain'?" Maaya asked, unable to hide her smile.

"Only if you're on my ship, and we might have to see about making that happen someday," Adelaide replied with a wink. "Oh, and… a little advice before I go. Stay inside at night, okay? Levien is usually safe, but some strange things have been happening recently."

"Things like what?" Maaya asked quietly, her blood running cold.

"I'm not sure exactly. I've just heard murmurings. Either way, it just seems best to keep to yourself while the sun is down, especially since you're traveling by yourself."

"Right. I'll do that. Thank you."

Adelaide nodded, and then her smile quickly returned.

"But while the sun is up, I hope you enjoy everything Levien has to offer! And I will see you again."

She tapped her finger politely to her forehead in farewell, then strode out of the restaurant.

Maaya watched her go until she disappeared into the crowd. She wasn't even aware that she was still standing, staring at the now-closed door, until Saber tapped her sharply on the shoulder.

"Hey. Lover girl. Your soup's getting cold."

"Oh, stuff it," Maaya mumbled as she sat down, refusing to meet the ghost's stare.

"What? Just pointing out that you're absolutely smitten, which is all well and good—and let's be honest, you could do a lot worse—but also, you need to hurry up and finish so we can find somewhere private to talk."

Maaya nodded, then turned back to her soup, eating as quickly as she could. She had no idea how anyone would still have room to try to eat the bowl after they finished their soup. She was already close to full.

As she finished her soup with Saber hovering impatiently nearby, she thought about Saber's comment. Sometimes it felt like Saber could see through Maaya just about as well as Maaya could see through her, so she wasn't sure how much of what she'd said was supposed to be taken in jest.

Whether or not Maaya cared was another story. Her mind kept drifting back to Adelaide, the sound of her voice, her confident stride, and her long beautiful hair. She didn't know anything else about her, but in terms of first impressions, Adelaide was off to an excellent start.

Maaya ate only a few bites of the inside of the bowl before she decided she couldn't eat another bite without making herself sick, pocketed the map and coins Adelaide had given her, then put her tray away. She waved at the man at the counter as she left, and he waved back with a smile, though she was sure he was only doing it to be polite.

She walked out into the street in high spirits, though after a few feet she realized she didn't have any idea where she was going. Nor was she sure where she would be able to find an isolated spot in a city this crowded.

Saber seemed to have a plan in mind already, however, and gently tugged on Maaya's sleeve. They walked into the narrow alley behind the restaurant, which wasn't quite out of view of the main street, but was far enough away that no one would notice Maaya talking to herself.

"Sorry about disappearing on you earlier. What are we—?"

"Spare me," Saber interrupted tiredly, and though she didn't raise her voice, Maaya could tell she was angry. "Do *not* do that again. This isn't up for debate, so don't bother explaining. Just don't do it again."

"Wait, what—?"

"I told you not to leave, and it wasn't because I wanted to make things difficult for you. This city is huge, and when I got back and you weren't there I didn't know if it was because you had gotten lost or captured. If we lose each other we have no way to find each other again, and I have no way to help you, do you understand? Not to mention you're supposed to be avoiding attention until we get out of here, so imagine my surprise when I look for you in a panic only to find you chatting with a *ship's captain* over lunch and having a good time!"

Maaya was stunned. She hadn't expected Saber to react like this.

"I didn't—"

"One last thing. I've followed along with all the things you've wanted so far, and while I'm not going to say you owe me one, I will say you at least owe me the respect of basic communication and reliability. If we're going to do this I need to know that you won't disappear every time a pretty girl shows up."

Maaya's face burned.

"That's not why I—"

"I don't really care, honestly. Just please, don't do it again, regardless of the reason. Okay?"

Maaya nodded, unable to speak. She had never felt so ashamed in her life. She wanted to protest, to say that she hadn't walked off because she was enamored by Adelaide, but she knew it was pointless. The reason really wasn't important.

But then she remembered something.

"Hey, Saber… that girl. She looks like she could be Krethan, don't you think? She's a sailor, too. And since we're looking for Svante's contact, who we know was supposed to take us back by boat…"

Even as she spoke she was afraid Saber might call the idea ridiculous, but Saber tapped her chin thoughtfully.

"Now that's a thought. I'm sure there's more than just the one Krethan here in this enormous city, but it's definitely worth a shot. I could see Svante hitching a ride with someone like that. When I look at the ship logs, I'll start with her. I don't suppose you stopped staring at her pretty face long enough to catch her name?"

"Oh, shut up," Maaya retorted. "Her name is Adelaide, and as I'm sure you heard, she mostly does local cargo shipments, but she's leaving for a two-week long expedition tomorrow. What you missed, though, is that she does long-term assignments frequently."

"What's your point?" Saber asked, trying and failing to hide her smile.

"If someone is just taking cargo anywhere else on the Selenthian coast they wouldn't be doing a long-term assignment, would they? I'm assuming 'long term' means going farther than Selenthia."

"If so, why would she talk so brazenly about it? Even if it was a code phrase, most people here are probably familiar enough with sailing to come to the same conclusion you did. Now, I'm not saying it's not a possibility," Saber added quickly as Maaya made to interject. "I'll look into it, promise.

If it turns out she's our girl, then your little lunch date just made things a whole lot easier on us."

Maaya glared, but said nothing.

"We should move quickly, though," Saber continued, suddenly looking more serious. "The captain wasn't specific with her warning, but I overheard something similar as I was taking some guy's coin. There's definitely something strange happening in Levien, and I think you know what I'm talking about."

"What? No… they can't be here already," Maaya gasped quietly.

"I don't know for sure, but I overheard some locals talking about people disappearing. Houses empty, everything still there, the usual. That sounds like our ghosts to me."

Maaya took a deep breath, running her fingers through her hair. If they were here, that could spell disaster. She guessed Levien's population was many times that of Sark and Anorath combined, and the city itself was a crucial part of Selenthia's infrastructure.

"Right. Let's get to it," Maaya said firmly. "You can start with the records and I'll start talking to the locals. Do you know where we need to go?"

"There's a big building near the middle of the dock where everyone seems to check in and out. I figured I'd start there. Plus, it's got a ton of windows in front to supervise the ships, so I can keep an eye on you while I work. Anyway, there's a *lot* of stuff in there, so I want to get started as soon as possible. Ready?"

Maaya nodded again, and they headed out toward the dock, a sick feeling growing in Maaya's stomach. Time was running out much faster than she thought.

19

A MYSTERY OF CARDS

HOURS LATER, just as the sun started to disappear behind the distant horizon, Maaya walked tiredly into the room of the hotel Adelaide had pointed out to her earlier, collapsing onto the bed with a groan. Saber followed close behind, looking both ways down the long narrow hallway, then closing and locking the door behind her. She then went over to the window to make sure it was locked and that the curtains were shut tight.

Despite hours and hours of searching, neither of them had found anything remotely useful. Maaya had spent some time getting to know some of the dockhands and asking about any interesting gossip, but either for lack of trust or lack of information they didn't have anything interesting to say. A few were able to confirm, speaking quietly and glancing around shiftily as they spoke, that Levien was home to many Krethans who lived there to escape their troubles back home, but if anything, that made Maaya's search harder. Now, instead of looking for a single Krethan, they were looking for one of many.

Saber's search had been just as fruitless. There were apparently no records of voyages to Krethus whatsoever, and so far every single ship and every mission it took on was accounted for with incredible accuracy, leaving no suspicious gaps. As they suspected, travel between the two countries was illegal, which meant that even if some ships did travel there, it wouldn't be documented anywhere Saber could find it. Further, much to Maaya's disappointment—though she didn't dare tell Saber—the ghost had discovered that Adelaide was nothing more than the captain of a merchant vessel who delivered cargo up and down the coast. She had taken a few trips to nearby islands, which explained her long-distance trips, but there was nothing more.

"We have to consider that some of these records are inaccurate; otherwise Svante wouldn't have been able to get here in the first place," Saber said, pacing by the bed now she had ensured the room was secure. "According to this office, no ship has departed for, or arrived from, Krethus in the last… oh, I couldn't even keep counting. But he made it here somehow."

"Could he have snuck in another way somehow?" Maaya asked as she sat up, but Saber shook her head.

"Not with the security this place has. Everything is kept pretty tight. Besides, Svante definitely said his contact was here. I suspect he had fewer problems because he had money, but still."

"So we just need to find out who could be lying to the office, right?" Maaya asked hopefully.

"That'd be one way to do it, but it could take months. Dozens of ships go in and out of that harbor every day, and even behind closed doors no one mentioned Krethus. Not *once.* Believe me, I was listening hard."

Maaya lay back on the bed, feeling thoroughly defeated. She hadn't expected finding Svante's contact to be easy, but she had expected to figure out at least something by the end of their first day. She thought the arrival of a wealthy Krethan in a city this big might cause at least some gossip, but no one seemed to know anything at all. Maaya had even attempted to pretend she knew about his arrival already and simply wanted someone else to talk to about it, but no one had taken the bait.

"It's all right. We'll get back to it tomorrow. Reading through the ship manifests and records all day got me familiar with how it all works, so I'll be faster tomorrow. I might actually go back tonight; it might be faster with only the night shift working. What do you think?"

"Are you sure you wouldn't get bored?" Maaya asked. "I'd feel bad sleeping while you're off working still."

"Don't worry about it. I need to use my advantage of being dead to… well, my advantage. Besides, there's much more interesting stuff in there than you might expect. Turns out there is a huge market for, uh, how should I say… products for adults."

Maaya burst into laughter as Saber grinned.

"Well, I guess it would be more efficient… it's bound to be more entertaining than watching me sleep. Just promise to be careful, okay?" Maaya said.

Saber nodded.

"Of course. I'll be back before sunrise. Also… I'm sorry for being so harsh with you earlier. I just want to make sure we're on the same page, and that if something goes wrong I can be there for you. Okay?"

"No, you were right," Maaya admitted with a sigh. "I shouldn't have just left like that. She could have taken me anywhere; it was lucky we only went so far."

"All's well. To be frank, I was slightly jealous. I went through all that effort of getting money to treat you to lunch and someone else beat me to it. But honestly, and I mean this with total sincerity, if we get back here and you find out she's single…"

Saber quickly disappeared through the wall, laughing as Maaya threw one of the bed pillows in her direction.

Maaya sat in silence for a few moments, deep in thought. The bed was so very comfortable and she was so very tired. But still, there was something else nagging at her mind, something she was sure would not let her sleep.

She stood up and walked to the desk across from the bed. Opening the middle drawer, she took out a piece of paper as well as the small inkwell and pen that came in every room.

If you come back early, going to watch city for hour or two. Want to see how bad ghost walks are. Will be safe, will return soon. Staying on roofs if you want to find me.

—Maaya

She felt slightly guilty for leaving, but the note would have to suffice. Besides, Maaya didn't plan on going far.

Maaya made sure the note was easily visible, patted her coat to feel for the key to the room, and then after a brief pause grabbed a dark washcloth from the neatly folded pile of towels on the dresser near the bed, stuffing it into her pocket. Satisfied, she walked silently out into the hall. She descended two flights of stairs to the lobby, where the man behind the counter gave her a friendly wave, and then she walked out into the night.

Almost immediately she ducked into a dark alleyway nearby, pressed a purple card to her leg, and then, with a surge of strength, leapt up to the roof of the hotel, moving swiftly out of sight from the streets below. Higher and higher she jumped, going from rooftop to rooftop until she could see the entire city around her. As she went, she took the washcloth out of her pocket, then tied it behind her head so that it covered her nose and mouth. Then, she pulled up her hair in a bun—or as much of one as she could make, anyway—and pulled her hood over her head. It wasn't much of a disguise, but it would have to do.

She paused a moment to take in the beauty of it all. On one side was the ocean, empty and dark save for the few ships out at night, their lights reflected in the small waves. On the other was an ocean of lights twinkling merrily as the night of the city came to life. She briefly forgot that anything else existed, that outside the city walls was darkness and cold, miles and miles devoid of all life. She forgot about Sark and the other small towns they passed, secluded and unknown to anyone who wasn't already there. Now that she had been here for only a day she couldn't imagine being anywhere else. The rest of the world was too isolated. She wanted to be somewhere she could see new faces every day, where exploring the city would take more than a day.

Somewhere people like Adelaide lived.

Maaya shook her head to clear her mind. She didn't know anything about the girl other than that she was the captain of a cargo ship, that she was outgoing and confident, and that she was almost unfairly beautiful. As much as Maaya appreciated all three of those things, she knew that wasn't enough to let the girl dominate her mind like that. Besides, Adelaide was leaving tomorrow, and with any luck, Maaya would be leaving shortly after, and it was unlikely they would see each other again. There was, perhaps, a chance that they could meet while Adelaide was on her way out. Maybe if Maaya got to the docks extra early—

Stop it, Maaya thought forcefully, turning her attention back to the city.

The thought of the tall faceless ghosts was enough to push any other thoughts from her mind. If they attacked here, it was sure to cause chaos. A panic in a place with so many people would cause damage and death all on its own.

There were two things keeping Maaya's fear at bay. The first was that the ghost walk in Anorath had been minuscule compared to the last few she had seen in Sark. The other was something more personal. Despite Saber's assurances, Maaya hadn't been able to forget what Rahu had said about the ghosts being attracted to her somehow, but if the attacks in Levien had happened before she'd arrived, as was the case with Anorath, this meant it was much harder to put the blame for their appearances on her. While the attacks were still horrifying, this fact at least helped soothe the guilt that constantly clawed at her insides, fighting tooth and nail to be noticed and suffered.

She also thought about Svante's theory that the use of *libris* attracted the ghosts. While it was certainly true that the ghosts had started to increase in number the more Maaya and the others fought, there was a definite delay. She and the others had used *libris* for years without seeing so much as a single one of the strange ghosts, and in cases where they were spotted, it had been days since any of them had been in the area. This, too, gave Maaya some hope—and an excuse to use her power. Now she was in Levien, she could fight off what ghosts she could, then get to Krethus as quickly as possible to destroy the machine before the effects caught up with her.

Just then, she thought of yet another bit of good news. If the ghosts were attracted so much to *libris* use, the fact that only a small number were only just now showing up in Levien meant that there were probably no other *libris* users in the city—or at the very least, that they were smart enough not to use their powers. While someday she hoped to meet others like her, for the moment she wanted any advantage she could take. Besides, other *libris* users could put Saber in danger.

The bright glowing lines flickered and then disappeared from Maaya's legs as she sat down. She let her feet dangle over the edge of the building she sat upon, and she watched the city below in silence. She wasn't entirely sure what she was waiting for, now she thought of it. She wanted to see if the ghosts really had made it to Levien, but if they had, she had come woefully unprepared to do anything about it. She had only a few blood cards left and hadn't bothered to make more, and if she had to be frank with herself, her heart just wasn't in it at the moment. Fighting the ghosts, traveling to Krethus, destroying the machine… it was all just so much. She was fully aware of how petty that sounded, but she couldn't bring herself to care. There was little motivation to be found for such a task when most of the people she cared to aid in carrying it out were already gone, or assumed to be gone.

Maaya thought of Roshan, and her heart ached. He probably had no idea what was going on… if he was still alive. Had he and his father made it out? Did they see what happened to Svante? Did they think Maaya had been killed? That was all possible, if Sark was even still on the map. Maybe Rahu had convinced everyone to stay. Maybe the ghost walks had gotten even worse and the town was now completely devoid of life. If that were true, it would be months before anyone discovered its fate given how often people traveled inland these days. She thought of her home, of the streets she used to walk every day and night, empty, silent, dead…

She fought the urge to throw up. That was too much to think about, and there was no proof of any of it. She forced her brain to push those thoughts back into a corner, promising herself that if she found any opportunity to send a message to Sark before leaving Levien, she would do so.

Just as she was wondering how long she was willing to wait before going back to her comfortable bed, she heard a scream.

She leapt to her feet, searching the streets below frantically for any sign of white lights, but she couldn't see anything out of the ordinary. This didn't mean the ghosts weren't there, of course; there could be too few to stand out against the lights of the city, or they could have passed through nearby buildings, temporarily out of sight.

Maaya gripped her card pouch, then dashed in the direction of the scream.

She heard nothing further as she leapt from rooftop to rooftop, but it wasn't hard to find the source of the cry. A few streets over she saw a woman leaning over a body in the street, and Maaya's heart sank.

She dropped silently to the ground as a small ground of people gathered around the couple, her *libris* lines flickering away before she stepped into view.

"He's alive, it's all right," someone said loudly, and sighs of relief followed.

"What happened?" Maaya dared ask as she approached.

"I'm not sure. My husband and I were walking home from dinner together, and then he suddenly just… stopped. Stopped moving, stopped talking, just stared straight ahead like he was sleepwalking. And then he fell!"

Maaya took a step back and scanned the nearby streets and buildings. She still saw no sign of the ghosts. Was it possible they would have appeared and then disappeared again so quickly? They usually didn't disappear after such a short time unless Maaya or the others used a blood card on them, regardless of how many there were.

"The medics are on their way," said one man, dressed in a fine suit and sporting a gold pocket watch. "Lucky I had a bird on me."

"Thank you. Thank you so much," the woman replied gratefully, cradling her husband's head in her lap.

"There's a silver lining, too. If you'd both kept walking you might have been struck by one of those fireworks," another woman said disapprovingly.

"Fireworks?" Maaya asked curiously.

"Fireworks indeed. Only a few feet in front of them, there was a burst of red sparks! No idea where they came from or who set it off—they probably ran for fear of getting in trouble—but if these two hadn't stopped they might have gotten hit. Probably a child. They're so reckless with these things. I tell them, I keep telling the parents, these things aren't *toys*, but they still…"

Maaya didn't hear the rest. This was too familiar a situation to be coincidence. This man had almost certainly had an encounter with one of the ghosts, but that wasn't what scared her. A shower of red sparks, combined with the fact that the man was still alive, meant that someone *else* had used a blood card to get rid of the ghost.

A distant siren slowly became audible, coming in their direction. There was nothing else Maaya could do here, and she didn't much like the idea of being seen near any trouble.

"I think I'm going home now. I hope your husband recovers quickly," Maaya said kindly, trying to hide the anxiety in her voice.

"Thank you, dear. Please be safe!"

Once she was sure no one was looking in her direction, she disappeared into another nearby alley, burning another card and making her way swiftly back to the rooftops.

She searched her surroundings agitatedly. This attack had just happened, which meant that whoever had used *libris* couldn't be far—unless, of course, they were part of the group below, but she doubted that. Throwing a card wasn't exactly a subtle action, and surely someone would have seen it.

After a few minutes of searching, she realized she was thinking about this the wrong way. If she wanted to find this *libris* user, all she had to do was make sure she got to the next ghost walk first.

She didn't have to wait long. Out of the corner of her eye she saw a white glow suddenly appear a few streets ahead of her. She currently stood at the base of a steep hill, and the buildings on each street stood several feet higher than those on the streets below. This presented something of a challenge, but it also gave her a chance to gain high ground.

Maaya moved as quickly as she could. The ghosts weren't far away, and she had a definite advantage of speed over—

She ducked suddenly as a dark shape passed her in a blur. It moved so swiftly compared to Maaya, even with her enhanced strength and speed, that Maaya couldn't immediately make out what it was. Then, to her immense surprise, she realized it was a person.

They wore a dark cloak that reached almost to their ankles, and their head and face was covered by a dark veil. The bright lines of *libris* covered their legs and arms, but Maaya had never seen patterns like those before. While she recognized the colors, there were many more lines than what Maaya was used to, and more tightly compressed and jagged in their appearance. Whenever she and her friends had used *libris*, the patterns were always exactly the same. This was not only different from anything she had seen before, but clearly more advanced.

The stranger darted toward the ghosts with more speed than Maaya could even hope to match, so she settled for simply trying to gain a good vantage point on a nearby roof. She pulled out what blood cards remained in her pouch, prepared to assist the stranger in whatever capacity she could. There were only about two dozen ghosts, but that was more than what she could deal with in a single volley.

A moment later, however, she saw her help would be completely unnecessary.

She saw a handful of cards streak through the air toward the ghosts, and only a moment later they detonated on impact with force Maaya had never before seen. Despite the fact that the stranger had used only a few cards, every single one of the ghosts instantly disappeared in a shower of sparks and a loud bang.

All this happened before the figure even landed.

They hit the ground lightly amidst the shower of sparks, glancing around with as much concern as one might check their garden to see how their plants were growing after a rain. Evidently satisfied with the results of their assault, they leapt up to a nearby balcony, and from there to the roof of an apartment complex.

"Wait!" Maaya cried, though in her fear, it came out almost as a whisper. If the stranger heard her, they didn't show it. "Hey, who are—?"

She broke off as she was suddenly blinded by a white light. She stepped back in surprise, wondering for a split second what could cause such a glare —and then felt a wave of horror wash over her as she realized what was happening.

She reflexively lowered her gaze to the ground, then jumped backward with as much strength as she could muster. A group of ghosts was materializing right on top of where Maaya had just stood, and she desperately fought the swell of panic that rose within her. If she had waited for even a moment…

With reflexes born of a lifetime of flight, she flung her remaining blood cards at the materializing ghosts. The cards erupted as they struck their targets, causing the ghosts to vanish before they had even fully appeared.

Maaya took a moment to verify they were gone, then fell to her hands and knees, her whole body trembling. *I almost died. I just almost died.*

A small part of her mind frantically tried to get her attention, reminding her that she was out of blood cards and that she needed to escape, but she couldn't bring herself to move. Breathing was about all she could muster, and that in itself was a challenge.

But when she heard a soft noise from immediately behind her, adrenaline took over once again, and she whirled around —finding herself staring directly at the cloaked figure.

Maaya gasped in fear, then struggled to push herself backward. The stranger had her in a compromised position, and while ordinarily Maaya would have been able to use *libris* to her advantage, this newcomer had already demonstrated that they were far faster, stronger, and more adept at *libris* than she was. What's more, the figure stood much taller than Maaya—which, admittedly, wasn't entirely out of the ordinary—and had what looked to be a full deck of cards at their disposal.

However, it seemed like the stranger had no intent of causing Maaya any harm. They raised both hands in a sign of peace, then slowly reached out a hand to Maaya. After a moment full of uncertainty, Maaya took it and was pulled effortlessly to her feet.

"Are you well?" the figure asked. The voice was deep, mechanical, and distorted, and even up close Maaya couldn't make out any distinguishing features of the person's face. Her inability to discern any of their features made her uncomfortable, and she was glad she had decided to cover much of her own face as well.

"I'm fine," Maaya said shakily. "Who are you? How do you know—?"

"No details. You must get away quickly. Do you have enough *libris* to get home safely?"

"I have some, but I'm out of blood cards. But I—"

"Then you must go. Take some more blood cards so you can defend yourself. Here." The stranger opened their pouch and took out a half-dozen cards marked in red and handed them to Maaya. "Until you can make more. Now, go. Be safe."

Just as the stranger was turning to leave, Maaya saw a small glimmer as the lights from the nearby buildings reflected off something shiny on the stranger's coat.

Maaya started. Fastened to the stranger's coat was a pin—one that looked almost exactly like the one Emil had given her.

"Hey! That pin, you—wait, don't go!"

The stranger stepped off the side of the building and disappeared. Maaya rushed to the edge and looked over, then glanced frantically up and down the street, but they were gone.

Maaya couldn't help but stomp her foot onto the roof in frustration. She had finally discovered someone who might have been able to give her answers or assistance, and she had let them get away before even finding out who they were.

She spent another minute looking up and down the nearby streets in a vain attempt to catch another glimpse of the stranger, then decided to head back the hotel. It only took her a few minutes to reach the alley by the hotel. She landed quietly, the lights on her legs flickering and then disappearing. After checking to make sure no one was watching, she walked back into the street, around the corner, and back into the lobby. All the while, she clutched the cards the stranger had given her tightly in her hand.

It wasn't until she was safely back in her room that she dared to look at them. She placed them on the bed, then did a double take.

These were definitely blood cards, but they were unlike the ones she and her friends had used. In fact, she couldn't remember seeing this particular design at all. The cards were all cut at the same size as though specifically made for this purpose, and the material was thicker and more durable. The designs written in blood were far more intricate and the lines more crisp. While the lines on Maaya's cards were fluid and curved, these were jagged and sharp, much like the glowing lines of the stranger's *libris* augments.

Maaya ran her finger softly over the cards, feeling the tiny ridges where the blood had dried. Whoever the stranger was, they were clearly skilled in a way Maaya could never hope to match. She took a moment to be thankful that they, whoever they were, had decided to assist Maaya rather than fight her. Maaya wasn't sure that she and Saber combined could defeat such a strong person, even if they were well rested and had a full deck of cards.

Her mind drifted back to the pin she had seen on the stranger's cloak. This raised even more questions. Maaya's first suspicion was that the pin identified users of *libris*. This would explain both why Emil had given it to her and why he hadn't wanted her asking around about it. From there, she hypothesized that Emil had planned for her to make connections with other users of the magic in order to bolster her strength. Maaya imagined fighting alongside the stranger as they worked their way toward the machine and couldn't help but smile with excitement. That would definitely be preferable to making their way alone.

She pulled the pin out of her pocket, toying with it absently as she stared off into space. While the thought of making such allies was appealing, she realized she was no further along than she had been that evening. She still didn't know for sure what the pin signified, nor how to find anyone else who might have one. The one person she had seen escaped before she could ask them any questions, and unless Saber came home with good news, they still had nothing in terms of a contact or ride.

She flipped off her shoes, then went over to the desk, crumpling the note she had written for Saber. She didn't have to know about that until Maaya woke up.

Hoping that her friend was having more luck than she was, Maaya turned off the lamps in the room, double checked that the door was tightly locked, then climbed into bed.

20

THE BLACKFINS

Maaya was vaguely aware of someone gently shaking her awake. She opened her eyes slowly, then smiled as she saw Saber looking down at her.

"Good morning, sleepyhead. How do you feel?" the ghost asked.

"I slept wonderfully," Maaya replied, sitting up and stretching. Her sore muscles finally seemed to have mostly healed, and she felt refreshed. She had also had some very pleasant dreams, but she knew Saber would make fun of her until the end of time if she told her what they were about. Not that it would have been hard for her to guess after the day before. "How was your night?"

Saber sighed, looking as tired as it was possible for the dead to look.

"It was all right, I suppose. I didn't find anything substantive, but at the very least I think I managed to narrow down our options. I set aside at least fifty ships that I'm absolutely certain have no business with Krethus or even anything in that general direction."

"How many are there total?" Maaya asked tentatively.

"Hundreds," Saber said dully. "But if I can keep going at this pace, it should only take a few days at most to at least get us a very good guess."

"You should rest your eyes some!" Maaya protested. "Besides, I have to tell you about what happened last night…"

Maaya told the story of everything she had experienced the night before, keeping a wary eye on Saber's expression in case the news of her nighttime walk made her angry. However, as Maaya reached the end of her story, Saber only looked puzzled.

"You know, that could actually be valuable information," the ghost said.

"So there are other *libris* users in the city who also know about the ghost walks, and they have the same pin you've got. It seems like there are connections we're definitely supposed to make here and our only job is to find out how."

"Do you think one of them might know Svante's contact?" Maaya asked.

"Possibly, but that might not matter. There has to be more than one way to get to Krethus, and who better to ask than people who have a stake in defeating the same ghosts we're after? Honestly, that's probably why Emil gave that thing to you. You have a much better shot of finding more people like you than a person with no name and no description and no idea we're coming."

"Yeah, you're probably right. Only trouble is, I can't imagine any of them wearing that pin out in public. I might have to wait until nighttime to do some more exploring of my own. If I can meet that person again…"

"What do you mean exploring of your own? Am I not coming with you?" Saber asked, raising an eyebrow.

Maaya faltered.

"I'm not sure if it would be safe," she said, and Saber scoffed. "I mean it! You didn't see how easily this person got rid of those ghosts. There were over a dozen of them and that stranger destroyed them like they were nothing. I'm worried that if we meet someone like that and they decide you're a target, I won't be able to stop them from hurting you."

Saber opened her mouth to argue, then closed it again, looking thoughtful.

"That's… actually a good point. I'm not sure how much I feel like meeting my untimely end here before we even get started. I would assume they're only after those specific ghosts—I have met other dead here who have been here quite a while, after all—but… you're right. I think it'll be safer for me to just continue my work in the office."

"Sorry. If I find out they're friendly I'd definitely introduce you. I mean… they have to be friendly, right? If Emil is the one who recommended them."

"Emil's recommendation does them absolutely no favors, but I understand where you're coming from," Saber said. "Now this doesn't mean you're off the hook. I expect you to play this as safely as you can, too. If I find out you're taking silly risks…"

"I know, I know," Maaya smiled. "I should be fine. They helped me. They even gave me some of their blood cards to make sure I got home safely. Here, look. Have you ever seen anything like these?"

Saber peered down at the cards Maaya held out for her, examining them from multiple angles.

"I haven't. This is definitely a unique design. And you say they got rid of the ghosts effectively?"

"Very. That person couldn't have thrown more than a few cards, but they hit with as much force as an entire deck of mine. Their other cards must be just as powerful; they were faster and stronger than me and it didn't seem like they were even trying."

"Seems like you need to get back to your studies," Saber suggested with a grin.

"You're telling me. Also, there was something else… if there's time, can we look for a way to send a message to Sark? I… I want to see if Roshan is okay over there."

Saber's expression softened.

"That'll be hard to fit into our schedule when we're working day and night, but we can definitely try. Though you know we might be gone before we get a response. The police are sure to get word of us here eventually."

"That's true," Maaya sighed. "At the very least, we can let him know we're okay and that we're still going on with our mission. We don't have to give details about where we're going; he'll already know. Maybe it'll give him some comfort to know we're still—what?"

Saber had snapped her fingers suddenly, looking as though she'd had an epiphany.

"Sorry. I just thought of something. When we go out today, let's ask some of the ghosts about that pin of yours."

"Didn't Emil tell us specifically not to ask about it?" Maaya asked pointedly.

"Sure, but what are the dead going to do? Rat us out? The only people who can see and hear them are likely the people we're looking for anyway, so if they do decide to tell, all the better for us."

"Okay, we can try. You do the talking, if you don't mind. Someone's bound to notice me talking to thin air."

Saber waited patiently as Maaya got dressed and put on her shoes. Maaya double and triple checked to make sure she had the stranger's blood cards and her pin before starting for the door. Saber followed wordlessly as Maaya walked down the hall and to the lobby and as Maaya returned her room key. But as Maaya stepped determinedly out into the street in the direction of the docks, Saber gently tugged on her shoulder.

"What?"

"I admire your work ethic, but I'm willing to bet you didn't get a snack in during your escapades last night," Saber said. As if on cue, Maaya's stomach growled. Saber grinned. "Thought so. Let's grab some food."

. . .

An hour later, Maaya's appetite temporarily sated, they walked the streets of the city near the docks. Maaya had been able to convince Saber to spend up to an hour searching for a place that would let them send a message. She figured it wouldn't take long given how well organized the buildings were, not to mention an abundance of signs and advertising.

But as they walked slowly up and down each street in succession, she realized she had absolutely no idea what she was looking for. She had heard people vaguely talking about sending messages to others, but didn't know how they did it. She expected the city itself to have couriers, but none who would be willing to travel all the way to Sark, and she didn't own a mechanical bird. Even if she did, she doubted it would fly that far.

Finally, however, they stumbled across a large building that seemed to have what Maaya was looking for. A number of metal boxes sat outside into which passersby occasionally dropped envelopes and packages. Inside the building she saw a long counter with several people behind it handling letters and boxes. The roof of the building had several vertical slots, and as Maaya watched, dozens of mechanical birds flew in and out of it, moving in all directions.

"If anything has what you want, it'll be this place," Saber commented, looking quite impressed.

Maaya nodded, took a deep breath, then entered.

For a moment, it was difficult for Maaya to reconcile the sheer amount of activity in the building with how quiet it was. The people behind the counter stamped, shuffled, organized, and more at speeds that demonstrated years of experience all while talking calmly to customers. Behind the workers, several metal machines clanked clumsily as they moved large containers full of letters or sorted parcels by size. On the far-left wall stood a several shelves filled with mechanical birds of all different shapes and sizes. Maaya watched as a customer selected a bird, paid one of the workers, then quickly entered one of several small private stalls to record their message.

"Now what?" Maaya whispered.

"Get in the queue, and when you're called up, just say you'd like to send a message to someone in Sark and you'd like to know what your options are," Saber instructed.

Maaya stepped into the line, suddenly feeling very self-conscious, but no one so much as passed her a second glance. The line moved steadily, and Maaya was just starting to get comfortable when she realized she was missing something important.

"We're going to have to pay for this somehow!" she whispered urgently, but Saber sigh in mock exasperation.

"You don't have to panic over *everything*, you know. Find out how much it'll cost, then step to the side and pretend to be counting your money. In the meantime, I'll get what you need."

"If you're sure…"

No sooner had she spoken these words than the customer in front of her walked away from the counter and the smiling man behind it beckoned to her. Maaya walked up nervously.

"What can I help you with? Are you here to pick up?" the man asked cheerily.

"Oh, uhm, no, I'm actually hoping to send a message to someone I know in Sark. Is that possible?" she asked, and as she spoke she imagined the man laughing at her for such a ludicrous request. But he kept smiling.

"I can definitely do that for you. I'll just need some information. What's the recipient's name?"

"Roshan Kulkarni."

"Got it. And their address?"

Maaya froze. She knew vaguely where Roshan lived, but had no idea what his address was. She wasn't even sure she could name the street he lived on.

"I… uh…"

"If you're not sure, that's all right. What we can do is send the message to Sark's local office and they'll send out a letter saying he's got a message waiting for him. It'll take a little longer, but he'll still get it. Would that be all right?"

"Yes, of course!" Maaya replied, remembering to breathe. This wasn't so bad.

"Great. Now, how would you like this message sent?"

"What are my options?" Maaya asked.

"We've got a few. Let's see here… it does seem like Sark has a wireless telegraphy office, so if you want the fastest method possible, you can use that. It's a bit pricey, though," the man said, briefly looking Maaya up and down. "We do have some long-distance birds which are a little cheaper and take a little longer. Finally, we can send something via our quarterly courier. It's the cheapest, but it also takes the longest."

"And when would that arrive?" Maaya continued intently.

"Unfortunately, it'd be a few months. Our last quarterly went out only three weeks ago."

"Okay. How much would the telegraph and bird be? I need to think about it."

"Certainly, miss. The telegraph would be one hundred rial, and the bird would be sixty. When you've made your decision, just come back up to me here; you don't need to wait in line again."

Maaya thanked the man, then walked over to a row of benches near the wall of mechanical birds, her head spinning. One hundred rial was ridiculously expensive, and while sixty was nearly half that, it would still be a challenge for Saber to come up with without anyone noticing. Maaya had been able to rent her room the previous night for only twenty five, and the meal Adelaide had bought her had been only three or four.

"Well, we're not doing telegraphy, that's for sure," Saber said idly. "And we're certainly not going to wait for months. We'll be back by then. Looks like I need to get us sixty rial."

"Are you sure? That's so much money…" Maaya whispered.

"It is. Even I'm feeling a little guilty at the thought of it. I think we should bite the bullet and do it, though. Sixty rial is worth the price of letting one of your best friends know you're alive and safe, and that we're still going to save the world, right?"

Maaya nodded almost imperceptibly.

"It's better than a hundred, anyway… why do you think telegraphs are so expensive?"

"From what I understand it's still an emerging technology. The equipment is expensive to set up and operate, the lines need to be set up and maintained, and the longer the message is, the more work it takes. The price you pay for instant communication to almost anywhere, I suppose."

"How did you know that?" Maaya whispered, impressed.

Saber paused.

"That's a good question. Probably another fact from my past that's managed to slip through my amnesia. I certainly didn't spend any time studying it. Anyway, I'm going to go get your money before I lose my nerve."

Without hesitation, Saber disappeared through the windows and out into the streets.

While Saber was gone, Maaya tried to think about what she wanted to say to Roshan. Sure, she wanted to let him know she was safe and that she was about to depart for Krethus—she wasn't going to say she had no idea how yet—but how could she tell him that she was scared? That she missed the sound of his voice and his comforting optimism? That she was terrified she would never see him again?

She did her best to shake these thoughts from her head. There was no point worrying about that. She was going to deliver something short and concise. The rest could come later. She *would* see him again no matter what it took.

Only ten minutes later Maaya felt her coat pocket suddenly get heavier, accompanied by the quiet clink of coins.

"The bird's all yours," Saber said proudly.

Maaya stood up and walked back to the counter, placing the coins on top of it.

"I'd like a bird, please."

The man counted the coins, then smiled at her again. This somehow put her at ease. She had been expecting him to say something judgmental, to ask where she got the money, or to question its legitimacy, but he simply put the coins away in a drawer under the counter and motioned for her to meet him over by the wall of birds.

He came out from behind the counter and brought her attention to a small section on the right side. These birds were slightly larger than the others, the metal used to form their bodies thicker and sturdier. They appeared to be modeled after some kind of hawk or falcon, though Maaya didn't know enough about birds to tell.

"You can pick any one of these. Have you ever used one before?"

"Only to answer messages I already got," Maaya admitted, and the man seemed slightly relieved that he wouldn't have to start from scratch.

"All right. Just hold out your arm in front of one and wait until it climbs on, then take any of these stalls here to record your message. It's mostly the same process as sending a response. This model will hold up to half an hour of speech. When you're finished, bring it over to me so I can input the destination and you'll be good to go!"

"Thank you," Maaya said warmly, and the man departed.

She held out her arm to one of the birds on the lowest shelf, which came to life immediately, climbing delicately onto her arm. Once she was sure it was secure, she walked over to an empty stall and locked the door securely behind her. Saber followed, staring with great interest at the bird.

Maaya sighed. Now that it was time to speak, she felt silly. This was only a recording. This was nothing compared to seeing her friend in person. She wasn't even sure if he was alive. To spend so much money on an errand like this suddenly seemed incredibly stupid.

Saber interrupted her thoughts by putting a comforting hand on her shoulder as though she understood Maaya's hesitation.

"Don't overthink this. Just tell him what's going on, then we'll be out of here and we won't even have to think about it. Okay?"

Maaya gave her best attempt at a smile, then turned to the bird, tapping it twice on the head as she had before.

"Record," she said, and the bird's eyes lit up. "This message is for Roshan. It's Maaya. I don't know when you'll get this, if you get it at all, but I wanted to let you know that I'm okay. I can't say where I am or where I'm going in case someone else hears this, but Saber is here with me and we're still going to do the job we set out to do. Everything is going to be okay, I'll make sure of that."

Maaya paused, and the bird tilted its head expectantly. There was more she had to say, she knew that. This was her one chance to communicate anything until she returned, and so regardless of how it made her feel, she had to make use of it.

"I hope everything is okay over there," she continued slowly. "It feels like it's been so long and I have no way of knowing what's going on. I'm afraid, Roshan. I'm so afraid I'll come back after all this time and all this work and nothing will be there. I'm afraid I'll never see you or hear your voice again. I'm afraid of this mission, of being captured, of everyone I meet… I'm miserable, really." She laughed, wiping her eyes that were suddenly brimming with tears. "But we're going to be okay. Everything is going to be okay. I'm not going to stop until this is done no matter what I have to face. Be strong, okay? Keep Sark in one piece for me. You won't be able to answer this, but if you have anything to say, write it down so you can tell me in person. Because I'm coming back. I promise. I… I miss you. Stay safe. Message complete."

The lights in the bird's eyes flickered, then shut off. Maaya glanced at Saber, who gave her an encouraging smile, and then stood up to exit the stall.

The man behind the counter greeted her as she approached.

"All set?" he asked, and Maaya nodded. "Fantastic. I've already got all the details of the destination here, so you can just leave it with me and I'll see to it that it's sent by the end of the day. Thank you!"

Maaya thanked him in kind, and then before she knew it, she was standing back on the street outside the post office. She thought she might feel a sense of relief after being able to send a message to Roshan, but now her mind was plagued by all sorts of new doubts. She wondered if anyone left in Sark was still alive, and even if they were, if Roshan would get the message once it got there. Perhaps it would be intercepted, giving authorities a tip as to where she was before she'd gotten away. Maybe Roshan would try to meet her and they would miss each other. There were so many new possibilities fixable only by Maaya returning to Sark to investigate in person that she didn't feel much better at all.

Fortunately, Saber didn't let her languish in her doubt for long.

"Hey, let's get to talking to some ghosts, yeah?" she said somewhat impatiently.

"Right, yes, sorry. I was thinking we'd start in the neighborhood I was in last night. The person I saw was obviously familiar with it, so maybe the ghosts there will recognize this."

"Good idea," Saber affirmed, and they walked quickly toward the neighborhood at the base of the hill.

It took a little longer than the previous night, as they were forced to traverse the crowded streets rather than the rooftops. Once they arrived, it didn't take them long to find what they were looking for. Two ghosts, a man and a woman, stood close together, talking to each other in urgent hushed whispers as though worried anyone nearby might overhear. Their mix of outfits was a sight in itself; the woman wore elegant ruffled clothes that were at the height of fashion a few hundred years prior, while the man was dressed in a fine well-tailored suit of modern days. They hardly gave Saber a second glance as she approached, but once they caught on to the fact that Maaya could see them, they turned to face her, suddenly looking interested.

"You can see us!" the man exclaimed. He was old and short and had a slightly hunched back, and his well-pressed clothes were a sign that he was someone wealthy enough for a proper funeral.

"Yes. Are there not many here who can see ghosts?" Maaya murmured, pretending to dig in her pockets as a group of living people passed.

"Hardly any. I was beginning to think the rumors of the living who could see the dead were all lies," the man said. "But you've come at a most fortuitous time."

"Why? Has something happened?"

The ghosts glanced at each other.

"We were hoping you'd know. There's been strange things happening in Levien lately. We saw some new ghosts, some kind we've never seen before. They aren't natural. 'Course they disappeared as quickly as they came, but something's not right about them. But no one we talk to seems to have any idea what's going on."

"I do," Maaya whispered. The ghosts leaned in, watching her intently. "It's a long story. They don't cause any harm to anyone who's already dead, but if they touch anyone who's alive, they kill them. And they seem to be spreading. I'm here because they started coming to the town I live… the town I used to live in."

The ghosts shared frightened glances.

"It's okay, though. I know what's causing them to appear and I'm going to stop it," Maaya added quickly.

"How? I don't suppose you're the one patrolling the streets at night, are you?" the woman asked.

"No, but I have the same powers they do. Just… not quite as strong," Maaya admitted, feeling a little embarrassed. "But I know where I have to go to put an end to this. Actually, speaking of that, I was wondering if you could help me…" She reached into her coat pocket, glanced around to make sure no one was looking, then held out the pin for the ghosts to see. "An acquaintance gave me this, and I'm trying to find any others who might know this sign. The person you mentioned also had one, but they ran off before I—"

She broke off as the ghosts looked down at the pin in alarm. The woman even took a step back.

"What? What's wrong?" Maaya asked.

"Oh, dear child. Who gave you that?" she asked fearfully. "Put that away now before someone sees."

"What is it?" Maaya repeated urgently.

"That's the symbol of the Blackfins. Do you really not know?" the man asked incredulously.

"I was told its name but I don't know anything else about them. What's wrong with it?" Maaya asked, feeling suddenly self-conscious.

"It's a good thing you decided to ask us rather than anyone else. You'd probably get arrested on sight for carrying that."

"Why? What are the Blackfins?" Maaya pressed.

"From what I understand they started out as a simple band of pirates, thus the 'fins' part of their name. They've been in business for a few hundred years, and since then they've become an entire criminal empire. They're still in the sea business, of course, but they do all sorts of other things, too. I wouldn't exactly call them mercenaries or hitmen, but they're about as close as you can get."

Maaya gaped.

"Why would Emil give me something like this? That's horrifying!" she breathed.

"This acquaintance of ours gave her this pin and said it would help her," Saber explained to the inquisitive ghosts. "He said we would be among friends if we found others who knew the symbol."

"He couldn't have meant for us to get involved with a group like that, could he?" Maaya asked.

"Hang on there, let me see that pin a little closer," the man continued, adjusting his spectacles. Maaya held out the pin for him to see, and after a moment, he nodded. "Ah, yes. This makes slightly more sense. This isn't an insignia of membership; it's one of obligation." At Maaya's blank stare, he continued, "This isn't what you own as part of the organization. It's what you use when you need to call in a favor."

"Which invariably leads to membership in most cases," the woman sniffed. "You don't just get a free favor from the Blackfins and then go on your merry way!"

"Maybe that's what Emil wanted," Maaya said slowly. "He wants us to find the Blackfins and ask them to take us to Krethus as a favor."

At this, the ghosts looked even more shocked than before.

"You're going where now? Are you mad, child?" the woman cried.

"That's where I have to go to stop these ghosts. They're everywhere over there and spreading fast. If I don't take care of them at the source they'll overrun Selenthia."

She wasn't sure if this argument made her appear any less mad, but the ghosts seemed satisfied and didn't press the issue further, for which Maaya was grateful. She was having a hard enough time convincing herself of all the details.

"Anyway, where can I find the... you know, these people?" Maaya continued quietly. "It's quite urgent."

"Now that I don't have an answer to," the man answered, shaking his head. "They don't exactly go around wearing name tags, and I don't know any personally. They could be anyone, and they could be everywhere or nowhere. Mostly you keep your ear to the ground, and if you listen long enough you'll pick up a clue. They leave enough of them out there to find."

"Great," Saber said sarcastically. "I guess we'll just have to go wandering around the city for hours every day hoping that eventually—"

Suddenly, a third ghost ran into view through a nearby building, looking quite excited. He dashed over to the group of ghosts, and without so much as a hello, pointed vaguely in the direction of the city's main gates.

"You'll want to see this!" he announced. "A big military force just entered the city. They're apparently looking for someone, some wanted criminal, and they think she's here!"

"Oh, how exciting! It's been a while since we've been able to witness something like that," the woman said as they all perked up.

Maaya and Saber looked at each other in a panic. They were out of time.

"If you have any ideas, now's the time," Saber urged.

"I... I don't... let's go to the docks," Maaya suggested helplessly. The other ghosts seemed too engaged in their gossip to notice their sudden change in demeanor.

"We should get out of the city, not get ourselves locked between the ocean and the police," Saber argued.

"We can't keep running. We'll have a better chance of staying ahead of the police if we take a ship, and if we want to do that, we—"

"If we do that there's a chance we'll end up somewhere even farther away from Krethus, and we don't even know what ships we need to look for!" Saber protested.

"One thing at a time. For now, we have to get out of here. Come on!"

Saber relented and flew swiftly after Maaya as she ran down the inclined street toward the docks. She saw nothing out of the ordinary, but she assumed it wouldn't be long. The police probably wouldn't charge the streets to look for her, not in a city this big. Rather, they would probably start by blocking all the exits and trapping her inside. If Maaya could only make it to a ship...

She stopped running as she reached the floating docks, then scanned the ships frantically, hoping for an opportunity to jump out at her. She thought for a moment of trying to sneak aboard, but the security was simply too tight. Besides, she thought, based on how the ghosts had just reacted to the mere insignia of a law-breaking organization, she doubted captured stowaways would be treated with much respect—especially if they fit the description of a wanted criminal.

"Now what?" Saber asked quickly.

"Look for a ship we can get on. Any ship, it doesn't matter, we just—"

Suddenly Saber grabbed Maaya and pulled her roughly behind a stack of boxes. Before Maaya could speak, Saber put her hand tightly over Maaya's mouth.

"Keep quiet and still. Look," Saber muttered.

Maaya felt a wave of dread pass over her. A few officers walked slowly down the dock and, to her horror, were placing posters with her own face on it on signposts and bulletin boards. After a few moments passed they turned out of eyesight and earshot, but Maaya remained where she was.

"How did they get here so quickly? Was it the message for Roshan?" Maaya whispered, her voice shaking.

"Doubt it. It's not even supposed to go out until tonight. And even if the man we gave it to listened to your message, there's no way he would have been able to contact the police in that time. No, they were already on their way here."

"We can still find a ship somehow, we just need..."

"Oh, stars," Saber gasped. "I think they're closing the harbor."

"What?!"

"A few of the officers, they're talking to the harbormaster, and he doesn't look pleased. They've got a document. Looks like the ghost was right. They don't just have the police after us; they have the Selenthian military now," Saber breathed.

"Don't panic. We'll figure something out," Maaya said, even as her voice shook with nerves.

They both quieted as they heard the clomp of boots directly on the other side of the boxes they hid behind. Maaya didn't even breathe. She felt for her card pouch in desperation, ready to do anything necessary to escape. It couldn't end like this.

"Now see, I told you something like this would happen," drawled a casual voice, sounding thoroughly unconcerned with the sudden military presence. "Everyone wants to relax, but like I keep saying, you never know when the bronzies will show up."

"This doesn't suddenly make you right, you know," another voice replied quietly. "They aren't coming for the Blackfins, so it's neither here nor there."

Maaya perked up at the mention of the name, and even dared to lift her head slightly to hear better.

"It is, though. They're going to prevent any ships from leaving, just you watch. And when they do, they're going to search the ships. Every ship. That means ours, too. Now, we've prepared for this eventuality as always, but they look pretty serious. Deck-by-deck-search serious, if you get me."

"Wonderful. Guess that means we'll have to leave ahead of schedule if we want to beat the news."

"Have we got everyone?"

"I think our commander's still out grabbing pastries for our sendoff lunch. But I feel like the crew wouldn't be too broken up if we were to accidentally leave him behind."

"I thought you were too much a man of protocol to go talking like that," the first man laughed.

"I'm only suggesting a possibility," the second man said lightly.

"Once we get back he'll have all our heads."

"I'd deal with that just to see the look on his face," the second agreed, and they both snickered.

"Anyway, let's inform the rest of the crew. We're all going to have to pretend to be law-abiding sailors again."

The sounds of their heavy boots started to depart. Maaya tensed. The police were closing in, the harbor was closing, and she was still in need of a boat. If she waited even a few minutes, all could be lost.

"Maaya, you can't possibly be thinking—" Saber started, but broke off in alarm as Maaya suddenly stood.

"Remember? It's a time to be bold," Maaya murmured. She hoped she looked bold, because her nerves were about broken.

Fighting the urge to throw up or panic, she jogged after the two men, catching up to them just before they reached the ramp up to their ship. They both wore the coats and collar pins of officers, and high-ranking ones as well. One of the men wore an ocular implant, and for a moment Maaya worried he might be able to see Saber, but he had eyes only for Maaya as she approached. They both turned to face her inquisitively, and she realized it was now or never. She reached into her pocket, pulled out the pin Emil had given her, and showed it to them.

"I need to get to Krethus," she said firmly, staring intently at them. The two men looked at her in shock, then at each other, and then back at her. For a split second she was afraid she had just showed her pin to the wrong people, that she was only mere seconds away from being taken into custody—but then they seemed to relax.

"Well, this hasn't happened in a while. What do you think, Gunnar?" said one of the men, turning to his partner with the implant.

"A pin's a pin, Halvar. A nice one, too. Should be a done deal as far as

I'm concerned," Gunnar said, and she recognized his voice as the second man who had spoken.

"Hold on now, look at that," Halvar exclaimed, pointing to a place right behind where Maaya stood.

Maaya turned around, and once she realized what he was pointing at, she thought she might faint from dread. There, immediately behind her on a post, was one of the wanted posters, her face printed on it as clear as day. For a minute that seemed to last an hour, all three of them stared at the poster, and Maaya was painfully aware of how accurate this print was. They would know it was her beyond a doubt.

Then Halvar broke the silence.

"Ha! I love it," he chuckled. "No wonder you want out. But you're cutting it a little close, don't you think?"

"I… I didn't—"

"No worries, friend. Here, put that away and come along. We need to get you some kind of disguise. Hey Gunnar, think we've got any coats for someone this tiny?"

"Doubt it. Maybe someone can ask David to bring back a kid's uniform."

Maaya opened her mouth, but no sound came out. Were they really accepting this so easily? And were they *really* poking fun at her height in this situation?

"We'll figure something out," Halvar said. "Worse comes to worst, kid, you're the cap'n's niece. Or sister. Or something. We'll make it up as we go."

Before she knew it, Maaya and Saber were on the deck of the ship. It was a beautiful craft. It stood about three hundred feet from bow to stern and fifty feet amidships. It had three tall masts with traditional square and angular sails with too many ropes between them all for Maaya to count. When she took a quick peek over the side of the ship, she noticed a whole row of what looked to be fin-like oars near the waterline folded neatly against the hull and connected to a long copper pipe that ran just above them. What purpose they served, Maaya couldn't guess.

The hull itself was made of redwood and dull orange metal, and a set of double stairs rose up the quarter deck leading to what Maaya assumed was the captain's cabin. There was another set of doors level with the main deck, and two more before the stairs of the forecastle.

"Come on now, you can see the sights all you like after we're safely out of here," Gunnar chided gently, and he led her to the set of double doors toward the stern.

As they walked in, Maaya noticed a man and a woman dressed similarly to Gunnar and Halvar, wearing identical coats and collar pins of silver and bronze. Maaya realized she must be in the officers' quarters, and try as she might to avert her eyes, she couldn't help but stare.

"We got any spare coats that might fit this one?" Gunnar asked them as he gestured to Maaya, who suddenly felt very small under the gaze of so many officers.

"I might. I'll check my stores," said the woman. She was tall and imposing, with auburn hair in a severe bun and steely grey eyes. "Who's this again?"

"No idea, but she's got a goldpin and needs to get to Krethus."

"I see. It's been a while since we've had that kind of excitement. She looks uninitiated."

"I know! My favorite kind of person," Halvar grinned, and the woman walked off through a nearby door. "Hey kid, give me that pin, yeah? I need to let the captain know you're here."

"Will the captain be angry?" Maaya asked quietly, and the other officers laughed.

"Not for a goldpin, absolutely not. Also, fellas, they're closing the harbor, so we need to get out of here on the double."

The remaining officer, a broad-shouldered man with unruly white hair, hastily set down his drink as he coughed.

"Were you just going to save that for last, Halvar?" he said irritably, wiping his mouth on his sleeve.

"Nope! What I'm saving for last is that our dear commander probably won't make it back in time."

The two men paused as they stared at each other, then burst into laughter. The white-haired officer patted Halvar on the shoulder as he walked out toward the main deck, still chuckling.

"You're a good man, Halvar."

"All right, stay here," Halvar told Maaya. "Inga will get you properly dressed while I let the captain know what's going on, and then we'll be out of here."

He gave her an exaggerated sweeping bow, then departed. Gunnar followed closely after him.

Maaya had so many questions she wasn't sure where she would start even if she could speak. She felt some relief now that she was successfully on board a ship with people who appeared to want to help her, but that relief was replaced with further fear. She was on a ship full of Blackfins, and while they seemed friendly for now, she wasn't sure if that would change during a long trip overseas.

"You, my dear, are absolutely mad," Saber said quietly, though she was grinning widely.

"What?"

"You just marched up to a pair of uniformed officers, waved your Blackfins pin in their faces, and demanded passage to Krethus, all while standing directly in front of a wanted poster with your face on it. That is probably the bravest and also the stupidest thing you have ever done."

"I didn't have a choice! I was terrified," Maaya protested, but Saber waved her hand dismissively.

"Hey, being brave doesn't mean not being afraid. Besides, think back to Maaya a few months ago. Even under dire stress, do you think she'd ever do something like that?"

Maaya paused. Saber was right. While Maaya had always taken on more stress than she probably should in order to keep herself and her friends safe, she couldn't fathom being put in a position like this in the past. Granted, the circumstances were entirely different then, but she had a feeling she would have simply taken Saber's suggestion to flee the city and hide somewhere rather than attempt a daring escape on a ship full of strangers.

The last officer, Inga, walked back out a moment later holding a coat much smaller than the one she was wearing. She walked over and held it up to Maaya, staring the girl up and down, and then handed the coat to her. In her other hand she held a black cap, which she also gave to Maaya.

"Put these on. Put your hair in a bun and put it under the cap. We'll have to find you more suitable shoes eventually, but for now we'll just have to hope the police aren't paying close attention. Oh, and be very careful with that coat. It belongs to my daughter, so if it gets damaged at all…"

"I-I'll take care of it," Maaya stammered. Inga seemed pleasant enough, but also not someone she wanted to irritate.

"Have you ever been sailing before?" Inga asked. Maaya shook her head nervously, but Inga didn't seem bothered. "I figured. Note the lack of collar pins on your coat. This is what you wear when you're the guest of an officer on board. You have no rank. If it becomes necessary you will be a relative of mine. I will speak and you will be too unwell to answer questions. In case you need to demonstrate any knowledge whatsoever, the only ranks you need to know are as follows. Gold pins for the captain, silver for commanders and lieutenant commanders, and bronze for lieutenants. Commanders have three pins; lieutenant commanders have two. Have you got all that?"

"Yes," Maaya affirmed quickly. Inga, evidently, was a lieutenant commander, and Gunnar and Halvar were lieutenants.

"Good. Now hurry up and get dressed. I need to make sure the crew is ready for departure and possible inspection. Oh, and… I assume this is your first time with the Blackfins, yes?" Maaya nodded meekly. "Ignore anything you may have heard and make your own judgment. You're safe with us. What happens from here is up to you."

Without another word she swept from the small cabin, letting the doors close softly behind her. She heard loud voices calling to each other from outside, though she couldn't make out what they were saying.

"What do you think she meant?" Maaya asked, puzzled. "That sounded awfully friendly for someone who's a part of a big criminal organization."

"It's not uncommon for rumors to surpass truth, but you're right. That's suspiciously friendly. I can only assume it has to do with this goldpin of yours they keep mentioning."

"I don't remember Emil and the others calling it that. What do you think it means?" Maaya continued as she struggled to button the coat.

"I'm not sure, but remember how that man mentioned how the pin was for calling in a favor? I'm assuming the pins are like rewards, and that you get more important ones for more important services. A goldpin sounds like it means something pretty significant."

"What if they find out I'm not the one who earned it?" Maaya asked.

"I don't think they will, if only because their policy on asking questions seems to align pretty well with ours," Saber answered nonchalantly, helping Maaya put up her long hair. "It shouldn't matter anyway. Seems to me if you earn a favor like that you can give it to whoever you please. It'd be your loss. Anyway, I'll go put your old coat in Inga's quarters for safekeeping."

No sooner was Maaya dressed than Halvar jogged back into the cabin, gesturing to Maaya.

"We've been given permission to leave on the condition that we let the police check out every person on board. Unfortunately, that includes you. Come on out and stand by Inga; she'll talk for you."

"Yeah, we covered that," Maaya replied, and Halvar grinned.

"Of course you did. I'm guessing she went straight to giving directions rather than, you know, saying hello."

"Basically."

Halvar laughed and led the way out to the deck. For a moment she felt somewhat at ease. Halvar's easygoing attitude in the face of this danger helped her feel more confident.

And then she saw the soldiers, and it was all she could do not to run and hide.

It was easy to see why the crew called them "bronzies." Their uniforms were all black but for the bronze insignias on both their jackets and hats. Each also had an eye patch that looked something like an ocular implant; they too were bronze, fastened by a black leather strap that wrapped around their heads. Maaya felt intimidated under their gaze. It felt like they were staring right through her. But then she felt a faint glimmer of hope as she noticed two of them look straight at her, then glance somewhere else.

"Oh, good. They don't recognize you," Saber said quietly, taking her place at Maaya's side. "We'll get through this okay. Just remember not to open your mouth."

The ship's crew was lined up on deck, staring straight forward with military discipline. Maaya quickly found Inga and stood next to her, fighting the urge to lower her gaze. If she was a relative of this important officer, she had to look the part.

"And this is everyone?" one soldier inquired. "You seem to be missing a commander."

"You see, sir, that's because our first officer's an idiot and is currently distracted buying food," Halvar explained, and Maaya heard snickers from the crew. "We'd wait for him but we have no way to tell him to hurry up, and we need to get moving."

"What's the rush?" the soldier continued suspiciously. He was tall, with neatly trimmed raven-black hair and a thin mustache.

"Two things, mostly. First, we had a last-minute change of schedule; turns out at least a few customers want their cargo ahead of the projected delivery date and they're paying handsomely for it. The second reason is we just don't like our commander and this is our chance to get rid of him."

This time Maaya heard open laughter on the deck, but the soldier didn't so much as twitch.

"Funny," he growled, then turned to look at one of his men who was coming up from below. "Is that everyone?"

"That's everyone. Rest of the ship is clear," the man affirmed.

For a moment Maaya thought they were safe, but then the soldier with the mustache turned and looked directly at her. She was so surprised that she couldn't even look away, which she belated realized probably worked in her favor. They stared at each other for a few full seconds, and then the soldier glanced at Inga.

"Who's this?"

"This is my niece. She's wanted to go on a long voyage for some time now, and since she cannot stay at home at the moment, this was the perfect opportunity."

"I see. Unfortunately, this is a dangerous time to be traveling; there's a criminal on the loose, one we suspect is here in Levien. Anyone who isn't officially part of the crew will need to remain behind until we find them."

Maaya's heart pounded in her chest. Not now, not when they were so close.

"That won't be possible. Her parents are away and I was instructed to take charge of her. She's been unwell as of late, so to leave her home alone could bring trouble. There is no one else available to watch her."

"I… see. I will see if we can make an exception. Is she on the manifest?"

"Not yet. This was last minute. It will be a brief addendum."

In the midst of her fear, Maaya took a moment to admire how Inga seemed absolutely unintimidated by the soldier in front of her. She stared at him, expressionless, until finally he looked away.

"Fine. What's your name?" he asked, turning again to Maaya.

Maaya, caught completely off guard, said the first name that popped into her head.

"Adelaide," she blurted. A few of the officers and crew looked at her in slight surprise, but Maaya was too anxious to pay them any mind.

"No, *your* name," the soldier clarified irritably.

"I... er, my name is Kim," Maaya answered, her cheeks burning.

"Like I said, feeling unwell," Inga said, looking completely unperturbed. "She's supposed to be resting. If you'd be so kind as to hurry this up, she can get back to it."

The soldier glared at her, but said nothing, instead turning on his heels and walking away. He gestured impatiently at his men, who started to leave the ship.

Maaya let out a quiet sigh of relief. They hadn't recognized her, and even her momentary blunder hadn't made her look suspicious. Watching the soldiers depart, she suddenly felt weak. She was going to make it. She was actually going to make it.

Inga patted Maaya strongly on the shoulder, then turned to the others.

"Inspection's over, ladies and gentlemen. Finish getting the ship ready for departure. I'd like us out of berth in ten minutes."

The deck was immediately full of activity as the crew and officers returned to their stations, securing the last bit of cargo, sweeping the deck, and double checking every line and sail.

After a brief period of silence, Inga glanced down at Maaya, an amused expression on her face.

"Where did you come up with the name 'Adelaide'?" she asked wryly.

"She was someone I met yesterday," Maaya explained hastily. "We didn't see each other for long, but when that man asked me my name I just... my mind blanked and I just chose the first name I could think of."

Inga chortled.

"Cute. Now, I'll remember the name Kim for if it becomes necessary, but since I assume we won't meet anyone else of any importance until we reach Krethus, might I have the pleasure of knowing your real name?"

Maaya hesitated uncertainly, but Saber nodded encouragingly at her side.

"I'm Maaya. Maaya Sahni," she said.

"A pleasure. I'm Lieutenant Commander Inga Strand, though I suppose in the absence of our unfortunate first officer, his rank will fall to me."

"Commander Strand, then?" Maaya asked, and Inga nodded approvingly.

"Good, you remembered. Now, because you aren't of rank, you aren't technically required to refer to anyone by theirs, but it's good ship etiquette.

It's also not my ship, so I would just do that unless the captain tells you otherwise."

"Okay," Maaya agreed. "So… what should I do now? Is there anything I can help with?"

Inga raised her eyebrows slightly in surprise.

"I appreciate the offer, but with as little as I assume you know about sailing, you would probably get in the way. No offense. If you'd like, we can find some odd jobs for you, but you're traveling as a favor and a hefty one at that. You aren't required to work."

"I suppose. Actually, I was wondering—"

"Well, this is a surprise!" interrupted a voice from behind them. Maaya's eyes widened as she realized she recognized it. "I know I said I hoped to see you soon, but I wasn't expecting you to appear on my ship the very next day."

Maaya whirled around. There, walking down the stairs from the captain's cabin, dressed in her long black coat with golden collar pins, her long red hair blowing freely behind her in the breeze… was Adelaide.

She walked over to Maaya, who was too dumbstruck to move or say a word. Adelaide laughed, then held out her hand.

"So, my new friend has a favor from the Blackfins! You are just full of surprises, Maaya. We'll have to catch up, but in the meantime… welcome aboard."

21

SECRETS OF THE LSV WINDFIRE

Maaya stared, fully aware that her jaw had dropped in surprise. She had so many questions, so many things she wanted to say, that all her thoughts became tangled and messy in her mind. Left with only one option, she held out her hand hesitantly, nearly jumping in shock as Adelaide took it firmly and shook it.

"I know Inga said you were ill, but I assumed that was just a cover story. Are you all right?" Adelaide snickered.

Maaya wasn't sure. Finding her way onto a ship bound for Krethus with the assistance of a mysterious and possibly dangerous group of people she hardly knew anything about was almost too much to process, but to find out that *she* was the captain only increased her confusion. That meant Adelaide was bound for Krethus as well, and that she played a major role within Blackfins—whatever they were.

"Well, say something already!" Saber urged, and she seemed torn between amusement at the expression on Maaya's face and her own concerns over what they had just discovered. "Say you're fine and that this is just unexpected."

Maaya repeated these words to Adelaide, and the captain smiled.

"The feeling is mutual. Give me a moment to set course and make sure we're well on our way and then you and I can talk. We both have some explaining to do, it seems."

"Don't worry, ma'am; we can take care of steering our own ship out of port," Gunnar said.

"Yeah! Let Commander Strand do it, she's got her shiny new rank and everything, she must want to put it to good use," Halvar agreed.

Adelaide looked Inga up and down, her own cheerful demeanor contrasting mightily with Inga's impervious expression. Inga was noticeably taller than the captain and appeared to be roughly a decade older. She had broad shoulders and muscular arms that were evident even beneath her officer's coat.

"You know, just because our commander got left behind due to his own ineptitude, that doesn't mean you all get to shuffle your ranks without my approval," Adelaide said in what Maaya assumed was supposed to be a strict tone, though her expression was anything but.

"We just thought we'd save you some time, is all," Halvar explained casually. "We take care of all the boring rank stuff, maybe fight over who gets the best pips, and you just keep giving us orders. You're the captain! Easy job, you know."

"All the more difficult when I have to babysit you children," Adelaide shot back with a grin, then waved vaguely at the open ocean. "Fine, fine. Commander Strand, take us out and head in that general direction. Please try not to hit anything unless it's wearing a bronze hat. I'll be in your quarters with our new guest."

Inga bowed slightly and then swept off toward the bridge, already delivering orders. Maaya expected the sails to fall, but instead she heard a burst of pressurized air and saw a cloud of steam emanate from near the rear of the ship. The sails hadn't moved, but the ship started slowly forward nonetheless. Commander Strand stood at the helm, guiding the ship with great precision through the boats and docks that surrounded them on both sides.

Adelaide gestured for Maaya to follow her and walked to one side of the ship, pointing down at the water below. Maaya peered over the railing, and her eyes widened. The fins near the water line, which had been motionless when she made her way on board, were now moving. Each rotated smoothly in its socket, pushing against the water to move the ship forward. Rather than moving all at the same time, each fin was slightly delayed in its movement than the one ahead of it; Maaya thought of the way a centipede walked—only this didn't scare her like centipedes did. The horizontal pipe just above the row of fins rattled slightly with each rotation, and Maaya guessed it provided the air pressure needed to keep everything moving.

"Cool, isn't it?" Adelaide said proudly. "This system is a recent addition. Ours is the first ship to get it!"

"Did you special order this one, too?" Maaya teased, and Adelaide nodded eagerly.

"Actually, yes! When you travel farther out than most other ships you find out you need certain tools to tackle some more unique challenges. Like when we're shipping cargo to Malenia, an island sat right in the middle… oh, hold on. That's my 'I'm an innocent merchant' speech."

Maaya smiled, but she suddenly felt uncomfortable. Apparently her discomfort was evident in her expression, because Adelaide immediately shrugged apologetically, then beckoned toward the door leading back to the officers' quarters.

"Here, come with me. We'll talk in private."

The captain led the way through the double doors and into the room Maaya had watched Inga disappear into before they departed. It was lightly furnished with only a small writing desk, a chest of drawers, and a bunk bed. Bright sunlight filtered in through the room's only window, and Maaya spotted two lanterns sitting on the writing desk that would be more than adequate for lighting the room at night.

Saber floated in after them, and she did not seem impressed.

"If I'm right, this room has one piece of furniture for every time Inga Strand has smiled in her life," the ghost said. Maaya snorted before she could stop herself, quickly turning it into a cough as Adelaide glanced at her concernedly.

"As you may have guessed, this is Commander Strand's quarters, but you'll probably have it mostly to yourself. She's never been one to take advantage of the comforts of her rank," Adelaide explained, sitting comfortably on the bottom bed.

"Wait, you want me to sleep in Inga's room?" Maaya asked in surprise.

"Sure! I'd give you your own quarters, but this ship isn't quite big enough for that. Even our previous commander had to share his quarters with one of the lieutenants. But Inga prefers sleeping… oh, wherever she happens to be when she's tired. Most often it's in the crew quarters. She's a social one, our new commander."

"Really? Her?"

"Well, not social in that she has a lot to say, but in that she enjoys being around people. Which, I must say, is a necessary trait when cooped up on a ship this size for weeks at a time. But I digress. This room is yours, and hey! It even has a bunk for if you want to invite a friend over!"

Maaya laughed, and for a moment she almost forgot the situation she was in. But then her mind drifted back to the way Adelaide had so easily introduced herself as part of the Blackfins, and her discomfort returned.

"So… what's going on here?" Maaya ventured tentatively. "Who are the Blackfins? And why are you one of them?"

"You sound disappointed," Adelaide replied with a guilty smile. "Listen, the Blackfins aren't all they're made out to be. I mean, they used to be, from what I've heard, but it's complicated. They're so old as an organization and have spread so far that every group you meet will be different. Some are very heavy into the organized crime while others simply find a sense of community with a little sprinkle of illegal activity on the side. Traditionally there's also been some other *interesting* requirements for membership, but it's not strict. Not anymore."

"Requirements like what?" Maaya asked suspiciously.

"There used to be a supernatural element to the whole thing. How that and crime go together I have no idea, but needless to say that isn't a universal requirement anymore," Adelaide continued, and then stared at Maaya almost pleadingly. "Listen, Maaya… I don't know what you've heard, if you've heard anything at all, but I don't want you to think poorly of me. Or anyone else here, for that matter. We use cargo delivery as a front, but it's a front for travel, nothing more."

"Wait… you got involved with the Blackfins so you could travel?" Maaya asked skeptically.

"I know. It sounds silly, right? But you know how it is. People can't go anywhere these days, not outside their own country, and it's frustrating. It's a big world out there and sometimes… well, sometimes where you grow up doesn't feel like home, so you need to find a home for yourself. Does that make sense?"

"More than you know," Maaya replied quietly. "So… you're not pirates or anything?"

Adelaide burst into laughter.

"Not like the kind you're familiar with, I'm sure, but it's a title we've adopted easily enough. We've all earned our positions and keep fair and square. I'm pretty sure the only thing any of our crew has ever stolen has been a few pastries; when we get back to Levien, I'll treat you to some and you'll understand why." Adelaide winked, and then her expression became serious. "But there's a little more. I hesitate to tell you this because I don't know how you feel about people like me, but… I'm from Krethus. Born and raised. That's one of the reasons we're going now. I haven't seen my family in a while and I… well, recent events have necessitated I go back."

"Right, all of the gho—" Maaya broke off as Saber elbowed her hard in the arm. "The war, right?" she corrected hastily.

"That's one aspect of it, I suppose," Adelaide said with obvious relief. "So… you're not upset?"

"Of course not. I want to go there too, don't I? I'd be some idiot trying so hard to travel to a place full of people I didn't like. But now you mention it… I don't suppose you knew a man named Svante, did you?"

"Svante, Svante… what's their last name? That's pretty common where I —oh! You knew another Krethan, did you?" Adelaide asked excitedly.

"I did. It's a long story," Maaya answered. "I don't know his last name, though. But he was going to help me get to Krethus, and said he had a contact in Levien who could get us there. I wondered if that might be you."

"I wish I could say I was. But how fortuitous we met, then! I'm even happier to be of assistance."

"Speaking of… what's a goldpin? And what does it mean?" Maaya continued.

"Oh, you really are new to all this, aren't you? It's cute," Adelaide grinned. "It used to be that if you weren't in the Blackfins but did special favors for them you'd get something in return so you could call in a favor later. A goldpin, well, whoever earned that probably did so by doing something very meaningful or helpful, like saving a high-ranking Blackfin's life, assisting them in something incredibly illegal, or providing them with lots of funding. Big stuff."

"I see…" Maaya said. She felt slightly dirty for having carried the pin earned by someone who had potentially committed some terrible crime.

"On that note, I think it's my turn to ask some questions. Where did you get this pin?" Adelaide asked intently.

"I… er… a friend named Emil gave it to me for helping him out. I did him a big favor. Nothing illegal, of course," Maaya added hastily. Adelaide's eyes widened slightly.

"Emil? I don't suppose you mean *the* Emil from Anathor?"

"Anorath?"

"That's the one. I haven't been there for at least ten years so I get it mixed up with its twin city sometimes. Really, who names two cities so similarly? Anyway, how is he?"

"He's… fine!" Maaya replied, hoping she sounded convincing.

"Apart from being dead and everything," Saber added.

"That's good. I've really meant to get back to Anorath someday. What did you do for him? It must have been pretty big to get him to give this up for you," Adelaide continued.

Maaya struggled to think of a good excuse, but came up blank. There was only so much storytelling she could do at once. Luckily, as she so often did, Saber came to the rescue.

"Emil's an intelligence broker, so you helped him get ahold of some very valuable information concerning why people were disappearing in, and fleeing from, Anorath. You discovered there was something serious going on and gave him what he needed to deal with it," Saber suggested.

Maaya passed this along, and Adelaide only looked more intrigued.

"Oh, now *that's* interesting. What's the secret?"

"You aren't allowed to say," Saber continued shortly.

When Maaya relayed this message, Adelaide appeared disappointed, but not upset.

"I'm not surprised, but it was worth a shot. So this explains how you got your pin and where you came from, but not why you're traveling to Krethus. What business does a good Selenthian girl like you have there?"

"It's kind of… personal," Maaya said before Saber could jump in. "But that man, Svante… we became friends, and one night when we were talking he told me all about his family. He seemed so ready to get back to see them. Unfortunately, he… he isn't alive anymore. But that's why I want to go. I want to find them and tell them what happened."

Maaya hadn't thought about it before, but as she spoke she thought of Svante and how happy he had been when talking about his family, and she knew suddenly that this was something she needed to do. She felt a wave of grief wash over her as she remembered their conversation on the roof. He had been a strange man, but a genuine one, one she was happy to have called her friend even for a very short time.

"I… oh, stars. I'm sorry, Maaya. I didn't mean to make you get into that. Really, I—"

"Don't worry about it," Maaya replied quickly, forcing a smile. "It's only right I tell you my business when I'm on your ship. Besides, I feel like I can trust you."

Adelaide seemed heartened at these worse.

"I'm glad. And hey, if you've got personal business, so long as it doesn't end up harming the ship and crew, that's all yours. We've all got our secrets."

"That may be an understatement," Saber offered.

"That's true. But too many secrets don't make for great friendships. Maybe… maybe someday I can share more of mine with you," Maaya said, and even as she finished her sentence she was aware of just how silly she sounded. Saber made a gagging noise from her side.

"That'd be great! I always like making new friends, especially close ones. They're rare finds. I feel like that could be you and me someday. We just need to make sure we have a little more in common. I, for example, don't fall over when a small wave hits, and that's something I like to share with anyone I'm in a relationship with."

Maaya spluttered in protest, and Adelaide laughed. Behind her faux outrage, however, Maaya's heart had skipped a beat at the captain's choice of the word "relationship."

"Now for the most important question, and I say this with some measure of seriousness," Adelaide continued, crossing her legs and staring intently at Maaya. "Gunnar told me there are wanted posters with your face on them all over the city. In fact, I think it's safe to say you're the reason we barely got out before the soldiers shut down the harbor. I may be part of the Blackfins, but it doesn't seem like your history is entirely clean, either. What's your story?"

Maaya's gaze fell to the floor. She was hoping she wouldn't have to talk about this, but it was a completely fair question, and Adelaide had been open with her. After a moment, she realized that what she was feeling was not fear of getting in trouble—it was of Adelaide being disappointed in her. Or worse, outright disliking her.

"I told you I came from Sark and that I was traveling alone, right?" Maaya said. Adelaide nodded politely. "The reason I left is because something horrible happened there. People started disappearing and a powerful man there blamed it on me. He turned the town against me, so I had to run. That's… how Svante died. He was trying to help me, and they killed him."

Adelaide's eyes widened in shock.

"Why would he try to blame you? Did you know him before he betrayed you?"

"I used to work for him, sort of," Maaya answered, the old bitterness already returning to her voice. "I was as poor then as I am now, and he offered food in exchange for doing some odd jobs for him. He always made it clear that I was disposable, and making me his scapegoat was apparently worth it for him."

"So… you didn't do what they're blaming you for," Adelaide stated matter-of-factly.

"I didn't, no," Maaya said, hoping with everything she had that the captain would believe her. "I didn't always do the most legal of jobs when I worked for him, but I never hurt anyone. I had to put food on the table so my friends and I weren't put out on the streets and starving to death. That's all I ever tried to do."

Adelaide shook her head in disbelief.

"Well, I'm glad you managed to escape. We'll make this a quick trip so you can get back to your friends soon, yeah?"

Maaya felt a lump in her throat. If the previous subject had been uncomfortable, this was downright unbearable.

Luckily, Adelaide seemed to understand.

"Oh, no… oh, I'm so sorry. It was that man's fault, wasn't it?" she asked. Maaya nodded, and anger flashed briefly in Adelaide's eyes. "I see. And his name?"

"Rahu. Everyone loves and trusts him, so they believed him immediately."

"Rahu. I'll remember. I'll have more questions about him later, I'm sure, but if I'm ever back out in that direction I may need to stop by to meet him."

"Oh, no. Please don't do that," Maaya begged. "He's really powerful and he has the whole town at his back—"

"I've faced down far more frightful opponents than simpletons masquerading as men of power and intellect," Adelaide interrupted, her voice hard. "Such men are always put in their place eventually, and I happen to take great satisfaction from doing just that. Don't make the mistake of thinking I'm incapable of such a thing. Besides, he is responsible for the death of one of my countrymen. It's hard to let that go unanswered."

Maaya decided not to argue, and not just because Adelaide's tone intimidated her. She imagined Adelaide leading her entire crew into the streets of Sark, rescuing Roshan, then finding Rahu, and… what came next Maaya wasn't sure. The Adelaide she pictured in her mind carried a sword and stood triumphantly above Rahu, the point of her sword at his throat, and Maaya smiled inwardly. If ever such a thing were to happen, she would have absolutely no problem with that at all.

Maaya was partway through wondering if Adelaide had ever fought someone when suddenly she caught the glimmer of something moving out of the corner of her eye—and when she turned to look, she nearly screamed.

An enormous spider, larger than her entire hand and then some, was crawling slowly across the writing desk. It stood tall on spindly legs and seemed to have its eyes set on one of the lamps. Maaya was so shocked that it took a moment for her to realize that the spider was made entirely of metal, and that its body was made of a curious intricate clock face.

"Oh! Chronis! There you are," Adelaide scolded. "I see what you're doing, so don't even think about it. Get over here."

The spider turned to look at the captain, glanced back at the lamp with what Maaya could have sworn was an expression of longing, then climbed its way down the desk, across the floor, and up the bedpost. When it crawled up Adelaide's arm, Maaya couldn't help but shudder. Metal though it might have been, its movements were so realistic that Maaya didn't really care.

"Not a fan of spiders?" Adelaide asked as the spider wrapped itself around her lower arm. Its legs fit perfectly into the smooth metal curves of Adelaide's augment, and after a moment Maaya couldn't tell where the spider ended and her metal arm began. Only the new presence of the clock on her arm gave any hint that anything had changed.

"N-no," Maaya stammered foolishly. "What…?"

"This is Chronis. He's the timekeeper of this ship, but he likes knocking things over just for the fun of it sometimes. And no, before you ask, I didn't special order this. He's been in my family for a few generations now. Take a look!"

Maaya stepped slowly closer, afraid the spider might suddenly leap off the captain's arm and attack, but nothing happened.

"He won't bite," Adelaide said encouragingly. "He occasionally leaps onto people's faces from above, but not if he likes you."

Maaya shuddered, and Adelaide laughed.

As much as the spider frightened her, she had to admit it was a gorgeous piece of machinery. There were three separate, circular sections to what made up its "body," each a slightly different size. The first, near the front of the spider, was simply a small compass, but on the side of the dial were eight small jewels that looked like eyes.

The middle medium-sized dial appeared to be a normal clock at first glance, but upon closer inspection Maaya saw that there was a smaller clock inside the first with two separate hands of its own, set to a time many hours into the future.

The largest part of Chronis' body was what truly fascinated Maaya. The dial was a beautiful picture of the night sky, glittering brightly with hundreds of tiny lights. There were more hands than Maaya could count at a glance, and these were of stars and planets of various sizes.

Even Saber now seemed impressed, and she put both hands on Maaya's shoulders as she peered over her to get a closer look.

"It's beautiful," Maaya murmured, pointing at the third dial. "What is this for?"

"Just for keeping track of the positions of stars and things. For directional purposes, you know," Adelaide explained. "I rarely look at it. I prefer looking at the actual sky. It's a dying art, but so much more beautiful. Have you ever looked at a clear ocean sky through a telescope? It's the most wonderful thing, far more beautiful than any human recreation. No offense." Adelaide said this last to Chronis, who responded by making a rude clicking noise. Adelaide stood up, smiling brightly, and smoothed the front of her coat. "Well, I think that takes care of everything. At least for now. Are you satisfied?"

"I think so," Maaya replied. "So… you believe me, right? About everything I said?"

"Until I've been given a reason not to," Adelaide answered bluntly. "I'm sure you haven't told me everything, but we've only really been acquainted properly since earlier today, so that's to be expected. Now, I need to get back to it. Feel free to walk around; this isn't a man-of-war so there's really not all that much to see, but better you familiarize yourself with it. If you need anything urgently, talk to one of the officers—just know they may not have time for you unless it's really important."

"Is there anywhere I shouldn't go?" Maaya asked. The last place she wanted to be caught somewhere she shouldn't be was on a ship in the middle of the ocean.

"Just my quarters. And probably everyone else's quarters, but that's just good manners. Apart from that you can basically go anywhere. Just don't expect anything exciting."

"I've never been sailing before! This is all exciting," Maaya said, and Adelaide winked before heading to the door. "Oh, uh… does this ship have a name?" Maaya asked quickly, hoping to keep Adelaide there for as long as she could.

"It does! You're aboard the LSV Windfire, one of the fastest ships in the fleet. Well, our excuse for a fleet, anyway."

"What is 'LSV'?" Saber asked, puzzled. Maaya repeated the question.

"Levien Speed Vessel. It's pretty silly when you hear what it stands for, but they're all about their designations. I had to start using it if I wanted to be able to work here. Anyway, I'm off. Let's have dinner together sometime, yeah?"

"Of course!" Maaya agreed enthusiastically, and with another friendly smile, Adelaide departed.

Adelaide had only been gone a moment when Saber turned to face Maaya, a wide grin on her face.

"Don't say a word," Maaya muttered, but her threat fell flat as her cheeks burned.

"A dinner date with the captain! And on your first day, too. She's remarkably accepting considering you almost brought the might of the Selenthian military down upon her and her illegal operation here. She's a keeper, that's for sure. Anyway, come on; we should go exploring, and you should meet more people. If you only spend time with the officers people will start to think you're an elitist or something."

Saber started to head for the door, but Maaya held out her arm to stop her.

"Hang on. I just thought of something."

"What?"

"It's about the Blackfins," Maaya continued as she took off the coat Inga had loaned her and put on her old one in its place. "The person I saw last night… they had a Blackfins pin, and they could see ghosts."

"So?"

"And remember what Adelaide said. There used to be *supernatural* requirements to get into the Blackfins."

"Maaya, do please get to your point already," Saber said exasperatedly.

"I'm saying, what if I'm not the only person on this ship who can see you?"

Saber paused, but didn't look troubled. If anything, she seemed almost excited at the prospect.

"Well, that would definitely make things less boring for me—"

"Saber! Take this seriously, won't you?" Maaya pleaded.

Saber averted her gaze upon hearing the sharp tone in Maaya's voice.

"All right, fine. How about we go explore and I'll keep my distance? We'll see if anyone reacts to me being around, but if they do I'll be far enough away to escape while you bring the wrath of the captain down on whoever causes trouble, okay?"

Maaya wanted to refuse, to tell Saber that she wasn't allowed to leave their quarters until Maaya had figured everything out for certain, but she knew the ghost would have none of that. She thought desperately for any alternative to Saber putting herself out in the open, but could think of nothing. After almost a half a minute of silence, she sighed in defeat.

"Fine. Just let me make sure I have some cards ready."

Ten minutes later, Maaya and Saber walked back out on deck. Now they were on their way, Maaya already felt much freer—and safer with a partially replenished deck of cards concealed in her pocket. She scanned the deck warily, looking for any sign that someone would notice the ghost hovering in plain sight, but no one so much as gave her a second glance, though a few did offer a smile and wave.

For the most part, everyone appeared too busy to talk. There were still several other ships nearby, and Commander Strand was steering the ship expertly toward the open ocean. Gunnar and Halvar were on deck near the bow speaking to a small group of men in plain white shirts. Adelaide herself was nowhere to be seen.

"Imagine everyone's surprise if I flew up and just released all the sails?" Saber said happily, then grinned mischievously as Maaya shot her a dark look.

As there wasn't much to see on deck, Saber suggested they go below to see what else the ship had to offer. They walked through the forecastle, the stores, the gun deck, and the mess hall, but none of these contained anything of remote interest—especially to Saber.

Maaya was almost too distracted to look around as they walked. She remained vigilant, so much so that at times she realized she was holding her breath due to tension. She kept her right hand close to her chest, ever ready to draw a card at a moment's notice and provide an escape for her friend. But though nearly everyone she met glanced up at her from their work, some of them giving her a friendly greeting, not once did anyone look at Saber.

Saber, for her part, was disappointed.

"Not that I don't enjoy your company or anything, but this is going to be a long trip, especially when half the time you won't even be able to answer me," Saber groaned.

"On the plus side this means we don't constantly have to worry about anyone being out to get you," Maaya replied, though she knew this would be little comfort to her.

"Do you want to look around the captain's cabin?" Saber suggested as they passed back through the gun deck on their way back.

"Absolutely not," Maaya answered shortly. "I know you're bored, but we're not allowed there."

"*You're* not allowed there. No one else on board knows I exist, apparently," Saber said bitterly.

"Even so, I don't like it. We can't just invade people's privacy because we can get away with it."

Saber let out a long dramatic sigh, taking care to be as loud as she could.

"What am I going to do? There isn't even anywhere to fly to out in the middle of the ocean! And I don't suppose there are many dead people out here, either. I could die all over again."

"Oh, relax," Maaya responded playfully. "We'll figure something out. Besides, you never know. Remember all those pirate stories where they would make people walk the plank? Maybe we… hold on."

Maaya stopped, then kneeled down to pick up a slip of paper pinned underneath a large wooden box.

"Fantastic! A cargo manifest, I assume. Now we can see what kind of extremely illegal… what? What's wrong?" Saber frowned.

Maaya held up the slip of paper between trembling fingers. It was a *libris* card—a purple one of exactly the same design as the blood cards the stranger had given her the night before.

"Oh, stars," Saber whispered. "That person you met… they're on board."

"Or at the very least, they've been here," Maaya replied, quickly tucking the card away in her pouch.

"What do we do?" Saber asked anxiously, her eyes flicking from doorway to doorway as though expecting an assailant to jump out at any moment.

"You should go back to our room to hide. In the meantime I'm going to talk to the captain," Maaya answered determinedly.

"I really don't think that's a good idea," Saber warned, but Maaya shook her head dismissively.

"I'm not going to tell her about this, not exactly. I just want to know if she's seen or heard anything suspicious. There's a chance it might not be the same person, but either way, if someone like this is on board she needs to know."

"What if she knows already? They were wearing a Blackfins pin and this is a ship full of Blackfins."

"True, but we've been walking around for a half hour now and no one can see you. That stranger wouldn't exactly fit in here, Blackfin or not. Also, what would someone with that kind of strength be doing on a cargo ship like this even if they knew it was going to Krethus?"

"So, what, are you saying the crew could be in danger?" Saber asked.

"I don't know. I just feel like the captain should know about this," Maaya replied tersely. "I don't want to think that we're making this entire trip with someone like that on board."

"All right. I'll go hide and you can tell me what Adelaide has to say. Try to be quick."

Maaya nodded and the girls split up, Saber floating up through the ceiling to take a more direct route back to their quarters.

Maaya made her way quickly to the main deck, glancing hurriedly around for the captain while at the same time trying not to make it obvious that she was troubled. Her gaze passed over various officers and crew, and her heart pounded in her chest. It could be any one of them and she would have no idea.

Finally, she spotted Adelaide standing near the helm, talking animatedly with Inga—or at least, the captain spoke animatedly while the commander simply nodded politely, occasionally giving brief responses.

Maaya jogged up the stairs, standing nearby so as not to interrupt their conversation, but Adelaide beckoned her over warmly.

"So! What do you think of my lovely vessel?" Adelaide asked eagerly.

"It's beautiful," Maaya replied distractedly, hoping she didn't sound rude. "It's a lot bigger than I thought it would be."

"Yeah, well, you won't be saying that for long," Adelaide chuckled.

"Sorry, do you have a minute? I was wondering if I could ask you something," Maaya pressed, uncomfortably aware of Inga's piercing gaze upon her.

"Sure! Excuse me, Commander."

Adelaide stepped away from the wheel and walked over to the side of the ship, safely out of earshot of anyone else. The fins along the waterline had resumed their places flat alongside the hull now they were out in open waters, and the ship rose and fell gently in the small waves, small bursts of water spraying from the bow and brushing against Maaya's face in a fine mist.

"What's up? You look a little nervous," Adelaide asked, still smiling.

"I just wanted to know… have you seen or heard anything strange going on?" Maaya asked slowly.

"Absolutely," Adelaide answered instantly. "The way Halvar's got his hat on makes me think he's wearing a wig under there, and one of the crew members I ran into earlier was wearing socks of two different colors. Strange things are afoot indeed. No pun intended." Adelaide managed a full three seconds before bursting into laughter at Maaya's utterly confused expression. "I'm sorry, I couldn't resist. Why do you ask, though? Have you seen something?"

Maaya froze. She should have guessed the captain would ask her where such a question came from, but she had been too busy working up the nerve to talk to her in the first place.

"Not exactly. It's hard to explain… I guess something's making me uncomfortable. Maybe it's because we're going to Krethus."

"That's very possible. And you've never been sailing before, have you? It could just be first-time jitters. Nothing to worry about, I promise. Even some of the crew who have been out on dozens of missions get those occasionally! It's that feeling which caused so many haunted ship stories: sailors got nervous, thought they were too strong and manly to feel that way, and blamed it on ghosts instead. I'd like to think we're a hardier sort here, but it's totally understandable if you're feeling nervous."

"I suppose," Maaya replied uneasily. She didn't want to let the subject go so easily. There was too much at stake to let a little social anxiety get in the way. "Is this ship… I don't know… safe? That is, if someone snuck on board, would you know?"

Adelaide raised her eyebrows slightly.

"I would, absolutely. We're a tight-knit family here; a stowaway would be noticed right away. Why? You didn't try sneaking someone else on, did you?"

"No! Of course not," Maaya objected, and Adelaide laughed again. "I just… I've learned to trust my instincts, and they feel off right now. It could be just the jitters, like you said, but…"

Adelaide put a hand on Maaya's shoulder and smiled encouragingly.

"Tell you what. I'll make sure the ship is searched high and low for anything suspicious. It couldn't hurt, especially not since our little visit from the military this morning. The Windfire is a small ship, but a determined stowaway could find a way to stay hidden just long enough to see something that could get us all in trouble. Does that help?"

"It does, yes! But… you aren't doing that just for me, are you?" Maaya asked tentatively.

"I am, yes," Adelaide chuckled. "Frankly, if we did find a military spy on board we'd make sure he didn't live to tattle on us. But don't you worry," she added quickly as Maaya's eyes widened in shock, "I sincerely doubt we'll find anything out of the ordinary."

"Why go through the trouble, then?" Maaya asked quizzically.

"Because you're cute, and I like you," Adelaide answered with a wink.

"You can't just keep using that as a reason," Maaya protested, though she couldn't help but smile.

"That it's repeated doesn't make it any less true," Adelaide contended. "I want you to feel safe on my ship—and that goes for everyone. So thank you for coming to me."

"Is it okay if I talk to you about things like this? I mean, am I disturbing you by coming to you right away?"

"You could go to any of the officers, but now you mention it, I would rather you just come straight to me," Adelaide answered thoughtfully.

"Why? Isn't that more work for you?" Maaya continued.

"Like I said, because you're cu—"

"All right, all right. Point taken," Maaya laughed. Adelaide winked, then headed back toward the wheel.

"Commander Strand, at your leisure, order a deck-by-deck search of the entire ship by the end of the day," she ordered. "If anyone finds anything even remotely suspicious have it reported to me immediately. Otherwise I'll accept my usual end-of-day report."

"Is there a problem, Captain?" the commander inquired, already looking more serious than usual.

"Not that I know of, but I'd like a confirmation all the same," Adelaide answered. "I'll be in my quarters. There's a lot of paperwork to be done."

"You? Paperwork? I thought you gave it all to Halvar."

"I did, but he still hasn't figured out how to forge my signature. Plus I need to look over all his math. If he's going to fake it he needs to at least do it convincingly. Anyway, I'll be off. Get us up to full speed as soon as we're able."

Inga nodded, then turned back to the helm as Adelaide disappeared through the double doors into her cabin.

Maaya immediately headed back down the stairs to her own quarters where Saber waited impatiently. After making sure no one was around to listen, Maaya quietly slid the door shut behind her.

"Well?" Saber asked quickly.

"The captain said she hasn't seen anything weird, but she's ordered a full search of the ship, top to bottom. If there are any people here who shouldn't be, we'll know by tonight."

Saber frowned.

"That's all well and good, I suppose, but that doesn't help us if the person we're worried about is part of the crew."

"That's true, but it's something, at least," Maaya sighed. "At least we'll know that the ship and captain aren't in danger. One thing at a time."

Saber shifted agitatedly, running her fingers through her hair.

"Don't get me wrong, I'm glad this is happening. Honestly, this is a lot more than I expected. But I would feel a lot more comfortable if we could get to the bottom of this particular mystery sooner rather than later—and not just because I don't fancy the idea of staying cooped up in here the whole time otherwise."

"What do you think we should do?" Maaya asked nervously.

"You don't have to look that scared! I was just going to say I think we should draw them out ourselves."

Maaya spluttered in protest.

"That's exactly a reason to be scared! Didn't we go over this? Didn't I tell you how dangerous they are?"

"Yes, and believe me, this isn't something I say lightly. But if you think about it, now that we're on a ship, I have the advantage. Everything is so cramped and small that all I have to do is float through a few floors and walls to escape."

"I don't like it," Maaya replied, shaking her head fervently. "What if they're too fast?"

"We can't just keep avoiding danger. Especially not out here. We need to realize that where we're going there's some unpleasant stuff ahead. And as long as we're traveling on this ship, we need to know that we can… maybe not trust this crew, but not constantly worry about being in danger. Don't forget, this stranger could pose a threat to you, too."

"I don't think so. If they're a stowaway they'll be found, and if they're part of the crew the captain wouldn't let them hurt me."

"Unless they tell the captain you have a ghost friend. And as much as she seems to like you I'm not sure how well that would go over—especially since the whole purpose of this trip is to visit her home country which is currently being ravaged by ghosts."

"You're not one of those!"

"She doesn't know that, and there's no way to prove otherwise since she can't see me."

"Okay, fine. So let's say we somehow draw this person out, *and* that we somehow doing it without any of the crew realizing. Then what?"

"We could always try to reason with them first," Saber replied, then raised her eyebrows questioningly at Maaya. "What? I'm not a barbarian; of course I think we should try to use words first. If not, though, we'd have to..."

"Yes?" Maaya asked meaningfully.

"I don't know. Do what we do best, I suppose. But look: we've been here for hours now, and before we realized another *libris* user was here we were standing around gawking at everything like tourists. Odds are probably good I've already been seen. If they somehow managed not to see me yet, then I question your recollection of their competence. All I want to know is who it is."

Maaya stared around the room helplessly, desperately hoping for an argument that stubbornly refused to present itself.

"You really want to do this, don't you?" she said finally.

"Yes. And I know you don't like it, and I know your logic is sound, but think about this." Saber floated closer, taking both of Maaya's hands in hers.

"I love you and I respect you, but you have done a lot of stupid things recently, and you said I get one free stupid decision myself."

"I feel like it's unfair to call that in when your life could be in danger," Maaya murmured, staring at the floor.

"Both of our lives are in danger, and they've been at stake since we had to flee Sark. I know it's just the two of us against the world right now, but that doesn't mean I'm going to hide until we make it to Krethus. I was scared at first, and I still am, I suppose, but… I had some time to think, and if this is going to be our last grand mission I don't want to go out like a coward. If there's someone on this ship who can see me, I want to know who it is. And if their experience is fighting ghosts like the ones we're up against, then they are in for a surprise when they meet me."

Saber said these last words with such conviction and confidence that Maaya couldn't help but smile.

"And I've got your back, you know that?"

"Never doubted it for a second," Saber replied with a grin.

"Do you have a plan, then?" Maaya asked.

"I figure we can take another walk around the ship and I'll get right in people's faces—be really obnoxious, you know—to the point where even if someone is trying to hide the fact that they can see me they won't be able to resist showing that they can."

"Okay… and that's different from usual how?" Maaya continued, then yelped with laughter as Saber pushed her onto the bed.

22

FINDING THE STRANGER

LATER THAT EVENING, with only an hour or so until sunset, Maaya and Saber stood near the bow of the ship with a few of the crew, watching the sky turn brilliant shades of purple and pink. A light wind was at their back, and though Maaya had been warned that nights at sea could get quite cold, she was comfortable for now. Lights began to flicker on all across the ship, giving it a distinctly cozy atmosphere. Maaya and Saber sat next to each other, their backs against the railing, along with six of the sailors and Gunnar.

Halvar stood facing them, his attempt at a serious expression on his face. After a moment, he cleared his throat.

"So it goes like this," he said. "The cap'n and then-commander and I were out in the dingy, and wouldn't you know it, we only had one oar. Commander David broke the other one trying to fight off some soldiers in a pursuing boat, and he got them well enough, but now we were stuck."

"Hold on, Halvar," Gunnar interrupted. "We're supposed to be telling made-up stories. Make David smarter in this one so we don't think you're telling the truth."

Saber snorted.

"The more they talk about this man the more imperative it is that I someday meet him," she commented.

"Fine, fine. So, the *captain* lost the oar trying to fight off some soldiers, and David was putting forth his most valiant effort to get us to safety," Halvar continued.

"There you go," Gunnar grinned approvingly.

"The captain was most distressed, having been injured grievously in the fight, so now it was up to David and me to get us back to the ship. Only trouble is we were fighting a headwind on top of only having the one oar, and on top of *that* we were taking on water. Between the two of us we had to get ourselves back to our rendezvous, keep the captain from bleeding out, and keep us afloat long enough for rescue. I've never worked so hard in my life."

"And not a day since, I'll wager," Gunnar interjected.

"You interrupt me again and I'll put *you* in this story," Halvar shot back as the others laughed. "Now, it was a struggle, but we got to the rendezvous… and the Windfire was nowhere to be seen. There was the shadow of a ship on the horizon, so we thought they might just be running late, so we started in their direction… and then suddenly there were two ships, then three, then four. Soon enough we realized we were facing down a small fleet of Selenthia's finest, and they had their eyes on us.

"Now we were in a bit of a bind, you understand. The army was behind us and the navy was in front of us, and we had one leaky boat with one oar and an injured captain. So now's about the time I started to worry, but David, cool as ever, kept his wits about him…"

"Moon have mercy, this is the most boring story yet," Saber complained. "The truth has got to be more interesting than this. We're supposed to be telling ghost stories and I have yet to hear anything remotely frightening. Or accurate, for that matter."

Maaya smiled. Evidently it was custom on the same night every week for some of the crew to get together and tell ghost stories, something Maaya had been happy to attend. She was interested to hear what kind of stories adventurers at sea had come up with over the course of their travels. An hour in, however, she and Saber found themselves somewhat disappointed.

There had been only one story that sent shivers down Maaya's spine. A young woman only a few years older than Maaya had told a story about a captain who went exploring a wreck with some of her crew in the dead of night, each carrying a lantern and rope. Through the course of the night, one by one the others disappeared, their lanterns flickering out as they went. A few hours later the captain found herself alone and lost inside the lower decks of the dark abandoned ship. For some reason, no matter how many stairs she climbed, she could never find her way back to the top deck—and always she was pursued by the sounds of whispers and maniacal echoing laughter. Finally, nearly delirious from fear, she made it to the top deck only to find her entire crew hanging by their necks from the mainmast, expressions of horror on their pale dead faces. Before the captain had any time to react, her own lantern went out.

While Maaya had been genuinely frightened, Saber had scoffed, explaining that ghosts were far too impatient to set up an elaborate ploy like that.

"Go on, Halvar! Tell us something that's actually scary!" Saber shouted. "Silence would be more terrifying than your story right now."

This, too, had been going on for an hour. While Saber had reluctantly agreed to join Maaya for the ghost story session, she had not done so quietly. She had shouted at nearly everyone, being as obnoxious as possible, and this only got worse as no one reacted to her.

"...then, just as we were within firing range, a great big ship exploded out of the water in front of us," Halvar continued emphatically, clearly into his story now. "It was an ancient ship, the kind you see in shipyard museums. Full of holes, too, and sails so ragged they were nearly gone. But wouldn't you know it, it rose right out of the water, blocking any of the navy's ships from firing at us. This by itself was already shocking, but then we saw that the ship wasn't empty. We had to do a double take, because right there on deck, before our very eyes, was—"

Maaya screamed.

Everyone immediately turned to look at her. Maaya leapt to her feet and away from the railing, staring wide-eyed at Chronis, who stood directly above where she had been seated.

"Oh, it's you, Chronis. Got my hopes up for a second there, I thought my story was just so downright scary it'd given the girl a fright. You weren't trying to help me, were you?" Halvar asked the spider.

In response, Chronis waved its right front leg and made a whirring sound.

"Well, I appreciate the effort anyway," Halvar chuckled.

"Sorry! I didn't mean to. It startled me," Maaya breathed, determinedly not making eye contact with Saber, who was doubled over with laughter.

"Not a problem! You gave us quite a scare too. And really, that's why we're here. But now you have to go next."

"I have to... what? Oh, no, I don't have any—"

"You've got a few seconds to think, I'm almost done. Where was I? Right, the ship appeared out of nowhere, and right there on deck..."

As the others turned to watch Halvar again, Chronis now included in his audience, Maaya chanced an imploring glance at Saber, who floated over to her, still chuckling.

"What? You want an idea for a story? Surely you can think of something yourself."

Maaya turned her head slightly away from the others so they wouldn't notice her mouth moving.

"I'm not good at talking in front of people, and I'm really not good at coming up with stories on the spot," Maaya whispered, pretending to be fixing one of the buttons on her cloak. "Besides, you're the one complaining about the stories we've heard so far. Give me something you'd like to hear."

"I suppose it would be appropriate for the new girl to shock everyone by telling the best story," Saber replied. "All right. Give me a few minutes and I'll come up with something that will give all these seasoned sailors a sleepless night."

Maaya nodded almost imperceptibly, and the slightest hint of a smile played across her lips. She had to admit, she was having… fun. The last few days had been filled with pain and uncertainty and stress, but now her biggest worry was coming up with a good ghost story to tell her new friends.

Friends. The word seemed to echo in her mind. She wasn't sure if she could actually call them friends just yet, but she got the feeling that such a thing was inevitable the longer she stayed on board. It didn't seem like Maaya shared much in common with any of them so far, but that hadn't mattered. They were all friendly and had been more than happy to include Maaya in conversation.

What's more, they were the exact opposite of the type of people she expected to find on a ship. She had always pictured the crew of a ship like this to be rigid and strict, shouting orders and constantly standing at attention with nothing but "yes, sir" and "no, sir" in their vernacular, but this crew was anything but. While they were efficient and clearly experienced, it seemed like their personal relationships were on the same level as their professional ones. Orders were given and followed and duties were performed quickly and proficiently, but were accompanied by the banter Maaya would expect from a group of long-time friends seated at a bar table. This openness put Maaya at ease, and before long she found herself actually trying to talk to the crew. Going out with the intention of communicating with strangers was something Maaya had always tried hard to avoid.

"…and then, once we could finally see again, we saw the navy—or what was left of it—in full retreat. But the strangest thing was that the ghost ships were nowhere to be seen. There wasn't the slightest hint they'd ever been there. Before we could think on it too long, the Windfire rounded the bend and came to pick us up. I managed to wake David up, but he didn't have any memory of it, the idiot. The captain was still unconscious, too, so there was no getting her to back me up. But to this day I mean to get back there someday, and I'll see if I can't take a dive and find out what's really down there."

The crew, which had now grown to about a dozen, applauded politely. From its perch on the rail, Chronis mimicked applause by lightly tapping its two front legs together.

"Well done, Halvar, the crew is all still awake by the end of this one!" Gunnar said jovially.

"Don't forget, you're still going tonight, and I know you're all out of ideas," Halvar retorted, then turned to face Maaya. "Anyway, your turn! You got something good for us?"

"I… I suppose," Maaya replied uncertainly, then gasped as Halvar pulled her to where he had been standing.

"Great! Take your time, but also, make it quick. Gunnar needs his ego deflated soon or he's going to float off into the sunset."

Saber rubbed her hands together delightedly.

"All right, I've got the perfect idea. Set the scene. It's an old cobblestone street on a cloudy night, the moon hidden behind the clouds, and there's not a sound to be heard. What little light remains casts down through the branches of dead trees, flinging skeletal shadows onto old dirty windows… hey, come on, you'd best start talking or I'm going to forget it all."

Maaya ignored her. Behind Saber facing the port quarter, out on the surface of the calm ocean waters, a light had appeared. It was still far enough away that it flickered gently, and had Maaya never seen such a thing before, she might have been forgiven for thinking she was seeing the reflection of the setting sun off a faraway ship or buoy.

But she had seen such a thing before.

Saber turned to look and then stepped back, visibly shocked.

"Oh, stars. Even out in the middle of the ocean? That can't be!"

A few moments later Maaya remembered she was currently supposed to be the center of attention. She turned back to face the others, who watched her with knowing stares.

"Nerves, eh? We won't bite," Gunnar said warmly. "Here, I'll get you started. It was a dark and stormy night, right? And you were home alone, your parents were supposed to be back hours ago…"

"We don't have time for this. Tell them you feel sick and you need to go. We need to figure out how to deal with this," Saber instructed from her side, not taking her eyes off the light in the distance.

"I… sorry, I… don't feel good," Maaya mumbled. Her voice trembled involuntarily, but this only seemed to help her case.

"Ah, fair enough then. Sorry to put you on the spot!" Halvar said. "Come sit back down with us. Guess that means you're up, Gunnar. And oh, I can't wait to hear this…"

As soon as Gunnar stood up, however, Maaya turned away and walked briskly back toward the stern. Halvar called to her, but she couldn't hear what he said.

"What do we do?" Saber asked agitatedly. "If they keep coming this way they'll put the entire ship in danger, but if you fight them you risk revealing yourself to the crew—and to our mysterious guest if they're still aboard."

"I have no choice," Maaya whispered. "There's no guarantee the stranger is here. I don't want to hold off and let the ghosts get too close on the off chance the stranger will reveal themselves or that the ghosts will disappear before they get here."

"I think we should wait," Saber objected. "It puts the pressure on them. If they're still here, as far as they're concerned they're the only ones who can stop those ghosts, and they face the same dilemma as you. They'll have to reveal themselves, and that's a better option than what we've got right now."

Maaya exhaled nervously.

"How many are there?"

Saber squinted at the light, which had already come much closer. Maaya could make out the vague shapes of the tall ghosts and see the dark shadows of their eyes, but couldn't see much beyond that.

"Looks to be only about a dozen or so. Have you still got the blood cards the stranger gave you?"

"I do, but I don't know if I can use them! They might be too high level for me," Maaya hissed.

"You haven't made any spares of your own?" Saber asked incredulously.

"I didn't think I'd have to already!"

"Okay, fine," Saber said as they climbed the stairs at the ship's stern to get a better look at the approaching ghosts. "We should have a minute or two; if we get back to our room now you can make one or two before they arrive. We'll need a backup plan, but I think I—"

Saber broke off as several thin white objects streaked from the ship toward the ghosts. Despite the distance that still lay between the ship and the ghosts, the objects hit their mark with incredible accuracy. The distant light immediately flickered out as the ghosts disappeared in a burst of red sparks. The sound of the bang that marked their demise arrived only a moment after.

Maaya and Saber stared at each other in shock, then sprinted the rest of the way up the stairs.

"Maaya... I think they came from the captain's quarters," Saber said, her voice dull with fright.

"What do we—?"

"I'll go take a look. Stay here."

"Saber!" Maaya whispered in desperate protest, but the ghost had already passed through the double doors to the cabin. Only a moment later, Saber returned, looking shaken.

"The stranger is there on the rear balcony. They didn't see me; they were still watching the ocean. But they're here."

"Go find Adelaide," Maaya said quickly. "I'll stay here; if anyone comes out, I'll try to follow them."

"Be careful," Saber said quickly, then darted off below deck, leaving Maaya by the helm.

Maaya suddenly felt a wave of fear wash over her. The stranger was here after all, and they were right on the other side of the doors she now stood in front of. Though the stranger had helped her the first time they met, Maaya had been in disguise then; if this person thought that Maaya was going to blow their cover…

Maaya forced the thought from her mind and remained firmly in place. She wasn't going to be intimidated. She had been through far too much to let some newcomer get in her way now. What's more, by entering Adelaide's quarters they had shown themselves to be a threat… and Maaya wasn't about to let someone endanger Adelaide without a fight.

Nearly ten minutes passed. Maaya paced the deck agitatedly. No one had come out of the cabin on this side, and she guessed that even with the help of *libris*, getting to such a vantage point would be difficult without taking the direct route of the cabin. Either that meant the stranger was even more adept than Maaya first suspected… or that they were still in there.

Just then, she jumped as she felt someone tap her shoulder. She whirled around to see Saber behind her.

"Gods, Saber, don't startle me like that!" Maaya gasped.

"Sorry. I didn't want to call to you in case that person is still hanging around."

"Did you find her? Did you find Adelaide?" Maaya asked urgently.

"Yeah. She's safe belowdecks down eating dinner with some of the crew."

Maaya breathed a sigh of relief.

"Okay. I didn't see anyone leave the cabin, so I think they got out another way. I couldn't watch both the front and back at once. Don't go looking again, though. I'll just have to talk to Adelaide before she… what?"

She trailed off, noticing the ghost's troubled expression.

"It's just… I have a suspicion as to who it might be," Saber said slowly.

"What? Who? How do you know?" Maaya asked as a fresh wave of dread spread over her.

"I searched the ship. The whole ship. Even after I found Adelaide I thought it'd be a good idea to find as many people as I could, just so I could say with certainty that they weren't in the cabin."

"To make sure no one was missing while the stranger was here," Maaya ventured, and Saber nodded.

"Right. And I found almost everyone. There was only one person I couldn't find no matter where I looked, and I looked everywhere except in this cabin."

"Who… who was it?" Maaya asked slowly.

"I never found Commander Strand."

Maaya shuddered, and her mind raced. As much as she didn't want to jump to conclusions, Inga would fit what she knew of the stranger so far. The stranger had been noticeably taller than her and hadn't spoken much when they'd met. They had also demonstrated accuracy and composure befitting a high-ranking and highly trained officer. Inga also wasn't someone Maaya could rule out; while Maaya had gotten to know many of the crew members, Inga remained stoic and mostly silent.

"Before you worry too much… I have no proof of anything, so I don't want us to fall prey to conjecture," Saber reasoned quietly. "I just thought that was an important detail."

"You're right. It was," Maaya replied shakily. "I need to tell Adelaide about this."

"And say what? We need to come up with something more convincing than a gut feeling, but at the same time we can't say anything that would give you away."

"I'm not sure that's the most important thing anymore at this point. She could be in real danger," Maaya protested.

"If this person is a member of the crew—especially if it's Commander Strand—why would they have any reason to hurt her?" Saber asked doubtfully.

"I don't know. But I know Adelaide trusts her, and if Inga is hiding something this big from her… I don't know. I just have a bad feeling about this. Adelaide was big on knowing my backstory and she didn't even know me. Imagine if one of her friends was exposed as being someone who thinks they can see ghosts and who trespasses in her cabin?"

"That's fair, I suppose. There's always the chance the captain knows, but we can't just ask that outright in case it's not true. Actually… I have an idea."

"What is it?"

"The commander needs to give a report to the captain tonight, right? I can hide in the cabin and wait for her to make that report and I can see what happens," Saber proposed.

"Are you insane?" Maaya objected, unable to stop her voice from rising. "If Inga *is* the stranger, and she sees you…!"

"If she sees me, she won't be able to do anything about it. Not without exposing herself to the captain. Besides, I wasn't going to hover around in plain view," Saber continued before Maaya could argue. "I'll keep just behind the wall or behind a piece of furniture so I can hear what's going on without being seen."

"I still don't think—"

"Oh, enough already, Maaya," Saber interrupted suddenly. "You're in no position to keep doubting me, not after everything you've done recently. If you're going to be such a coward about everything, you might as well just turn around and go back home. It's embarrassing, really."

Maaya fell into a stunned silence. She wanted to argue, but she was so taken aback by Saber's sudden callousness that she had no idea what to say.

"All right, it's settled, then," Saber continued as though nothing had happened. "You can head back to our room if you want and get some rest. I have no idea how long it'll take for those two to come back, but I don't want to leave in case I miss them. As soon as I figure out what's going on I'll come back and let you know. Sound good?"

Maaya nodded wordlessly, then turned away before the ghost could see her expression. As she headed down the stairs, she fought the urge to cry. What Saber had said hadn't even been that bad, all things considered; she simply hadn't expected her to snap.

She walked through the empty officers' quarters, then into her own, closing the door quietly behind her. She undressed slowly and climbed into bed. She was tired enough to sleep, and the bed was comfortable enough, but she knew she couldn't sleep. Not yet.

Was she really a coward? Maaya didn't think so. Just earlier Saber had praised her bravery for risking showing her goldpin to Gunnar and Halvar, but maybe that hadn't been enough. Maaya had to admit she'd been foolish lately, and Saber had taken it all in stride with only a little resistance. Saber had forgiven her for fighting Emil's battle, for wandering off with Adelaide, and for going out in the middle of the night in Levien after she had specifically told her not to run off. Maaya could admit all those things were foolish sure enough. But cowardly?

Whatever her reasons, it was clear there were some unresolved issues—at least on Saber's end. Maaya made a mental note to talk to her about it later, though for the moment she hoped the ghost wouldn't be back *too* soon. She was no longer in the mood to think about what Saber had said or anything to do with the stranger.

Maaya took a deep breath and tried to clear her mind. Her bed was comfortable and warm, and the gentle rocking of the ship was comforting in its own way. She turned to face the wall, and before she knew it her eyes felt heavy, and she drifted slowly off to sleep.

It was still dark when she awoke. She blinked, disoriented, wondering why she was awake at such a late hour. Then she heard a gentle knock, and when she turned over, she saw Commander Strand standing in the doorway.

"I apologize for waking you, but the captain has asked to see you," she said quietly.

"Wha… what time is it?" Maaya yawned, sitting up with difficulty.

"An hour until midnight. I expect she'll be going to bed soon, but she dallied on her paperwork again and wants to stay up to finish."

"Did she say what she wants me for?"

"No. I, however, am going to sleep, so she probably just wants company to help keep her focused."

Maaya stared.

"She would wake me up for that?"

"She is the captain, after all. If it's too much trouble, I can tell her you'd rather sleep than see her."

"No! No, it's okay, I'll… I'll get ready," Maaya stuttered.

The room was still dark, but Maaya swore she saw the commander smile faintly.

"You can see her whenever you are ready. She'll be expecting you, so just go right in. I'm going to sleep. Have a good night, Miss Sahni."

With that, Inga departed. Maaya listened to her soft footsteps as the woman walked back out onto the deck, and then there was silence.

Maaya shuddered. She had been so tired she had temporarily forgotten that Inga was the subject of their makeshift investigation. Further, if it was an hour to midnight and Saber was still gone, that could spell trouble.

She tried to remain calm as she quickly pulled on her clothes. If Inga was just now coming to get her, it was possible that she had only just finished delivering her report to Adelaide. That Adelaide was a chronic procrastinator seemed oddly in character, so her request for Maaya's company didn't seem out of place, either. Still, it was strange that Saber wasn't at least coming to tell her what happened before Maaya went to see Adelaide. Maaya guessed that whatever happened during the report wasn't important enough to justify the rush, or that Saber was still in a foul mood. Either way, Maaya found she was more eager to see Adelaide than the ghost.

The night air was cool even inside her room, and she knew that she would be shivering within minutes once she walked out on deck. She pulled on Nadya's cloak and then stepped out into the main room. It was dark except for a few candles, and no one else was there. The doors to the other officers' quarters were closed, so she assumed nearly everyone else was asleep. She walked quietly, but her heart pounded in her chest, heavy enough that for a moment she was genuinely concerned about waking up the others.

The cold struck her hard as she walked outside, and she instinctively hugged herself. The breeze was still gentle, but every tiny gust pushed the relentless cold through the fabric of her clothes.

There were only a few men and women on deck, and Maaya realized she had never thought about how a ship might operate at night. She suddenly felt guilty at the thought of having woken up any of the night crew while she and Saber took their walk through the ship earlier that day.

She walked quickly up the stairs, unsure if she was nervous or frightened or anxious, or if she was shivering from any of those things or simply the cold. As she approached the door, she hesitated. She couldn't wait to see Adelaide, but even every positive thought was marred by the memory of the stranger.

Finally, she knocked on the door.

"Come on in!" came Adelaide's cheery voice from the other side.

Maaya opened the door and stepped inside, immediately relaxing as the warmth of the cabin washed over her. She turned and shut the door behind her, eager to shut out the cold of the night.

"Oh, hey, Maaya. Nice of you to join us."

Saber's voice. Maaya felt a wave of relief pass over her at this sign her friend was okay. As she turned to face Adelaide, however, she cried out.

Saber floated motionlessly in the air next to Adelaide—and to Maaya's horror, the captain herself was holding a blood card to the ghost's throat.

"Have a seat, go on now," Adelaide said, gesturing with her free hand to one of the free chairs in front of her massive desk.

"Wha—?! N-no, please," Maaya stammered, struggling with her words as she attempted to process everything she was seeing. "Don't hurt her, please!"

"Easy now. We'll get to that in good time. Now have a seat so we can talk things over, yes?"

Maaya obeyed, trembling. The captain stood almost comfortably behind her desk, and Maaya suspected she wasn't going to take any action just yet, but she didn't want to tempt her. She couldn't tear her eyes from the scene, and an avalanche of questions overwhelmed her. Had Adelaide been able to see ghosts this entire time? Did she know the stranger was here? Had Inga perhaps told her?

"Let's start easy," Adelaide said, her voice hard. "Who is this?"

"Her name is Saber. She's a friend," Maaya answered mechanically.

"An unusual friend, but I've heard of stranger things. I would say that's your business, but then your friend decided to snoop around in my quarters this evening and eavesdrop on private conversations. That, unfortunately, is a serious breach of privacy. Do you have any idea why she would want to do that?"

Maaya opened her mouth, but no words came. Telling Adelaide that she only wanted to find out if Inga was the stranger sounded bad no matter how she could think to phrase it regardless of what her intentions were—what's more, she was already in a very bad position, and making an accusation against her first officer, whom Adelaide no doubt trusted, would only make her look worse.

At the moment, however, telling the truth seemed to be the only way to give Saber a chance.

"It's my fault. I asked her to do it. I thought you were in danger," Maaya explained desperately, trying to keep her voice level. "There were some ghosts out in the ocean earlier, and… someone stopped them, but they were in your cabin. They're the person I've been worried about, but I couldn't tell you because I didn't know you could see ghosts! Once I found out they were here, I… I wanted Saber to keep an eye on you in case something happened."

"You sent your dead friend to spy on me? That's not a very friendly thing to do," Adelaide mused.

"Not spy!" Maaya protested. "Don't you understand? There's someone here on this ship and they were in this room! And I thought…"

"You thought you might have me monitored to keep me safe. That's cute," Adelaide cut in. "I suppose your intent is noble enough even if I still have grievous concerns with the way you went about it. But that doesn't explain why your friend was inspecting my paperwork so fervently."

Maaya tore her gaze from Adelaide and stared at the ghost, who looked back almost guiltily.

"You what? Saber!"

"Look, I'm sorry. My curiosity got the better of me, and after years of not being seen by anyone, I… developed some bad habits," Saber said.

"And what interest do you have with the information in my paperwork?" Adelaide pressed.

"None. There was just very little else to do in here while I waited," Saber answered.

"Indeed. So I'm to understand that, purely of your own volition, you decided to look over some very private documents?"

"Yes. Maaya was the one who had a bad feeling about it, but I sort of snapped at her. Sorry about that, by the way," Saber continued. "I honestly had no idea what your paperwork was all about. I really don't care what you have to say to your parents—"

"All right, enough," Adelaide interrupted tiredly. "You realize how bad this looks for both of you. I'm interrogating two people who both take the blame for this, who each expect me to believe that they are at fault and that their friend is innocent. Maaya, when you came aboard my ship, I told you that I trust you because I had no reason to feel like I shouldn't… but now I'm afraid I have been given a reason."

"I'm sorry," Maaya pleaded quickly. "Part of it was I didn't know you could see ghosts, but the rest, I… I didn't mean…"

She trailed off as her eyes fell upon the card Adelaide was holding in her hand. At first glance, Maaya had been able to immediately identify it as a blood card—but now she looked closer, she realized the design itself was frighteningly familiar.

"Yes?" Adelaide said.

"That blood card… who gave that to you?" Maaya asked slowly.

"Why do you assume it was given to me? I see you must know at least something about *libris*, so why not assume I made it myself?"

It took only a few moments, but then it clicked.

"You… then… that was you?"

"Who was me? What are you talking about?" Adelaide said, looking genuinely confused.

"You were the one who got rid of the ghosts tonight!" Maaya cried, and despite her growing anxiety at the realization of who she was speaking to, she felt a flicker of anger. "You were the stranger I tried to warn you about. And you were the one in Levien!"

"Well, yes. I took you to lunch, and—"

"I'm not talking about that," Maaya interjected irately. Saber shot her a worried glance.

"Hey, uh, maybe watch the tone? My life is currently in danger, as it were—"

"Yes, you're right. Maybe there are some other things I should have told you, and maybe Saber shouldn't have been prying into your work, but I'm hardly the only one with secrets in this room."

Adelaide narrowed her eyes.

"What in the world are you talking—?"

"I saw you just last night on the rooftops in Levien. I saw you take down the ghosts, and after you were finished, you gave me *these*," Maaya said, taking the stranger's blood cards from the pouch on her arm and slapping them firmly on the desk between them.

For what felt like a full minute, there was silence. Maaya stared hard at the captain and watched as her eyes widened in shock. Adelaide's mouth fell open, and then her arm holding the blood card to Saber's throat dropped to her side. Saber took this moment to flee, moving safely to the other side of the cabin.

"That was *you*?" Adelaide exclaimed finally.

"Yes. That was me," Maaya responded breathlessly. She was terrified of the anger in her own voice, but there was no stopping now. "That's a big reason why I didn't tell anyone about Saber: because if a person who could get rid of ghosts so easily was *on this ship*, I didn't want to bring Saber to their attention. Also, I don't know about you, but where I'm from, people are killed or jailed for saying they can see things no one else can see. And beyond that," Maaya continued harshly as Adelaide tried to speak, "you introduced yourself to me as a normal ship captain, then I find out you're with the Blackfins, and *then* I find out that not only can you see ghosts but that you take to the streets of Levien at night to get rid of them! And you've been able to see Saber this whole time and haven't said a word! What am I supposed to think about that?"

Adelaide started to speak, then broke off. She did so at least twice more before her shoulders slumped, and she nodded. When she spoke again, her voice had lost its edge.

"Right. You're right. Okay, Maaya. It seems like we both have some explaining to do. I hope you can understand my reasons for keeping some of this to myself, but I should have been up front with you about being able to see your friend here. I'm sorry."

"Well… I understand that, anyway," Maaya said reluctantly. "Since no one else on board can see her it'd be a little strange to admit that, even if you only told me."

"Ah, well, that's the thing…" Adelaide said, and to Maaya's surprise she let out a guilty laugh, putting her hand awkwardly behind her head. "See… actually, everyone on board can see her."

Despite the situation, Maaya almost laughed at the expression of utter shock and confusion on Saber's face.

"I'm sorry, do you want to run that by me again?" the ghost said in a low voice.

Adelaide giggled nervously.

"Well, remember when I said that there used to be a supernatural element to the Blackfins? It's true that it's no longer a requirement, but in some circles it's still pretty popular. For those ostracized from their communities for their attachment to the supernatural, the Blackfins offer a source of companionship. And it so happens that every person on this ship can see ghosts. Believe it or not, it's mostly coincidence—"

"So are you telling me that this entire evening when I was making a total fool of myself, everyone on board could see and hear me perfectly fine and were content to let me just blather away?" Saber asked venomously.

"I'm sorry, I truly am," Adelaide replied quickly. "When you first came aboard, that was my decision on the crew's behalf. I didn't know what was going on and I knew little about Maaya, so I didn't want to make her feel as though this secret she was trying very hard to keep under wraps was in any way in danger of being exposed. Like I said, that was her business—her choice whether to tell or not. She already had to deal with all of us being Blackfins and all, there was no use adding to it."

Adelaide squirmed uncomfortably under Saber's intense stare for a few moments, and the ghost even moved a few steps closer to the captain, placing her hands on her hips. For a moment Maaya was worried that the ghost would lose her temper, but then Saber sighed.

"Do you have any idea how *bored* I've been? I thought I was going to have to go the entire trip with only one person to talk to! You have some nerve, really."

Despite herself, a smile fought its way onto Saber's face, and Adelaide and Maaya let out a simultaneous sigh of relief. Within moments the three of them were laughing together, and for the first time in a long while, Maaya felt like everything would be okay. Adelaide now knew the real truth about them both, and instead of turning Maaya away—or turning her in—she was laughing with them. Apologizing, even. Maaya would never tell, but she wasn't relieved because Adelaide's reaction meant she was no longer in danger—Maaya had been more concerned about Adelaide disliking her than her own safety.

"All right. Now that we're all sort of on the same page, I want to apologize again," Adelaide said. "To you, Maaya, for misleading you right after I expressed my desire for honesty regardless of my reasons. And to you, Saber, for, uh… threatening to kill you, I guess?"

Saber curtsied.

"Thank you. I've never felt truly threatened like that before, and it was quite an invigorating lesson. For my part, I'm sorry for appearing to spy on you. I assure you I was genuinely just very bored."

Adelaide snorted.

"And… I'm sorry about all of this," Maaya said. "I know I had my reasons, but I did say I trusted you. I want you to know I mean that. Maybe now I can prove it."

Adelaide waved her hand.

"You're fine! I understand why you wouldn't want to tell me about all the ghost stuff, especially when you're already by yourself on a ship full of alleged criminals. It was only when I thought you might be trying to dig into things that it became a problem."

"And if that's the reaction I can expect when doing so, you have my word I will not be doing so again," Saber said airily.

"So… we're okay, right?" Maaya asked tentatively. Adelaide beamed.

"Of course! Honestly, I was afraid you'd be terribly upset with me. But now we have oh so much more to talk about. Like the fact that you hunt ghosts, too! You're not so bad with *libris*, you know. There aren't many who know the art, and most of the ones I met who did know it were just awful. Who taught you?"

"I sort of taught myself. I found a book with ghosts in it, and at the time I didn't understand what was wrong with me, so I taught myself to read with Saber's help so I could figure it out—"

"You taught yourself how to read *and* the card system? Doubly impressive."

"Are you kidding me? You're so much stronger than I am!" Maaya exclaimed. "I've never seen designs like yours, and your cards are so powerful…"

"Yes, well, my family figured out my *gift* from an early age and spent quite a lot of money for a good tutor. If I was on my own, though, there's no way I'd get nearly as far as you have. Nobody does that on their own."

Saber grinned.

"I told you, Maaya, you're good at this. Give yourself some credit."

"The others picked it up so much faster than I did, though. Kim was already on my level."

"They also had the privilege of learning from someone who already knew it. You had to learn the hard way. Besides, I'm sure the captain would be more than willing to teach you what she knows," Saber added slyly.

"Oh, absolutely! I need someone who can keep up with me. The only other person on this ship who knows any *libris* at all… well, I suppose he's not here anymore, is he? My old first officer knew a little, but he only used it for physical boosts so he could do more around the ship. He was honestly so terribly boring. Anyway. I have to ask, Maaya. Now that I know this about you, I have to ask again why you're going to Krethus. Surely you must know what's going on over there."

Maaya and Saber shared a glance, and after a brief pause, Saber gave her the slightest hint of a nod.

"I do, yes. That's… actually why we're going," Maaya replied with effort. Even though she knew Adelaide wasn't likely to get angry over something like this, it was still hard to tell. "My friend Svante told me what was going on over there because he wanted me to help. He said he thought he had figured out a way to stop the machine that's causing the ghost walks."

"So they've reached even that far… but this man, he wasn't crazy, was he?" Adelaide asked suspiciously.

"Oh, no. He was a scientist. It was his job to figure out a way to stop them. His research led him to Sark, because there was a gem there he thought could protect whoever owned it against the barrier, or whatever is stopping people from getting to the machine."

"Really? I've heard of that as well. My government occasionally sends operatives off to search for just such a gem. Was it in Sark after all?"

"It was. That's what started to cause problems with that man I told you about, Rahu. Rahu and Svante actually worked together for a little while, but as soon as Rahu saw a chance to get ahead, he… he asked me to steal the gem and give it to him before Svante could find it."

"Did you?" Adelaide asked, unable to keep a flicker of irritation from her voice.

"No, not at all," Maaya said hastily. "It's… complicated. We ended up stealing a lookalike gem and giving it to Rahu because we couldn't find the real one, and that's because..."

"Here," Saber said simply, pointing to the gem on her forehead. It only took a few moments for Adelaide to figure it out.

"Stars, that *is* complicated. So the real gem does exist, but most people can't see it because it's attached to a ghost. Right, so what did that end up doing to Rahu and Svante?"

"Well, Rahu held what he *thought* was the real gem for ransom. He contacted the Krethan government and asked for a lot of money in exchange for it. By that time Svante and Rahu weren't talking anymore, and Svante asked me to come to Krethus with him instead because he knew the truth. And... we were so close, too."

"What happened?" Adelaide asked quietly, her tone softening.

"The night before we were supposed to leave, there were ghost walks all over the city. My friends and I—they knew *libris,* too—split up to try to protect as many people as we could. They... they ended up dying to the ghosts." Maaya looked away. She was *not* going to cry. "Once all the survivors gathered in the town square Rahu managed to calm them all down. He was almost nice to me for once, once he figured out what happened to my friends. But then Svante came by and thought Rahu was after me, so he tried to protect me, and... he..."

"That's when Rahu turned on them both and blamed them for the incident," Saber finished. Maaya shot her a grateful look. "Svante was publicly executed right in front of us, and we managed to escape using *libris*, but now all of Sark thinks Maaya brought the ghosts to Sark."

"I see." Adelaide placed both her palms on the large desk before her, her expression contemplative... and angry. "So this man is responsible for the deaths of your friends and one of my fellow citizens, he attempted to blackmail my government, and after he failed to kill you he sent the military after you?"

"He also made a living by pretending to be able to see ghosts; he just made Maaya and her friends get rid of them and took all the credit," Saber added helpfully. "Oh, and he burned our house down."

Adelaide's hands tightened into fists on the desk, and Maaya felt a rush of terror at the fury on her face. But then Adelaide relaxed, took a deep breath, and smiled.

"All in due time," she said brightly, then glanced back at Maaya. "I don't suppose Svante ever got a message to my government that you were coming along?"

"I don't think so. He meant to, but... well, he didn't get the chance," Maaya answered.

"That's fine. We'll take care of that once we arrive." At this, Adelaide walked around the desk and put both her hands on Maaya's shoulders, and Maaya felt a thrill of excitement at her touch. "You have my full support and the support of my entire crew in this endeavor. Once we get to Krethus, you can be assured that once my government knows what's going on, you will have their support as well, even if it's only the sanctioning of your efforts."

"Really? They won't hate me for being Selenthian?" Maaya asked hopefully.

"Of course not. Prejudices are for those privileged with enough comfort to develop them. We aren't in a position to deny someone's aid just because of where they come from. You could ooze out from under a rock for all they care as long as you can help us with our little problem. Anyway, speaking of the Krethan government..." Adelaide turned to face Saber now. "You must tell me about yourself. History was never my strong suit, but I know the robes of the old court when I see them. Who were you?"

Saber looked uncomfortable.

"I don't know. I have no memories of my past at all. Before Svante came along and recognized my clothes as well, I didn't even know I was Krethan. He did say he was going to help me figure all that out... I'm hoping that at some point that will still be a possibility."

"Of course! My family is well connected. We'll get that figured out for sure, don't you worry."

Saber smiled up at her appreciatively, and Maaya felt her heart swell with happiness again. Everything was starting to piece itself back together.

"So, speaking of you being in the Blackfins and everything... why were you wearing that pin that night I saw you in Levien? And the mask?" Maaya asked.

"The mask was simply a disguise. I have no qualms about anyone seeing me; I just don't want them to know who I am. That way if I get a negative reputation rather than a positive one, I'm safe," Adelaide explained. "As for the pin, it's for just in case I meet any others like me on the streets. There are other *libris*-capable ones out there, and some are trying to fight the ghosts in their own way. It's a much quicker introduction than trying to ask questions and explain myself if ever I meet any of them."

"Why are you going for any reputation? Shouldn't you be trying to keep *libris* a secret?" Maaya continued incredulously.

"Absolutely not. I can understand the thought, but my take on it is that if people never get to see the good of it they'll only ever know the bad. I'd rather Selenthia's minds be changed by positive exposure than by the necessity of disaster. Not everyone agrees with me, of course. My parents think it's a needless danger, and honestly I can understand that thought as well."

"No offense, but I have to agree with your parents," Maaya said with a light smile. "What are they like, anyway? Your family?"

Adelaide sat on the edge of the desk, swinging her legs back and forth.

"That's a little complicated, too. My family is of old Krethan money, and so they're pretty traditional in a lot of ways. I grew up living a very comfortable lifestyle with my two siblings, and my parents spent quite a lot of money on my education and career preparation. My older brother and younger sister had minds for numbers, so they were to be the bookkeepers and analysts of our family business' next generation. I… was a little harder to figure out. Eventually, once my parents realized there was no containing this personality of mine, they decided I should be the family's new face of the family when it came time. A high honor, you understand. My siblings were a little jealous. At least my brother was. My sister shared much of my impatience, and she was so young at the time she didn't really understand the gravity of it. Frankly, I didn't really, either."

"Did the ghosts stop all that from happening?" Maaya asked softly.

"Yes and no. Krethan's old money is very defiant in the face of disaster. With so much wealth tied up in various places it's hard to hit any of those families in the wallet. No, the family business is still alive and well, even if some of the family itself isn't. The ghosts killed my brother and I'm no longer involved, so it fell to my sister to learn to manage things on her own."

"Oh no… I'm so sorry," Maaya murmured.

"It's all right, I suppose. This was years and years ago. It wasn't until some years later that I decided to leave home to go adventuring in Selenthia. It sounds a silly reason for leaving, but it was… necessary. My parents and I haven't always seen eye to eye, we'll put it that way."

"Do you still talk to your family?" Maaya asked, hoping she didn't sound too tactless.

"Occasionally. We write letters back and forth every so often—that's what Saber saw me writing just now—and we're on good enough terms that I visit in person as well. They're pleasant people; we just get along better when my interactions with them are brief. Surprisingly, on top of me leaving the business, one of the things they always get on my case about is not bringing home a suitable husband or wife. Really, the pleasures they have time to worry about."

"Ah, so you're not currently seeing anyone, then," Saber said knowingly, and Maaya felt her cheeks threatening to flush.

"Correct. It's something I'd like to change eventually, providing my spouse-to-be is okay with my lifestyle. I'm not in the habit of changing myself that drastically for anyone, to the disappointment of many."

"I'm sure," Maaya said before she could stop herself. Adelaide raised her eyebrows with a smirk, and Maaya hastily continued, "So, is this what this trip is about? To go see your family again?"

"It is indeed. Evidently my sister's found someone to settle down with, and as you can imagine, my parents have been absolutely insufferable. I thought I'd drop by to see them now they're making some final preparations."

"Do your parents know you're with the Blackfins?" Saber asked curiously.

"They do. They weren't very happy with it at first, and I doubt they still are, but they have nobody but themselves to blame for my involvement. They were the ones who gave me this ship, after all." At the girls' surprised looks, she continued with a laugh, "Oh yeah. They had no idea what kind of bad habits they were encouraging with this, but it's all worked out. My family doesn't have any Blackfins in it besides me, but they are fairly well connected there, too. They've accumulated lots of favors from lots of donations."

"Are the Krethans not as afraid of the Blackfins as Selenthians are?" Saber asked with amusement.

"Not quite, but still some. My family's dealings were still mostly under the table, but you can imagine how valuable the Blackfins are as allies when there's a ghost problem. Commander David, who I'm sure you've heard all about by now, was actually the first person to serve under me. Through him we made other contacts, and soon enough we had quite a crew here. It was absolutely not what my parents intended, but it was too late by then."

"So how did you learn about *libris* during all this?" Maaya continued.

"It was a big part of my studies, actually," Adelaide explained. "As you may know, actually being able to use *libris* is a rare thing. Even many people with supernatural connections can't use it. On top of being rare, it's a valuable asset in Krethus given our situation. Oh, how times have changed. Anyway, once my parents figured out I could use it, they poured money into making sure I was as good as could be. It wasn't exactly broadcast, but they did brag about me at parties quite often. It was infuriating. But hey, they'll love to see that I've met another person who's so skilled at it. You'll keep me on my toes, they'll say. But I'm sure they'll love you in general. Who wouldn't?"

"Wait, what do you mean they'll love me?" Maaya inquired suspiciously.

"Well, you're going to meet them, of course."

"You could ask me first!" Maaya spluttered. "Is this something all your friends do after knowing you for two days?"

"No, you'd be the first in a long while."

"Why me?"

"Because you're cute, and I—"

"All right, forget I asked," Maaya interrupted wearily, and Adelaide laughed.

"Anyway, it's getting late. I'll finish my paperwork tomorrow; I am absolutely beat. I think I'll take a few minutes on the balcony before heading to bed. Would you two like to join me?"

"Thanks, but I think I'm going to go take a walk," Saber said immediately. "Now that I know everyone else can see me after all, I should go introduce myself properly. And probably give an awful lot of apologies. Oh, Maaya, you stay," Saber added as Maaya made to walk to the door with her. "You're tired, too. Stay here for a while, then get some sleep. If you come with me you'll be walking until you're dead on your feet."

Before Maaya could protest, Saber disappeared out the door. Maaya let loose a string of swears in her mind. Saber had definitely left her alone with Adelaide on purpose, and Maaya would definitely be talking to her about that later, too.

"Oh well. She can always join us another time," Adelaide said brightly. "Come on; it's so stuffy in here."

Adelaide walked across the cabin toward the door at the back, and Maaya followed, staring around her as she went. In the midst of the excitement from earlier she hadn't been able to get a proper look at the inside of the cabin. It wasn't as large as Maaya had expected from the outside; much of it was taken up by the large wooden desk in the center behind which Adelaide sat in her high-backed red velvet chair, but most of the walls were also covered with bookshelves enclosed in glass panels. Maaya spotted books and scrolls of all sizes behind the glass. A large bed was pushed against the far wall, and on the small table beside it sat a globe, a book, and a candle.

The next thing she noticed about the cabin was that, behind its initial illusions of grandeur, it was extremely messy. The floor rug was folded up at one edge as though someone had tripped upon it and had been in too much of a hurry to fold it back down again. A hat rested on one of the bedposts, and what looked to be nightclothes were flung unceremoniously in the general direction of the bed; only half of them had made it while the others lay in a crumpled heap on the floor. Multiple books lay open and scattered about on the large desk and across the floor, accompanied by multiple pairs of shoes. A long slender sword in its scabbard lay on the floor in one corner in a position that told Maaya it had, at one point, been propped up. The layer of dust upon it also told her it had fallen quite some time ago.

"I see you've finally noticed the personality I've added to this room," Adelaide said jovially. "Commander Strand keeps telling me to clean up after myself, but she doesn't understand. If I start cleaning this place up, I'll never finish my paperwork."

She led the way out onto the narrow balcony, taking one of the candles with her. The balcony was sparsely furnished with only a single lounge bench and a tiny table. Adelaide placed the candle upon the table and then sat down, inviting Maaya to join her. After a moment of hesitation, Maaya sat.

They spent a few long minutes in silence, staring out at the reflections of the ship's lights upon the calm waves of the water below, listening to the gentle creaking of wood and the flapping of sails,and the occasional unintelligible voice from the other side of the ship. The air was frigid but fresh, and Maaya inhaled deeply, letting it fill her lungs. She hadn't thought such a simple scene could be so beautiful. Or perhaps it was the company she currently held.

"So now we've gotten so many questions out of the way, I want to actually talk about you, if that's okay," Adelaide said, still staring out at the sea. Maaya stared at her, watching as the reflection of the candle's flame danced in her green eyes. "You've heard all the basics about my family… what's yours like?"

"I don't know. I grew up in orphanages—or at least, Sark's excuses for orphanages. I was always told that my parents are still alive, they just couldn't afford to take care of me. That's not a rare story where I'm from. I started living on my own when I was about twelve, and when I was thirteen, I met Saber. She helped take care of me from that point. I didn't always have a home, but I always had enough to eat with her help."

"That sounds really tough," Adelaide said sympathetically.

"It wasn't so bad. It was the only thing I knew, so it didn't bother me too much. The hard part was the ghosts. Lots of ghosts would just not leave me alone when they found out I could see them, so I had some close calls. Believe it or not, it was Rahu who saved me from some angry people once. He knew what I could see, so he offered to help me get by if I worked for him."

"Using you from the get-go. Disgusting," Adelaide said derisively. "And you were so young, too."

"I was really grateful at the time. And I suppose if it hadn't been for him I never would have felt the need to look for others who were like me. I never would have found my friends."

"What were their names?"

"Kalil, Sovaan, and Kim. They could all see ghosts, too. It was so nice to be around people who could see what I saw, you know? It made so much of what we went through worth it. So long as we had each other, everything was okay. And now… I don't even have anything to remember them by, except…"

Maaya reached into the pocket of her cloak and drew out Kim's diary, holding it in both hands. She hadn't looked at it since they had arrived in Anorath. Almost instantly she regretted taking it out to look at it as a fresh wave of grief swept over her.

As Maaya thought to put it back in her cloak, Adelaide put a comforting hand over hers, and Maaya stopped.

"A diary… have you looked at it?" Adelaide asked gently.

Maaya shook her head.

"I don't know if I should. It was her private writing. I think I'm happy just having something that she had."

"That's good of you, Maaya. If I may… is this the only thing she wrote in?"

"I think so. Even if not, it's the only thing left anyway. Saber only just managed to save this before our house burned down."

"In that case… I think you should read it someday. Not now, but someday," Adelaide offered. "She was dear to you, right? The way I see it is this: that notebook holds her thoughts and ideas never heard by anyone else in the world. That book may survive this world longer than you. If anyone should have this last glimpse into her world, and to decide what is shared and interpreted the way it should be—or what remains hidden forever—it should by all accounts be you."

Maaya choked on a sob, looking away hastily as she fought back the tears welling in her eyes.

"I'm sorry," she sniffed. "I don't mean to put this all on you so suddenly."

"Hey, it's okay. Promise." Adelaide put an arm around Maaya's shoulder and her free hand on Maaya's lap, pulling the girl closer. "I can't imagine the life you've led, especially when you've been alone for so much of it, but I can promise you that you will never have to worry about that again, okay? You've got friends here, and you've got me."

Maaya nodded and leaned her head on Adelaide's shoulder. It was all she could do to keep her emotions under control. She had been given hope and then had hope snatched away so many times that she almost didn't want to believe this was happening. This seemed almost too good to be true. Adelaide was a genuinely compassionate person, just like it seemed most of the others on this ship were. She was starting to think Nadya had been right. Maybe there didn't need to be a reason for this kindness. Maybe it could really be the way of things… and maybe it already was, and she had simply been around the wrong people for too long.

They sat in silence for a long while, and Maaya started to feel drowsy again. Evidently Adelaide felt the same way, for she soon stood up and stretched, yawning widely.

"If I stay a moment longer I'll fall asleep out here, and as much as I enjoy your company, that's just not a good idea for either of us."

She extended a hand to Maaya and pulled her easily to her feet, then opened the door back to the cabin. The candles inside were flickering at the end of their wicks, leaving the room darker than before, though this somehow made it seem all the more comfortable.

"Can you find your way back okay?" Adelaide asked, yawning again, and Maaya nodded. "Great. You get some sleep, and I'll see you tomorrow."

She led Maaya to the double doors that opened to the main deck and opened one for her.

"Thanks for listening earlier," Maaya said warmly. "It was really nice to spend some time with you."

"The feeling is definitely mutual. Let's do it again soon." Adelaide pulled her in for another hug, and then to Maaya's utter surprise, kissed the top of her head. "Sweetest of dreams to you. Now I'm off before I fall asleep on the floor again."

"What? Again?"

But the door was already closed.

Maaya made her way back down the stairs, nearly skipping in her happiness. There were butterflies in her stomach, but for once it was a feeling she hoped would last.

As she re-entered her room, she noticed Saber floating there, a knowing grin on her face.

"You're welcome," the ghost said simply.

"For what? You didn't have to leave, you know," Maaya insisted.

"Providing you aren't just being stubborn, you are the most adorably naïve person I've ever met," Saber countered.

"What are you talking about? I already know *you* know I like her. There's no hiding that from you."

"Yes, well, she's not exactly a master of deception herself," Saber rebutted innocently.

"What do you mean?"

"Oh, you poor innocent thing. She's quite infatuated with you as well. Are you really going to say you couldn't tell?"

"She is not," Maaya retorted, then hesitated. "…is she?"

"What's that thing she says every time you ask why she's done something for you?" Saber asked, clearly amused.

"What, the thing about liking me? People can be friends, you know."

"If you insist!" Saber surrendered. "Perhaps you're right. I suppose only time will tell."

"Oh, stop teasing me. You'll get my hopes up. It's not like you have any more experience with this than I do. Anyway, I thought you were going to be off talking to the crew," Maaya said, rolling her eyes as she pulled off her clothes again and slipped back into bed.

"I was, but since Adelaide didn't tell them they're allowed to talk to me now they're still pretending not to see me. I'm sure Adelaide will deal with that tomorrow," Saber sighed. "Besides, I needed to make sure I was here to gloat before you came back and fell asleep."

Maaya laughed, then lay back on the bed's thick pillow as Saber put out the candle on the small desk under the window. Before she could close her eyes and drift off, however, Saber spoke again, her voice quieter and more serious now.

"I really am sorry for what I said before. I… I don't know where that came from. It was a really foul thing for me to say."

"It's okay. You were kind of right. I've done my share of silly things recently. I deserve more than one stern talking to."

"I suppose." Saber sounded uncertain, as though there was something else she wanted to say. "Still. I can scold you without the insults. You really are brave, you know that?"

"I'm slowly starting to believe it," Maaya murmured, closing her eyes and smiling. Her heart felt lighter still now this loose end was being taken care of sooner than she'd expected. "We're all safe and okay, and that's what's important right now. After tonight I'm sure we can fix anything."

"I hope so," Saber answered simply.

Maaya turned over in bed, and then, her smile still on her face, she let sleep take her.

23

DEAD ZONE

The next morning, Maaya awoke rested and refreshed. She sat up to get dressed, humming absentmindedly, and at first she wasn't sure why she was in such a good mood. As she replayed the events of the previous evening over in her mind, however, she grinned.

Saber was nowhere to be seen, but Maaya wasn't concerned. The light of late morning shone through the small window over the desk, so Maaya guessed that Saber had left hours ago eager to see the captain as soon as she awoke, and that the ghost was now undoubtedly talking to everyone she could.

As Maaya finished putting on her shoes, her stomach growled, and she realized she hadn't eaten since near lunch the day before. She had been hoping to see Adelaide again, but she suspected the captain was busy finishing all the paperwork she had neglected the day before—and Maaya was already feeling slightly dizzy from lack of food. That would definitely need to be taken care of first.

She ran her fingers through her hair in an attempt to tame it, smoothed down her cloak, then took a breath and made her way out onto the deck.

The pleasant combination of the cool breeze and warm sun washed over her, and she closed her eyes to experience it all the better. The air was fresh, untainted by the smoke of industry and fog of the valley, and the sky was clear and vivid blue save for a few puffy white clouds. The Windfire cut smoothly through the low waves, and Maaya welcomed the occasional spray of ocean mist on her face. She was quickly coming to understand why Adelaide loved the ocean so much.

Suddenly, she heard a burst of laughter from the deck near the bow. Glancing over, she saw a small group of sailors standing in a circle. Saber was with them, and while the others were laughing, she looked perturbed. A moment later, Saber took one of the crew member's hats off her head and floated a few feet higher, making the sailor jump for it in vain as the others doubled over in renewed mirth.

"Hey, Maaya!" called Halvar from behind her. The officer waved down to her from where he stood at the helm, then beckoned for her to join him. "Cap'n wants to see you!"

Maaya trotted up the stairs, unable to hide her smile. At the top of the stairs she found Adelaide standing in the doorway to her cabin, stretching her arms with what appeared to be great effort.

"Morning!" Adelaide greeted her, relaxing with a sigh. "I am absolutely exhausted already, but all of our paperwork is officially done."

"What kind of paperwork do you have to do, anyway?" Maaya wondered.

"Some official things, some not. I have to keep track of the crew and the cargo we're carrying, the state of the ship when we left port, any supplies we need to pick up and repairs that may be necessary, as well as noting any complaints, reports, disturbances… oh, the list goes on and on. And then there's all the paperwork that makes us look like legitimate sailors, like fake trade agreements, fake receipts, all that good stuff."

"She's an absolute stickler about it," Halvar complained, relaxing with his elbows propped up on the railing.

"When it's done right, we don't get in trouble—and you, bless your heart, do not do it right," Adelaide chastised, then winked.

"Well, we can't *all* be the brains. I guess I make up for that with my talents in literally everything else."

"Don't you have some work to be doing?" Adelaide pressed.

"Probably. Give my poor little brain some time to figure it out."

Adelaide blew a raspberry at him, then stepped back into her cabin.

"Maaya, join me. I'm about to have lunch."

Maaya happily followed and took a seat in one of the comfortable chairs in front of Adelaide's desk. Adelaide had evidently done some cleaning during the course of her paperwork, as much of the desk was now visible—at least enough of it to fit Adelaide's food. There was a small platter of what appeared to be fish sandwiches and a second plate of various fruits and vegetables, some of which Maaya had never seen before. A small bowl of hummus sat in the middle of the fruit and vegetable plate, lightly garnished with chia seeds and thyme.

"I'm used to eating on my own, so I forgot to ask for extra dishes. We'll have to share," Adelaide said, taking a monstrous bite of a crisp pale-looking vegetable while at the same time taking a sandwich in her other hand. "I'm so hungry. I said I wouldn't distract myself with food until the paperwork was done. You seem like a disciplined sort, though."

"I don't know if I'd go that far," Maaya said lightly, taking a bite of one of the sandwiches. The bread was a little hard, but it was otherwise delicious--far more so than she expected from ship food. "I got everything done by the time it needed to be done, and that's all I ever cared to tell anyone."

Adelaide flashed her a knowing glance.

"A girl after my own heart, then. Too much, in fact. I was hoping you might be able to help keep me on track. Inga tries, but she seems so much like my mother sometimes that I can't help but rebel."

"I'm surprised! You seem so… put together, so organized," Maaya pondered aloud.

"On the outside, sure," Adelaide said, taking a deep scoop from the hummus bowl with another chunk of vegetable. "And it's true: as a whole I get things done, and I get things done well. It's just that the situation inside my head is an absolute mess most of the time. I find it hard to focus on most things, but then there are other things, just a few, that I can give my all and then some. Ask me to do paperwork and my brain will throw a tantrum like it's a child, but ask me to steer a ship and handle ropes and manage an entire crew and I can do it until I drop from exhaustion, and I'll absolutely adore every second of it."

"I can't imagine. When I was back in Sark I was in 'charge' of three, maybe four people—if you could call it being in charge at all—and it was so difficult," Maaya mused.

"Did you like it?"

"I suppose. I mean, I started doing it because it was necessary, but I think it grew on me. If I had to say, I think I'd rather be the one taking orders than giving them, though."

"Why is that?" Adelaide continued, deeply intrigued.

"Well, making decisions is hard, isn't it? When you tell someone to do something you're responsible for whatever happens to them."

"True! And there are times when you feel the weight of that responsibility on your shoulders. But then there are the times you feel a certain exhilaration to it, and you remember all the times you were the one taking orders and you told yourself, 'I can do better than this.' And then, suddenly, you get the chance to prove it. Oh, it's wonderful. Halvar is right: I am a stickler, and about many things at that, but I'll tell you right now there is no better crew and no ship better run on the ocean right now."

"Were you always like this? Being a leader and loving people, I mean," Maaya asked, finishing her first sandwich. She glanced down to take another, and with slight alarm realized there were already only a few left.

"Oh, no. Not at all. When I was younger I was terrified of people," Adelaide said. "I had always gotten the feeling I never quite understood social customs. Every conversation was a challenge that mentally exhausted me. Looking natural was difficult, so obviously I sought to avoid it."

"So what happened?" Maaya inquired, leaning forward slightly in her seat.

"I became jealous of how easily people were able to talk to one another, and I figured that it was something that could come with practice. Since I avoided conversation at all costs, obviously, I never got better. So I decided to start by complimenting one stranger every single day to get me more used to it."

"That's so cute!" Maaya exclaimed, grinning. "Why that?"

"I always had trouble starting conversations, so I figured what better way to start a conversation than by telling someone something nice? Either that opens them up to further conversation or they walk away feeling better than before. Either way, I slowly began to get over my fear of approaching people, and conversing became more natural. I still struggle with anything that isn't incredibly straightforward, so I don't know if I've gotten better at communicating, but I have gotten better at not caring what people might think of me."

"I suppose I've never given it much thought," Maaya admitted, chewing slowly on a jicama. "I've only really ever said what I thought was necessary and not much more. But you can probably tell I don't really like talking to others."

"Given the type of people you've had the option of talking to, I can't say I blame you at all. But we'll change that, just you wait and see," Adelaide winked. "Oh dear. I think I've gone and eaten too much. Here, you take the rest."

Maaya did a double take. She wasn't sure how Adelaide had managed to make so much food disappear, especially not with how much she had been talking, but there was hardly anything left.

"Next time, separate plates," Maaya said, raising her eyes to meet Adelaide's, and Adelaide let out a guilty laugh. "Hey… does it seem kind of quiet suddenly?"

The women fell silent, listening hard, and then the smile vanished from Adelaide's face.

"Oh no."

At once she was on her feet, heading to the door. Quite concerned, Maaya followed, leaving what remained of her food behind.

As she stepped back out onto the deck, the silence still seemed to surround her, but she couldn't figure out why. Nothing had changed visibly since she had gone into the cabin; much of the crew was still on deck doing whatever it was they normally did, and there didn't appear to be anything out of the ordinary about the weather.

"You noticed, eh, cap'n?" Halvar grunted disapprovingly.

"Maaya, actually," Adelaide responded. "How long?"

"Only about a minute. We're hoping it's a fluke."

"I hope so. All the same, make sure our fins are working so we can use them if necessary, and have the sails raised and secured just in case."

"Aye, cap'n."

Halvar swept off toward the lower deck as the other officers made their way toward him.

"What's going on?" Maaya asked concernedly.

"That silence. Have you figured out where it's coming from?" Adelaide frowned.

Maaya glanced around. The crew was a little quiet, but this wasn't enough to create this oppressive blanket of stillness. There was always *some* noise no matter what time of day or night it was. She glanced out over the horizon, looking for any possible weather disturbance that might somehow dampen the sounds she usually heard—and then she did a double take.

"There's no wind," she realized.

Sure enough, the sails hung limply from the yards and the ocean had taken on a glassy calm that was equally fascinating and unsettling. At first, the sight fascinated her. She had never seen or heard anything like this before, and the tranquil water was oddly inviting. But then another thought occurred to her: without wind, they weren't moving.

"Yep. Not an ideal situation," Adelaide said darkly. "We're sitting ducks like this."

"Is there danger out here?" Maaya asked nervously.

"Not often, but it's always best to be able to move if you need to. Besides, we have to think about what could happen if the Selenthians realize you've escaped. If they pursue us and we're stuck here, that's bad news."

"It's been a few minutes and nothing's picked up yet; my guess is we're stuck in a doldrum, ma'am," Gunnar said as he approached. Behind him, crew members were already working to raise the sails.

"This can't last too long, can it?" Maaya asked quietly, her heart starting to thump in her chest now she was starting to realize the gravity of the situation. She stared at the sea behind them, looking for any ships that might be chasing them, but she saw nothing.

"That's the problem. We have no idea," Gunnar shrugged. "This could last for an hour or a month."

"There've been stories of ships stuck out in doldrums for weeks, and everyone aboard died after they ran out of food," Halvar said, jogging back up to meet the rest. "Of course, that won't happen to us; we have our oar system, but that won't take us anywhere fast. It's usually just for easy maneuvering in port when our sails are down. And making everyone else jealous, of course."

"Where's the commander?" Adelaide inquired of Halvar.

"Helping the crew check the steam engine before we start 'er up. Figured we might as well do all our pre-docking maintenance now we've got to re-fill the tank and all. The longer we can run the engine without trouble the better for our sanity, I figure."

"Understood. While they work on that, I guess we're stuck," Adelaide sighed. "This hasn't happened to us in a good while; of *course* it would happen now that I want to get home quickly."

"You don't think anyone would realize I've come out here already, do you?" Maaya said uneasily.

"It's hard to say. As much as we joke about the bronzies, they're pretty bright, all things considered. And they did realize you were in Levien after only a short time. They might have realized their mistake not long after we left. Finding us out here on the ocean might be a bit more challenging, but they also have a lot of ships to play with," Adelaide replied thoughtfully. "To be clear, I don't think we're in any danger right *now*; I only worry if this continues for too long."

"We'll be fine," Halvar added reassuringly. "This is an inconvenience at most. Anyway, if we're stuck I'm off to have some fun. Holler if you need me."

"Do you need me for anything, or can I go babysit?" Gunnar asked. Adelaide smirked and nodded after Halvar, and Gunnar departed.

"So… we wait?" Maaya continued uncertainly.

"Basically. Until our oars are ready or the wind picks up we aren't going anywhere, and there's really not much to do then. If this only lasts a little while we're in good shape, but it can get pretty boring otherwise," Adelaide explained. She looked somewhat calmer, but Maaya still detected some nervousness behind her calm voice.

"Well, if anyone was following us, wouldn't they get caught without the wind, too?"

"Sure, but they come prepared. Their long-distance ships usually have teams of oarsmen on board specifically for instances like this, or for when damage takes out their sails. I love steam tech as much as anyone else, but a good old-fashioned team of oarsmen can go more than twice as fast as our system here."

Maaya quickly suppressed the swell of fear that threatened to overtake her and tried to ignore her mind's helpful reminder that every time she had been on the brink of escaping up until now, something had always happened to get in the way.

But then her thoughts were interrupted as she heard a scream from the deck below.

She snapped to attention and glanced around frantically, searching for the source of the cry, and then noticed a dark shape falling from one of the yards. A split second later, she recognized Halvar. What he had been doing she couldn't guess, but he was now plummeting toward the ocean below. A moment later he was gone, vanishing beneath the flat ocean surface.

Before she could react, everyone below burst into applause. Only a moment later, Halvar's head reappeared above the water, and he flashed them all a proud grin.

"Idiot," Adelaide laughed. "You all right, Maaya?"

"I… fine!" Maaya said quickly, turning away and clearing her throat awkwardly.

Halvar was soon joined by three others, then five, then a dozen, all of whom gladly took off their coats, hats, and shoes and leapt into the water with varying levels of grace. A few took to the mainmast, which they maneuvered expertly, and jumped, some doing tricks as they dove.

"That didn't take long," came a voice from Maaya's right. She turned and saw Saber floating idly toward them. "I was listening to a most interesting conversation about sea slugs—at least, that's what I hope it was about—and then my entire group ran off."

"Saber! Lovely to see you. How's the crew?" Adelaide beamed.

"Well enough. Their spirits are high; that much I can gather from their relentless taunting. Once I get past that, they're a charming lot, really."

"I'm so glad you like them. It means a lot. Anyway, I can't believe I haven't asked this already. Do you two know how to swim?"

"I know how not to drown, I think," Maaya offered.

"Why me?" Saber asked.

"I wouldn't want to exclude you just because you're dead," Adelaide said as though Saber's question was the silliest thing she'd heard all morning. "You can come with Maaya and me."

"I'm sorry?" Maaya asked, but by then the captain had already taken her by the wrist and was pulling her gently down the stairs and to the port side of the ship where a wide section of railing had been folded down.

"You, my friend, need some swimming lessons if you're going to be on this ship any longer," Adelaide insisted cheerily. "Here, I'll even go first, and then you can come to me."

The captain unbuckled her coat and shrugged it off while at the same time kicking off her boots. Once she was down to her pants and undershirt, she flashed Maaya another smile, then leapt off the side of the ship, diving into the water with such poise that hardly a ripple emanated from her point of entry. A few seconds later she reappeared, flinging her soaking red hair behind her, and she waved eagerly to Maaya.

"Hop in! I've got you."

Maaya was suddenly nervous. Her swimming experience was very limited, and she hadn't been in water apart from that which was necessary for hygiene for years. She was sure she could keep afloat, but beyond that she knew little of swimming. While the calm water had looked inviting from the safety of the top deck, its dark and seemingly endless depths now seemed frightening.

But, she reasoned, the ocean was where Adelaide was… and she wasn't about to let her fear get in the way of *that.*

Without allowing herself a second thought, she took off her outer clothes, and then she jumped.

Her landing was much less graceful, and she fought her instinct to kick and push with her arms as soon as she hit the water. Still, she was painfully aware of how she looked as her head broke the surface and she coughed. Almost immediately, she felt a supporting hand at her side.

"You're all right, there you go," the captain said encouragingly. "It's been a while, huh?"

"Most of the times I was in water like this, it was by accident," Maaya spluttered, kicking her feet to avoid floundering with her hands.

"I can tell," Adelaide laughed. "Here, come to the ladder so you can hang on to something."

Adelaide guided Maaya to the side of the ship where there were a number of parallel indents carved into the wooden hull. Maaya held on tight, relieved at the respite, then watched as Adelaide kicked off from the side of the ship, treading water effortlessly in front of her.

"Right. When you're in the water and you're inexperienced, your instinct might be to kick and flail and do whatever you need to stay afloat. What you need to remember is that even if you hardly move at all, you'll still float. If I lay on my back I might just fall asleep and I'll still be above water. We're naturally pretty buoyant. What you want to do instead is move your legs and arms only enough to keep you situated upright and your body will handle the rest. Watch what I'm doing."

Maaya observed as Adelaide swam a little closer, then continued treading water. Sure enough, her arms hardly moved; they seemed only to be there to stabilize her as her legs kept her head above water.

"We'll practice that first, because once you've got that down the rest is about as easy as you can get. It's staying comfortable above water and not panicking that challenges most people."

Maaya spent the next twenty minutes practicing, and through focus and Adelaide's encouragement, she found herself able to keep herself above water with no assistance for increasing lengths of time. She found herself quickly tiring, however, something Adelaide seemed to notice. The captain helped her back to the ladder, a knowing smile playing across her lips.

"Another thing about swimming: it works just about every muscle in your body, including about a dozen or so you didn't even know you had. It's one of the best ways you can build consistent strength. If you're a beginner, though, you don't want to spend too long in the water just practicing; the middle of the ocean is not a good place to run out of strength, you understand."

Maaya nodded shakily, suddenly feeling extra grateful for Adelaide's presence.

"Save some of your strength, Maaya. You should have at least one go at whatever the crew is doing now," came Saber's voice from above. Maaya looked up to see the ghost floating lazily a few feet above them. "I don't know about the swimming part, but you're definitely good at climbing and jumping. Look."

Maaya stared. About a dozen of the crew, including Halvar and Gunnar, were lining up on the topsail yard. As soon as everyone was in line, the man at the head of the line jumped, making a stupendous dive into the water far below. Almost as soon as he had reappeared safely away from the ship, the next person jumped, and then the next, each garnering applause as they did.

"I have to admit I wish gravity affected me the same way it affected all of you; I would be up there in an instant," Saber said with amusement.

"Oh, yes! Let's do that!" Adelaide exclaimed. "You aren't afraid of heights, are you, Maaya?"

"Only a little, but—"

"Great! I'll go first again and make sure you're all right once you hit the water. Just remember how little effort you need to stay afloat and you'll be fine. Oh, and don't panic."

"Right…"

Maaya followed the captain up the ladder with trepidation, and Saber followed close behind as they ascended the mainmast. Those already back on the ship, looking eager to get back above, stepped back to allow them passage.

Climbing the mast was much easier than Maaya expected, and she felt almost at home. This was what she was good at even without the assistance of *libris.* It was also much shorter than Maaya expected—until, that was, she looked down.

The view from the topsail yard was simultaneously awe-inspiring and terrifying. With no land or buildings in the way, Maaya felt as though she was seeing the world for the first time, and more of it at once than she ever had before. She remembered standing on the rooftop in Levien a few nights prior and how vastly different that had seemed. Now she thought about it, she couldn't decide which she liked more.

As they made their way to the very edge of the yard, Saber floated even closer to Maaya. Maaya was sure the ghost wanted to be there in case she lost her balance, but the way Saber looked at the back of Adelaide's head made Maaya think there may have been something more to her presence there.

"How are you feeling? Not too scared yet, I hope?" Adelaide questioned encouragingly.

"I don't think so," Maaya answered hesitantly. "If I jump from this high, won't I go far underwater?"

"You'd think so, but not really!" Adelaide said. "If you're nervous, bend your legs a little when you enter the water; it'll prevent you from going straight down. Oh, and… hold on."

"Hold on to what?" Maaya asked, bemused.

"No. Look."

She gestured to a point far in the distance off the port beam. Maaya squinted. A tiny dark shape was now on the horizon, one that hadn't been there before. After a moment, Maaya realized it was a ship—and it was headed in their direction.

"Ship incoming! All hands on deck!" Adelaide cried sharply, her tone changing in an instant. All at once, the crew below began making their way back aboard the ship, and those currently on board headed to their stations. Adelaide turned to face Maaya, her expression almost apologetic. "We'll have to have our fun another time, it seems. Let's get below."

Adelaide quickly leapt back to the mast and started her way down with expertise born of years at sea. Maaya and Saber watched her for a moment, and then shared a knowing look.

"Shall we?" Saber grinned.

"Like we haven't shown off enough already," Maaya retorted playfully, letting the ghost take her hands.

A moment later she was in the air. Not bothering to return to the mast, Maaya leapt directly off the yard above the deck. She felt a rush of adrenaline as she plummeted toward the deck below, but not quite fear. She heard scattered cries of alarm and couldn't help but smile. Saber held on, slowing and controlling her descent, but not so much that it didn't still look dangerous to someone unfamiliar with this tactic.

She landed firmly on the deck only a moment later, Saber letting her go just inches before her feet touched down. Once Saber was certain Maaya had her balance, she went off to pick up Maaya's clothes from the deck.

"Stars, Maaya, you just about had my heart," came Adelaide's breathless voice from behind her. Maaya turned to see the captain just reaching the last rungs on the mainmast, and felt oddly satisfied at having beaten her to the deck.

"Hey, you're going to have to do that again! That was impressive," Halvar called approvingly from the top deck, and Maaya grinned.

Before Maaya could reply, Saber returned with her bundle of clothes, and then swiftly flew off to get the captain's belongings as well.

"What do you make of it, Gunnar?" the captain asked, her tone once again all business.

"Let me see here," Gunnar murmured, his ocular implant whirring softly as he tried to get a better look at the ship. "It doesn't look like the usual navy ship, but it's still too far off to tell. Whoever they are, they definitely spotted us first. They're headed right for us."

"Can you estimate the radius of the doldrum?" Adelaide continued.

"My guess is about fifteen miles, ma'am, but that could be off. It's hard to tell from here."

"That'll do. How's our steam engine?"

"Ready and waiting on your command, Captain," Commander Strand answered immediately.

"Get us moving after a head count. In the meantime, Gunnar, make sure we're ready to defend ourselves," Adelaide ordered. Both Gunnar and Inga nodded, then hurried away. Adelaide sighed, then stepped over to the side of the ship and squeezed some of the water out of her hair. "What a day."

"You don't think they want to fight, do you?" Maaya asked fearfully.

"Anyone who puts their ship on a direct course for another often needs help badly or plans to attack. It's generally seen as a pretty aggressive move," Adelaide explained, shaking her head so that her long hair fell back into place behind her shoulders. "It's hard to tell at this distance, so for now we're only making sure we're prepared."

"That sounds scary. Have you ever had to fight before?"

"Only a few times. I prefer escape if I can, but I fight if I must, and we've always won. Using *libris* is cheating, really. Oh, but that reminds me. Crewman!" The man she spoke to immediately stopped and stood at attention, waiting for orders. "Get our peace flag flying."

The man rushed off, and Maaya couldn't help but admire Adelaide's unquestioned air of authority even as she stood mostly undressed and soaking wet. It was a look Maaya wouldn't mind seeing again, she thought before she could stop herself.

The steam engine came to life with a loud hiss, and a plume of steam rose up behind the Windfire. This was followed almost immediately by the sound of splashing on either side of the ship as the fin-like oars began moving.

The ship began moving slowly forward, and Maaya understood

Adelaide's concerns. As useful as the oars were, not to mention what a technical marvel they were, the Windfire wasn't moving all that quickly. The other ship, still miles off, was clearly moving faster with the wind in their sails.

The heat of the sun dried their clothes quickly, and after ten minutes Maaya felt comfortable enough to put on her coat and shoes. Adelaide soon did the same, though her thick hair was still clearly wet. Before long, there was hardly any sign of what had happened earlier.

"Anything yet, Gunnar?" Adelaide said quietly as they progressed. She stood with most of the other officers on the top deck, with Maaya and Saber close by.

"Definitely not a navy ship, ma'am. And from what I can see they're flying peaceful colors," Gunnar answered, squinting. "They've raised sails, though, so they must have lost their wind by now. Oh, but they've got oars, too."

"That's unusual for a non-navy ship," Halvar said thoughtfully. "Their complement must be impressive."

"There's that… or something else," Adelaide speculated. Halvar threw her a questioning glance, and Inga nodded as though Adelaide had just made an excellent point.

"That's about as vague as you can get, cap'n," Halvar grumbled.

"Would you like me to go out and get a closer look?" Saber offered, but Adelaide shook her head.

"I don't think so. Stay with us for now, just in case. Gunnar… I don't suppose you can make out what kind of ship we're looking at by now?"

In response, Gunnar grinned.

"I can now, ma'am. Looks like an old man o' war, rusted and rotted to bits, and it's got a mermaid with two tails as its figurehead."

Adelaide breathed a sigh of relief, and Halvar's face suddenly lit up with understanding.

"Oh, no kidding! It seems like it's been ages since we've seen them; I thought they'd finally sunk."

Maaya and Saber looked between them, waiting for some kind of explanation, but none came.

Luckily, they didn't have to wait long.

Maaya could hardly see it at first, but then she was able to make out three small shapes moving toward the Windfire from the other ship. Their forms were hazy and pale, and at first she thought they might be mirages, shimmering over the still ocean in the heat of the sun. But as they grew larger, coming ever closer to the ship at a speed no dinghy could ever hope to reach, she realized they were ghosts.

The three ghosts flew straight onto the ship and up to the top deck with such confidence that Maaya was almost certain they had been here before. This was only reaffirmed when the officers and some of the crew gave them friendly waves as they approached. They stopped in front of Adelaide, who smiled and shook the lead man's hand like they were old friends.

The ghost in front was a tall middle-aged man dressed in a tattered officer's coat in a style Maaya didn't recognize, but the way he stood slightly in front of the others made her think he was of high rank. Her attention was immediately drawn to a massive gash that traveled from his forehead down over his left eye and finally stopped just above his upper lip. The skin that wasn't covered by his wiry eyebrows or long unkempt mustache and beard was dark and ridden with wrinkles that told the story of a man who had rarely, if ever, changed his facial expression.

The others—a man and a woman—were at least two decades younger, and they wore the uniforms of sailors. They sported the same unkempt look as the man in front of them… and similarly gruesome injuries. They stood obediently by the first man's side, not moving and not speaking.

Before the tall ghost said a word, his working eye flicked up to stare at Saber for a moment, and then he looked at Adelaide. When he spoke, it was deep and gravely, equally strengthened and worn ragged by years of use.

"I know it's been a while, Captain, but I didn't think it had been so long your crew had the chance to start dying and continuing to serve into perpetuity."

"Oh, she's not part of my crew. She's a friend of a guest!" Adelaide explained with a grin, gesturing at Maaya. The girl suddenly felt extremely self-conscious, but the ghost hardly looked at her.

"You didn't do *guests* last time, either. But I suppose as long as you're always captain, I'll be able to deal with whatever else changes. It's good to see you, of course," the ghost rumbled.

"And you! Sorry I'm not around more often; I've been consigned to local deliveries for a while. I'm taking full advantage of this trip as I can, though it would be much nicer without this damned dead zone. Anyway." Adelaide turned to Maaya, pointing between her and the three others. "Maaya, this is Captain Skarin of the Nocte Cadenza. Skarin, this is Maaya. We met in Levien, and she's coming to Krethus with me."

Skarin raised his right eyebrow ever so slightly.

"Your guest is Selenthian? Times are changing faster than I can keep up. You're also getting shoddy in your work, Captain."

"What do you mean?" Adelaide asked.

"You were always so good about covering up after yourself. I did figure you were bound to slip up eventually, but I didn't expect it to happen so soon. You're still so young and full of promise."

"Still not following, Skarin," Adelaide replied smoothly.

"Hmm? Perhaps this wasn't your fault, then. Either way, I thought you ought to know there's a small fleet of Selenthian navy ships after you. They're a few hours out. If this dead zone doesn't fade soon they'll catch up to you by nightfall."

Now, suddenly, Adelaide looked concerned.

"What? How many? From where?"

"You'll see them dead astern when the light is right. There are perhaps eight or nine, and they're moving quickly. Now, if they aren't so desperately after you, perhaps you can tell me what they *are* after."

Maaya's heart sank, more out of guilt than fear. Her mere presence here threatened the lives of everyone on board and there was nothing she could do about it. She watched Adelaide, unable to tear her gaze away from the captain, who, despite her obvious fear, kept her expression neutral.

"Oh, they're after us all right," Adelaide replied. "But the reason is irrelevant. If we still have a few hours yet, we'll find a way to escape. Gunnar says the dead zone can't be *that* big."

"Which was perhaps true when he looked the first time, but had he looked again he would notice it's expanding in front of you," Skarin growled. "But not behind, which is important. They can still catch up with you, but you can't flee."

Adelaide shared a look with her officers, then glanced back at the ghost.

"What about doubling back to get our wind, then going around the zone?" she proposed.

"Won't work. They've spread out, so if you double back they'll surely catch you. What's more, you wouldn't get out of the zone even on the short side with this… ridiculous contraption," he said disdainfully, gesturing at the puffs of steam dissipating over top the Windfire.

Adelaide cursed.

"Suggestions?" she insisted of the group of officers.

"I've already got one," Skarin said. "The majority of their ships are small frigates at best; they're fast, but not all that effective in a fight."

"That doesn't matter when it's eight or nine against one," Adelaide responded sharply.

"True, if your hypothetical situation involved one ship on your side," Skarin said lightly.

"Fine. Two, then. Your ship is powerful, but not that powerful."

"Correct. That's why I brought more."

He gestured to the horizon behind him, and Maaya's eyes widened. Several tiny dots had appeared behind Skarin's massive man o' war, and they were growing slowly larger all the while.

"They too will be here by nightfall," Skarin continued. "We will cover your escape, but if you would so honor us as to lead the charge, we will fire upon every miserable ship in their pathetic fleet until all that's left of them is memory and smoke."

Adelaide looked undecided, but Saber's face lit up with joy.

"What are you so happy about?" Maaya murmured.

Saber opened her mouth to answer, then hesitated, suddenly looking thoughtful. Then her face fell.

"I just got excited by the prospect of a good fight, that's all. I forgot some people don't want to be dead just yet."

"It's generally a stage you want to let someone reach willingly, but we can't all be so lucky. Given that you and I are already there I think some excitement is only understandable," Skarin broke in, staring at Saber with approval.

"Oh? Is your whole fleet made up of ghosts?" Saber asked, intrigued.

"The whole lot. Getting together for something like this isn't common, but I have some sway and also a vested interest in doing as much damage to the Selenthian fleet as I possibly can."

"Why?" Maaya asked.

"They're the reason I'm dead," Skarin explained flatly. "I was a sailor, and a law-abiding one at that, but they saw I was from the wrong part of the world and that was all the reason they needed. They boarded my ship, killed everyone aboard while making me watch, took everything we had, and then set my ship ablaze to let me burn and drown. It wasn't a pleasant death."

"How awful," Saber continued, though her empathy was clearly overpowered by her curiosity. "So, what, you died mortal enemies and now in death you seek to continue your work?"

"Oh, nothing so petty," Skarin replied dismissively. "I did my time serving in the Krethan Armada, but I never fired on another ship. When I was killed I wasn't sailing to war as an officer. I was sailing home as a father and husband. My ship had no armaments, its complement was hopelessly low, and we flew a flag of peace. It meant nothing to them."

"How low and dirty," Saber seethed. "On your way home to see your family, even. Do you know what became of them?"

"Unfortunately so, as they were aboard my ship at the time," Skarin said darkly. "When you watch your wife and children die in front of you, you lose all sense of allegiance to your nation. When ideologies compete, patriotism loses to vengeance every time. Now, I've probably sunk enough ships to make most logical people think Selenthia has paid the price for their actions, but they clearly have not learned... not when they, after all this time, still dare to send more warships into my waters."

"My heart to you, friend," Saber said, bowing her head slightly.

Maaya said nothing. She felt bad for Skarin to be sure, but she was having trouble reconciling what had happened to him with his actions. She could only guess how long ago this had happened, but to her knowledge the navies of the two warring countries hadn't met in even a small skirmish in well over a decade. The war had simply been too taxing for anything more than posturing. If that was true, then Skarin likely was killing people who had no knowledge of, or indeed any involvement in, what had happened to him.

This doubt must have shown on her face, because Skarin peered down at her, a sneer on his face.

"And what does our ship's only Selenthian think about this? You must think me an awful man, but the years have tempered my ire, as evidenced by the fact that you're still alive."

Saber's sympathetic expression vanished in an instant, and she moved directly in front of Maaya, rising slightly until she was at eye level with the old captain, her face less than a foot from his.

"Watch yourself. This is my Selenthian, and I can promise you that if you harm her in any way I will give your *ire* some competition."

"Enough, both of you," Adelaide commanded sharply, her voice cutting instantly through the tension. "Skarin, this is my guest, and you will treat her with all the respect that position affords her. Know your place while you're on my ship. Saber, you will do well to avoid escalating things unnecessarily."

Saber slowly backed down, but didn't take her eyes off Skarin for a moment. Maaya, who realized she had unconsciously put her hand to the pouch on her arm, drew it away quickly.

"Not that I need to justify anything to you, but I don't have any love for Selenthia just like it doesn't have any for me," Maaya said, trying and failing to meet Skarin's gaze. "That's partly why I'm here, and why I'm so grateful to the captain for letting me come."

"I see," Skarin said slowly, looking her up and down. "She must see something in you that I don't. But I'm an open-minded sort. You and your friends have my word I pose you no threat. If you're so bold, or even stupid, perhaps, to try to flee Selenthia for Krethus, then you have at least enough heart to gain my favor. Let's see if you can do something with it."

Maaya would have offered a sarcastic retort had Adelaide not been there, so she settled with shooting him a scathing look, then turned her head away.

The ships were all closer now, and the Nocte Cadenza was now so near she could see just how impressive it was. It looked old—very old—and its wood and steel hull was pockmarked with holes and snapped and decaying wood, but it was still unquestionably sturdy. It was also *huge*. It completely dwarfed the Windfire, and Maaya felt like she was looking at a small fortress. It was a four-masted ship with three gun decks that held at least seventy guns between them. A crew of ghosts, which she could tell outnumbered the Windfire's crew at least four to one, was busy preparing the ship for battle, rolling out guns, clearing the deck, and reinforcing cargo.

As it neared it began to turn slowly so that it soon drew parallel to the Windfire, matching its course and speed. Maaya started to feel slightly dizzy as she stared, overwhelmed by the sheer size of the ship.

Skarin noticed her watching, and smirked.

"My pride and joy. She'll be on your side this night. The Selenthians have sent their best, and their best… will not be good enough."

"You're cheating just a bit, don't you think? With the being already dead part, I mean," Halvar pointed out.

"My crew can't die, but my ship can still sink," Skarin replied. "She just won't."

"So, what's the plan?" Adelaide asked, bringing everyone back on track.

"Our fleet against theirs. If we have time we'll position our ships between them and the Windfire so you won't get hit. If they decide to leave peacefully, I… will allow it. But should they try to interfere, we will need to defend ourselves."

"Of course. I hope they won't be that stupid," Adelaide replied.

"They've certainly come armed to the teeth with stupidity. Whatever the case, they're determined not to be outmatched in speed or firepower, but the former works slightly to our advantage."

"Right. They plan to trap us with their smaller and faster ships and wait until the big guns show up," Adelaide mused, and Skarin nodded. "They'll either have to make a daring attempt with their weaker ships or wait for the rest to get within firing range."

"By which point we would already hold the advantage," Skarin concluded. "But I must warn you, this is purely hypothetical. They have strong winds at their back while my fleet makes their way here with nothing. The Selenthians are hungry wolves chasing limping prey."

"We'll need some backup plans, then," Adelaide said. "Join me in my cabin. Officers, with me; Halvar, you're in charge. Maaya, I'm sorry, but this meeting is for officers only."

"That's fine!" Maaya said hurriedly. "I can do some preparing of my own."

"You don't think you'll be fighting, do you?"

It was not a question.

"N-no, I just thought… just in case, you know," Maaya answered meekly, very aware of everyone's eyes on her. Adelaide nodded.

"Do what you need to do. Just don't plan on fighting. If you need help with anything, talk to Halvar. This shouldn't take too long."

"I should hope not," Gunnar said suddenly. "Our friends are here."

Everyone turned in unison, staring west. Sure enough, Maaya could just make out the shapes of a small fleet of ships far behind them spread out wide like a net. Even as she watched, the ships farthest away from them began to turn slightly so that within minutes every single one of them was unmistakably headed right for them.

Adelaide grimaced, then gestured to the others.

"Everyone, with me. We have less time than we thought."

They all departed except for Halvar, who took the helm as the others disappeared inside Adelaide's cabin.

Maaya turned away, walking to the edge of the deck and staring at the oncoming ships. She wanted desperately to look away, but she knew she would feel even more anxious if she didn't have eyes on her pursuers at all times.

She leaned over the railing, suddenly feeling sick. Guilt and fear overwhelmed her with such force that she had to fight through the murk of despair to remember to breathe. She had hoped against hope that they would somehow manage to avoid running into trouble once they escaped Levien, but she should have suspected something like this would happen. It's what always happened. She was given hope and then that hope was crushed into dust before her. It didn't matter who came to her rescue; if it was one man, he was taken down by another more powerful man. If it was a ship and crew, they were chased down by an entire fleet. The world itself seemed to want Maaya, and nothing was going to stand in its way.

Saber sat on the railing next to her and put a comforting hand on her back. Maaya didn't even look up.

"We'll get out of this, you know we will," Saber said confidently.

"Will we? We're stuck in the middle of the ocean with an army after us," Maaya moaned.

"Sure, but we've got one too, and ours is dead already," Saber said encouragingly. "We're not alone this time."

"We weren't before, either," Maaya murmured. "I wouldn't be half this afraid if we *were* alone. At least then I wouldn't have to worry about anyone else getting hurt."

"Hey, have you *seen* your girlfriend fight?" Saber teased, and this was enough to earn a glare from Maaya. "Plus, Commander Strand looks like she could probably snap a tree in half. The two of them alone could probably take out half the fleet themselves. And then Halvar would just out-stupid the rest of them."

Halvar glanced over at her, raising his eyebrows.

"Hey, you know I can still hear—"

"My point is," continued Saber as though Halvar hadn't spoken at all, "in all other things we've been hopelessly outmatched. This time we stand a fighting chance. All things equal, who do you think is going to win? A bunch of uptight stiff-collars on boats just following orders, or a captain of the Blackfins who's mastered *libris* and who's leading a fleet of the dead into battle?"

Maaya finally let a faint smile reach her lips.

"I suppose. I just need *something* to work out. All of this has been to stop these awful ghosts and we haven't even made it to the continent the stupid machine is on yet. And... if anything happens to Adelaide..."

"I know. Let's not sit around moping, then. We've got a fight to prepare for."

"I wish I could, but Adelaide said—"

"Adelaide is a very busy woman who doesn't have time to micromanage your life in the middle of a battle," Saber hushed. "Besides, she'll need all the help she can get, and who better than someone who can handle *libris* like you can? We can make some healing cards too, just in case."

"Good idea," Maaya affirmed. "It's been so long since I made any I'm not sure I remember how."

"Well, you'll be happy to know I have a book on *libris* from Adelaide's library, then," Saber said proudly. "It's got some high-level stuff in there. It should be effective."

"Did you ask her to borrow it?" Maaya asked, narrowing her eyes in suspicion.

"I did, actually!" Saber contested, starting back toward the officers' quarters, and Maaya fell into step beside her. "I mean, sort of. I wasn't specific which book I wanted. But anyway, that's not the point; we don't have a lot of time left. Let's get a good deck going. You'll need to make some for me, too, so I hope your writing hand is ready. As for fighting, well, we'll just fight somewhere she's not and she'll never know the difference."

"Hey, I can still... hear you..." Halvar attempted, but neither of the girls gave him any response.

Four hours later the sun dipped low in the sky, half of it concealed behind the calm ocean. Storm clouds miles and miles away glowed orange in the dying light and the roll of distant thunder boomed, but over the Windfire there were only empty skies over windless seas. As night loomed, it brought with it all the apprehensions and exhilarations of war.

The Windfire and Nocte Cadenza floated side by side, all guns pointed at the oncoming fleet. The Selenthians had slowed, struggling against the lack of wind, but they were close enough now that any attempt at fleeing would be dangerous. On the other side of the Windfire, the dead fleet was just as far away, trying with all their might to close the distance before the Selenthians could.

Adelaide and her officers stood on the bridge with Skarin, who stared down the oncoming ships with blatant contempt.

"Well, my ship is sandwiched in between two groups of warships who want to destroy each other," Adelaide said in a clipped tone. "I'm glad we planned for a worst-case scenario, because it looks like that's what we've got."

"Yes, not ideal," Skarin rumbled. "But not the worst. My fleet is close enough that your pursuers must be cautious. It's clear they did not expect you to have friends."

"They can still fire at us," Halvar said uneasily.

"At great risk to themselves. The living instinct of self-preservation will work in our favor."

"Not to mention we aren't even completely sure what they want yet. We may be able to talk ourselves out of this yet," Gunnar pointed out.

"Maaya, get to your quarters, okay?" Adelaide said, a hint of warmth in her voice now. "Stay there and stay safe until this is all sorted. We'll try to handle this peacefully, so don't be afraid."

Maaya wanted to protest, but she couldn't. As much as she wanted to fight, she couldn't forget that they were only in this position because of her. Any risk she took would be undermining every effort Adelaide had made to transport her safely thus far.

And so she obeyed wordlessly, so weighed down by fear that she could hardly walk straight. Only weeks before she would have been frightened if a single law-enforcement officer looked at her suspiciously, and now a powerful arm of the Selenthian navy itself was pursuing her. To think she had started her day having a lovely lunch with the captain, thinking that everything was all right. It was too much for her to process, and she still wasn't sure that she wasn't dreaming.

She sat down on her bed, thinking it almost amusing that two fleets of warships were lining up outside while she was simply sitting about in her quarters. Beyond this she felt completely numb, all her emotions that fought with her and each other running themselves ragged until none of them meant anything anymore. Every urge to fight, to hide, to run, to cry, to scream and choke and throw up and hit something and give up and surrender all fought desperately for her acknowledgement, and she gave them none.

Saber sat with her, and though the ghost didn't appear nearly as bothered, she did seem to understand the tremendous burden her living friend faced.

"I know what you're going to say," Maaya said finally, uncomfortably aware of the sound of her own voice breaking the silence. "That everything will be okay and that we'll make it through this."

"I wanted to, but I didn't think you wanted to hear it," Saber replied softly. "Words only mean so much sometimes."

"But you believe it?"

"I do."

"How?"

"Just based on our track record," Saber said, staring up at the ceiling. "Not that we haven't had our share of setbacks and all, but think about it. We escaped Sark when the entire town wanted you dead, you made it to Anorath in the bottom of a fishing boat, stayed in an underground hotel run by ghosts until you escaped after destroying a few dozen walkers, and then took a horseless carriage all the way to Levien where you walked straight up to a pair of high-ranking officers and demanded they take you across the world so you could save it. I know things have been difficult and scary, and I know we've suffered greatly for it, but ask Maaya from a month ago if she thought she could ever make it this far. Hell, ask her right now."

"I guess… I feel like it was more under my control then. I could always run if I had to. I didn't like to, but I could. But I can't run now."

"So don't run. Fight," Saber said, kneeling down in front of Maaya. "You're so very good at it when you do."

"I've only ever fought the walkers and a few angry ghosts. I don't think I'm all that good at fighting, and I hate doing it," Maaya protested.

"Right, and if I can be honest, I don't think you ever really had a reason to."

"What? What about our home? What about Kim and Kalil and Sovaan, what about—?"

"Oh, I'm not saying you never had motivation or the will to survive and protect the others," Saber interjected gently. "But that manifested in your ability to run, to hide, to scavenge, to retreat. Because that's how you kept all of you safe. But now things are different."

"How? All I can think about is running; that hasn't changed," Maaya sighed.

"Oh, but it has," Saber continued intently. "When you left Anorath, you were running toward Levien. When you got on this ship, you weren't running *from* Selenthia, you were running *toward* Krethus. You've had a destination in mind the entire time."

"Does it not still count as running away if there's an enemy behind you?"

"Only if you let them dictate where you go. Otherwise they're just helping you get where you want to go even faster. You've had Krethus on your mind this entire time, and now look at you. You're fighting to save the world, and if you don't care about that right now then remember *who* you're fighting for. I'd like to think I'm included in there somewhere, but I do know you've got someone else who means a lot to you, and I *know* you don't have a full deck of cards on your arm right now because you're thinking about running away. Fight for me, fight for them, fight for the world, I don't care—but fight. Now's the time more than ever, because every single reason you have to fight is on board this ship right now, and unlike before, we aren't too late. We're right on time, and all you need to do is decide."

Maaya let out a shuddering breath. It wasn't fear. It was... anticipation. As much as she was loath to admit it, Saber's motivational speeches worked well on her.

Maybe the ghost had a point. Sure, her schedule had mostly been dependent on whether law enforcement showed up, but now she thought about it, they had always been a secondary consideration. Not just for this, either; even back in Sark when she led the Ghost Hunters on their missions they avoided officers like an artisan might avoid foot traffic on his way home from work, but they always made it to where they wanted to go.

And it was also true that Maaya usually fled danger, but maybe that was because she was only too afraid to find out if she could win if she stood her ground. Maybe she could. Maybe she only needed to find out.

She heard shouting from a distance, and she glanced out the window for any sign of trouble, but she couldn't see any movement. Halvar's voice came next, and he shouted something back, but though his voice was loud, his tone was not angry.

"Negotiations, I presume," Saber said idly, watching Maaya out of the corner of her eye.

Maaya nodded distractedly, already lost again in her thoughts. She thought of the friends she had lost and the ones she left behind. Kim, Sovaan, Kalil, Roshan, Nadya and those from farther back in her past who had been lost too early, too young. Even Emil might make the cut, though she'd never tell Saber. They were the ones who had taught her there were people worth trusting in the world after all, that the world wasn't just a cesspool of deception and ill will. It was because of them that she was even here now, and why she had met Adelaide and gone farther on this wild adventure than she would have ever thought possible even a week ago.

Now, perhaps, it was time to give something back in her own way. It was unlikely that Roshan or Nadya or any of her other friends back home would benefit from the defeat of a Selenthian fleet... but it would help Maaya and Adelaide, and Halvar and Gunnar and Inga and all the other people she had so suddenly come to care about. She had to start somewhere, after all.

She glanced up at Saber, who had been staring at her expectantly.

"There are a lot of soldiers out there on those ships. What do we do about them if they decide to fight?"

"Fire up your best cards and crush them with your bare hands," Saber answered simply.

"And there are a lot of ships. What about them?"

"Ships are easy to burn."

"A lot of our friends are out there, too. They'll be in danger."

"Indeed. Seems only reasonable we should be there to protect them, seeing as how we're good friends and all."

"And Adelaide? She doesn't want me to fight… what if she sees me?"

"Then, my dear, you fight so hard you take her breath away."

Maaya grinned and got to her feet, shrugging off her coat. Saber floated up to meet her, looking as though she had expected this all along.

"Will you forgive me for this stupid decision?" Maaya asked playfully.

"Are you kidding? I've been trying to convince you to do this all evening."

Suddenly, there came cries of alarm from the deck, followed by the frantic ringing of bells. And then Maaya heard a sound, a sound so loud and horrifying that it rooted her to the spot in fear.

Thoom. Thoom. Thoom.

This was followed shortly by screams of terror and then the splintering of wood and shattering of glass. Maaya gasped as the Windfire suddenly began to move, and then she nearly fell over as the ship shuddered with the force of a full broadside attack. Almost immediately there came a second much louder volley from beside them. The Nocte Cadenza had unleashed its first assault, and it was so powerful that Maaya thought the very sea itself was joining the fray.

Her head ringing, she stumbled to the door and then out into the empty main room. She heard frantic shouts from the deck and the sound of gunfire from all directions. The ship trembled again as it launched another strike while at the same time turning sharply. Above the din she heard Adelaide's powerful voice, calling out orders with confidence and composure.

"Got everything?" Saber asked, looking Maaya up and down. "Cards, shoes, coat…"

"I'm not worried about catching a *cold*, Saber," Maaya remonstrated.

"Just making sure! Now, whatever you do and wherever you go, I'll be right behind you, okay? If you run into trouble, I'll make trouble turn tail. We've got this."

The girls shared a look for a moment, and then Maaya nodded determinedly.

"No more running."

Then, with all the confidence she could muster, she pushed open the doors and walked out into war.

24

AHEAD OF THE WAVE

As soon as Maaya walked out onto the deck, the small flicker of courage she had so desperately been holding onto disappeared instantly. The air was filled with smoke and the sea around them was a mass of sails, masts, and flashing lights of gunfire. The lack of wind made it difficult to maneuver, so evidently both fleets had decided the next best thing was to simply get as close to each other as possible and fire at close range. If this were a normal fight, Maaya thought, it wouldn't be such a bad strategy—especially for the Selenthians, whose had more ships on their side. Being so close meant they could trap their enemies in the crossfire and also board their ships if necessary.

For the moment, however, the Selenthians seemed content with simply doing as much damage as possible, and as terrified as she was, Maaya also felt confused. If the navy was after her, why they want to risk killing her? Unless, of course, those were their orders. But if she was an important enough person to justify sending several ships after, she thought, she must also be important enough that they should attempt to verify they had done their job properly.

"Hey, Adelaide's leaving," Saber called to Maaya over the noise.

Maaya whirled to look up at the bridge just in time to see Adelaide's limbs light up with *libris* lines, and then, with inhuman speed, she leapt off the deck in the direction of one of the Selenthian ships. Maaya barely had enough time to notice she had her sword buckled to her belt before the ship rocked so violently from a detonation that Maaya lost her balance and fell to the deck.

Saber offered her hand and quickly helped Maaya to her feet as a few crewmen ran toward the source of the blast.

"Burn your cards before that happens again," Saber suggested. "Oh, and give me a few. If I don't get a chance to cause some mayhem before Skarin kills everyone I'm going to be a little upset."

Maaya quickly took out a handful of cards from her deck, and within seconds, green and purple lights flickered brightly to life above her limbs. She felt her tiredness wash away instantly, her sore muscles unhindered and ready to fight.

"What do you want?" Maaya asked.

"As much orange as you can spare," Saber answered, grinning widely. "Have you got your healing cards?"

"As many as I can carry."

"Good. You ready? No time to—"

"Miss Sahni? Where do you think you're going?"

Maaya flinched, then turned slowly to look up at Commander Strand as might a dog who had just been caught stealing food.

"I, uh… nowhere, exactly, I just wanted to…"

"Remember what I said when we first met, Miss Sahni," Inga continued as she approached, and the faintest hint of a smile teased the corners of her lips. "You are without rank on this ship. If we want to get into technicalities that means you don't have to listen to a word I say. If I may make a recommendation, however… take this with you."

Inga pulled a sword from behind her back, then handed it to Maaya, who stared up at her in astonishment.

"I… I've never used—"

"Aim the pointed end at the people you don't like, then swing," Inga advised with a straight face. "Don't worry if it breaks; we've got dozens of them in our stores. Just make sure you don't hurt yourself, yes?"

"If I may, Commander, she's never been able to follow that order," Saber said airily, and Inga chuckled.

"I give the same advice to my captain and am similarly ignored. Perhaps you two can look out for each other; I would look out for her, but she goes where I cannot follow. I must be on my way, however; good luck to you both."

With that, Inga swept back up to the bridge, and Maaya felt a new surge of confidence. She stood up, and with some difficulty, fastened the sword at her waist. Then, with a few powerful leaps, she reached the top of the mainmast and looked around, scanning the area around her.

It was a disaster. Multiple ships on both sides were already taking on water, and there was so much smoke in the air that she could hardly see. Any remaining light from the distant sunset was no longer visible. She heard cries of pain and fear from all directions, as well as the clanging of swords.

What she could not see, however, was any sign of the captain. She guessed Adelaide was lost in the smoke somewhere, but she still felt a flutter of nervousness.

Beside the Windfire, the massive silhouette of the Nocte Cadenza stood out in the smoke like an augury of the apocalypse. Between flashes of gunfire she saw Skarin standing at the helm, calling out orders to his crew with glee as three levels of guns rained hellfire down upon his enemies. It looked like the ship had been struck several times, but to no effect. One Selenthian brig had already made the mistake of trying to get close in order for its soldiers to board, and the resulting barrage had torn the ship to shreds.

"If you don't get started soon I'm leaving you behind," Saber said menacingly, and a burst of flames flashed in her hands and spread up her arms.

"Right. Let's start disabling these ships. If you see any of our ship's people in danger make sure they make it out safely, okay?"

"Oh, boo. You're no fun," Saber replied. "But it's better than nothing. Lead on!"

Maaya took a moment to figure out where she wanted to go, and then leapt off the mainmast.

This time, with the aid of her augments, she didn't need Saber's help. She landed on a mast of a nearby friendly ship, and then, using all the momentum she could, took another great jump. This time she landed on a small Selenthian ship, and for a moment the crew was too distracted to notice. She pulled her sword from its sheath, then set to work cutting as many ropes as possible, watching in delight as the ship's sails started to flutter to the deck.

"Maaya, please. Be more imaginative!" Saber called from above.

Maaya looked up—and barely had enough time to dodge out of the way. A tremendous surge of flames erupted from the ghost's hand down toward the ship. Multiple sails immediately caught fire, and the flames spread quickly to the masts and started to work their way hungrily down the wood.

By now the crew had definitely noticed their presence, and after a moment, Maaya heard whistling. She quickly realized the crew was firing arrows at her, and positioned herself so that the mast was between them. But the wood was burning fast already, and the heat soon pushed her away.

Maaya thought frantically. She didn't want to use fire; the battling ships were all so close to each other that setting ships aflame presented the risk of damaging friendly ships as well. She also had very little experience with hand-to-hand combat, and even less with a sword. Even if she had, she didn't think she would be capable of killing anyone or even severely wounding them. But there had to be something…

Suddenly, it came to her. She was no great shakes at fighting anything that wasn't a ghost, but she didn't have to defeat anyone herself—she only needed to make sure her friends could win, and the best way to do that would be to take away the enemy's ability to fight at all. The crews she couldn't do much about, but disabling the ships' guns would be a good start.

"I'm going in, cover me!" she called to the ghost, who looked only too happy to help.

Maaya grabbed hold of a nearby rope, then dove off the mast, letting the rope slip through her loose grip. When she was nearly level with the deck, she tightened her hold on the rope, swinging right past a group of confused solders and right over the side of the ship. Using her momentum to her advantage, she ran almost horizontally along the side of the ship, using the rope to keep her upright for as long as it would last.

The ship's guns fired over and over, but Maaya quickly noticed a pattern. As soon as one gun fired, there was a short period of time when it was being reloaded before it could fire again—and when it did fire, the force of the blast pushed the gun backward, leaving a small gap in the port. That was exactly what she needed.

A gun just in front of her went off, and without hesitating even a moment, Maaya took another jump and swung right through the open port. She knocked over a sailor on her way in, and with her augmented strength sent him sliding across the floor. Saber sailed in immediately after, dragging a second man down as he fumbled to draw his blade.

"Whatever you're going to do, do it quickly!" Saber shouted as she beat the man's head repeatedly against the floor.

Maaya quickly looked over the gun. She was sure she could move it with her temporary strength, but she knew she would wear out before she had even finished this side of the gun deck. Upon closer inspection, she noticed that every gun was set upon a moving wooden carriage. Never having seen a gun up close, she had to take a moment to admire its ingenuity; a moving platform absorbed the majority of the gun's recoil and also made it easier to swab the inside after every volley. It also, however, presented a definite and easily exploitable weakness.

With much less strength than Maaya thought would be necessary, she pulled the gun away from the port, sending it rolling backward until it collided heavily with a support beam. She then raised her hand to the carriage and set it ablaze, pleased with how quickly it began to burn.

"Saber, can you keep everyone off my back?" Maaya asked as the other sailors on the deck stared up at her in alarm.

"My pleasure. Give me a holler when you're on your way out."

The ghost soared ahead, knocking every sailor she encountered to the ground, leaving them moaning in pain and, Maaya guessed, incredible confusion. She left them only injured, leaving Maaya with precious few seconds to disable each gun in turn.

Maaya rolled each gun away from its port and set its carriage on fire as she went, and before long all sounds of weapons fire from the ship ceased. She hadn't disabled them all just yet, but the other sailors, upon discovering her attempts at sabotage, decided it was more important to stop Maaya than to keep firing. A few sailors managed to make it past Saber, only to be thrown roughly aside as Maaya continued her work.

Within just a few minutes, every gun on the deck had been disabled. Some sailors had attempted to put out the flames, but by the time they did the carriages had been too badly burned to continue to function, rendering the guns almost entirely useless.

By this time, some of the armed soldiers from above had made their way down, and though they couldn't fire any weapons at her because of the risk of hitting their own crew, they were closing quickly, and would soon block her escape if she didn't move quickly.

"Saber, I'm out!" Maaya called, shoving the last gun aside and dashing to a nearby open port.

Maaya quickly discovered that getting out would be more difficult than getting in; luckily, it seemed Saber had already thought of this, and within moments, the ghost grabbed Maaya hands and helped pull her upward to the deck. From there Maaya jumped up to the relative safety of one of the masts, her eyes flicking back and forth to assess the situation.

The ship she was currently on had stopped firing, and multiple sections were severely burned. As the crew rushed to put out the fires, Maaya hoped she had done enough. In retrospect, it had been a lot of effort just to disable a single ship's guns. It was effective, but a method she could see tiring her out quickly.

"Thoughts?" she asked Saber, who floated impatiently nearby.

"Effective, but not worth it," the ghost said, tapping her chin with her finger. "We can try for the same effect by sabotaging every ship's supply of gunpowder."

"How would we do that without blowing ourselves up?"

"We don't have to burn it. We can soak it and that'll do the same thing. Even if it'll work again after it dries, that still gives us the advantage short term."

"Works for me," Maaya replied, taking a few blue cards from her pack and giving them to Saber. "In the meantime I'll see what I can do to stop the guns that are already loaded."

"Just make sure you aren't hit by one, okay?" Saber grinned.

"Gee, Saber, you think I should stay away from the end that goes 'boom'?"

The girls laughed, and then it was time to take action. Saber dove toward the ocean below, and at the last second veered through the hull of a nearby ship and out of sight. Following close behind, Maaya leapt from the mast, searching for any free ropes on the ship she had just entered. Unable to find any, she cut one free herself, letting a sail plummet to the deck below much to the shock of the crew. She let herself fall, and then, just as she reached the side of the ship, held on tight.

Her momentum carried her forward, and she ran along the side of the ship just above the gun deck, drawing her sword again. Here she had easy access to the gun port hatches—and the ropes that held them up. As she ran, she cut the ropes holding the hatches open, causing them to shut hard with a *clang*, subsequently blocking the guns inside from firing. She knew the hatches were light and that it wouldn't be much effort to re-open them, but every minute of delay she caused was invaluable.

As she reached the end of the gun deck she heard a thudding sound behind her. She turned to see an arrow embedded in the hull where she had been running just moments before. Without hesitation, she launched herself off the hull just as more arrows flew in her direction. She held onto the rope as she jumped, and the strength of her jump carried her high and away and out of danger. At least for now.

She took another great leap and landed on the ratlines near the bow of the ship, then jumped again, setting her sights on another craft. Before she even landed, Saber was beside her, looking quite proud of herself.

"Did it work?" Maaya asked, landing lightly on the deck of a friendly ship.

"Oh, it worked marvelously," Saber beamed. "You should have seen the looks on their faces. How'd you do?"

"I knocked all the hatches closed. They'll have to find a way to keep them open again if they want to keep shooting," Maaya said breathlessly.

"Oh, good idea. Let's do it again, shall we?"

Maaya agreed, and soon they were on their way again. They managed to temporarily sabotage one more ship, and then another before Maaya finally had to retreat. By now the soldiers on board the ships had become aware of Maaya's game and were targeting her with everything they had. As quick as Maaya was, her *libris* lines made her an easy target to spot, and she only barely dodged a number of arrows.

Saber rushed over to join her, and soon they found refuge in the high masts of a Selenthian frigate that had been almost completely abandoned due to damage and the fact that it was slowly burning and taking on water. When they paused, Maaya stared around at with a keen eye; the whole time she and Saber had been working to sabotage the ships, she had kept an eye out for Adelaide, but she hadn't seen the captain anywhere.

Just then, something rushed by her that was not an arrow. She whirled around to see a thin slip of paper streak up into the sky and vanish in the smoke, narrowly missing Saber. Saber, who had been happily throwing fire down at the ship below, paused in confusion.

Maaya glanced around hurriedly, then noticed a figure standing on one of the masts nearby, their arms and legs glowing with a variety of colors. Maaya's heart leapt, thinking she had finally found Adelaide—or that Adelaide had found her—but then her blood ran cold as a momentary break in the smoke revealed the figure wearing the uniform of a Selenthian navy officer. He was several years Maaya's senior, and from the designs of the lights on his arms and legs, she knew he had mastered *libris* at a higher level than she had.

"Saber! Behind me!" Maaya shouted in a panic, and the ghost dashed for cover just as another card shot through the air, missing her by inches.

"Since when do they have someone with *libris* on their side?" Saber shrieked.

Without thinking, Maaya jumped hard, straight at the officer. She knew the danger she was in, but there was no fleeing this battle. Every moment he was allowed to continue fighting was another moment Saber was in mortal danger, and if he was allowed to flee he would sure pose a severe threat to the entire crew of the Windfire—and Adelaide.

The officer, apparently not expecting such a direct move so quickly, tried and failed to move out of the way; Maaya collided with him hard, forcing him to grab onto a nearby rope to avoid falling. Maaya grabbed the mast to steady herself, then jumped at him again. This time he was ready, and blocked her with both arms. He struck back swiftly, and while she managed to dodge the blow aimed at her face, she stumbled as he hit her hard in the stomach.

She didn't allow herself to fall. She had no choice but to beat him, and she would take whatever he threw at her. Maaya dropped to her knees, dodging another blow aimed at her head, then pushed off from the yard, striking him roughly from below. As he fell back she delivered a swift kick with all her strength to his lower legs that sent him falling right through one of the sails below.

Maaya made to follow, but then leapt suddenly to the side as a burst of fire shot toward her. She jumped from yard to yard, staying ahead of the flame; she knew she had to get close again so he couldn't use his elements, but she was running out of space. The masts behind her were burning, and that left only the decks and whatever ratlines hadn't yet been destroyed.

Then, she had an idea. Burning a water element card across her forearm she leapt straight at the officer again, and at the same time let a burst of water fly immediately in front of her. The brunt of the officer's next attack dissipated in the water, and while the droplets of heated water seared her skin, it was enough. Before he could strike again, she was upon him, and once again they fought, each trying to disable the other while keeping their balance.

Though the officer's *libris* was more advanced than Maaya's—even if he was nowhere near Adelaide's level—Maaya's plan of staying close was working; unable to use any of his elemental cards at this range, he was forced to go toe to toe with her. Maaya quickly discovered that he was not quite as fast as her, and that her small stature and lower center of gravity gave her a minor advantage.

The fight continued, their field of battle becoming smaller with every passing minute as the flames began to consume the ship. She was only thankful it had already been mostly abandoned, as this spared her the threat of the crew attempting to attack her as well.

Maaya was starting to get nervous. The longer the fight went on, the more of an advantage her opponent gained. She was able to defend herself for now, but she had already used much of her strength when she attempted to disable the enemy ships, and she was certain she didn't have as much stamina as this officer had. And so, as the fight proceeded, her tactics became more desperate. More than once she attempted not only to strike him, but to grab him, hoping to force him off the edge and into the ocean below, but he refused to budge. She fought as hard as she could, thinking only of protecting Saber.

As her fighting became more erratic, however, the officer landed blow after blow. While at first Maaya didn't feel any pain, his strikes quickly began to take their toll on her body. She clawed at his face, but this only served to make him swing harder.

Finally, with a strong kick to Maaya's chest, he sent her flying off the yard and down into the smoke and fire.

Maaya landed hard on the deck far below. Pain seared through her entire body, and she would have cried out if not for the fact that her landing had also knocked the wind out of her. She stared down at her body in growing horror as her *libris* lines flickered, then disappeared.

From above, the officer jumped into the air, and then, with another kick, sent the burning mast they had just been battling upon falling right toward her. Maaya attempted to crawl away, but the pain that stabbed at every part of her body left her unable to even move. She whimpered and raised her arms, attempting to cover her head as the heavy mass of wood and fire fell swiftly toward her.

And then, suddenly, she was moving. She was vaguely aware of someone picking her up, and then of being encircled in a pair of strong arms as her rescuer rolled out of the way of the falling mast just in time. A shower of sparks flew upward upon impact, but the newcomer's body shielded Maaya from them. A moment later they let Maaya go, and Maaya realized her rescuer was none other than Inga.

"Are you all right?" Inga asked hurriedly. By now, Maaya's breath was starting to return, and she coughed.

"I'm fine. Only hurt a little. But be careful, there's a man—"

"I know. He's being dealt with." She then lifted her head and called, "Make sure everyone's off the ship, then sink it. Make it fast!"

Maaya watched a dozen of the Windfire's crew steal quickly onto the ship, heading immediately down toward the lower decks. Then she turned to look back up toward the sails, but there was so much smoke that at first Maaya couldn't see any sign of the mysterious officer.

Then, suddenly, she saw him, standing silently on one of the remaining yards like a phantom. At first it looked like he wasn't moving, but then she realized he was holding a card in his hand—and that he was staring directly down at her.

Inga slowly lay Maaya down on the deck, then stood up, putting herself between Maaya and the stranger.

"Inga, wait," Maaya coughed. "He's got *libris*, he's stronger than—"

"Unfortunately I am not the one who will be dealing with him, but I appreciate your warning," Inga said without taking her eyes off the man.

"Then who—?"

Before she could say anymore, she saw movement out of the corner of her eye. Turning her head quickly, she saw another figure leaping toward them with incredible speed. Maaya's eyes widened in surprise and delight—she recognized those *libris* lines.

Before Maaya had even fully registered she had arrived, Adelaide slammed both feet hard into the mast the stranger was standing on, causing him to lose his balance. There came a horrifying snapping and splintering sound as the mast began to tip. Without even waiting a moment, Adelaide jumped above the stranger and hit him as hard as she could square in the chest. Maaya wasn't sure whether the snapping sound she heard was the falling mast or the man's ribs, but his cry of agony was enough. He fell from the yard, but Adelaide wasn't done. Even as he fell she pursued him downward, delivering one final tremendous kick that sent the man crashing straight through the deck itself and down into darkness.

"Maaya!" Adelaide gasped as she landed, rushing over and helping the girl to her feet. "Are you all right? Are you hurt?"

"I'm fine," Maaya said quickly, stretching her limbs. She had gone past the limits her magic allowed, but there was no point making Adelaide or

Inga worry. "I'm so glad you're okay; I was looking for you this whole time! Are you okay?"

"I'm well, but I can't do much more," Adelaide said. "I had no idea they had another *libris* user with them. It's a good thing I saw him before I ran out. Are you all spent as well?"

Maaya nodded.

"Saber and I were disabling the ships as best we could, so I burned out pretty quickly, but I think we… wait. Where's Saber?"

She stepped back, her eyes darting all over the deck, but Saber was nowhere in sight.

"No… oh, please, no. Saber!" Maaya cried, but there came no answer.

Adelaide and Inga shared a troubled look, and then Adelaide put a hand on Maaya's shoulder.

"It's hard to see out here; she's probably just lost. We need to get back to the Windfire. This ship is going to be sinking soon, and it looks like the navy is diverting the rest of their ships for a last push toward mine."

"But what about—?"

"Once this is over I promise we will look for her and find her if she hasn't returned already, but right now we need to defend my ship or it could well be the end of it. Okay?"

Her voice was stern but understanding, and Maaya had no choice but to agree. Adelaide gave her an encouraging grin, then motioned to Inga, who departed quickly.

They started across the deck, stepping nimbly around burning wood and the hole Adelaide had created in the deck by sending the unfortunate officer through it. As they got closer to the side, Maaya realized someone had placed a wide wooden beam between the decks of this ship and the next, allowing the Windfire's crew easy access. Adelaide led Maaya across quickly, then continued on.

The Windfire slowly came into view, and though it looked to be in no immediate danger of sinking or burning, Maaya suddenly saw the problem. Two ships had moved so that the Windfire was between them and the Nocte Cadenza, pinning Adelaide's ship in with no escape—and navy soldiers were now attempting to board. One wide wooden beam stretched from each ship to the Windfire, and with the weight of soldiers already on them, the crew of the Windfire was unable to push them away.

"They must really want you badly," Adelaide commented nervously, walking faster still with greater strides, but then she stopped suddenly. "I need to leave you here. If they're after you, taking you aboard the Windfire wouldn't be a good idea. Stay here and out of sight; if they realize you aren't on board the Windfire, they'll chase you."

"I can't just stay here while you're fighting!" Maaya protested.

"I appreciate the thought, but right now you're too worn to use *libris* and you have no experience with a sword. If you want to help, stay hidden and safe. As long as you're safe I won't have anything to worry about while I'm fighting. And," Adelaide said more intently as Maaya opened her mouth, "you've already done a great service by disabling as many ships as you did. You have been a wonderful help to us so far. Now, I'm going. I'll send for you once this is over, and you have my word… this won't take long."

A steely, confident look in her eyes, Adelaide turned and dashed away, making the leap over to her own ship in a single bound, the others moving quickly toward the ship in turn.

Maaya stomped her foot in helpless frustration, then looked for a place to hide. There appeared to be a small empty cabin at the stern, and so she stepped inside. It looked like it hadn't been used in years, which was perfectly fine with her.

She found an old wooden chair and sat down, then covered her face with her hands as she tried to stay calm. Her anxiety was returning, and at the most inopportune time. Saber was gone, Adelaide was in danger, and there was nothing she could do about any of it.

Useless, a voice in her head said scathingly.

She tried to ignore it. She wasn't useless. She had managed to accomplish more than she thought when she first agreed to fight, and she had even gone toe to toe with a trained military *libris* user. She hadn't won, but it was a much more equal match than she would have ever expected. Now the navy was making its last attempt at finding her. They would fail. They were losing.

But they're only here because of you, the voice returned.

Maaya shook her head, squeezing her eyes shut tight in an effort to block out these intrusive thoughts. If it hadn't been for the dead zone, which was certainly not her fault, the navy would have never caught up to her to begin with.

But it happened anyway, and now Saber is gone, and Adelaide is soon to join her.

"Enough," Maaya breathed aloud, standing up and pacing the room. Everything was going to be fine in the end. The Selenthian navy was losing, many of its ships were disabled, and its soldiers were running in circles trying to fight enemies they could not see. Everything was going to be *fine.*

But still, the thought of Adelaide in the center of the battle made her nervous. Adelaide was good, as was her crew, but they numbered few against the combined forces of multiple navy ships. What's more, while the Windfire was swift, that speed meant nothing in the dead zone, and if the navy decided to cut its losses and flee they could take down the Windfire with relative ease.

The thought was like a hot brand against her skull. She might be out of *libris*, but that was no reason to sit helplessly in a cabin while others fought her battle. She didn't know what she could do just yet, and she certainly wasn't going to put herself in danger and risk worrying Adelaide, but she had to do something.

Finally, unable to hold it any longer, she threw open the cabin doors and headed below deck. She had an idea.

She found the gun deck bustling with activity, but despite how many ghosts were there, none of the guns were firing. The captain of the ship, who was standing nearby investigating one of the guns with a few other sailors, immediately noticed Maaya and walked over to meet her.

"Can I help you?" she asked pleasantly, as though Maaya had just walked into a quaint bakery.

"Are we able to hit the ships attacking the Windfire from here?" Maaya asked.

"Not quite. They're just out of reach, but if we turn our ship so our guns can hit them, we risk running into the sinking frigate off our starboard beam, and I don't have the manpower to fight fires or floods. We're stuck for the moment."

"But we're close, right?"

"We are. Why?"

"I don't want to hit the ships themselves. I just want to stop their soldiers from boarding the Windfire," Maaya explained, walking over to a gun and peering out the port. It was small, but if the gun could be moved just far enough…

"That's a heavy risk. Not to mention it would take some very accurate aiming, and these weapons aren't built for precision," the captain said uncertainly.

"Let's try," Maaya said encouragingly. The captain struggled to speak for a moment, then shrugged.

"Fine, but you're aiming. Just tell us what you need."

Maaya walked down the length of the gun deck, stopping at the very last port that was closest to the Windfire. Through it, she could see she had a clear shot to try to hit exactly what she wanted.

"Help me move this," Maaya grunted as she pushed in vain against the heavy gun.

"Which way?" the captain said, directing four of her men to assist Maaya with a quick gesture.

"To the left. Keep going… there," Maaya said triumphantly. She pushed down on the gun slightly, causing the other end to rise. She kneeled behind it, staring with one eye down the length of the gun, lining up her target.

"Even if you do that, the gun's position will change the instant it fires," the captain said pointedly. "Like I said, there's not much point to—"

"We'll need to stabilize it, then," Maaya interrupted. "I just need this one shot. Can we find a way to hold it down?"

"I… suppose," the captain replied slowly. "You might damage my ship in the process, so this had better be good; I won't give you more than one."

Maaya nodded, and the ghostly sailors quickly went to work, fastening the carriage to the deck and locking the gun into to its current position.

"We'll hold on when you're ready," a burly sailor said.

Maaya leaned down again to check and double check. There was no wind, so she didn't need to account for that, but she did need to consider that the gun would sink quickly as gravity overtook it, and even that the gun might not fire perfectly straight. Her positioning had to be exactly right so that even if the gun didn't fire exactly how she planned, she would still hit her mark.

All the while, soldiers streamed across the beams from both ships, and Maaya's heart sank as she saw dozens of soldiers still waiting to join the already high number of soldiers aboard the Windfire. It was now or never.

She stepped back with a nod, and the four men held on tight to the gun, preventing it from moving up or down as it went off. Maaya took a deep breath, then grimaced.

"Fire."

The entire deck shook as the gun went off, accompanied by the sound of splintering wood. The four ghosts holding on to the cannon were thrown backward, but the carriage remained firm. The shaking subsided in an instant, and Maaya was immediately at the gun port, holding her breath as the agony of time passed slowly by.

The projectile seemed to move in slow motion, and as it moved, Maaya was afraid that she had aimed too low, that it would fall harmlessly into the water before reaching her target. For one horrifying moment it looked like it was turning slightly to the right, and she panicked, thinking it was going to hit the Windfire.

But then, miraculously, the projectile struck true—it blasted upward through the wooden beam of the first ship, and then, as it began to fall, struck the second beam as well. Under the weight of the soldiers on top, both beams snapped in two, sending wood and sailors falling into the sea below.

"Yes!" cried Maaya, pumping her fist.

The captain looked at her in astonishment, then gave a conceding nod.

"That was… quite a shot. Well done."

Maaya watched as the enemy sailors left on board the Windfire suddenly became nervous, both at the fact that a projectile had passed so close to them and that their escape and reinforcements had instantly been cut off. The battle continued, and suddenly she saw Adelaide on the Windfire's bridge clashing swords with her opponents. Her *libris* lines had faded, but this seemed no impediment to her. She carried her sword in the hand of her augmented arm, the device's additional strength helping her overpower her opponents with ease. She parried one man's strike, then drove the tip of her blade through the lower leg of another, who cried out as she dropped to the deck in pain. Maaya saw a glint on her augmented arm, followed by the terrified screaming of a man Adelaide hadn't even touched. A moment later she realized Chronis had leapt from Adelaide's arm and latched itself around the man's face. The sailor dropped his sword, clawing at the metal spider that refused to let go.

Near the bow, Inga and her group had made it back aboard, and were now fighting their way across the ship toward their captain. When one particularly stubborn sailor stood in Inga's way, she simply hefted him into the air and threw him overboard.

Maaya realized she was holding her breath as she watched the battle unfold. It was a beautiful thing to watch Adelaide fight; her movements were more powerful than elegant, but she deflected the attacks of soldiers much larger than her, and at any given time had her eye on at least two opponents. She fought them over to the side of her ship, pinning them against the railing; one of them dropped her sword and put her hands in the air. Maaya saw Adelaide smile.

But then the unthinkable happened. As Adelaide reached for the surrendering sailor's weapon, another man reached up from behind her and struck the hilt of his sword against Adelaide's head. Adelaide immediately went limp, and then the sailors she had just pinned to the railing threw her over the edge.

"NO!" Maaya cried, and before anyone could say a word, she bolted for the stairs.

She sprinted up to the deck then dashed over to the side of the ship. She could still see the ripples on the water where Adelaide had fallen, but the captain herself was not reappearing. What was worse was that though the fierce fighting continued on her ship, and her crew appeared to be driving the Selenthians back, no one had seemed to notice that Adelaide had fallen —or if they had, they were unable to assist her.

Without hesitation, Maaya ran as fast as she could, jumped on top of the railing, then dove straight into the sea.

The first thing Maaya realized was that swimming with her extra clothes on—not to mention her sword—was very difficult, and she quickly found herself struggling to stay afloat. She quickly kicked off her shoes and pulled off her outer shirt, then unbuckled her sword and let it sink into the dark depths below. This great weight off her, she swam as quickly as she could toward the Windfire. She still saw no sign of Adelaide, and she began to panic. She stared around helplessly, and then, taking a deep breath, plunged underwater.

She opened her eyes and almost immediately regretted it. The seawater stung her eyes fiercely, but she forced them open. After a few seconds of frantic searching, she saw the captain just a few feet under the water. She wasn't moving.

Maaya surfaced, took another great breath, then dove down again. She kicked with all her strength until she reached the captain, and then, one arm around Adelaide, she swam desperately for the surface.

Holding up another person, especially one who had fallen limp, was much harder than Maaya anticipated, especially with as tired as she already was, and she choked on seawater as she struggled to stay afloat.

"Help!" she cried, but she wasn't sure anyone could hear her over the sound of the fighting above. She tried to shout again, but coughed instead. Only now did she remember she wasn't actually a good swimmer; in her desperation to save Adelaide she had done whatever she thought was necessary, but now she was here, she realized she would soon be in trouble herself if no one noticed them.

That was a dilemma for later, though. Right now she had to make sure Adelaide was alive.

"Hey," Maaya said, brushing the captain's hair from her face as she tried to see if she could feel her breathing. "Hey, come on, wake up!"

Adelaide's eyes fluttered, and focused with some difficulty on Maaya.

"Sorry… dizzy," the captain uttered. "Can't…"

"Don't worry, I'm here," Maaya said in what she hoped was an encouraging tone. "Just try to stay above the water, can you do that?"

"Need help, but… yes," Adelaide said breathlessly.

Maaya tightened her grip on the young woman, then stared around, hoping for another set of steps or a stray rope, anything to hold on to while Adelaide recovered, but there was nothing. She fought the urge to panic, trying to remember what Adelaide had told her about how little effort it took to tread water. Unfortunately, she also remembered something else the captain had told her about swimming: *The middle of the ocean is not a good place to run out of strength.*

A few minutes passed and Maaya's breathing became ragged. Every muscle in her body burned in protest, and more than once, under the weight of the captain's body, her head dipped underwater. She cried for help again, but her pitiful voice was lost in the sound of clashing swords and booming guns.

Just when Maaya thought she might not make it, a loud and shrill horn sounded from one of the ships nearby. It blasted a few times in succession, and then fell silent. Maaya had no idea what such a horn could signify, but then a deafening cheer went up on the deck of the Windfire and surrounding friendly ships. Maaya glanced upward to see that the few soldiers left standing were now pressed against the railing, their hands in the air. The sound of guns came to a stop, and she heard cheering from multiple other ships as well. As she looked on, she saw the remaining navy ships hastily raising white flags on their masts. They were surrendering. The battle was over.

Maaya hardly had time to celebrate. Her muscles continued to weaken, and she struggled to stay afloat. She no longer had the energy to call for help, even if they might have heard her then.

Then, even as her grip began to loosen, she heard multiple splashes in the water around her. She whirled around in a panic, ready to use whatever strength she had left to fight off anyone who might try to hurt Adelaide, but then Halvar and Inga's heads appeared above the water.

"I've got her," Inga said, taking the captain into one strong arm.

Maaya let go gratefully, then finally let herself relax a little as Halvar put his own arm around her.

"You all right, kid?" he asked, then smiled as she nodded wordlessly back at him. "Great! Gave us a bit of a scare, you did. All right fellas, bring us up!"

Maaya then noticed that both officers were holding on to ropes in their other hands. The crew above quickly pulled on the ropes with all their strength, pulling all four of them swiftly upward. Only a few moments later, they collapsed onto the deck. Inga and Halvar quickly got to their feet as the other crew members rushed over to check on them.

"The captain's stunned and hurt," Halvar said, visibly concerned. "She's got an open wound on her head. Where's our doctor?"

"Down at the bow treating sword wounds; we haven't got many, but they look serious," a crewman replied, and Halvar cursed.

"Get her up here as soon as she's certain none of her other patients will die," Halvar ordered, and the crewman nodded, running hastily down the stairs.

Just then, Maaya had another idea. She reached into her sopping card pouch and peeled off a healing card. The designs and paper were still all intact, so she saw no reason why it wouldn't work… but there was only one way to find out.

"Here, let me," Maaya said, fighting her way to her knees and leaning over Adelaide.

The captain didn't look good. She was half conscious but still hardly able to keep her eyes open, and now that she was out of the water a fresh trickle of blood dripped down her face.

Maaya placed the card against an exposed part of Adelaide's skin, and to their credit, neither Inga nor Halvar attempted to stop her. She closed her eyes as she prepared to energize the card, but then stopped. Adelaide was already weak. Using a healing card with Adelaide's own energy might leave her bedridden for days from weakness—and that was one of the better possible scenarios Maaya had in mind.

Maaya thought hard. From everything she had read about healing cards, nowhere had it been specified that the energy had to come from the body of the person being healed—the only requirement was energy itself, not where it came from. This was one reason ghosts couldn't use them, as they had no energy to start the process themselves. So, in theory, it might be possible for Maaya to use *her* energy to heal Adelaide. It was worth a try.

She closed her eyes and imagined her own energy flowing into the card at the same time as she activated it. The card suddenly felt pleasantly warm under her palm, and she could feel her own energy depleting as though she were falling unconscious. She fought to stay awake, refusing to break contact until this was over.

And then the warmth faded. Maaya opened her eyes.

The captain took a deep breath, then coughed violently, her body twitching with the effort. Inga hurriedly helped her sit up and patted her on the back as Adelaide coughed up seawater.

A few moments later, Adelaide was left breathing hard, but most definitely awake and alert. She peered around, then tried to stand up, but Inga held her back.

"Easy, Captain. Stay still until you've regained your bearings."

"Status?" Adelaide inquired hoarsely.

"The battle is over; we won," Inga said, a soothing tone amidst her usual professionalism. "We're doing a head count now and assessing our situation. There are no reports yet of any deaths, but the Windfire did sustain moderate damage, so we'll need to wait until some repairs are finished before we get under way."

"Good. Commander, I'm relying on you to make sure things are organized. I… I feel very weak."

"Understood, Captain. You sustained a head injury and spent several minutes overboard before we could reach you. I will need to ask you to rest until we can further assess your situation. I will handle it from here."

Adelaide nodded, then gasped and looked around fervently. When her eyes landed on Maaya, she visibly relaxed and then smiled.

"Maaya! Thank the stars. Are you all right?"

"I feel like I might sleep for a few days straight, but I'm fine right now," Maaya answered, and Adelaide laughed weakly.

"I'm glad. Say… that was some good swimming there. What did I tell you?"

"You were right about it hurting so much... but maybe next time you'll be pulling your own weight," Maaya teased.

Adelaide reached over and gave Maaya a playful shove, and they both fell over, laughing as they did.

"What would you have me do with the sailors from the Selenthian ships, Captain?" Inga asked, unable to hide her amusement.

"See to it that any surviving sailors returned to any working ships they have left. We don't have room or time here for prisoners."

"Understood."

Maaya and Adelaide lay on the deck, too comfortable in each other's company and relief from fading adrenaline that they wouldn't have got up even if they wanted to. They lay close, their heads nearly touching, and then Maaya felt the captain's hand seek hers, holding it tightly. Maaya's face immediately flushed.

"I guess I have you to thank for saving my life, then," the captain said. "That was a really brave thing you did. Where did you come from? You didn't sneak aboard, did you?"

"No! I was on the ship where you left me. After I destroyed the boarding platforms I saw—"

"*You* fired that shot?" Adelaide asked in disbelief.

"I did. I didn't know if it would work, but... I'm glad it did."

Adelaide whistled.

"That was a hell of a shot. It probably saved our skins, too. I was hoping Skarin and his crew would join in but they apparently had some problems of their own to deal with. But... really, thank you. I hope I can repay the favor someday."

"Are you kidding? You already have!" Maaya said, rolling onto her side to see Adelaide better. Adelaide stared back, and Maaya was suddenly captivated by her bright green eyes only a few inches away. "The whole reason I'm alive right now is because you let me stay on your ship, because you trusted me. You saw who was after me and you took me with you anyway. You could have spared yourself all this if you'd just turned me in."

Adelaide scoffed.

"Unthinkable. Even right now I am more sure than ever I made the right decision. You, Maaya... you're incredible. And I would face them all down again if it meant keeping you here."

Maaya smiled, pulling her eyes away from Adelaide's as her face turned even redder.

"And I would do all this again, too."

"I figured," Adelaide said, brushing a stray hair from Maaya's cheek. "Say, was that a healing card you used on me just then? I'm not in as much pain as I feared, and I'm not even near as tired as I thought I would be."

"It was. I… I tried something new. I know how they usually work, but I didn't want to exhaust you even more; you'd already been through so much. So I tried making the card use my own energy instead. And I don't know if it worked completely, but it at least worked a little. I'm completely exhausted right now," Maaya laughed.

Adelaide raised her eyebrows.

"Really? You're not in a great state, either; why'd you do that for me?"

"Oh, I don't know," Maaya replied before she could stop herself. "Because you're cute, and I like you."

Adelaide was speechless for a moment, and for the first time Maaya could remember, she saw the captain blush. She opened her mouth to speak, but then a blinding light swept over the deck.

"What the—?" Adelaide uttered, struggling to sit up.

Everyone had stopped what they were doing to look at the source of the light. At first Maaya thought it might be the sun breaking through the smoke, but then she realized that it was far too bright for sunrise, and that the light was much too bright and too close. She got shakily to her feet, hoping against hope that her suspicions were wrong… and then she felt her stomach drop.

The ghosts had arrived. Hundreds and hundreds of them floated slowly over the ocean, heading straight for them. More and more were appearing every second, a white blanket over the dead sea, their ranks stretching wide. While they had not appeared directly on top of the ships, Maaya knew they had only a few minutes before the ghosts arrived.

"It's them," Maaya cried, and Adelaide snapped to attention, struggling to her feet.

"Stars, this isn't good. Our ships are dead in the water and trapped, and there are way too many ghosts to get rid of ourselves. I… I don't know what to do," Adelaide stammered.

"Leave it to me, Captain," came a deep rumbling voice from beside them. They turned to see Skarin floating there, looking unimpressed by the oncoming ghosts. "My ship will clear a path for your escape."

"But there are other ships in the way, how will we—?"

"No time for explanations. Just follow my lead," Skarin said, then floated back to his ship. Maaya heard him calling orders to his crew, and though she couldn't hear exactly what he was saying, the massive ship soon began to turn until its bow faced east. And then, with all the power her oarsmen could muster, the Nocte Cadenza started to push forward.

Adelaide stumbled to the helm and flipped a switch on the small brass panel in the center of the rudder wheel post. Maaya heard the hissing of steam and splashing sounds from either side of the ship, and the Windfire slowly began to move ahead as well. Adelaide spun the wheel, taking the Windfire directly into the wake of the Nocte Cadenza.

Maaya glanced behind them. She felt better now that they were moving, but the ghosts were still easily catching up, as slow as they were. Maaya's breath caught in her throat. If they made it out of this, it was going to be close. Very close.

"Do you have any bloods?" Adelaide asked, focusing intently on the task in front of her.

"No; I haven't had time to make any more of my own."

"Okay. Here, reach into my left coat pocket; my deck is in there. Take however many bloods you need and keep those ghosts off us."

"What? But these are too high level, I can't use—"

"Focus, Maaya. You've done some great things already, and you are far better than you give yourself credit for. You have to *feel* that you can. I believe you can; now you just need to do the same. Okay?"

Maaya nodded, then gulped. She pulled out Adelaide's deck of cards, taking a moment to admire the slick high-quality material of her cards; unlike Maaya's, these did not stick together when wet, and seemed to be at least somewhat water repellant.

She flipped through the deck quickly, taking every blood card Adelaide had. She didn't feel the connection to these cards that she felt with her own; they were but mere slips of paper in her hands. She took a deep breath and steeled herself, then walked to the side of the ship to get a better view of the ghosts below.

They were still a few minutes out, but closing quickly, and even as the Windfire gained speed, she knew it wasn't enough to outrun them.

Suddenly, there was a horrendous sound of shattering glass and splintering wood from ahead of the ship. Maaya spun around to see the Nocte Cadenza plowing full speed into a small navy warship that hadn't managed to move out of the way in time. The smaller ship crumpled from the impact and started to take on water immediately. Its crew immediately began to abandon it, swimming desperately for safety.

"That crazy man," Adelaide muttered, a grin on her face. "Looks like we're going to make it out after all. How are they coming, Maaya?"

"They'll be on us in a minute!" Maaya said nervously, her voice starting to tremble.

"We've got this; just hang on and keep them off our tail," Adelaide ordered confidently as the Nocte Cadenza pushed another ship out of the way.

They continued on, Adelaide deftly weaving her way through the debris and other ships. The ghosts followed all the while, silent and slow like the evil in Maaya's worst nightmares.

And then, just when Maaya thought they were about to break through, the Nocte Cadenza suddenly came to a grinding, shuddering halt dead ahead.

"Damn!" Adelaide swore. Skarin's vessel had collided with a sinking ship that was too big to force through, and was now stuck. Unfortunately, with as fast as the Windfire was going and the short distance between them, stopping the Windfire wasn't an option. "We're going hard to starboard, everyone brace yourselves!"

Maaya frantically looked in both directions. Starboard definitely seemed the right way to go; to port was another sinking ship, but there was still enough above water to damage the Windfire badly if she tried to push though.

But then her eyes widened. To the right of Skarin's ship, barely visible just under the dark water, were the jagged remnants of a battleship's steel mast. If the Windfire struck it they would be stuck and start flooding for sure. Maaya's mind racing, she decided to see if her last idea would work as well as the others.

"No! Go left! Mast in the water!" Maaya cried. When Adelaide opened her mouth to argue, Maaya continued, "Trust me!"

Adelaide hesitated, then pulled hard on the wheel, sending the ship turning sharply to port. Maaya heard another sickening grinding noise as the bow of the Windfire barely scraped the Nocte Cadenza's stern, and for a moment she feared they had cut it too close, but then the noise stopped, and the Windfire moved out hard to port.

Maaya breathed a quick sigh of relief. They had avoided that danger, and were now going to safely pass Skarin's ship on the left, but that still left the sinking ship directly in front of them—and as comparatively small as the Windfire was, there was no way they could fit through. Now it was time for phase two.

"Get Skarin to fire on that ship! If he breaks it up, we can pass!" Maaya called. Adelaide looked at her in shock, and then smiled. She passed on the order to Halvar, who called it ahead to someone farther down the ship. So it went until an officer at the very head of the ship shouted something to one of the ghosts aboard Skarin's ship.

Maaya hoped against hope that they heard correctly, and that if they did, they would act quickly enough. They were approaching quickly. If they tried to stop they would be overwhelmed by the ghosts, but if they didn't make it through they would collide with the sinking ship.

Closer and closer they came, and still nothing happened. Maaya couldn't breathe. She could already hear the gut-wrenching twisting of metal and snapping of wood in her mind. This was it. She shut her eyes tight, bracing for impact.

Thoom. Thoom. Thoom.

A deafening burst of gunfire caused her to open her eyes. A huge cloud of smoke billowed out in front of them as the Nocte Cadenza unleashed a broadside attack on the sinking vessel from what guns were left in front of the Windfire, practically disintegrating the Selenthian ship. The burst was so loud that Maaya almost had to cover her ears, but before she knew it the guns had stopped again, just in time to let the Windfire pass.

As the Windfire sailed past the Nocte Cadenza, Maaya scanned the water frantically for any sign debris that might still pose a threat, but she could see nothing through the smoke that blanketed the ship and everything around them. She held her breath in terror, expecting any moment to feel the Windfire come to a jolting stop.

But then, suddenly, finally, they were free. The Windfire sailed out of the smoke and into clear waters. They had made it.

"YES!" Adelaide shouted triumphantly, and before Maaya knew what was happening, the captain left the helm and pulled Maaya into a tight hug. "Maaya, you are brilliant and insane. Absolutely completely insane."

"Before we celebrate too much, we've still got one problem chasing us down," Halvar reminded them quickly, having taken over the wheel.

"Right, our ghost friends," Adelaide said, letting Maaya go and turning to face the wave of oncoming ghosts.

The ghosts were close now, within range of her cards. Maaya prepared to throw one of her bloods, then faltered.

The Selenthian men and women, still busy trying to pull their fellow sailors out of the water and onto the few ships that still floated, didn't notice the ghosts as they approached. Even if they had, Maaya thought, the ships of the dead fleet had blocked them in. Maaya knew what would happen next.

Some of the crew who were unfortunate enough to look in the direction of the ghosts suddenly stopped short, then fell to their knees, staring blankly ahead. Before anyone could make sure they were all right, the wave of ghosts began to pass over the navy ships.

Even in the open water the Windfire couldn't outrun them on the power of its oars alone. Maaya took up one of the blood cards in her hands, focused as hard as she could, then flung the card at the oncoming wave.

The card sailed a few feet, then fluttered uselessly into the water below.

"That's okay, give it another go," Adelaide said encouragingly even as she leaned against the wall of the cabin for support.

Maaya took a deep breath, trying with all she had to suppress the panic that welled violently inside her. She closed her eyes again, trying with everything she had to feel beyond the paper in her hand. She focused hard, letting the sounds of splashing water and screaming fade behind her. It was just her and the card now. Really, it was a *libris* card like any other. Why should she not control it? It might not be her blood, but that meant nothing. Maaya had far too much of her own to be beaten by a slip of paper now. This was her domain, this was what she excelled at, and for the love of everything in the world, if Adelaide believed she could do it, then she wasn't going to take no for an answer.

The card suddenly felt warm in her hands. Fighting her surprise, she opened her eyes again, taking care to avoid staring the ghosts in the eyes. They were so close now that they would be upon the ship in seconds.

Maaya threw her card.

This time the card soared through the air with the precision and aim Maaya had learned over years of practice. It collided with the first ghost in the wave, and with a powerful burst of sparks, it and half a dozen others vanished instantly.

"There you go!" Adelaide cheered. "Now again! Send them back to the void!"

Maaya took another card, and this time there was no resistance. Its warmth comforted her, almost like it was reassuring her they were on the same side. She flung this too, with similar results. Before long she noticed that a gap had opened up between the Windfire and the deadly wave, and though the ghosts continued on, the Windfire was in no danger so long as she held her course.

Then, out of nowhere, the ghosts flickered and disappeared… and then the sky went black.

Cries of horror erupted on deck, but Maaya couldn't speak. She was only too familiar with this horror. The great red scar of the gaping maw in the sky had opened once again, and Maaya fell to the deck, shutting her eyes tight as dizziness overwhelmed her.

For only a moment all was silent, save for the utterances of shock and fear from some of the others, but then came the part Maaya dreaded most. As the screaming began, Maaya opened her eyes.

Behind the fleeing Windfire, hundreds of ghosts, all of them sailors from the Selenthian fleet, were being pulled skyward by a force beyond any Maaya could imagine. Despite the fact that she knew it only affected ghosts, she held on tight to the deck just in case this mysterious power suddenly changed its mind and decided to take her with the rest of them.

But, just like before, the invisible wind that carried the ghosts of the dead sailors with it pulled only the newly dead, even as the ghosts from Skarin's fleet looked on, some in anger, some in horror. The sky was filled with the ghosts, fighting the invisible power in vain. The memory of Maaya's own friends desperately struggling against the void returned to her in force, and she shut her eyes tight and held her hands to her ears.

And then it was gone. The void in the sky sealed itself up in a matter of moments, leaving only the red scar behind. The stars slowly faded back into the view as though nothing had happened. The last echoes of the sailors' screams rang in Maaya's mind, and she shook her head, dazed.

"Maaya, you okay?" she heard Adelaide ask, then felt the captain's powerful grip on her arm.

"Yeah… I… f-fine," Maaya whimpered, getting to her feet. Her first thought was to make sure the ghosts hadn't reappeared, but there was still no sign of them.

From below, Inga rushed up to meet them, looking extremely concerned.

"Captain, are you—?"

"Fine, just exhausted. The ghosts are gone so let's not ask questions. Cut the engine and bring us around; let's stick near our allies until we've got everything sorted. Continue with our damage assessment and assisting the wounded. If we're in good enough shape I'd like to get us out of here as soon as possible."

"Of course, Captain. Should I help you to your bed first?"

Adelaide looked ready to object, but when Inga raised her eyebrow, the captain relented.

Inga effortlessly helped the captain to her feet, and then, putting an arm behind her back for support, helped Adelaide walk to her cabin. Maaya hung back. She knew the captain was safe now, but after what they had just been through she didn't want to leave her side.

The instant Inga helped Adelaide out of her heavy coat and into bed, Adelaide looked up at the commander, all her usual authority in her gaze.

"You're in charge while I recover, Commander. I trust you, as always."

"Of course, Captain," Inga said with a slight bow. "You should consider bed rest as well, Maaya."

Maaya agreed, thinking she'd like nothing better than to lie down and give her aching body some rest… but then she gasped.

I need to find Saber!" she exclaimed.

Inga's eyes widened slightly, her expression much like that of someone who left home on a trip only to remember something they had accidentally left behind.

"I'll see to it she's found," Inga responded immediately, then flagged down a nearby officer through the still-open doors to the cabin. "Have the entire ship searched and find Saber," she commanded. "If she's nowhere on board get word out to the rest of the fleet that she's missing and needs to be located immediately. For future reference, *please* remember that both Saber and Maaya are part of our head count."

The officer saluted, then departed quickly. Inga stared down apologetically at Maaya.

"I am sincerely sorry for the oversight, Miss Sahni. I will ensure she is located as quickly as possible."

"Thank you," Maaya said weakly. She felt the desperate urge to search with everyone else, but her exhausted body furiously demanded respite, and it threatened to collapse any minute. She knew, however, that until her friend was found, she wouldn't not be able to sleep a wink.

Only after a few minutes, however, a sailor came jogging out onto the deck.

"Commander, Saber's here. She's in your quarters."

Inga dismissed the sailor, then nodded encouragingly at Maaya, who suddenly felt as though she might burst into tears with relief.

"Go make sure your friend is all right," she said warmly, and Maaya nodded.

By the time Maaya reached the doors to the officers' quarters she was nearly sprinting, and when she tore open the door to her quarters, she saw Saber floating there. The ghost looked mildly confused, but otherwise unharmed and undisturbed.

"Oh, hey Maaya. I was wondering where— oof."

Maaya hugged Saber with all the strength she had left, and now she was definitely crying. Even as she held the ghost in her arms, she made sure she was aware of her presence, afraid that if she didn't feel her there for even a moment, she might disappear.

"Nice to see you too," Saber continued in slight alarm, escaping Maaya's grip. "Are you all right? Why are you crying?"

"I thought… I thought you had gone! I thought maybe the officer had hit you," Maaya cried, wiping her eyes on her sleeve. "You disappeared and none of us could find you, and I thought…"

"Maaya, you're worrying me a little," Saber continued. "Nobody hit me. I'm fine! I promise. I've been here for a while just wondering where everyone's been off to."

"You were here this whole time? Why didn't you try to find me?"

"I… don't really know. I figured you were out with the captain and that you'd be back soon. I didn't want to interrupt. Did you have a good time?"

Maaya stared.

"I wouldn't exactly call this fun, no… but we won. Adelaide got hurt but I managed to heal her, and the ship wasn't damaged too much. Oh, and she let me use some of her blood cards, and it turns out I can use them after all."

"Wait, hang on. She got hurt doing what? What damaged the ship? What kind of crazy game were you playing out there? I can only assume it was Halvar's idea."

"I… the battle? With the Selenthian navy? The one where you were setting ships on fire?" Maaya said incredulously.

Now it was Saber's turn to look confused.

"You guys crossed the Selenthian navy? How did I miss that? I was right here."

"Saber, you're scaring me. If this is some kind of joke this is not the time—"

"I'm not joking! Sorry, Maaya, I just… I don't know what you're talking about. I'm not trying to be difficult."

"You were *just* out there with me. We were fighting together, we destroyed guns, we fought an officer on the opposing side who also knew *libris*, and he attacked you!"

Saber looked genuinely troubled.

"And… this happened just now, you say?" the ghost asked slowly, and Maaya nodded. "I… I see. I don't recall any of that. You said there was a man who knew *libris* who attacked me?" Maaya nodded again. "Right. I don't know if this is a possibility, but if he went after me there's a chance that whatever he did knocked me out of sorts for a while. I'm still here, so clearly he didn't seal me, but… maybe something else happened. But I'm here, okay? And I'm not going anywhere. In the meantime, you look absolutely exhausted. What say you get some rest and we can catch up and figure things out tomorrow?"

"Why can't we figure it out now? I'm really worried about this."

"I don't know how to figure it out!" Saber protested. "I don't have any answers for this. All I know is that I'm here now and I'm okay, I just apparently don't remember what happened. Maybe it was being exposed to *libris,* maybe the whole thing was just all sorts of traumatic for me somehow and I blanked, it could come back to me later… I don't know. I wish I did, but I don't know what to say otherwise. Considering I didn't know anything was amiss until a minute ago I have very little to offer in the way of answers."

There was a long pause, and then Maaya relented.

"That's fine, I suppose. I'm just glad you're okay. And tomorrow everything can go back to normal."

"You think so?" Saber said.

"I hope so. We beat the entire enemy fleet, and then… well, let's just say there's no one left to follow us."

"A whole fleet!" Saber said in awe. "I'd ask you for the details now but you look exhausted. I can always ask someone else if I get too impatient. Get some sleep, okay?"

"You got it," Maaya smiled. Then, as she crawled into bed, she remembered something. "Can you go see Adelaide and let her know you're okay? She was worried about you, too."

"Of course. And then I'll come straight back here to spend the night with you, so don't you worry," Saber said gently, helping Maaya pull up her bedcovers.

"Oh, and go easy on her, will you? I healed her but she's still exhausted," Maaya yawned.

"What, Adelaide is capable of tiredness? You learn something new every day I guess," Saber quipped, then grinned. "I'll be back soon."

With a cheerful wave, Saber disappeared up through the ceiling.

Maaya stared at the silhouette of the bed above her in the darkness. She was concerned over Saber's apparent lack of memory about what had just happened, but maybe Saber was right. Maybe there was some side effect to almost-but-not-quite being struck by a blood card. It was also possible that this could be temporary and that tomorrow things would be back to normal. This had definitely been an unusual experience, and she consoled herself by thinking it would not happen again.

She sighed, finally letting herself relax. The last source of her dread had disappeared now she knew Saber was safe. With this in mind, it was as though the floodgates of fatigue opened, and within seconds, she was asleep.

25

ATTRACTION

Maaya awoke the next morning to the sounds of banging and loud voices. She sat bolt upright in bed, fearing the worst, but then realized that there were people laughing as well, and that the banging sounded more like the steady movements of hammers than of weapons. She gazed longingly back at her pillow, still feeling plenty of exhaustion from the day before, but begrudgingly accepted that she would never get back to sleep with that kind of noise going on.

She slipped lightly out of bed and got dressed, then made her way out to the deck. By the position of the sun she guessed that it was close to midday, which meant she had slept for over twelve hours. Then, as she slowly climbed the stairs to the top deck, she felt a light breeze gently blow her hair from her face. She had never been so happy to feel the wind.

"Morning to you!" Halvar called cheerily from the wheel. "Come here and take a look at this."

He led her over to the starboard side of the ship and gestured to the sea in front of him, and Maaya gaped.

"It's a beautiful disaster, isn't it?" Halvar continued with a smile.

Where just the evening before there had been several gleaming battleships of the Selenthian navy, what remained was a mess of broken hulls, many of them still burning. Immense dark plumes of smoke rose from the wreckage and high into the sky before the wind began to carry it away. In the water surrounding the wreckage, Maaya saw all manner of debris: torn sails, splintered wood, cabin furniture… and bodies.

"Should we worry that anyone will see that smoke?" Maaya asked, turning away so Halvar wouldn't see her shudder of discomfort.

"Not likely. No one from the mainland will see it, that's for sure. If there is anyone else out here they wouldn't dare come near once they got a glimpse of our fleet."

"We can't just leave it there, can we?" she continued skeptically.

"Probably not, but Skarin said he'd take care of it so we can be on our way. Seemed pretty delighted at the prospect, really, but I'm not complaining. The sooner we can leave the better. We just need to finish a few quick repairs and then we'll be set! I'm not usually one for cabin fever, but I said a few prayers of thanks for this wind coming back."

"Yes, thank goodness," Maaya said gratefully. Now that the wind was back it was doubtful any other ship would have the time or the means to catch up with them. "How bad is the damage?"

"Not so significant we're dead in the water, but we're in no shape to fight again. Our repairs are just to ensure we can make it safely back to port without sinking in the final stretch," Halvar said. "After all we've been through that'd be nothing short of embarrassing. Anyway, we don't have the resources or time to make solid repairs out here; we'll have to wait until we dock, and I can bet you anything the cap'n is going to want to oversee every tiny detail; this ship is her baby."

"I've noticed," Maaya replied with a smile. "How is she?"

"Much better after a full night's sleep, but I'm worried she might have fallen ill."

"What? How?" Maaya asked.

"She woke up looking and feeling much better than yesterday, but rather than insisting she resume command as she usually does, she agreed to let Commander Strand keep handling things."

"I'm not sure I follow."

Halvar leaned over, relaxing on his elbows on the railing as he stared out at the burning wreckage.

"Adelaide just likes being in control. Or maybe it's more accurate to say she can't stand *not* being in control. She trusts us, mind you; she just likes being on top of things, and she's very picky. If something's even slightly out of place or not as it should be, it'll bug her until she fixes it. She's usually so eager to get back to work that she'll resume her duties before she's actually ready. It drives Inga absolutely batty."

Maaya smiled. That sounded like her captain all right.

"Anyway, I can't imagine what might have come over her. All I know is she said she was going to take today to rest and that she had some other plans as well. What those could be I can hardly imagine—"

"Miss Sahni, there you are. It's good to see you awake and well."

Inga strode over to them, a rare smile on her face.

"Thank you," Maaya said cheerily. The return of the wind had put her in an excellent mood. "I haven't slept that long in a while. How is everything? Are we going to be leaving soon?"

"Within a few hours at most, I expect," Inga answered. "After we complete our repairs we'll need to finish checking in with the other ships, and the captains of every ship still need to convene to decide what our next course of action is to be. For us, regardless of the decision, we will soon be departing for Krethus."

"Does that mean you'll be going, then?" Maaya asked.

"Indeed it does. Though I suspect the captain is physically well enough to deal with such matters, she's made it clear that she has no desire to do so today, so I will be taking her place. Before we get there, however, I do come on behalf of the captain with a personal request."

"What is it?" Maaya questioned, her imagination already leaping helpfully into action.

"She requests that you join her this evening for dinner and that you keep your entire evening free for practice."

"Practice for… what?" Maaya said, bemused.

"I haven't the slightest idea. Before I could ask her to clarify she had already moved on to another completely unrelated subject. If you haven't already guessed, this is the norm, so I'm afraid you'll have to find that out for yourself tonight."

"I'll be happy to," Maaya said, unable to hide her silly grin from her face. "Is there anything I can help with before then? I still have some healing cards left."

"That won't be necessary. The injuries our crew sustained were minor in the grand scheme of things, and you wouldn't want to tire yourself out too much to answer the captain's request."

"That's… fair," Maaya relented. "So what are we—?"

"Ah, there she is. The unexpected hero of the LSV Windfire," drawled a voice behind her. Maaya turned quickly to see Skarin, flanked again by two ghostly soldiers. "I am quite impressed with how you handled yourself, especially against ships of your home country. Perhaps you were telling the truth after all."

"I told you," Maaya replied in a clipped tone. "Maybe you shouldn't be so judgmental."

"Naivety didn't get me far in life, but perhaps I simply didn't execute it correctly. It does seem to be working so far for you," Skarin retorted amusedly.

"I prefer calling it not being bitter and miserable, but agree to disagree," Maaya said icily, and Skarin laughed.

"You'll do. I can see why Adelaide chose to bring you aboard."

"Is there something you need, Captain?" Inga interjected politely.

"I wanted to check on the progress of your repairs myself since some of my crew is assisting you. They occasionally have difficulty meeting my standards, and I wanted to ensure they weren't slacking."

"They're doing a fine job, I assure you. How fares your ship? She took many more hits than the Windfire."

"She did, but she can handle it," Skarin said dismissively. "Besides, we have much more time for repairs; you, on the other hand, need to be ready for travel within hours. Speaking of, I also wanted to check on your captain. Is she well?"

"She's recovering well, thank you. I expect she'll be resuming command tomorrow morning."

"After the beating she took? She's even hardier than I remember," Skarin said, clearly impressed.

"She has definitely earned her position and our respect," Inga replied. "She will unfortunately be occupied for the remainder of our voyage, but she asked me to pass along her respects and hopes that she will have the pleasure of seeing you again soon."

"I sincerely hope so. As much as I adore the thrill of battle and consider it a privilege to fight beside her, I would prefer a more peaceful venue for our next meeting that we might catch up. Much has happened in the world since last we spoke. But I won't bore you. You're standing in for the captain this afternoon, correct?" Inga nodded. "Good. I will see you then."

Skarin and his guard left back toward the Nocte Cadenza. Maaya hadn't noticed before, but the colossal vessel had been badly damaged in the battle. One of the masts tilted dangerously, frayed and broken ropes hung limply all over the ship, and there were dozens of fresh breaks and holes in the hull. How it was still floating was nothing short of a miracle, Maaya thought as she watched the ship's crew scramble to salvage and repair what they could before anything got worse.

"Now, as I was saying," Inga continued as though there had been no interruption, "the captain has also suggested you refresh yourself with a bath before joining her for dinner."

"A… bath? In what?" Maaya asked foolishly, imagining trying to take a comfortable bath in a bucket of cold seawater. Inga laughed again.

"We're not so primitive as you might think. We keep a supply of fresh water on board for cleaning ourselves and our clothes. It's quite refreshing, especially after a day like yesterday."

"That… sounds nice, actually," Maaya said, suddenly very aware of how dirty she felt. She felt uncomfortably sticky, especially under the weight of clothes that had been soaked by seawater the night before. "I think I'd like that now."

"Follow me then, if you please," Inga instructed, and Maaya followed.

Along the way, Saber caught up with Maaya, waving merrily at her as she approached.

"Off to the baths then? Good, good. Not that I can smell you, but if I could I imagine it would be awful. Your hair still looks nice, though."

"Thanks," Maaya grumbled, and Saber beamed. The ghost was definitely feeling well again. Still, the thought of what happened the previous day ate at Maaya. "How are you feeling? Do you… remember anything?"

"Not a thing. It bothers me a lot, to be honest, but I feel fine otherwise. I'm thinking I should consider myself lucky a single memory is all I lost given how close I came to no longer existing, but… well. Let's talk happier things and try to avoid getting into any more fights with *libris* experts, yeah?"

They proceeded two decks down, then toward the stern. Inga opened the door to what looked like a small closet; it was narrow enough that Inga would likely be able to place her palms flat against the parallel side walls at the same time, and only long enough that she probably could not lay down on the floor with her legs straight. A small tub took up most of the room, only large enough that most people could probably fit into it with some squeezing.

For Maaya, however, it was perfect. The water was clean and still and the lightest wisps of steam rose off the surface. A thin slat was cut into the wood near the ceiling to provide ventilation, which kept the room from becoming overwhelmingly humid. Beside the tub on a narrow bench was a small bowl with a few small soap containers inside, a large towel, and a smaller hand towel.

"If you'd like, leave your clothes outside the door when you undress, and someone will clean them for you," Inga said.

"Does everyone do this? I've never heard of something like this on a ship before," Maaya asked in fascination.

"There are similar facilities on many ships, especially larger ones. Most of the crew is limited to short showers to conserve water, but being a favorite guest of the captain comes with certain… benefits," Inga smiled. "Do enjoy yourself."

With that, Inga closed the door, and Maaya heard her footsteps fading down the hall.

Maaya stared back at the tub with some trepidation. She had never taken a bath like this before. Indeed, she had hardly ever had a proper bath at all; keeping herself clean in Sark usually involved taking a bucket of cold water from the tap and scrubbing herself as quickly as she could before all the water ran out.

She proceeded to undress, and then, while Saber turned away to put her clothes outside the door, took a careful step over to the tub. Steam rose in gentle wisps from the calm surface, and the clear water looked delightfully inviting. Maaya dipped her toe in to test the water—and then recoiled with a yelp.

"What's wrong?" Saber asked, trying and failing to hide her laughter.

"It's so hot!" Maaya gasped, kneeling down and submerging her hand into the water.

"That's the idea. It's so much more comfortable than a cold bath, that much I know. Oh, and it's good for you, too. Heat eases the pain of sore muscles, and I have a feeling you'd appreciate that right now."

"But… how do I get in?" Maaya asked helplessly.

"Quickly. You'll get used to it. Trust me."

Maaya steeled her nerves. She had just spent the previous day battling a fleet of Selenthian ships *and* a small army of ghosts. Was a little warm water really going to get in her way?

She stepped in and submerged herself up to her chest, and immediately regretted doing so. She gasped as the warmth seemed to envelop her very being, and she made to step out again, but Saber held her gently at the shoulders.

"Deep breaths, Maaya. It's not as bad as it feels."

Maaya breathed, and sure enough, within a few moments the shock had passed. The water was still hot, but not unbearably so. In fact, it already felt soothing. Once Maaya was sure she wasn't going to start hyperventilating, she let herself ease back onto a small stool that was submerged in the tub. It was slightly too short to keep her mouth and nose above the water, but Maaya didn't mind.

She leaned back and rested her head on the side of the tub, closing her eyes as the comforting warmth washed over her. Then, after taking a breath, she let herself sink completely underwater. Unlike the cold salty ocean, being underwater in the tub was like wrapping herself in a thick blanket from head to foot, muffling the sounds of the outside world.

When she could hold her breath no longer, she poked her head out from under the water, brushing her hair back.

"You like it?" Saber asked, clearly amused.

"I might never move again," Maaya sighed happily. "You'll just have to go on without me."

"Fat chance. You still need to tell me everything that happened yesterday. Here, wash up while you're at it. Your hair's so long now you might actually finish the story before you're done washing it."

Maaya snickered as she took one of the soap containers from the bowl and began to tell her story. Saber's expression changed from impressed to amused to vindictive to horrified, and when Maaya finished her story, she didn't seem to know how to react.

"Wow, that's… really something," she finally said. "I can't believe I don't have any memory of this. That must have been terrifying for you."

"I only thought I was going to die twice," Maaya joked as she washed the suds from her hair. "There was just so much going on all at once, but… we all made it through. It turned out better than expected, and you know what? I think that's because of you."

"What? Why me?" Saber asked suspiciously.

"You gave me one heck of a motivational speech last night. I was sitting in my room like a coward and you got me to get out there and give it my all. If you hadn't gotten me to do that, who knows what would have happened? Adelaide might have drowned, the Windfire might have been taken over…"

"Oh, do give yourself credit for something at least once in your life," Saber interrupted. "You're telling me that you did all these amazing things, but I get credit for them? Not this time, my friend. You're a hero, and this is all on you. Sorry, I don't make the rules."

"I'll accept the fact that I helped, but I'm nowhere near ready to accept the label of hero. No way," Maaya refused. "But… you were right about what you said. I guess I can do more than I thought when I choose to stand and fight."

"You bet, and I am going to make sure you never forget it for an instant," Saber continued happily. "Now, speaking of overcoming hardship, there's one more matter we need to talk about."

"What's that?" Maaya asked, taking the hand towel and scrubbing her face and body.

"Confessing your crush to the captain, of course."

Maaya dropped the hand towel in surprise, then quickly picked it up, looking determinedly away from the ghost.

"No. Absolutely not."

"Why not? This is the perfect time! And you know she likes you back."

"*You* think she likes me back. Besides, it's a little weird considering she's the captain and everything. If we were back in Levien and she wasn't on duty, then maybe—*maybe*—I would say something, but there's no way I could right now!"

"What, so the fear of getting rejected by your crush is greater than the fear of the Selenthian military chasing you down?" Saber teased.

"Yes, it is!" Maaya answered immediately. Saber sighed.

"One day soon the both of you will be holding hands and making googly eyes at each other, and I will float above both your heads and scream 'I told you so' at the top of my lungs."

Maaya stammered helplessly, then sighed and closed her eyes, leaning her head back in the water.

"It really is weird, though. She's the captain right now, on duty and everything. I'm just a guest. It feels weird when there's that difference. Even if she felt the same way about me that I do about her, that might affect how she reacts. What if… what if I wait until we get to Krethus? Maybe we can go somewhere, somewhere she's not a captain in charge of a crew or anything like that. Just a girl that I really really like."

Saber pondered this for a moment, then appeared, at least for the moment, satisfied.

"Fair enough. But if you reach that point and still don't confess, I will do it for you."

"You wouldn't."

"Try me."

Maaya and Saber stared intently at each other, and then finally Maaya broke off, rolling her eyes in frustration. Saber smiled gleefully at her small victory.

Then there came a light knock at the door, and an unfamiliar voice from outside said, "Your clothes are ready, ma'am."

The girls stared at each other with raised eyebrows.

"'Ma'am,' huh?" Saber observed. "Well now, aren't you fancy? A right proper woman you'll be in no time, I dare say."

"Oh my dear lady, please don't speak so out of turn. I have a most important dinner I must attend and have no time for tomfoolery," Maaya said, raising her nose in the air. Then she snorted with laughter and both girl fell into a fit of giggles.

"I'll get your clothes while you dry off," Saber offered, and flew over to the door and out of sight.

Maaya submerged herself one last time to make sure she had cleaned off all the soap, then stepped out onto the dry floor. The towel she picked up was much larger than she expected, falling down to below her knees once she wrapped it around her. As Saber brought in her clothes in a neatly folded pile, Maaya quickly dried herself off as best she could, running her fingers through her hair in an attempt to tame it even though she knew the wind would undo all her work in mere moments.

Her clothes were dry and fresh, and putting them back on felt like she was putting on new clothes entirely. She sighed happily as she looked down at herself—it was a definite improvement.

"Let's get back up top before they send a search party. After you, my lady," Saber teased, opening the door for Maaya. Maaya glared at Saber as she passed, unable to keep a straight face.

When she stepped out onto the main deck, she immediately noticed the distinct lack of officers on board. Only Halvar and Gunnar remained, and Inga was nowhere to be seen.

"Maaya, up here!" came a familiar voice, and Maaya smiled as she looked up to see Adelaide waving down at her. "Come join me."

Maaya happily obliged, taking the stairs two at a time. When she reached the top, Adelaide scooped her into a hug in an instant.

"You smell good!" she said bluntly. "Enjoy the bath?"

"That's an understatement," Maaya replied, nodding emphatically.

"Great! I thought you might. I just had one earlier myself, and oh, it was so very satisfying after yesterday. Even managed to wash my bedclothes, too, since they were soaked with seawater last night. Your hair's all a mess, though. Here, come in, and I'll take care of that. Saber, you can tag along!"

"Thank you, Captain, but I need to tell some of the crew I'm still alive. Ish," Saber said sweetly. "You two have a good time!"

Maaya didn't even bother glaring this time. She had already figured Saber would find some excuse to leave.

She joined Adelaide inside the cabin, which somehow looked much cleaner than she had seen it had. She had been prepared to walk into a near disaster considering the battle, but she couldn't find a single item out of place.

"I know. Don't worry, it'll be a mess again soon. It's just that since I'm not back on duty I had nowhere else to divert my energy but cleaning, and when I get focused I get *really* focused," Adelaide explained, smirking at the expression on Maaya's face.

"Are you feeling okay? Did the healing card miss something?" Maaya asked attentively, looking the captain up and down.

"Still feeling a little tired, but none the worse for wear I suppose. But after yesterday I just… I don't want to deal with any of this," Adelaide sighed. "We won, and it went better than expected, and that's great. But there was so much death, and then there was that walk, as you say… it just took a lot out of me mentally, you understand. So that's what today is for—last night I rested my body, and today, my mind. Now, come here! Let's get that hair taken care of."

Adelaide jumped onto her bed, then invited Maaya to sit in front of her. Maaya hesitated, then sat down with her feet tucked under her, her back to the captain. She felt the gentle tug of a brush as Adelaide pulled it slowly through her long hair.

"So much politics, too," Adelaide continued. "I expended all my energy on paperwork, and now I'll have to come into port with an explanation as to why it looks like I sailed us through hell and back. I'll figure out a way to get that done, but Inga will have to handle the rest. I personally just want to sit in here for the rest of the journey and only come out when it's time to disembark. Someone else can handle the paperwork, the repairs, all of it."

"Can they do that?"

"Oh, yeah. Inga can handle everything, and she knows me well enough by now to know what I want. I just usually insist on being involved in everything. Not this time, though. I actually sort of look forward to being off the ship for a while."

"Seriously, do you feel okay? You sound kind of… agitated," Maaya pressed concernedly.

"I am agitated, possibly a little depressed, but I'm okay. I should stop talking about the stuff I'm trying to avoid, though; that'd probably help," Adelaide chuckled. "What about you? How are you holding up after all that excitement?"

"I hurt a lot less than I thought I would, but I think the bath had something to do with that," Maaya said contentedly. "Otherwise… I think I'm all right. It's just been one thing after another, and I'm not sure if I'm getting better at dealing with it or if I'm just numb to it all by now."

"This is a lot for any one person to deal with. Even those of us who have spent years out here don't deal with that kind of thing often. Or… at all, really. I know shore leave is going to be good for everyone."

"What does a captain do in her time off?" Maaya smiled.

"Lately I've started seeing my family more, and this time is no different, though it will be the first time I've actually come home in a while. I'm not too fussed about our schedule, but I'm anxious to be home. Otherwise I just like relaxing, taking walks, training and going on patrols, maybe working on a puzzle or three, things like that. I don't usually keep in contact with much of the crew during shore leave, and this time I'll be spending plenty of it with you!" Adelaide finished.

"I really do appreciate you inviting me along, but I have to try to take care of this whole ghost thing first…" Maaya said, and it was hard not to let her disappointment carry on her voice.

"There will be plenty of time for that! An extra day or two won't make things any better or worse, and besides, you have earned yourself a break. If you keep going at this rate, constantly running and fighting and looking over your shoulder, you're going to burn out. It's a wonder you haven't already, really."

Maaya bit her lip. She didn't want to say that she felt like she had burned out a long time ago, and that the only reason she continued on was because she had no choice if she wanted to survive. This wasn't a hobby or a job she could quit when she started feeling overwhelmed. She was slightly jealous of Adelaide's ability to get away from it all whenever they docked. It seemed like her troubles ended where the water began.

Almost immediately, she scolded herself. That wasn't fair at all. Adelaide had grown up under different circumstances to be sure, but she had her own fair share of hardship. Maaya had seen glimpses of Adelaide's vulnerability, and in those moments she knew that while Adelaide appeared to have everything in her life organized and planned down to the last tiny detail, there were things she truly struggled with underneath.

"But anyway, that's why I think you should spend some time with me," Adelaide continued. She sounded calmer already, and her movements were smoother, something Maaya's scalp appreciated. "I can show you around, we can get some nice things to eat, we can get you some new things to wear, it'll be great! And you can sleep in a bed that doesn't rock back and forth all night, too. Then when it's time for you to go, well… we'll see what happens."

Maaya thought she detected a hint of sadness in Adelaide's voice, much like the one that currently filled her heart. *Come with me,* she wanted to say, but she knew now wasn't the time. Not when Adelaide was feeling so drained.

She fought the urge to tell her anyway. Everything she had been through recently told her that she couldn't wait for the right time for anything. Whenever she tried, something always happened or got in the way. For all she knew there would be another disaster right when they started off. Maybe the ship would be more damaged than they thought and it would sink and they'd have to go their separate ways. Maybe Adelaide would fall ill, or maybe she would get killed, and Maaya would never have the chance to—

Maaya shook her head roughly. She was absolutely not going to let herself go down that path. Everything would work out this time. It had to.

"Hold still," Adelaide scolded softly from behind her. "Almost done."

Maaya remained silent, listening to the sound of the brush working its way gently through her hair. She could forget the rest of the world existed in a moment like this. She suddenly realized how lucky she was, relaxing on a comfortable bed on her way to Krethus while the girl she had become so enamored with sat behind her, brushing her hair. She smiled slightly as she imagined going back in time to only a few days prior and telling herself that the attractive woman who was taking her to lunch would soon be taking her across the world.

She let her mind wander. It had been a while since she had allowed herself to do that properly. The struggles of her journey had begun to make her feel like dreams weren't allowed anymore, or that if she wished for anything she would receive the opposite instead. The last time she dreamed, she had imagined buying a big house for herself and her friends away from the world that ignored them at best and tried to kill them at worst. She had seen how that dream turned out. But now, perhaps, it was time to start dreaming again.

"What about you? Have you thought about what you're going to do once this is all over?" Adelaide asked.

"Not… really," Maaya answered uncertainly. "I haven't really thought about anything except what I'm trying to do now. I suppose I would try to find work somewhere and make a new life for myself. Honestly, my goal is to eventually find a place I can stay for more than a few nights and to not worry about going hungry again. I want to go someplace people don't hate me and I can actually just… live."

"That's a lot to have on your shoulders. But try not to worry about that right now, okay?" Adelaide said encouragingly. "Whatever happens after, whether you make it or you don't, I'll help you."

"Really?" Maaya asked before she could stop herself.

"Of course! Did you think I'd just disappear after we got to Krethus?" Adelaide teased.

"I don't know! I guess… I guess I thought this would all be temporary, just like everything else," Maaya answered softly, then gasped as Adelaide hugged her tightly from behind.

"You, my dear, are stuck with me. That's how relationships work. Isn't that how it is with you and Saber?"

"Well, yes, but—"

"No buts, then! The only way I'll leave is if you tell me to, and I have to admit that would make me very sad." Suddenly, Adelaide stepped off the bed, then sat down immediately in front of Maaya, staring at her directly. "You wouldn't, would you?"

"Wha— no! Of course not," Maaya nearly cried. "I was thinking you'd be the one who would have to tell *me* to go away eventually."

"It seems we're in the same boat then! Er, no pun intended," Adelaide said. Maaya snorted, and they both burst into laughter.

When they had calmed, Adelaide stood up, holding out her hand to Maaya to help her up.

"Where are we going?" Maaya asked curiously as Adelaide walked toward the doors.

"Saber has something of mine and I need to get it back, just for this evening," she said brightly. "And then I have to send us off!"

"I thought you weren't supposed to be on duty," Maaya said, raising an eyebrow.

"I'm not, but with this, I can never resist."

With that, she opened the door and stepped out onto the deck, the wind catching her open coat and her long red hair. As she and Maaya walked out onto the bridge, everyone on deck stopped what they were doing to look up at their captain.

"Report, Commander?" Adelaide said to Inga, who was already at her side.

"Skarin and his fleet will finish taking care of the wreckage shortly before going on their way, our temporary repairs are complete, and the wind will be at our backs," Inga stated succinctly. "We're roughly a week and a half out from Krethus if this keeps up."

"Seems like now would be an awfully good time to get under way, ma'am," Gunnar said, and Halvar nodded enthusiastically beside him.

Adelaide smiled widely, looking refreshed.

"Agreed." She stood tall and raised her voice, calling to the crew at large, and Maaya couldn't help but admire her in that moment. She was every inch a captain who loved the sea and this group of oddities she called her family. "Everyone to your stations, take us around, and make all sail! We're running before the wind and our homeland calls!"

A cheer erupted across the deck as everyone got to work. The ship began to turn, and as the sails dropped, they caught wind, sending the ship lurching forward. Maaya had missed this. She had almost forgotten just how swift a ship the Windfire was.

Once they faced west Inga straightened their course, and the Windfire began its speedy trek home. Maaya stared off to port, where in the distance the Nocte Cadenza was starting to make her way north, leaving now-clear seas behind her. The other ships that had joined them in battle headed north as well, but on their own headings, so that within hours she knew they would all be on their own again.

"Are you sure you wouldn't like to take over, Captain?" Inga asked, a knowing smile on her face.

"For once, I am. Maaya and I have some important things to do tonight, but don't you worry. I'll be up annoyingly early tomorrow to take charge until the instant the Windfire has made berth. On that note, Halvar, there's a book of mine in Inga's quarters; could you get that for me? Quickly, now."

"You got it, cap'n."

Without hesitation, Adelaide turned and started back toward the doors to her cabin. Maaya followed again, slightly disappointed that they weren't going to spend a little more time outdoors, but she wasn't about to complain.

Halvar came running back up the stairs and into the cabin only a minute later, and Maaya recognized the book on *libris* Saber had borrowed from the captain earlier. Maaya peered down at it expectantly, and Adelaide smiled.

"Thank you, Halvar. Please make sure no one disturbs us for the rest of the evening unless it's to bring food." When Halvar bowed and then departed, shutting the doors behind him, Adelaide turned her attention back to the book and opened it in earnest. "I thought we might give you some practice with *libris,* what do you say?"

Maaya started, already intrigued.

"You're… going to teach me?"

"I thought I might. You seemed a little impressed with my skills back in Levien," Adelaide grinned.

"That's one way of putting it, yeah."

Adelaide laughed, then flipped through the book to one of the first chapters, but instead of reading from it she pushed it away momentarily and sat on top of her desk.

"Now, Maaya… how exactly did you learn? That is, the first time you made use of *libris*, how did you do it?"

"I just… copied the symbols from the book and then did what it told me to do," Maaya answered uncertainly.

"Okay! You don't need to worry about giving me the wrong answer or anything. I'm just trying to figure out where you are so I know where to take you. It sounds like you're a very by-the-book sort of person, then; am I right in guessing you haven't really experimented before?"

Maaya shook her head.

"I didn't even know that was something you could do until last night. I learned that there are three different levels, and I basically just kept copying symbols at higher levels until they didn't work anymore."

"Ah, I see! You read a very introductory book, then," Adelaide said thoughtfully. "Not that that's bad; if anything, it makes it all the more impressive that you can do what you do. Anyway, have you ever wondered how it works, how one might improve? For example, if you were to go to school to learn to read, at the end of every year you could say that it was practice that made you better. But what about *libris*?"

"I… I don't know. The book never really said. I guess I thought practice made that better, too. That is, the more I pushed myself to my limit the greater my limit would be."

"That's a good thought! Unfortunately, it's also completely wrong." Maaya glanced up at her in surprise, and Adelaide nodded. "Sure, our limits can gradually increase as long as we keep practicing, much like we can gradually run longer distances if we exercise often to increase our stamina. But that doesn't increase our power or change what we're capable of doing—only how long we can do what we already know."

"How does it work, then?" asked Maaya, leaning closer. "Is this the part where I forget everything I ever knew?"

"Oh, stars, no! Nothing so cliché," Adelaide remarked. "You've got incredible skill as it is. No, we're just going to build on that foundation. See, introductory books will tell you that there are levels to *libris*, but that's not exactly true. What happens is that, as you become more attuned to the practice, you find that you're able to do more—but that in order to do more, you need more complex cards. To the layman it might seem like better cards make for better skill, but in reality it's the other way around. Once you really discover where your power lies, the card becomes the bottleneck, and the way to get around that is to make your own cards."

"I'm not sure I understand… I already make my own—"

"No, you make what the book told you to make," Adelaide corrected gently. "What I mean is… think of the blood cards I use. They have a totally different design from yours, right? That's because this is the design that works for me. It took me a while to find it, but now, when I create my cards, I just focus and let my hand go. You'll find this is the case with all elite users; everyone has their own unique style, a little flair to the practice of *libris* that really lets them make it their own."

"I see… I think. So if I want to get better I need to find my own style?" Maaya asked slowly.

"That's kind of a simple way of putting it, but that's the gist of it, yes," Adelaide affirmed.

"How can I do that?"

"Well, let's see. It's kind of hard to explain, but I'll give it a try. You know that feeling you get when you pick up a card and it feels warm to the touch? Like it's connecting with you instead of just being any old slip of paper?"

"Yes! I feel that all the time with my normal cards. And then just last night when I was using your blood cards on the ghosts. The first one didn't work, but then I really concentrated on the second and it just… suddenly became warm. And then with every card after that I didn't have to try as hard. And it was the same with the healing card design I got from your book."

"Ah, that's good! They caught onto you fairly quickly, then. That's the feeling you're after. It'll still be different once you finally find your own style, but to know you can get this far already is a good sign."

"What do I need to do?" Maaya asked curiously, excitement welling within her.

"We're just going to need paper, and lots of it," Adelaide said, shuffling around with the papers on her desk. "Luckily, I keep plenty of that around for work, but this will be much more fun."

The captain sat down a stack of paper in front of Maaya, then picked up a quill and multiple inkwells, all with different colors.

"I want you to forget the symbols you've learned so far, but hold on to that feeling of warmth and connection. Everything else is still the same. I want you to try drawing a physical augment card. Instead of thinking back on any designs you already know, think about what you want to accomplish and combine it with that feeling you experienced last night. Then just let your hand go. It might feel like just a bunch of pointless scribbles at first—

and they probably will be—but both components are there. You're just helping them connect."

Maaya stared at her.

"So I'm just… letting my hand go and hoping for the best?" she asked skeptically as she prepared the purple ink.

"Basically, yeah!" Adelaide replied cheerfully. "Honestly, if you want the secret to figuring out *libris* like the masters, this is the key part. Once it clicks in your mind, you won't need books or designs anymore. It will all come to you like instinct, like it's been there all along. That's where your power comes from. Go on! Close your eyes, that's it…"

Maaya started slightly as Adelaide took her hand in both of hers and guided it across the paper, then let it go. Maaya kept going, unsure of what exactly she would see when she opened her eyes again, but she tried her best to focus. She thought back to the night before, to the comforting feeling from when she grasped Adelaide's blood card in her hand. There had definitely been something there, something she hadn't felt before… but she wasn't completely sure what it had been, so she wasn't sure how to recreate it.

Nevertheless, she tried her best until finally Adelaide gently stopped her.

"You're almost out of space. Why don't you take a look at what you've got?"

Maaya opened her eyes, and after her eyes adjusted to the light of the room, she stared down at the paper in front of her—and it was an absolute mess. There was no consistency whatsoever between the different patterns on different parts of the page, and half of them she couldn't even remember drawing. Her shoulders slumped slightly as she stared, but Adelaide smiled encouragingly.

"No, this is good! This is really good."

"It's chaos," Maaya mumbled.

"Yeah, it's a disaster!" Adelaide continued joyfully. "That's a good step!"

"How is that a good thing?" Maaya asked in frustration.

"Because if it's a mess, it means you're not holding back. You aren't falling back on old habits or letting muscle memory get the better of you. This is true free handing, and that's where you need to be to get to the next step. Here, let's get you a new paper and you can try again…"

Maaya took a deep breath, closed her eyes, and set her quill to the paper once more.

Maaya had no idea how much time passed, but it felt like hours. As time went on and she filled up sheet after sheet of paper, she had to focus harder in order to prevent her mind from wandering. She wondered how Saber was doing, what Skarin was doing, and how long it might take the Selenthians to realize that their fleet and all of its sailors weren't coming back. But still she tried as hard as she could for only a taste of the warmth she had felt before.

Suddenly, she realized that she had been so focused on trying to remember the warm feeling she sought that she was no longer paying attention to her writing—but that her hand was still moving. Something was connecting somewhere. She grasped this moment and refused to let go, and as she did so, her imagination seemed to take on a mind of its own. She wasn't just seeing scribbles anymore; she was seeing definitive shapes and colors. They didn't mean anything by themselves at first, but when Maaya saw them in their mind, they had the feeling of being distinctly *hers*. Her mind had made these. This was her design.

She heard Adelaide clap her hands gleefully behind her, and chanced opening her eyes. The page before her was mostly more aimless scribbles, but then, near the bottom right corner, her writing had taken a sudden and definite shift. There were mostly circles, smaller ones inside larger ones interconnecting with each other, but there was a distinctive pattern of three slightly wavy lines that moved from the upper right corner to the bottom left. No matter where on the page she looked, the designs all started to take the same form.

"Oh, look! You're getting it! Did you feel it?" Adelaide asked excitedly.

"I… I don't think so. Not yet. But I feel like I'm close," Maaya murmured, worried that getting involved in conversation would distract her.

"I think so, too. Okay, one more try. You ready?"

Maaya nodded. Adelaide slipped another paper in front of her, and Maaya tried again. This time, she slipped back into drawing her patterns with ease, and she felt every stroke of the quill on paper as though she had been doing this same thing all her life.

And then, finally, it hit her. The paper felt warm under her fingertips, as though some of her own energy was passing through the quill onto the designs on the paper, and it was responding in kind. This was similar to what she had felt when handling Adelaide's blood cards, but there was something different to this. While Adelaide's cards had given her the impression that they were allies working together against a common enemy, this felt more like it was an extension of herself.

"That's perfect!" Adelaide exclaimed, pulling the paper away and investigating it closely. "Yes, very good. It seems like you've found what you're looking for. Now, the next step is to turn it into something that will actually work. These are all pretty, but they won't do anything. So maybe we can… oh, speak of the devil."

Maaya glanced up in confusion to see what Adelaide was talking about only to see that the captain was now striding across the room to the doors at the rear of her cabin. When she threw them open completely, Maaya stood up in shock.

About a hundred yards off the ship's stern, a bright white light had appeared. Maaya hadn't noticed it at first, so focused was she on her work, but now they were impossible to miss against the quickly darkening sky. Unlike the night before there were only about a dozen ghosts this time, their blank eyeless gazes set firmly upon Adelaide's ship. Despite the urgency that suddenly filled her heart, she couldn't help but be surprised that she and Adelaide had been practicing for so long that it was now nearing sunset.

"They're not going to catch up to us—not with the Windfire going at full speed," Adelaide said. "This is a perfect opportunity, though. What say you try making a blood card of your very own?"

Maaya tore her gaze from the ghosts to stare up at the captain.

"What? You mean right now?"

"Of course! You've got your connection down, and you've found your style. I suggested the physical augment first, but now I think the circumstances require something a little different."

"How do I do that? If I'm not going by the book, how do I know what I'm making?" Maaya asked impatiently.

"It's all about writing with a goal in mind. Not to mention, your choice of ink will help you. I mean, if you're writing cards with your own blood there are really only so many things you can accomplish," Adelaide chuckled. "Just have your purpose in mind when you begin and it will come naturally. Just do what you did before! And you'll need this."

Adelaide took away the stack of paper, then replaced it with a single slip of paper made of the same high-quality material as her own cards. Then she took out a bronze device from her pocket, as well as a smaller clean inkwell. The device was round and small, almost like an egg, but with two visible unmarked buttons in the center. Adelaide handed both to Maaya, then stood back, gazing down at the girl expectantly.

Maaya held the object cluelessly in her hands.

"What am I supposed to do with this?"

"Oh! Have you never used one of these before? No problem. Hold out your hand, that's it. Now place this narrow end over your finger, like so, and you might feel a little—"

Maaya gasped in pain and jumped, more out of surprise than anything else as she felt a sudden sharp prick on her finger. As she pulled her hand away, however, the pain seemed to fade almost immediately, and she saw only a small drop of blood welling at the tip.

"Sorry! I should have warned you sooner," Adelaide said quickly, taking Maaya's hand in hers and holding her finger above the small inkwell. "I use this device because it sure beats cutting up my hand every time I need blood cards. It's just a little prick, but you get a surprising amount from it."

She gently squeezed Maaya's finger, and though she felt only a slight throbbing pain, enough blood dribbled from her finger within moments to completely cover the bottom of the vial.

"How many should I make?" Maaya asked, still trembling slightly from the shock.

"Oh, just the one. This should be fine. Now here, this is the fun part." Adelaide again held the device to Maaya's finger, and Maaya tensed, preparing for another jolt of pain, but instead she only felt a slight shock, much like what she occasionally felt when she touched a metal object. When Adelaide pulled the device away again, her finger had stopped bleeding. "Isn't it great? Seals up the wound nice and tight. It doesn't heal you completely, but it's good enough to let your body do the rest on its own, and so much more convenient than using a whole card to heal yourself or having to wrap your finger in a. bandage. Anyway, hurry now, before your blood dries."

Maaya took a fresh quill, dipped it into the inkwell, then took a deep breath, closing her eyes. The patterns were still there in her mind, as fresh as if she had never stopped drawing in the first place. As her mind drifted to the ghosts, the patterns began to shift and turn red. Without hesitation, she began to draw.

She didn't know how she knew she was done, but after a few moments she set down her quill again. On the card before her were patterns of orbs and curved lines, circles that were partially shaded like small overlapping eclipses, and three small sets of three dots each that rested between them like stars.

Adelaide peered over her shoulder, staring down at the card in total fascination.

"Now this is interesting… very interesting. That's quite a design you have here. While I'm not at all surprised, this does make me happy."

"What? Why? Does it mean something?" Maaya asked blankly.

"Not exactly. Some people think you can tell a lot about a person by their styles, and I'm not sure how much I buy into that, but… here." She reached into her card pouch and pulled out one of her own blood cards. "See the difference?"

Maaya stared. She hadn't noticed before as she was too busy worrying about being able to use them, but now that she was finally getting a closer look, she could see the source of Adelaide's captivation. While the lines on Maaya's card were fluid and wavy, Adelaide's were hard and jagged. And while Maaya's card had patterns that looked much like moons and stars, Adelaide's contained what was almost unmistakably a sun with sharp lines for beams of light casting down from it.

"They're so different… in almost every way," Maaya observed, and Adelaide nodded thoughtfully.

"Not just that, though. I've never seen anything quite like this. Some people have similar styles, and some are so different they might be considered opposite, but these… I would call these complementary, even. I'm not sure what it means, but I think it fits us well, don't you?" she said happily.

Maaya didn't reply. She stared down at her card, but she was already too lost in her imagination to see it. Of *course* something like this would happen. The sun and moon together between them? If this wasn't a sign, she didn't know what was—and Saber was going to be absolutely thrilled.

Before that train of thought had gotten too far from its station, however, she remembered that the whole reason she had created a blood card in the first place was because there was something slightly more pressing going on. She stood up, taking her card firmly in her hand, then stared back out the rear doors of the cabin.

The ghosts were about the same distance away as before, if not a little further, but something about this particular walk made her more uncomfortable than usual. She couldn't immediately pinpoint why, but as she watched them travel along their slow methodical path, she realized they were chasing after the ship. They were *turning*. They had never done that before. They had always gone completely straight with absolutely no regard for their surroundings or what lay in their way, but this time they were definitely following the ship.

"Have you ever seen them do that before? Turn like that?" Maaya asked nervously.

"I haven't, no," Adelaide muttered, narrowing her eyes at the ghosts. "It could be I've just never seen it before; if they seek out the living it's only natural they might do this on the ocean where we're the only living ones for miles. Still…"

"Do you see them out here often?"

"Never. So I won't worry just yet. I have no frame of reference, so this could be normal. All the same, best get rid of them as quickly as we can. Are you ready to give it a go?"

"What if it doesn't work?"

"Oh, it will. This is yours, a creation of your literal being. There's no need to test this one. Go on then! Throw it out and see what you've got."

Maaya stepped outside onto the deck, staring slightly to the side of the ghosts. Even from there she could feel the strength of their dead stares pulling her in. She resisted, but she could already feel her limbs growing weaker.

Without any further hesitation, she held her card up between her first two fingers as she had done so many times before, and flung her card out across the open ocean. It flew straight and true, and a few moments later, connected with its targets.

A great shower of red sparks erupted from the contact point, far wider and brighter than Maaya had ever seen from one of her old cards. A split second later she heard a loud *crack* from the direction of the sparks as sound caught up to light. When they faded away into the water, Maaya was astonished to see that every single one of the ghosts had vanished.

Maaya could hardly react before Adelaide let out a whooping cheer and hugged her tightly from behind.

"That was great! Look how strong that card was! You see? The cards were putting a limit on you, not the other way around. That's why finding your style is so important, because it… oh! Careful!"

Maaya fell suddenly to her knees, overcome by weakness and dizziness, and she would have fallen over completely had Adelaide not been there to catch her. She fought with everything she had to stay conscious, knowing what usually came next after making eye contact with the ghosts… but nothing happened. The dizziness began to fade and her strength slowly began to return only moments later.

"Looked a little too close, huh?" Adelaide asked. "It's okay. You had a lot to focus on, so I understand getting a little distracted."

Maaya paused.

"Speaking of distractions… weren't we going to have dinner?" she asked with a smile.

AN HOUR later Maaya and Adelaide sat comfortably on the deck outside Adelaide's cabin, full and content after a delicious meal and warm under a cozy blanket Adelaide had brought out with them. Maaya had curled up under the blanket on the bench, and though Adelaide was too tall to do the same, she didn't appear too bothered by the chilly breeze.

They stared out over the water as they had done before, and it felt even better the second time around. The soft rocking of the ship combined with the gentle lapping of waves against the hull and creaking of ropes began to lull her into a state of drowsiness despite how hard she fought to stay awake. She was so used to taking any opportunity to sleep that she could, partly because she never knew when she would suddenly need to do a job for Rahu, and partly because the real world had never been worth staying awake for. Now, however, it was… and in a way she had never expected it to be.

She sighed contentedly. It had been weeks since she felt like this: full after a solid meal, in the company of someone she really liked, and *safe*. She had always felt like the world was against her but for the few people who were brave or stupid enough to stand on Maaya's side in the face of it all. There had only been a few of those, and hardly any of them were left alive—the ones who hadn't been dead to start with, anyway.

But now, here, she could stare up at the night sky filled with far too many stars to count, sitting next to an absolutely gorgeous young woman who was charming, intelligent, and witty—not to mention a woman who could see ghosts and was incredibly skilled with *libris*. Even their styles complemented each other, in the captain's own words.

It was in that moment that she finally told herself the truth she had been so anxious about acknowledging: she had fallen hopelessly in love.

As if on cue, Adelaide reached over, put her arm around Maaya's shoulder, and pulled her close so that Maaya's head rested on Adelaide's shoulder. Maaya caught the faint scent of soap from her red hair as it fell gently around her.

"Honestly, this is going to sound silly, but whatever stars aligned and fates brought us together, I'm really, truly glad you ended up here," Adelaide said softly, the sound of her smooth voice music to Maaya's ears. "I know there was a lot of confusion and we had kind of a rough start, but… I'm so glad things worked out. I can't imagine things going any better than this."

I can, Maaya thought, but thought it better not to say so. Instead, she said, "What's so special about me? I mean, I'm really glad this all happened too, and I wouldn't trade it for the world, but… you have so many friends here, and probably more back home. What's another?"

In response, Adelaide pulled Maaya tighter, hugging her with both arms. Maaya did not resist, thinking that she could stay here in her arms forever and be perfectly happy.

"Don't be ridiculous. I have a lot of friends, sure, but many of them also serve under me, so it's a little different. I also don't have many friends my age, and the few who are I can't really connect with. We get along on a superficial level, I suppose, but it's really rare that I meet a person I feel like I really want to get to know beneath the surface. It's not just about what you can see and what you can do—it's you as a person that intrigues me. I don't know. I just love having you around, I guess. Seeing your face and hearing your voice brightens my day, and when you're gone I think about when I'll get to see and hear you again. I hope I'm not coming off too strong or anything, by the way."

"Oh, no, not at all!" Maaya said hastily, resisting the urge to add, *keep going.* "Since the day we met I was hoping we'd get along. I didn't expect to run into you again this soon, but if I hadn't I had planned to come back to Levien so that I could try to find you again."

"Really?" laughed Adelaide, and were it not so dark outside, Maaya might have caught the pink tinge in her cheeks. "That means a lot. When I said I hoped we'd meet again, I meant it. The world is so dull and dark and frightening these days; it was a pleasure meeting someone who really exemplifies the opposite of all that."

"You thought that of me?" Maaya asked, amused. "What do you think now you've gotten to know me and realize I'm just as scared as everyone else?"

"Oh, my dear, you stand out from the rest of the world even more than I first thought," Adelaide said delightedly. "Everything I've seen from you since the moment I saw you on board my ship has done nothing but demonstrate that. I just… I'm glad you're here. I'm really, truly glad of it, and I hope we can stay friends through all the rest of the hell the world is going through."

Maaya couldn't help but feel a flicker of disappointment at the word "friends," but she nodded earnestly.

"I'd like that. I really would."

And she meant it.

A comfortable silence fell again, and they returned to watching the ocean and sky together. Maaya still couldn't help but reflect on where she had been and where she was now. It seemed like forever ago that she had fled Sark, lying half-conscious in the bottom of a boat. Now here she was, days away from Krethus on a ship full of friends and in the arms of a gorgeous Krethan captain. How quickly things had changed, and how much closer she was to finishing her mission than she thought she'd ever be.

But even as she let herself relax, a disturbing thought nagged at the back of her mind, one that had persisted intermittently ever since before she had even left Sark. Rahu's words echoed in her mind, and the clarity of his voice in her memory frightened her.

Look here at this one they call Ghost. Who better for him to employ than one who calls upon the spirits themselves? She attracts them with her mere existence!

Maaya closed her eyes, willing his voice away. At the time she had discounted this statement as Rahu simply saying anything he thought was necessary to rile people up, to make them angry and afraid… but as she traveled, the more concerned she became that there might be some truth to what he had said. In many of the places they had shown up, the presence of the ghosts only seemed to intensify—and that was before Maaya had even used any of her *libris* cards. Even if it was purely coincidence, the fact that it kept happening made her extremely uncomfortable. And then there was what happened earlier when the ghosts had appeared to change course to follow the ship, something even Adelaide said she'd never seen before. Besides, what were the odds of multiple ghost walks happening out in the middle of the ocean?

"You all right, Maaya? Are you cold?" Adelaide asked, and Maaya suddenly became aware that she was trembling.

"No, it's not that," Maaya said, and when Adelaide glanced at her curiously, she instantly wished she'd answered differently. "I'm just thinking about back home, that's all. So much of it still makes me nervous. I… I'm afraid to go back. Even with as far away as I am, some of that fear still follows me."

"Like Rahu," Adelaide murmured, and Maaya glanced up at her in surprise. "I thought so. I'm sure the rest of it is scary as well, but it all goes back to him, doesn't it? I understand that fear. Not even putting an ocean between you will make that go away, even though I wish it could. But you're safe with us, I promise."

Adelaide hugged her again, and Maaya had never felt safer in her life.

An hour later, when both girls were nearly falling asleep, they decided it was time to head to bed. Maaya, despite how much she was enjoying Adelaide's company, thought it was probably best if she fell asleep in her quarters rather than out on a bench in the cold. Even Adelaide seemed to be feeling the effects of the chilly breeze, and she quickly bundled up the blanket before folding it. Then they went back inside together, eager to get out of the cold.

The warmth of the cabin washed over her like she was putting on clothes fresh from in front of the fireplace, and it was all she could do to stay awake. When they reached the door, Maaya turned around, expecting to say goodnight there, but instead the captain took her arm in her own, then gestured to the stairs with her free arm.

"May I escort you to bed, my lady?" she asked teasingly. Her accent was so terrible that Maaya burst into laughter, and Adelaide soon joined her.

"You're so weird when you're tired. But yes, you may."

They walked down the stairs together, arm in arm, and if at first Adelaide had intended it to be a joke, Maaya didn't intend to pull away until she did—and Adelaide didn't seem inclined to do so either.

Unfortunately for Maaya, getting to the officers' quarters took all of half a minute, and soon they were standing outside the door to the small room where Maaya slept. Maaya looked at it reluctantly; even though her comfortable bed was just on the other side of that door, she didn't want to sleep. Not yet.

"Anyway, I wanted to spend this little bit of extra time with you because I may not get to see much of you tomorrow," Adelaide explained quietly. "Since we'll be arriving soon I have some more work to do; I need to explain where all this damage came from somehow, and since I won't be mentioning the Selenthians in the official report it's going to take some dedicated and detailed fabricating."

"Why wouldn't you mention them? They were the whole reason for all this."

"I'll explain later," Adelaide said tiredly. "Long story short, it would lead to investigations and conflict and calls for war, and we absolutely do not have the strength for that at the moment. It's easier to make something up and skip weeks, potentially months, of bureaucratic headaches. Not to mention we'll have to go back to Selenthia at some point, and if my government thinks I'm in any way a target of their military they'd never let me leave port again."

"That's understandable," Maaya yawned. "I'll see you before we get there, though, right?"

"Absolutely. You're coming with me anyway, and as friendly as Krethus is I wouldn't ask you two to set out immediately by yourselves. But for now I need to sleep, so I'll see you the day after, okay?"

She gave Maaya another hug and kissed the top of her forehead again, sending chills of excitement down Maaya's spine. And then she was gone.

Maaya didn't wait. She opened the door to her cabin and closed it tight behind her. She thought about searching for Saber before she fell asleep, but the ghost was in plain sight, hovering upside down near the ceiling and looking bored out of her mind. When Maaya entered, the ghost flipped over and waved.

"Goodness, that was a long dinner date," she exclaimed. "What in the world were you doing up there?"

"I spent most of the day practicing *libris*, believe it or not. I know, so romantic," she said as Saber made a face. "But she taught me a few things..."

She relayed the story of how she had figured out her own unique style, how the ghost walk had appeared near the end of their lesson, and how they had seized the opportunity for Maaya to make her first unique blood card.

"It was so strong, Saber. It was so much more powerful than any card I've made and used before. It felt almost too easy."

"Why do you not look excited, then?" Saber pressed, a wide smile on her face. "I'd be over the moon about it. Heck, I already am, and I wasn't even there."

"They did something strange. The ghosts, I mean. They started off behind the ship, but then... they turned and started following us. It was like they were actually trying to chase us down."

Saber's smile disappeared, and she looked disturbed.

"That *is* strange. I wonder why they would start doing that now when they've never done it before. Maybe they just get a little more creative as we get closer to the machine that created them."

"I don't know... I have to admit I'm worried that what Rahu said about me might be true after all. I know what you said, and I still don't really believe it myself, but... if these strange coincidences keep up..."

"I know. But listen—you're nearly to Krethus now. The entire country has been ravaged by these things. You can't look at their appearances as anything to do with you. Rahu was a conniving, manipulative, and disgusting man, and he said those things to turn people against you and that's the end of it."

"I hope so. I hate the thought that I would ever have to admit even to myself that he was right about anything."

This elicited a chuckle from Saber, and Maaya was starting to feel better already. Rahu's story was over now, which should have meant the same for his influence over her. Perhaps someday soon that would be true. Despite his best efforts she had survived, escaped, and was now feeling better about her life and future than ever before.

"Anyway, come to bed. You look exhausted," Saber said. "When you wake up I can tell you all about *my* exciting day…"

Maaya slipped into bed, and she felt an underlying current of excitement as she did. She would only be sleeping in this bed for less than two more weeks… and then, finally, she would be in Krethus.

26

KRETHUS

The next week and a half passed more quickly than Maaya would have ever imagined. Adelaide had been right that the Windfire was deceptively large; after long enough on board Maaya quickly became aware of just how small a space it was to share with roughly sixty other people, and she felt grateful that she had a place of her own to sleep.

While at first Adelaide had been busy with paperwork, she had gone to great lengths to finish as quickly as she could. In addition, while she took over some of her old duties, she made it clear that Inga was to handle the bulk of the ship's operations until they returned as she still needed to recover from their ordeal. All this combined left much more time for Adelaide and Maaya to spend together, something Maaya was all too happy to take advantage of.

They spent some of their time practicing with Maaya's new *libris* cards, but the small area of the ship provided little room to work with much more than blood cards, and so they turned to simply enjoying each other's company. They shared most of their meals together and spent long hours of downtime talking, sharing stories, or simply watching the ocean.

The more time they spent together, the more Maaya allowed herself to entertain the idea that Adelaide liked her the same way she liked Adelaide. It was a tempting thought, and some reflection allowed Maaya to see Saber definitely had a point, but part of her still almost refused to believe it. It was too good to be true. After all the misery she was used to she was looking for evidence that supported her desires, not what was actually there. Besides, even if she was somehow right, there was no way she'd be brave enough to admit it. Not yet. And so, for now, she remained content to simply stay with Adelaide and enjoy what time they had together.

Finally, early one morning, Maaya caught her first glimpse of Krethus. It started out as nothing more than a dark shimmer in the distance, so formless and lacking in detail that for a few moments Maaya played it off as nothing more than a mirage. It wasn't until others began to catch sight of it, causing a sudden uproar of excitement, that Maaya realized what she was looking at. Once Gunnar was called to confirm and stated that they were right on course, Maaya began to feel nervous.

"I guess there's no going back now. We finally made it," she murmured to Saber, who floated placidly by her side.

"And not a moment too soon. As wonderful as this ship is, as well as everyone on it, I'm unreasonably bored here."

"I just hope we won't run into any trouble once we're there," Maaya continued apprehensively.

"You'll be fine. You know Adelaide would defend you in a heartbeat; she already did it once against the Selenthians."

"Don't remind me," Maaya sighed. "Do you know how hard it is to think up a good way to repay someone who basically went to war for you?"

"Give her a big ol' kiss," Saber said seriously, then laughed as Maaya playfully shoved her away.

As they came closer to shore, Maaya began to see the shapes of buildings and the silhouettes of other ships in the mid-morning sun. This port, whatever it was called, wasn't nearly as populated or busy as Levien, something Maaya was extremely grateful for. The slower she could ease herself into this new country the better.

Evidently, Maaya was the only one feeling nervous. Everyone else seemed nearly beside themselves with excitement. More than once Inga had to remind them to pay attention to their work, and it seemed she was fighting the urge to celebrate as well.

"Home sweet home," Halvar said delightedly, walking over to the bow to join Maaya and Saber. "Well, sort of. My home's a few cities away, but I always love coming in here. Spare me the rush and chaos of the big city; give me a good cozy shore town like Unshala any day."

"I did expect a busier entry point, especially for someone like Adelaide, but I suppose even the most social among us have their limits," Saber commented.

"Oh, I'm sure she'd prefer a place like Levien; she absolutely adores the busy city life. But she's got a special affinity for Unshala here, and as such, most of us do as well." At Maaya's questioning glance, he smiled and continued, "Well, this is her hometown, in'nit? Did she not tell you?"

"We hadn't actually talked about that," Maaya said distractedly, already squinting to get a better look at the town. "Anyway, maybe she wanted it to be a surprise. She's also been really distracted; we've been focusing on fun things mostly."

"Yeah, that battle really threw her for a loop. I haven't seen her that off in a while," Halvar grunted. "She has to come up with a good excuse for all this damage, make sure everyone's on the same page, then get through all the red tape for repairs, resupplying for our next trip, and then she's getting a bunch of people together for—"

"Careful, Halvar, before you go sharing things that ought not be shared," Adelaide's cheery voice came from behind them. "Good morning, you two. How's everything? Sleep well?"

"Well enough, I think," Maaya replied, greeting the captain with a smile. "How about you? You look exhausted."

"I am *incredibly* exhausted, thank you, but that's nothing a short jaunt around town won't fix. As soon as we're all settled and I've made sure they don't need me for anything else, we're off to town."

"Am I coming with you, then?" Maaya asked with amusement.

"Of course! There's so much we need to do, but we'll go over that later. I can't resist surprising you; you're so cute when you're surprised." She grinned mischievously, then turned back to face the wheel where Gunnar stood at the ready. "We're coming in fast; raise the sails and switch to oars, and take us light to starboard to offset the wind and current!"

The crew sprang into action and Maaya heard the sound of the steam engine starting again, then looked out ahead of the ship. They were close enough now that Maaya could see individual people on the docks and in the streets behind them.

Unlike Levien, here there were only a few streets that branched out from a sprawling cobblestone town center. Everything was pleasantly spread out, with neatly trimmed vegetation growing between and in front of buildings. Some appeared to be stores while others looked like apartment buildings. There were only a few dozen people out and about at most despite it being almost midday. Behind the town rose a trio of hills covered in leafy colorful plants, and Maaya saw tall wooden poles sticking out between the trees, holding cables up over the trees and high into the hills and out of sight.

As the ship approached the dock, it continued to slow, until it was running under only the power of the oars. Gunnar expertly took the ship in, and soon enough the oars were shut off as well. As they floated the last short distance to the dock, Adelaide paced the deck, making sure everything looked absolutely perfect.

And then, finally, the LSV Windfire came to a stop. A cheer erupted from the deck as dockhands jogged forward, taking hold of ropes and helping secure the ship. On the starboard side a long solid plank was already being extended from the dock, and people on board the Windfire started to line up for dismissal.

"Halvar, get over here. We disembark last, you know how it goes," Adelaide chided, and laughter erupted from the crew as Halvar, who had been making a very poor attempt at blending in, reluctantly stepped out of line. "Officers, give me one final check and deck sweep, then we can be off. How are you feeling, Maaya?"

"Nervous," Maaya answered quietly. A small crowd of people had gathered to see the Windfire pull into port, some of them staring aghast at the sight of the ship's damage. She unconsciously took a step back, hoping no one would notice her. "Do you think anyone will have a problem with me like Skarin did?"

"I sincerely doubt it. Like I said, we don't have time for those kinds of attitudes here. Besides, if anyone does have a problem with you and is stupid enough to verbalize it within my earshot, they'll regret it very quickly. Stick with me while I take care of some quick things and then we can go into town, yeah?"

Maaya stood awkwardly on deck until the officers walked over from various parts of the ship and stood in a straight line in front of Adelaide with the rest of the crew. The captain stood before them, smiling widely.

"All set? Great. Ladies and gentlemen, it's been a pleasure as always, and I formally declare our shore leave in effect. Commander Strand, please remain with me so we can take care of any outstanding business, and the rest of you are free to go. I expect we'll be ready to set back out again in about a week and a half, so have fun, but stay nearby so I can reach you."

The officers and crew happily departed, with the exception of Inga, but to Maaya's surprise, Halvar hung back as well. He flashed Maaya a smile when he noticed her staring, but said nothing.

"I feel like I'm missing something… oh, yes! Chronis, where are you?" Adelaide called. The ship was silent for only a moment before the spider came climbing swiftly down a nearby mast. Adelaide held out her augmented arm to it, and it immediately climbed on. "Fantastic. Now we're ready. And yet… now that we're here, I almost don't want to go."

Adelaide rested her palm on the railing of the ship, a sentimental gleam in her eye. But this lasted only a minute before dockhands and repair crews began to board the ship, and she was pulled from her reverie, leading the way down onto the docks.

"Where does everyone go between trips?" Maaya asked curiously, watching as the familiar members of the crew disappeared into the crowd or into side streets or into nearby carriages.

"Depends," Halvar said. "Some folks live local, so they check in with friends and family. If we're on shore leave long enough, some will travel farther away to visit people. That's where Gunnar's going; he hasn't seen his wife in a good few months. The rest usually just find an inn nearby and spend their free days meeting locals and getting drunk until it's time to head back out again."

They stopped at the end of the dock as Adelaide and Inga met with the harbormaster; Inga carried a stack of papers while Adelaide gave the man a summary of their trip and important reports.

"So do you travel all the time, then?" Maaya continued.

"That also depends. Sometimes we've got plenty of shipping missions and other times we've got more downtime than we know what to do with. Altogether I figure we spend about ten months of the year sailing and the rest we've got to ourselves. Never all at once, of course. Then there's everything in between. It's a good gig, honestly. Especially since Adelaide gives us hazard pay."

Maaya and Saber shared an amused look as they tried not to laugh, and turned away quickly as Inga raised her eyebrows.

While they waited, Maaya took a moment to admire Unshala. The first thing she noticed was that it was peaceful. Sark and Anorath had been quiet—and maybe even somewhat relaxing—but there had always been an undercurrent of fear and anxiety there, especially in Sark where most people thought she was a hardened criminal. She was sure some of her experiences had been marred by the fact that she was being pursued while also trying to get to the bottom of the ghost mystery, but here, all the way across the world, she felt much more at ease. She realized that her primary concern was someone recognizing she was from Selenthia and giving her grief; otherwise, however, she felt perfectly content to walk about in public. At least so far.

"You know, maybe it's because I just spent nearly two weeks on board a ship full of people who can see me, but I feel like everyone is staring at me," Saber said suspiciously, glancing around at the people gathered nearby. Most had come to watch the Windfire come in, and only a few paid any attention to Maaya—and even then, it was fleeting.

"I wouldn't worry too much. Being able to see ghosts is just as rare here as it is in Selenthia, if not more so. It just doesn't have near as much of the stigma that comes with it anymore," Halvar explained. "I'd wager no one in town apart from the crew can see you. Come to think of it, I haven't seen any other ghosts in Unshala for a while, either. But Krethans, at least around here, are much more aware of *libris* and ghosts and all, so you'll find that our captain is a bit of a… local celebrity, you might say."

"Wait, so even if they could see me, they wouldn't be afraid?" Saber asked, sounding almost disappointed.

"Most likely. As long as you're not one of the walkers you should be fine.

Just don't get to causing any trouble just because you're invisible; that's still not quite accepted here," Halvar chuckled.

"I'll have you know I have never caused trouble a day in my life," Saber replied indignantly.

"Is that so? You must have a high threshold for trouble. Or maybe it's common practice on Selenthian ships to scream bloody murder in the faces of everyone you think can't see you," Halvar continued, laughing harder as Saber protested.

A few minutes later, Adelaide stepped back from the harbormaster with a friendly wave, looking exhausted and relieved.

"Well, that does it! I'm officially off the hook," she said brightly. "Inga, you'll oversee the rest of the ship's business for the afternoon?"

"Yes, Captain. Should I return directly to your estate when I'm finished?"

"Couldn't hurt! Just make sure everything's checked and double checked as usual. Don't leave without an estimated completion date on those repairs. Oh, and…" At this point, Adelaide leaned in and stood on tiptoe to whisper something into Inga's ear. Maaya couldn't make out what it was, and Inga's expression didn't change, but then the commander nodded and walked away. "Perfect. Now, Halvar… I need you to run ahead to my estate before anything else so you can get a message to our government representative. They need to be made completely aware of the situation as quickly as possible."

"You got it, cap'n," Halvar said enthusiastically. "Will you be long?"

"We'll probably be out the entire evening; we have much to do."

"That all being fun, I hope?"

"I wouldn't be sending you to do my work if I had any intention of doing it myself," Adelaide answered with a wink. "Saber, you're more than welcome to join us if you'd like, but I'm afraid much of what we'll be doing won't appeal to you very much."

"No? My tastes are pretty broad, for the record," Saber said.

"Great! We're going to get some lunch first and then probably go window shopping." She laughed as Saber groaned.

"You finally make it to land and *that's* how you're going to spend your time? Forgive me, but I'm going to do something more exciting. Say… where and when should I meet you?"

"You could go with Halvar if you'd like!" Adelaide offered. "He can show you around my place, and it's quite a lovely ride to get there as well."

Saber and Halvar stared at each other, and for a moment it was hard to tell if Saber was intrigued or disturbed by the thought, but then they grinned together and glanced back at the captain.

"That sounds like a wonderful idea. I think I'll take you up on that. I'm sure Halvar here and I will have plenty to talk about."

"Have a good evening, you two," Halvar added. "I'll have our message sent within the hour. Oh, cap'n, is Commander Strand taking care of the—?"

"Yes, Halvar," Adelaide interrupted slowly in a tone like she was talking to a small child. "And since you still have not mastered subtlety in any respect, I suggest you simply not talk to anyone until you arrive. Just to be safe."

"I may be able to offer lessons, Captain," Saber offered, a mischievous glint in her eye.

"Thank you, but I'm afraid that if you speak subtly to Halvar it will simply go over his head. Just make sure he doesn't get too distracted on the way home."

Saber gave her a mock salute, then followed Halvar as he led the way off in the direction of the hills. The two of them were already chatting animatedly, and Adelaide smiled as she watched them go.

"It's nice to see them getting along so well. I was worried Saber might be a little selective of who she chooses to be friends with."

"She's definitely gotten better about that since we left Sark," Maaya explained. "I also think being stuck on the ship with literally no other choice had something to do with it. I'm a little jealous, actually. She ended up making more friends than I did, and she had a whole day where she didn't think anyone could see her."

"That's all right! You got to know a lot of my favorite people. Besides, it's partly my fault anyway for keeping you to myself for so long. Anyway, let's keep talking over food."

Adelaide led the way down one of the nearby streets which was lined with small cozy shops. Maaya saw a barber shop, a tailor, a small clothing depot, a gearworks, a store filled with tools, and a number of restaurants. As soon as she began to catch the scents drifting from the open doors and smoking chimneys, her stomach growled loudly. She had been so focused on watching Krethus as they approached earlier that she had forgotten to get something to eat.

They turned into a small café where smells of cooking meat and fish and baking bread reached her nose. It was much different than what Maaya was accustomed to, but her philosophy on food was that she was willing to try almost anything once—and even if she weren't she didn't think her stomach would allow any objections.

Half the tables were full when they walked in. A few people glanced up as they approached, and Maaya almost froze, but while a few smiled or nodded at Adelaide, the rest simply turned back to their food and conversations. Adelaide snapped up a single menu from the small desk at the front, and then, with an exaggerated gesture, invited Maaya to sit at a nearby table.

"I don't know if you've ever had Krethan cuisine before but this would be a good place to start. Lots of basic meals here," Adelaide said, handing the menu to Maaya. "I already know what I want."

Maaya stared down at the menu, a glossy double-sided page bordered with fake leather, and she felt a twinge of nervousness and guilt. She discreetly put her hand to her coat pocket, feeling for how many coins she had left, and almost felt sick when she realized she had none.

"Uhm, I'm actually not really that hungry—"

"I'm paying, and I always planned to, so order whatever you like," Adelaide interrupted kindly, seeing the look on Maaya's face. "You'll get used to being treated eventually. Today will be a good exercise in that."

Maaya stared up at her, narrowing her eyes slightly.

"What's that supposed to mean?"

"You'll see! I don't want to give anything away lest I ruin your appetite," Adelaide answered with an infuriating smile. "You like seafood? Here, you can't go wrong with the shrimp sandwich; I know the real name's a bit odd so I can order it for you if you'd like…"

Maaya wasn't sure about ordering a dish she couldn't pronounce—and that didn't have any picture to go with it—but as soon as their plates were delivered to their table she could see Adelaide had made an excellent recommendation. Maaya's lunch was an open-faced sandwich on lightly toasted rye bread topped with a light layer of butter, then mayonnaise, crunchy lettuce leaves, egg slices, and a generous layer of hand-shelled shrimp garnished with dill sprigs, a few diced tomatoes and cucumbers, and a slice of lemon.

Adelaide, on the other hand, faced down a plate of fried fileted herring seasoned with salt and ground white pepper and a light layer of breadcrumbs sprinkled on top. To the side was a generous helping of mashed potatoes with butter and cheese and a small dish of jam.

It all looked and smelled so delicious that Maaya even forgot her guilt for a few moments as she dug in. It was definitely very different from what she was used to back home, but if everything Krethus had to offer was like this plate of food, she could see herself becoming comfortable with it very quickly.

Maaya thought that at some point their eating would slow and they could get back to conversation, but Adelaide was undeterred by the limitations of a human stomach, and ate with gusto until finally she was left mopping up the last of her mashed potatoes with a spoon. Maaya stared, wide eyed, holding the remaining half of her sandwich halfway to her mouth.

"What? I was hungry," Adelaide said, looking completely unapologetic. "Hurry and finish up so we can move on to our next stop."

"At some point I'd like to know more about this agenda of yours, especially if you're going to be taking me all over town when I've only been in Krethus for all of half an hour," Maaya said pointedly, taking a large bite from her sandwich.

"Of course! Our next stop is to get our hair done, and then finally, we're going to get you a new wardrobe."

"A wardrobe? What would I do with furniture?" Maaya responded, completely befuddled. Her confusion only grew when Adelaide burst into laughter.

"Oh, no, dear. I mean we're going to get you some new clothes! And plenty of them."

Maaya stared at her again, then turned back to her food, unperturbed.

"Okay, now I know you're joking. Lunch is one thing, but if you expect me to believe—"

"May I remind you that you literally saved my life? I think a few pieces of fabric would be just the start of giving my thanks."

"And you saved mine, so we're even!" Maaya protested.

"Yes, well, you looked much more amazing when you did it. I don't make the rules," Adelaide smiled innocently.

"You're literally making rules right now."

"I guess you're right. In that case, as the rule maker, I hereby establish that we're going to get you some *fantastic* outfits, and I also add that you aren't allowed to complain more than three times. Ah, don't start yet!" she said cheerily as Maaya opened her mouth. "Don't use your first complaint when you haven't even finished eating."

Adelaide giggled as Maaya glared silently, her cheeks burning.

After lunch they moved on to an establishment Maaya would have never given a second glance back home. Getting one's hair done was something reserved for people with money and free time, and Maaya never had either of those two things concurrently. The thought of sitting down to let someone *else* wash and cut her hair when she was perfectly capable of doing such a thing herself with a trusty pair of scissors was mind boggling. The wealthy really did have such strange pastimes.

When she saw customers sitting in plush chairs talking animatedly with the people trimming their hair, as well as getting what looked to be extremely relaxing massages while their hair was washed, she began to have doubts. This doubt only increased when she saw a woman from a nearby chair pay and walk out of the building with an absolutely stunning haircut, something Maaya would never be able to do on her own.

"Afternoon, ladies!" a woman said warmly from the front desk. "My, I hope you're both in for a trim today; you have such lovely hair."

"We are, absolutely," Adelaide beamed. "This one's new to both town and haircuts, so make sure she's only given the best."

Maaya suddenly felt nervous as both women stared at her, and she momentarily thought about making a dash for the door before she let either one of them near her head with sharp tools.

Twenty minutes later, however, as they stepped back out onto the street, Maaya felt like staying for the experience was the best decision she'd ever made. She ran her fingers repeatedly through her hair, which was now several inches shorter and completely free of knots or tangles. It fell behind her like a sleek shimmering wave, and it was all she could do to avoid stopping and looking at her reflection every time they passed a store window.

"My head feels so… light," Maaya said in awe.

"I know! Isn't it great? Now imagine doing this on a regular basis and feeling this amazing all the time."

Adelaide, for her part, didn't look much different. As she had explained to Maaya, this was part of regular maintenance; trimming her hair frequently helped it stay long by preventing damage from getting too far. This had fascinated Maaya, who had always thought it contradictory that trimming one's hair *more* often means it would get longer.

Their next stop was a deceptively large clothing store. Adelaide stopped to examine the signs hanging above the various racks before turning to stare Maaya up and down.

"You're pretty tiny so that limits your options just a little, but we'll find something for you!"

"Hold on. No matter what your definition of 'wardrobe' is, that doesn't change the fact that I don't have anywhere to put any of this."

"My house, of course. You're staying there, remember?"

Maaya stared.

"You only said I was meeting your parents, not that I was sleeping over!"

"Semantics, really," Adelaide said dismissively. "Besides, did you think I'd just say goodnight and leave you to just find a place to stay in a different country with no money?" she continued with a laugh, and when Maaya struggled to respond, Adelaide took her lightly by the arm and pulled her over to one of the many racks before them.

What followed was an experience unlike any Maaya had ever had, and by the time a few hours passed she was still struggling to decide whether or not she had actually enjoyed it. Adelaide seemed much more excited than Maaya was, even if Maaya was incredibly grateful for the opportunity to have more than one article of clothing to choose from. While Adelaide was more focused on the details—like which dress Maaya would look best in or if she should just buy them all—Maaya was too busy coming to terms with the fact that this was actually happening. She was too overwhelmed by the luxury of having options to care about what those options were.

Still, at Adelaide's encouragement and over-the-top enthusiasm, Maaya slowly began to enjoy herself. Then, while trying on a particularly nice dress, she paused, looking at herself in the mirror. She hadn't done this before. She had seen what she looked like in the various clothes Adelaide picked out, but she hadn't actually *seen* herself. There had never been a reason to do so before. So long as she didn't stand out and didn't look like a complete disaster, her appearance had never been all that important. But now things were different, and she couldn't help but stare. Now that her hair had been done and she was clean and wearing a dress she had to admit was gorgeous, she saw herself like she never had before. Was this what the world saw on the rare occasion it thought to acknowledge her existence?

"You all right in there?" came Adelaide's voice filtering in through the grated door of the changing rooms. "It's okay if you're stuck in all the straps and things, it's happened to me more times than I can count—"

"I'm fine, sorry. I… got a little distracted," Maaya said as she stepped out, suddenly feeling very self-conscious. Adelaide let out a low whistle.

"My goodness. Now I'm distracted, too. You look amazing! We'll definitely go with that one for special occasions. Do me a favor and help me get everything up to the front? I got a little something for myself while we're at it; I figure we can both change and spend the evening dressed more comfortably."

Maaya quickly changed back into her regular clothes, then helped Adelaide fold everything and take it up to the front. All in all there wasn't nearly as much as Maaya had been expecting from Adelaide's gung-ho attitude, but now she had at least one outfit for every day of the week, and that in itself was something she never thought she would achieve in her wildest dreams.

"And this comes out to… let's see here… two hundred twenty rial," the woman behind the register said, her nails clacking on the heavy plastic keys of the device in front of her.

Maaya was floored. She had never heard of anything being so expensive in her entire life. For a moment she couldn't breathe from fear, and she imagined Adelaide getting angry and turning to scold her for trying to buy so much, for being so selfish and taking advantage of her kindness—but instead Adelaide simply reached into her pocket and counted out a handful of large coins, then happily handed them over.

"What a steal. Thanks very much," Adelaide said with a smile. "Can I get bags for all but this one and have them sent to my address? I'm changing right now. Maaya, dear, pick what you want to wear tonight and meet me back here when you're done."

She quickly scribbled down her address on a piece of paper the woman offered her, then trotted off to change, leaving Maaya behind to look through what she had just purchased. Maaya was suddenly acutely aware of the woman behind the counter looking her up and down, though she said nothing. Maaya couldn't blame her if she weren't at least a little judgmental. Maaya had worn these clothes almost every single day for years, and it showed.

When Maaya chose her clothes—a relaxed pair of dark slacks and a sleeveless teal top with a black cardigan to match—she took care to tuck Kim's diary safely within Adelaide's bags and then hurried off, eager to escape the awkward silence.

Adelaide was already at the counter when Maaya returned, chatting energetically with the woman at the counter. She had picked out a calming yellow dress shirt that drew even more attention to her red hair, a knee-length skirt, and a pair of low heels that made the height difference between the two of them even more noticeable. It was also the first time Maaya had seen her in anything other than her captain's uniform, and Maaya thought she pulled it off *very* well.

"Get a load of us, huh?" Adelaide said as Maaya walked over, pulling her into a quick one-armed hug. "All ready for an evening on the town. It's so nice to get out of that coat; it's one of my favorite parts of coming home."

"Pleasure to have you back," the woman said approvingly. "All your things will be delivered to your address by tomorrow morning. Also, is this book yours? It was in your bag."

She held up the diary Maaya had slipped into Adelaide's things.

"Oh, yes. That's mine, sorry. I didn't have anywhere else to put it," Maaya explained hastily, hoping the woman wouldn't hold or examine it for too long. Adelaide met Maaya's eyes for a moment, but said nothing.

"Fair. Just wanted to make sure I wasn't mixing up customers' things. Got a lot to deliver down here and this looks important. Can I do anything else for you?"

"I think we're set. Have a good evening!" Adelaide finished with a smile, and then she led the way to the door.

Maaya had evidently lost track of time, because when they stepped back out into the street the sun was only an hour from setting, and it cast a comfortable glow over the town. Adelaide looked absolutely radiant in the warm light, and she seemed happier than she had been in a long while. Maaya wasn't sure if it was the feeling of being home, relief at having escaped their trials and arriving safely, or that Unshala was simply a charming place to be, but whatever it was, it was contagious. Maaya hadn't felt this good in a long while either.

"It's a little early for dinner yet, but I think I know where we can go next," Adelaide said.

"Not more shopping, I hope?" Maaya groaned teasingly.

"Oh, there will be plenty of time for that later. This is something a little more special."

They walked down the cobblestone street back toward the small town center. As they got closer Maaya could hear the sound of gently splashing water from the fountain, and she watched a small group of children playing happily around it. There were more people here now than before; Maaya guessed this was a popular evening destination as much as it was a shopping center. The seaside views and comfortable atmosphere certainly did no harm. In the distance she saw the Windfire floating in the harbor. It was easily the biggest ship there, which surprised Maaya all the more; nearly all the rest were small fishing boats.

Adelaide led the way into a two-story building at the end of the street. Maaya realized quickly that it was another restaurant, but instead of going to sit down, Adelaide turned immediately right inside the door and up a flight of carpeted stairs. The building was dimly lit, with most of the light on each table coming from a trio of candles in the center. Most of the patrons looked like they had put some effort into getting dressed to go out, and those serving tables wore collared and buttoned shirts. Maaya suddenly felt very glad she had changed before coming.

Upstairs there were more tables, and Adelaide ignored these as well. Instead she took Maaya through a narrow door near the end of the room where wide glass windows presented a wide view of the docks and beyond. Through the door was a terrace with only a few small tables, all of which were unoccupied, and it was here that Adelaide finally took a seat, enthusiastically inviting Maaya to join her.

"So! What do you think?" Adelaide asked, leaning her elbows on the table and propping her chin in her hands.

"Er… about what?" Maaya asked lamely.

"This! Krethus, Unshala… everything, I guess," Adelaide continued. "It's nice, right?"

Maaya opened her mouth to tease her, but then paused. She knew what Adelaide was feeling. She wasn't just excited because she was back home and because that was simply her attitude about everything—though the latter was definitely true. She clearly loved her home, but it was also very important to her that Maaya liked it as well. Adelaide's eyes held all the hope of someone who dared take the risk of showing something she was proud of to someone she cared deeply for.

"It is. I love it," Maaya affirmed happily. "It's beautiful here. It's so quiet and calm. I thought I would be terrified once I got here, but instead… I just spent the whole day without feeling like I had to look over my shoulder all the time or worrying that something bad was about to happen. I don't feel like I have to hide here."

"And you don't. Of course you don't. I never want you to feel like that again. But honestly, that's why I like it here. No matter where I go, this always *feels* like home. The people may change and it may look different sometimes, but I always know I'll be safe and welcome here," Adelaide said affectionately.

"Hey… Halvar mentioned he hadn't seen a ghost in Unshala for a while. Are other ghosts uncommon here, too?" Maaya asked.

"More so in recent years. There used to be plenty."

"They weren't… sealed, were they?" Maaya pressed nervously, thinking of Saber.

"Oh, no. Not at all. I think most simply went looking for safer places. They know the walkers can't harm them, but they know the expanding radius can. And some I assume wanted to go to a place with more people to talk to. Unshala isn't exactly a bustling city, and it can get lonely when no one can see you. I completely understand, but at the same time it feels lonely not having them here. Maybe someday they'll be back once this is all over."

For the next few minutes they simply stared out at the ocean together. The setting sun painted a beautiful picture as it touched the distant horizon. From their vantage point on the terrace she had an excellent view of the streets below, where people strolled about casually as if they hadn't a care in the world. The cool breeze wafted wonderful scents in her direction, and she heard music as a man with a strange string instrument set up near the fountain and began to play.

The sight before her was everything of paradise she had ever imagined. It wasn't a luxurious flat in a bustling wealthy district like she had seen on postcards, and it lacked the sweeping grand avenues filled with glittering shops and marvelous attractions. But here more than any place she had been in the world so far, she felt comfortable and safe. She doubted the Selenthians would try to pursue her this far, but it was beyond just that. Here should start fresh—and she couldn't ask for better company while doing so.

"You know, none of this is at all like I expected," Maaya said quietly. "The first time I ever saw a Krethan I thought he was trying to kill us. When I thought about trying to get here I thought everyone here would be out to get me. And when I heard what was happening here… I guess I expected people to be more afraid, but I haven't heard anyone mention the ghosts at all."

Adelaide nodded.

"You may soon enough. Unshala sees very little ghost activity comparative to other places, but it still happens. Besides, you have to understand: people can't panic forever. When the world's end seems imminent for decades, being afraid all the time gets exhausting. It's in the back of all our minds but it's not new anymore. We've all grown up with this fear."

"That makes sense. I guess that's how I felt when I was in Sark; there was just so much danger and stress all the time that I sort of became numb to it."

"That's it, exactly. What's more, even before the machine the government was trying to make Krethans afraid of everything, too. When I was growing up and I'd study our history I'd see the propaganda the government put out ages and ages ago. They really tried hard up until the end. But eventually people just lost interest. The war had just been going on too long and everyone was too exhausted to be angry anymore. So then they briefly changed tactics and put out a whole new campaign, said they would search the entire country for Selenthians and execute them, all sorts of things."

"Did they?" Maaya asked, horrified.

"Of course not. They didn't have the resources for that. Besides, by that point so many Krethans knew at least one Selenthian personally that the fearmongering was almost completely ineffective. The 'enemy' isn't as scary when they're the people who live next door, go to temple with you, teach your kids… no, it was over then. The war of weapons might have gone on, but the war of ideas was over. Defeated by, of all things, apathy and exhaustion. Not to mention that what was left of the court, though it had little power by then, strongly disapproved—and people loved the court over the government. Then, of course, before the government could try anything new… the machine happened."

"Do you know anything about it? I only know that it exists, but there has to be more to it than that, right?" Maaya continued, intrigued.

"I know what I was taught," Adelaide shrugged. "It's allegedly on the estate of someone who used to work for the government. I don't even remember his name. He wasn't very important. He lived alone with his daughter there in the time leading up to the start of the ghost attacks. I don't know if he something to do with it or if he was simply their first victim, but I'm not entirely sure. I do know the government should have notes on it, and I'll be seeing if I can get ahold of them before we go."

"I see…" Maaya murmured disappointedly. She had been hoping for more. Technically its location *was* useful, but if even Adelaide had little more than that, then Maaya would be going in woefully unprepared.

"I'm sure we'll find plenty of history after we shut it down, though," Adelaide continued thoughtfully. "Hardly anyone's been within miles of the place for over a hundred years save for the military, and they just guard the borders; there's bound to be some interesting stuff there."

"I'm just worried about shutting it down in the first place," Maaya sighed. "If it's basically been in your backyard this whole time and your government still… hang on, are you saying 'we' again?"

Adelaide grinned.

"Yeah! That's okay with you, right?"

"I didn't… I thought we were… you said we'd see what happened once we got here!" Maaya spluttered.

"And we're here, aren't we? I admit I said that just now because you're cute when you get flustered, but I also think we could work really well together on this. You've got Saber to keep you safe when you go into the barrier, but I figure it couldn't hurt to have company."

"I suppose… you know, you can talk to me about these things. You don't have to just decide."

Adelaide chuckled sheepishly.

"Right. Sorry. Bad habit. I just really want to do this with you and I didn't think you'd see a problem with it."

"I don't! You just move so fast it's hard to keep up sometimes," Maaya smiled. "How do you do that? Where do you get the energy for it all?"

"I don't know. A good diet and exercise, I suppose, or just loving life. Maybe even harboring an unnatural disdain for hesitation regardless of circumstance. Maybe some of it is genetics, too; it's impossible to tell."

"Is your whole family as… uhm…?"

"Energetic? Relentlessly optimistic? Easily distracted? Not in the slightest," Adelaide said without missing a beat. "They're like me in that they have plenty of stamina, but it manifests in their work, not in their personality. It's why they're so good at the business thing. But they're nice enough people anyway, even if they're a little too traditional for me. They might be glad I'm teaming up with you to try to shut down the machine."

"You said there were others like you, right? People who grew up training with *libris* to figure out how to destroy it?"

"We weren't trained to destroy the machine, not exactly," Adelaide explained. "We're just supposed to be the strike force to deal with the ghosts when they inevitably show up. By the time I was born everyone figured there was no hope of getting to the machine anymore, so all we could do was keep the ghosts themselves at bay."

"So no one's tried to shut it down in all this time?" Maaya asked, astounded.

"Oh, there are still attempts all the time. The government has a reward for anyone who can stop it, so plenty of people try, but I think most people go into it expecting to fail."

"What's been tried so far?" Maaya gulped.

"Just about everything I can think of. The government tried using their own weapons, but anything mechanical just stopped working once it entered the barrier. Any people who went in disappeared. Others tried to be clever and dig up from underneath, but the barrier goes underground, too. They tried making fast vehicles, but they were almost immediately limited in their selection of drivers because they had to be able to see ghosts. Not to mention the terrain prevents a straight shot. And after losing several very expensive pieces of equipment the government decided it was no longer a viable thing to keep spending money on."

Maaya fought the despair that sought to well up within her. None of this should have come as a surprise to her. She should have known that the Krethan government and its people had been trying for years to shut it down, and that they obviously hadn't been successful, which is why she was here. Besides, she had something that no one else had: Saber's gemstone. That was, of course, if Svante had been right in what he said about it.

"I think we'll be able to do it," Adelaide said quietly, studying the expression on Maaya's face. "We've got a unique advantage and we've got each other. That's worked out well so far, hasn't it?"

"It has. I guess that's why I'm even more afraid than I was when I was alone," Maaya murmured.

"What do you mean?"

"I mean… every single time things have started to go well, they always ended up worse in the end. No matter how certain I was that things were going to get better, something always happened at the last minute. I've had almost everything taken from me more than once, and… I'm really afraid it's just going to happen again with this. With you."

Adelaide's expression softened, and she reached over across the table, taking Maaya's hands tightly in hers.

"It's not going to end like that this time. Obviously I can't tell the future, but I've got a good feeling about this. There can only be so much bad in the world. I'm not sure I believe in karma, but I think that if you work hard enough for something you'll eventually find it. Fate isn't cruel enough to waste its time on temptation; you aren't fighting the world, just the few awful souls in it. Once you get past them there's a whole lot of good waiting on the other side."

Maaya forced a smile. She didn't want to go down this road again; too many times now she had let herself show weakness and doubt and left others with the job of trying to console her. This wasn't a bad thing in itself, she thought, but occasionally she wanted the positions to be reversed. Her friends—and Adelaide especially—had done so much for her over the past few weeks alone. For someone who had previously been used to being in charge of taking care of others, this was an uncomfortable situation.

"I know you're right. I just have a hard time remembering it sometimes,"

Maaya said as cheerfully as she could. "I imagine you're probably not coming along just for me, though."

Adelaide didn't answer right away. She looked conflicted, as if she wasn't sure how to say what came next.

"You're right. Obviously I want to go with you because you're cute, and I like you," she said, then laughed as Maaya gave an exasperated sigh. "But I also want to go because—and please don't take this the wrong way—you represent kind of an opportunity for me. This is something I've always wanted to do. With you and Saber, I think we can do this, and I'd like to be part of it."

"I understand. Even if you didn't grow up preparing to destroy the machine you still have to fight what it creates," Maaya said sympathetically.

"There's that, yeah. After fighting this for years and experiencing all the loss that's come with it, I'd like to see this over and done with as much as anyone." Adelaide took a deep breath, then looked back out over the ocean. The sun was nearly gone now, and the light from the candles between them flickered in her eyes. "When I think of Krethus, this is what I see. There are so many cities that have been permanently abandoned, that have fallen into ruin, because of this machine. My country has its faults, but I can't stand to see it like this, nor its people. That's what I'm after. I'll do this for the world—hell, I'll even do it so my parents might be a little prouder of me—but mostly it's because I'd like to see my whole country like this again."

It was Maaya's turn to take Adelaide's hands in hers, a gesture not lost on the Krethan woman. Maaya smiled at her, genuinely this time, and where despair first came, confidence now rose. This was what she could do for Adelaide, how she could repay her for everything the captain had done. Of all the ways Maaya was uncertain about herself, this was something she knew she and Saber could do. She was, after all, the leader of the Ghost Hunters.

"You will. And soon. They've taken a lot from us, but we're still here and we can still fight. And I didn't travel across the world just to fail in the last stretch. I've only been here half a day and I can see why you love this place so much. We're going to win, I promise."

Adelaide stared back at her, and for a moment Maaya thought she might cry. Then she quickly rose to her feet, pulling Maaya along with her, and hugged her tightly, resting her cheek against the top of Maaya's head.

"You are such a wonderful human being, and I'm so very glad I met you. See what I mean about fate and temptation? If it were so cruel it wouldn't have brought you into my life."

Maaya blushed furiously, thankful that Adelaide couldn't currently see. But then the embarrassment began to fade. In the interest of bravery, it was about time she started showing her feelings as well.

"I'm glad I met you, too."

Maaya could have stayed there in Adelaide's embrace for the rest of her life, but after a few moments Adelaide stepped back, glancing down at the street below.

"Well, that's about it for this part of Unshala. Is there anything else you want to see, or do you think you're ready to come home with me?"

"I think I'm ready to call it a night," Maaya said happily. "But… does your family know I'm coming?"

"Hmm. Maybe. If they saw Halvar he might have told them. If not, I'll let them know once we get there. I'm not entirely certain they're home yet, though. They were off seeing extended family while preparing for the wedding, and they might still be doing more. It's been weeks since I got their last letter."

"They won't mind that the first time they hear about me is when I'm showing up on their front door?" Maaya asked, raising an eyebrow.

"Not at all. They'll enjoy I'm bringing someone home of my own volition, and they make a habit of keeping the house eternally guest friendly. Besides, I think they're still hopeful that me bringing someone home will eventually translate into a romantic relationship. Meeting the parents is a big first step, right?"

"Oh no. Are they the type of parent who tries to get you together with your own friends?" Maaya asked with a knowing look. She remembered Roshan's father who, for the first month after he realized his son was friends with Maaya, had not been subtle about his idea that a boy and a girl becoming friends meant something more was to come later. Roshan and Maaya thought it was too amusing at first to stop him, but eventually decided to tell him it would never work, if only because Maaya wasn't into men at all.

"Not exactly that. They tried to be a little more proactive in that they tried to set me up with other children from wealthy families. It never worked, but they also never gave up, and they were close to insufferable. That was actually what got me to leave in the first place. It was the cherry on top of the disastrous sundae of my childhood, I suppose. Anyway, let's go get a carriage."

They walked back downstairs together. It was much warmer inside the building and even more crowded than it had been before. This part of Unshala was definitely where the night life was to be found. Maaya made a mental note to come back when she had money of her own to spend.

Once they were out on the sidewalk, Adelaide waited patiently until she saw a horse-drawn carriage coming toward them. She waved her arm to get the coachman's attention, and he tipped his hat in her direction to let her know he'd seen her. The carriage stopped a few feet from them, and the doors opened, letting out no fewer than half a dozen people. They laughed loudly, saying things Maaya couldn't quite understand, then walked into the building Maaya and Adelaide had just come out of.

"Well, look-y here! If it isn't the captain herself, back from the lonely sea. How are you doing?" the coachman exclaimed as he glanced down at them again, making an exaggerated gesture of taking off his glasses to wipe them on his coat.

"Even better than usual! How about you?" Adelaide said cheerily.

"Can't complain! Not much has changed since I've seen you last, but our son's off to school in a few months so we're looking into taking a vacation before then. How long are you back in town?"

"Oh! Wish your son the best for me, please. I'm only in town for a few days, but I imagine I'll be back much sooner next time. Oh, by the way, this is Maaya; she's new in town. Maaya, this is Asmund. He's been a friend of my family since before I was born."

The coachman tapped two fingers to his forehead in greeting, giving Maaya a once-over.

"A pleasure. What brings you to Unshala?"

"I... er..."

Maaya hadn't actually thought about what she might say if someone asked. She hadn't really planned on being in a position where she talked with anyone long enough for them to ask questions, and *I'm here with my dead friend to save the world and fulfill the desires of a Krethan my old employer had murdered across the sea, and in the meantime the girl I like is taking me to meet her parents* was currently her only explanation.

"She's staying with me for a few nights. She's never been to my place before," Adelaide jumped in smoothly. "Figured my parents would want to meet her sooner or later. Oh, and she's absolutely amazing with *libris*, so I want to take her to the gymnasium while we're here."

"Really! Another *libris* user. How fascinating. May I ask where you're from?" Asmund continued.

Maaya breathed a quiet sigh of relief. She had momentarily forgotten that knowing *libris* was not something that was likely to get her killed here. That was definitely going to take getting used to. Telling people she was from Selenthia, however, was a different matter entirely.

"You can tell him; it's okay," Adelaide said quietly as Maaya's uncertainty returned.

"I'm... from Sark. It's a little town in Selenthia a few days from Levien, if that helps," Maaya said, and even as the words came out of her mouth, they felt wrong, as though even speaking the name of her home country aloud was forbidden. But Asmund merely nodded, looking nothing if not impressed.

"That's quite a long way to travel to see a friend. I don't suppose you arrived with Adelaide, then?"

"I did! It was… an interesting trip," Maaya said lightly.

"Of that I'm sure. Nothing is ever uninteresting with her around," Asmund nodded. "At any rate, it doesn't look like I'm picking anyone else up at present, though things will start to get much busier in about an hour or two. Can I get you ladies home?"

"I would be so honored," Adelaide replied, and she let herself into the carriage. Maaya followed quickly, secretly eager to have another ride in a carriage even if this one was led by actual horses.

The girls talked the whole way there, though Maaya was somewhat distracted by the view from the carriage windows. Adelaide quickly caught on to this and switched to pointing out important landmarks, or, as was the case when it became too dark to see, explaining what would be visible if they were to take the same route in the daytime. Maaya soon gleaned that Adelaide's house wasn't terribly far away, but that it was a bit of a challenge to reach on foot because it was near the top of one of the hills she had seen earlier.

Still, when the carriage came to a stop less than half an hour later, Maaya couldn't help but feel disappointed. She wasn't sure if riding in a carriage would ever get old.

However, this disappointment quickly disappeared when she saw Adelaide's home. It was a wide two-story house of wood and brick set on about an acre of flat land in between growths of tall colorful trees that were nothing more than intimidating shadows in the night. Its architecture looked old, but the entire house was in immaculate condition. It had a sweeping porch at the front and a wide balcony that surrounded the entire second floor. It was clearly the house of someone with wealth, but at the same time it seemed more comfortable than extravagant, nothing like the marble pillars and ornate decorations of the wealthy of Sark whose wealth was only useful if they could flaunt it. This was a home of old money, one that didn't need to show off because its reputation, and that of those who lived within, spoke for itself.

From the brightly lit gate where they stood the house was about twenty yards away down a stone walkway lit by electric lamps. When Maaya noticed lights on in multiple rooms she began to feel nervous, and she wasn't immediately certain why. She didn't like meeting people regardless of who they were, but something about the fact that this was Adelaide's family gave her extra pause. Then she realized that it wasn't the prospect of meeting them that frightened her—it was the idea that they might for some reason dislike her. Despite not knowing any of their names or what they looked like, Maaya realized she was already eager to please them.

Maaya cleared her throat, stopping her imagination before she could get too far lost in it.

"That's that, then. Tell your folks I said hello," Asmund grunted from atop the carriage. "If you want a quick ride to the gymnasium just send me a message ahead of time. I work all this week but I'll be happy to go out of my way for you."

"Thank you, as always," Adelaide said, reaching into her pocket, but Asmund waved her off.

"You're absolutely not paying me a cent for your first ride home in months, don't you even think on it," he said sternly. Adelaide looked like she wanted to argue, but Asmund wasn't having any of it. "Just promise to see me more than once or twice before you head back off."

"Of course! I always try to see you when I'm in town. Have a good night," Adelaide replied, giving him a friendly wave. Maaya waved as well, and then Asmund was gone, riding quickly into the night and out of sight. "Anyway, Maaya! What do you think?" she continued, starting forward down the path.

"It's so beautiful. I can't believe you actually live here," Maaya breathed in astonishment.

"I technically don't, but that's beside the point. I'm glad you like it. Let's just say if my parents decided to ever give it to me one day I wouldn't turn it down."

"Speaking of your parents… is there anything I should know before I meet them?" Maaya asked nervously as they approached the front door.

"Honestly, I hadn't thought about it. Nothing important enough to jump out at me right away. Besides, I think we're too late to meet them; if they're home they're probably in bed already. You'll get to see them tomorrow once we're back, I'm sure."

Maaya didn't say anything. She was utterly blown away at the concept of a house that was so big that multiple people could be in it for hours and not actually see each other for almost a day.

Adelaide fumbled in her pocket, then produced a small key which she used to unlock the large front door. It opened into a dimly lit foyer that contained a few chairs, a small table, and decorative plants, but otherwise the foyer's main feature was a wooden staircase that went straight up to the second floor and the chandelier that hung above them. To its right was a doorless entry to what looked like a wide hallway; directly to Maaya's left and right were two more doors that she suspected were either closets or bedrooms.

Maaya jumped as she suddenly noticed movement at the top of the stairs, and then grinned as Saber flew down speedily to greet her, hugging her tightly.

"Welcome home! Stars, have you *seen* this place? It's huge! I've already been into every room, including what I suspect will be your bedroom while you're here, and you are going to sleep very well I can tell you that much."

"Good to see you too, Saber," Maaya laughed. "Did you have fun with Halvar?"

"Until we got here, anyway. Then he went off to send Adelaide's message, and it was taking him forever so I decided to do some exploring. This is an absolutely beautiful place. Speaking of beautiful, you two are looking gorgeous this evening."

"You're too kind," Adelaide said, placing her hand to her chest. "I'm so happy you like it here. Where did Halvar end up going?"

"About three rooms thataway," Saber answered, pointing down the hall to Maaya's right. "He went right to bed only a short while after sunset. Said something about how you work him too hard."

"I'm sure he did," Adelaide chuckled. "I'm feeling pretty tired myself. Is there anything else I need to know?"

"I don't think so. The people I assume are your family got home shortly after we arrived, and they're all in high spirits and greatly looking forward to seeing you, so there's that. Halvar also informed them Maaya is coming, so they're already prepared for that, too. Other than that… honestly, they really didn't have anything interesting to say."

"Was it that or were you just impatient to look around?" Maaya asked, amused.

"Well I *never.* Such implications of my character," Saber huffed, but faltered immediately under Maaya's stare. "Okay, yes, basically. You'd do the same, I guarantee it."

"Maybe I'll have the chance tomorrow," Maaya suggested, and Adelaide smiled.

"Of course! We'll be busy for at least a small part of the day, but otherwise there will be plenty of time for that."

"I hope you're not busy in the evening," Saber commented airily. At the girls' questioning looks, she continued, "Oh, I forgot to mention: Adelaide, your parents are having a big dinner tomorrow night to celebrate you coming home and they want you and Maaya to come."

Adelaide raised her eyebrows in surprise.

"Huh. I wasn't expecting that. I wonder if they're putting on airs because my sister is home."

"They want *me* to come to dinner? Isn't that… I don't know, a special family thing?" Maaya inquired.

"Usually it is. I guess they just really want to meet you," Adelaide said brightly, and Maaya was slightly impressed at how easily she'd accepted this information. "Now… anything else, Saber?"

"Just a question. Am I allowed to go exploring at night or would that be dangerous for me here?"

"Oh, you can definitely do that! This area is very ghost friendly. I don't think there's anyone else in town who would be able to see you, but if for any reason there is and you want to say hello, feel free to say you're a friend of mine. Anyway, if we're set, I'm very much looking forward to bed. I was hoping we'd have time for dinner together but I am completely exhausted. Maaya, come with me and I'll show you your guest room."

Adelaide led the way up the stairs, and Maaya and Saber followed. The hallway was narrower than Maaya expected, though she soon found out why. When Adelaide opened one of the doors along the hallway, she led the way into one of the biggest bedrooms Maaya had ever seen—though admittedly that wasn't saying a lot. It was sparsely furnished with a hefty bed, a writing desk and chair, a wardrobe and chest of drawers, a bedside desk, and a large mirror. On the other side of the room were two more doors, one which clearly led to the balcony and another that Maaya couldn't quite figure out.

"That's the bathroom," Adelaide explained, answering Maaya's unspoken question. "If your experience on the ship was agreeable, you should like this one even more."

"How about that? I was right," Saber grinned. "Come here and feel this bed, Maaya; I need you to tell me if it's as comfortable as it looks."

"You've been here all day; I don't know how you're still more excited about this than I am," Maaya remarked, then turned back to Adelaide. "So… I don't know how to properly thank you for what you did tonight—"

"Just saying 'thank you' will do," Adelaide smiled. "It was no trouble, and I had a lot of fun treating you. It's worth it for me if I get to see you smile."

Saber made a gagging sound from across the room, and the other two laughed.

"I hope I can do the same for you someday," Maaya said.

"What, make me smile? You already do that every day."

They hugged again, Maaya fully aware of the silly grin plastered on her face. Then Adelaide stepped back, stretching and yawning at the same time.

"Oh, before I forget. There's a nightgown in the wardrobe if you'd like. Have a lovely night, both of you, and I will see you tomorrow morning!"

She gave a little wave, then walked back out into the hall, closing the door quietly behind her as she went.

Maaya stood still for a moment, relishing the feeling of joy that washed over her. Then she turned and went over to the wardrobe to find that there was more than just a nightgown inside; there was also a robe, a brush, an umbrella, and a pair of slippers. She took out the nightgown and prepared to change, but before she could do so, Saber came over and placed her hands on Maaya's shoulders, staring fixedly at her.

"Wh-what?" Maaya stammered, taken aback by the intensity of the ghost's gaze.

Saber took a deep breath and closed her eyes as though praying for patience, then opened them again.

"Okay. I need you—I *need* you—to tell me that you just saw what I saw."

"What? Saw what, where?"

"Adelaide. The way she talked to you, the way she touched you, everything."

"I guess? If you're going to tell me this is proof of what you said before—"

"Then I would be right. Maaya, sweetheart, if her flirting were any more obvious she would be down on one knee."

"Really, Saber," Maaya protested, feeling her cheeks turning pink as she averted her eyes.

"What? You know I'm right, don't you? This was too obvious even for you to miss."

"I… I suppose," Maaya said uncertainly. "Don't make fun of me. I think you're right, I just… what if I'm only seeing what I want to see? And you know it's been years since I've had any sort of romantic feelings, and we know how that went, so I'm really nervous, is all."

To Maaya's relief, the ghost only smiled.

"I know. I'm nervous for you, but only because I want this to work. Anyway, I just wanted to get you to admit the possibility existed. If you still didn't notice what she was doing I was going to start tearing my hair out. And don't ask how, I would find a way."

"Well, now I've admitted it, so there," Maaya grumbled as she started to change. "I suppose next you'll want me to plan what I want to say to her."

"If you really think planning is necessary, then sure. Just take care to do so quickly; my threat of telling her for you still stands." Maaya stared daggers at her, but Saber was unmoved. "It does! But we'll worry about that later. You need to tell me what you did today, and I hope you're not too tired because we have a serious deficit of friend time we need to make up for."

As tired as Maaya was, as she looked around the room, she thought she might be too excited to sleep. She couldn't believe she was here. In *Krethus.* She had made it, and it was so much more beautiful and friendly than she had ever expected or hoped for. In fact, for the first time in her life, Maaya thought it would be almost impossible for things to get any better than they were now.

And so, even after climbing into the large bed—which was almost indescribably comfortable—she stayed awake for hours, filling Saber in on everything that had happened earlier that day and listening to Saber tell her own stories. Saber seemed to be in a better mood than she had been since even before the ghost walks had started occurring in Sark, and Maaya too was nothing short of elated. The thought that this might only be temporary attempted once or twice to break in upon her happiness, but upon failing each time, resolved to sulk miserably in a corner of her mind she cared not to explore.

Finally, Saber stopped and patted Maaya's pillow meaningfully.

"You look like you'll collapse if you stay up a moment more. Get some sleep! I'll be out having a grand old time. Oh, and wherever you're going tomorrow, I'm coming too. I was happy to give you both some private time to get things going, but now that you know what you need to do I need to start tagging along again. Maybe I'll even give you some helpful tips and reminders—"

"Saber, I'm going to hit you," Maaya threatened tiredly, but her warning fell flat against Saber's gleeful expression.

"Fine, fine. I'll give you a few days to think on it. My little Maaya, all grown up."

"Do you think you were this annoying while you were alive, too?" Maaya said, attempting and failing to keep a straight face.

"Who knows? It might have been what got me killed. Frankly, upon some deep introspection I can't say I'd blame whoever did it," Saber replied nonchalantly. "Joke's on them, though, they just made me and my infuriating attitude immortal. But you love me anyway."

"I do, weirdly enough," Maaya relented, hugging the ghost tightly. "Go have fun! You can tell me all about it tomorrow."

"Oh, I will. I'll be back in the early morning. Stars, Maaya. I'm so happy right now. We did good, both of us."

After making sure Maaya was comfortable, she flew through the wall and out into the night, smiling all the way.

Maaya sighed contentedly. She hadn't seen Saber this joyful in a long while—and she hadn't felt that way herself, either. This was definitely what her past self would have called too good to be true, but here she was. And now that she was here she was going to do everything in her power to keep it that way. She thought back to what Saber had told her on the ship before the battle, and the ghost had been right—Maaya finally had a reason to fight. And fight she would.

27

TRAINING FOR GHOSTS AND FAMILY

Maaya awoke the next morning warm, comfortable, and incredibly well rested. She remembered where she was almost immediately and smiled to herself as she snuggled deeper underneath the covers. From the light outside she could guess it was mid-morning, and while she knew Adelaide expected her later, for now she was free to relax—and right now she wanted nothing more than to simply lie in bed and do absolutely nothing. This had always been her favorite part of waking up on days she had little to do, and in a bed this comfortable it would take a lot to convince her to leave any sooner than she had to.

She dozed for about an hour, drifting in and out of sleep filled with flickers of pleasant dreams until finally she heard a gentle knock at the door. Maaya got up quickly, rubbed the sleep from her eyes and ran her fingers through her hair, then opened the door. To her surprise, Inga stood on the other side, holding a large bag in her hand.

"Miss Sahni," the tall woman said with a polite smile, placing the bag down on the floor in front of her. "The rest of your clothes arrived. Did you sleep well?"

"I slept *wonderfully*," Maaya replied happily. "What about you? I don't think you were here when we got back last night… you must have got in pretty late."

"I only arrived half an hour ago, and I have yet to sleep," Inga said, then chuckled at the shocked expression on Maaya's face. "Don't worry; I'm off to rest now. Before I go, Adelaide would like me to pass on her request that you join her for breakfast before going to the gymnasium. She requests you wear something comfortable and easy to move around in. Oh, and be sure to bring your cards."

"What exactly is the gymnasium? We're surely not going to spend the day exercising and lifting weights?"

"Not exactly, no. But I believe that's something she wishes to explain herself. Is there anything else?"

"Oh! No, nothing," Maaya said hastily, and then, as Inga turned to walk away, added, "Sleep well!"

Inga paused, and Maaya suddenly realized how awkward she sounded. This was the first officer of the Windfire she was talking to; to be so casual was surely overstepping some kind of boundary, especially for someone Maaya had hardly spoken to.

Maaya's doubt must have been evident on her face, because Inga simply smiled and said, "We aren't aboard the Windfire anymore, so it's fitting we become familiar with each other in a different capacity. Your intent is appreciated, and I hope you have a lovely day."

With that, Inga departed, leaving Maaya conflicted, albeit pleasantly so. Inga still intimidated her, but she didn't think she would mind getting to know her better. Inga definitely had an air of mystery about her, and it intrigued Maaya greatly.

"How sweet! You two are getting along so well," came Saber's voice suddenly from immediately behind Maaya, and she jumped, then turned to glare at the ghost. "Sorry. That still hasn't gotten old. Did I hear right? Adelaide wants to take you out to a gymnasium? I know she's got a lot of energy but I still figured she'd take you somewhere romantic over dragging you along to share in her workout regimen."

"Yeah, I don't know what that's about, but she's done a good job so far," Maaya grunted as she picked up the clothing bag with difficulty. Inga had made it look so easy. "Anyway, did you have fun last night?"

"The best night I've had in a long long time. I used to feel lucky when I could explore a new street and now I'm on a wholly different *continent.* It's a dream come true," Saber answered excitedly.

"Was there anyone out there who could see you?" Maaya asked, carefully pulling her clothes out of the bag and laying them on the bed to sort through.

"Not a one, but I was only a little disappointed. Otherwise it was just like the way things used to be. I went wherever I pleased and no one saw me at all. It just felt… right." Saber sighed reminiscently.

Maaya giggled.

"I'm surprised you didn't run into anyone from the Windfire. Then again, even if they did see you I don't suppose they could have admitted as much. I guess *libris* is more acceptable here than in Selenthia, but I still can't imagine it going over well for anyone who decided to talk to thin air."

"You never know. They could all be like Roshan and accept it. Granted, he accepts basically everything because he just assumes you're always doing something weird, but I'm more than happy to provide demonstrations for a whole crowd. What do you think would scare people more? A floating chair or a piano playing itself?" Saber asked thoughtfully.

"The piano, but you don't know how to play. Also, don't you dare," Maaya remarked firmly as she slipped out of her nightgown and into a pair of leggings and a tight sleeveless top.

"Exactly how many pianos have we encountered that you know what my skills are? Anyway, now that I'm coming with you again I should be distracted enough so as not to cause any trouble," the ghost winked.

A few minutes later Maaya was ready to go. Saber had pulled her hair up into a bun while she slipped on her shoes and then fastened her card pouch to her left arm. On her way to the door she couldn't resist looking at herself in the mirror. Apart from her hair and clothes she didn't look all that different, but when she saw herself she saw a completely new person staring back at her. And she liked it.

Halfway down the stairs Maaya realized Inga never specified where Adelaide wanted to meet her, and so she spent the next few minutes peering nervously into each open room, hoping to find Adelaide and not someone else who might think a stranger were spying on them. Then she spotted Adelaide sitting by herself at a small table on the back porch, a small book in one hand. Every so often she would glance around expectantly, then return to reading.

Maaya took a breath, then opened the back door and stepped lightly out onto the porch. Adelaide glanced up at her and smiled delightedly, quickly putting down her book and leaping to her feet to hug her.

"Great, you're ready! Feels good, doesn't it? So many of my other clothes are so stuffy; it's nice to be able to just move around. How'd you sleep?"

"It was lovely. How about you? …you did sleep, right?" Maaya asked skeptically, and Adelaide laughed.

"If it wasn't obvious already, it will be soon. Anyway, come sit down! I figured we shouldn't eat a big meal just before going to the gymnasium, but we have enough to give us some energy and hold us over until later."

Maaya sat, taking in the view of the yard as she did so. The back porch led down onto a sweeping neatly trimmed lawn with a white picket fence separating it from the trees beyond. A small creek passed through the yard, carrying cold clear water down toward the ocean behind them. Through the trees she could see the rooftops of some of Adelaide's neighbors, though they were so far away that Adelaide might as well be living in the wilderness.

The wide porch was sparsely furnished; apart from the elegant metal table and chairs they sat in, which themselves were slightly rusted, there were only a few other cushioned chairs that looked like they hadn't been sat in for a long while.

And then there was Adelaide. She was dressed simply, much like Maaya, with her long red hair pulled up behind her in a ponytail, but Maaya could still hardly look away. As Adelaide turned briefly back to her book, Maaya couldn't help but stare at her bright green eyes, vivid in the morning sun.

No matter how Maaya saw her, she was stunning. As quickly as they had become friends, and as comfortable as Maaya now felt around her, one thing had remained the same from the first moment Maaya had ever laid eyes on her—just seeing her took Maaya's breath away.

"Hey. Eat," Saber said suddenly, elbowing Maaya lightly in the shoulder and winking. Maaya glared, then picked up a scone.

"You're going to be joining us today, right?" Adelaide asked Saber as she put down her book.

"Of course! As fun as it is bothering Halvar, you're still my two most favorite people. Besides, if Maaya is going to be doing anything physical I could not in good conscience let her go alone; she's prone to hurting herself, see," Saber explained seriously.

"It's not my fault! The danger comes with the job, especially when I'm after ghosts like you," Maaya retorted.

Adelaide laughed.

"I'm glad! I think you'll both like what's happening today."

"What *is* happening today?" Maaya asked. "Why are we going to a gymnasium?"

"I know what you're thinking, and it's not like that. Not exactly," Adelaide grinned. "There's a reason I asked you to bring your cards with you. We're going to be practicing some *libris* while we're there! Now that you've figured out your style, I thought it would be neat to see what you're capable of."

"Are you sure that's okay? To do something like that in public?" Maaya asked nervously.

"Of course! We'll probably be the only ones doing it, but it's still part of the gymnasium's intended purpose. It's just a much better place to practice; there's stuff to break and a wide-open area for us to play around in. I used to train there all the time with my tutor. On that note, I brought you something!" Adelaide reached down and pulled out a small stack of paper of the same material her own cards used, as well as an inkwell and several different small tubes of ink. "You looked like you needed better paper after all your cards got soaked. Just make yourself a few each of the important ones. We shouldn't need any bloods today."

"What, was I not coming along for target practice?" Saber quipped.

"If you want to make our aim worse, be our guest," Maaya replied, taking half a dozen slips of paper from the stack and getting to work. "I'm a little nervous; I already felt so strong and fast when using *libris*, and that was just with the basic cards. I can't imagine what using these new cards will feel like."

"You'll have to be careful, that's for sure. The first time I experienced a sudden increase in speed I went right into a wall," Adelaide chuckled. "But you catch on quick. Your mind and body are pretty quick to figure out your new limitations. That's the point of today: helping you find those limitations."

"I still can't believe *libris* is so accepted here that you two can practice in public. In a building *designed* for just that, no less. How remarkably open-minded," Saber commented.

"I'm not sure if I would call it open-mindedness. This came out of necessity, not because people suddenly became nicer of their own volition. There are still people out there who are skeptical, if not downright frightful of it. Some think humans just shouldn't possess this kind of power. Still, we're getting there. Unshala is one of the friendlier places about it, too."

"That wouldn't have anything to do with the fact that you're from here, would it?" Maaya asked with a grin.

"Not to sound conceited, but… probably," Adelaide said brightly. "Anyway, hurry up and finish; Asmund is here."

Maaya was just about to ask how Adelaide knew, given that her entire house sat between them and the front walk, but then she saw Chronis hanging on one of the porch posts, waving a mechanical arm at them. Adelaide stood up and walked over to it, holding out her augmented arm, and the spider leapt gracefully onto it, almost immediately disappearing into the winding metal.

"Remind me to get back home at a decent hour so we have time to rest, okay?" Adelaide murmured to her arm, and Chronis responded with a polite clicking sound. "You ready, Maaya?"

Maaya quickly took up her cards and placed them safely within the pouch on her arm, then she and Saber followed Adelaide around the side of the house to the front walk. Down on the street just past the gate, Asmund stood casually by his carriage, not looking at all annoyed at the wait. He opened the door for them as they approached, then hopped back up top without hesitation.

"Good mornin' ladies. Hope you don't mind if I hurry on; I need to get back for the lunch rush. The gymnasium, right?"

"That's the one," Adelaide confirmed as they sat down. "If you need to go full speed ahead that's fine with me; Maaya's never seen how fast one of these things can go."

"You've got it, Captain."

"That's really quite all right—" Maaya started to protest, but then shrieked as she was thrown back into her seat as the carriage took off. Adelaide burst into laughter as Maaya struggled to sit up, and Maaya would have made a snappy retort had she not been more concerned with holding on for dear life.

Though Maaya knew they made good time, the tumultuous nature of their trip somehow made it seem even longer than the ride to Adelaide's house the night before. Now, when the carriage finally stopped, it was with great relief and not disappointment that Maaya stepped out of the carriage.

"Sorry 'bout that, Maaya," Asmund grunted from his seat on top of the carriage. "There are certain people you just can't say no to."

"One of you tell him your ghost friend wants him to do that again sometime," Saber said delightedly. Adelaide did so, and Asmund raised his eyebrows.

"Really! I had a third passenger this whole time and didn't even know it? Well, so long as she likes my driving, I can't complain. I don't know where you are, miss, so forgive me for only looking in your general direction, but it was my pleasure. Now then, I'll be off. What time should I be back?"

Adelaide glanced down at Chronis. The hands on the clock face suddenly whirled around rapidly, stopping at a point a few hours in the future.

"Two in the afternoon, apparently," Adelaide relayed.

"So early?" Asmund inquired.

"We're going to be worn out so I want to get us back in time to nap and clean up; we've got a dinner with my parents tonight."

"We?" Asmund asked, and then his eyes fell on Maaya. "Oh, I see. In that case, I'll be back at two sharp. Don't wear yourselves out too much, now; I'm not legally allowed to carry you."

He put two fingers to his forehead again and then directed the horses onward, taking the carriage off toward the coast.

Maaya glanced around. She could see the ocean nearby, but she didn't recognize anything else. She tried to look for the hills where Adelaide's house was, but a low blanket of clouds blocked much of them from view. In the distance, dark clouds loomed, threatening rain and lightning.

In front of them was a massive building made of marble, steel, and wood, all put together like the dream project of a budding and slightly over-enthusiastic architect. It was smooth and modern, and curved metal fixtures looped through the higher walls and roof, arched over the building, then came back down again. It was both elegant and a little confusing, but Maaya loved it already. All around the building were massive windows, and inside Maaya could see all kinds of equipment; some she had seen before in books or at the tiny makeshift gymnasium in Sark, but others were so foreign and strange to her she knew she would injure herself trying to use them.

Adelaide led the way in, and as soon as they passed through the glass double doors she felt a wave of artificial coolness wash over her. She shivered involuntarily, though she knew it must feel wonderful for those in the midst of heavy training.

They walked up to the counter just inside the lobby where a woman in a long robe greeted them with a polite smile.

"Is the open outdoor field free?" Adelaide asked as they approached.

"I believe so! Not many interested in going outside with the threat of rain… ah, yes. Looks like it's completely empty, actually," the woman said, flipping through some papers on the desk.

"Wonderful. Can we reserve the entire thing for two hours?"

"The whole thing? That's unusual," the woman said, frowning. "Do you have a group coming with you?"

"No, it's just the two of us, but we're going to be training with *libris* this afternoon," Adelaide said undeterred.

At once, the woman's face brightened with recognition and excitement.

"Oh yes, of course! Forgive me, it's been a while since you've trained here. I can do that for you. I'll just need the holding fee. Did I hear right that both of you know *libris*?" she asked as she took the coins Adelaide already had at the ready.

"That we do," Adelaide replied. "This one's superbly talented, but we're going to be trying some new things today so I want to make sure we have space."

"Of course! I absolutely understand. How wonderful; it's so rare to see more than one of you in the same place when there isn't elite tutoring going on. I guess Unshala is in good hands. We haven't had any attacks in the area for months that I know of, but… better safe than sorry, you know," the woman said, unable to keep a hint of concern from her voice.

"Without a doubt. It would definitely be a mistake on their part to come here now," Adelaide said warmly. "Anyway, I'd like to get started so we can make the most of our time."

"Of course! Please follow me."

The woman led them around the corner and into a hallway behind the lobby. Through the small square windows in the hall, Maaya could see all kinds of shiny and well-maintained equipment. Everyone seemed so focused, so dedicated. Maaya had to admire them, and she could see why Adelaide would fit in so well here. Were Maaya's life ever to stabilize, Adelaide in particular was the kind of person she aspired to be.

No, that wasn't quite right, Maaya thought. She didn't aspire to be *like* Adelaide. It was more that Adelaide's skill and attitude motivated her. Maaya had been accustomed to leading the way, to showing others how to get things done, but now she was in a position where it was she who had much to learn. Whenever Maaya was around Adelaide she felt pushed to her limit, as though if she didn't try her very best at all times, she would be left behind. Rather than feeling jealous or demotivated, however, she felt even more eager than before to improve, to catch up. Adelaide brought out the best in Maaya, and she quite liked the feeling.

Before long they reached a heavy door that led outside, and Maaya found herself a little underwhelmed. She wasn't sure what she had expected, but what she saw before her amounted to little more than a multipurpose track. A ring around the entire field was clearly meant for jogging, and in the center there were a few sets of bars, rings, and climbing ropes. There were also a few piles of weights, some of which looked too heavy for any normal human to lift, and a few balls, discs, and training dummies. Beyond that, there was little else of any interest.

"I'll come alert you when it's five minutes until your time is up," the woman said kindly. "If you need anything, anything at all, please don't hesitate to let me know."

With that, the door closed softly behind her, and the three of them were alone on the field.

"I must admit, I was expecting… oh, what's the word… *more*," Saber said idly, staring around at the empty field.

"There's usually a little more out here; I imagine they've started moving things in because of the threat of rain," Adelaide replied, and as though on cue, there came a roll of distant thunder at her words. "But what do we need special equipment for? All we need is right here." She patted her card pouch, then smiled.

"What should I do? I've never really trained for this before," Maaya asked uncertainly.

"You've got all new cards now, so our first goal is to get you situated. Make sure you're comfortable, you know," Adelaide answered, taking a few cards from her pouch. "Once we do that, we can move on to more fun stuff. But before anything else, do some stretches! It's best to be at least a little warmed up before you start using magic."

Adelaide sat on one of the mats and began stretching her arms and legs. Maaya, who had never sat through an actual routine before, tried to mimic Adelaide's actions as best she could. It was clear she was going through something she'd done many times before, and Maaya thought it was probably a good idea to pick up on that if she was going to start using magic at an even higher level.

They were finished before she'd had time to start wondering just how long it would take, and as she got to her feet she already felt much more prepared and ready.

"All right! Let's start with speed. Burn your card and let's see what you can do," Adelaide encouraged.

Maaya hesitated, then took one of her new cards and applied it to her right leg. The paper dissipated under her palm, replaced by bright glowing lines in matching patterns. As soon as the lines began to hover over her legs, she gasped. Her old cards had offered her a feeling of greater speed and agility, but this was a new feeling, one that immediately put her old cards to shame. As she stared around at the field, she felt like she could be anywhere in an instant, as though she only had to think of her destination and she would be there before she could blink.

"Feels good, yeah?" Adelaide asked with a knowing smile. "Let's start slow so you don't end up running face first into a fence. Start at a jog, then work your way up to speed so you aren't caught off guard. Do that a few times and then you can try going from a standstill to your very fastest. Good?"

Maaya nodded, then after taking a deep breath, started to jog slowly around the track. Her slow pace was agony; she felt like she was in a race against time itself, and a marked impatience began to well within her, one that almost frustrated her. But she resisted the urge to take off, instead working her way slowly up to a run, and then to a sprint, which to her new legs still felt as though she were only moving an inch every hour.

And then, finally, just as she started her second lap, she pushed forward with everything she had.

The effect was instantaneous. She didn't even perceive herself as moving; she had been staring at a point on the opposite side of the field, and before she could even register what had happened she was already *there*. She stopped abruptly, then turned around to spot Adelaide and Saber waving from the other side of the track.

Maaya stared at the distance she had crossed so quickly, then braced for the exhaustion she was certain was coming—but it never came. Instead, she felt like she was only getting started.

"Again!" Adelaide called happily.

After another moment spent catching her breath from surprise, she started moving again. This time her slowness was even more agonizing than before. Every step felt like it took minutes, and she wasn't sure she could handle doing this repeatedly. Besides, she had already done it once already and managed perfectly fine. What harm could come from going a little faster?

She focused on her destination back on the other side of the field, and then dashed forward as quickly as she could. Then, almost immediately, she gasped, coming to a stop as quickly as she could—and narrowly avoided smashing right into the metal gate surrounding the track.

At once, Adelaide was at her side. Maaya noticed the flicker of her own *libris* lines on her legs.

"You okay? Did you hurt yourself?" Adelaide asked, and Maaya shook her head quickly, thoroughly embarrassed. "Great! That's why I suggested taking it slow; when you try to jump right to it without easing yourself into it you underestimate the sheer power you've got at your disposal. Though, I have to say… I've never seen anyone move that fast before."

Maaya stared up at her.

"What do you mean? You move that fast all the time."

"Me? Oh, no. I'm quick, sure, but what you just did was something else. You might as well have teleported from one place to the other; I could barely even see you move."

"You ready to give yourself credit yet, Maaya?" Saber asked pointedly, having floated over to join them. "That was incredible. Honest."

"That's definitely going to take getting used to," Maaya replied uncertainly, though she couldn't deny she felt excitement rising within her. "I guess I've always been good at running, though."

"Everyone's got things they're better at," Adelaide explained encouragingly. "My strength, for example, is… well, strength. I can't move quite as fast as many of the other elites, but if a fight ever comes down to pure power, I'm hard to match. Anyway, try again! Do that a few more times until you've got the hang of your speed, and then we'll work on your accuracy."

And so Maaya ran, again and again, back and forth across the field. Each time she began to feel a little more control, and after half a dozen runs she was able to pinpoint exactly where she wanted to move to and could guess roughly how much power it would take to get her there.

"Wonderful! I think you're ready to move on to the next stage," Adelaide cheered, walking over to the rack of discs on the field. When Maaya stared at her curiously, Adelaide smiled. "It's easy to move when you can focus completely on where you're going, but what about when you can't? It helps to be able to move nimbly even when other things have your attention."

"What are we going to do with those?" Maaya asked.

"Catch."

Adelaide threw one of the discs, sending it sailing high across the field. Maaya stared for a moment until she realized exactly what Adelaide was after.

With a sudden burst of speed she traversed the entirety of the field, arriving under the disc just in time to catch it—but with her attention focused on the disc, she had forgotten to check her surroundings, and she subsequently slammed into the metal gate. A sharp pain seared through her body, and she blinked rapidly, slightly dazed from the impact.

"Next!" Adelaide called, and threw another disc—in the complete opposite direction.

Maaya shook her head to clear her vision, then rushed off after the disc, taking care to drop the first one by Adelaide's feet as she passed.

This went on for some time, and again Maaya soon found herself regaining control. All in all, though she was certainly traveling faster than she ever had before, the method was exactly the same as it always had been. This was just another *libris* card that worked like the others, and she needed only to master it like she had every one before it. Slowly, her body and mind began to work in sync until her augmented speed felt as natural as if she had always been able to do it.

Back and forth she dashed, catching the discs Adelaide threw no matter how high or far she sent them flying. After catching a particularly difficult low-flying disc sent spinning near the ground close to the wide windows of the gymnasium, Maaya smiled as she handed it back to Adelaide.

"Can you give me something a little more challenging?"

Adelaide raised her eyebrow wryly.

"As you wish."

No sooner had she spoke than she took one disc in each hand, and in one smooth movement, flung them both hard in opposite directions.

Maaya was off in a flash, chasing the disc that was flying slightly lower to the ground. If it was flying lower she could catch it sooner, Maaya reasoned, giving her enough time to get back to the other one before it fell.

She snatched the first disc out of the air, then whirled about to face the other, sliding several inches in the dirt at this abrupt change in direction. Then she took off again as she watched the second disc begin its decline. Adelaide had thrown it far, and for a moment Maaya wasn't sure she'd be able to reach it in time. But then, with a final push, she grabbed the second disc before it hit the ground.

She turned back to Adelaide, a proud smile on her face, but the smile disappeared as she saw a third disc soar straight into the air above Adelaide, and then begin its sharp descent straight toward her head.

Maaya pushed forward as hard as she could, watching as if in slow motion the disc fall close and closer to Adelaide, and she couldn't help but notice the faintest traces of a smile on her lips. As Maaya reached her, she leapt into the air, seizing the disc from just above Adelaide's head. She twisted in the air, hoping against hope to regain her balance before she fell—and then she landed with both feet firmly on the ground.

Adelaide applauded, as did Saber, but to Maaya's utter surprise she heard the sound of other people clapping as well. She turned to see roughly a dozen people gathered near the door leading back into the gymnasium; there were several others inside as as well, staring out at Maaya and Adelaide through the windows.

Maaya suddenly felt extremely self-conscious. Attention was bad, that much she had learned, and she fought the urge to run.

"Well, what do you know? You've got some admirers," Adelaide said happily, putting a comforting hand on Maaya's shoulder. "They're all right. Just pretend they aren't there. What say we try some different cards? You've definitely gotten the hang of your speed already."

"What's next?" Maaya asked, panting and looking purposefully at Adelaide to avoid seeing any of the people watching her.

"Strength, but let's only do that briefly. That'll sap your energy a lot faster than anything else. We'll help you find your limit and then we'll move on the to the elements; that should be fun! Here, let's use these dummies."

They walked over to the short line of dummies. Adelaide applied a purple card to her upper arm, and when her jagged bright *libris* lights flickered to life over her arms, she gestured to one of the dummies.

"The reason we're using these instead of weights is because they're a lot more practical for our purposes," she explained. "Weights are for *building* strength, and we've already got that with our cards. Besides, we're not going for endurance here; the way we typically use our strength, it will come in short bursts. We can get a more accurate gauge of our threshold by hitting stuff rather than lifting weights. Does that make sense?"

"I think so… wouldn't endurance be useful, though?" Maaya asked curiously.

"It can be, but that's not typically how we operate. You should know this more than anyone: we work best when we aren't standing still. To be still is to be vulnerable. We get in, strike, and get out, all the while making sure we're aware of our surroundings and aren't getting hit. Here, give it a try. Just punch this guy," she finished, patting one of the dummies on the shoulder.

Maaya burned a purple card of her own, stepped up to the dummy, planted her feet solidly, then hit the dummy square in the chest with her fist. She felt a rush of adrenaline as her fist connected, transferring power she had never come close to unlocking straight into the dummy's body. It rocked back immediately, but its heavy and sturdy base kept it from toppling over. It swung back, then wobbled until it finally came to a stop.

"You're holding back," Adelaide noticed. "Don't be afraid. Step forward, lean into it, and hit that thing with everything you've got. If it helps, pretend it's Rahu. If it doesn't… do it to impress me."

Maaya scoffed until she heard this last sentence, then gulped. There was certainly nothing for it now.

She took a deep breath, and then in one smooth move took a step forward, leaned into her strike, and hit the dummy as hard as she could. She felt the shock of the impact as the dummy slid backward several inches. To Maaya's surprise, however, she felt nothing in the way of pain or tiredness—a strike like that, which likely would have disabled any human, had hardly affected her at all. If anything, she felt ready to go again.

"Better! Much better," Adelaide encouraged. "Go ahead and try again. Show these dummies who's boss."

Maaya stepped down the line, pausing before each dummy and putting everything she had into each strike. At first she was out to impress Adelaide, hoping that her precision and power would have as much of an effect as her speed. But as she went on, the thought of Rahu began to filter back into her mind. She hadn't thought about him for days, but now that she had been reminded of his existence, she felt anger bubbling up inside her. She imagined his face on the dummy, and she clenched her fists harder as she hit it. She liked Krethus, and she liked being here with Adelaide, but he was the reason she had been forced to flee in the first place.

Wham.

He was the reason her hometown feared and hated her and the reason the military was after her, pursuing her because of his lies.

Wham.

He was the reason she had spent so many years of her life hiding, stressed, hungry, and tired, and the reason she constantly worried she couldn't take care of her own friends. Her family.

Wham.

He was the reason she and her friends had been used and then discarded like tools. He was the reason she didn't know if Roshan was still alive. He was the reason Svante, Kalil, Sovaan, and Kim were dead—and that they had been deaths she had been forced to watch.

Wham. Wham. Wham!

"Hey, okay, I think that's enough," Adelaide said hastily, taking Maaya gently by the shoulders and guiding her away from the dummies. "Don't wear yourself out. You all right?"

Maaya blinked, staring up at Adelaide. She had been so lost in her anger that she had momentarily forgotten where she was and who she was with. She smiled quickly, not wanting Adelaide to know what was on her mind.

"I'm fine! I guess I got a little carried away. This is just so fun; I didn't expect I would see this much of an improvement. Hey, you haven't shown me what you can do yet!"

Adelaide grinned.

"We're working on you, not me. But since you've shown me your strength I suppose it's only fair I show you mine."

She stepped up confidently to one of the dummies, stretching casually like she was about to start on a comfortable morning jog. Saber and Maaya backed up slightly, unsure of what to expect.

And then she struck. She hit the dummy dead center with a punch that looked like it took her almost no effort, but upon impact a loud *crack* echoed across the field. The dummy was sent flying back several feet, its heavy base sent completely airborne, and the dummy somersaulted twice before hitting the ground again in a bent heap.

Maaya and Saber stood speechless and in awe as Adelaide jogged over to pick up the dummy and return it to its place in the line. From behind her she heard a few quiet gasps of apprehensive admiration.

"And that's that," Adelaide said proudly. "I may not be the swiftest or most graceful of fighters, but if I get to land even one solid hit it'll be over just like that. Satisfied?"

"I… y-yeah," Maaya stammered, her eyes still wide with surprise. "I'm definitely glad you're on my side."

"Of course! And I'm happy to put my talents to use for you. I already sent one man straight through the deck of his own ship for you, so just imagine what will happen when we get back to Selenthia and run into some of your old friends from Sark."

Adelaide smiled, but there was an icy dangerous tone in her voice. Maaya suppressed a shiver.

"So what's next? Elementals?" she asked hastily.

"You got it. Let's try fire; we'll take it by itself first, and then we'll combine it with some of your other cards. If you can use both physical augments and both elements at once you'll be in great shape. Let's begin!"

Their practice resumed, and this time Adelaide joined in, teaching Maaya where and how to direct her new elemental powers. Maaya soon learned that there was so much more to her elements than simply creating a barrier; combined with her speed, she left trails of fire winding across the field behind her like footprints. When they moved on to water, she quickly learned how to control streams of water so that they darted around her like snakes, stretching and bending at her mind's command.

Once she had practiced the elements on her own, Adelaide and Maaya practiced together. At first they mirrored each other's movements so Maaya learned how to switch quickly between techniques on the fly, and then Adelaide began slowly sending bursts of fire and water in Maaya's direction; she had the choice either to dodge or to retaliate with her own elements, nullifying Adelaide's attacks as they came. Before long Maaya felt nearly as comfortable with her new cards as she did with her old ones, and she couldn't help but smile as she ducked and wove between Adelaide's assaults as they came. It certainly helped that Saber was on the sidelines the entire time, cheering on Maaya and taunting Adelaide, trying in vain to distract her.

Finally, Adelaide stopped, calling for a time out. Maaya gladly obliged. Though she still felt fine, she was sure she would feel the effects of their training as soon as she let her *libris* fade. What's more, there was now a sizeable crowd standing outside the gymnasium watching them train. Though they all appeared to be in high spirits, Maaya was growing more and more uncomfortable with their presence.

"That was excellent. You picked everything up faster than I expected! How do you feel? Ready to take on some walkers?"

"I feel like I could take on an army of them," Maaya answered excitedly. "Does it always feel like this?"

"What, the feeling that you could take on the world? There is a bit of a honeymoon period once you get your style down, but some of it is always with you. When I've got my *libris* going, I feel like I'm at my very best and that nothing in the world can stop me. It's wonderful, really. I'm glad you get to experience this with me."

Suddenly, from Adelaide's augmented arm, there came a beeping sound. Adelaide glanced down, and her eyebrows rose in surprise.

"Goodness, is that the time? We've only got about fifteen minutes before we're due to head back."

"I suppose you two can rest now considering Maaya's gone and learned everything too quickly," Saber suggested, but Adelaide tapped her chin thoughtfully.

"It's true. Maaya definitely appears comfortable with her new style. To be fair, though, that's only been against plastic opponents. There is one more thing I think we can do with the time we have left to really see how well she's really mastered her cards."

"What's that?" Maaya asked cautiously.

"I propose… a duel. You and me," Adelaide said brightly. "That way we can see how you work when both your body *and* mind are put to the test."

"What?! Y-you want me to duel *you*?" Maaya stuttered, taking a step back. The image of the broken and bent dummy flashed into her mind. "I'm not that good!"

"Hey, easy," Adelaide laughed. "We're not going to hurt each other. I just want to test your speed, your strength, and your reflexes. Remember what I said about always being on the move and quick thinking? I want to see you in action."

"How do you know who wins, then?" Saber asked, amused.

"How about… whoever disables the other?" Adelaide suggested. "Not by way of injury, of course. Whoever can pin the other down wins."

Almost immediately Maaya's brain helpfully jumped in with images of

Adelaide pinning her to the ground, strands of her red hair falling gently into Maaya's face as she smiled down at her.

Maaya shook her head furiously. *Stop it stop it stop it.*

"What do you think, Maaya?" Saber smirked, evidently at least partially aware of what was on Maaya's mind.

"Fine," Maaya said shortly. "But if I *do* get hurt—"

"Then I promise to stay at your bedside and take care of you until you're better," Adelaide finished, a sudden warmth in her voice.

"Right. Let's just do this then," Maaya said, completely flustered.

"Burn whatever cards you need and then we'll start on the count of three. Ready?"

Maaya made sure she had all four cards burning, then nodded, already thinking ahead. Adelaide had definite advantages in strength and experience, but Maaya was faster. She glanced around at the field, looking for any tools that might aid her in disabling the girl; she didn't immediately spot anything she could pick up, but there was a chance she could put some of the objects between them to act as an obstacle while Maaya gained more advantageous ground.

"One… two… three!"

Adelaide ran straight for Maaya at great speed, but Maaya, who had been expecting this, dodged immediately to the left, then straight ahead. For now it was important to keep some distance between them. Adelaide couldn't catch Maaya in an open sprint, so she would depend on Maaya getting close; if Maaya was going to do that, she needed to make sure she had the upper hand. She also knew she had to get a better feel for the lay of the land so her environment wouldn't take her by surprise and throw her off at a crucial moment.

Adelaide pursued her, and Maaya kept backing away. Just in time she realized that Adelaide had been moving in such a way as to trap Maaya in a corner. Upon this realization she pushed with all her speed directly past Adelaide, who looked surprised at such a bold move.

Maaya made for the center of the field, but upon noticing Adelaide was right behind her, changed direction immediately, searching around her for anything she could use to her advantage. She spotted a few trees she might be able to climb, as well as a wide rocky area near one corner. If necessary she could attempt to lose Adelaide there; from all her years spent leaping over rooftops, in narrow spaces, and around tight corners, Maaya was confident in her agility and steadiness on her feet.

Adelaide dashed to her side, and from behind her came an impassable trail of fire. Every so often she would fling a ball of fire in Maaya's direction, and Maaya was forced to dodge it or block it with water of her own, causing a great burst of steam—this effectively blocked Adelaide's attacks, but it obstructed her vision temporarily, something she imagined Adelaide would try to take full advantage off. She couldn't stay within striking distance, nor could she retreat and let Adelaide continue to create a wall to box her in.

In response, Maaya decided to try to use Adelaide's tactic against her. Sprinting as far away from Adelaide as she could, she used her own water to douse the flames, then ran to the opposite side of the wall, successfully putting Adelaide's own barrier between them. She knew Adelaide would be forced to douse the flames if she wanted any chance at getting to Maaya, which would subsequently open up more of the field for Maaya to use to her advantage.

Suddenly, she noticed an object sail right past her head. She turned quickly to see Adelaide, a few discs in her hands, throwing them at Maaya with dangerous precision. Maaya ducked another quickly, and then smashed another into pieces as it soared by her. The first disc had taken her by surprise, but now that she knew what Adelaide was trying to do she was able to dodge them easily. What's more, Adelaide's aim wasn't perfect; the next disc soared several feet to the side, so far off that Maaya didn't even have to move. She watched it fly by, and then a split second later realized her mistake: Adelaide hadn't missed by accident.

She turned just in time to see Adelaide making straight for her, and Maaya barely had enough time to dodge out of the way, scraping her leg in the dirt as she made her narrow escape. Adelaide, more nimbly than expected, turned sharply and pursued her. With only a few feet between them, Maaya leapt off the ground with as much strength as she could muster in the direction of one of the climbing ropes. Her new strength carried her just far enough to grab hold of the rope, and she made use of her momentum to send her swinging away from Adelaide.

This, however, presented a new problem. So long as she was on the rope, Adelaide could easily figure out her trajectory and place herself in just the right position to meet her. Maaya also simply couldn't jump off the rope, as she would lose all her momentum and make an easy target.

Thinking fast, Maaya remembered her fight with the soldier up in the masts of the Selenthian ship. She called fire to one hand and water to the other. Then, in one swift motion, she projected as much of each element as she could muster, then let go of the rope and clapped her palms forcefully together.

A tremendous burst of steam exploded from around her, temporarily blocking her view of Adelaide—and vice versa. She looked to the ground below, fully prepared to launch off at full speed as soon as her feet touched down.

When she hit the ground, she launched herself toward Adelaide. Her distraction appeared to have worked, for the girl momentarily seemed caught off guard, staring around the cloud of steam above. By the time Adelaide caught sight of Maaya, it was too late.

Maaya ducked below Adelaide's outstretched arm, then swung her left leg out, catching Adelaide's ankles. The taller girl fell, and for a moment Maaya thought she had done it until Adelaide sent a burst of water into Maaya's face, momentarily blinding her.

She leapt away as she tried to clear her vision, but the damage was done. She soon felt Adelaide's grip on her arms, a grip so powerful she knew she had no chance of escaping even with her augmented strength, and then felt Adelaide sweep her legs out from beneath her. She fell hard to the ground on her back, and before she could even try to get away, Adelaide sat on top of her, holding her at the wrists.

From the edge of the field a tumult of cheers and applause erupted from the crowd, which had now grown substantially. But Maaya had eyes only for Adelaide, who stared triumphantly down at Maaya, an expression of absolute joy on her face.

"Maaya! That was fantastic!" she exclaimed, letting her *libris* lines flicker and then fade. Maaya did the same and was suddenly overcome with a wave of exhaustion. "Absolutely brilliant, using your elements together like that. Did you learn to move like that in Selenthia?"

"I learned some of it there. Ghosts were unpredictable and I had to be able to keep up with them even if they could pass through walls or fly up high," Maaya panted. "Not to mention I had to be able to escape just about anything and anyone. I just kind of learned as I went."

"That would explain it. I can see where you got your strengths. It really suits you. You might not have as much physical strength but you're clearly a quick thinker and faster than anyone I've seen before. How do you feel?"

"Like I just ran to Selenthia and back," Maaya groaned.

"Excellent work, Maaya. Both of you, really, but that was a sight to see!" Saber said happily. "You really picked up your new style quick. Looks like we need to get you some training in hand-to-hand combat next. You think your commander would be up for that?" she finished, glancing at Adelaide.

"Don't give her any ideas," Maaya said quickly. "Anyway, are you going to let me up now?"

"Oh, I don't know. I kind of like this view," Adelaide said airily, then laughed as Maaya blushed furiously.

She stood with some effort, then took Maaya's hand to help her up. Then she led the way back toward the door, glancing down at Chronis as she did so.

"Right on time. I don't know about you but I can't wait to get home and take a long hot bath."

"I'm with you there," Maaya said tiredly. She hadn't pushed herself to her limit, but the hours of practice had definitely taken their toll on her.

As they approached the gymnasium, Maaya realized they'd have to go through the small crowd of people watching them. She tensed suddenly and lowered her gaze, hoping that if she appeared uninteresting enough they would turn their attention to Adelaide instead. Saber hovered protectively nearby, scanning the crowd for any sign of trouble.

Maaya had no such luck, however. If anything, the people seemed far more interested in her than in Adelaide, and as she approached, a small handful of them clamored for her attention.

"I've never seen you before! Are you new?"

"What's your name? Are you here to protect Unshala with Adelaide there?"

"I heard there were only a few elites in the area! Does this mean there are more than we're being told?"

"Everyone, please, give us some room," Adelaide requested, her sharp voice ringing above the excited crowd. They indulged her reluctantly, taking a few steps back. "This is a friend of mine from out of town. She'll be joining me on an important assignment within the next few days. She's not accustomed to this kind of attention so please go easy on her."

Maaya stopped abruptly as an older man stepped up to her, and to her utter surprise, gave a deep bow.

"Thank you for your service to our country, miss," he said kindly. "You and the others make sure my family can sleep soundly at night."

"I've never felt safer now we've got two elites here in little old Unshala. Next time you two are in town I'll treat you to lunch, how's that?" another suggested eagerly.

Adelaide took Maaya gently by the wrist and led the way through the crowd. Maaya was too nervous to hear the others as they continued to speak, terrified that as soon as they realized who she was or where she was from they would become hostile. But none of them did any such thing, and as Adelaide and Maaya passed into the hall, the spectators held back to let them leave in peace. Maaya let out a silent breath of relief.

"I hope you don't mind a little fame, because you've now got quite a reputation here in Unshala," Adelaide chuckled as they walked down the empty hall.

"I'm not sure… developing a reputation has never been a good thing for me. And I guess I'm still a little worried they'll react differently when they know where I'm from. I know most people don't mind *libris* here, but I'm from the country Krethus is at war with. Not to mention Rahu has accused me of all sorts of horrible things, and if that reaches anyone here…"

"Most people couldn't care less where you're from, and if for any reason they do hear what you've been accused of they'll know you're innocent in an instant. Those things the Selenthians are so terrified of we've been dealing with for decades. If anything it will just make the Selenthians look more foolish, what with how they're chasing away one of the only people who could help them."

"That'd be presumptuous of our people, considering Krethus suffered some severe catastrophes before this new era of open-mindedness came about," Saber commented.

"That's true. I'm hoping we can put a stop to this before Selenthia learns the same lessons the way we did," Adelaide sighed.

They walked out the front doors and down toward the street just as Asmund pulled up in his carriage, waving politely at them.

"You look exhausted. How'd it go?" he asked as he jumped down to open the door for them.

"Wonderful. Maaya's a natural, but I already knew that," Adelaide said, flashing Maaya a wink. "But you're right, we're exhausted. We're ready to go home and collapse if you don't mind."

"We'll be off on the double, then," Asmund affirmed, shutting the door behind them and jumping back up to the top of the carriage.

There was silence for a few minutes as Asmund's horses started off down the street, broken only by the sound of rolling thunder that was getting closer by the hour. The skies were growing darker, and Maaya stared out the window at the dark clouds and distant flashes of lightning. She had always loved storms. While the rain could be inconvenient, the sounds of a thunderstorm calmed her like little else. She often daydreamed about reading a book next to a rain-spattered window in the evening, looking out at the soaked streets and dripping trees as the last light of the sun faded away. A candle sat on the table before her, and a fire crackled quietly in the background.

But there was too much on her mind to be intrigued by a storm that hadn't yet arrived. She was somewhat comforted by Adelaide's words, and she did feel safer in Unshala than she did anywhere in Selenthia. Even if someone did figure out who she was, she reasoned, what were they going to do? Turn her in? To whom? The Krethans had no issue with her, and the Selenthians couldn't come to get her. In that respect, she was safe. But what she couldn't stop thinking about was the life she had left behind her in Selenthia… and she wondered if she would ever be able to go back.

"You look pretty pensive there. Rial for your thoughts?" Adelaide asked, focusing her bright green eyes on Maaya.

"I'm just thinking about what my life will be like after all this is over," Maaya explained. "I do love it here but there's a lot I'd like to go back to in Selenthia… but I know that even if we manage to destroy the machine here, nothing will have changed back home. I'll still be a wanted criminal."

"Not necessarily," Adelaide replied, and when Maaya stared up at her in curious surprise, she smiled. "I've been thinking about that too. This is just me dreaming, but once this is all over I'm hoping we can get our governments to communicate. I'm sure at least some Selenthians know about our situation, but they may not have connected you to it. Once we explain how you're involved I'm sure your government would let you off the hook."

"You think they would do that? Just talk to each other while they're at war?" Maaya asked, astonished.

"Oh yeah. They may not talk much because they're *supposed* to hate each other, but the truth is most of the top brass on both sides are probably just as tired of this as the rest of us are. Most of what happens right now between our militaries is just posturing. There are still some lines of communication open, and if our government makes an announcement in good faith for the benefit of yours, we could even start spurring some peace talks; you never know."

"They're stuck, then," Saber mused. "Nobody wants to be involved anymore but they're all too proud to take the first step themselves."

"Naturally. That'd mean defeat, even if we haven't really had any skirmishes for decades," Adelaide said quietly. "The fact of the matter is we're all stuck. Being in the war isn't working for nationalistic purposes anymore, but at the same time no one wants to bow out. Everyone is equally tired and afraid, torn between caring too much and too little. Our countries are economic disasters and we focus on the war only as much as is necessary to forget our own problems at home." She paused, then gave Maaya another grin. "But we'll get through this. Big things are happening here, things that should change the world as we know it for the better. I know it'll all be okay in the end."

Maaya smiled, unable to resist Adelaide's contagious optimism. "I hope so. I kind of like the sound of that, you know? Saving the world and all."

"It'll definitely be nice to talk about. Something I can hold over my parents' heads until the end of time, anyway," Adelaide chuckled. "But speaking of my parents… let's talk about dinner!"

Maaya felt a surge of nervousness. She had completely forgotten that she was to have dinner with Adelaide's family that very night.

"Ah, so… that's still happening, is it?" she asked slowly, and Adelaide smirked.

"Absolutely! You don't get to escape something as important as this. It'll be okay! I promise. I was just thinking we could go over a few quick things so we spare ourselves any awkward moments."

"Do I have to worry about saying the wrong thing in front of them?"

"Not exactly. You're kind of special in that, since you work with *libris* too, that's a whole lot of stuff we don't have to try to explain away—the fact that you can see ghosts and use *libris* will be totally normal to them."

"That's good. That's usually what people would find the worst about me," Maaya said, smiling nervously.

"You won't have to worry about that. We can even tell them about Saber if you'd like, though for the sake of simplicity, I would recommend just avoiding that for now," Adelaide suggested. "But as my parents' priorities are ever the strangest I've ever encountered, I would also avoid mentioning your home life too much. That you're from Selenthia isn't a big deal, though they may have some reservations. What they'd have more of a problem with is finding out you were poor and don't know your parents."

"What? Why?" Maaya asked, befuddled.

"Family is a big deal to them. Honoring the family name, things like that. They don't necessarily look down on orphaned or adopted children—they have no problem with the concept, really—it just isn't something they're used to because everyone in their circles values the family legacy nonsense so much. Likewise with the money issue. As open-minded as they claim to be, there's still that part of them that gets uncomfortable around poverty. It's so much a foreign concept to them they just have no idea how to deal with it even if their hearts are in the right place."

"I… I see," Maaya mumbled. "So what should I tell them? I don't want to lie."

"You don't have to. Just say your home life is personal and that you don't want to get into it. Trust me, wealthy people have their fair share of drama and gossip as well, so my parents will understand. If they press you for any details on what you do for work, you can always just say you were employed as an assistant to a wealthy person from Sark. That's technically true, no?"

"I suppose. I just… I'm honored to meet your parents, I really am, but if they would have such a problem with me for things I can't even control, would it be so wrong of me not to care if they liked me after all?"

Adelaide sighed, looking like she was struggling for words.

"You're right, of course. I know if our positions were switched I would probably be refusing to see them. I am who I am, and if someone doesn't like me that's entirely their problem. This is me being a little selfish, actually. I'm sure you'd like them to like you, but… it's also really important to *me* that they like you."

"Why? You're the one who rebelled against them and went your own way, right?" Maaya pressed.

"Because you're cute, and I like you," Adelaide replied slyly, then held up her hands innocently as Maaya made to protest. "It's the truth! I want my parents to like you because I like you, and I would love for you to be accepted and welcome in my home. Wouldn't you want the same?"

Maaya faltered. In that, Adelaide was right. It was hard for Maaya to imagine the situation being reversed—mostly because she had no family to bring Adelaide home to—but she thought about Kim and the others and how much she would want them to like Adelaide. It would mean everything to her.

"Fine," Maaya relented, and Adelaide smiled brightly. "Is there anything else I should know? This seems pretty easy so far."

"There's just one more thing," Adelaide said, and to Maaya's surprise she turned away, looking embarrassed. "Can I ask you a silly favor? When we're talking about *libris* and how we practice together… can you tell them I did a good job, too?"

Maaya stared at her, and then burst out laughing.

"Are you kidding? That's your big request? To tell your parents you impressed me?"

"I'm sorry!" Adelaide protested, her face bright red. "I know it's silly, I do, and I know this is bad timing after you did such a good job back there. It's just that my parents invested so much into my training and they were always so critical of me, and now that I'm taking you home with me I want them to know I'm still—"

She broke off as Maaya smacked her lightly in the shoulder.

"You're such a kid," Maaya interrupted, still laughing. "I'll do it. Besides, it wouldn't be a lie anyway; you *are* better than me."

"Thank you," Adelaide replied awkwardly. "I'll make it up to you, I promise."

"You don't have to! Besides, you won't feel much like paying me back when you find out I'm going to tease you about this for the rest of your life," Maaya continued, then cried out and devolved into a fit of laughter as Adelaide embraced her tightly, ruffling her hair.

"Don't push your luck," Adelaide said, though her intimidating tone was somewhat marred by her own fits of laughter and bright red cheeks.

As the horses pulled up in front of Adelaide's house, Maaya began to feel nervous again. She and Adelaide made to get out of the carriage when Saber suddenly floated past them, her palm to her forehead.

"You two go ahead, I'm going to take a walk; I'm not feeling so well," Saber muttered quietly, as though she were suffering from a headache.

"What's wrong?" Maaya asked concernedly. She made to step closer to the ghost, but Saber floated away, keeping some distance between them.

"Not sure. I felt like this on the ship before, remember? But it went away then. I'm just going to walk to clear my head until it stops again."

"Okay… please find me if you need me, all right?" Maaya said softly.

"Yeah. Whatever. See you later," Saber continued distractedly, then vanished from the carriage.

Maaya and Adelaide shared a glance, but before they could say anything the door opened to reveal Asmund, gesturing grandiloquently toward Adelaide's house with his free arm.

"Home sweet home. Hope you don't mind if I rush off; no one is going to want to get anywhere on foot with the rain coming. I'll stop by and say hello to your parents soon if it's all well and good. I imagine everyone's busy with the wedding coming up."

"I have no idea, actually. I have yet to see them. We'll probably talk about that at dinner tonight," Adelaide said. "All I've read in my letters is that this marriage is definitely happening in the near future."

"Hmm. They could do to inject a little more excitement in something that's supposed to be such an important moment," Asmund harrumphed. "Anyway, just let me know when I should be receiving my invitation. You ladies have a good night."

He tipped his top hat to them, then started off immediately. As the sounds of the horses' hooves and carriage wheels on the gravel road faded into a roll of thunder, the first raindrops of the oncoming storm began to fall. They landed with a quiet metallic ring on the front gate and rustled the leaves of the bushes and flowers lining the front walk. It was calming and peaceful, and Maaya wouldn't have minded standing out in the rain, but at the moment she was too concerned about Saber to enjoy the moment.

Adelaide, however, seemed eager to get inside, and so they headed quickly down the walk as a much louder crack of thunder echoed overhead. By the time they made it to the door it was already raining hard enough to dampen Maaya's hair. She grimaced. That was the one part of storms she could do without.

"Now I'm definitely looking forward to that hot bath," Adelaide yawned as she shut the door behind them. "And sleep. Plenty of that."

"Do you think Saber is okay?" Maaya asked worriedly, walking to a nearby window and staring out at the empty front yard.

"I think so. I think that as we get closer to the machine she may feel more uncomfortable; this wouldn't ordinarily affect ghosts, but she's a special one what with that gem on her forehead. But once this is all over she should be just fine," Adelaide answered reassuringly.

"I hadn't even thought about that… I hope she comes back soon so I can tell her. Even if it's not true it might help her to think about it that way. She must be really scared; ghosts don't feel uncomfortable," Maaya mused.

"She'll be all right. Besides, if she needs anything at all, she knows where to find us," Adelaide continued encouragingly. "In the meantime, you should get some rest. My parents are pretty relaxed, but falling asleep in your soup would probably raise some eyebrows."

Maaya laughed despite herself, trying to think positively. This had happened before, as Saber pointed out. And if Saber could find her way back and feel better after disappearing in the midst of a huge battle at sea, taking a simple walk in a safe neighborhood should be much better.

"How will I know when it's time to wake up or where to go?" Maaya asked, suddenly remembering her lack of directions from earlier that morning.

"Inga will come by to make sure you have time to get ready, and then when it's time I'll come get you. I wouldn't make you walk in all by yourself," Adelaide winked.

After sharing a quick hug, they went their separate ways. Maaya's exhaustion seemed to grow with every step she took, and when she entered her bedroom it was all she could do not to collapse on her comfortable bed right away. She proceeded resolutely to the bathroom where she began to fill the spacious tub with warm water.

She sank into it gratefully, impressed with the sheer variety of soaps sitting on a narrow shelf on the wall above. This was definitely something she could get used to.

The silver lining of her nerves about dinner that night was that they helped keep her awake long enough to finish bathing and prepare for bed. All the while, scenes of their coming meal played in her mind; every daydream that started with she and Adelaide sharing a romantic moment over dinner soon turned into a daymare where her parents immediately hated Maaya and told her to leave and never return.

Maaya returned to the bedroom, hopeful that she might see Saber there waiting for her, but the room was empty. She sighed, trying to ignore the panic her brain tried to instill in her. She already had enough to worry about with the dinner ahead; she didn't need to become anxious over Saber on top of that.

The bed was even more comfortable than she remembered, and the combination of her soothing warm bath, the soft sheets, and the gentle pattering of rain outside was enough to cause her eyelids to droop almost immediately. There was nothing for it, Maaya thought. These things would all resolve themselves one way or another, and there was no point in worrying about them just yet.

In deference to her resolve, her mind gave her only the sweetest of dreams when she slipped into sleep, ones that had even her unconscious self eagerly awaiting the night ahead.

28

THE FAMILY SOL

It felt like only a few minutes had passed before there came a knock at the door. Groggy and disoriented, Maaya took a few moments to realize what the sound was—and when she did, she had no idea who could possibly be knocking. It was dark outside; who would be trying to wake her up in the middle of the night?

"I've got it," Saber said quickly, floating over to the door. She poked her head through the door to see who was on the other side, then came back in immediately, opening the door wide.

"I've just come to make sure Maaya is awake; dinner is in an hour," came Inga's voice.

"Well, her eyes are open, but I'm not sure she's actually awake yet. I'll make sure she gets up," Saber grinned.

Maaya sat up drowsily, rubbing her eyes, and then she snapped to attention.

Dinner. Right.

"I would appreciate it. I've also been asked to remind her that Adelaide will meet you both shortly before it's time to eat. I will not be joining you as it is a private family affair, but I hope we can catch up soon."

"Shame," Saber said sympathetically. "Hey, no one else in this family can see ghosts, right?"

"Correct, and you are thus more than welcome at dinner." Maaya heard a note of amusement in the commander's voice. "In anticipation of this question, however, Adelaide has requested you try your best to behave yourself, and would like me to express her acknowledgement of how difficult that is likely to be for you."

"Oho, I see how it is," Saber cackled. "I will do my best, but beyond that I can give her no guarantees."

"Of that I'm sure. I'll see you both soon," Inga said warmly, and then she departed, the sound of her footsteps fading down the hall.

"All right sleepyhead, time to get up," Saber said in a sing-song voice. "Oh, you're awake enough to glare at me, good. Sleep well?"

"It doesn't feel like it, but it's probably better that I did," Maaya yawned, taking a long stretch.

"Good. We've got a whole hour until dinner, so let's get you looking pretty. You need to make a good first impression on your girlfriend's parents."

Maaya only rolled her eyes as she got out of bed, stumbling to the wardrobe. She already knew what she wanted to wear; the rest was just a matter of mustering up the confidence to leave the room.

As she pulled out her black dress and lay it on the bed, she suddenly remembered what had happened earlier that day.

"Oh, Saber… how are you feeling?" she asked cautiously. Saber's face fell slightly.

"I'm all right. I don't feel weird anymore, if that's what you're asking. But my mood was definitely soured a little. This has happened twice now and I really would appreciate it if it didn't happen again."

"What is it like?" Maaya continued, running a brush through her hair.

"It's hard to explain. I suppose I'd liken some of it to feeling anxious and needing to escape, but that's only a small part. The rest is… too strange to describe. I feel like I'm being pulled this way and that, like if I don't focus I'll lose my grip on this world and get sucked away. Whenever that happens the world just turns hazy, like I'm here but also not here, and I lose all sense of whatever's going on around me."

"That sounds… horrifying," Maaya murmured, stepping closer to the ghost. Saber didn't move.

"It is, but in that introspective crisis sort of way. I'm not really afraid of anything in particular, I just feel this sense of looming dread on top of the fact that I get this distinct feeling of not existing. It's… unpleasant. I wish I knew why this was happening because I'm actually starting to get very concerned."

"Adelaide has a theory on that, actually," Maaya said, and Saber looked up at her hopefully. "She says it's probably because you're getting closer to the machine and because of the gem. But she also says that as soon as we destroy the machine it should all go away."

"I see… so I can expect this to only occur more often the closer we get?

That's encouraging," Saber mumbled, but she seemed satisfied for the moment. "Oh well. It's good to know I'm not actually in danger. The sooner we can get rid of this thing, though, the better."

"Of course! I'm sure Adelaide will want to talk about it soon. I have to admit I'm already getting impatient; it's nice being here and all, but this is what we came here to do, and I don't think I'll be able to truly relax until this is over and done with."

"I understand. This is bound to be the easy part, though. Adelaide's well connected and wealthy, so actually getting there shouldn't be any trouble. But we'll worry about that later. For now, get dressed! I'll see if there's anything in the bathroom we can use to fix your face."

"My face is fine!" Maaya protested, and Saber paused, looking her up and down.

"If it makes you feel better, sure," she said, then laughed, retreating to the bathroom as Maaya threw a pillow at her.

Maaya slipped off her nightgown and into her black dress. It felt even better the second time, even as she struggled to zip up the back. Saber came out of the bathroom quickly, just in time to help, then held up a fine-toothed comb.

"Turns out there is some stuff in there, but nothing for a complexion like yours. Not unless you want Adelaide thinking you're suddenly ill of blood loss. Anyway, let me do your hair. What are you feeling: up or down?"

"Down, I think. It's been up for exercising all day," Maaya said, obediently sitting down on the bed as Saber guided her to it and began brushing her hair. "You know… we're going to figure this out, okay? All of this. Maybe we can even put an end to this before you start feeling bad again."

"Don't even worry about it. We'll think about that once we start planning, but for now, this is your night and I don't want you to mess this up because your mind is elsewhere," Saber murmured as she started a small braid.

"What do you mean? Where should my mind be if not on the job we came here to do?"

"A little closer to home. At least for tonight. You two are getting all dressed up to go to dinner, so this is your chance to make a good impression on everyone at the table. Myself included, of course."

"How can I make a good impression if you're hanging over my shoulder?" Maaya grumbled.

"Oh, I'll behave. Just think of my presence as a little positive pressure nudging you in the right direction."

Maaya rolled her eyes.

"I'm absolutely not doing what you want me to do in front of her *parents*. Especially not when her sister is going to be married soon!"

"Hey, you heard Adelaide. Her parents are always wondering when she'll bring someone home. Don't worry about me. I'm just there to observe. I need to get to know these people better if I'm to give you any sort of advice in the future."

Saber finished a second small braid on the other side of Maaya head, then pulled both gently behind, bringing up a small part of her hair into a half ponytail, the braids coming together like a circlet. She used the comb to make sure everything was straight and smooth, took a brief but careful glance at Maaya's face to make sure all was well—running her fingers over Maaya's eyebrows in the process—then stood back looking quite satisfied.

"Come take a look!"

Maaya stood, then walked to the mirror. She couldn't help but smile at what she saw. What she had seen the day before in the dressing room hadn't been an illusion. This was really who she was. The girl she saw in the mirror… she could definitely see her standing next to Adelaide.

She took a deep breath and let it out, then couldn't help but do a little twirl in front of the mirror. This was a confidence booster for sure.

"You're welcome," Saber smirked. "Now get your nice shoes and let's go. We've still got time, but I want to make sure we don't get lost again."

Maaya slipped on her shoes that sat by the door, and then, after a brief pause to gain her bearings, opened the door.

The hallway was empty, but Maaya was suddenly very aware of her surroundings. She had never before dressed for the specific purpose of being seen before. That went against everything she ever knew. This part would definitely take getting used to.

Just as she reached the stairs, someone else came walking up quickly, and for a moment Maaya stepped back in surprise, eager not to start her night by running into someone she'd have to spend an awkward dinner with later. And then her jaw nearly dropped.

Adelaide stood before her, staring down at her with a bright smile on her face.

"Well, don't you look absolutely stunning tonight?" she said, staring Maaya up and down. "You're going to turn some heads at dinner that's for sure. Saber, nice to see you! I'm glad you'll be joining us."

Adelaide was dressed in a white button shirt under a black blazer, both rolled up to just under her elbows and unbuttoned casually at the collar around which a fine gold chain with a small green stone at the bottom was draped. Well-ironed slacks fell over sleek black shoes with tiny gold buckles, and her long red hair was pulled up tight into a clip behind her head leaving not a single strand astray. Her augmented arm even looked shinier than it usually did, and Chronis had taken its usual place upon it. As Maaya remembered to breathe, she noticed a faint cozy and musky smell like a mix of clean linens and new books.

"I… uh… wow. You too," Maaya said, scolding herself inwardly for sounding so silly. Saber snorted quietly from behind her.

"If I've taken your breath away that's all I need to know," Adelaide said, then extended her arm. "We're a little early, but there's no harm in getting to eat sooner. Are you ready?"

"I think so," Maaya said nervously, even as she took the taller girl's arm. "You're sure they're okay with this? And that I won't embarrass myself?"

"Well, I can't promise the latter; that's up to you," Adelaide laughed. "But you'll be fine. You look absolutely gorgeous, we already went over the little you need to know, and they're good people who are looking forward to meeting you. Don't let what I said before scare you; we have our disagreements, but I will always call this place home and will always call them family."

Temporarily comforted, Maaya let Adelaide lead her down the stairs. She wondered what kind of people Adelaide's parents would be like. Adelaide cut an imposing figure all by herself as the captain of a ship, one who had an entire unquestioningly loyal crew of Blackfins at her command. Then she had turned out to be a *libris* elite from a family of old wealth with political influence and contacts—and she was just the rebel child. Maaya could only imagine what kind of people stood beside the force of nature that was Adelaide, the ones responsible for the family's incredible wealth and power.

She pictured a massive dark room with a long table covered in expensive foods she had never seen before. Candles were the only source of the room's light, and Adelaide and Maaya sat together on one side while her family, imposing and faceless in the shadows, sat on the other, an aura of intimidation and disapproval emanating from them all the while. And Adelaide's sister, of course, fuming at Maaya for coming to steal her spotlight.

Once down the stairs, however, they walked only a short while before coming to a set of double doors on the side of the house facing the backyard. Adelaide turned to Maaya, gave her an encouraging nod, and then knocked twice, opening the doors immediately after.

What Maaya saw was nothing like what she had seen in her head. The room was almost cramped and brightly lit, and the sounds of clinking glasses and laughter already filled the room. In the center of the room was a round table with chairs around it for six. A small chandelier hung directly over the table, small enough that Maaya was almost disappointed… but only almost. The table, made of deep red wood, was covered with a simple white tablecloth that was several inches too short—a design choice, perhaps—and while there was plenty of food, it wasn't the overwhelming smorgasbord she had envisioned.

At the table was a man and a woman, both in their early forties by the looks of things, and beside them, a younger woman. The man was dressed in a proper suit and tie, but the tie was already loose, the top button of his shirt undone in a statement of comfort over fashion. Thick blond hair was slicked back on his head, but in the way that suggested it had taken quite a battle of brushes and gel to make it stay put; already a small patch was fighting to free itself from its prison. He had a friendly face and jovial air about him, with light wrinkles on his face that came from years of smiles.

The woman beside him carried herself more elegantly, though Maaya could see this came from practice, not from desire. Her red hair, somewhat darker than Adelaide's, fell to just below her shoulders around her round and gentle face. She was the type of woman whose voice was soft in all manner of conversation, but whose sharp reprimands could put military personnel to shame. She wore a navy-blue dress that fell to her ankles, with a slit halfway up one side for just the right amount of intrigue.

Adelaide's sister, Maaya guessed, looked every part their daughter. She had gotten her father's hair, a wavy light blonde that she had with some effort put into a ponytail and adorned with tiny silver chains. She wore a slender maroon dress that contrasted her sky-blue eyes, which were bright with mirth.

As Adelaide and Maaya stepped in, Maaya worried that all conversation would cease and that they would be left in awkward silence, but Maaya's father beckoned them over quickly, standing up at once to greet his daughter. He hugged her tight and planted a kiss on each cheek, then held her at the shoulders as he stared into her eyes. This, Maaya thought, was love, and oh did she desire it so very much.

"My little Adelaide, it's so wonderful you've made it here. You look amazing as always. Life at sea treating you well? No trouble in your delays, I hope?"

"Only minor delays from weather, that's all, and you know I wouldn't let something as small as that get in the way of seeing you," Adelaide said cheerfully, though Maaya thought she detected the slightest hint of reservation. "How are you? How is everyone?"

"Oh, we're doing well. Just tired, you know, from all the traveling," her father continued as he stepped back to allow Adelaide's mother and sister room. "We were all over the northern province picking up orders and trying to meet with some of our more stubborn family, you know how it goes."

"An absolute mess, that's what it all was, until the last few days," Adelaide's mother broke in after a more formal hug. "The train broke down twice on the way up, it was terribly cold, and we tried three times—three!—

to meet with your aunt and uncle, but they always seemed to be busy. Then we found out your uncle's father had just recently fallen seriously ill, and so the family weren't even in the area the entire time."

"Oh, goodness. Is he okay?" Adelaide asked, while at the same time pulling her sister into a tight hug and lifting her an inch off the ground, much to her sister's protest.

"Seems to be. He'd gone to a hospital for serious pain in his chest, but they eventually found out he was just cheating on his diet. No one's ever been able to convince that man to stop eating chocolate," Adelaide's mother sniffed.

"But everyone's alive and well, and they said they'd love to make it down for the wedding, and to see *you*, of course," Adelaide's sister said. Now that they were standing next to each other, Adelaide had only a small advantage in height. "How's life, you dunce?"

"All the better now you're back in it, you egg," Adelaide retorted with a grin.

"I can feel the love," Adelaide's father chuckled. "Now let's sit and eat before the food gets—oh, hold on just a moment now, we have a guest! I've completely forgotten, how rude of me."

He walked over to Maaya and extended his hand politely. She shook it quickly, suddenly nervous again now that they had all noticed her standing there. Adelaide's mother and sister were soon to follow, and they were all smiles as they did so.

"My name is Felix Sol, this is my wife Cajsa, and our youngest daughter Marit. It's such a pleasure to meet you; Adelaide hasn't brought a friend home in so long."

"Maaya Sahni. Thank you so much for having me here with you tonight," Maaya replied, hoping she sounded confident. Then she turned to Adelaide. "Your last name is Sol?"

"Yeah! Fitting, in'nit?" Adelaide answered proudly.

"You have a lovely accent. Where are you from?" Cajsa asked as they took their seats.

"I'm… from Selenthia, actually," she started. This was not the way she had intended to start the evening. "From a place called Sark, if you know it. I'd spent my life there until I met Adelaide."

"Ah, I see! How interesting," Felix replied genuinely, though he sounded slightly disappointed. Cajsa didn't say a word, but her lips held the faint lines of a grimace. "Terrible business, what's going on in the world between our countries, you know."

"Yes, it's sad. I'd like to see all this put behind us," Maaya answered diplomatically.

"You can say that again," Marit nodded, raising her glass slightly. "Anyway, how'd you two meet over there?"

"I was in Levien, and I wasn't used to the docks; I fell over and Adelaide started teasing me," Maaya answered, smiling at the thought.

"Really? Is that how you meet all your friends, Adelaide? By making fun of them?" Marit chuckled.

"On the contrary, I'm still doing that thing where I give someone a compliment every day, especially if they look like they could really use it. By the way, I love what you've done with your hair," Adelaide shot back, and Marit bowed her head slightly, covering her grin with her hand.

"I was new in Levien, and apparently it was obvious, so she invited me to lunch. It was a very nice introduction to a new city," Maaya continued, already trying with great difficulty to keep a straight face.

"Ah, so you got around a bit, that's nice," Felix said, looking slightly relieved. Maaya could only assume that, in his eyes, the ability travel meant wealth—and to be fair, under normal circumstances, he wouldn't be wrong. "What do you do in Selenthia?"

"Just give him the answer you gave the street vendor in Sark," Saber said quietly. "You were an independent contractor. If you want to spice it up a bit, say you were trusted with very specialized jobs that dealt with the security of the town."

When Maaya relayed this information, the other three looked impressed.

"That's not bad for someone your age. Where did your parents send you to school? It must have been impressive," Cajsa continued.

"I, uh…"

"She was educated and trained privately," Adelaide broke in smoothly. "There's a good reason for that, which I'll get to in a moment, but that's why she was in a quiet place like Sark. She needed to be somewhere isolated and quiet."

"Whatever for?" Cajsa asked in surprise.

"Well, as it turns out, Maaya here is actually quite an expert with *libris*," Adelaide finished with emphasis.

All eyes were on Maaya now, and any trace of disappointment their gazes might have previously conveyed was gone. Maaya swallowed anxiously.

"Are you really? Now that's quite fascinating," Cajsa said, her eyes now alight with interest.

"Oh, very," Adelaide continued. "So now you see why she had to keep things private; Selenthia isn't nearly as friendly when it comes to *libris* as we are."

"I should say not! It's a travesty. Backwards, really, the whole society," Felix said suddenly. "No offense, of course. But I imagine that's why you're here, yes? To continue your studies?"

"Actually… it's something else," Maaya said slowly. "When I was in Selenthia I met a man from Krethus. He worked in the government studying the ghosts and trying to figure out a way to get rid of them. Shortly before he arrived I started seeing the ghosts in my town, too. So once he told me what was going on, I thought… I thought I might come here to see what I could do."

"The ghosts have reached Selenthia? That far? Oh, stars…" Cajsa breathed. "That must have given you an awful fright; Selenthians are so underprepared for something like this."

"It wasn't so bad," Maaya responded, slightly defensively. "Any of the ones that showed up in my town, I destroyed. But I learned they'd just keep coming, that I'd have to get rid of them at the source if I really wanted to keep my town safe."

"I admire your goal, even if it is lofty," Felix said. "Getting here alone must have been a challenge considering we technically aren't allowed to travel to each other's borders. I congratulate you for making it this far, however."

"Unfortunately, Adelaide must have told you by now what the situation is and why it cannot be fixed," Cajsa said, a note of genuine sadness in her voice. "Had we known of a solution at any point up until now we would have stopped this problem a long, long time ago. Selenthia's best hope for survival is to take advantage of those who know *libris*. It's not perfect, but we adapt, as we always have."

"Ah, yes, most unfortunate," Felix continued. "On that note, will you be staying with us for a time or heading back?"

"I'm staying," Maaya replied firmly. She didn't like the way they were talking to her. It was sad, almost condescending, as though the problem was both the impossibility of the situation and her own inability to fix it.

"Actually…" Adelaide began, toying with her fork, "we thought we might go try to destroy the machine together."

Now all eyes were on Adelaide, who seemed no worse for wear under their intense stares.

"You want to what?" Marit asked, dumbfounded. "You're going to try that again, are you?"

"Again?" asked Maaya and Saber in unison.

"Later," Adelaide stated, then continued undeterred. "You know I wouldn't try unless I thought I had a good shot at it. I wouldn't just go try to make the same mistakes I made last time. This time I'm pretty confident we can make it."

"That's… certainly ambitious," Cajsa said thoughtfully, a glint of anticipation in her eyes now. "What's your plan? Even if Maaya here is adept as *libris* as you say—"

"Are you better than Adelaide?" Marit asked Maaya hopefully. "Did you learn some secret tricks in Selenthia to give you an advantage?"

"Talk yourself up enough to avoid disappointing them, but remember Adelaide's request," Saber instructed, winking at the red-haired girl.

"Unfortunately not. I was the best in my town, and I can hold my own for a little while against her, but she's the strongest between us," Maaya explained.

Marit looked disappointed, but Felix clapped his hands.

"I hope you take no offense to this, Maaya, but I am quite proud of my daughter's skills for being able to best someone so talented as yourself."

"Oh, not at all. I really hope I'll be able to learn from her as we go," Maaya said, and Felix nodded approvingly.

"Hopefully there will be just enough for both of you to learn from each other. Like I say, if you're the smartest person in the room, you're in the wrong room. Now then, what about this Krethan fellow you met? Did he come back with you?"

"He, uhm—"

"He stayed behind to conduct a little more field research. To find out the severity of the problem, the time between pulses, that sort of thing," Adelaide interrupted. "He wants to see if that can tell us how fast the radius is spreading."

"Oh, heavens. Is he safe there by himself with no eyes for ghosts?" Cajsa asked, her eyes widening.

"He had— er, he *has* an ocular implant that lets him see the ghosts," Maaya answered uncomfortably, and her heart sank. "He should be fine."

"Ah, good. I should have guessed our government wouldn't just send him into dangerous territory unprepared," Felix grunted approvingly.

"Now, dear, will you be needing any assistance for this new venture of yours? Passage, money, anything else?" Cajsa asked casually, as though these were resources she assigned away every day. She probably did, Maaya thought in retrospect.

"Thank you, but no. I've already got it all taken care of. A few of my officers have already made contact with the government to secure passage and have taken care of all the broad details. We'll be going over the rest later, but I've been assured the most important things are already secured."

"I see… well I'm glad you're self-sufficient," Cajsa said, and though her voice kept its pleasantness, she seemed dissatisfied.

"I just didn't want to concern you, that's all. Not with my little sister's big plans in the works," Adelaide smiled, smooth as ever. "Speaking of which, give me some details! What have I missed?"

"Well, it's all going very well," Marit answered, and to Maaya's surprise, she suddenly sounded more reserved. "Vilmar is staying with his parents for a few weeks while we all get our affairs in order. We don't have an exact date yet, that much is still true, but we're hoping for sometime five or six months from now. Right when spring hits, you know, so all the trees will be turning green, the weather will be nice and warm…"

"So what's he like now it's coming down to it?" Adelaide pressed eagerly. "You get to know a lot about a person when they're under stress."

"Oh, I'm not sure he's ever felt stressed in his life," Marit answered. It didn't sound like a compliment. "He's not quite as hands on about all this as I'd like, but then again I've heard that's the case with a lot of husbands. Isn't that right, mum?"

Cajsa smiled, but didn't say a word.

"Well, I'm excited to finally meet him," Adelaide continued. Maaya thought she detected a flicker of concern in her voice. "I'm excited for you, sis. The time leading up to the big day will be kind of intense, but it'll all be worth it, I'm sure."

"Thank you," Marit returned warmly. "Though that would mean slightly more if you had similar experience under your belt. No offense."

"That's fair. I am the older sister! I should be the one telling you all about my knowledge, the lessons I've learned… things of that sort. I'm not entirely lacking in romantic experience, though, so I'll offer what I can."

"Oh really? Who's the last person you really felt anything for? And actually confessed to, at that?" Marit continued compellingly.

"Don't be silly, Marit. She visits her love all the time," Felix chuckled. "What was her name? Windfire?"

Adelaide snorted as Marit and Felix shared a grin.

"Windfire and I have a close but purely professional relationship. If you want to know who I'm really interested in, think about who I went through all the effort to bring to dinner."

It took a moment for Adelaide's comment to sink in, but when it did, Maaya choked on the water she had just been sipping. Saber patted her back gently as she quickly regained her composure, dabbing at her eyes with her napkin.

"Don't go teasing her like that, dear. She needs to become more familiar with your sense of humor first," Cajsa scolded lightly. "Really, you've broken a few hearts that way. Are you currently seeing anyone, Maaya?"

"I, uh… no, not right now," Maaya replied, forcing a smile. Adelaide was smiling at her, but she couldn't tell what it meant. Had that really been what it was? A joke?

"That's probably best, what with you traveling so far away, and for who knows how long," Cajsa said airily. "But I'm sure you would have the hand of anyone you liked after you return. You're making an honorable effort, and any smart young man or woman would notice."

The rest of dinner passed smoothly, and Maaya supposed that she enjoyed herself, though if she were to be entirely honest, she didn't remember much of what happened after that. She was moderately sure she took part in conversation, and was vaguely aware of the desserts that came out after dinner, and was even mostly certain that they tasted good, but a haze hung over her mind. Her heart pounded so loudly in her chest she was worried the others would notice and ask who could possibly be walking loudly upstairs at this hour.

And so she took part in conversation for the rest of their meal, and afterward while they lounged about and simply talked. About what, Maaya couldn't remember, but she did eventually realize she no longer needed Saber's guidance and that Adelaide's family seemed to genuinely enjoy her company.

All the while, she both dreaded and couldn't wait for the end of dinner. While she couldn't remember much else from their dinner, as everyone's words seemed to go in one ear and out the other, she remembered Adelaide's words with perfect clarity, as well as the calmness and confidence with which she had spoken them. It was so like Adelaide to talk that way even about something so serious, and even in a situation that requested more tact than she was willing to give… but that was her sense of humor as well. Her jokes were delivered straight to the point and with a smile, so much like every truth she ever told.

Maaya almost jumped as she suddenly felt Saber's arm on her shoulder, and her low voice in her ear.

"I know you know this already, but you should talk to her tonight. This opportunity isn't just presenting itself, it's throwing itself at your feet and begging."

Maaya nodded imperceptibly, then straightened up. She was overthinking things, as she often did. Regardless of what Adelaide had meant, she would soon find out. Everything she had felt and wondered and feared and hoped would be answered soon enough.

After what felt like an eternity, dinner was over. Everyone stood up and hugged one another as a uniformed man bustled in to begin clearing the table, and to Maaya's relief, the family made a great effort to include her as well.

"It was just wonderful to meet you, dear," Cajsa expressed warmly. "I'm glad Adelaide has a friend like you in the world. I look forward to seeing you again, even if you must be rushing off."

"It was great to meet you, too," Maaya replied, and she meant it. While Adelaide's family might have their points of disagreement, as well as certain ideologies Maaya had trouble accepting without comment, this was family. This was what it meant to have a family, to love, and to be loved. In that moment Maaya felt a pang in her heart, one she had never felt before. It was the pain of loss, but for someone she had never met. "I'll definitely be around for at least a little while."

"Have a good night, my loves," Felix said jovially. "I'm off downtown early tomorrow morning, so don't fret if you don't see me around."

"G'night, dad," Adelaide said, kissing him on the cheek. "I expect to be home tomorrow, but two of my officers will be with me and we'll be working pretty heavily. But oh! Before I forget… are you still friends with that painter from the next town over? What was his name… Demryn?"

"Ah, yes, that's the one. We haven't spoken in a few months, but that's the norm with our busy schedules. Why?"

"Could you ask him to come over tomorrow for a job? I'll pay him extra for travel and the short notice, but it's kind of important."

Felix looked somewhat taken aback, but nodded earnestly.

"Of course. Anything for you, my love."

The rest of the family finished their goodbyes, and before long it was just Saber, Adelaide, and Maaya. Maaya opened her mouth to speak, but Adelaide gently took her by the arm, leading her out the door and toward the stairs.

"If it's important, let's wait until we're somewhere a little more private."

They headed wordlessly upstairs and down the hall. The silence bore down upon her suddenly, the weight of all her unspoken words almost too much to bear. She hoped Saber would say something, anything, but the ghost was silent and expressionless.

When they reached Maaya's bedroom, Adelaide let herself in, and Maaya followed. Then, Adelaide glanced at Saber almost apologetically.

"Could we have a moment, please? I won't be long."

"Of course," Saber said immediately, then turned away and floated through the wall.

Adelaide turned back to Maaya, but before she could say a word, Maaya spoke.

"Did you mean it? Did you mean what you said?" she asked softly. She had meant to sound much firmer in her request, but now that they were actually here, it was harder to follow through.

The smile partly faded from Adelaide's lips, and she opened her mouth to speak, but no words came out. After a few moments, she sighed, then walked over and sat on the bed. Maaya remained where she was, uncertain if this was an appropriate time to try to comfort her or to be more determined in her demand for answers.

"This is where it gets a little hard for me. You're a wonderful friend, Maaya. I've really loved spending time with you and getting to know you, training with you—"

"That doesn't answer the question," Maaya interrupted hesitantly.

"Right. Look, I… I'm sorry. I guess I wasn't as clear as I tried to be, and now I've created confusion where I really didn't want to. I didn't mean to string you along or anything, so…" Adelaide stood up again and walked over to Maaya, then placed both hands on her shoulders. "Regardless of what my mother says about my sense of humor, I want you to know I would never lie about something like this. I've been saying this all along, only this time I mean it in more than just a friendly way, and I hope you understand what I mean when I say that I really, *really* like you."

Maaya froze. Adelaide's last words immediately began echoing through her mind, which immediately began analyzing every enunciation, every movement of her lips as she had spoken them. Maaya was floored. These were the words she had dreamed of hearing for many nights now. Was this actually happening?

Suddenly, she realized she should probably say something. Adelaide was staring at her and starting to look uncomfortable, but when Maaya tried to speak, she could only stutter. A million possible responses and questions all fought to be first, but Maaya's brain had completely locked up. And so, when she finally managed to speak, she could only say one word.

"Why?"

Even as this one syllable left her mouth, she chastised herself, already hearing Saber's voice in the back of her mind. *Oh, good response, very good! Not, 'Oh that's so romantic,' or, 'I like you too.' No, you went with 'Why.' Honestly, Maaya, it's like you're trying to fail.*

Adelaide sighed and stepped away, pacing nervously.

"I know. It's kind of strong, isn't it? I really didn't want to make you uncomfortable, especially if you don't feel the same way, it's just… it's not any one thing, you know? I've been thinking about it, trying to see if there's one thing in particular. I wanted to know so I could tell you just that, but… it's just you! You as a person, as a whole, everything about who you are. It's everything all the way up to how whenever you leave I'm stuck thinking about you until I see you again. Sure, we have things in common, which is a great start, but it's the way we bonded so quickly, the way you understand me without judging me, and I mean *really* understand. It's your open mind and open heart and the way you smile and laugh and want to do good for the world, your optimism and bravery, the way you can go from giving me a passionate speech on how the world should be to telling me off for buying you lunch. It's just… you."

Maaya wished that Saber were there to translate her stunned expression and helplessly malfunctioning vocal cords to a clearly distraught Adelaide. It was starting to sink in. The more Adelaide went on, the more Maaya was beginning to realize this was the real thing. It was actually happening. This was the moment she had been hoping for, the one she thought would never come because she was too afraid to start it herself—and it was going to pass her by if she didn't do something.

Adelaide wrung her hands, looking extremely apologetic.

"Stars, I'm so sorry. I went way too far, didn't I? We had a good thing going and I guess I maybe read more into it than I—"

She broke off as Maaya suddenly stepped over to her and took Adelaide's hands in hers. Maaya stared up at the taller girl, and then, with every last semblance of bravery and arguably foolishness she could muster, she stood on tiptoe and gave her a quick kiss on the cheek.

"Hush. I was just about to tell you the same thing."

That was all it took. A look of shock passed over Adelaide's face, followed closely by relief, and then utter joy.

Maaya still had so much to say and so much to ask—as she was sure Adelaide did as well—but all her words were lost to the moment as they kissed. It was so simple a thing, and even held remnants of their uncertainty and awkwardness, but these she could ignore. It was unlike anything Maaya had ever expected, and yet still so much like what she had always dismissed as just stories. There was no way real life could ever match the pages in her books; that was what she used to think. It was all artistry, all made up by wordsmiths who took a dull concept and turned it into poetry, the hopeless ones lost in the throes of young love who thought every first kiss was a sign of forever. There was no way a simple touching of lips could mean that much.

And yet, here she was, feeling as though she would never have to talk again, because everything she could ever hope to say, even had she an eternity to place every word in perfect order, would still fall miserably short of what she was saying right now without speaking at all. *Really,* a thought muttered quietly from the depths of her mind, *the stories don't do this justice at all.*

When they broke apart and stared at each other again, Maaya felt like she was seeing Adelaide for the first time. There was a new understanding between them, one that didn't need to be clarified or reaffirmed in any other way than by the words Adelaide had so bravely spoken—the ones Maaya knew she would soon return in kind.

"Really? You were going to do that tonight?" Adelaide asked, looking barely able to contain her excitement.

"I was! You're going to think I'm silly, but I've been trying to figure out how to tell you I liked you for days and days now. Saber started threatening to tell you herself if I didn't do it quick enough. But after you said what you did at dinner… well, I thought it was now or never."

"I'm sorry about that, really," Adelaide laughed, scratching the back of her head awkwardly. "I didn't mean to put you on the spot, it's just… I only ever know how to be straightforward with everyone. I can't do subtleties; I don't really understand how they work. I suppose I knew my parents might think I was joking since I was being so direct, which is part of why I said it, but I guess I also hoped they would believe me. Ask questions, you know? And if they seemed like they were into it, then… well, the next step would be to talk to you. But I guess the first step should have been to just talk to you first, huh?"

"To be fair, if I didn't already have some clue when you got me dressed up to take me to dinner with your parents, you might've wanted to rethink how much you were into me," Maaya laughed, and Adelaide snickered. "Speaking of having a clue, I should go get Saber… she's going to want to tell me she told me so."

Maaya practically skipped over to the door and opened it quickly, looking out to see Saber floating lazily nearby, peering uninterestedly at a painting on the wall. When Saber caught her eye, it took only a moment for the ghost to catch the expression on Maaya's face, and she grinned broadly.

Not bothering to fly all the way to the door, she passed through the wall, then stopped before Adelaide and Maaya, crossing her arms innocently.

"Sorry, did you need me for something?"

"I… we, I mean, have to tell you something," Maaya started, but paused as Saber held up her hand.

"Well, it will have to wait. As luck would have it, I need to be off. Super important ghost business, you see, and I'll be out for a few hours at the least. Considering how late an hour it is, the two of you had better spend your evening alone with each other. So very unlucky I can't join you, but I'm sure you'd only be talking about boring things anyway—unless something I have absolutely no knowledge of just happened. If it did, you'll have to fill me in tomorrow when you're both rested. Okay?"

"Oh, my. That is unfortunate. Not to mention incredibly spontaneous," Adelaide replied seriously. "You must be in a rush, so I won't keep you, but I do want to let you know that if anything *did* happen, it likely went very well."

Saber nodded in understanding, then flashed them both a quick wink before floating over to the door leading outside. Just before she disappeared into the night, she turned back to glance and Maaya and said, "Oh. Yes, I did tell you so, didn't I?"

Before Maaya could respond, Saber had dashed outside and out of sight. Maaya and Adelaide stared at the door she disappeared through for a moment before Adelaide walked hesitantly over to Maaya's side.

"So, here's the thing. I spent all my time figuring out how to confess to you, so I have absolutely no idea what to do now."

Maaya laughed.

"I think I have an idea. Come outside with me?"

Maaya opened the door and stepped out onto porch, followed closely by Adelaide, who shut the door with a quiet *click* behind her. Maaya placed her hands on the ornate metal railing and stared up at the sky. The storm clouds had started to clear, exposing wide areas of the vast starlit expanse behind them. She closed her eyes, enjoying the soft ocean-scented breeze on her face. Adelaide stood by her side, and in that moment Maaya felt closer to her than she had ever been before. To her surprise, her nervousness had all but completely abated; now, somehow, she felt comfortable, or at the very least surer of herself than she'd ever been.

"Before tonight, you once told me why I was special to you. Now that we're here… I want to have a chance to do the same thing."

"Oh, so that's how this is going to go. I'm glad it's dark out so you can't see how red my face is."

Maaya grinned.

"When we first met, I thought I wanted to be just like you. You're so confident, outgoing, optimistic… everything I wished I was. But I realized that wasn't quite right; it's more that you make me want to be a better person. You sort of gave me a purpose beyond just what I'm fighting for. That's all my life was, just doing what had to be done, but now I can focus on more than that. Being around you brings out the best in me, and I love that about you. I think that's how it should be, you know? It's not just about how you feel about another person, but how you feel about yourself when you're around them. And when I'm with you… I've never felt better."

"You know, I think that's an amazing way to look at it," Adelaide said, and she broke her gaze from the moon to stare at Maaya. "I think that's part of why I was so eager to meet you. Back in Levien I had been walking around that morning, and when I saw you… I knew you were the one I had to speak to that day. And the reason for that is because the thought of talking to you absolutely terrified me."

Maaya stared back, then burst into laughter.

"What? Terrified you?"

"Yes!" Adelaide replied, slightly flustered. "Remember how I said I started giving a compliment to one person each day to help me get better at speaking and feeling braver? Before that morning, I was feeling pretty good about myself; I could walk up to most people I saw and start chatting no problem. But then you came along, and when I saw you at first my heart just sort of fluttered with nerves. It was that feeling I used to get all the time when I'd look at someone I thought was way out of my league, the kind of person I'd go out of my way to talk to so I could get over that feeling."

"Me, out of your league? Please, now you *must* be lying," Maaya teased.

"I'm serious! I couldn't put my finger on why at first. I mean, it's not like you've got an imposing figure or anything." Adelaide laughed as Maaya lightly smacked her arm while trying and failing to look irritated. "But then, as I got closer, I realized it was the look in your eye. You were someone who knew what you wanted, who would go through hell and back to get it, and who probably already had. You had the natural confidence that I struggled for years to even pretend to have. You were where I could only dream of being, because once you get past my act, that's it. But you? That's who you are as a person, who you are every day, and I thought you'd see right through me. And that's why I had to make you the person I talked to that day."

Maaya's cheeks burned. To hear that she came off that way to someone like Adelaide was one of the best compliments she'd ever gotten, even if Adelaide hadn't intended it that way. Her first instinct was to deny it, to say that she was pretending too. But then, she thought, there could be different types of confidence. Maybe Maaya wasn't all too sure of herself like Adelaide was, and maybe she avoided people rather than seeking them out on purpose, but she was definitely confident in her principles and her goals. She hadn't made it this far because she was a timid and frightened person who had just gotten lucky through it all. Before their battle at sea, Saber had reminded her that being brave didn't mean not being afraid—which was good, because Maaya was unquestionably afraid. But here she was all the same, where others had tried and failed to reach.

"I think you gave me too much credit," Maaya said finally. "But there's a reason I didn't see through you… there's nothing to see through. What you're doing isn't an act. It may have been when you started, but it's not anymore. I've seen the way you talk to your crew, to your friends, to your family, to *me*. I might be naïve about some things, but you are right; if you were just acting I probably would have seen it right away, and that's because I've known so many people who did just that."

"Uh huh, okay. You didn't even realize I was hitting on you for a whole week."

"And you couldn't even tell I liked you back!"

"Neither could *you* from the sound of things!"

They devolved into fits of giggles, and Adelaide pulled Maaya close, kissing the top of her head as she had done before. They breathed deep the night air and silence fell, the comforting silence Maaya knew so well.

They stayed out on the porch until the moon had risen high and started to fall, and while at first they focused on the night sky while they sought courage to speak what secrets remained in their hearts, after only a short while they had eyes only for each other. They spent the night and early morning hours in each other's arms, some spent in silence while others were spent sharing so much Maaya thought she would run out of air in her lungs before she could finish talking. And then, when their words were temporarily spent, they kissed instead, each time becoming more familiar and delighted with the feeling.

At last, and only when they could hardly keep their eyes open, they decided it was time for bed. Sunrise was a few hours away yet, but Maaya soon remembered that when the next day came they would be getting back to work on the task at hand. For the first time since she had spotted the single ghost on the river with Styx and the others, she had forgotten that the rest of the world and the ghosts within it even existed, and she marveled that any one person had the power to do that to her. Still, it was about time they got back on track.

They shuffled sleepily back in to Maaya's room together, hand in hand as they had been for hours, and Maaya glanced longingly at the bed she was soon to sleep in. Adelaide led her over to it, but though Maaya invited her to sit, she refused.

"If I sit down I won't get back up," Adelaide said, a yawn breaking her smile. "I don't know how I'll manage to get up early tomorrow. Or later today, as it were."

"Sleep in a little, just this once. It's a great feeling," Maaya persuaded, and Adelaide put her finger to her chin thoughtfully.

"I suppose I could give myself an extra hour or two. I mean, I have an excuse; it's not like all this happens every night, does it? Anyway, you can relax as you'd like, but the sooner you join us the better; we've got lots to plan and we definitely need your input."

"We?" Maaya asked.

"Inga and Halvar are coming with us, at least to start. We won't be able to get the rest of the way without their help. We'll especially need Saber on the same page, too. I'm getting even more tired just thinking about it."

"Yeah… I'm definitely ready to call it a night," Maaya murmured, and she was just about to collapse onto her bed when she realized she was still wearing her nice dress. "Oh, uh, could you…?"

Adelaide chuckled and helped Maaya zip down the back of her dress. Maaya slipped off her shoes, then stretched, almost immediately regretting it as a wave of drowsiness bordering on dizziness nearly overwhelmed her.

"See you tomorrow then?" Adelaide said, and Maaya nodded happily. "I can't wait. Sweetest of dreams to you, and… thank you. For tonight, and for all of this."

They shared one last quick kiss, and then Adelaide departed, smiling once at Maaya before shutting the door quietly behind her.

Maaya immediately stepped out of her dress and let down her hair, running her comb quickly through it to smooth it out before getting into bed. She was vaguely aware of a slight pain in her cheeks, the kind that came from a smile that just wouldn't go away, and the thought certainly did nothing to make it stop any faster.

I can't believe it, a voice said in her mind, the same one that had said the same thing at least once every hour the entire evening. Even after all this time she only knew she was awake from her near certainty that she never felt this tired in any of her dreams. Still, she thought, all the more reason the morning couldn't come soon enough.

As Saber hadn't yet returned, Maaya decided to wait to see her until morning. And for the first time in a long, long time, she didn't think even once of all the dangers and sorrows of the world as she drifted off to sleep.

29

THE WAR ROOM

When Maaya awoke later that morning, she was vaguely aware of someone shaking her gently by the shoulders. She opened her eyes blearily to see Saber floating above her, looking relieved.

"Good, I thought you'd never wake up. I would have let you sleep longer, but it's almost midday and everyone's been up and ready for a while now. I thought you might want to join them before it gets too late. Also, I heard my name brought up a few times and I'm getting impatient to see what's going on."

Maaya sat bolt upright in bed.

"It's that late? And they're already all together? For how long?"

"Only an hour, I'd say. They would have gotten started sooner, but Adelaide accidentally fell asleep on Inga's shoulder and got sent back to bed for a nap. What in the world did you two *do* last night?"

"We were up late talking, that's all," Maaya said, getting out of bed and picking through the pile of clothes she hadn't yet put away. "I figured you'd wake me up when it was time for everyone to meet."

"I am ever your loyal alarm clock," Saber quipped.

"Sorry. What did you do, anyway?" Maaya asked as she pulled on a pair of pants and short-sleeved shirt.

"The usual. Exploring! I've only really had one night to do that so far, so there's still so much I'm missing. This won't get old for a while; it'll be a shame when we have to leave. But that's not important. You need to tell me *everything* about last night."

"Didn't you just say you were impatient to see what the others were talking about?" Maaya continued meaningfully, raising an eyebrow.

"Not enough to miss this. Go on, start talking."

Maaya stared at the door, then grumbled.

"Fine. But only for a few minutes. We really need to get down there."

Maaya sat back on her bed and began recounting the events of the previous night as she brushed her hair. Saber listened intently, and by the time Maaya finished her story, she looked positively delighted.

"I'd planned to tease you, but after hearing all this I'm just so happy it all went well. This is the most disgustingly romantic story I've heard in a long time. You know, I never expected her to be as clueless as you when it came to this sort of thing; you two must have been the only ones on the entire ship who weren't aware you'd fallen head over heels for each other."

"Yes, well, we got there eventually," Maaya retorted, her cheeks flushing ever so slightly. "Anyway, I'm just looking forward to you not pressuring me to confess to her anymore."

"Oh, I wouldn't get too comfortable. There's still marriage to think about, you know," Saber joked, and Maaya rolled her eyes.

A few minutes later they headed downstairs, Saber leading the way to a large room at the side of the house with floor-to-ceiling windows and a sunken sitting area around which a number of incredibly comfortable sofas were positioned. Some of these had evidently been moved in order to face a low wide table between them. The table was scattered with a few maps and notepads, though Maaya wasn't close enough to see what was written on any of them.

Adelaide, Inga, and Halvar were already there, as well as another man Maaya didn't recognize. He sat somewhat apart from the rest of the group, looking bored. He was a portly well-dressed man with neatly combed hair, a pair of wire-rim spectacles, and a bushy mustache. When Maaya and Saber entered the room he suddenly sat up in complete surprise. At first Maaya didn't understand what about her arrival could have shocked him so much, but then Saber drew in a quiet breath beside her.

"Oh. That one can see me."

"Well, good morning, you two!" Adelaide said cheerfully, springing up from her position on the sofa to greet them. She gave Maaya a quick hug and then stepped back to gesture to the stranger. "This is Demryn. He's a long-time friend of the family and an excellent painter. He's been working with realism for, what, thirty years now?"

"Thirty-two, if you can believe it," Demryn said, unable to take his eyes off Saber. "Is this the one?"

"She is indeed. Her name is Saber, and she's a good friend of Maaya's.

Er, that's her, by the way," Adelaide said, nodding to Maaya. "Anyway, what do you think?"

"I think I've never had so fascinating a subject in all my years," Demryn replied, carefully looking Saber up and down.

"Someone explain what's going on before I break this man's nose," Saber said, narrowing her eyes at him.

Demryn stepped back immediately, clearing his throat nervously.

"Ah, I'm sorry, Saber," Adelaide jumped in quickly. "I wanted this to be a bit of a surprise which is why I didn't mention anything until I was sure Demryn would be here. As you can obviously tell, Demryn can see ghosts, and he's also an amazing painter. What I'd like to do—with your permission, of course—is commission him to paint your portrait."

"Why? Not that I necessarily mind, but this seems an odd thing to do when we have so many more important tasks to focus on."

"True, but this isn't just to give you something to hang in your foyer," Adelaide smiled. "I know you've been trying to discover your past identity. As of yet there are no cameras that can reveal ghosts to those who can't already see them, and in order to discover who you once were, the experts will need to know what you look like. Thus, I've asked Demryn to get a portrait of you. What do you think?"

Saber's eyes widened in shock.

"You… you would do that for me?" she asked slowly.

"Absolutely I would," Adelaide replied instantly. "I know we're here for the machine, but there's no reason we can't do this as well. This is important to you, so it's important to me."

"I… I don't… thank you," Saber said, looking completely stunned. "What do I need to do?"

"Mostly just stay still until I'm finished," Demryn offered, hesitantly stepping closer.

"You think you can handle that, Saber?" Maaya teased.

"Are you kidding? I would do a lot more than that if it means figuring out who I was," Saber said joyfully. "All right, Demryn. Lead the way and show me your skills."

"O-of course, miss," Demryn said, turning and leading the way back toward the hall.

When they disappeared, Adelaide guided Maaya over to the sofa where she had been sitting, and no sooner were they sitting down than she gave Maaya a very obvious kiss on the cheek.

"So, my darling, how did you sleep?" she said, smiling at the look at Maaya's face.

"I think it's safe to assume everyone knows, then?" Maaya asked, embarrassed.

"She wouldn't shut up about it this morning," Halvar chuckled. "If there's anyone you want to break the news to first, better get on it before Adelaide tells everyone on the continent."

"Don't be silly. She can have Selenthia if she wants," Adelaide said airily. "But alas, business calls; time is short. Inga, Halvar, how go your efforts?"

It was Halvar who spoke first, his tone suddenly as businesslike as Maaya had ever heard.

"I've been in contact with our representatives, and while they can't offer any direct assistance, they did say we'll have secure passage all the way to Nalmar. We've got a train route already prepared and they're in the process of informing everyone on the line. In the meantime,they're sending a courier with our passes; they should be here by late evening."

"As of early this morning I've been assured we'll have half a dozen *libris*-capable Blackfins on site once we arrive in Nalmar. We have ten to twelve others who will be there to ensure our route is clear of any and all obstacles and to help provide backup if and when the machine goes down," added Inga.

"Not bad. They might not be elites, but that's definitely better than nothing," Adelaide mused.

"What are you talking about?" Maaya asked, completely lost.

"In short, we've been trying to figure out how to get to the machine and how many people to bring with us. We've established what route we're taking and to where, and roughly who's going to meet us there," Adelaide explained.

"We're looking at about three days' travel on the train, and then a decent walk on foot to the border of the radius," Halvar added.

"The radius?" Maaya said slowly. "I think Svante mentioned that once… he said that anyone who passes through it is killed instantly."

"That'd be it, though that's not *entirely* accurate," Adelaide said. "It's true that if you're inside the radius you'll probably die, but only if you're in there when a pulse hits. And a pulse is… well…"

"The radius isn't so much of a wall as it is a marker where it's not safe to be," Halvar offered helpfully. "Every so often the machine will send out a shockwave of sorts, emanating at the machine and extending until a certain point where it fades. That point almost never shifts, so we've taken to calling that point the radius. If you're outside it, pulses will fade before they hit you, and you're safe. If you're inside, you're dead."

"It also appears as though every time a new pulse is emitted, the radius expands just slightly. At the moment we're talking a matter of inches," Inga continued. "For that reason we have been trying to complete some calculations that will aid us in our strategizing."

"What kind of calculations do we need?" Maaya asked, intrigued, and stared down at the notepads that she could now see were covered in formulas and messy scribbled notes.

"Since we'll be passing through the radius we'll inevitably encounter at least a few pulses. We expect to be protected from the pulses by Saber's gem, but since we don't know how far her own protective aura spreads, it will help us to know how often the pulses occur and how quickly they move. The pulse frequency is more erratic than it used to be, we can make at least rough predictions by measuring the increase in the size of the radius in time, combined with how long a pulse takes to get from the center to the edge. It won't be perfect, but any little thing helps."

"Is there a way to figure out how much protection we can get from Saber?" Maaya continued, highly impressed.

"For that, we can only wait and see," Inga finished grimly. "There's also the possibility that, as we get closer to the machine, that protection may diminish. If that's the case, we will need to make a plan to accommodate for going in with fewer people than we expected."

"The good news is that once we've tested it a few times, we won't all need to be huddled together in fear the whole time; we just need to make sure we're together when a pulse hits," Adelaide said cheerfully.

"But the bad news is the likely small area of effect of Saber's protection means we can't bring many people with us inside, which is doubly bad considering there are bound to be machine-created ghosts swarming the place," Halvar grumbled.

Maaya gulped. She hadn't considered that part. Of course they wouldn't just get a free shot at the machine even with Saber's protection.

"I'd argue that's a good thing. If we have a small group that makes it easier to keep track of anyone, and if anyone gets stunned by one of the ghosts they won't get lost in a crowd," Adelaide countered. "We'll also be able to move more quickly."

"So… how big is this radius right now?" Maaya asked slowly.

Adelaide glanced down at one of the pages in front of her.

"At the moment, roughly twenty-five miles," she said. At Maaya's look of shock she continued hastily, "That's not bad! It's a two-day's walk if we hit some resistance, maybe a little less if we're lucky. And it's only within the past few years that it really started to expand, and it's still pretty slow."

"If you don't count the acceleration," Halvar said pointedly. "As of now it's only a an inch or two per pulse, but the amount it increases by goes up every time, too. You've seen what our calculations have found."

"We're going to destroy the machine by then so the calculations are irrelevant," Adelaide answered.

"Wait, what do the calculations say?" Maaya asked worriedly.

Halvar sighed.

"When the radius started expanding, it was almost imperceptible. When it was finally noticed and measured, scientists found that the amount by which it was increasing grew with every pulse. Double one, you get two. Double two, you get four, and so on. So right now it's not moving fast, but someday it will be. And based on what we've figured out, well…"

"Our estimates show that at its current rate of growth, the radius will circle the planet entirely in three years, give or take a few weeks," Inga finished.

Maaya felt her breath leave her. Three years? Was that really all it would take? With as long as the machine had been operating while the world struggled to exist despite it, she couldn't imagine only having three years left before it consumed everything. She hadn't even known it existed until she met Svante. She shuddered at the thought that Svante might never have made it to Sark, that she would have gone on with the rest of her life blissfully unaware of the machine's existence until it was too late.

"Does anyone know why it started expanding like that?" Maaya inquired uneasily.

"Not a clue. It was mostly steady for decades and decades, but then just a few years ago it suddenly started moving. As far as we could tell, nothing inside or outside changed; all we know is that it's moving," Halvar explained.

"Might it stop?" Maaya pressed.

"Maybe, but we have no frame of reference. Nothing like this has ever happened before."

"Again, irrelevant, because it will be destroyed long before then," Adelaide repeated firmly, glancing quickly at Maaya.

"Well, you definitely stand a better chance than last time, that's for sure," Halvar admitted.

"Oh, that's right… you never told me you had already tried once. What happened then?" Maaya asked, eager to move the subject away from how little time they had.

Adelaide sighed dejectedly.

"A whole lot of nothing is what. I wasn't given clearance at the time, so I snuck my way in. I thought I was good enough and fast enough to get in and destroy the machine before I was hit by a pulse. I felt unstoppable. I was an elite, after all. But I made it a mile or two in and destroyed a few dozen ghosts before my *libris* faded. Had it not been for a few officers who spotted me and got me out before the next pulse arrived, I… well, you can imagine."

"I… I'm sorry it didn't work out," Maaya said softly. "But you weren't hurt, right?"

"Mostly my pride. My family hasn't let me live it down since. They still take me seriously, but every so often they'll bring it up again just to remind me."

"That's not fair!" Maaya protested. "Haven't they seen what you're capable of? Don't they know how good you are?"

"Yeah, but they want to keep me grounded, I suppose. It's part of why I was so eager to escape them when I was younger; keeping me 'grounded' always meant kicking me down a peg whether it was deserved or not. Either way, once we succeed here I'm sure they'll never mention it again. And if they do, I'll be too happy to care."

"We'll definitely make it," Maaya smiled. "Especially now your government knows what you're trying to do and can help."

In response, Adelaide merely shrugged.

"The first part is true, but not the second; we're on our own on this one."

"What? Why?" Maaya asked in surprise. "Aren't they helping us get there? Can't they do anything else?"

"They're only helping because I'm an elite; most people don't even get transportation or approval. They're the last ones to provide help. I know it must sound silly, but please understand, we have people trying to go destroy the machine a few times a week. They're all absolutely miserable attempts, too, given how impervious it is. At first the government tried to sponsor anyone brave enough to try, but it was far too costly. To them this is just another attempt by a group of people who will fail before they've even started."

"But it's not! We have Saber, and—"

"And if they knew about Saber, they would immediately try to take over this mission, and to take her as well," Adelaide interrupted gently. "They would absolutely not let such a powerful tool be wasted by a group of, in their eyes, amateurs."

"Speaking of Saber, I believe there is one other thing we should discuss before any final decisions are made," Inga said meaningfully, and the others shared an uncomfortable glance.

"What is it?" Maaya asked, sounding almost impatient. Their expressions didn't bode well.

"You know our plan is to use Saber's gem to protect us as we proceed through the barrier, right?" Halvar said, and Maaya nodded. "Well, the thing is… er…"

He faltered, then broke off, staring at the floor with his mouth hanging open as he tried and failed to figure out how to explain himself.

"We aren't completely certain that Saber's gem will actually work," Adelaide sighed. "All the research, all the information, and all the experts who researched this say it will, and it sounds very convincing. It's just that nothing else has worked before, and there's only really one way to find out for sure if this will."

"What?!" Maaya sputtered. "So you're saying Saber could just disappear like all the others if she goes in there?"

"No! Well… I suppose what I'm saying is it's not completely outside the bounds of reason. We have no frame of reference, that's all. But everything we've read says it should work—"

Maaya scoffed.

"Yes, well, your government has had a hundred years to work on this and hasn't found a solution yet, so I don't see why I should put much faith in—"

"Maaya, please listen," Adelaide urged quietly. "This *is* the solution. I'm not saying success and failure are equally possible. All I'm saying is there is only a sliver of doubt so barely significant that I think it fair to mention. It's something Saber should factor into her decision. It's only fair to her. But beyond that, everything we know tells us it will work."

"Think of it this way," Halvar added. "You study *libris,* right? Say you read up on a new type of card. You know the design by heart, the theory makes sense, and the book is written by experts who have done it before. So you're pretty sure you can use it. The only thing is, even though you're almost completely sure, you can't *really* say it's a guarantee until you've tried it yourself. It's like that."

"Krethus would not have spent so long seeking the gem if we were not sure it would work. It's part of the machine's schematics—at least, what schematics were salvaged. We are confident it will work," Inga finished.

"I… I suppose. This just seems like a very dangerous possibility, and I don't want my friend to be put in danger," Maaya said uncertainly.

"That's understandable, which is why we thought to mention it. Saber will know too, and she can decide whether she wants to go or not. We won't make her; it's her choice," Adelaide said with an attempt at a comforting smile.

Maaya pursed her lips, then nodded begrudgingly.

"Right. Let's assume it will work, then. What about the other elites like you? Can't some of them help?" Maaya asked in frustration.

"Unlikely. There really aren't that many of us. They're all over Krethus at the moment; most are contracted out to protect important establishments or high-traffic areas. Remember, our work is most commonly defense, not offense, and there's an entire country for just a handful of people to protect."

Maaya spluttered in protest, then fell silent, fuming. It wasn't that she minded going with a small group of people—in fact, she agreed with Adelaide that it made things easier—but it was the principle of the thing. How could a government that wanted this machine gone so badly refuse to provide meaningful assistance to those willing to try? Adelaide was no amateur; she had been trained as one of the *libris* elites, she came from an old and powerful family, and she had an entire crew at her command. Surely that had to amount to something.

"Hey, we'll be all right," Adelaide said comfortingly, moving over to sit closer to Maaya. "To be honest, I didn't want any of their help anyway. If they tried to help they'd insist on being in charge, and… well, you know how I feel about that."

Maaya broke a small smile.

"I know. I'm just annoyed that your own government wouldn't even try to help you with something that's this important. You know they'll try to take the credit for all our work once we do it."

"I don't think they would. They're not always the brightest bunch, but they're not malicious," Adelaide replied.

"I hope so," Maaya sighed. "I guess I'm a little bitter at the thought of doing work other people can take credit for. When I was in Sark with the others that was an everyday thing."

"Ah, yes, the lovely Rahu," Adelaide said sourly, then cleared her throat, speaking louder to the room at large. "Halvar, Inga… may I have a moment with Maaya?"

The other two bowed slightly and then left the room, taking their paperwork with them.

"What's going on?" Maaya asked, staring around at the empty room before looking back at Adelaide.

"I just wanted to ask if you've had a chance to look at your friend's diary yet," Adelaide said gently.

"Oh… I… I haven't, no," Maaya admitted.

"Have you thought about it?"

"Not too much. I guess I've been too busy thinking about everything else," Maaya said uncertainly. "I'm still not sure if it's something I'm comfortable with. Even if she's not here anymore… she wrote it only for her to read, and she never told me otherwise."

Adelaide nodded.

"That's fine. In the end it's up to you; I just know how important she was to you, and since you have this piece of her with you I wanted to at least make sure it was something you thought about. We can't let these chances pass us by without thought, you know?"

"I know. Thank you," Maaya smiled.

"Speaking about thought… have you thought about going back to Sark when all this is over?" Adelaide continued.

"Oh, no. Never. Even if all of Selenthia didn't think I was a traitor and they let me back in, if I step one foot into Sark I'll be killed," Maaya said nervously.

"You don't know that. Maybe by then things will have changed. Once everyone here finds out what you've done it's only a matter of time before it spreads back home."

"You don't know Sark. It's so isolated that for a few years I thought it was the only place in the world. The people can be nice if they don't hate you, but they have no idea what's going on outside its walls. It's… it's an ignorant and scary place."

"What if you weren't alone?" Adelaide asked pointedly.

Maaya stared at her in shock.

"No, absolutely not! They would kill you too, they wouldn't care. You remember what they… what they did to Svante. Please… don't even think of such a thing. Don't make *me* think of it. When this is over we should stay as far away from there as we can," Maaya pleaded.

"Fair enough," Adelaide surrendered. "Though I'm still so curious about the place. It's where you spend most of your life, after all. I just want to hear more about it! Did you have other friends there besides the three you told me about? What else was it like? Indulge me just for a bit, won't you?"

She looked at Maaya with such an innocent and inquiring stare that Maaya couldn't help but laugh.

"Okay, fine. You know, apart from some of the people, it wasn't too bad. They were easily scared, but if I met someone who'd never heard of me before, they were nice. I had a few friends there too, yeah. Some were dead, but most were alive. There's Roshan, a friend I've had since I was little, and he's one of the best people I know. Then there's Sylvia, who's kind of strange, and she's always got a crow on her shoulder, but she was always friendly. She liked taking walks with us. Then there was Styx, and you will never meet a man with a bigger heart—or a bigger man in general, for that matter…"

Before she knew it she was explaining everything she could, from all the people she had gotten to know for better or worse, all the adventures she and her friends had been on, her favorite places in town, and how she had come by the nickname Ghost. She talked about how she had met Saber, how they had become friends so quickly, and how they had eventually found the others to eventually become The Ghost Hunters.

"Honestly, if things were a little different I probably would have stayed," finished Maaya with a sigh. "It wasn't perfect, but it was home. Now I'm thinking about it, I actually kind of miss it. I wish I could go back at least once to see any of my friends who might be left, and… hey, is this why you got me going down memory lane?" she suddenly shot at Adelaide, who giggled mischievously.

"Hey, if you don't want to go back, you don't have to. But if you choose to avoid it, don't do so because you're afraid of the trouble you'd be in when you got there. I'd make sure that wouldn't be an issue," Adelaide said warmly.

Maaya imagined walking back to Sark months after she left. She, Adelaide, and Saber walked fearlessly down the main street. A few people nearby caught sight of her and opened their mouths in anger, but backed away in fear as they met Adelaide's steely glare. Roshan would be there, as would Styx and Sylvia, and perhaps others. And Rahu too, of course, but he had lost all his power; without the aid of Maaya and her friends he had been unable to keep up his act and had fallen from grace. Yes, that could work. Maybe it was okay to go back.

Then, out of nowhere, the memory of Svante being held down by the police before being shot in the head in front of a frenzied and cheering crowd entered her mind—only this time it was Adelaide. Maaya heard the crack of a gun and watched her fall motionless to the ground, her eyes blank and sightless, as a pool of blood grew slowly under her head.

Maaya stood up suddenly, drawing in a sharp breath.

"No. No, we can't go. I won't," she said shakily. She had been stupid to think for even a moment that something like that would work. It didn't matter how talented or powerful Adelaide was or even the two of them combined; against an entire town they would stand no chance, and they would meet the fate that Maaya by all respects should have met just a few weeks before.

Adelaide was immediately at her side.

"Okay! I'm sorry. I shouldn't have pushed it. You all right?"

"Yeah. I just remembered… well, it's not important. I'm fine. I'm sorry, it's… it's just so dangerous there, both for me and for anyone who's seen with me. I watched people die, and I can't… not with you."

Adelaide pulled her into a tight hug.

"That's all right. As curious as I am I'd never ask you to put yourself in danger for it, and I certainly wouldn't take the risk if it's something you weren't comfortable with. Here, let's move on to something else. Maybe instead of the past we can focus on the future. How's that?"

"How?" Maaya asked as they sat back down.

"You know. Dreams, goals, plans, where you see yourself in a few years, things like that. I want to know what kind of dreams a beautiful mind like yours has."

"Oh, stop," Maaya laughed. "I haven't thought about that in a while, either… it used to always be my dream to someday get a big house out in the country where all of my friends and I could be free of Rahu. We would each have our own room, always have food on the table, and everything would just be peaceful. And… well, that didn't exactly work out. But I have… how to say… I've had some new dreams in light of recent events."

"Oh?" asked Adelaide with a teasing grin as she pulled Maaya closer, bringing their faces just inches apart. "How so?"

"Well, I'd still like a nice house. Only, instead of out in the country, it could be right on the shore in the city. And it doesn't have to be so big. In fact, maybe I'm okay with sharing a room depending on who's with me..."

"Oh, that sounds lovely. Keep going," Adelaide hummed, brushing her lips against Maaya's neck, smiling as Maaya squirmed.

"Or we'd be in a nice place on a high floor facing the ocean so we could wake up and feel the breeze on our faces, then we could watch the ships sail in and out... and at night we can light candles on the balcony, then sit under a cozy blanket to watch the sunset as the city lights up below us, and *stop it that tickles.*"

Adelaide laughed as Maaya cried out and tried in vain to push her away, and Adelaide kissed her from her chest to the nape of her neck. Finally, she relented, hugging Maaya tightly.

"Like I said, you have a beautiful mind. I love it," she said happily. "It'll happen someday. You know that, right?"

"To be honest, I've tried not to get my hopes up. Every time I started dreaming I'd get reminded why I shouldn't. But... I would really love it," Maaya murmured. "Now it's your turn!"

"To tell you about my dreams? Oh, I don't know," Adelaide said thoughtfully. "For a while I thought I was living them. Like I mentioned once, anyone who loved me had to be content with my lifestyle of always being on the move. But I've been thinking about that lately, and I'm not sure I'm so confident about that anymore. I think I was just saying that because I didn't think I would ever find anyone who was more appealing than the life I already lived, but... the thought of settling at least a little has come to mind. I'd still love to be out on the ocean and live for adventure, but it'd also be nice to have a cozy home to come back to every so often. Something that isn't my parents' house, I mean."

Maaya smiled.

"And I used to think I only ever wanted to settle and relax for the rest of my life because I was so used to being on the move and never being *able* to settle, but... if I had that stability I think it'd be nice to get out more. I've also found that I actually really like sailing."

Adelaide sighed contentedly and rested her head on Maaya's shoulder.

"Yeah. Whatever happens in the next few days, the future beyond that looks pretty bright. At least as long as you're here with me."

"And I don't plan on changing that," Maaya said softly as her heart leapt.

"Hey. I really like you, you know that? I'm glad we're in this together," Adelaide continued, brushing Maaya's cheek softly with the back of her hand.

"I'm glad, too."

Maaya had expected the day to be full of planning and people bustling about, but while Halvar and Inga double and triple checked their calculations, communications, and personnel, Adelaide and Maaya were left creating cards. Maaya quickly discovered that this was to be a painful process; she had never carried more than a handful of blood cards before, but this time Adelaide was insistent that they each carry no fewer than five or six dozen. And while each card didn't take that much blood to create, the real problem was needing to make fresh incisions every few minutes.

"Do we have enough yet?" Maaya moaned pitifully as she finished yet another card. She had long lost track of how many they had. While Adelaide's device had been useful to start, she had drawn blood with it so many times that her skin was feeling very tender. It was now late afternoon, and the sky was starting to turn orange as the sun turned down toward the hills.

"Almost!" Adelaide said brightly as though this process didn't bother her at all. "Cheer up, love. We're doing this all at once, so after we're done here, we're set."

Just then, Saber floated slowly into the room, stretching her arms high above her and then behind her back as she feigned a yawn.

"Hey Adelaide, the next time you decide to go get a custom-made anything, have someone invent a camera that can see me. This was pure torture," she complained.

"Oh! Are you all finished?" Maaya asked excitedly, leaping to her feet as the ghost approached.

"My part's done. Demryn needs a few more days to finish the actual painting, but he did a whole sketch. Let me tell you, his reputation is not without reason. Hopefully he'll let you see before he goes home. …what happened to your hand?"

"We're making enough blood cards for an army is what happened," Maaya grumbled, gesturing down at the growing stack of red cards on the table.

"I just don't want us to run out!" Adelaide objected.

"Maybe you won't need to hit the machine after all; I assume you'll just be able to destroy every ghost that's ever existed," Saber teased.

"If the machine wouldn't just make more, you'd probably be right," Adelaide chuckled. "Oh, Saber, now you're here there's something important I need to tell you that could affect where we go from here."

Saber took a seat next to Adelaide while Maaya finished up the rest of her cards. Adelaide repeated her concern that there was no absolute guarantee the gem would work, and that they were going off the assurances of what Krethan scientists and *libris* experts had been able to glean from their research. Maaya watched the ghost from the corner of her eye as Adelaide went on, but the ghost's expression was imperceptible.

When Adelaide finished, Saber tapped her finger thoughtfully to her chin.

"I see. So the only way to know for sure is to send me inside this barrier when a pulse arrives, at which point I may be completely fine or disappear completely, yes?"

"Correct," Adelaide answered apologetically.

"I appreciate you being up front with me about this. You didn't have to, so your intention is noted. Unfortunately, this is just too much of a risk for me. I can't do it. I quite like existing and don't want to risk changing that. Maaya, pack up your cards and get your clothes; we need to find a way back to Selenthia." Saber waited a few moments as everyone's shocked eyes fell on her, and then she burst into laughter. "The looks on your faces! You must not know me as well as you think. Really, now. To think I'd call this entire massive expedition to a halt because the gem has a tiny chance of not working."

"I… but… doesn't this bother you? At all?" Maaya protested.

"A little, I suppose. I wasn't lying about how I like existing and don't want that to change. But the risk is minimal, and even if it weren't it wouldn't make much sense to quit, would it? If I wouldn't disappear now, I'd just disappear later when the machine start killing off the entire world. Might as well give it a go now and see what happens." Then, seeing the hurt expression on Maaya's face, she continued more gently, "I don't mean to sound so tactless; being dead just gives me a different perspective on things. I would hate to disappear on you. But I knew going into this that there'd be a risk, even if I didn't think it'd be this. I'm not scared. And if this works, it will have been worth it."

Maaya only nodded. She was relieved Saber seemed to have taken it so well, and she knew the ghost had a point. Still, it was hard to imagine putting her in any danger at all. If it came down to it, she'd rather face the danger herself than subject her loved ones to it—though she knew Saber would say exactly the same thing.

"I guess that's that, then," Adelaide said after a moment's silence. "I'm glad you'll be with us. And we'll do everything in our power to keep you safe."

Saber bowed graciously.

"Likewise. I know I can't hurt these ghosts myself, but I do hope there's some opportunity for me to cause a little mayhem."

"If not, I'm sure you'd make one," Maaya said, wincing as Adelaide's device made a new incision in her finger.

"Without a doubt. But that will soon be irrelevant, because they're only going to exist for a few more days," Saber said determinedly.

"That's the plan!" Adelaide exclaimed. "All right, I think we're done drawing blood. Cards are just about done! Inga, Halvar, have you got everything prepared?"

"You bet. We managed to fit everything you'll need into two packs," Halvar said proudly. "We'll have to wear most of our clothes more than once, but I figure that's all right if we're saving the world and all."

"As long as we're allowed to bathe before doing any interviews," Adelaide chuckled. "Oh, Maaya, make sure you're wearing what you want to wear for the trip, okay? And bring a coat."

Maaya paused. She had been so caught up in preparing and planning that she hadn't thought about the clothing aspect of the trip.

She packed her cards into her card pouch with some difficulty, then picked up a healing card, but Adelaide stopped her.

"Let's wait until we're on the train to do that. I don't want us to feel too tired until we're settled in for the night."

"Is it really going to take three days? Are we making any stops?" Maaya asked, setting the card back down and getting to her feet.

"Only a few stops to my knowledge, but only very brief ones," Adelaide said, starting to gather up her own cards. "We won't be getting off until the final stop so we don't need to worry. And yes, unfortunately it will take three days. If it's anything like my last trip it will pass quicker than you think, but I also get serious cabin fever. My apologies in advance."

Maaya snickered, then jogged upstairs to get ready. She pulled on the tight clothes she had used during training, strapped her card pouch to her arm, slipped on her shoes, then grabbed Nadya's cloak. Finally, she pulled her hair back into a tight ponytail and stared at her reflection in the mirror. Already she felt nervous, as though simply getting dressed was the proof her body and mind needed to realize that they were actually going to do this.

But while she was nervous, she was not afraid. This was no armada, nor was it a town of angry and frightened people she faced. These were ghosts, and this was the territory she knew best. What's more, with her new cards, she felt more powerful than ever. She had seen what they were capable of, what *she* was capable of, and she eagerly awaited the chance to extinguish as many of the foul spirits as she could. Then, finally, she could set her sights on the one thing she had fought so hard and traveled so far to reach: the machine.

She headed back downstairs just in time to hear a knock at the door. Halvar rushed over to open it, revealing a slender man in a courier's uniform carrying a blank brown envelope. Without a word, he handed it to Halvar, then departed immediately.

"Our passes?" Maaya asked as she hopped down the last few stairs, and Halvar nodded.

"Yep. Now we're officially good to go. Could you take these in to the others? I need to send a message to Asmund."

Without waiting for a response he handed the envelope to her, then disappeared quickly down the hall.

When she stepped back into the room where everyone else had gathered, she saw that Demryn had joined them now, looking a little overwhelmed. Saber had a large piece of canvas in her hand, showing it excitedly to Adelaide, who seemed, if it were at all possible, almost as excited as Saber was. Inga stood at the window, her hands clasped behind her back, staring pensively out at the yard as it began to grow dark with fading sunlight.

As soon as Saber noticed Maaya, she flew swiftly over to her and held up the canvas in front of her.

"Look! Isn't it great?" she exclaimed proudly, as though it was her own creation.

Maaya stared with fascination at the canvas. It was a sketch of Saber, one more detailed and realistic than any piece of art Maaya had ever seen despite being obviously incomplete. Her face was expressionless but for the slightest hint of a smile, and her long hair was pulled back behind her shoulders and tucked behind her ears.

What most impressed Maaya, however, were her eyes. They were serious and intense as ever Saber could be, but Demryn had also managed to capture the mischievous fire behind them.

"You look… beautiful," Maaya said finally, unable to take her eyes off the canvas.

"Thank you. This sketch isn't terrible, either. Anyway, he's going to go back and make an actual painting from this reference here, and he says that should be even more impressive," Saber said excitedly. "You know… it gives me a weird feeling, this sketch. Not unpleasant, but I've never seen myself not dead before. This doesn't show me being all see through and flying, this… this is really me. I'm having kind of an existential crisis just looking at it."

"Stop looking at it then!" Maaya teased, handing the canvas to Demryn gratefully. "Thank you so much for this. I can't wait to see the finished piece."

"Oh, no, this one is for you," Demryn said, and Saber glanced up hopefully. "I have my own much messier sketch with color references and other important notes, but I thought you might want a little something for yourself to keep in the meantime."

"Wouldn't I *ever,*" Saber exclaimed, floating past the canvas Demryn was holding out to her and hugged him tightly. "You beautiful, remarkable man. After the good you've done for this world I hope you can join me in the next."

Demryn's conflicted expression showed he clearly wasn't sure how to interpret Saber's last comment, but luckily, Adelaide walked over just then and pressed a handful of coins into his hands.

"Thank you so much, Demryn. This will be so helpful. You have my note about who to send this to, yes?"

"That I do. They may take a little longer on the search and analysis than I will on the painting, but at least it should surely be in the system by the time you all get back."

"How sure are you they'll be able to figure out who she was?" Maaya asked, intrigued.

"Very," Demryn answered in a way that hinted he had answered this many times already today alone. "Our historians have quite extensive records. I also imagine they will be excited to take this on; to my knowledge they've never done anything like this before."

"Really? Never?" Maaya continued in fascination.

"Well, you see, a ghost losing their memories is actually completely unheard of. The only ones who don't remember who they are are the ones who have been around so long that finding this information wouldn't do them any good. This particular case—coupled with the fact that their subject had a position on the high court—should excite them," Demryn explained.

"I do hope they can tell me how I died as well. And I hope it was at least some sort of exciting," Saber said enthusiastically.

Demryn opened his mouth to reply, then apparently thought better of it; instead he simply bowed in farewell, then picked up his belongings and left the room.

"Right, that's that. Are these the passes?" Adelaide said, turning her attention back to Maaya and the envelope she carried while Saber carefully rolled up the canvas Demryn had given her.

"Yes. Halvar said he's going to send for Asmund, too," Maaya replied as she handed the envelope over to Adelaide.

"Great! We should be on our way within the hour, then. How are you feeling?"

"Nervous," Maaya answered truthfully. "I know I had always planned to do this as soon as I could, but… I guess now that we're actually getting ready to go I can't believe we're finally getting started."

"I completely understand, and I've done this once already," Adelaide said with a smile. "But I'm excited this time. I feel like it's not a matter of *if* we succeed, but *when.*"

"I hope you're right," said Halvar casually as he walked back into the room, his arms stretched behind his head. "I need this in my work history, and while you may be content to go one for two, I set only the highest standards for myself."

"Work history? You plan on going job hunting, Halvar?" Adelaide asked, amused.

"Oh, stars, no. I've got the best job in the world and I know it," Halvar replied seriously. "But if I'm ever at the pub and need to impress some people, well…"

"Uh huh, sure," Adelaide interrupted with a grin. "How long will Asmund be?"

"Oh, he's on his way already. Maybe ten, fifteen minutes?"

"Perfect. Go help Inga move our things to the street and then triple check we've got everything."

"You got it, cap'n."

No sooner had Halvar turned away than Felix, Cajsa, and Marit stepped into the room together. They looked hesitant, almost nervous to disturb Adelaide, but the moment she saw them, she rushed over to greet them.

"Are you off so soon, my darling?" Felix asked, not bothering to hide the sadness in his voice.

"Unfortunately. I wish I could stay longer, but the sooner we finish this the sooner we'll be back; I need to get back to you three, of course, as well as my work," Adelaide replied comfortingly.

"If you do actually manage to pull this off, I'm thinking about uninviting you from my wedding; how is my lame ceremony supposed to compete with the girl who saved the entire world?" Marit said in mock vexation.

"Don't be silly, that'll make it even better for you," Adelaide returned. At Marit's inquiring expression, she continued, "All you have to do is point to me and go, 'Look, she saved the world, and I'm still the one getting hitched first. What does that say about me?'"

The sisters laughed, then shared a tight hug.

"Really, I hope you manage to do it. Nothing would make me happier," Marit mumbled. And then, to Maaya, she continued, "Take care of her, please? She's an idiot and you look smart enough to balance that out."

"That'd make her a world-renowned genius, then," Adelaide grinned.

"Please be safe, my child," Cajsa said, hugging her daughter next. "Don't try to do the impossible; if it comes down to it, I would rather that you escape alive having failed."

"I know. Don't worry; I like living too much to sacrifice myself," Adelaide replied with a half smile.

"Ah, come here. Yes, both of you," Felix grunted, and to Maaya's surprise, he wrapped his arms around both of them. "You are both strong, intelligent, and talented young ladies. Together I'm sure you'll make wonderful things happen. Regardless of the outcome my faith in you remains unshaken."

"Stars, dad, I won't look good if I set out on my mission with wet eyes," Adelaide chuckled. "I promise we'll do you proud. At the very least we'll kill a few hundred of those things for you."

Felix let them go, then patted Adelaide strongly on the shoulder.

"I know you will."

Ten minutes later, Maaya, Saber, and Adelaide led the way down the front walk, followed closely by Inga and Halvar. Asmund's carriage and horses sat in the street, ready and waiting for them. Behind them, Adelaide's family stood on the front porch together, watching them go. Along with her family stood Chronis, who, to the spider's great distress, had been asked to stay behind. After an initial protest, Chronis relented, waving after them with the saddest expression it was possible for a creature of metal to make.

As Inga effortlessly loaded the carriage with their belongings, the rest of them hopped inside. There was plenty of space for the five of them, but Maaya still felt slightly claustrophobic; there was definitely a difference between a carriage with just her and Adelaide in it and one with five people.

"How long will it take us to get to the train?" Saber asked curiously.

"About an hour, an hour and a half, thereabouts," Adelaide estimated. "We'll arrive well after dark, but it should be already waiting for us."

"No kidding? We get a train all to ourselves?" Saber asked incredulously.

"Not exactly. This train is one of the military trains that goes to the 'front'—that is, to the radius. We just ensured we'll get transport on it. We will, however, have our own carriage."

"The privileges of *libris*, of course," Halvar said proudly, as though it was he who had bestowed this benefits upon them.

"Any stops we make along to way will be to pick up additional personnel, including some of our own, but it's basically just a straight shot to the machine. Or rather, the town closest to its border on this side of the country," Adelaide continued, smiling.

Inga soon stepped inside the carriage and sat next to Halvar just as Maaya heard Asmund climb up top the carriage. Within moments, they were on their way. Maaya stared out the window of the carriage at Adelaide's house, and at her parents and sister who still remained outside. A sudden swell of loneliness rose within her. She felt like she had only just arrived, and now she was leaving again. Though she didn't travel alone, she somehow felt as though she were leaving something behind.

Family, a voice in her mind said quietly.

. . .

Just over an hour later the carriage pulled into a dark steam-filled train station off a dirt path. Maaya stared. It looked very… temporary, she thought. The low platform was clearly a hasty setup, with one wide set of wooden stairs leading up to it; the sides hadn't even been covered, exposing the framework underneath. Instead of any roof there was only a canvas tent spread above where she assumed passengers would get on and off the train.

The area in front of the platform, where Maaya guessed carriages and horses might be parked, was nothing more than a small dirt clearing. At the moment, they were also the only ones here. The platform was lit with lanterns that Maaya might expect to see at construction sites. Everything else around them was dark, and she felt slightly nervous.

"All right ladies and gentleman, time to catch our next ride," Adelaide said, suppressing a yawn.

Inga opened the door and stepped out. Halvar followed, then Maaya, then Adelaide. Saber, too impatient to wait in line, passed through the carriage immediately, scanning the area intently.

"Say, does your military know I'm coming along?" she asked.

"Yes, but they don't know who you are; as far as they're concerned, you're just an ordinary ghost. Please try not to contradict that," Adelaide said with the slightest hint of a smile.

"Hey, hold on a moment," Saber said suddenly. "If I can go inside the radius of this machine, can't they just send any old ghost over to the machine to shut it down?"

"They can't. Any ghost that's caught in a pulse disappears just like any living human," Adelaide said darkly. "You're a special case, but they don't know that."

"Drat, that's right. Well, I suppose they'll find out as soon as we destroy this thing."

"I just realized I'm trying more new things in the span of these few weeks than I have during the entire rest of my life so far," Maaya mused as they began taking their things off the carriage. "My first time on a ship, in a horse-drawn carriage *and* a horseless carriage, on a train…"

"Really? You'd never been on any of those before?" Adelaide asked disbelievingly.

"Really. I'm not even sure we had any of those things in Sark. Maybe a carriage or two for the really rich, but they never wanted to travel outside their rich districts anyway."

"Ah, this should be fun for you then. Just a note about these trains: they go very fast."

They walked up to the platform where Maaya noticed two people she hadn't before: two soldiers dressed in full military gear. Maaya unconsciously stepped closer to Adelaide, who put a subtle and comforting hand around her waist.

"I take it you're Adelaide and company," one of the soldiers inquired.

"We are indeed," Adelaide affirmed, holding out their passes. After only a brief glance, the soldier waved her through.

"Safe trip to all of you," he said as they passed.

The train sat motionless in front of them, long and cold, its cars stretching out into the darkness beyond the platform. The engine at the front was massive and intimidating, made of black metal folded and bent in sharp aerodynamic designs, and a bright light placed at the front illuminated the ground for a hundred feet ahead. Steam billowed from it, obscuring it slightly and making the light seem like a giant eye on the body of an immense shadowy giant. There were lights on in each car, and the doors to each car were open, but as far as Maaya could tell they were all empty. She shivered. Something about being on a train completely alone made her deeply uncomfortable.

Adelaide led the way confidently onto the train as though she had done this dozens of times before, and the others followed close behind. As soon as they entered, Adelaide turned left, taking them to the door at the back of the car.

"We're going to take the very last car, just for privacy," she explained. Maaya wasn't sure whether that made her more or less comfortable.

As they walked, Maaya noticed that each car looked almost identical. Some of these cars had clearly been used for leisure in the past and had been hastily retrofitted for military purposes; gone were spacious seats, wide tables, and comfortable beds. Instead, half of each car was dedicated to cramped sitting space while the other half was cramped with smaller cots. It was efficient, but didn't look particularly comfortable. Every so often they passed through a car that served a different purpose; one looked like an entire kitchen and another served as a washroom.

Their walk to the final car seemed to take forever. When they finally arrived, Adelaide immediately began pulling down the shades over all the windows while Inga and Halvar organized their things in a corner.

"Home sweet home for the next three days," Adelaide said cheerily.

"Hey, do you think if I race the train I could beat it at full speed?" Saber asked, already fidgeting.

"I wouldn't recommend it. When I say this train goes fast, I mean it goes *very* fast. If you got left behind there'd be no catching up until the train stops, and that could be for hundreds of miles," Adelaide answered sympathetically. "You'll have to stay cooped up with the rest of us."

"Fair enough. How fast do you think I can drive Halvar insane?"

"It's only a race if I try to do the same thing in kind. May the best of us win," Halvar smiled, extending his hand.

"Challenge accepted," Saber said, shaking his hand and grinning wickedly.

"If the children with us must play, I suggest they do so in another car, especially when we are trying to sleep," said Inga pointedly.

"Yes, Commander," Saber and Halvar answered in unison.

"Of all the people I expected Saber to get attached to, Halvar was not the one," Adelaide said thoughtfully. "I feel like I should be disappointed. Anyway, I'm going to get ready for bed because I am worn out something fierce. These beds are so tiny, though; Maaya, help me push these together, won't you?"

"Two beds just for you? Where am I supposed to sleep?" Maaya asked, crossing her arms.

"With me. I don't snore, promise. I just might accidentally knee you in the stomach if I have a bad dream. Anyway, come here."

Adelaide said this with such casual finality that Maaya couldn't think to argue; as it was, she was halfway over to the bed before she had processed what Adelaide said, and felt a sudden fresh wave of excitement. This was going to be interesting.

Just as they finished, Maaya heard a distant whistle.

"Oh, you may want to sit down for this," Adelaide suggested, gently pulling Maaya down to the bed next to her. "If you have trouble with a dock you'll be no match for this train."

Maaya made to argue, but when she noticed that Halvar and even Inga had taken a seat, she thought better of it.

They started off slowly, and continued on at this speed for so long that it took nearly a full minute for the last car to pass the platform they had boarded from. Maaya was starting to wonder whether Adelaide had been playing a joke on her when, suddenly, the train lurched forward.

Faster and faster it went, accelerating with such speed that Maaya nearly fell into Adelaide. She gasped, holding on tightly to the taller girl as the train continued on, the sound of its metal wheels on the tracks growing louder and louder, the car rumbling as they went.

"Is it going to be like this for three days?" Maaya yelped, and Adelaide laughed.

"It'll get better once we're up to speed, then you'll hardly notice we're moving at all, trust me," she said comfortingly.

Half a minute later, the force of the acceleration began to diminish and Maaya regained her balance. The others stood and got back to setting up their beds and preparing for sleep.

Maaya pushed aside one of the window shades and looked out in fearful fascination. They were moving almost too fast for Maaya to comprehend. She watched as the lights of distant towns passed by and as plants growing near the track whizzed past in nothing more than a blur. She couldn't help but wonder just how far away this machine was if traveling at this speed would take them three days.

"All right, lights out in a minute. You coming?" Adelaide asked.

"I… actually, not yet. There's something I want to do first," Maaya replied, struck with sudden inspiration. When she had taken Nadya's cloak with her, she had come across something else she wanted to bring along, too. "Don't worry; I'll go into another car so I don't disturb you."

"Sounds good! Don't worry about waking me when you come in; I'm not a light sleeper." Before Maaya could get up, Adelaide leaned over and kissed her on the cheek. "Good night, my dear."

"And sweetest of dreams to you," Maaya murmured, kissing Adelaide firmly on the lips.

Leaving Adelaide looking positively ecstatic, Maaya stood up, picked up her pack from the floor, and walked out of the car to the one in front of it.

She almost immediately regretted this decision as soon as she saw the completely empty car, but before she could turn back, Saber floated through the wall beside her.

"Would you mind if I kept you company?" Saber asked, and Maaya shook her head quickly. "Great. Everyone else is falling asleep and I don't feel like exploring just yet."

"I'd love to have you. This train is spooky," Maaya said quietly, and Saber nodded happily.

"I know, it's great! Anyway, how have you been?"

"What?" Maaya laughed, taken aback by her casual question.

"It's just been a while since it's been just the two of us together, you know? I don't exactly count our guest room at Adelaide's house or on her ship; besides, we were awfully distracted then. I sort of feel like I've been neglecting you as a friend, I suppose."

"What are you talking about? We've been really busy, it's understandable," Maaya said consolingly.

"That's true. It's just been a while since we've had quality time together. We haven't really had that since Sark, and I figured… since we're not really doing anything for a few days…"

"Oh, come here, you sap," Maaya laughed, pulling Saber down to sit next to her on one of the benches and putting her arm around the ghost. "I know just what we can do."

She set down her bag on the bench next to her, then pulled out Kim's diary, setting it on the narrow table in front of her.

"What's all this?" Saber asked curiously.

"Adelaide and I have been talking, and she thinks I should read it," Maaya said softly. "She thinks that since it's the only thing left we have of our friends that we should know what's in it. At the very least, we can know Kim's stories. We don't have to share them, but… I don't know if I could go my whole life knowing there's something left of her right in front of me. These are her words, you know?"

"I've actually been thinking about it myself," Saber pondered. "On one hand, it's her private writing. On the other… she's not around anymore, and this is just a guess, but I imagine she'd be okay with it."

"I'd like to think so. She was pretty private in general, but when we were together she always opened up. She told me about who she liked, asked me for advice, all sorts of things. I guess I really want to see what was in her head when she was living with us. And I guess… I guess I want it to take me back. I didn't like Sark, but I liked what we had there. And maybe it's selfish, but… I want to relive the good days, at least for a little while."

"It sounds like you've made your mind up then," Saber said, and Maaya nodded.

"I'm actually glad you're here. Do you want to read with me? It could be our time, just the three of us."

"Yeah. Yeah, I'd like that a lot."

Maaya settled back in her seat and Saber leaned against her. She placed her hand on the cover, thinking hard about what she was about to do. It seemed almost surreal; this notebook was the only reminder the world had of her friends' existence, and the words inside had never been read by anyone but Kim. Maaya almost dreaded starting to read it, knowing that eventually she would reach the end where there would be nothing new left to discover about her beloved friend; the sense of mystery was comforting, in a way, telling Maaya that there was still something left, still something new and unexplored she could hold on to if ever she needed to.

But she knew she couldn't let that last forever. To do so for such a purpose would be selfish, too.

Slowly, Maaya opened the cover, and they began to read.

30

TO THE MACHINE

The next morning, Maaya awoke slowly to the gentle rocking of the train car and sound of metal wheels gliding smoothly over the tracks. Thanks to the curtains over all the windows, it was still mostly dark. Maaya had no idea what time it was, but it didn't sound like anyone else was awake, so she allowed herself to relax. If anything, she was disappointed she was awake already; with how long they were going to have to be on the train, she figured sleeping would be one of the best ways to pass the time.

She was also surprised that her body allowed her to wake up this early. She and Saber had been up for at least an hour reading through the diary, and then to finish things off, Maaya had finally gotten fed up with the throbbing and stinging in her hand from drawing blood earlier in the evening and used a healing card to patch herself up. After that, she had been so exhausted that Saber had to help her to bed; she didn't even remember getting into bed, much less if she had disturbed—

Maaya's eyes snapped open. She had forgotten where she was sleeping—or rather, who she was sleeping with.

Sure enough, Adelaide's peaceful sleeping face was just inches from hers. Maaya's entire body tensed before she caught herself and remembered to breathe. There didn't have to be anything strange about this. Besides, they already knew they liked each other. What was the harm?

Maaya slowly relaxed, unable to take her eyes off Adelaide. She had never seen Adelaide asleep before, and she was beautiful, so very beautiful, even then. It was as though the fire and vigor that coursed through her veins every moment she was awake finally let her be at peace, and she lay still, breathing slowly and softly without a care in the world.

Before she could stop herself, Maaya reached over and gently brushed a few locks of hair from the sleeping girl's face, tucking them behind her ear. Her touch helped drive home something that she had been reminding herself of ever since she had gone to dinner with her two nights ago: this was real.

As she stared at Adelaide's calm face, she tried to imagine how the future would look with Adelaide in it, and what she herself needed to do. Maaya had never been in a relationship like this before. Was it possible to move too fast? Too slow? Should Maaya be more forward or leave that to Adelaide? What were her boundaries? How would she know if she were crossing them?

Maaya wasn't sure whether she had started to doze or if she were simply that distracted, but she didn't notice that Adelaide had woken up until the girl had wrapped her in a hopelessly tight embrace, pulling Maaya so close that she could hardly move.

"Well, good morning," Adelaide murmured, nuzzling her cheek against Maaya's own. "Have you been awake long?"

"I-I don't think so," Maaya stuttered, momentarily overwhelmed. She would have to work on being more forward later.

"Mm, good. I woke up once during the night and you still weren't here, so I started to get worried. Where did you go? Walking the train?"

"Oh, no. Saber and I… we were doing something else. I'll tell you about it later," Maaya said quietly, feeling the tug of tiredness on her mind. She felt more comfortable and safe in Adelaide's arms than she had all night.

"I look forward to it. You want to get some more rest? We've got all the time in the world at the moment."

"No, that's okay. If you're up, I'll get up," Maaya said, hoping her disappointment wasn't evident in her tone. She already couldn't wait for the coming evening.

"Suit yourself! I guess we can have breakfast and go over what little intelligence we have about our little adventure here."

"Intelligence? I thought hardly anyone knew anything about it," Maaya said, stretching as Adelaide released her and sat up.

"Most of what we know are unimportant details, but I feel like I should share them anyway; the more people know, the better. Besides, if my government has been actively seeking the gem Saber has, you two might be able to connect some dots I'd never know about before. That could help us."

They sat up and Adelaide clicked on the small light overhead. As Maaya's eyes adjusted to the light, she saw that the two beds previously occupied by Inga and Halvar were empty.

"I remember Svante saying something like he believed the gem had the ability to cancel out whatever the machine was doing," Maaya said thoughtfully. "He wasn't sure how, but he seemed pretty confident. Or hopeful. One of the two."

"Interesting! I'm learning new things already," Adelaide commented. "Let's wait until we get the others to keep going; I'm sure they'll want to hear this as well."

They didn't have to wait long. As soon as Maaya and Adelaide were up and about, Halvar and Inga came in from the adjacent car. Halvar held a large plastic bag in his hand that was full of something Maaya couldn't quite make out.

"Morning, cap'n. Maaya," Halvar greeted them. "I brought breakfast. It should still be hot."

"It's only eight in the morning; I'm surprised you're up this early," Inga added.

"Yes, well, we have an awful lot of sitting around to do," Adelaide remarked. "Where's Saber?"

"She said she was off to explore the train. I told her most of the cars look the same, just like last night, but she wouldn't hear it. Anyway, I just walked all the way down near the front to get food, so I don't think I'll be going all the way back to search for her if that's all well," Halvar said.

"That's fine. Maaya's here, and that's all we need for now," Adelaide said brightly. "Let's eat, and while we do I'll fill you in on everything I know and everything the government sent me, then maybe we can have some fruitful discussion."

They sat down at one of the narrow tables and Halvar began pulling small boxes out of the bag, giving one box to each person. Maaya opened her box to find a breakfast sandwich, still slightly warm, with a small helping of vegetables on the side. Compared to what she had been eating recently it didn't look appealing at all, but her growling stomach made it clear that it was going to be eaten or else.

Adelaide and Inga opened a few of the curtains, letting in some of the bright sunlight from outside. Maaya squinted, but couldn't resist staring. The ocean was still visible, though it was several miles away at least. They were currently passing through a hilly vibrant landscape dotted with quaint wooden houses, each with its own large unfenced yard. She saw small corner markets, a handful of street vendors, and beautiful white rolling sand dunes that led to the clear waters of the beach. There was no trace of the big city here, and Maaya suddenly wished they could stop to enjoy it.

Adelaide pushed her breakfast box to one side after taking a massive bite of her sandwich, then pulled out a small sheaf of paper.

"Right, so if you aren't interested in history, here's the important stuff. The train will make its final stop on the north side of Nalmar. We'll be meeting most of our associates there and going through the city. It's not a terribly long walk, but it's not insignificant. Nalmar is abandoned, but we'll still need to be careful. The closer we get to the machine, the more of those ghosts we'll see. At the south exit is the military base in charge of guarding the perimeter, so we'll have to check in with them, and then we're good to go."

"Who's coming with us?" Halvar asked.

"The five of us will comprise the main group. The rest will be there to give us more sight and cover if we need, providing the gem can provide them sufficient protection," Inga explained. "They'll spread out in a wave ahead of us to seek vantage points, and the few who can use blood cards will try to clear us a path."

"Once inside, we know that the pulses emanate roughly every hour with occasional deviations, and they are visible to us, so as long as we keep Saber close, we should be in good shape," Adelaide added. "We just need to be careful about zoning, but that's what our associates are for; they'll make sure we aren't cornered or caught in a bad position when it's time to dodge a pulse."

"So, I'm curious about something. Your government knows all this about Saber's gem... does anyone know how she got it?" Maaya said slowly.

"I have no idea. No one in our government even knew where it went for certain," Adelaide said. "They eventually got a lead as to who it might have passed to, but it had simply passed through so many hands that everyone lost track."

"Svante said that they suspected it had gone to Selenthia—to Sark, I mean—and they were right, weren't they?"

"From what I can see, that was one of many leads. Svante was one of many Krethans sent to various places in the world to try to retrieve it. I'm surprised even one of them turned up anything, to be honest," Adelaide admitted. "It's also likely that Svante wasn't told everything; I'm sure they impressed upon him the need to return the gem, but not exactly how everything worked."

"You're right... he wasn't able to explain a whole lot," Maaya sighed. "So, we have the gem, and we're mostly certain it works. Does the fact that it's attached to a ghost change anything?"

"It shouldn't. It was never alive, so it could never die; as far as we're concerned it's the same as it always was—just invisible."

Maaya remembered Saber flicking Svante on the nose to prove how real she was, and couldn't help but smile.

"I just hope we can find out what the bloody machine was designed for. From what I've heard, these ghosts weren't its intended purpose. Seems like one hell of a side effect if you ask me," Halvar grunted.

"From what I've been able to decipher from the creator's notes, it was designed to take in energy and then transfer it elsewhere. We think it might have been an attempt to be some sort of power generator. We just don't know what *kind* of power, though. It's related to *libris*, that much we know, but all these other effects, as well as the machine's intended purpose, are a mystery," Adelaide said thoughtfully.

"And this gem has the same type of energy in it..." Maaya murmured. Something about that fact troubled her, but she couldn't put her finger on what it was.

"Right, which should work to our benefit," Adelaide continued. "The problem obviously isn't the gem itself. We just need to get it there."

"Do we know how to turn this thing off once we get there? If it's been powering itself for this long, I imagine it's not as simple as just unplugging it," Halvar said.

"No, but we can smash it, I'm sure," Adelaide answered brightly. "I've looked over these blueprints, and I see no reason we can't just break it to pieces."

"Great. So what's the hard part? If we've got cover and don't get lost, are we good to go?" Halvar continued.

"Hopefully. We'll play it safe, and we'll be up against a lot more of those ghosts than usual, but the hardest part is finding safe passage through the pulses. That's what we've got Saber for. We stick with her for every pulse, avoid the walks, and we're good to go."

"I want to be skeptical, but then, I suppose we have a tool no one else has," Halvar pondered aloud. "I'm just baffled at the thought of what the machine could have been originally designed for that a malfunction meant shooting out waves of ghosts that kill everyone."

Adelaide shrugged.

"I'm hoping we'll have time to find out, but our priority is shutting that thing down. Our scientists will do the best they can with the machine's broken remnants."

"Say, I know we're going to be getting some protection and all, but I don't suppose you guys want to do any warmup for fighting against the ghosts before we get there?" Halvar asked.

"Not particularly. I think we're as ready as we'll ever be. Why?" Adelaide returned.

In response, Halvar turned his gaze back to the window.

"The opportunity is there if you change your mind."

The others followed his gaze. Sure enough, a few miles from the train, a wide rank of the tall faceless ghosts was making its way across the hills. Maaya frantically scanned the area, looking to see if anyone was in danger, but the ghosts appeared to be moving through uninhabited lands. A busy town street was less than a mile from them, in between the ghosts and the train, but the ghosts were moving parallel to it. Maaya sighed quietly with relief. This time, at least, it seemed there would be no danger.

Maaya relaxed, but Adelaide seemed to have other plans. She hopped to her feet and then gestured at the locked door at the end of the train car with a smile.

"Fancy a walk outside, Maaya?"

Before she knew it, Adelaide was leading her toward the door at the back of their car. Maaya pulled back reflexively when Adelaide opened it, expecting a sudden rush of wind, but none came. Still, when she saw how quickly the ground was moving underneath the car, she suddenly felt a little queasy.

"What's out here that we can't see from in there?" Maaya asked nervously.

"A better vantage point. It will give us better reaction time if the ghosts head our way. I'd rather the relative freedom of outdoors than the confines of a train carriage. It's all right! I'll keep you safe."

Maaya wasn't sure how she felt about taking a walk on the outside platforms of a moving train, but her desire to try to take down some of the ghosts overpowered her fear.

Adelaide went first, stepping out easily like she had done this dozens of times already. She offered her hand to Maaya, who took it gratefully and held on tight.

The wind whipped at Maaya's hair, and for a split second she panicked, thinking she would be thrown over the edge, but after a moment she realized it wasn't as strong as she thought. Just like inside the train, once she became accustomed to the speed, keeping her footing took little effort. The rough metal grate below provided plenty of traction and there was railing on all sides just in case. It wasn't large, but it was enough that she could take a few steps in any direction, and this comforted her a little.

Once she was certain she wasn't going to be flung off the train, she stared around her, taking in her surroundings. The view wasn't much better—though it was certainly better than what she got through the windows—and the fresh air felt wonderful on her face. She would have enjoyed the moment had it not been for the ghosts that now occupied Adelaide's attention.

"It doesn't look like they're going to run into anything important," Adelaide said thoughtfully. "If they keep going the way they are they'll stay out of our range, and then it's miles and miles before they hit the next town; they aren't likely to hurt anyone this time."

Maaya turned to watch the ghosts as the train sped past. They would pass the ghosts completely within minutes at their current rate of speed.

Maaya couldn't help but think that out here the ghosts seemed mostly harmless. In the middle of a street full of screaming and trapped people in the middle of the night they had seemed like her worst nightmare. Here out in the open in broad daylight, however, with nothing of value in their path, they seemed almost a passing attraction.

"Hey… have you ever seen these ghosts out during the day before?" she asked.

"Not nearly as often as I do during the night, but it does happen, unfortunately. Makes them much harder to fight, I'll say that; they're much easier to see at night. I hope we don't see too many more on our way. A train is hardly a good vantage point to… wait, what are they…?"

Maaya's gaze darted back to the ghosts just in time to see them start to turn. Slowly, ever so slowly, their path changed until they were headed directly for the train—a path which would take them directly through the bustling town.

"Oh, stars, no!" Adelaide breathed, then quickly pulled out some augment cards and made to burn them.

"Wait! You can't be thinking about leaving the train?" Maaya cried, taking Adelaide's arm.

"Those ghosts are going to pass right through that street and kill everyone in it if we don't do something," Adelaide replied sharply, trying to pull away.

"You'd never be able to make it back!" Maaya protested, holding on tighter, worried that Adelaide would leap off the moving train right then and there. "Even if you did you'd be in no shape to do any fighting once we got to the barrier. Adelaide, please, maybe we can get a message to them instead—"

"If we don't go to them now, *they'll all die*. This is my job! I have to protect everyone I can," Adelaide hissed, finally pulling her arm from Maaya's grip. Maaya flinched, her instincts warning her that Adelaide might strike her, but instead Adelaide ran her fingers agitatedly through her hair, her voice trembling now. "Why, why are they turning…? I can't…"

Maaya dared not speak. It was true they needed to be rested and well for their final part of their trip, and it was also true that if Adelaide did somehow manage to make it to the town, defeat the ghosts, and then make it back to the moving train, she would be too exhausted to move for probably a few days—but Maaya couldn't bear to argue. To protest Adelaide's attempt to save her people would make her come off as though she was arguing in favor of their death, no matter what her reasoning was.

Adelaide was visibly distraught. She paced back and forth, looking as though she might cry, all the while never taking her eyes off the ghosts. Any chance she might have was quickly slipping away as the train passed by the town, and she seemed to realize this. Her hands were balled into fists at her side, and she bit her lip hard.

Maaya prayed with all she had that the ghosts would simply disappear as they had done so many times before. There was still time, still plenty of space between the ghosts and the town, enough that maybe…

But the longer Maaya watched, the more she realized what was about to happen.

With the ghosts right on the border of the town, Adelaide's body tensed, and Maaya thought again that she might attempt to leave the train, but instead she let out a scream of helpless rage and sorrow, stomping her foot hard on the metal grate below. Her cry was a sound Maaya couldn't bear to hear, and she winced and glanced downward, wanting nothing more than to turn invisible.

Without so much as looking at Maaya, Adelaide passed her, then disappeared into the train car.

Maaya did not follow. She remained frozen in place as a tumult of emotions overcame her. She could only stare at the grate beneath her, fully aware of what was about to happen just nearby, and even more painfully aware that she, even with all her new power, could do nothing about it. Not if she wanted to be able to fight her way to the machine.

She couldn't imagine what Adelaide was feeling. Maaya had her own experiences from Sark, and she had tried to keep her town safe, but part of that had only been because she felt obliged, and much of the rest came from following Rahu's orders so she and her friends would have enough to eat. Adelaide, however, had been trained from childhood to destroy these ghosts and grew up in a country ravaged by the death and terror they brought upon everyone. And here she was on her way to try to save her world, having to turn her back on the people she was supposed to protect. That she would not have been here otherwise was immaterial; she had been presented a choice, as awful as the options may have been, and she had chosen to leave them to their fate.

Maaya knew it wasn't fair to blame herself, but she couldn't help it. If she hadn't held Adelaide back, maybe she could have made it. Maybe they could have figured something out. There was no way to tell now.

As logic slowly began to wrest control of her mind from her emotions, a wave of dread washed over her in their place. Maybe it was her fault… just not in the way she had originally thought. More than once now these ghosts, previously thought to be mindless and directionless beings, had changed direction—and each time, always, they came for her. She fought this thought desperately, frantically scouring her mind for any evidence to the contrary. She had never been alone when this happened, she reasoned. They could be after anyone.

But then she remembered the ghost in Sark, the first ever to show up in Selenthia. And then how they had almost overwhelmed Sark until she left, at which point Emil had informed her the attacks had lessened. She remembered how the first attacks happened in Anorath, and how they happened again in Levien. It was almost too much to believe it could possibly be a coincidence. She wondered briefly if they could be after Adelaide, but that couldn't be right either; Adelaide had seemed so confused at their actions that Maaya guessed she had hardly seen it happen before.

Maaya considered telling Adelaide her theory, but Adelaide's cry of anguish helpfully replayed itself from her memory, and Maaya shuddered. On her long list of bad ideas, that was near the top.

She let out a shaky nervous breath, then walked as quietly as she could back into the car, then through to the one she and Saber had sat in the night before. If any of the others saw her, they didn't try to stop her, and that was what she wanted right now.

She would have to talk to Adelaide later. Still she felt numb, both with the knowledge of what was about to happen nearby and the possibility that it was her fault. She pushed forward, fighting the dead weight of sick horror in her stomach, hoping they were far enough away that she wouldn't hear the screams.

When she entered the second car and looked up, she noticed Saber hovering nearby, and Maaya breathed a sigh of relief. If anyone could talk her down from this, it was her.

"Saber, I need you," she said, painfully aware of the crack in her voice that made it obvious she was trying hard not to break down. "I think… I think the ghosts might be after me, and I just made them… Saber?"

The ghost didn't move. She was so still and silent that Maaya wondered if she was playing a game. But then she turned and glided noiselessly to the other end of the car, her expression completely blank as though she wasn't actually seeing anything before her.

"Saber…?" Maaya asked hesitantly.

She reached out to touch the ghost's shoulder, but before her fingers touched, the ghost whirled around and grabbed her tightly by the wrist. Maaya gasped in pain and tried to pull away, but Saber held on, twisting her hand slightly.

"Who are you? What makes you think you can just walk up and touch me?"

"S-Saber, it's me!" Maaya whimpered, trying desperately to pull free, but the ghost's grip was like a vice. "Don't you remember—?"

"I don't care who you think you are. *Don't touch me,*" Saber growled coldly, then flung Maaya from her grip, sending the girl crashing hard against the wall.

Maaya saw stars. She was vaguely aware of Saber floating nearer to her, and she held her arm in front of her face in case the ghost tried to attack her, but then Saber was gone.

Maaya tried the fight the tears she knew were coming, but quickly gave up. Her pain, the shock of Saber's reaction, and everything she had just experienced outside with Adelaide all overpowered her easily within moments, and she broke down, her body shaking with her sobs. She hugged her knees to her chest and lowered her head as she cried. Adelaide was probably furious with her and had likely told the others what happened, and Saber… Maaya could only assume that the machine was affecting her again. How long it would last she had no clue, but she hoped it would end soon.

Worst of all, despite being one of only five people on an otherwise completely empty train, Maaya once again felt like she had nowhere to run or hide. She thought momentarily that she wanted only to be home before quickly remembering that the only place in recent years she could call home had been burnt to the ground.

Maaya wasn't sure how much time passed, but gradually she began to calm. She stood up slowly, feeling slightly dizzy as her head throbbed dully with pain, but she otherwise felt fine. She brushed her hair from her face and looked around the empty car. She wanted to move, but she didn't know where she could go. All the other cars looked basically the same, so there was nothing to explore; further, she didn't want to risk running into Saber or any of the others.

Suddenly, she remembered that she had left her pack in this car when she and Saber had been reading Kim's diary the night before. If nothing else, she could occupy her time with that until she was able to figure out if it was safe to seek anyone else's company.

As she walked across the car to grab her pack, she stared out the window. Hardly any time had passed, of course, and the sun still shone brightly and cheerfully as ever. She grimaced. It was going to be a long day.

She found Kim's diary just where she had left it. She sat down quietly and then pulled it over to her, opening back to where she had left off the night before.

I think I'm getting the hang of this. I can actually read my letters. That sentence only took a minute to write. Anyway, we're going out again tonight. Everyone is excited. Maaya looks tired. I hope she's okay. I just hope we go where Anrik lives. I know it's bad we can see ghosts, but I think it would impress him. But maybe before I'm brave enough to tell him I can see ghosts, I should be brave enough to tell Maaya he even exists. Everyone else would make fun of me, but I know she wouldn't.

Maaya couldn't help but smile as she remembered Kim's confession and request for advice. She hoped Kim had read back over this entry and felt proud of herself. She also felt a swell of pride that Kim knew she could come to her with this kind of thing. At least in that regard she had accomplished what she always wanted to.

As she turned the page, she heard a voice from nearby.

"Getting started without me, huh? Honestly, I leave for five minutes and you're so bored you start to read for fun."

Maaya glanced up in surprise as Saber floated over to her, stretching widely.

"Saber…?" she said timidly.

"The one and only! I was wondering if you wanted to come explore the train with me. I know it's a whole lot of nothing, but at the same time there's something appealing about having an entire train all to ourselves, especially if it's going to fill up with boring soldiers later. I'm giddy like a schoolgirl. You game?"

"I… I think so," Maaya said hesitantly, setting the diary aside. "How do you feel?"

"No worse for wear I suppose, but I definitely think I'll be able to give Adelaide's cabin fever some decent competition. You? Hey, why are your eyes all red?"

"It's nothing," Maaya said dismissively, but Saber floated in close until their faces were only inches apart.

"Don't be silly. Was it the diary? If you read something important I don't want to leave until I get a chance to see it, too."

"It's not that, Saber. Just… don't worry about it. Let's go," she said, sidling around the ghost and getting to her feet. She started walking down the car, but then she heard Saber's voice from behind her, suddenly quieter and more serious.

"Maaya… was it me? Did I do something and not remember it again?" Maaya turned to face her, temporarily lost for words, and Saber's face fell. "Oh, no. Maaya, what did I do? Did I say something?"

"Saber, please, don't worry about—"

"Maaya, *what did I do?*" Saber asked pleadingly. She made to place her hand on Maaya's arm, but when Maaya flinched, she pulled back. "Oh, no… I didn't hurt you, did I?"

"Saber, it's okay. I know you weren't yourself, so—"

Saber moved forward again like she wanted to give Maaya a hug, then pulled back, her face full of guilt.

"Maaya, whatever I did, I am so, so sorry. I don't remember a thing. Please tell me it wasn't bad."

"It wasn't; it just took me by surprise, that's all," Maaya assured her. "Everything's fine, I promise. I just… something else happened earlier, something horrible. I wanted to find you to talk to you about it, and I can't get it out of my head."

"What happened?" Saber asked, sitting down on a bench nearby.

Maaya sat next to her, took a deep breath, and then told Saber what had happened outside with Adelaide. The scene replayed itself in her mind as she did so, and she shuddered at the memory.

When she finished, Saber took a deep breath, then let it out slowly.

"That's... mighty heavy, yeah," she said. "I can see how you'd be afraid you're attracting these ghosts, but this isn't your fault, okay? None of this is your fault. I said it before and I'll say it again as many times as I have to."

"But... how can you explain any of this? The ghosts following me or showing up more often in places only after I arrive?" Maaya asked desperately. "That night when we saw the ghost on the hill for the first time, even then it was after me!"

"We don't know any of that for sure," Saber said firmly, resting a hand on Maaya's shoulder. "Those ghosts could have always sought out people and we just didn't know it; there were so many people in every direction every time we encountered them that they could have just appeared to be going in random directions. So of course when we were alone it'd look like they were chasing you."

"But those ghosts out there, the way they turned—"

"They could have been going toward the town for all we know. It was between you and the ghosts, right?"

"I... I suppose, but—"

"And on the ocean, they turned toward the ship because you were the only living beings for miles. Even out on the hill, the one ghost went after the two men living there, not after you. We only happened to see it because we literally tried to find it. So I even have doubts about Svante's claim that they show up where *libris* is used, because they seem to just chase down anyone they can find—and considering they chase down *libris* elites and move about as fast as you do when you've just woken up, they aren't even all that bright."

Maaya snorted despite herself, and Saber grinned widely.

"Listen," Saber continued intently, "I promise, this is not your fault. They aren't after you. They don't care about you any more than they do anyone else. No offense, but in this case you are nothing special at all."

Maaya smiled.

"Honestly, that's exactly what I want to hear."

Before either of them could say anything else, the door opened suddenly and Adelaide stepped swiftly through, visibly concerned. Maaya tensed, expecting the worst, but when Adelaide saw Maaya relief washed over her face, and she hurried over to her.

"Maaya, thank goodness, there you are. Where have you been? I missed you coming back inside so I thought you were still out there, but then you weren't outside so I worried you'd fallen off, or… I shouldn't have left you out there, not after dragging you with me. Are you all right?"

"Yeah, I'm fine, all things considered," Maaya answered uncertainly. "But… about earlier, when I tried to stop you, I didn't mean—"

She broke off as Adelaide waved her hand.

"Don't worry about it. I wasn't upset with you. I may not have even made it in time to save them had I tried. It's just a terrible, terrible position to be in. But look at me, saying this like you don't understand; you've been there yourself, haven't you?"

Maaya stood up and pulled the taller girl into a tight hug. She felt Adelaide tremble as she fought to keep her own tears at bay.

"I guess I have. It never gets easier, but all we can do is our best. We can't be everywhere at once. Even with *libris* you're still only one person. We have to choose between saving the world and saving everyone in it, because we can't do both." Maaya let go and stepped back, her voice growing quieter still. "That's why I'm here. I couldn't save the people I wanted to, and I left the rest behind. But I… I don't regret it. Once this is over I think it will have been worth it."

"Frankly, I think you should both be proud of yourselves," Saber said suddenly. Maaya and Adelaide turned to face her in surprise. "You're facing that age-old dilemma of which terrible option to choose. Most people shy away from such a conundrum, content that they'll never have to face it. They never choose. They say it's a silly thought experiment. But you've both made that choice. Be proud of yourselves for being strong enough to make the choice no one else wants to, and for following through. You aren't choosing who dies; you're choosing who you risk your lives to save. It could be nobody. You *could* give up and hide at home and wait for someone else to solve the problem. The fact that you're doing this anyway says everything about you. And only good things, in my view."

Adelaide was silent for a few moments, and then she sighed deeply and smiled.

"You two are wonderful. Thank you. I guess I'm being unrealistic for complaining that a world-ending catastrophe isn't as peachy as I'd like it to be. But you're right, Maaya. I think this will be worth it. And we're doing our best, right? You've crossed the world just for this."

"And you've tried to do this more than once now, not to mention you grew up preparing for it," Maaya returned. "Honestly, you're one of the most dedicated people I know, and the world is lucky to have you. *I'm* lucky to have you."

"Funny, I was thinking the same thing about you," Adelaide laughed.

"You both are lovely, but if you're going to get sappy on me I'm going to leave," Saber interrupted, flashing them a subtle wink.

"Right, of course. There are plenty of empty cars for Maaya and I," Adelaide said airily, and Maaya coughed. "Speaking of which, how was exploring the train?"

"I don't know. We were just about to get started when you came in," Saber said.

"You haven't started? Halvar said you left hours ago," Adelaide said, confused, and then a look of realization slowly passed over her face. "...oh."

"'Oh' indeed," Saber sighed, similarly vexed. "I guess that explains why I came to my senses in an empty car. Lovely."

"This needs to end soon," Maaya murmured.

TWO DAYS LATER, late in the afternoon, the train began to slow down. It was hardly noticeable at first until Maaya realized it was quieter than usual. When she looked out the window, she saw that their surroundings were not flying past them as quickly as they had before.

The sky was clear and bright, and puffy white clouds dotted the sky. The distant trees and nearby shrubbery swayed gently in a light breeze and flocks of birds glided slowly across the sky. It was not the picture of the apocalypse Maaya had imagined. Even though there was no good reason for it, Maaya had imagined a dark scene, one she supposed was almost like a war zone. The sun had been blocked by clouds of smoke in her imagination, and Nalmar had been ablaze, with enemies lurking around every corner.

As she stared out the window, she almost thought she would have preferred her version of things. The environment here matched the ghosts they were about to face so well—just like they seemed to have no awareness of their surroundings, killing with abandon while simultaneously expressing no emotion and flickering in and out of existence like an unpredictable sun shower, the bright sky and cheerful sun seemed almost to mock them. This was the end of the world they were up against, and while such a thought was everyone's worst nightmare, it came under the guise of their vision of paradise.

Adelaide stepped into the car not long after, looking mildly perturbed.

"Inga, how many stops has this train made since we left?" she asked.

"None, Captain," Inga verified immediately.

"That's what I thought. That doesn't bode well," Adelaide mused, staring out the window as well. "Either way, it looks like we've arrived safely."

"What's wrong with that?" Maaya asked curiously.

"Nothing in itself, I suppose. It's just that usually the train will make a few stops at other bases along the way to pick up supplies and soldiers to take to the perimeter. Maybe there just weren't any ready to go," Adelaide explained, not breaking her gaze from the window.

"For our specific mission, the lack of stops is not a problem," Inga added. "Our associates will have arrived through other methods of transport. We will see them shortly."

"I just can't wait to get off this train!" Saber exclaimed impatiently. "No excitement at all, not a lick of it. I counted every car on this train and got halfway through counting every seat."

"Agreed. Let's make sure we're all packed up and ready," Adelaide suggested, and they immediately got to work.

As the train continued to slow, Maaya's heart pounded in her chest. More than once she patted her arm to make sure her pack of cards was still there and ready to go should the worst happen.

Once they had double checked everything in their possession, they started the long walk down the line of train cars. The train was chugging along slowly now, and from the windows in each car Maaya could see buildings and roads and electricity lines, though it was hard to see what state their surroundings were in as they walked.

They entered the first car just as the train finally came to a stop, and Maaya heard a loud hiss from the engine not too far away. The doors to the platform opened, and for the first time in days, Maaya walked out upon solid ground.

Unlike the makeshift station from which they had departed, this looked like it had always been meant for train travel. There was no shaky wooden platform; instead the tracks had been laid into the ground and the station built around it, making it easy for large numbers of people to get on and off. The station also had a dedicated roof, and was all around much larger, providing access to more than just a few cars.

In terms of people, however, the station was almost completely empty. Only three people stood clustered several feet away; there weren't even any soldiers, which Maaya had expected to see.

"Say, Inga… our friends got the word that they were supposed to meet us here before we arrived, right?" Adelaide asked just loudly enough for the other four to hear.

"They did. I made sure of that."

"And how many were supposed to be here?"

"Ten to twelve at my last estimate."

"That's what I thought. Maybe they're waiting for us outside the station. Let's get moving," Adelaide said assertively.

Before they had gone even a few feet, however, the three strangers nearby suddenly turned to face them. One of them, a young man, stepped forward.

"Commander Inga Strand?" he asked. Inga nodded. "I'm Corvin, the LC of my group."

"LC?" Saber asked quietly.

"*Libris*-capable," Halvar answered under his breath. "Technically able to use the magic, but nowhere near the skill of the elites. One LC typically leads each group."

"Are there others?" Inga asked tersely, and Corvin shook his head.

"We've been the only ones here for at least a day, ma'am. Are we expecting others?"

Inga turned to Adelaide, but while she said nothing and her expression hardly changed, Maaya could tell Inga was displeased.

Adelaide let out a long, slow breath.

"We have little time to wait. Corvin, you and your group stay here to meet anyone else that might come in the next hour. My group is going ahead to the perimeter. We'll have a little time to hang back as we wait for a pulse, but I can only give it an hour."

"What's the harm in waiting?" Saber asked. "Wouldn't the odds of our success be higher if we have more people with us?"

"Perhaps, but the question then becomes how long we should wait," Adelaide answered, clearly troubled. "They should have already been here by now. If they aren't here already, I can only assume they won't make it at all. If that's truly the case, we need to question why—and I think you may know the answer."

Maaya swallowed nervously. All those people were supposed to be their protection… so if they had somehow been stopped or even delayed by the ghosts, she worried suddenly that she was underestimating the specters even now.

"To the outpost then?" Halvar suggested, patting his pockets and pulling out their passes.

"Correct," Adelaide affirmed. "Inga, I assume you still know Nalmar best; lead the way. I'm afraid I was too tired last time to remember our route. Maaya, keep a few bloods ready. Just in case."

With that, they walked out of the station and into the town known as Nalmar. Though there were no other people around, no sign of any ghosts, and no sign of trouble in general, the sight of the town's empty streets made her incredibly uncomfortable. It was only after they had walked about a block that she realized why.

This town is almost exactly like Sark.

There were minor differences in architecture, as one might expect from a town in an entirely different country, but otherwise the similarities were uncanny. She had become familiar with Sark's shoddy infrastructure, the way every neighborhood seemed to be built onto itself and so very different from the next, and this town was the same way. The cobblestone streets were narrow and claustrophobic, while buildings that were much taller than was safe leaned precariously over them.

What disturbed her the most were the signs that this was a town that had seen death, and that those who escaped—if indeed any had—had done so at moment's notice in a panic. Doors and windows, left open long ago, creaked in their frames. Pairs of shoes were left lined up outside front doors, clotheslines hung across yards with some clothing still hanging pitifully from them, and children's toys sat on porches, rusting into perpetuity. If not for the few signs of wear and decay, as well as the fact that nature was doing its best to slowly reclaim the land, Maaya might have thought it was simply a very quiet day in a town that would have otherwise been bustling with people.

As they kept moving in silence, Maaya imagined herself back in Sark on streets nearly identical to these. She could almost see herself walking down these streets in the middle of the night with Saber, Kim, Kalil, and Sovaan, or running into Roshan in the early morning as she went out to fetch water. Despite all she had been through recently, that life hadn't been all so long ago. A matter of weeks at most. Still recently enough to make her pine for her life back home, to feel as though she could simply go back in time and fix everything that had happened.

She shook her head determinedly and stared back at the road, ignoring as much of Nalmar as she possibly could. She would never have that life again, and that was for the best. There was no use wishing for it now.

"If we don't get interrupted we should reach the outpost in a fairly short time," Adelaide said quietly. "Saber, how are you feeling about this? Do you still want to press on?"

"Unquestioningly," Saber said immediately. "We did not come all this way to fail from such a stupid oversight. All the better if it goes as planned… looking around this town has reminded me of every reason we came here."

"You see it too, huh?" Maaya continued, and Saber nodded.

"It's unsettling. I'm expecting Rahu to come walking down the street at any moment. What angers me the most is that he was the one left alive. Looking around this town reminds me that he's back home in the lap of luxury and that he's remained there at our expense. I am so very eager to pay him a visit on our return," the ghost finished darkly.

"Planning on playing his piano and scaring him to death?" Maaya smiled.

"Hardly. Though I've heard piano wire is an excellent tool for decapitation."

Inga laughed, and Maaya realized it was the first time she had ever heard her do that so openly.

"I should like to work with you more often," Inga said with an approving smile.

They continued on without incident. Nalmar was so peaceful that Maaya started feeling suspicious. With as close as they were to the machine and how much trouble the Blackfins had evidently run into on their way here, she thought it odd they hadn't seen a single ghost. But still, onward they went, with hardly a sign that the ghosts existed at all. Only the ghost town around them was any indication that something was, or had ever been, wrong.

Finally, however, Maaya spotted something in the distance over the roofs of some of the nearby buildings. A curved line, ever so faint like a faded grey rainbow, arced high into the sky, so high that it passed out of sight before the top was anywhere near visible. Maaya guessed at its size based on the curve she could see, and put it at over twenty miles at least.

"The radius," Adelaide informed her grimly. "The outpost should be—ah, there it is. Let's keep moving."

As they rounded a corner, Maaya saw the dark green wood and metal of the military outpost in the middle of the street. It was made almost entirely of tents, with ropes blocking off the street and running between them. A thin barricade of sheet metal had been set up in front of the tents, though Maaya couldn't guess for what purpose. She wondered for a split second why the camp would be set up in such an odd place until she realized that everything past the outpost must currently be inside the radius of the machine. The outpost itself looked easily moveable, and she was sure it had been gradually moved back as the radius expanded. She speculated that at one point it must have been at the very end of the street on the edge of town, if not further.

Adelaide slowed as they approached, taking out a handful of bloods from her own card pouch.

"Something isn't right here…"

As they walked closer to the outpost, Maaya suddenly realized she hadn't seen a single person, soldier or otherwise. It was also deathly quiet where she had expected to hear at least light chatter.

"I was expecting somewhat more of a presence on the infamous border of the machine's barrier," Saber commented, searching the area around them. "I don't suppose they all take lunch breaks at the same time?"

"They most certainly do not," Inga replied shortly.

"I would have thought they'd be expecting us, or someone else at least. It's not every day the train comes in," Halvar thought aloud.

"Anybody home?" Adelaide called, but the only response was her own echo and the sound of cloth from tents and flags flapping lightly in the breeze.

Adelaide made to enter the outpost, but Inga suddenly reached out and pulled her back.

"Wha—?!"

"Look. Evidently it is expanding faster than we thought," Inga said in a low voice.

It took a moment for Maaya to understand what she was talking about. She had been so focused on trying to see if anyone was inside the outpost that she hadn't seen the faint grey line of the radius… and with growing horror she realized that nearly the entire outpost was *inside* it.

"Oh… oh no," Adelaide breathed. "You don't think…?"

"I think our military was caught off guard," Inga stated gravely. "My guess is it overtook them, likely in the night while most of them slept."

"But… they must have had a watch posted," Adelaide protested, horrified.

"The radius is difficult to see even during the day; perhaps they did not expect it to move so quickly."

"Is there any chance they just ran away?" Maaya asked shakily.

"It would be unlike them, but it's not out of the question. What does make that scenario unlikely is that if even one had escaped the area would be swarming with personnel," Inga said, and though she was clearly trying to keep her expression neutral, Maaya could tell she was agitated.

"This means there's a hole in their wall and they don't even know it yet," Halvar said in a low voice. "I'm sure they'll figure it out eventually, but for now…"

Adelaide paced back and forth, biting her lip as she fell deep in thought. All eyes were upon her now, ever in deference to their captain.

Maaya felt like she should be afraid. Everything about the situation was telling her she should be. The sudden disappearance of the military presence, their almost complete lack of reinforcements, the ominous absence of any of the ghosts that were supposed to be plentiful, the radius that was expanding faster than any of them had thought… all signs of an expedition doomed to fail.

But she wasn't afraid. She couldn't be. She had come so far and fought so hard against enemies both living and dead, that this was just another obstacle. They were almost there. Weeks ago she had heard whispers of the mysterious Krethan weapon, and now here she was, standing at the brink of its ill-omened aura. Against all odds she had made it here, and now it was time to get through the one last hindrance in her way.

Adelaide stopped, then turned back to her small company. They watched her attentively, waiting for orders.

"I understand this is not what any of us expected or planned for, but it looks like this is our reality now," she said firmly. "We're going to need to pick up the slack. Inga, Halvar, I need you to get back to the nearest camp and get word to them of what's happened here. Bring our friends from the station with you to help spread the word to our associates. Tell them Maaya and I are inside and need immediate backup, and ask them to keep a lookout for any of our friends who might have been held at bay."

"You three are going in alone, cap'n?" Halvar asked incredulously.

"Yes. If you're swift enough we won't be alone for long, but it's vital you spread the word. If it's expanding fast enough to take the perimeter guards by surprise here, there's a chance it could have done the same elsewhere. Oh, and Inga, I know I've asked a lot of you already, but… could you make sure all of our other plans are still proceeding without issue?"

"Leave it to me, Captain," Inga said, bowing slightly. "I sincerely apologize for my lack of results here, but it won't happen again."

"This wasn't your fault," Adelaide assured her. "I know I can rely on you just like I always have."

"It's okay, you don't have to say it; I know you trust me, too," Halvar grinned.

"Of course! Whatever would I do without you? Saber, don't answer that."

Saber closed her mouth and simply winked at Halvar instead.

"Will that be all, Captain?" Inga inquired.

"It will," Adelaide said heavily. "I apologize for this abrupt separation, but we *will* see each other again soon, and that's an order. Sound good?"

"It will be my pleasure to carry that out," Inga replied, and without another word she walked over and swept both Adelaide and Maaya into a tight hug.

"Good luck in there, you three. I hope by the time I'm standing here again it's with a grand party to welcome you back after your success. Take care, friends," Halvar said.

"Be safe, please," Maaya said, realizing this was the first time she would be away from them since she had boarded the Windfire back in Selenthia. "And… hurry back."

"Not too quickly, though. I just spent three days on a train with Halvar's ugly mug; I need a breather," Saber teased, but then the two clasped hands firmly, staring at each other as only good friends could.

"Give them hell for me, yeah?" Halvar smiled.

"I will take great joy in sending them straight back to it."

With that, Inga and Halvar departed, heading swiftly back toward the station. Maaya sadly watched them go. She had always envisioned them being a part of this, and now… now she was one of only three.

Adelaide grimaced, then turned back to face the outpost. Maaya looked on from beside her, focusing her eyes on the faint grey border, the only thing that separated relative safety from certain death. It wasn't moving now, but it would inevitably do so again, inching toward her where she stood. This was how the world would fall if they failed: not from any single powerful catastrophe, but from the long slow progression of an unstoppable force sweeping over the world like a disease.

"Look there," Adelaide said suddenly, pointing past the abandoned camp.

From a point far, far inside the perimeter, Maaya saw movement. A wave of light seemed to be erupting from some unknown point miles and miles away, expanding quickly every minute. At its current speed it would hit the perimeter in less than a minute.

"A pulse?" Maaya asked, and Adelaide nodded.

"I guess this is my time to shine," Saber said nonchalantly, though her expression betrayed her agitation.

"Maaya, stand back; I don't know how far the radius will expand once the pulse hits," Adelaide said nervously. "Saber… how do you feel? You all right?"

"As well as I can be considering I may not exist in a few moments," Saber replied, staring straight ahead at the oncoming wave.

Maaya watched with growing nervousness as it approached. It wasn't very bright, nor in any way particularly intimidating in any other way than its size and speed. But it signified only the swift and immediate termination of existence of both the living and the dead. She tore her gaze away from the wave to look at the gem on Saber's forehead, the gem people had died and been killed over. The gem she had lost friends over, and the one that was now supposed to protect them against a power so formidable and unrelenting it had brought an entire nation to its knees. Was something so small really capable of deflecting such a force?

"Maaya, just in case this doesn't work out for whatever reason… I love you, okay?" Saber said meaningfully. "Everything is going to work out no matter what."

"It will, so don't you start that," Maaya said, gripping Saber's hands tightly in hers. "Don't even think about it."

"What, you aren't going to get sappy with me? That's fair; it is a pretty new thing for you—oof."

Maaya pulled her into a tight hug, and for a moment she feared that she would never let go. This was happening almost too fast for her to absorb.

"You've always been the bravest one of us," Maaya said, her voice muffled slightly in Saber's robes. "And if it hadn't been for you I wouldn't have made it even halfway here. So… thank you, for being my best friend, and for everything else."

"Anything for you, darling," Saber grinned. "Now, stand back; if this doesn't work I'd feel really bad if you died because I pushed you into a heartfelt moment."

It took every ounce of will Maaya had, but she let go, then walked over to Adelaide's side. Adelaide took her hand and they stood silently together as Saber turned slowly again to face the pulse that was now mere seconds from them.

"Once more unto the abyss, it seems," Saber murmured, and then, after a moment's hesitation, she stepped forward to meet the wave.

PART III

31

ACROSS NO MAN'S LAND

Time seemed to slow almost to a stop. Maaya saw the wave coming and Saber floating defiantly in its path. All the things she wanted to say ran wild through her mind. She had been here before, back in Sark, watching as hundreds of ghosts had converged on her friends, being close enough to see them but too far to do any good. Would this be how things ended with Saber as well? And could Maaya really say that she learned anything when yet again she found herself wishing she could reverse time to say all the things that were now too late to say?

The wave passed over Saber, and it crashed over an invisible barrier before and around her as the ocean might throw itself hopelessly against a rock. Saber didn't move, and though angry the wave appeared to be, it converged upon itself harmlessly several feet behind her. Maaya couldn't tell if Saber was in any way harmed, or even if she was still there; she had lost sight of the ghost behind the oncoming pulse, which was now set to hit the barrier in less than a moment.

And then it hit. The result was somewhat more anti-climactic than Maaya had expected; there was no sound or burst of light or pressure when it arrived. It simply dissolved as though it had never been. The only difference was the radius itself, which had almost imperceptibly expanded by a few inches. It did not seem the intimidating weapon of the end of the world she had been picturing; it was slow and silent, it had been trying for decades to consume the world, and it had taken this long to reach just this far.

Then she saw Saber, who had turned around to stare at Maaya and Adelaide, not bothering to hide her proud grin.

"Hey, would you look at that? It works! Who knew my tacky jewelry was a greater weapon than anything the mighty Krethan government could ever develop?"

Maaya dashed over into the barrier and hugged the ghost tightly. She didn't have to say a word.

Adelaide followed close behind, a smile on her face, one of distinct and overpowering relief.

"That answers our most pressing question," she said. "How do you feel? Did it hurt?"

"It felt like nothing at all. I was expecting a little nudge at least, but had I not been watching it with my own eyes I wouldn't have been able to tell anything passed over me at all," Saber informed her. "To be honest I was a little worried that I'd suffer some adverse effects from it, but I'll definitely take this comfort."

"I'm so glad," Maaya exclaimed. "It looks like there should be plenty of room for Adelaide and I to hide behind you whenever a pulse comes up."

"Indeed. Just stay behind me, fair maidens, and I will protect you," Saber said valiantly.

"That didn't take long to go to your head," Maaya snorted.

"My head is literally the source of your salvation, what did you expect?" Saber returned without missing a beat.

"Kids, let's focus," Adelaide interrupted gently, fighting to keep a straight face. "Before we go too far I'd like to take a quick detour along the radius to see if there are any other camps that might still be populated."

"Wouldn't they check on each other?" Maaya asked, trotting to catch up with Adelaide as the taller girl strode forward.

"They do. Or at least… they should. Either way, it would give me some peace of mind to be able to speak with someone else out here. That we're the only ones so far makes me very uncomfortable."

"I'm having trouble understanding just how empty it is out here," Saber commented. "Being caught in the expanding radius while asleep is one thing, but what about everyone else outside it? Don't tell me your soldiers can't actually see these ghosts."

"Most can't, but they have implants," Adelaide explained. "There are few LCs, even, but seeing the ghosts coming is usually enough. Our soldiers have been trained to stay clear of them for decades. Typically the only way a soldier is caught off guard is if the ghosts appear right on top of them, and even then they can usually get out of the way in time."

"How very odd, then…" Saber murmured.

They carried on in silence, walking to the end of the empty road and beyond. To Maaya, it was like walking into another world. These houses, though weathered by storms, were otherwise untouched by nature; life of any kind had no place here, so it had never had a chance to begin taking back the land the humans had built upon so long ago. Everywhere Maaya looked, death stared back at her. She remembered that night back on the hill in Sark, feeling as empty as the world looked, and she suppressed a shudder. This feeling was just like that, but magnified.

Nothing changed as they walked, save for the fact that they were now passing into what Maaya assumed used to be farmlands. There were even fewer buildings here, which only made the empty feeling inside her worse. The only evidence that anything other than dirt had ever been here was the skeletons of long-dead trees, fragile and hollow, delicate enough that they might break under someone's intense stare.

Suddenly, in the distance, Maaya saw them. At least two dozen walkers floated slowly, silently, aimlessly. She nudged Adelaide lightly in the arm, then pointed, unwilling to speak lest she drew their attention somehow. Adelaide narrowed her eyes at the ghosts, then shrugged.

"Not to worry; they aren't headed our way. We'll be seeing a lot of those as we go, and I know we made a lot of blood cards but we need to save them only for when we're in real danger. Otherwise we need to keep track of their movements so we can stay out of trouble."

Maaya bit her lip. She was concerned about the ghosts and whether they would turn to pursue her like they had in the past. The more this happened, the less she was convinced of Saber's determined assertions that the ghosts weren't after her.

The more she thought about it, the more she wondered if the ghosts were actually smarter than she had previously given them credit before. They had somehow managed to pin her three friends down despite their years of knowledge of *libris* and fighting ghosts. It was also possible that they knew what she was planning to do and were thus doing what they could to stop her. Despite how slowly they moved, their efforts had proven much more effective than Maaya would have originally thought.

Something about the atmosphere inside the barrier drove them to walk in silence. Maaya fought for words to break it, but she couldn't think of any. It was as though the pall of death and fear of everything that stood in her way prevented her from thinking of anything else. So stifling was it that it was hard to avoid feeling alone even as Adelaide and Saber walked directly beside her.

Half an hour later they reached another military outpost. Adelaide's shoulders drooped as they approached and they saw that this camp too was empty, and well within the barrier.

"Damn. I can only assume this is the case for most of the others, but we don't have time to find out," Adelaide muttered. "It looks like it's the three of us going through No Man's Land together."

"Is that what they call this? How cheery," Maaya said dully.

"I can hardly think of better circumstances under which to spend some quality bonding time," Saber said airily. "Relationships develop so much faster when both parties are risking their lives together. Or so they say."

"Who says that?" Adelaide asked, a small smile playing across her lips.

"I don't know. *They*," Saber repeated, gesturing vaguely before her. "They have a point, though. I mean, we saw how fast you two fell for each other when Maaya was on the run from the military."

Maaya snorted.

"That had nothing to do with it."

"You mean to tell me you didn't feel even a flicker of that desire to throw caution to the winds and sweep your lady love off her feet when you were already doing so many other crazy things?" Saber teased.

"If anything, that made it worse. It's hard to think about how to confess a crush when you're worried about an entire country trying to hunt you down," Maaya laughed.

"I'm with you, Saber," Adelaide said as they started away from the radius. "Maaya was moving so fast I thought I'd lose her if I didn't make some effort to hold on to her."

"What are you talking about? I'm the one who has a hard time keeping up with you," Maaya protested.

"See? It's happening already," Saber interjected with a grin. "Soon you'll be arguing like a married couple, and with as often as you two are risking your lives for this endeavor that could be a reality soon. Not that I'm dropping hints or anything—"

"*Saber*," Maaya groaned, and the other two laughed. Before Saber could reply, however, Adelaide suddenly straightened, holding up her hand.

"Another pulse. It's coming a little sooner than I expected. Ready, Saber?"

"Ready," the ghost said determinedly. "My protective aura is larger than I thought, but stay close behind me just in case."

Maaya and Adelaide huddled close behind Saber, unable to tear their eyes from the oncoming pulse. Maaya already knew they would be safe, but there was something about being inside the barrier that suddenly made it all the more terrifying. The pulse was vast, stretching as high as the sky itself, and she suddenly felt very small.

And then the wave washed over them. Maaya gasped and shut her eyes tight, but felt nothing. There wasn't even a sound to indicate that it had passed them by or that Saber's own protective barrier had caused any disruption.

"You guys okay?" Saber asked quickly.

"We're fine. Didn't feel a thing," Adelaide answered. "That's one less thing to worry about."

"We're not safe just yet," Maaya said suddenly, reaching for her pack of cards.

Nearby, a small group of ghosts had appeared out of thin air. While at first they moved away from Maaya and the others, they soon began to turn. Slowly, ever so slowly they turned, until finally they were unmistakably coming straight for the girls.

"They're doing it again," Adelaide growled, reaching for her cards.

"Why does this keep happening?" Maaya asked worriedly.

"I don't know. I only saw this once before on the ship, and nothing I've read has suggested they've ever done this, either. I can only imagine it's because we're getting closer to their machine."

"I'll take these. Save your cards," Maaya suggested, taking a step forward while fighting the paranoia that swelled within her. That Adelaide, a Krethan *libris* elite, had never heard of this phenomenon happening before was definitely not a good sign. At the very least, Maaya figured that if the ghosts were really after her, she ought to be the one to dispose of them.

She waited until the ghosts were comfortably within striking range. All the while, the ghosts did not alter their course even a little. Regardless of who they were after, it was clear these ghosts, unlike their Selenthian kin, had enough awareness to attempt to chase down their prey.

A few blood cards streaked through the air, followed by a torrent of red sparks, and then Maaya and the others were alone in No Man's Land once again.

Maaya let out a quiet breath of relief. Even if these ghosts were smarter, they were still equally susceptible to her newly empowered cards. With as many cards as she had, she could take down a few hundred on her own. She just hoped she wouldn't have to.

Adelaide relaxed, but she was visibly uneasy.

"I wasn't expecting to have to worry about those things chasing us," she said tersely. "Let's keep moving. The sooner we stop this thing the better."

"Do we have a plan? I can't imagine you expect to reach the machine in a day," Saber inquired.

"We're going to find some shelter to rest during the day. The ghosts are easier to see at night, so we'll move then. It's also cooler, which should be less taxing on our bodies. Maaya and I can sleep in shifts," Adelaide explained.

"At least shelter shouldn't be too hard to find out here," Maaya said quietly. She gazed around at the houses and buildings that were left in No Man's Land. It was hard to imagine that these buildings hadn't been occupied for at least a century.

Onward they trudged, leaving the visible radius behind them. A shroud of quiet and loneliness hung over everything Maaya could see and hear, and she started determinedly straight ahead. If she was right, they were the only human around for miles and miles, and they were heading straight for the birthplace of the deadliest force in the world. There would be no help for them out here.

"Oh, if Svante could see us now," Saber said cheerily, completely unaffected by the misery of their surroundings. "Not that I expect he would make it too far even with his neat little augments. He'd probably bumble around nervously while stuttering about how dangerous this is, but he'd be overjoyed."

"Don't forget trying to get home for tea on Wednesdays!" Maaya said.

"Oh, I do miss that man. He was so very odd, but a genuinely nice person. He stuck out like a sore thumb in Sark. I hope he's having a pleasant death," Saber sighed.

"I suppose what happened to him was better than the ghosts getting him," Maaya added softly.

"Too right. I almost wish he'd come back, though. There was still so much he could have added to the world. Is that a weird thing to say?"

"Yes, but I get where you're coming from," Adelaide smiled. "I haven't forgotten about him or what you'd like to do for him. We'll work on that once we're finished with this, along with everything else."

"I was hoping it would all be over after this, but I guess it will be nice to tie up all these loose ends without the threat of the ghosts ever again," Maaya said.

"We'll be fine. We destroy the machine, we set things right with Svante's family, and then we get to setting up our new lives. What more is there?" Saber continued airily.

"What more indeed," Adelaide said delicately, but at Maaya's inquiring look, she only smiled and glanced away.

"Honestly, Maaya, if you're so inclined, I think we should just stay here," Saber said as though she hadn't heard. "You can be yourself here, and people love you for it—or at the very least they don't try to kill you. If we never so much as point our noses in Selenthia's general direction again we'll be none the worse for it."

Maaya fell silent. Despite being here in Krethus and enjoying the safety and security it had to offer, she couldn't keep thoughts of Selenthia out of her mind. She couldn't forget what friends back home who might still be alive. She still feared returning to Sark, but she would have to go back to her home country eventually. That much she knew. She had made her friends a promise.

Her heart throbbed with pain as she thought of Roshan. Despite his concerns, he had done nothing but support them the whole way even when

Maaya and the others had decided to run off across the world with someone they all previously thought had been trying to kill them. He had always been so patient, so forgiving. She had promised him she would come back once this was all over. Was he still alive to remember that promise? Had he gone to bed that night thinking he would see his friend soon and then never woken up again? Or had the ghosts taken him after Maaya left, too far away to protect him?

A flicker of doubt passed through her mind, and she blinked, trying to clear it. Thinking about returning to Sark was dangerous. Even if the rest of the world slowly learned what had happened here and somehow left behind their irrational fear and anger, Sark was no place for Maaya. The reputation she had there was too great for even a miracle to do away with.

It didn't take them long to find a place to rest. Outside one nearby neighborhood only a few small houses and sheds dotted the otherwise barren and rolling landscape. They walked toward one of the sheds, made of three walls and a slanting roof. Maaya didn't like the wide open space—it was too easy to be seen and too hard to hide—but it gave them an excellent view of their surroundings. Strangely, Maaya couldn't see even a single ghost no matter which direction she looked. Their strange absence unnerved her, but it was better than the alternative.

"We can stay here until dusk," Adelaide said, letting down her pack with a sigh of relief and rolling out a thin blanket. "We can take naps in turn before setting off."

"Sounds like a plan," Maaya replied comfortably, settling down next to Adelaide and stretching. She wasn't tired, but she had many years of experience resting during the day to prepare for nighttime excursions.

When they were both comfortable, Adelaide draped her arm around Maaya's shoulder, pulled the girl close, and kissed the top of her head.

"I know this isn't the most romantic of situations, but I'm glad you of all people are with me. I feel so much better now than when I tried to do this alone," she said softly.

"I'm glad you're with me, too," Maaya giggled, twisting so she could plant a kiss on Adelaide's cheek. "It's hard to be afraid when you're here. I wish we had a little more time for ourselves, though."

"Oh, once this is over I'm going to shower you with so much attention you'll get sick of me for sure," Adelaide grinned. "I've yet to take you on a proper date."

"I guess we'd better finish this quickly, then. But next time I'm paying," Maaya said.

"Whatever makes you feel better, dear," Adelaide chuckled. "If you don't mind, I think I'll nap first. Are you okay with taking first watch?"

"That's fine!"

"You know, both of you can rest while I keep a look out. I don't need to sleep," Saber said pointedly.

"I appreciate the offer but I think it would be safest to have two pairs of eyes on our surroundings at all times," Adelaide replied. Saber nodded, then positioned herself a few yards from the entrance to the shed.

"I'll wake you toward late afternoon," Maaya said, leaning over and kissing Adelaide's forehead.

"Or sooner, if you get lonely," Adelaide teased. "Be careful out there, okay? Don't hesitate to wake me up if something happens."

Maaya stepped outside and sat near Saber on an old overturned bucket, already missing the shade. It wasn't particularly hot, but the glare of the sun off the miles and miles of dirt around them hurt her eyes. Luckily, there still seemed to be no sign of the ghosts. She tried not to think of the fact that they could simply appear out of thin air.

She turned as she heard the sound of rustling paper and saw Saber unrolling the portrait of herself, staring at it intently.

"It's still so strange to look at myself this way. I don't think I'll ever get over it," Saber said, almost to herself.

"He captured you well," Maaya smiled, peering over the ghost's shoulders.

"Absolutely he did. You know… I'm glad we came here. I know it was out of necessity, but I want to be selfish and take some joy from this. I spent years thinking I would never know who I was or anything about my past, and now it's almost assured. They're trying to figure that out as I speak, and that's… that's a powerful feeling all right."

"Hey, you deserve it," Maaya replied, flinging her arms around the ghost's shoulders. "You're allowed to have things for yourself sometimes, and I can't think of anything better for you. I just wish I could have done something for you back in Sark."

"You made my existence great enough to make me forget this even bothered me," Saber said, her voice wavering ever so slightly. "I know our situation wasn't great, but the people were. Even when it was just you and me, I wouldn't have given it up for anything if it meant you wouldn't be there. But look at us now. We're going to save the world, I'm going to find out who I used to be, and you've got yourself an attractive lady pirate captain on your arm."

"Yeah… look at us now," Maaya sighed contentedly. There was a short pause, and then Maaya continued uncertainly, "Hey… what do you think about ever going back to Sark?"

"What in the world for?" Saber asked, raising her eyebrows.

"I don't know. Just in general I guess. Adelaide mentioned it a few times.

She's mentioned Rahu, too. I think she wants us to go back and take care of our unfinished business."

"We have no unfinished business," Saber replied flatly. "Rahu isn't our problem. I know I mentioned wanting to behead him but that was in jest. The only thing we have to do that's in any way related to Sark is to get back in touch with our old friends and otherwise stay as far away from it as possible. It's far too risky to do anything else."

"She seems to really hate him, though. She offered to come with us," Maaya mused quietly.

"We all do, but there's no facing him down. Not with Adelaide, and not even if she had her entire crew at her back. He's brainwashed everyone. Sark is a small town compared to Levien, but there are still thousands of people there. If you stepped foot in that town again you'd be dead, as would be anyone who tried to defend you."

"Yeah… you're right," Maaya exhaled. "I guess I've been dreaming of a perfect end to all this, one that sees justice being done to Rahu for everything he's done."

"That's the thing about justice, unfortunately. It's fallible, inconsistent, and susceptible to temptation and corruption," Saber said sympathetically. "But let's not dwell on such things. You escaped and you're making a much better life for yourself in a place no one can touch you. So let's talk about something more important: what do you think my name was? I don't know many Krethan names so I can't even begin to guess."

They spent the next few hours hypothesizing about Saber's past and coming up with many increasingly ridiculous names. Maaya loved every minute of it. Beyond providing a distraction from keeping watch over the seemingly endless and empty expanse around them, it was clear it made Saber happy. Saber had always been in high spirits even if her sense of humor was a little crass, but she had always been the one using her unique talents to help Maaya. Maaya had always had trouble thinking of what she could possibly do for a ghost. Now, even though find out who Saber had been was not Maaya's doing, she was glad to be a part of it. Saber really did deserve every bit of it.

Three times more did the pulses come, and each time Maaya and Saber huddled close to the shed, making sure that the girl sleeping inside was properly protected as well. Already Maaya was becoming less and less afraid of them; so long as Saber was nearby the pulses might well not have been there at all.

Eventually, when the sun started to fall and the landscape turned orange, Maaya stepped inside the shed and gently shook Adelaide awake.

"That time already, huh?" Adelaide yawned, immediately taking her nearby card pouch and fastening it to her arm. "Anything noteworthy happen while I was asleep?"

"Nothing. Nothing *not* noteworthy, either," Maaya replied. "It was as dull as could be out there and I'm not sure if that's a good sign or a bad one."

"These things have never seemed like ones for omens; so far they've been fairly straightforward about their intentions. My guess is they're still about as brainless as we think they are. Anyway, get some sleep. I'll wake you when it's time to eat and get moving."

"You going to be okay out there?" Maaya asked, settling down where Adelaide had just been sleeping.

"I'm far more afraid of boredom than I am of any ghost. I may have to wake you early if Saber doesn't provide sufficient company," Adelaide chuckled.

"You won't have to worry about that. She talks enough for two people."

"That's the problem. So do I."

The girls laughed, then Adelaide stepped out into the late afternoon sun. Maaya quickly felt a wave of exhaustion wash over her now that she was lying still in the shade. It wasn't the bed from Adelaide's guest room or her comfortable couch back home, but it would have to do. Maaya hadn't yet been so spoiled that she had lost her ability to fall asleep just about anywhere.

Before she knew it, she felt herself being nudged awake. When she opened her eyes, all was dark. It only took her a moment to remember where she was.

"You were so far gone I felt bad to wake you, but we should get moving," Adelaide said quietly. "I made us some food."

Maaya sat up slowly and rubbed her eyes. She was no stranger to waking up in the dark. Maaya had expected it to be far worse; with no one around for miles and the military now gone, she had expected to wake up in the total absence of light. Instead, when she opened her eyes, she noticed her surroundings bathed in the soft white glow of moonlight. Just outside, a small lantern Adelaide had brought with her lit up a tiny makeshift stove upon which was stretched a short length of foil. A few slices of bread were warming upon it while a few eggs cooked slowly.

"Eggs and toast for dinner? That's a new one," Maaya said as she stood up. Before anything else she made sure she had her cards on her, and then she slipped on her shoes.

"It's breakfast for us!" Adelaide said, and there was a tone to her voice Maaya couldn't decipher. "By the way, when you step out here… keep your head down."

"What? I'm sure your cooking isn't that ba—" Maaya started, but then her breath caught in her throat as she left the relative safety of the shed.

Now she could see the source of the light. And it wasn't the moon.

The tall faceless ghosts, thousands of them, floated slowly in all directions as far as Maaya could see. While none of them seemed to be headed in their direction, Maaya immediately understood the threat. Staring at them for too long was bound to cause her to make eye contact with one of them eventually.

She glanced away quickly before she could become overwhelmed by the sheer number of them, but not being able to see them was almost worse—she knew they were there just outside her field of vision. She consoled herself, thinking that if Adelaide were unconcerned enough that she could be making a hot breakfast while the ghosts paced around them they couldn't be in mortal danger. Still, images of her last night in Sark replayed themselves in her mind, accompanied by ringing memories of screams and terror. There were countless more here than there had been even on the worst night back home, and she felt almost dizzy as she tried to suppress the urge to panic.

"You kids take it easy and enjoy your food; I'll keep an eye on these things," Saber said from nearby, her attempt at sounding bored slightly ruined by the tremor of nervousness in her voice.

"Where did they all come from?" Maaya asked, aghast.

"As the sun set they just started appearing. I imagine this is what we can expect all night," Adelaide grumbled, shutting off the small fire. "We might make better time if we travel during the day at this rate."

"While true, I think your point about it being safer to travel at night is even more true now we're seeing just how many of them apparently wander about in the dark," Saber commented. "Trying to sleep during this would just be asking for trouble."

"Agreed. We'll just have to do our best with what we've got," Adelaide sighed. "Come eat up, Maaya. It's only an hour after sunset, but we should get moving soon."

"I don't suppose if we attacked any of them the rest would notice us?" Maaya asked, doing her best to scoop food into her mouth from the foil without spilling it everywhere.

"I don't think so, but considering what else they've been doing lately I don't want to tempt them. We'll save our cards only for situations where they're absolutely necessary. At least I know we can still outrun them if it comes down to it."

They finished quickly and packed up their few belongings in minutes. Saber floated nearby, keeping a wary eye on the nearby ghosts. Maaya fought to avoid staring; she felt distinctly uncomfortable not being able to see where any of them were moving.

After one final sweep of the area in and around the shed, Adelaide started off with Maaya keeping step beside her. If Adelaide still had any of her maps with her, she wasn't using them, though Maaya wasn't overly concerned about this.

A few attempts at conversation were made, but they faded quickly. For her part, Maaya found it difficult to focus on anything other than her immediate surroundings. It wasn't just that they were passing through unfamiliar territory in the dark; it was the ever-present but silent threat of the ghosts. She tensed, feeling like she did when she shut her eyes when someone was about to strike her, but without knowing when—only this feeling never went away. It followed her, an invisible force constricting around her chest that made it difficult to breathe and focus.

More than once they had to stop or change course to avoid the ghosts. In a few instances, several lines of ghosts had headed straight for them; they froze as the ghosts passed within just a few feet of them, not daring to move or fight lest they decide to turn and attack. Miraculously, none of the ghosts turned toward them, eventually leaving them free to move on.

As the hours passed, gradually and mercifully, the number of ghosts seemed to lessen. Maaya wasn't sure how far they had traveled, but they had moved at a slow pace the whole night, constantly delayed and redirected. Despite their slow pace, Maaya felt more fatigued than she had in a long while. She had spent the entire night tense, afraid, and on high alert, and it was beginning to weigh heavily on her.

Maaya gripped Adelaide's hand as they pressed on, suddenly wishing they had the help of the Blackfins Inga had promised. As of now they were but three faces in a sea of thousands, all of which appeared to want them dead. As grateful as Maaya was not to be doing this alone, she felt anything but safe.

32

FRAYING OF MIND AND BODY

By the time the sun started rising, Maaya and the others found a safe place to stay in the skeletal remains of a two-story building near a cluster of boulders and long-dead trees. It looked like it could have been someone's vacation home at some point long ago, but now very little remained except its brick walls. It wasn't quite tall enough to provide protection against the ghosts if they passed through the area, but it gave them good vision of their surroundings. Maaya felt much more comfortable keeping watch from above rather than on the ground.

"You should rest first, Maaya; you look completely beat," Adelaide said, letting out a sigh of relief as she sat down with her back against one of the crumbling walls.

"I'm fine. I'm just not sure I breathed the entire night. It was so eerie walking through so many of them like that," Maaya replied as she sat down next to her, grateful for the weight off her tired feet. "How far did we get, do you know?"

"Not as far as I would have liked. I'd say maybe a third of the way? I'll see if I can think of a way to make better progress tonight. I'm just worried the ghosts won't be quite as nice to us the closer we get."

"Pulse incoming," Saber reported, floating casually over to them. It had already become routine for them.

The pulse arrived and then passed over them without incident just as it had done a dozen times during the previous night. Maaya didn't even bother to watch it go.

"Just imagine: when this is all over, you won't have to babysit us anymore," Maaya teased.

"Right," Saber answered dully. "I'm going to take a walk."

"You okay?" Maaya asked concernedly.

"Only if you don't ask any more stupid questions. I'll be fine, I just need to walk this off."

Maaya glanced away toward the floor, biting her lip. She knew Saber wasn't herself when the machine affected her like that, but it didn't make her words hurt any less.

"Take as much time as you need. Just stay nearby in case there's another pulse, all right?" Adelaide said calmly.

"No, really? I thought I'd just leave you both here and see what happens," Saber replied sharply, then took a breath, running her fingers through her hair. "Sorry. This is why I need to go. I'll be around."

Saber turned and left immediately, floating down through the floor and out of sight. Adelaide and Maaya shared an uncomfortable glance, and then Adelaide gave her best attempt at a smile.

"She'll be all right. Do you want to get some sleep?"

"I'm fine!" Maaya repeated, though part of this protest came from her eagerness to prove her strength to Adelaide. "I just needed to get off my feet and rest, that's all. What about you? You don't look so hot yourself."

"Excuse me?" Adelaide teased, shoving Maaya lightly. "I'm all right. If you wouldn't mind taking watch, I'll get an hour or two in. Completely flipping my sleep schedule like this is wreaking havoc on me."

"I can do that. I want to do some more reading, anyway… and be here for Saber when she comes back."

"It's awful, what this thing is doing to her," Adelaide sighed. "I hate that we can't do anything about it until we destroy the machine."

"I've been thinking about that, actually… you don't think it was these ghosts that killed her in the first place, do you?" Maaya asked slowly.

"That's an interesting question… what made you think that?"

"It's just strange that the gem that has the power to get us to this machine is on her forehead. Meaning, she was wearing it when she died. Why her of all people? How did she get it? It makes me think she must have been in the area, or maybe even working on the machine itself when things went wrong."

"It is odd, I'll grant you that. She definitely didn't have it by accident, not if she was wearing it proudly on her head like that. But I don't think the machine killed her, or the ghosts. For one, if she were killed by the ghosts, she'd just disappear like everyone else they kill. Second, this gem seems to negate at least some of the machine's energies. Apart from that gem, she's an ordinary ghost. Lucky for us, that."

"I suppose. I'm still so curious as to how she got it. It's such an odd thing for her to have, especially when she ended up all the way in Sark."

"Hey, maybe we'll figure that out when we get there or when we figure out her real identity. As far as I know there was only one of those gems, so there's bound to be documentation of it somewhere. That said… I've been doing some thinking of my own, and my theory is a little darker."

"What is it?" Maaya asked, leaning forward slightly.

"I… I just wonder if maybe she's the reason the machine went haywire," Adelaide said quietly, as though she were admitting a terrible secret. "If the gem is such a powerful tool against this machine, but it died with her, maybe that took away the only real failsafe its inventor had."

"But… that's…" Maaya stammered. That couldn't be true. Even if it didn't mean Saber was at fault, it was still hard to think that she could have had anything to do with it.

To Maaya's growing discomfort, however, the more she thought about this theory, the more it made sense even if she still wasn't ready to accept it. Her initial reaction was that this couldn't be true, because even if Saber had died the gem would still exist on her body… until Maaya remembered that she herself had possessed the real gem. She had taken the circlet from the abandoned mansion in Sark, and with it, Saber, who had been trapped inside. This meant that there was no difference between the ghostly version of the gem Saber wore and the real one—they were one and the same.

"Please don't get the wrong idea," Adelaide added hastily. "I don't think she's at fault for any of this, even by accident. I just think she may have held the key to stopping it if it ever got out of control, and that her death meant it disappeared when it was needed most."

"Assuming this gem was meant to be a failsafe. We don't have any idea what it was supposed to be," Maaya murmured.

"Also true. Like I said, a dark theory, but just a theory," Adelaide said, almost apologetically. "The details don't matter. Whatever led up to this, that machine is getting destroyed as soon as we get there, and all will be well when this is done."

"Let's not tell Saber about this theory of yours, yeah?" Maaya suggested, and Adelaide shook her head emphatically.

"Absolutely not. Even if I'm right, the poor girl doesn't need that on her conscience. Not after everything else. Anyway… I'm going to get some sleep. Wake me up around midday, okay? We can switch off once before we start our night."

Adelaide set down her small sleeping mat and rested her head on her pack, and within minutes was fast asleep.

Maaya smiled, then quietly pulled Kim's diary out of her own pack. She hadn't had the chance to make much progress on it since their ride on the train, and it was about time she got back to it.

She flipped slowly through the pages that were filled with progressively longer entries with increasingly neater handwriting. Maaya felt a swell of pride. Kim had clearly put a lot of effort into this, and it was showing.

Sylvia isn't coming over as much as she used to. It feels a little lonelier here. I hope she isn't dying. I want to think that she'll be around forever. Maybe Sovaan was wrong and she's just a regular ghost. Maybe it's our fault for not going to visit her as often as we used to. I wish we could, but I'm so hungry I feel weak. Maaya and Saber are doing their best, but it's hard for them to feed four people.

Maaya felt the pain of an old guilt wound reopen deep within her. She had tried for a long time to live life without regrets, but that hadn't quite gone according to plan. She missed Sylvia and Styx, and promised herself that when she got back to Selenthia, there would be no more going weeks without seeing her own friends no matter what the circumstances were.

She continued on to the next entry, her curiosity suddenly piqued when she saw Rahu's name.

Rahu hasn't come by for a long time. I've almost forgotten what he sounds like. Not what he looks like, though. He's the only rich person who ever comes here. I hope he hasn't forgotten us. We need to eat. Maaya doesn't like him, that much I know. I didn't used to understand why, but now I think I do. The more I think about what he's doing, the worse it seems. It's not fair. I don't think the boys understand, but they don't care about where the food comes from as long as it tastes good. Does he really care about us? I know he's not perfect, but he wouldn't lie about that… would he?

Maaya turned the page roughly. Kim had been a little more perceptive than Maaya had thought; she had always hoped her personal grudge with Rahu would stay personal, at least until her friends were a little older. She hated that Kim had slowly started to find out the hard way what kind of a man Rahu was on her own.

Truth be told, she had never wanted her friends to hate Rahu, or even to dislike him. She knew what it was like to be alone and to have so little faith in the world. She wanted them to be appreciative of Rahu, to think that there was good and charity in the world, and that it was possible for a stranger with power and wealth to love someone like them when he had no reason to. She wanted them to think that such people existed. By the time they learned otherwise, she hoped, they would be older and more prepared to deal with the evils of the world on their own terms—not by necessity and through hard lessons as Maaya had.

She set the book gently aside, a whirl of emotions running through her mind already. It turned out such people did exist, and that they were far more numerous than Maaya would have ever guessed. While her few friends back in Sark had been wonderful, the nature of their relationships made acts of kindness less surprising. Nadya, however, had been a total stranger, and had been the first one to persuade Maaya to think that there didn't need to be a reason for someone to be kind to another. And then there was Emil, in his own strange way. He had asked for much, but given much in return, making and fulfilling promises to her that he would suffer little from breaking. Then there was Halvar, Gunnar, Inga… not to mention Adelaide.

She sighed, closing her eyes as she felt tears threatening to surge forward. This was the world she had wanted her friends so desperately to know, and they had all been so *close.* They had spent years fighting to make the world that much better, hoping one day to seek out those better parts of it themselves, and they had died just hours before they would have realized that world existed just outside the borders of the home they had lived in for so long.

Maaya stood up and walked over to part of the wall that had fallen away, exposing most of the landscape around them. In moments like these she was reminded that she could never truly escape the weight of her experiences. She could promise herself all day and night that she was doing the right thing, that she was fighting through tragedy and hardship to make the world a better place for those who were still here… but she had her doubts as to whether she would still be around to enjoy the world she was trying so hard to save.

Before enough time had passed for Maaya to start concerning herself with the next pulse, Saber floated slowly back into the room looking utterly exhausted. Maaya glanced at her hesitantly, but said nothing in case the ghost was still upset.

However, Saber came over to her immediately, tugging gently on her sleeve and nodding toward another room away from where Adelaide was sleeping. They had hardly left when Saber paused and looked Maaya straight in the eye, clearly hurt.

"Maaya, listen—"

"Don't worry about it," Maaya interrupted softly. "Please. You don't have to apologize every time it happens. I know it's not you."

Saber opened her mouth and closed it again several times before giving up. She let out a long breath and stared into an empty corner of the room.

"It's still unfair. It hurts me that I'm doing this to you, and now to Adelaide. This has to stop."

"And it will! We're so close. I hate that it's doing this to you, but we're almost there, and after that you'll never have to worry about this ever again. Just don't add guilt on top of what you're already feeling," Maaya pleaded.

"Easier said, but… I'll try," Saber sighed. "She's not upset with me, is she?"

"Not even close. She understands this just like I do."

"Good. I'll still make it up to you both, but that makes things a little easier. I'm surprised you're still awake, though."

"I'm keeping watch while Adelaide sleeps," Maaya explained, but Saber didn't look convinced.

"My emotions might be running wild, but my eyes still work fine, you know."

"I know! I think she's right, though. Better safe than sorry, especially if they appear right on top of us; better that one of us is awake already to—"

"It's fine," Saber interjected easily. "I'll take a small blow to my pride if it means my two favorite people in the world stay alive. Oh, and speak of the devil…"

Maaya whirled around to see a group of about twenty ghosts making their way straight toward them. There wasn't an intimidating number of them, but they had suddenly appeared uncomfortably close—if they weren't stopped one way or another, they would arrive in less than a minute.

Maaya immediately opened her card pouch and pulled out a handful of blood cards. She was confident that she could banish them all with only a few strikes, but it had to be done quickly.

"I'll go wake Adelaide," Saber said hurriedly, but Maaya stopped her.

"We don't need to wake her for this. If we wake her up every time a small group comes our way she'll never get any sleep."

"If you say so," Saber said uncertainly.

Maaya led the way, heading swiftly downstairs, her blood cards in hand. As much as she preferred the high ground, she didn't feel safe doing any sort of battling on the second floor of a building with already questionable stability.

Careful not to look the ghosts in the eyes, she took aim and then flung her cards out across the dirt field. The cards struck true, and with a shower of sparks, a number of ghosts disappeared instantly. Maaya let loose another volley, taking out all but a few of the remaining ghosts.

Before she could start thinking that her job of banishing ghosts had become too easy, Saber tapped her on the shoulder urgently.

"More coming from the left."

Maaya instinctively threw another card, the movement in her peripheral vision all she needed to hit her mark accurately. Before Saber could even warn Maaya she had flung another card, this time toward a third group that had appeared to her right. Each group was smaller than the last, and they were all coming from the front, which meant Maaya hardly even had to move to hit them all.

But it didn't remain simple for long. Suddenly, Maaya was aware of a blinding white light right beside her, though she couldn't immediately discern from which direction. She felt a flicker of panic at not being sure where to flee, but then gasped as Saber pushed her roughly forward. Maaya collapsed into the dirt, then sent a blood card flying directly behind her. The sparks were so close that they bounced harmlessly off Maaya's body where she lay.

"Behind is clear!" Saber called. "Careful in front!"

Maaya scrambled to her feet, hastily slipping more cards into her hand… and in her haste to ascertain how much distance remained between her and the oncoming ghosts, she glanced directly into their blank and empty stares.

Maaya had only enough time to feel a sliver of regret before she felt her strength leave her. Being pushed forward had definitely saved her, but it had also put her even closer to the ghosts. This might not have been a problem had Maaya an easy escape route, or if she were wearing any of her physical augments, but she hadn't thought them necessary at the time. All of that would be irrelevant once she made eye contact anyway, she thought dimly.

She was vaguely aware of Saber's scream of alarm as she fell to her knees, her cards falling uselessly to the ground beside her, and then the world went dark.

Maaya felt herself being shaken awake, and she opened her eyes slowly; even though she was in the shade, the bright light of the mid-morning sun bore into her, and she could feel a headache coming on already.

"Maaya? Are you all right?"

She recognized Adelaide's voice, frantic and concerned. She blinked, clearing her eyes, and she realized she was back in the abandoned house on the second floor where they had rested. Adelaide's shoulders fell as she sighed with relief, and it took a moment for Maaya to recall what had happened.

"The ghosts? Are they gone?" she asked, struggling to sit up.

"All gone, yes," Adelaide replied. She bit her lip, clearly agitated. "Are you sure you're all right? They didn't touch you? You aren't hurt?"

"I'm fine, I think. It usually goes away quick—"

"Good. Now we've established that, why didn't you wake me? Why did you try to deal with them yourself?" Adelaide continued severely.

Maaya faltered, surprised at the girl's tone.

"There were only a few to start, and you had just gotten to sleep, I didn't want—"

"You didn't want what? Didn't want to slightly inconvenience me? Risking your life so I might wake up to find you dead and gone was preferable, was it? How long did you think about what you were doing—or did you think at all?"

Maaya's eyes widened in astonishment and fear at the anger in

Adelaide's voice. She tried to find the right words, some possible way to deescalate the situation, but she was too stunned to speak.

"Listen, Adelaide," Saber attempted, looking almost frightened to intervene. "I know we made a mistake, but the ghosts are gone now, so—"

"Yes, because *I* got rid of them. And only just in time, too," Adelaide shot back, not breaking her stare from Maaya even once. "Don't you *ever* do that again. There is no room for stupid mistakes here. If there's danger, no matter how inconsequential, we face it together. Understand?"

"Y-yes," Maaya stammered. "I'm sorry, I—"

"You of all people, Maaya. After everything you've been through I thought you'd be the last person to play games with your own life by underestimating those things. Do you think I'd like to wake up to a world that doesn't have the girl I love in it anymore? Especially when you might still be here if you'd just asked for help but were either too proud or too stupid to do that?"

Maaya stared at the ground, her face burning with shame and guilt. She had gotten careless and taken a needless risk, just the thing she had always cautioned her friends against doing, and she knew it. But almost having died wasn't what caused her grief—it was hearing Adelaide talk to her with so much anger and hurt in her voice and knowing she had only herself to blame.

Unbidden, Maaya's mind flashed back to Sark where she had been forced to watch her friends die in front of her—only this time she saw herself where her friends had been, staring helplessly across the sea of ghosts to Adelaide, who could do nothing as the wave of dead swept her away. Maaya shut her eyes tight, willing this image to leave her be.

Adelaide sighed, then got to her feet, pinching the bridge of her nose. Maaya didn't dare speak; she wished she could sink through the floor like Saber could. From the look on the ghost's face, she was evidently considering doing just that.

"We need to be more careful in the future," Adelaide said finally, her voice softening slightly. "If you want to get some sleep and rest off that attack, I think you should. We can switch off once more before heading out for the night."

Maaya nodded meekly, then stood up and walked over to the corner of the room where Adelaide had been sleeping. Adelaide seemed calmer already, but Maaya wasn't willing to say anything yet. She wasn't sure she could even if she wanted to. She was too overwhelmed by shame to even think straight. She wasn't sure what there was to talk about anyway; there was no excusing what she had done, and she knew that.

She removed her card pouch from her arm and slipped off her shoes, keeping both next to her and ready just in case, then lay down, curling up with her back to the wall that faced the empty expanse behind them. Maaya wasn't sure she could get any sleep now. Her mind was far too busy recalling Adelaide's anger and disappointment in great detail—every expression on her face, every flash of her eyes, every tremor in her voice.

There was no point in dwelling, Maaya knew that; she would simply have to do better next time. She knew that, had their positions been reversed, she would have reacted just the same. If anything, she was surprised Adelaide had been so pleasant.

Maaya closed her eyes resolutely, fighting away the guilt and shame that wanted to pull her down into its abyss. If she knew Adelaide, what they had was stronger than something like this. Or so she hoped.

She wasn't sure when she fell asleep, or for how long. She felt like she had only blinked before she was being shaken awake again, this time with significantly more urgency than before. Before she could so much as yawn or rub her eyes, she felt herself practically pulled to her feet. Maaya gasped, pulling herself back to reality immediately.

Adelaide stood in front of her, and while she didn't look afraid, Maaya wasn't sure she liked what she saw any better.

"Ghosts incoming. A few dozen this time, about a minute away. Get your cards."

If Maaya hadn't already been awake, that would have done the trick. She snapped to attention, scanning the horizon for the ghosts. It didn't take long to find them.

This time, rather than floating at them in narrow columns, then ghosts had spread themselves out in rows only two deep, forming a long pale line against the dirt as they approached. Maaya did a double take. This was new, too, and she realized how dangerous it was. By spreading themselves out, they drastically increased their prey's chances of accidental eye contact, and made it that much harder to get around them.

Maaya grimaced, steeling her mind against the fear that sought to freeze her before she'd even begun. She would not be bested again. These were ghosts. They were *her* prey. She had spent the last several years of her life actively hunting them down, and now was no different.

She slipped on her shoes and attached her card pouch to her upper arm, drawing a handful of blood cards from it as she stepped over to the broken wall. They felt warm in her grasp as though impatient to be used. Maaya wouldn't make them wait long.

"You take the left, I'll take the right?" Maaya suggested, and Adelaide nodded, a small smile playing over her lips.

"I bet I can take down more than you."

"You're on."

In a single movement, they raised their arms and then flung their blood cards out over the empty wasteland. Before they had even struck their targets, the girls attacked again. Maaya's cards burned hot against her fingertips, and she let them fly, sending them toward the enemies they so clearly sought.

The ghosts disappeared in bursts of red light, and within seconds they had all been banished without a trace. Maaya squinted, searching quickly for any other groups that might be trying to take them off guard, but she could see none.

"Okay… I think we're safe," Adelaide breathed. "That was less trouble than I expected."

"How long was I out?" Maaya asked.

"Only a few hours. It's early afternoon. I wasn't planning on waking you for a while yet, but then they showed up. It could be just me but I feel like they're starting to show up more often now, even during the day. I *really* hope this isn't representative of what we'll be facing tonight."

"Do you need to rest now?" Maaya asked concernedly. Now that they were out of harm's way, at least temporarily, what happened just hours earlier started to come back to her.

"If you don't mind. Now that you're up, I'm realizing how tired I am," Adelaide said, and she looked it.

"Of course! I can wake you up when it's time to go tonight. Hopefully they'll leave us alone long enough for you to sleep for a while.

"I hope so. I'm still adamant about being united against emergencies, but I'd prefer we just not have any. Speaking of, though… I wanted to apologize for earlier."

"For what?" Maaya asked in surprise.

"For being so harsh with you. And I shouldn't have called you stupid. I was just… emotional. The thought of losing you, it— well, I'd rather not get into that, but suffice it to say I was not in a good headspace. I hope you aren't angry with me," Adelaide said, her calm tone betrayed by her pleading eyes.

"Oh, no! I appreciate the apology, and I understand why you were upset. I really should have been better than that. I *have* to do better, especially now. There really is no place for silly mistakes like that. So please, don't worry. Get some sleep! Hey… where is Saber?"

"Right here, m'dear," Saber announced, floating casually up the nearby stairs. "I was just taking a look at what we'll likely be walking through tonight, and the answer is buildings. Lots and lots of buildings. I don't know if that's a good thing or a bad thing."

"Good, I think. We'll use a little more energy moving between buildings but we'll have better vantage points and places we can escape if we need it," Maaya answered thoughtfully.

"Agreed. Unless of course we find that out of their sudden desire to follow us they've gained the ability to float *upward* as well," Adelaide added darkly. "Anyway, I'm going to get some shut-eye. How are you doing on bloods, Maaya?"

"I still have most of mine left. You?"

"Same. I'd say we should keep saving them, but it looks like we might have to be a little more liberal with their use tonight," Adelaide continued, staring out across the empty land behind them. As Maaya followed her gaze, she saw multiple groups of ghosts already starting to appear in the distance.

The hours passed slowly, though part of that was due to there being no further attacks. Though the ghosts appeared and disappeared, some very near to the house, none of them came in their direction.

Maaya began to relax, and even to watch the ghosts as they passed by. She thought about the first time she had ever seen one back in Sark and how terrifying it had been, but how so much exposure to them made her feel almost at ease around them.

Every so often a pulse would pass swiftly overhead; Saber was always there when they came, but she always departed as soon as she established Maaya and Adelaide were safe. The few times Maaya had tried to engage her in conversation, Saber simply shook her head and left. Maaya had taken to simply nodding in thanks whenever Saber came by to shield them, but nothing more. She would never admit it, since what was happening was outside Saber's control, but it hurt, and it hurt badly. That Saber felt too unwell to even be near Maaya tore at her heart. She missed her friend, and wanted nothing more than to end this so everything could go back to normal and that Saber could be well again. Despite Adelaide's presence, she felt oddly alone without her best friend by her side.

As night approached, more and more ghosts appeared. The sheer number of them was unnerving; though the sun hadn't entirely set there were already more of them than there had been the night before. Maaya decided it was time to get ready. She dug through what few food items they had brought with them and set about creating a crude meal. She was no chef, and the meager portions they had brought with them hardly helped, but she finally managed to put together something that was both edible and filling.

Setting the food aside to cool, she walked over quietly to Adelaide, who was still fast asleep. She had hardly shifted the entire afternoon. Maaya nudged her slightly, afraid that Adelaide might be in a sour mood from lack of sleep, but she smiled before she even opened her eyes.

"Something smells good. Is it time for breakfast?"

"My attempt at it, anyway," Maaya smiled, and then she became serious.

"I think we should hurry. There haven't been any more attacks, but there are more showing up every second, and they're bound to start coming at us."

Adelaide sat up, watching the ghosts beyond with a scowl.

"I think you're right. Let's get going."

THE SECOND NIGHT was far worse than the first. Maaya had been right in that the buildings provided them temporary escapes, but Adelaide's fear that the ghosts would pursue them vertically had come true. They were forced to defend themselves more than once, and in some cases were forced into precarious positions due to the sheer number of ghosts surrounding them. Adelaide had recommended against using any of their physical augment cards unless absolutely necessary to avoid exhaustion, but Maaya soon learned that their definitions of 'necessary' varied quite a bit. Even after only barely escaping a ghost's touch by mere feet, Adelaide still refused.

With sunrise only an hour away, the ghosts finally began to fade, leaving only a small pockets of them here and there, most of which did not approach them. Maaya was grateful for the reprieve; she wasn't sure how much longer she could continue on the way they had been going.

Once they had established they were mostly safe, Maaya, Adelaide, and Saber returned to ground level. Walking normally took much less effort than jumping from building to building, though Maaya's legs still felt weak beneath her. She hadn't been getting enough sleep, and the food they had brought with them provided enough energy to survive, but not for this level of physical activity. What's more, both of them had suffered minor injuries during the night, mostly from trying to navigate the precarious and dangerous terrain in the dark; these buildings hadn't been maintained in a century, and some of it definitely showed. They had mutually decided that healing cards would take too much energy and weren't worth it for cuts and bruises, but Maaya questioned this decision as her arms and legs stung and ached with every step she took.

One thing Maaya didn't feel was fear. She was vaguely aware that they could not continue this indefinitely, that given long enough the ghosts would drive them to exhaustion and starvation, but she knew that wouldn't be an issue. They could be defeated, and the machine would be destroyed before the ghosts could hunt them down. And for all the ghosts' efforts, Maaya and the others had made steady progress through the night, moving ever closer to the machine. They would make it there before their supplies and bodies gave out.

For Saber's part, the ghost seemed to be in a better mood than the afternoon prior. She had been at their side the entire night, shielding them from pulses and helping them strategize and flee safely without getting cornered or caught out of position. Now that things had apparently started to settle, she was back to her usual talkative self.

"The machine couldn't have been set up in a downtown area, could it? You could have had some abandoned luxury hotels to sleep in, but no, it has to be out smack in the middle of farm country," she reasoned.

"A lot of wealthy people had vacation homes out here. I can only guess this machine was actually this man's side project, something he tinkered with in his spare time," Adelaide said.

"How dense do you have to be to just *accidentally* create a doomsday device when you're tinkering with something on holiday?" Saber asked, shaking her head. "Then again, I remember some of Kalil's cooking experiments, and I suppose those meals could qualify as accidental doomsday devices—"

"What I wouldn't give for a proper bed right about now. Or even a floor that doesn't leave me covered in dust when I stand up," Maaya moaned. "Just thinking about a nice bed is putting me to sleep."

Adelaide nodded emphatically.

"I'm with you. I like being up and about more than most people, but when this is over I'm going to stay in my bed for a week. Oh, but it's a big bed, Maaya. You should join me."

"Hardly the time to be proposing a thing like that, don't you think?" Saber asked, raising an eyebrow.

"I meant to sleep, but I'm always open to suggestions."

They both laughed as Maaya groaned and buried her face in her hands.

Suddenly, Maaya stopped. Beside her, Adelaide paused as well, listening intently.

"What is it?" Saber asked urgently.

"I don't know. Something feels… different," Maaya muttered distractedly.

To all her senses everything was the same, but there was something slowly filling in the silent void left by the dissipating ghosts—something coming closer with each passing second. It was a feeling she had never experienced before. If she could liken it to anything, it was the feeling of dread that came before a bout of pure panic where she knew what was coming and knew equally that she was powerless to stop it, but in this case Maaya didn't know what manner of enemy she was facing, be it real or psychological.

"Augments out," she said shakily, and she quickly burned cards for speed and strength on her limbs.

Adelaide did the same, staring around nervously as she did so. The street remained dark and empty, not a sound could be heard, and the only signs of movement came from the ghosts too far away to do them any harm.

And then Maaya's world turned white.

"Jump out! Roof to your right!" Saber cried.

Maaya jumped with all the strength she could muster, and her blood cards were in her hand before she knew what she was doing. Her own cards were accompanied by Adelaide's, and they struck the ghosts that were appearing right where they had previously stood only a moment before.

Many of the ghosts fell, but before Maaya had even gained a solid foothold she again found herself surrounded by a blinding white light.

"They keep landing on top of us! Split up!" Maaya shouted as she leapt for safety again, leaving a burst of red sparks in her wake.

Again and again, groups of ghosts appeared out of thin air right on top of Maaya, forcing her to jump out of the way. So fast were they appearing that Maaya spent more effort getting out of harm's way than looking where she was going, and she quickly found herself perched on a high roof with most of her escapes cut off. Adelaide seemed to be managing against the ghosts pursuing her, but by now she was too far away to come to Maaya's immediate aid.

Finally, at least for a moment, it seemed there were no more ghosts to come. Maaya turned her attention to striking down as many of the remaining ghosts nearby as she could. Still, with as many as there were, they soon drove her to the edge of the roof as they slowly approach. She quickly scoped out an escape on a nearby balcony, then sent a few blood cards streaking down to the street below. If she was going to continue her escape, the street would need to be clear.

Another flash erupted before her eyes. Momentarily distracted, Maaya whirled around, prepared to throw a card—and found herself inches away from a ghost that had been floating right behind her.

Maaya shrieked and instinctively leapt backward, flinging her card toward the ghost, hitting it hard. Only a split second after relief coursed through her body did she realize her mistake. Having already been on the edge of the roof, jumping back had sent her straight over it.

As she fell, she had only one thought in her mind: she needed to make sure wherever she landed was safe. She twisted in midair and threw the last card she had in her hand at the few remaining ghosts in the street. They too disappeared, leaving Maaya with the sickening realization that she had been given time to position herself to land properly or to get rid of the ghosts that threatened her—but not both.

She crashed hard into the portico over the building's entrance, rolling twice before falling again and landing roughly on the ground below. The force of her collision caused one of the old wood pillars to snap, sending part of the portico crumpling down on her as she fell. Though her *libris* protected her temporarily from fatigue, it did not do so against injury; the glowing lines on her limbs flickered, then faded, and she cried out in pain as the full weight of her exertion returned to her body.

She whimpered as she struggled to her feet. All things considered, it wasn't nearly as bad as she thought it would be; at least that she could tell, nothing was broken.

She quickly drew another blood card, but as she stared around the street she saw no more sign of any of the ghosts.

Or of Adelaide.

"Adelaide?" Maaya called weakly, her voice cracking. She repeated herself again, her voice stronger this time, painfully aware of the sound of her voice echoing down the street.

"I'm here! I'm here," came Adelaide's voice from nearby. Maaya searched the street frantically for her and saw her stumble out into the street, looking as worse for wear as Maaya was, if not worse.

"Oh gods, are you okay?" Maaya gasped as she rushed over to her. A small trickle of blood fell down the left side of her face, and she gingerly held her augmented arm in the other; Maaya noticed that some of the delicate metal frame had snapped and bent.

"I'm okay," Adelaide said unconvincingly, wincing as she attempted to remove her arm augment. "Believe it or not, I've had worse."

"Let's make sure you don't set any new records," Maaya said soothingly, helping Adelaide unfasten the metal frame.

Once free of the broken metal, Adelaide put it gently into her pack with a look of regret.

"I was hoping that wouldn't happen. Repair time will be a good week or more with something this complex."

"We'll have all the time in the world once this is over," Maaya said reassuringly. "Do you want me to heal you? I'm in better shape, and—"

"Absolutely not," Adelaide refused flatly. "Don't think I didn't see you fall from the roof. Frankly I'm not sure how you're still standing. Besides, this is superficial, I promise. As soon as we have time to rest and recoup our strength I'll consider… hold on, another pulse is coming."

Maaya didn't so much as give the pulse a second glance until she realized something that made her heart drop.

Saber was gone.

"Oh, stars," Adelaide said in a hollow tone, quickly realizing the same thing. "Saber! Saber, where are you?!"

Maaya tore her eyes away from the pulse, frantically scanning the buildings and alleys around her for any sign of the ghost, but she could see nothing.

Her mind reeled with horrible possibilities. Had she fled from the ghosts?

Had either Maaya or Adelaide accidentally struck her with a blood card while they were fighting? Had she gotten lost?

"What do we do?" Maaya gasped, taking an unconscious step backward. She pulled a speed augment from her pouch, wondering if her new speed would be enough to carry her to safety with the pulse in hot pursuit.

"SABER!" Adelaide shouted desperately, then turned quickly to Maaya. "It'll be here in seconds, we can't make it that far!"

"Is there anything the pulse can't go through? Buildings, metal?"

"It goes through everything! Maybe… maybe our bloods can break it up just enough for us to be safe. Throw with me!"

They both pulled blood cards from their pouches, immediately throwing them toward the wave. Maaya held her breath as the cards sailed swiftly toward the wave—and then she whimpered as they passed harmlessly through.

"We have to try to run, we can't just give up," Maaya cried.

"It's here!" Adelaide said, her trembling voice full of dread. "Maaya, I-I don't want to di—"

And then it washed over them. Maaya held her breath. This was all happening too fast for fear to set in, and she didn't know what to expect. She had never died before.

Moments passed, and she felt nothing. She hesitantly attempted to breathe, and found she could do so easily. Maybe dead lungs didn't suffer from exhaustion.

Then, suddenly, she heard a familiar voice behind her.

"You two auditioning for a play? You've got the unnecessary drama bit down like a science."

Maaya whirled around.

"Saber!"

"See, you keep saying my name like you're surprised to see me and it's throwing me for a loop," the ghost said nonchalantly, but she wavered under Maaya's intense stare. "What? Do I have something on my face?"

"Saber… where were you? The pulse, it…"

"Yeah? I got us through safely like all the others, what of it? You two need some rest; we've dealt with dozens of these already, I don't know why you're suddenly worried again."

"Because you *left*," Adelaide said scathingly. "Don't swoop in at the last second and then act confused. Was that your idea of a practical joke?"

"Was what a joke? I've been here the whole…" Saber started, then trailed off, looking troubled. Rather than appearing in any way apologetic, however, she only seemed more irritated.

"Saber, it's okay," Maaya said, letting out a deep breath. It really wasn't, truth be told; now that she'd had time to process what had almost happened, she felt like she might throw up, pass out, or both. But she didn't want to add to what she was sure Saber was already feeling. "Whatever happened, it doesn't matter, as long as we're all—"

"Don't give me that, please," Saber interrupted tiredly. "I know. Best we not think about it. We move on, we finish this, we talk this out when we've got spare brainpower to handle this. Right now I don't. Let's keep moving and find someplace safe."

"Right, well… I'm glad you're okay," Maaya attempted, but Saber didn't so much as look at her as she passed.

Fighting tears, Maaya followed a few paces behind, Adelaide walking wordlessly beside her. Adelaide took Maaya's hand in her own, but it provided little comfort. She could feel Adelaide trembling, and she knew the girl must be exercising an impressive amount of patience to avoid saying anything.

THE SUN HAD BEEN in the sky for almost an hour by the time Maaya and Adelaide finally settled on the fourth floor of an old hotel. The years hadn't worn away too much at its stability, even though some of its walls were missing and most of the windows were broken, so they chose a pleasantly secluded old room with a decent view of the ground below, but one that was safe from the glaring sun.

Adelaide tore the dusty comforter off the ancient mattress in the center of the room, revealing old but mostly intact sheets below. Maaya was briefly afraid that there might be something living inside it before she remembered that nothing lived out here at all. After testing it cautiously, she relaxed, letting herself lie back upon the bed. It was definitely better than sleeping on the floor.

"Does that mean you'll be taking your sleep first?" Adelaide grinned.

"No, but I might need help getting up," Maaya chuckled.

"Nonsense. I am putting my foot down, both of you," Saber said severely, and the girls stared at her in surprise. "You are both exhausted beyond reason and injured on top of that; I *implore* you to both get some rest. If you keep trying to pull shifts you'll eventually push yourselves too far, and we are not yet close enough to take that risk."

"I understand your concern, Saber, I just…" Adelaide started hesitantly, then averted her eyes. Saber grimaced.

"You're just concerned that with my erratic mental state I might not be here to protect you when it's most important," she said bluntly, and Adelaide nodded. "That's understandable. I'm painfully aware of that myself, which is why I haven't said anything until now. But you and I both know this can't continue. At the very least, give yourselves a few hours. I can guarantee you that much at least."

"But… Saber, what if something happens and you have to leave, or—" Maaya started, but Saber cut her off.

"If I leave you'll be out of luck whether you're awake or not. It hurts me to see the state you're both in and I refuse to let my temporary impairment interfere so much that I cannot also do my part. I promise you, you are both safe with me. Now, see to your wounds and get some rest. I won't be far."

Without waiting for a response, she floated out of the room.

"What do you think?" Maaya asked Adelaide nervously.

"I think I'm too tired to argue and that's not something I'm used to saying," Adelaide said weakly. "I hurt all over and I desperately need sleep. I'm still concerned, but I'm in no position to fight. How are you feeling?"

"Well enough to stand watch, if that's what you're asking," Maaya replied, then gasped as Adelaide pulled her close.

"It's not. You're sleeping with me. I just wanted to know if you were okay. I saw your nasty fall back there, and… I know what's going on with Saber must be hard on you."

"It is. It really is," Maaya said softly as Adelaide took Maaya's face gently in her hands. "She's been my best friend for years, and we've been through just about everything. I feel like part of me is being slowly torn away."

"I know, love. I know. This is hard on us all. But she'll be back to normal once this is all over, you'll see," Adelaide murmured, gently kissing Maaya's forehead.

"What about you? How are you holding up?" Maaya asked concernedly.

"To be honest, my body's feeling better than my mind right now," Adelaide admitted. She sat up, and Maaya joined her, wrapping her arms around the taller girl's waist. "None of this is going how I planned. I didn't think that we'd go into this alone and barely coming out of multiple encounters alive. I'm at wit's end. Sleep should help, but I just… this is so hard, and I don't want to fail again—especially since that means you would get hurt, too."

"Hey, we aren't going to fail," Maaya said soothingly, leading her head on Adelaide's shoulder. "We've made it this far, haven't we? We're just tired, that's all. With some decent sleep and some more food we'll be ready to go. And I have to admit, resting with you makes me feel a lot better than taking a quick nap by myself."

"What, you don't prefer going to sleep knowing I'm watching out for you?" Adelaide purred, kissing Maaya tenderly on the cheek. "I understand. It's just not the same when you're not with me. Maybe this is reckless, but I'll take the risk if it means I can wake up to you next to me."

"You're in luck; I've been told I'm pretty reckless, too," Maaya giggled.

They fell back onto the bed, wrapped in each other's arms, taking each other in every way they could. This was what Maaya had truly missed and desired. They had all been so caught up in their plans and their mission that even when they had nights to spend together it was all spent in sleep, so tired were they from the goings-on of the rest of the world. That hadn't changed, but she was determined to get every second she could, even if it was here out in the world where nothing lived and love was as likely to perish as life itself. But not if Maaya had anything to say about it, she thought as they kissed.

Maaya ran her fingers through Adelaide's long hair as she felt Adelaide's hands run smoothly down her back and to her waist. Her body tensed, her mind already lost to the moment as Adelaide trailed kisses down her neck. Her pain, her tiredness, that all didn't matter. She was alive, she knew that much—how else could she experience this? And she would do it all again for this.

Time soon lost all meaning, but eventually passion was no match for exhaustion, and they soon succumbed to tiredness and injury, drifting off to sleep in the safety of each other's arms.

33

DEAD ON ARRIVAL

"MORE FROM BEHIND, ground level and rising, watch your eyes!"

"On it. Can you finish these last few?"

"I'm fine, go!"

A shower of red sparks erupted near the roof of the building Maaya and Adelaide stood upon, raining down to the ground below. Another burst followed as the ghosts attempting to make their way up toward them were obliterated, and then there was silence.

Maaya, panting and holding her arm, trudged over to Adelaide, who spat on the ground below where the ghosts had disappeared.

"How are you doing on bloods?" Adelaide asked between heavy breaths. She sported a fresh deep cut on her cheek and held her right foot gingerly just above the ground.

"A little under half left. If this keeps up I'll run out in a few hours. You?"

"Less than you. We might have to try to pick up the pace, but I don't know how I'll do that with my busted ankle."

"Let me heal you; I can take care of that at least," Maaya suggested.

"I can't let you do that, you'll be too tired to—"

"That wasn't a question. Sit down."

Adelaide protested as Maaya pushed her gently to the ground, but Maaya was hearing none of it, and with only one good leg Adelaide didn't put up much of a fight. Maaya pulled a healing card from her card pouch and placed it against the skin on her ankle, then closed her eyes.

At first Maaya hadn't thought it was possible to focus healing on a particular part of the body; it seemed like it was all or nothing. After experimenting with a few, however, she had discovered that it was not only possible, but simple. This allowed her to take care of more serious injuries without wasting energy on healing the entire body.

Maaya let out a breath as the healing process completed only a few seconds later, the card dissipating in her hand in a golden glow. Despite her narrow focus, it had still taken a lot out of her. Not that she was going to show Adelaide that.

"Better?" she asked pointedly, and Adelaide relented with a smile.

"Better. Thank you. Can you still move?"

"I'm fine, don't worry. I've had pain like this before; it goes away quickly. Saber? Everything okay?"

"Coast is clear for now, but the sun's about to set so we'd best cover as much ground as we can. It looks like there's another group of buildings not far from here, so let's try to make it there before the swarms really come out. Oh, don't move. Another pulse."

Saber floated over to them, standing defiantly in front of the oncoming pulse, and it washed harmlessly over them. Saber looked bored, as she usually did now after dealing with so many pulses, but there was something else there, too. Maaya couldn't immediately place it, but if she had to guess, it was… confusion.

"That's a good idea. Let's head out," Adelaide said, taking Maaya's hand and getting to her feet. She shook her leg, glancing down at it contentedly.

"Should we eat anything first?" Maaya inquired as her stomach growled.

"I think it can wait until after we get there; I just don't want to be caught on the open ground because we had any delays," Adelaide answered nervously. "We're getting close. If we make good time we'll reach the machine long before morning."

There it was. Adelaide had mentioned they were getting closer a few times, but this was what Maaya had been waiting to hear. They really were close—and Maaya knew she could expect all the resistance the machine had to offer before they reached it.

Saber had woken the girls up in the middle of the afternoon, and rather than waiting until nightfall to leave, they decided to start out immediately. With as many ghosts that were showing up during the night, they had agreed it would be better to start traveling by day even if it was more exhausting. With any luck, they wouldn't need to risk sleeping again until their mission was complete.

As they quickly found out, however, daylight provided much less of a refuge from the ghosts as it had in the past. There were far more of them now, and many of them now directed themselves right at Maaya and Adelaide. This meant more energy spent on escaping, more blood cards used, and more injuries. All the while, Maaya fought a growing panic inside her. There was little doubt about it now. The ghosts had to be chasing her. She couldn't fathom why, but there was no other explanation for it. They had pursued her ever since Sark. She knew it couldn't be Adelaide; she had fought them her entire life and had never seen them chase anyone before. Then there was Saber, who wasn't affected by them at all. This meant that they were after Maaya, and it also meant that if her friends got hurt, it would be her fault.

This thought bounced around Maaya's head as they walked. Along with this growing realization came the idea that she should tell Adelaide. She didn't know exactly what it would accomplish, but since it had to deal with the ghosts and the machine, she felt it was important for her to know. Perhaps she could be used as a distraction; if the ghosts really were following her she could draw the ghosts away from Adelaide while she handled the machine. Still, she hadn't yet mustered up the courage to say anything. She wasn't sure if she'd be able to by the time they were done.

The silence continued for a full ten minutes before Adelaide spoke.

"Hey, you've still been reading your friend's diary, right? Has it been worth it, do you think?"

"I think it has," Maaya replied, surprised by the suddenness of the question. "There's nothing very unusual or exciting in there, but… I feel like I'm getting to know her all over again. She was such a sweet girl; I wish you could have met her. She didn't have any of my cynicism even though she lived a life that was a lot like mine. She really loved and cared about us and she really believed in the good in everyone. She was only starting to realize what kind of a person Rahu was."

"Does she talk about the others much?" Adelaide continued interestedly.

"A little. We all got along, but she wasn't quite as close to the others as she was to me. Besides, they were teenage boys; you know how they can be," Maaya smiled. "But she was looking forward to us all getting out of there and having a better life together. However much they annoyed her, they were family."

"She sounds like she was a lovely person," Adelaide said softly. "I want to hear more about all of them someday."

"And I want to tell you. I want to tell everybody, really. They were just… such good people. I hate that the world doesn't even know they existed. I want to change that."

"After this, you will," Adelaide replied encouragingly.

"Hey, not to interrupt or anything, but I think I have some bad news," Saber said warily from ahead of them.

"What is it?" Maaya asked, instinctively putting her hand to her card pouch.

"Another pulse is coming already. I think… I think they're starting to happen faster now."

Sure enough, another pulse was already on its way, making its way toward them with frightening speed. Saber again shielded them from it effortlessly, but Maaya stopped. It hadn't been that long since the last one. They were safe with Saber's protection, but if the pulses really were increasing, that meant something much worse. If the barrier increased with every pulse, and the pulses were coming faster…

"Stars, this isn't good. This will accelerate the growth of the radius much faster than we originally thought," Adelaide cursed.

"Has it ever done this before?" Maaya asked hurriedly as they quickened their pace.

"Never. There have been some variations more than usual in the past few years, but nothing like this. It has to be because we're getting closer. If that's true, we can't waste any time getting there. We'll have to eat and rest later."

"Augments?" Maaya suggested.

"We can try, but we'll have to be sure Saber can keep up at all times. Let's get some speed."

In a single motion they applied one green card each to their legs, and their glowing *libris* lines soon flared above them as the paper burned away. They shared a glance and a nod, then started to run.

Night fell quickly, and with the onset of darkness came hordes of ghosts, all of which now seemed only too eager to pursue their living victims. Multiple times Maaya and the others were forced to change course or take a dangerous route through a building they weren't sure had an exit, or to exert themselves dangerously to avoid being closed in. Whenever possible, they spared their blood cards. They each only had a few left, and they knew they would likely face even more ghosts near the machine itself.

They only had to defend themselves with blood cards twice over the next few hours, but they still paid a heavy price. They were both weakened too much to use any healing cards, which had now become an issue due to the increasingly severe injuries they both suffered during the night. Saber tried her best to direct them safely, and the girls did their best to protect each other, but there were simply too many ghosts and the terrain was only getting more dangerous. On top of the rickety unstable buildings they fought their way through, they were now coming upon an area that by the looks of things once been heavily forested. Skeletal dead trees were everywhere, as well as tree stumps and sharp jagged branches that had either fallen or hung dangerously low in their path.

As time wore on, Maaya found herself desperately hoping for a break, any relief at all, but it didn't come. She feared that it wouldn't be the ghosts that killed them, but that instead they would be driven to exhaustion. Even with *libris* they were only human, and there were seemingly infinite ghosts, all of which were now pursuing them slowly but surely. They didn't need speed. All they had to do was wait until Maaya and Adelaide couldn't take another step—and after that, once they had used the rest of their cards, leaving them utterly defenseless.

Just when Maaya didn't think she could take it anymore, however, they found safety in a nearby building. With what strength they had left they rushed to the top floor some three stories above the ground, and with immense relief, Maaya noted that the ghosts were not following them upward, at least for the moment.

She collapsed onto the floor, taking deep wheezing breaths, and her *libris* lines faded from her body. Every part of her body seared with pain, and now that she was lying down for a moment to recover with nothing to distract her, it only felt worse. Adelaide lay on her back and closed her eyes, looking like she was doing everything within her power to stay conscious.

"You two okay?" Saber asked, her tone laced with concern and fright.

"Just… need a few minutes," Maaya gasped weakly, and Adelaide nodded.

"It looks like you have it for now. The ghosts are walking in circles below us; I think it'll take them a little while to figure out where we went. Stay put and rest. I'll let you know the instant we need to get moving."

"Thank you," Maaya panted, fumbling with her card pouch. Her heart sank as she looked inside. She had three blood cards left.

Another pulse passed over them. Maaya tried not to think about it. It had only been five minutes since the previous one. She thought of Halvar, Inga, and the others, and she hoped they were okay. She knew Adelaide's friends would be doing everything in their power to make sure that everyone outside the barrier was safe, and that they were smart enough to know what to do now that it was increasing in size much faster than they had anticipated.

But then the sight of the abandoned military outpost in Nalmar flashed back into her mind. The barrier had taken the Krethan military by surprise, and they had been guarding the barrier for decades. If even they could be caught off guard…

She tried not to think about it. Adelaide's friends weren't the military. They were the Blackfins, and they were used to the unconventional. They had also been led by one of the most brilliant and skilled captains Maaya had ever seen. If anyone could make sure everything in the outside world was okay, it was them.

Adelaide seemed to be thinking along similar lines. As her breathing slowed, she sat up with effort, staring out at the dark lands surrounding them and the hordes of ghosts that floated mindlessly below.

"Maaya, I…" she started, and then stared away, embarrassed.

Maaya shifted closer to her and leaned against her, letting out a soft sigh. "I know. It's all a mess."

"I just feel… weirdly alone out here. Not offense," Adelaide added hastily. "There's a whole world out there we're trying to save and I have no idea what's going on. It's so quiet here. It's making me uneasy. It's just so… desolate, and I feel myself running out of strength. I haven't thought much about dying, but I never thought it would be like this."

"Hey, don't say that," Maaya said suddenly, staring up at her. "We're not going to die, and our friends are fine out there. You know it would take more than a slow-moving barrier to get the better of them. Remember how they helped take down a whole fleet of sailors trying to kill me?"

Adelaide gave her best attempt at a smile.

"I know. I have the utmost faith in my friends and their abilities. I suppose now that we're here in the thick of it, I'm feeling… overwhelmed. I'm just very aware of my limitations, and I'm afraid my body will give out before we make it there."

"You? Never," Maaya persisted, and as she spoke, she felt that protective side of her coming back. It was the side of her that always came out when her friends were worried or scared or when she needed to assuage any doubts they had about what they had set out to do. "We're hours away at most, you said. That's all. Everything we've been trying so hard for is less than half a day away, and the only thing in our way are things we've both been fighting for years. As soon as this is over we can sleep in the wreckage of the machine for all I care, but we're *going* to make it there. If nothing else… do it to impress me."

Adelaide laughed, and pulled Maaya close, kissing the top of her head.

"You're right. The world is fine, and we'll be fine. We're doing everything we can and trying our best; there's no point worrying about anything else. Anyway, now I've caught my breath, I'm almost starting to feel better, so I… hang on…"

Adelaide suddenly got to her feet and squinted out at a point far off in the direction they were heading. Maaya followed suit, though she couldn't tell what Adelaide could be looking at. There didn't seem to be anything of note out there—only a few more buildings.

But Adelaide was clearly interested in whatever it was she was looking at, and after another moment, she drew in a sharp breath.

"The house. It's there."

"The house?" Saber asked curiously, floating up to peer over Adelaide's shoulders. "Oh. *That* house."

"We're that close?" Maaya asked in astonishment, standing on tiptoe as though that would help. It was still hard to see what she was looking for, and she soon realized she didn't even know what the house looked like in the first place. Still, it had to be among the buildings she was looking at—there were simply no others in sight.

"What a sight for sore eyes," Adelaide said, her shoulders slumping with relief. "I'm definitely feeling motivated to—"

"Time's up. Ghosts are coming," Saber interrupted sharply.

A short wave of ghosts was now making its way up toward them, and more were appearing behind them. To make matters worse, as Maaya looked on, even more started making their way toward them from multiple directions.

"Where do we go?" Maaya asked hurriedly.

"Straight down. From there, head right; you should be able to drop right under them and get out before they chase you down," Saber replied urgently.

Maaya and Adelaide didn't waste a moment. Rather than taking the stairs back down they headed straight for the open wall. An old creaking fire escape provided their way down, and through it groaned dangerously under their weight, it held until the girls were safely on the ground below.

Already equipped with new *libris* augments, they ran quickly away from the ghosts and directly toward a new pulse that was already coming their way.

"Saber!" Maaya cried, and from the corner of her eye she saw the ghost swoop in front of them just in time to cause the pulse to burst harmlessly around her and leave them behind.

Just when Maaya thought they were in the clear, a new wave materialized just in front of them and another to their left. With no other way to go, they were forced to turn sharply to the right—which sent them straight down a steep incline toward what looked like an old garden. Maaya quickly lost her footing and she crashed hard onto the ground below, Adelaide landing right beside her. Adelaide let out a gut-wrenching cry of pain that sent shivers down Maaya's spine, but they weren't done yet. The ghosts pursued them still, floating slowly and silently down the incline toward them, only seconds away.

"Adelaide, come on, we have to go," Maaya said urgently, but Adelaide shook her head. She was breathing heavily and her eyes were shut tight with pain. Maaya couldn't immediately discern how she had been hurt, but she could tell it was too much for Adelaide to get up and run again.

Maaya had no choice. She pulled one of her only remaining blood cards from her pouch and flung it wildly at the oncoming ghosts. Luckily, there were few enough that they all disappeared with the force of one card, but this still only left Maaya with two cards.

As the ghosts and red sparks vanished, Maaya stared around quickly to search for any more ghosts that might be on their way, but to her mild surprise, there were no other ghosts in the immediate vicinity. That didn't mean much given how they could appear out of thin air, but she would take whatever time she could get.

She turned and knelt next to Adelaide, who was still gasping and wincing from the pain. Now that Maaya had time to look, she could see what had happened. While Maaya had landed safely away from much of the debris below, Adelaide hadn't been so lucky. She had collided roughly with the jagged trunk of an old and long-dead tree, and it had left a vicious scrape all the way from her left knee to her left ankle, all but completely tearing away the fabric that previously covered her lower leg, as well as much of her skin along with it.

Maaya bit her lip. She'd had this kind of wound before, albeit not nearly as serious. While it was a relief nothing was broken, she was familiar with the sharp and unrelenting stinging that came from having one's flesh ripped away.

She took a deep breath, trying to assess her own condition. She didn't want to use another healing card, but Adelaide was in no condition to move at all now, much less fight on toward the machine. If she wanted Adelaide to live through this, she had no choice.

Adelaide was in too much pain to notice what Maaya was doing, and by the time she opened her eyes, the process was complete.

"Maaya… did you…?" she stammered, fighting to sit up.

"I did. There was no other way; your leg was completely ripped up," Maaya replied weakly.

Adelaide stared, and for a moment Maaya thought she would be furious, but then she nodded.

"Thank you. Again, I should say. This is twice now you've used your energy to get me back on my feet. I owe you for this. You all right?"

"Fine," Maaya breathed, fighting the wave of exhaustion and dizziness that passed over her. She needed to eat something soon or she wouldn't have any energy left.

But she wasn't fine, and it had nothing to do with any of the fresh wounds she had sustained during her fall. She had never heard Adelaide cry like that, and it was a sound she never wanted to hear again. Beyond just being disturbed by the sound of the woman she loved in pain, however, the fact that she herself was responsible for it was looming over her more than ever.

There was nothing for it. Maaya had to tell her.

"Adelaide, I… I have to tell you something," Maaya started, her voice trembling. She was already too afraid to make eye contact with her. "I think I… I think the ghosts are chasing me."

"Yeah, I've never seen them chase people before. It makes our job that much harder," Adelaide replied, but Maaya cut her off.

"No, I mean, they're after *me.* I don't think they chase after anyone but me. It's happened so many times now."

"Maaya, don't be silly," Adelaide said, and though she tried to smile, she seemed concerned at Maaya's distraught tone. "They're after both of us because we're trying to destroy the machine, that's all. I've never seen them do this anywhere else."

"Haven't you?" Maaya asked. "Remember that night on the ship when I made my first new blood cards? And then again on the train? You said you'd never seen that happen before, but who was with you both times?"

"That… that doesn't mean anything, the machine has been doing all sorts of new things—"

"And this is what I saw them do in Sark and in Levien. The very first ghost I saw headed straight for me, and I was the only person for miles apart for my friends, but they were never directly attacked. Every single time the ghosts have done this, they've come for me. Not anyone else, not even when they were in the middle of a crowded city or in the middle of the ocean. It was always me."

"But why you? What could they want with you? I mean… this isn't to say you aren't special, but you're just as human as the rest of us," Adelaide asked almost pleadingly.

"I have Saber," Maaya said softly. "I have the gem that lets me in where no one else can go. I was the one who touched it, who let Saber out of it. I tried to find some explanation, and so did Saber, but I realize they've been chasing me this entire time. And the first place they show up in my entire country is the little town I live in? I just… there's too much there for me to think it's a coincidence anymore."

Adelaide fell silent. Maaya could tell she was struggling to find the words to tell Maaya she was wrong, that the ghosts weren't after her, that this was all somehow still a coincidence… but she knew those words wouldn't come. This was too much even for Adelaide and Saber to deny.

"When did you start figuring this out?" Adelaide asked slowly. Maaya couldn't read her expression, but it made her suddenly nervous.

"Over the past few days, I suppose. I mean, I've been afraid of it for a long time ever since Rahu said I attract them, but there was always at least some reason I could believe it wasn't true. Now, though…"

"I can see why you wanted to dismiss that possibility, especially if Rahu was the one who planted it in your head, but… this is…"

Adelaide stood up, pacing back and forth. Maaya didn't dare move. Adelaide hadn't raised her voice—she didn't even look angry—but Maaya knew that what she was saying was a lot to take in, and she had no idea how Adelaide would process it. She had always been confident in their relationship, but she remembered Adelaide's reaction on the train after being unable to save the people in the nearby town. This was something she took extremely seriously. As well she should, Maaya thought. She had been trained for this since she was a child.

"So… we still don't know if this is true. There could be any number of explanations as to why the ghosts are acting the way they are," Adelaide continued, struggling over every word. "But you knew this was a possibility, do I understand that right? You had considered the possibility that these things are drawn to you?"

"I… I did," Maaya answered.

"Did you know about this when you stepped on board my ship? When you walked into my hometown? Into my house where my family lives?"

"Adelaide… I had no choice, getting Saber here was the only way we could get to the machine," Maaya said, and she was shaking now. Fear wasn't the right word. Dread was more like it.

"I understand that," Adelaide said, and Maaya could tell it was taking her much effort to keep her voice level. "Logically it makes sense. But I'm still coming to terms with the fact that you suspected you attract these things, my sworn enemies. And you walked amongst my friends and into my country, into my *home*, despite that. Why didn't you tell me about this? Why?"

"I didn't think it was real!" Maaya pleaded desperately. "I thought it was just Rahu trying to turn everyone against me—"

"And yet you just tried so hard to convince me he was right," Adelaide interrupted. "I… I don't know how to take this. I don't know what to say."

"Adelaide, please believe me, I came here to try to stop all this. If I stayed back home all of my friends would have been killed—"

"So you let your presence endanger my loved ones instead," Adelaide said coldly. "Look. Even if you didn't know for certain, and even if this ends up not being true at all, you knew there was a chance and you didn't think to let anyone know. And you walked around freely with no thought to what might happen if this were true."

"I didn't have a choice! They'd follow me no matter where I went, so I had to come to Krethus. I'm the one with the gem—"

"*Saber* is the one with the gem," Adelaide interrupted again. "That being the case, maybe you should have just… no, never mind. I'm not going to say something I'll regret."

"Adelaide, I promise, I never—"

"Don't, please. Maaya, I… I'm disappointed. This isn't some small thing to keep from me. And the ramifications of this if it turns out to be true, the lives that might have been put at risk, the risks we ourselves have undertaken because of this possibility… I… I don't know where to go from here. I need a moment alone."

Adelaide turned and walked away into the shadows of a nearby building. Maaya knew she wouldn't go far, not with the pulses happening so quickly now, but she still felt as though Adelaide were already a world away. Her heart ached in her chest and she could already feel the tears dripping down her cheeks. Adelaide hadn't once raised her voice, but the hurt and the betrayal Maaya heard in it was too much to bear.

She knew it would be inevitable. Every time something good came into her life it was torn cruelly from her—and she was usually the one at fault. She had always been a second too late, too slow, too hesitant, and she had paid for it over and over again. She had told herself that she would get better, that she would learn from her mistakes, but they kept happening anyway, and now it seemed unlikely Adelaide would want anything to do with her after this was over. There was no taking this back. Adelaide had been right. The fact that the ghosts might be pursuing her was almost immaterial. It was the fact that she suspected something so serious and so deadly might be happening and refused to tell anyone, choosing instead to spend her time around people she knew full well might be killed because of her mere presence.

Maaya stood up slowly and walked in the opposite direction, her tears blurring her vision as she looked for Saber. She had never felt hurt or shame in her life no matter how badly she had been beaten or how much she pushed herself to her limits. Somehow even the deaths of her friends didn't quite reach the depths of her heart this pain did. She felt as though if one of the ghosts approached her now she would let it take her willingly, but she shook off this thought quickly as a new wave of guilt surged through her. She couldn't let the world suffer because of her own heartbreak. At the very least she would see this through until the end. After that, well… she would have to decide that when the time came, providing she was still alive to do so.

Fortunately, none of the ghosts were nearby. Maaya hardly had time to reflect on how uncharacteristic this was of them before she saw Saber floating nearby, ever vigilant.

"Saber, I need to talk to you," Maaya sniffed as she approached, painfully aware of how pitiful and broken her voice sounded.

The ghost didn't move.

"Saber?" Maaya repeated, louder and clearer this time. When Saber didn't reply, Maaya's hurt slowly started giving way to dread.

No. Not now.

Saber turned to face Maaya, a blank stare on her face.

"Hello. Do you know where we are?"

Maaya covered her mouth as a sob threatened to escape.

"Are you all right?" Saber continued. "I suppose this is getting to us all. I feel strange, and I don't know how I got here. This place is familiar but I'm hopelessly lost. Something… something is calling me. Can you hear it?"

"I can't hear anything. Saber, listen, we need to stick together, there's bound to be another pulse soon, and Adelaide is down there—"

"I'm sorry? I think you've mistaken me for someone else. I don't know an Adelaide or Saber. Peculiar name, that. I hope you find your friends, but I need to go see who's calling me."

"Me! I'm calling you," Maaya protested, but Saber didn't so much as give her a passing glance as she turned to leave, floating off toward the house. "Saber! Come back, you—"

She broke off as a large wave of ghosts materialized nearby. They started moving instantly, and then, as always, they began to turn.

Maaya took a step back, pulling out the two remaining blood cards she had left. These wouldn't be enough, not by a long shot, but if she could just get back to Adelaide…

Then, Maaya froze. The ghosts were turning as they always did… but this time, they were moving away from her. As she watched, the ghosts shifted slowly, turning away from Maaya like she didn't even exist. They continued on until they straightened their course, setting them right toward the house.

And Saber.

They were after Saber.

Immediately, a flood of images flashed through Maaya's mind. The night on the hill. On the ship with Adelaide. On the train. In Anorath. Every moment here in Krethus. Adelaide had been with her for a few of those moments, but not all, and so Maaya had thought she was the only one the ghosts could possibly be after, but she had been wrong. Someone else *had* been with her every time from the very beginning. Someone with a solid connection not just to Krethus but to the machine itself.

They had always been after Saber.

Maaya felt as though the wind had been kicked out of her. All this time, all those painfully long days she had spent terrified that she was unconsciously attracting the harbingers of the end of the world to her, and it had been Saber all along.

It made so much sense now. The machine and the gem were inextricably linked even if Saber herself had nothing to do with the machine's creation. She still didn't know how the gem functioned or what its purpose had been, but of *course* the ghosts would be after it.

Partway through this realization, Maaya snapped back to reality in time to realize two things. One, she had to tell Adelaide. Two, their only protection against the pulses was now making her way toward the house without them.

Maaya raced back down the incline, nearly falling again, but caught herself quickly. She dashed over to where she had last seen Adelaide, searching the area desperately for any sign of her.

"Adelaide!" she cried, and her voice echoed into silence. "Adelaide, please, come quick!"

There was no response. Maaya fought the panic welling in her chest. They had very little time; they couldn't all be split up like this.

Maaya ran down the line of buildings, glancing into every alley. Adelaide couldn't have gone *that* far, which left only two possibilities: either Adelaide was ignoring her or she could not respond.

Ignoring the pain in her legs, she ran faster, still searching, still calling Adelaide's name.

And then she saw the one thing she had thought would remain only in her nightmares.

Adelaide had fallen to her knees in front of a wave of oncoming ghosts, her eyes blank and emotionless. Only a few yards away at least ten ghosts floated slowly closer and closer to her.

"NO!" Maaya screamed, and before she knew it her cards were back in her hand and she was sprinting with everything she had toward the ghosts. They were within striking distance, but with only two cards left Maaya had to make absolutely sure she would hit her mark.

Not again. I won't be too late again. Not again!

With only a few feet left between Adelaide and the ghosts, Maaya threw her cards with every ounce of strength she possessed, and they streaked across the old broken street, colliding with the ghosts just as they were about to touch the helpless girl. So close were they that as they disappeared the red sparks that signaled their demise bounced harmlessly off Adelaide's shoulders.

Adelaide collapsed as the ghosts disappeared. Maaya fell to her knees at Adelaide's side, holding back frantic sobs.

"Please be okay, please be okay…"

She shook the girl's shoulders roughly. For what felt like eternity, Adelaide did not respond but then fresh tears fell down Maaya's cheeks as Adelaide opened her eyes.

"What… how… oh, stars. I got caught, didn't I? Are they gone?" Adelaide asked quickly, sitting up in a flash.

"It's okay, they're all gone," Maaya managed, her voice wavering.

Without a word, Adelaide took Maaya into a tight hug, and it was all Maaya could do to avoid breaking down completely.

"That's a second time you've saved my life. Probably more if we count all those healing cards," Adelaide said with a smile, and Maaya could see tears threatening to escape her eyes as well. "Listen, I thought about what you said a little, and I—"

"You were right about everything," Maaya interrupted gently. "We don't have time for that, though; Saber's run off. We need to catch her before another pulse comes."

The color drained from Adelaide's face.

"She what? Where?"

"Toward the house. She isn't going fast so we can catch her if we hurry, but we have to go now. And the ghosts, they… they're following her."

Adelaide paused, and then she slowly blinked in understanding.

"I see. So that's how it is. Right. We'll deal with that later, then. You good on augments?"

"Yes, but I'm completely out of bloods."

"I've got four left; that should be enough to get us there. Let's go!"

For what Maaya hoped was the last time, she placed a green-patterned card to her skin, feeling relief as temporary strength once again coursed through her. Adelaide did the same, and then they were off.

At the top of the incline, Maaya saw Saber far away now, still floating casually toward the house. She didn't seem to notice the ghosts behind her; that much was a good thing, Maaya thought, as there were now at least a hundred behind her, their numbers growing with each passing minute. If Saber were to see them in her current condition she would surely make a run for it.

This unique situation gave Maaya and Adelaide surprising freedom; with all the ghosts after Saber, they didn't have to worry about fighting through any attacks. They just had to avoid the few ghosts in their way. The ghosts, who had previously followed them with the determination and persistence of seasoned hunters, were now ignoring them completely.

However, Maaya soon realized a problem. If they were trying to catch up with Saber, these ghosts would eventually, inevitably, become a big problem. With only four blood cards left and hundreds of ghosts, and with Saber's inability to leave their side given the frequency of the pulses, she knew they would have to destroy the machine very quickly—and that they would likely only have one shot.

"Saber!" Maaya called as she and Adelaide ran toward her.

If the ghost heard her, she didn't show it. She continued determinedly onward. Even through her fear, Maaya was puzzled. Saber had never acted like this before even when the effects of the machine made her behave erratically. This time it seemed she was moving toward something with purpose.

Maaya's heart pounded in her chest. It must have been the gem. Now that it was so close it was likely pulling her in.

Unfortunately, that meant Saber would not be helping close the distance between herself and Maaya. The girls ran on, and with the help of their *libris* Maaya estimated it would only take half a minute to reach Saber. Whether that would be long enough, Maaya could only hope.

Saber disappeared inside the house. Curiously, the ghosts did not pursue her inside. They stopped immediately like a line of soldiers during marching exercises.

And then, just when Maaya thought this would give them easy access to the house, every single one of the hundreds of ghosts turned slowly to face Maaya and Adelaide.

And then they surged forward.

"Oh no, ohhh no," Maaya gasped. "What do we do?"

"We can't stop now. Keep going! I've got bloods, I'll cover for you. Get inside and destroy that thing! Go!" Adelaide called, and before Maaya could argue, Adelaide dashed off to the right, using one of her cards to clear a small space for Maaya to reach the door.

Maaya ran as fast as she could. She didn't know where Saber was, and even if she found her there might not be time to get her back to Adelaide to keep her safe—if Saber was even in her right mind by then. No, the machine had to be destroyed right now, or she and Adelaide were both dead.

Adelaide flung another card which burst right next to Maaya's left shoulder, clearing a wider path. Maaya was painfully aware that Adelaide only had two left, and that after she used them she would be utterly powerless against the ghosts.

From inside the house a light suddenly glimmered. Brighter and brighter, faster and faster it flickered. Maaya didn't have to guess what was happening. She had to hurry. A quick glance over her shoulder showed her Adelaide being quickly overwhelmed, and though she tried to distract the ghosts and pull them away from Maaya, many of them split away from her, returning their attention to Maaya.

Maaya's vision blurred, and the world swayed. She had gone too long without food or decent sleep, and she hurt everywhere. But she had to make it. If she could just get inside before the next pulse…

Maaya reached the front door and flung it open, but as she made to dash inside the pulse erupted from the house, and Maaya's world instantly went dark.

34

WHERE WORLDS COLLIDE

Breathe. Remember to breathe.

Maaya opened her eyes, disoriented, then blinked. Whether her eyes were open or shut, everything around her was just as dark. She reached out around her, but felt nothing.

It couldn't be due to the night. Even if there were no ghosts—and Maaya noted curiously that they had suddenly vanished—the light of the moon and stars was the only other thing the barrier could not kill. But she saw nothing.

As the seconds passed, however, the world around her began to take shape like she had just stepped into it from sunlight and her eyes were only now beginning to adjust. She squinted, scanning the dark silhouettes of whatever she saw around her for any sign of Saber, of Adelaide, of the ghosts… but she was alone.

Am I… am I dead?

She thought frantically back to what had just happened. The pulse had been about to erupt, her hand was on the doorknob, and then the flash of the pulse…

Her heart sank. She hadn't been inside. Even if she had there was no guarantee she would have been safe. Saber had disappeared inside too far ahead of her for Maaya to be safe at that distance. Besides, if she weren't dead… where was everyone? Where had Adelaide gone?

Unless she was the one who died.

Maaya thought she might be sick. She fell to her knees on the porch, trying to work up the strength to call Adelaide's name, but her breaths came too quickly and too erratically.

She couldn't be dead. Neither of them could be dead. They had come too far for it to go wrong now. It simply wasn't possible. Maaya wouldn't let it be true. If there was any chance in the world that sheer will could reverse or prevent death, she would make it happen.

"Say, miss? Are you all right there?"

Maaya whirled around. A young man in his late 30s stood awkwardly in the doorway, staring down at her concernedly. He had a neatly trimmed mustache, short tightly cropped white hair, and vivid ice-blue eyes. He wore an immaculate black suit of the kind men wore when they would meet their ladies at the door with outstretched hands and a small bow, ready to take them into their waiting carriage. He was tall but not imposing; his demeanor was that of someone who was trained in the art of giving orders but didn't enjoy doing so.

"I... uh..."

"My, you don't look well at all. Here, let me help you."

The man extended his hand and Maaya took it automatically. His grip was decided and strong, born of many practiced handshakes. He pulled her effortlessly to her feet, and when she wavered he held her shoulder until she was stable. Only now did she see her surroundings in greater detail. She stood on the front porch of a house, one that looked familiar but different at the same time. She realized with some surprise that this house, unlike all the other buildings they'd passed, looked to be in perfect shape with not a single sign of damage or wear. At first she thought it might be the house they had been trying to get into, but she had seen it clearly, and it has been as ruined as the rest. How this one had remained in this state given where they were, she didn't know, but at the moment this was the least of her concerns.

"I hope I don't sound rude, miss, but how is it you came here? I haven't seen another person here in quite a long time."

"I..."

How could one adequately retell the long story that this was? How could she explain that she had come from across the world after watching her friends die in front of her, that she had crossed the ocean after taking part in a massive battle at sea—half of which were controlled by the dead—in the company of the woman she loved, that she had spent three days on a train only to find that the military presence there had been wiped out, and that she had crossed the barrier safely because of the magic gem on her dead friend's forehead?

Before she could even begin to formulate a response, however, the man spoke again.

"Ah, I see. You're not used to being dead."

Maaya froze.

"What did you say?"

"Oh, sorry. Did you, uh, not know you were dead? I've never had to break the news to someone before, so I apologize for my tactlessness…"

Maaya turned away, covering her mouth in horror. The man didn't look like a ghost, but there was no other way he could be out here. This explained why the world looked so different, why Adelaide was gone, and everything else. She had been outside Saber's protection for too long, and she had been hit by the pulse.

She had died.

"What… but how? How am I dead? I can't be dead," Maaya gasped, feeling her heart pound within her chest. Could the dead feel their hearts? She had never thought to ask.

"You must be, I'm afraid. The living simply don't come out here anymore. And I'm quite certain I would recognize another ghost. To be fair, I haven't seen all that many apart from myself, but I have had quite a long time to let my fate sink in," the man said gently. "Now then, you mustn't panic. Death happens to us all, sometimes just earlier than we expect or desire. But now you're here…"

"No, I… I can't. I can't, there was so much I had to do, and Adelaide…"

"Ah, the burden of unfinished business. I understand. But don't fret, miss. I promise you the good far outweighs the bad. Did you have a friend, then?"

"I did, she… we were more than that. She was just with me, she was *right there*, I don't understand…"

"Easy, easy. If she was here then she died with you, and you'll see her again soon I'm sure. At least, I have to assume as much if you both managed to make it out here. She's probably just wandered off in the dark, that's all. She'll come back! Now… would you like to come inside?"

Maaya couldn't reply, so the man gently led her inside the house. She was used to ghosts being very blunt about death, but she had never had that bluntness directed at her before. She now started to understand why it caught the newly dead off guard.

You failed.

The voice whispered callously from the back of her mind, sounding more bitter than malicious. It had failed, too, for it was her voice, after all.

You got so close, but you failed.

She couldn't argue this time. After all, she was dead. She was still here, but she was dead. It didn't seem like she was in her own world, either. The house inside looked just as perfect as the outside. There was no rot, no decay, no mess—no sign at all that the building had been sitting here abandoned for a hundred years. It didn't make sense.

Your best friend is dead, the girl you love is dead, and the machine lives. Now it will consume the rest of the world because you had one chance and you failed. Everyone alive now will die. Styx, Roshan, Inga, Sylvia, Halvar, Gunnar, Felix, Cajsa, Marit, they'll all die. They'll die running for their lives, seeking solace at the ends of the earth, and death will close in on them after they've lost everything but each other. And then they'll lose that, too.

There it was. Maaya could handle the guilt of her own failures, albeit barely, so long as she was the only one who suffered from them. But, as they so often did, her failures had repercussions for the people she loved. Because of her failure, because of her death, all of her friends would die. There was no second chance.

This was far too much for her to bear, and she broke down, unable to withstand the flood of cruel images her imagination played for her. She saw the total erasure of life across Krethus as the barrier spread, and then as it passed across the ocean, wiping away all life from Levien, from Anorath… from Sark. She saw her friends fleeing before it, hoping to find some place it would not touch, but falling one by one from injury, lack of resources, and lack of will. Eventually, the machine consumed everything, leaving a completely dead and silent husk of a world floating dark and abandoned in space, this one tiny glimmer of life and all of its history in the vast universe snuffed out forever.

Every sob shook her body, and through the heavy veil of sorrow, she realized she felt no pain. There was no pain anywhere except her heart, and she knew that no matter how dead she was, there was no escaping that.

She thought of Adelaide and how they had sat on the sofa together in her house sharing their dreams for the future. Maaya had seen them growing old together, as friends or otherwise, sharing their adventures and ambitions, always coming back to find each other no matter where their own paths took them. She had dreamed their paths would merge someday; Saber had jokingly mentioned marriage, and while it was too early to think about anything like that, it hadn't taken Maaya long to realize she wanted Adelaide in her life permanently, whatever that entailed. But now… now there was no life to keep anything in. She supposed there was always the afterlife, but even that was now limited since the barrier made ghosts disappear as well. Besides, there was no guarantee Adelaide had even made it here. Not everyone returned to the living world after their death.

A small part of her still didn't want to believe she was dead. Everything still felt too similar. There were clear signs that things had changed—the ghosts disappearing, the house looking like new, the presence of this man, her lack of pain and tiredness—but it wasn't enough. Not yet.

Maaya wasn't sure if this thought gave her hope or simply suppressed something that definitely needed further thought, but whatever it was she found a thread of resolve deep within it, and she hung on desperately. She wiped her tears from her eyes, then took a deep breath. One step at a time.

"Oh, I just realized I completely forgot to introduce myself!" the man said awkwardly, looking eager to avoid directly dealing with the issue of a crying girl in front of him. "I'm Isak. Isak Astrom. I, uh, I haven't seen another human for quite a long time, so please forgive me if I forget my manners."

Maaya almost had to smile. He seemed so genuine, friendly, and eager to please, but unsure of just how to do that. He reminded her of Svante almost, and there was certainly nothing bad about that.

"Maaya. Maaya Sahni," she said monotonously. If she really was dead, it couldn't hurt to start making friends.

"A pleasure, an absolute pleasure. What were you doing so far out here if you don't mind my asking? You must have noticed everywhere around here is completely abandoned… I don't suppose you were exploring."

"Oh, no. My friend and I, we were here to…" *To get rid of ghosts.* She wasn't sure she wanted to tell her new ghost friend that she had spent her life hunting ghosts. "We were looking for something. Something specific. I don't know if I'm ready to talk about it just yet."

"Fair enough! I won't pry. But I am surprised you got this far, you know. You must have been on some errand indeed to come this far out into the wilderness."

"You could say that," Maaya said uncomfortably. There had to be something, anything, better to discuss than the way she had died. "It's not important anymore. Not now that I… that I'm like this."

"I understand," Isak said solemnly, then brightened. "Here, let me show you around. This is my home as it was a century ago. Quite a lovely place, and I do miss it. It was such a nice escape from work."

"What did you do?" Maaya asked, her curiosity growing quickly.

"I served in the lower courts. I was wholly unimportant, but it was steady and honest work. It gave me enough to live comfortably and to support my daughter. She never wanted for anything growing up, and that's all I could ask for. A life serving my country and making my daughter happy. Freja, that was her name. Very gifted, bright young girl. She grew up with a sharp and perceptive mind and an icy wit, and I dare say she frightened off almost everyone who was interested in her. But if you got her in the right mood you saw all the warmth and heart underneath. It was a struggle adjusting to things after my wife passed, but we made it work."

"It sounds like your daughter was a wonderful person," Maaya said quietly. "I… I'm from Selenthia, actually, so I don't know much about your courts. How did they work?"

"Ah! You came an awful long way then," Isak answered, fascinated. "I have so many questions for you, but first, to explain: there were three levels to our courts, and to be frank, it was a bureaucratic nightmare. The emperor led the country, as did your Selenthian lord I believe, and surrounding him was the high court. Those were the lords and ladies, kings and queens, princes and princesses, as well as anyone ambitious enough to fight their way up there. They didn't rule supreme, but came close to it.

"The middle courts were our judges and lawyers, the ones responsible for upholding our legal system, but because they answered to the high court their authority was limited and often biased. It was a shame, but there was no getting around it. If you weren't a part of the high court by rights of lineage you'd have to push your way through the middle court, and it was a slog indeed. Then, finally, the low courts were comprised of clerks and other officials—not servants, but only really welcome in any court by the direction of those we served. It wasn't all bad. Our high courtiers weren't all stuffy and pompous as you might expect; it could be cutthroat, but not otherwise unpleasant."

"That's… really interesting, actually," Maaya answered intently as pictures of men and women wearing long flowing robes and golden crowns flashed through her mind. "What did you do? Did you work for a really important person?"

"I worked for the estate of one Lord Rasmus Lundqvist. I actually saw him quite often because I was in charge of all of his finances and assets," Isak explained proudly. "More than once he suggested I apply for a position in the middle courts, but Lord Lundqvist, he was too kind and generous to leave behind. There were few others like him and I was very aware of that. He was always so kind to Freja, too. He didn't have to be—he didn't even have to let her visit—but he was, and he did."

"It must be nice to work for someone you like that much," Maaya said. "You were definitely a lucky man."

"Indeed. I did try not to brag, but I spent so long hearing negative gossip from my peers that I couldn't help myself. But what about you? What did you do?"

Maaya hesitated. She supposed there was no point lying; she didn't need to justify anything now.

"I was sort of employed by a wealthy man in my hometown. It was a small and poor place, and the people were easily spooked. He would wait for something strange to happen and then go to fix it. Of course, I would do all the work because I was the one who could see ghosts, and he just took advantage of—"

"Hold on now, what was that you said? You could see ghosts? When you were alive?" Isak interrupted, his eyes wide.

"Yes. Me and three of my friends, actually. And we… we knew how to use *libris*, so we were basically hired to get rid of ghosts. But only the ones that were really mean, of course," Maaya added hastily.

"Ah! You could see ghosts and knew *libris*, and this whole time I've been talking to you like you have no idea what's going on! Please forgive me, Miss Sahni. I feel we have even more to talk about now; I was quite adept with *libris* too back then! But that is most fascinating… and strange, now I think on it. So this man, he couldn't see ghosts? How then did he know what to do?"

"He couldn't see them, but he knew they existed. And I was poor so I had no choice but to help. If I crossed him he'd kill us. So that's what we did."

"Well, one does what one must to survive, I suppose," Isak continued, and Maaya was relieved to see that he didn't look at all displeased. "So tell me, what was Selenthia like? I've never been, and I'm also a hundred years out of date!"

"To be honest, I don't know much about it. All I knew was my small little town. The other places I traveled to seemed nicer, though. The bigger the city, the friendlier people were. I could never stay long since I was in a rush to get here, but I did meet some nice people in each one. I had to get away in the end, but if I had a chance to live there on my own terms I suppose I would have actually liked it. Krethus, though… it's so much friendlier. I've only been here about a week and already I was thinking of staying."

"You have no idea how well that does my heart to hear," Isak said happily. "I am of course glad you found some satisfaction from your own country, but Krethus, well… all I knew of it was beauty, and I wanted to share that with others. Besides, what with the war and all, I often wished I could show the world I knew to people from Selenthia. Then perhaps they could see this was not a war worth fighting."

"Oh, believe me, we were as sick of the war as you were. Hardly anyone talked about it, and given how paranoid and easily angered the people from my town were, that's saying something," Maaya answered. The more she talked, the more she found she was successfully fighting off the misery of death—and the more her sense of duty was returning. "I'm sorry to change the subject, but… I don't suppose you know of a machine in the area? That's what my… my friend and I came here to find."

"A machine…? Hmm. The only machine of any kind I'm aware of in this area is the one I was working on, but I didn't spend much time with my neighbors; any one of them could have had their own side projects as well."

Maaya's heart began to pound in her chest.

"Could… could I see it?"

Isak shifted, suddenly looking uncomfortable.

"I… I suppose that's not entirely out of the question. You must forgive me, it was a very personal project and something that I invested a lot of time and money into. It's also a source of shame for me as it completely failed in its one purpose. But… well, I suppose you would understand more than most, given your background. I only ask that you hear me out before condemning me. I've had a long time to think on my actions."

Maaya agreed, puzzled by his reaction. She remained silent as he led her down a brightly lit hallway and then to a door at the very end which opened to a basement staircase. If the machine had failed in its purpose then its purpose was obviously not to create a ghost-spawning death factory. He also hardly seemed the type of person to design anything remotely close to that. The way he spoke of it, it was as though he had tried building a horseless carriage in his basement and was embarrassed to admit it wouldn't turn on.

Frowning, she descended the stairs after Isak—and as her eyes adjusted to the dim light, her jaw nearly dropped.

The entire basement was draped in cables, odd glass fixtures, vials, meters, dials, switches, and levers. The phrase "mad scientist" immediately came to mind, and she paused on the stairs to take it all in. Tubes criss-crossed the ceiling, light flashed intermittently from odd glass cases with electrical current buzzing inside, and red liquid bubbled in vials connected to two large horizontal capsules that looked almost like metallic coffins. To her utter surprise, she also felt the hum of *libris* magic, much like she felt when she used it herself. What purpose it served Maaya couldn't even begin to guess, but it was clear that Isak had been building something much more complex and important than a horseless carriage.

As Maaya looked on she felt a growing horror rise from the pit of her stomach. This was it. Without a doubt, this was the machine they had been after. She was standing in the room of the creation responsible for the deaths of millions of people over a hundred years.

She stepped slowly down the stairs, gazing at the dials and switches with abject terror.

"What… what was this for? What were you building down here?" she whispered.

"It looks frightening, I know," Isak said apologetically. "It… well, there's somewhat of a backstory to this, but the goal of this machine was to… well, to bring the dead back to life."

Maaya stared, frozen to the spot.

"How? Why?!"

"It was Freja," Isak answered nervously. "My daughter, she… she was so smart, so ambitious. She held a position on the court despite her unimportant lineage. She was destined for greatness, and she was such a sweet girl. But then she came down with something. I think she suffered the same immune disorder my wife died from. She fell ill quickly, and within a week, well… she was dead."

"So… so you made this to bring your daughter back to life?" Maaya spluttered. "How does that even work? That's not possible!"

"That's what I thought!" Isak exclaimed, and though he still looked uncomfortable, his voice was now filled with excitement. "But I had to try. I owed it to her to try. So I decided to take what I knew of *libris,* and that's where this machine came from. It was supposed to take the very essence of my life and transfer it to her. I wasn't stupid; I didn't think I could bring back a life without paying a price. Everything must be equal, you know. I designed this machine to take my life and give it to her."

Maaya fought to stay calm. She could understand the plight of a man who had lost his family, but she couldn't reconcile his grief with what he had attempted to do here. Using *libris* to seal away ghosts or gain physical enhancements for brief periods of time, that was one thing. There was some overlap between the two worlds and there always had been. But to play with that boundary between life and death was something else. It was unnatural. She had seen the sky grow dark and peered into the abyss, feeling as though this other world they tread so cautiously in might pull her away without a second thought. This machine sought to purposefully cross the boundary between worlds, an act of hubris that had now thrown everything into chaos.

"But… but it failed. The machine failed. So why are you dead? And why is it still hurting people?" Maaya asked tenuously.

"What do you mean, hurting people? The only person it ever harmed was me and I designed it to do so," Isak replied defensively.

Maaya paused in disbelief. Could he really not be aware?

"The ghosts this machine creates, they've been attacking people for decades. They kill anyone they touch. And anyone who gets killed by them… their ghosts and their bodies disappear completely. It's unlike anything I've ever seen."

"What?! What ghosts? This wasn't designed to have anything to do with ghosts, much less create them," Isak protested, aghast.

"Okay. Tell me more about this machine. How *exactly* was it supposed to work?" Maaya pressed, feeling herself trembling with nerves.

"It… well, here. Come look," Isak faltered, beckoning over at one of the metal capsules. As she approached, Isak wiped at the glass on its lid.

Maaya leaned over to look through the glass—and then leapt back with a gasp. There, lying inside the capsule, a perfectly preserved mirror image of the man standing before her, was Isak.

"That… that's you!" Maaya said shakily.

"It is. This was designed to take the essence of my life and transfer it to my daughter. A life for a life. I combined *libris* and modern science to do it: *libris* as the power and the machine as the method of conveying it."

"And? Did it work?" Maaya continued sharply.

"It did not. I would have tried again but I had only one life to give. The machine killed me, but where my life went I don't know. All I know is that it didn't go to her."

"So then why is it still running? Why is the machine still going?" Maaya continued, painfully aware of the shrill desperation in her voice.

"Only because I was never able to shut it off. Since its energy is the life force of *libris*, I no longer have any to give in my current state. But it's harmless, I assure you. It was only designed to take one life, and it took mine, so its purpose has been fulfilled."

"But it's still going," Maaya repeated. "There are ghosts everywhere because of this thing, ghosts that kill everyone they touch. It's also sending out pulses every hour, pulses that kill anyone *they* touch, and they're spreading farther every time. Eventually they're going to consume the whole planet, do you understand that?" she finished, almost angrily.

"I'm sorry, that just can't be possible—"

"That's how I died!" Maaya cried. "That's how Adelaide died. The world is in a state of disaster because of this machine! Haven't you ever wondered *why* there's no one else out here? Because it's uninhabitable. And soon the whole world will look like this!"

Isak gaped at her, and she could see acceptance slowly starting to seep into his mind.

"I see. Tell… tell me more. How do these things happen? What do these ghosts do?"

"They appear out of nowhere. They don't chase anyone, but anyone who makes eye contact with them falls unconscious, and anyone they touch disappears."

"D-disappears?"

"Yes. Their ghosts, their bodies, everything. And sometimes, if enough people have died at once, a great red scar opens in the sky and pulls them all into it. Do you have any idea why this might happen?"

"That… I don't understand, this was never designed to…"

"Think, please! There has to be a reason why it would do this."

"I never gave it one! It was only ever supposed to take my life. That's all. Since I died, the machine shouldn't be doing anything else."

Maaya thought hard. And then something clicked.

"It wasn't just designed to take your life, though," she said slowly. "It was also designed to give life to Freja, right?"

"Right. But I don't understand how—"

"The machine only did half its job." As Maaya spoke, she felt a sickening fear permeate every inch of her body. "You died, but Freja didn't come back to life. Is there any chance the machine might think its job isn't done yet?"

Isak stared at the ground, deep in thought, and then, slowly, he drew his hand to his mouth. He stepped back and gripped the edge of a nearby table, then gazed up at his machine as though he were seeing it for the first time.

"Its job isn't done…" Isak whispered. "It… it was supposed to take a life and give it to her. So… if she didn't return, and the machine no longer had my life to take…"

"Then it started taking others," Maaya finished. She felt sick to her stomach. This explained everything. It didn't change the way the machine worked, but somehow hearing an explanation made it all the worse. Millions of innocent lives had been taken for the sake of this one girl, because one man thought he could cheat death.

"But I don't understand!" Isak continued frantically, running his fingers through his hair. "Surely… surely it would have worked by now if the machine has been taking the lives of so many others. Surely it would have stopped!"

"The dead can't come back. At all. I'm sorry, but they can't. You didn't know that, and your machine doesn't know that. It's going to keep fulfilling the only part it can do, and it will keep going until there's no life left on earth to take."

Isak froze in horror.

"That… that explains it all, then. The people disappeared because their life force was being stolen, and the scar… that's the barrier between our worlds manifest. Red like blood, like the force of life that can send the dead from our world into the next. I saw such a thing on a much smaller scale when I died; if more people are dying it only makes sense a larger opening to the other world would result…"

As he spoke, Maaya realized there was one thing left she didn't understand. She had only just realized that the ghosts weren't chasing her, but that they were chasing Saber. Hearing Isak's explanation definitely helped her understand why the machine was doing what it did, but not why the ghosts were after Saber.

The gem, Maaya realized. The ghosts were made from a machine that combined itself with *libris*, and while Maaya didn't understand exactly how, the gem was also infused with the same power. That was why it had gone through so many hands, but why Saber hadn't appeared until Maaya, someone with access to the magic, had touched it. This also didn't explain why the ghosts were drawn only to the gem, and not to any *libris* use at all, but Maaya felt as though she were already a step closer. There had to be a connection somewhere.

Suddenly, however, she heard the sound of the door to the basement opening. She whirled around, and to her complete surprise, saw Saber floating down the stairs.

When Saber saw Maaya, the ghost's eyes lit up, and she dashed over to her. They hugged tightly, and Maaya had never been more grateful and more relieved to hold her friend close to her now. Whatever had happened, her friend was back. At least for now.

"Saber, thank the gods," Maaya sniffed, fresh tears already flowing down her cheeks. "I don't know what's going on, and you disappeared, and I…"

"Hush, it's all right, I'm here," Saber replied soothingly. "You made it this far; don't go giving up on us yet. We still have to—"

The sound of shattering glass interrupted her, and she and Maaya turned to see Isak staring at Saber with a mixture of wonder, excitement, and uncertainty. Whatever it was about her that surprised him had caused him to back up into the table behind him, knocking over an empty vial.

"The last time someone looked at me like that I almost broke his nose," Saber started, but stopped short, floating back in surprise as Isak walked slowly over to her.

"It's… it's you," he said, barely audibly. "It's really you! You've come back! After all this time… I'd started to lose hope, but you've come back, my Freja!"

35

A HUNDRED YEARS OF HISTORY

Maaya froze, her mouth hanging open. She had been broadsided by all sorts of surprises and coincidences over the past few weeks, but this was easily the biggest one. The machine had been designed to bring life back to a Krethan girl who had died a hundred years ago—and that girl had spent the last few years across the world, living with Maaya on the streets of Sark with absolutely no idea about any of it.

Everything began to connect. Saber's clothes, the fact that she had come from Krethus, her lack of memory about who she had been, the gem that miraculously served to protect them against the effects of the machine when nothing else could, the way Saber acted so strangely the closer they got… it all fit. She wasn't Saber. She was Freja. Freja Astrom.

Saber, however, looked only mildly annoyed at Isak's words.

"I'm sorry, I think you have the wrong person. I also don't mean to be rude, but we're very much in a hurry right now." Then she turned to Maaya. "You look an absolute mess. Are you all right?"

"I don't… Saber, this…" Maaya stuttered. There was too much to say, and her brain was still in the middle of processing everything.

"Oh, is this the machine? Is this what we're looking for?" Saber asked, and Maaya could only nod. "Well, I don't blame you for being a little out of sorts, this is… not at all what I was expecting. Did you make this?" she added, staring at Isak.

"I did! This was all for you! I made it so—"

"Fantastic. Not at all creepy," Saber interrupted distractedly, hardly giving him a second glance as she gazed around the basement. "Unfortunately, Freja won't be able to appreciate whatever it is you've built here. My friends and I have come to destroy it, you see. If it helps, we have a good reason. Speaking of, Maaya, we'd best get a move on. There aren't any ghosts left out there, but Adelaide's in bad shape. Let's get this over with."

Maaya's heart leapt at the mention of Adelaide's name, only to quickly sink again as she remembered her situation.

"I... Saber... I can't."

"Why? What's wrong?"

"Saber, look at me! Look around us. I... I didn't make it in time. The pulse got me. I'm... dead," she said pleadingly, hoping Saber would understand without Maaya having to explain any more.

Instead, however, Saber raised a questioning eyebrow.

"Dead? Says who?"

"Isak. Er, him," Maaya added, gesturing at the very impatient Isak. "Besides, everything's different. I don't feel any pain even though I'm hurt, and I shouldn't even be here, and the house doesn't look damaged, and..."

"Maaya, don't be ridiculous. You are absolutely not dead. Believe me, I would know. No, unfortunately, you are still very much alive, which means that once we're out of this bizarre place and our job is done you'll assuredly feel everything. As will Adelaide, I might remind you, who is also very much not dead. And as disappointed as I am that we can't frolic about in the afterlife together—"

"I'm... alive? Adelaide's alive?" Maaya breathed, placing a hand to her chest. Then she cried out in pain as Saber floated over and pinched her on the arm.

"Definitely alive. Er, sorry about that. Anyway, I would assume you're in shock and that this place is having some strange effect on you. Nothing seems right here. More on that later, though." She took Maaya's chin gently in her hand and turned her face to stare at a nearby panel of dials and buttons. "Machine. Destroy. Ghosts-be-gone. Remember?"

"Saber, listen..." Maaya started, steadying herself on the table as she spoke. Relief flooded through her at Saber's words, so much that her legs threatened to give way, but there was no time for that now. If Saber was right, she had to focus on the task at hand. Still, there was something that needed to be explained first. "I... I think you should listen to this man. He built the machine and he made it for a very specific purpose. You might want to hear this."

Saber turned back to Isak, who appeared as though he might burst if he couldn't speak soon. She threw him a withering look.

"If Maaya vouches for you, you get sixty seconds to explain yourself. Your time starts now."

"Freja... you don't remember, do you? You don't know who I am?" Isak asked, looking crestfallen but not entirely without hope. "I suppose that would make sense. This all went so terribly and it's all my fault. But now you're here, so I can show you! Freja, you… you're my daughter. I made this machine for you to try to save you."

Saber's eyes widened slightly.

"That is an incredible claim to make. The next words out of your mouth had best be some evidence."

Isak nodded enthusiastically, then walked swiftly over to a desk crowded with papers and book. From it he pulled a photo frame, which he brought over to Saber. Maaya stood on tiptoe to peer over her shoulder, as it seemed Isak had already forgotten about her completely.

The photo looked like it had been taken on the front porch of the house in which they now stood. In the center of the photo were two people: one of whom was clearly Isak, and the other a girl who was almost indisputably Saber. Saber looked at most a year younger than she did presently, and was clearly not dressed for a day at court; rather than her long flowing robes and hair full of ribbons, she wore a relaxed short-sleeve shirt and her long hair was pulled up in a messy ponytail behind her. Isak had her arm around her shoulder, looking every part the doting and adoring father.

Saber stared in silence, and Maaya knew it would be hard even for her to dismiss this.

"This was taken about a year and a half before… well, before you died," Isak explained gently. "We were taking a short vacation before we both went back to court. Oh, and here…"

He picked up another photo and held it in front of her. There were three people in this photo: along with Isak and a much younger Saber, there was a woman with long dark brown hair. She stood behind Saber, both her arms draped around the girl's shoulders. They looked so… happy, Maaya thought.

She was so intrigued by the photos that it took her a few moments for the realization of what she was looking at to wash over her. This was it. This was Saber's identity, this was her past. This was everything she had been searching for, everything she had been trying so hard to find.

Saber, meanwhile, looked hesitant.

"This… this is not what I expected to find here," she said slowly. "Still, I… I'm having trouble accepting this. All this shows me was that we were acquainted, but I don't see how…"

"There's more," Isak answered quietly, his features suddenly grave. "For that, you need to understand why I built this machine."

Isak repeated his explanation to Saber, who could not hide the shock from her face as she listened. He paced as he explained his story, clearly uncomfortable explaining the purpose of this machine to the girl it was supposed to save—a girl who had no memory of who he was.

"…so, please understand, we were never supposed to have this conversation. Not like this. I know it would have been hard for you, but I wanted so badly for you to have a second chance at life that I was willing to give you mine. I'd had decades to live; you hadn't even had two. You deserved more than that. If all else fails, then believe me based on what I tried to do, something that could only be done out of the kind of love I had for you. And if you still need more, look here." Isak pointed at the glass panel of the capsule he had showed Maaya. "My body lies inside, as it has for a hundred years. It was what killed me, and even now I don't regret that I died. I only regret that it didn't save you."

Saber covered her hand with her mouth in surprise.

"So… so if that's you in there, then that means… there, in the other one, that must be…"

Maaya felt a chill run down her spine. She hadn't thought of that.

Isak nodded seriously.

"Yes. I won't ask you to look, but if you need any more proof than you already have, well…"

He said no more. He didn't have to.

Saber appeared nervous, almost afraid, but slowly, cautiously, she made her way over to the capsule. She peered inside, and then a split second later pulled back with a gasp, turning away from the capsule in fright.

"Saber?" Maaya uttered concernedly.

"Th-that's… that's *me* in there," Saber stammered, horrified. "My body is in there."

"Are you all right?" Isak asked, taking a nervous step toward her.

"Fine. Just an existential crisis, you know," Saber said, and then she took a deep breath and let it out slowly. "I don't suppose it's often a ghost gets to see their body as it once was. Not perfectly preserved like that, anyway. It's like looking into a mirror, but… not."

"Believe me, it never stops being strange. Even after all this time, I still glance into that capsule and realize that's me in there. Or rather, where I used to be. People can say all they like about the body simply being a vessel for the soul, but when the soul looks back over its shoulder at the vessel it used to inhabit, it's a strange feeling indeed."

"So… you're him. You're my father. And I'm… Freja?" Saber said, and the name sounded familiar on her lips, as though she was slowly becoming reacquainted with a very old friend.

"You are. Freja Astrom, born at the height of winter one hundred and seventeen years ago. You were so ambitious; you put your mother and I to shame, you know. The first ever member of the high court by the age of sixteen who hadn't been given a free pass from their family name. Do you… do you remember anything? Anything at all?"

Saber's gaze fell to the floor, her eyes darting back and forth as she processed everything she had heard. She opened her mouth twice to speak, then closed it again, instead running her fingers over the capsule where her body lay. Maaya wanted to help her, to comfort her, but this was beyond her.

Finally, Saber slowly stared back up at Isak.

"I… I feel something, but I can't reach it. It's like it's all there, just out of reach. I've felt this way for weeks now. But… enough is there for me to know that you're telling the truth." She paused, then stared at Maaya, managing a smile. "So, this is me. Freja Astrom. I like the sound of it."

Isak smiled.

"You were named after the goddess of love, beauty, and war, for you held all that and more in your eyes. You made me so very, very proud to be a father. Your mother made me want to live in the present, and you… you made me want to fight for a better future."

"My, a mad scientist *and* a poet," Saber chuckled, and Isak appeared beyond relieved that Saber was taking this well. "So… how exactly was this supposed to work? I understand its purpose, but what was its design?"

"Ah! For that, look no farther than the gem on your forehead," Isak answered brightly, and Saber reached up to feel the gem sitting inside the circlet. "You might've already guessed it's no ordinary jewelry, but that was supposed to serve as the transfer point for an immense amount of *libris* energy. Taking a life, that's nice and easy, but to take the energy of a life and transfer it elsewhere? Now, there's a feat. I had infused that gem with all sorts of *libris* energies; that was how the machine would know where to send all the energy it took from me. It was supposed to absorb everything it took from me and give it to you."

"How strange," Saber said thoughtfully, and then she peered down into the capsule again. If she still felt any discomfort from looking at her own body, it no longer showed. "Well, something must have happened, because the gem isn't on my body anymore."

"Ah, something happened indeed," Isak said awkwardly. "I died as planned, and the energy did go to you, but… something went wrong. What, exactly, I don't know, but I suspect it had something to do with the fact that I came back as a ghost. I don't think that was supposed to happen."

"This is just a guess, but I'm assuming it's because you can't bring people back from the dead," Saber answered bluntly, and Isak looked embarrassed.

"I thought there had to be a way. If we could see ghosts, if we could interact with them, if we could harness the very power of the other world, why could we not also reverse death? If we can so freely walk into that world why can no one come back from it?"

"That's a dangerous way to think," Maaya interjected softly. "I've gotten glimpses of just how huge and unfamiliar this other world is. We think we understand it, we think we've mastered it, even... but we don't, and we haven't. Not even close. Some things are permanent and should be left alone."

"Right, so this answers who I am, who you are, how we died, and what the machine was for," Saber continued, holding up a finger for each item as though she were checking items off a grocery list, "but this doesn't explain where the ghosts come from or why the barrier or pulses exist. Not to mention why the ghosts follow me."

"You noticed that too, huh?" Maaya asked, and Saber nodded guiltily.

"It simultaneously made a lot more sense and confused me more than I already was," she admitted. "What's more, since I found myself in this house I haven't seen a single one of them. Nor have I seen another pulse."

"Well, I haven't seen these ghosts you're talking about, or these pulses, so you may need to catch me up," Isak said inquiringly.

"Did you really not see a single one in all this time? They're everywhere," Maaya asked pointedly.

"We're not exactly sitting in reality here. It's like this part of the world is frozen in time," Saber replied, then turned to Isak. "Let me fill you in."

She told him about the tall faceless ghosts that gradually increased in number, how they killed everyone in their path, and how every trace of life in their presence disappeared. She recalled how the sky itself seemed to open after their larger attacks and how Krethus had been experiencing attacks from these ghosts for a hundred years.

As she spoke, Isak paced, rubbing his chin. He did not speak, and after Saber finished her explanation he remained silent, deep in thought.

Maaya and Saber shared a glance, not wanting to say a word lest they interrupted his thought process.

"This unfortunately seems to be in line with what Maaya and I were talking about before you arrived. We hypothesized that because you did not return to life, the machine felt its job was not complete, and so it continued attempting to take more lives until it could restore yours and fulfill the second part of its objective."

"That would explain a lot, I suppose," Saber replied, frowning. "But something doesn't make sense. I remember Adelaide saying that the machine only started suddenly increasing the size of the barrier in the last few years. The ghosts had always been there, but the barrier had hardly moved. If I've been dead and gone for a hundred years, what changed within this short time to make it change?"

"I think I may have the answer to that," Maaya said suddenly, feeling the sense of dread returning. She had been thinking about the same thing ever since she heard Adelaide mention it and hadn't been able to come up with any sort of reasonable answer—until now. "You know what happened a few years ago, Saber? I found that gem in the abandoned mansion, and I brought you out of it when I touched it."

Saber whistled.

"That's it! Of course, that makes sense. Well, sort of. Why exactly would it kick the machine into overdrive, anyway?"

"You know, now you mention it… the machine wasn't always active after it killed me," Isak said, raising his hand before him as though holding onto an idea that was threatening to flee before it could be verbalized. "And the reason the gem isn't on your body anymore isn't because it disappeared due to the machine. No, I remember… a few weeks after I died, some thieves broke into the house and stole it."

"Wait, really?" Saber asked in disbelief. "That's what the case of the great disappearing gem mystery comes down to? Thieves looting an abandoned house?"

"Unfortunately. But the reason I remember that is because once the gem disappeared the machine suddenly became active again. It had been dormant up until that point. Yes, I remember now… up until then I had thought it a complete failure. I hadn't even entertained the possibility that you were still in this world in any form! But once the gem disappeared, suddenly it turned back on again. Now I understand why the gem seems to hold the machine's power at bay. The energy of my life was transferred to the gem as it was supposed to be, and while the gem was in the capsule, the machine thought its job was done. So once the gem was gone the machine suddenly thought it still had work to do."

"And when I touched the gem and brought you out of it, that must have… I don't know, activated it somehow. It must have given the machine some idea as to where you were. That's why the ghosts seemed to appear wherever we went," Maaya theorized.

"And they did *that* because this gem was designed to absorb power. So all the life they were stealing from all the people they killed, they were trying to transfer into the gem. Just like the machine was designed to do," Saber continued darkly. "I have to assume these ghosts were the manifestations of the machine's power, likely because this whole thing was designed with *libris* as a foundation."

"What of the barrier, though? What an odd thing to happen," Isak continued, befuddled.

"Self-defense? Maybe the machine was trying to stop anyone else from stealing anything?" Maaya suggested, but Saber looked skeptical.

"My guess is the machine got confused when it realized the gem was so far away because it had been designed with the gem right here inside it. So to compensate it decided to simply expand its reach," Saber shrugged, then turned to Isak. "But I'm hardly educated enough to say with any certainty. You built this thing. Any insight?"

"I'm afraid not," Isak admitted, staring downward and shoving his hands into his pockets. "None of this was supposed to happen, so this is all beyond what I had even considered possible."

"That's convenient," Maaya sighed. "But these ghosts… they must come from somewhere. I assume that every time a living person is killed by this machine they come back as one of the ghosts that have been following Saber—er, Freja—everywhere. But how did it even start?"

"Upon my death, I assume," Isak said mournfully. "I fear I might have unwillingly become the catalyst for this entire feedback loop. And at the time, no one yet knew this place was dangerous. And so came the police, and then the military, medical personnel, all sorts. They came in limited numbers because of the lack of visible danger, and so they… they all died. Each and every one of them. A few did get messages off, but it took a while for the government to put two and two together. That's all it took to get started. And by then the gem was all but lost. Not many can see something like that and leave it behind, and there was no reason for them to assume it was at all related to the machine."

"Not until they finally started looking at your notes. Then they became really interested in it but they had no idea where to find it," Maaya mused.

"And by then it had crossed the world and made it to Sark," Saber added. "I remember Adelaide saying the gem seemed cursed, and no wonder; anyone who took it was pursued by the ghosts, so they all died. Since no one could see the ghosts they likely just assumed anyone who touched it would die. That's probably why the wealthy family in Sark left. They probably thought their house was haunted."

"It's a wonder anyone managed to track it as far as they did even if they'd realized there were many different places it could be," Maaya sighed.

"Yes, well, I suppose a gem with a reputation like that becomes a little easier to monitor. I wish I could remember; I'm vaguely aware of having traveled great distances, but more in the way that I might remember parts of a dream I had weeks ago. Nothing concrete," Saber said, then turned to Isak. "Out of curiosity, do you feel any guilt? Any at all?" she asked directly, though not unkindly.

"Guilt? With all possible respect, my heart has been blackened by it," Isak replied heavily. "If I seem unmoved it's only because I've had a hundred years to sit here alone dealing with the repercussions of my failure, and when I finally meet others who can see me they tell me it was so much worse than I ever imagined. So, guilt? Yes… yes, I have felt that. That and much more. It's enough to drive a man to death, but as luck would have it, I'm already dead."

"So… why can't we just turn this machine off somehow?" Maaya interjected nervously. This wasn't a discussion she wanted to get sidetracked with. "Saber obviously isn't coming back to life—no offense—and in the meantime this machine is wreaking havoc on the world out there. We need to shut it off."

"Like I said, that isn't possible," Isak answered awkwardly, staring away again. "The machine was designed to automatically shut down after it had completed its task. There's no way to manually shut it down, but I never thought it would have to be. It was designed to run only once, and I was going to be dead after that, so how would I use such a mechanism even if I created it?"

"The tunnel vision of brilliance," Saber replied dully. "Why don't we unplug it? Or smash it? No matter how tough this thing is it's bound to be vulnerable to a good old-fashioned mallet."

"I don't think that's possible either. Like I told Maaya, this doesn't run on electricity or water or anything tangible—it runs on the very force of life and death itself. Of *libris*! That's why I can't touch it in my current state. I have no more life force in me. What's more, the machine started again once it was tampered with by thieves. I'm afraid that any attempt to destroy it might similarly make things worse!"

"In which case we'd just smash it harder," Saber suggested.

"It's not so simple! We have no impact over this at all, not since we're dead. I don't want to risk it, especially not if Maaya's friend is alive just outside," Isak said feverishly.

"Do you think there'd be any way to cut off that power? Since you used *libris* in its design you must have some idea," Maaya pressed, but Isak shook his head in frustration.

"With the positive feedback loop that's in effect now, the only way to cut off *that* power would be to end all life on the planet, and I don't think that's a good idea. No, but… there may be one way."

"What is it?" Maaya and Saber asked in unison.

"I need to think. Since the machine seemed to think it had done its job while the gem was still in the capsule, perhaps that means it only needs the gem. That is, it doesn't need Freja to be returned to life—it only requires the gem to be back in its rightful place. Yes, that would make sense!"

Saber crossed her arms.

"And… how do we test this theory of yours?"

"We can try it right now! If you wouldn't mind, could you please enter the capsule? If I'm right, the machine should turn itself off the instant it detects the gem inside once more."

"What, float inside a metal coffin with my own dead body? Not strange at all," Saber replied. Without hesitation, she floated toward the capsule and then disappeared inside.

Maaya held her breath, staring around at the blinking lights around her. Nothing seemed to have changed, but then, she had no idea how it worked. She wasn't sure what the machine turning off would even look like. Instead, she turned to watch Isak's face, searching for any sign of hope or relief—or disappointment.

After a minute, she heard a knock from the inside of the capsule, followed by Saber's muffled voice.

"Say, dad—can I call you dad?—is anything happening out there or what?"

"It… doesn't appear to be working," Isak answered miserably, and Saber immediately floated out again.

"A shame. I was becoming well acquainted with myself in there."

"I don't understand… I need to think, is that all right? I feel like I'm onto something."

As he walked over to his desk, Saber floated over top the second capsule, then stared down at Maaya.

"Hey, Maaya. Check it out. Now I can say 'over my dead body' and mean it."

Maaya choked and started to cough, and Saber beamed, then flitted happily over to her.

"Sorry. Couldn't resist."

"Is there anything dead humor doesn't consider incredibly inappropriate?" Maaya asked, wiping her eyes.

"I'm not even sure what that means. Anyway, isn't this great? We're on the path to figuring out how to shut this thing down, and on top of that, I've started figuring out who I am! Freja Astrom… it's really not a bad name, is it? And I was on the high court after all. Looks like Svante was right. I'm sure this guy has plenty to tell me, but I'm not sure I'm ready. I'm still getting over the fact he was my father, and I'm slightly distracted by this death machine. What do you think?"

"I think I'm trying to think of so many things at once my brain is overloading," Maaya said, forcing a smile. "I thought I was dead, but I'm not. I thought Adelaide was dead, but she's not. I thought you were gone, but now you're here. And now we're here with the machine, and it was supposed to bring you back to life, and you're his daughter, and… there's so much!"

"Yeah. When it rains, it pours," Saber nodded. "To be honest, I'm not as excited as I thought I would be. My brain's being pulled in about four directions at once. Once we get this machine out of the way, though, we can start focusing on more important things. Me and my identity, and you and your girlfriend."

"Honestly, it wasn't being dead that made me miserable… it was the thought that I'd lost her and the life we'd talked about together," Maaya murmured. "And I'm relieved, but also scared. Just before I thought we'd both died, I'd told her I thought the ghosts were after me. She was so upset. She thought I'd willingly brought danger to her friends and her home, and even though that's not true… she was still right. I went and did all that even when I thought it was a possibility. The way she spoke, I… I'm afraid she won't want to have anything to do with me anymore."

Saber sighed and placed both hands on Maaya's shoulders.

"Listen. None of us have been perfect. We've been doing our best, but let's not forget that you are a *teenager.* A special one to be sure, but you had the weight of the world thrust upon your shoulders. And for all Adelaide's training she's not much older than you, and she carries the same burden. You can't train yourself for this. It has hurt, and it will hurt, for a long, long time. It's possible you won't recover from some of this. I don't say that to scare you, I say that to impress upon you just how big this all is and how small you are. And no, that's not a short joke," Saber added, and Maaya, caught by surprise, burst into laughter. "All you have done during all of this is your very best. So sure, acknowledge your mistakes, but please, please try to forgive yourself. If not now, then eventually. The last opponent you need when this is all over is yourself."

"What about you and Adelaide, though?" Maaya continued softly. "We're together now, but our job isn't done. When we aren't together because we have a job to do anymore… do you think we'll stay together?"

"Maaya, I say this with everything I am: I am never going to leave you. Not until the day you die or the day I'm accidentally hit by a stray blood card because your aim is terrible. No, I'm with you for life, and Adelaide will be too. She said what she said when she was angry, so be willing to hear the other side of things."

"People are more honest when they're emotional, aren't they?"

"No, the only thing people are when they're emotional is emotional," Saber replied flatly. "Don't put extra weight on someone's words because they said them loudly or tearfully. What matters most is what they've said after they've had time to think. You get to know the true measure of a person, not by what they say when they're inhibited, but by what they say after they've had every chance to think. So let her think. Let her come to terms with everything she's seen and heard, and then see what she has to say. You can take this time to do some thinking yourself. And while I might not know her as *intimately* as you do—don't look at me like that—I have a feeling you two are stuck together for life as well."

Maaya sniffled and then smiled—the first genuine smile she could remember since she and Adelaide had rested together the day before.

"Thank you. I'm sorry, I've made this all about me, but you helped me anyway," she said, blinking away at her stubborn tears. "But we'll fix this. One thing at a time. And then after we do we can learn all about you. Are you going to want some private time with your family or do you think I can listen in?"

"Oh, I want you there. Maybe it's because we've spent a hundred years apart and I have no memories of my past life, but I don't really feel anything for him. He's a friendly man, sure, but when it comes to family... well, that's you. Besides, with as much history as we have to catch up on, it'd be a pain to retell it."

"I won't complain!" Maaya grinned. "So, Freja Astrom of the high court of Krethus... I guess that means I can call you a princess after all."

"I like the sound of that. Though after all this time I must have been promoted to queen by now. Or empress, even. That's how promotions work, right? I, Empress Astrom, hereby order the death of a certain Rahu of Sark in the most humiliating and painful way possible. Also, to my dear friends Maaya and Adelaide, by the powers vested in me by the Krethan Empire, I hereby pronounce you—"

"Oh stop," Maaya interrupted, feeling her face burn. Saber laughed.

"You know, I probably actually have the ability to do that. I'll have to find out. But oh, this is wonderful! Maaya... I still don't remember who I am, and now I have even more questions than before, but now I know! I... I don't know how I feel. I feel a little bit of everything, I suppose. This is a lot to take in. But my name, my family, my history... it's all here. And even if I don't really feel anything for this Isak fellow, the fact is, he's my father. I'd never expected to be able to *talk* to my family, but here he is! And now... oh, if I had working tear ducts I would be making a mess right now."

Maaya smiled and hugged her tightly. This was what Saber had wanted for years, and they had finally made it.

"I'm so happy for you, Saber," Maaya murmured as they held their embrace. "I used to be so afraid we'd never find out, but now we're here. And we'll find out everything! There's Isak, there's all the history the Krethan government has, there's your picture... and we have all the time in the world."

"Just don't start actually calling me Freja, okay?" Saber chuckled. "That sounds strange, and I'm not sure I'll ever get used to it. Besides, the name 'Saber' has gotten a certain reputation, and I don't want to have to start all over again."

"Of course. You're my Saber until you get sick of it," Maaya answered cheerfully.

She heard Isak clear his throat from the other side of the room, and they both turned to face him as he walked over to them. As he did so, Maaya felt her happiness start to seep away when she saw the expression on his face. He did not look pleased—if anything, he looked afraid of whatever he was about to say.

"So, I have good news and bad news," he offered, unable to meet their eyes. "The good news is that I *think* I've discovered a surefire way to shut down the machine."

"How?" Maaya asked.

"It still involves the gem. According to my theory, the energy taken from my life was directed to the appropriate place, and it *did* enter the gem like it was supposed to. For whatever reason it didn't bring Freja to life, but the energy did enter it. The only problem is, when you touched the gem and brought Saber out of it, that energy was displaced. To fix this, the energy must be returned to the gem and then returned to the capsule. Then and only then will the machine shut down again."

"Okay, and how do we do that? We don't have to take any more lives, do we?" Maaya continued uncertainly.

"Oh, no! Not at all! Well… ah, not exactly," he said, and his voice began to tremble. "The displaced energy is still there, but it exists as Freja herself. She's not a normal ghost, either. As a matter of fact, she wouldn't be able to exist without the gem there. She doesn't exist because her body died; she exists because the gem's energy allows her to. Think of her as a projection of sorts using the gem as a battery."

"So… what are you saying?" Saber asked slowly. "What type of ghost I am doesn't matter, does it? We just need to get the energy back into the gem."

"Right, but right now, the gem isn't tangible. When you were brought out of it, it materialized as you did: invisible and untouchable. In order for this to work, the gem has to be tangible again. And to do that… well… the process has to be reversed."

"What process? Just get to your point already," Saber said sharply.

Isak took a deep shuddering breath, and then finally met their eyes.

"The gem isn't tangible because you exist. So, in order to change the gem into the form it needs to be to shut the machine down, well… you can't exist."

36

THE PRICE OF VICTORY

Dead silence fell, pierced only by the thrumming of the machine all around the room. Saber appeared too surprised to speak, and Isak had lost his nerve, his gaze falling to the floor again.

Maaya didn't know what to think. Her brain, already well beyond capacity for the number of life-changing events it could handle at any given time, struggled to process what Isak had said. Saber couldn't exist? What did that mean? Clearly she already existed, so was that a statement about a hypothetical situation that would need to be true in order for this to work? Or was it a call to action?

"Do you… want to run that by me again?" Saber finally said. "What do you mean I can't exist?"

"I mean, you would need to stop existing. At that point the dispersed energy would return to the gem, which would then return to its original state. Think of the battery example—"

"How are you talking about her like this?" Maaya asked, stunned. "Talking about her like she's a battery? Like she's nothing more than one of your scientific gadgets—"

"Don't think this is easy for me, Maaya!" Isak interrupted harshly. "I have spent a very, very long time thinking about this, all while thinking I would never see my daughter again, that I had killed myself for nothing! And now I see her again only to realize our brief company can't continue if we're to spare the world any more of the side effects of my own creation. There is no respite for me; every option is a terrible one, and dead I may be, but it still hurts me more than anything."

Maaya fell silent, tearing her eyes away from Isak while panic bubbled within her. She tried to console herself by thinking that there had to be another way. There was no way to reverse death—they had already gone over that—so there was no way to make Saber suddenly not exist. Even if it was the only option it wasn't something any of them were capable of doing.

"Right. So get rid of me, recharge the battery. Or… however this works in your analogy, I honestly haven't a clue," Saber said, keeping her voice level with great effort. "And I suppose after we do that, we can chuck the gem inside my metal coffin and the machine will stop?"

"That's the idea," Isak replied quietly.

"Fantastic. Now, how do we go about making me not exist? I only half exist already, and I don't suppose your machine was designed to reverse the process of me being ghost-ified from a piece of jewelry."

"It was not. But it isn't that complicated. Ghosts can be sealed… right?"

Maaya jerked her head back up to stare at him.

"So by not existing you mean we have to destroy her," she said, her voice cracking.

"Not destroy! Sealed ghosts are hardly destroyed. It's just that their connection between worlds is severed. It's something many dead eventually seek willfully. I know it doesn't sound wonderful, but—"

"Doesn't sound wonderful? I've spent years sealing ghosts away, watching them disappear in front of me, and now you want to do that to my best friend? Are you *completely* out of your mind?"

"It's the only thing that will work! I'm sorry that the answer isn't sunshine and rainbows, but this is the only way," he answered aggressively, then turned to Saber. "Freja, please don't be upset with me. If there was another way, any other way…"

"I… I'm not sure I can believe this," Saber answered distractedly. "I just found you, my home, my name… we're so close to ending this, and I'm so close to my past. Why now? Why does it have to end now?"

"Oh, my dear, it's not the end!" Isak exclaimed, and he crossed the distance between them and flung his arms around her shoulders. Saber seemed too stunned to react. "If there was an end, death would be it, but as we all know that's hardly it at all. There's a whole different world out there waiting for us. We'll both be going there, you and I."

"We can't do this! There has to be another way, any way," Maaya cried. "Saber, I can't… not you too. Please. We can find something else, we always have, I can't—"

"Hey, don't start crying on me," Saber interjected gently, floating over to her and looking her in the eye. "I know this sounds bad, but… all things considered, if you had to lose anyone else to this, why not someone who's already dead? Isn't that better?"

"No!" Maaya protested, tears already brimming in her eyes. "It's not! You're my best friend, you've been there for everything, and even if you're dead already I can't watch this happen. We came all this way, you and me, trying to save Sark. What about Roshan, Styx, Sylvia…?"

"I know. I know," Saber said, biting her lip. "And if we had more time I would probably second guess myself. I can't even imagine the idea of not existing. I always have in some form or another. But… the world is still in danger right at this very moment. We don't have time to waste looking for a way to save my life—that'd be ironic anyway, considering all this is about me being dead."

"What are you talking about? There's always time for you," Maaya pleaded.

"I appreciate that, but these are other people's lives we're talking about. Your girlfriend, for one; she's still out there. All your friends, the whole world, it's all out there. We need to make sure they stay there."

"You can't be agreeing with this!" Maaya said helplessly.

"Not yet. I mean… I don't want to, of course. I would give almost anything to stay here with you forever… but I wouldn't give up your world. If I stay, it wouldn't be a great world for you much longer anyway."

"That's… I… hold on. Isak… what the machine did the first time, could it be done again?" Maaya asked desperately, turning to face the man. "Could you make it so the machine has something else to direct energy into, like another gem or something, and we can leave it there instead of Saber's gem?"

"Unfortunately not," Isak answered helplessly. He looked as though every time he had to refuse a suggestion it broke his heart a little more. "I would have to infuse the object we chose with *libris*, and I can't do that now I'm dead. What's more, I'm afraid that the old rules would still apply. It would still need to take a life to transfer that energy in the first place. And right now there's only your life to take."

"Could you teach me? Is it something I could do?" Maaya continued, her voice cracking with emotion. She was vaguely aware of what she was suggesting, acknowledging dimly she had taken no time to think about it at all, but it was all she could think of doing. There was no other possible solution.

"Absolutely not!" The voice wasn't Isak's. Saber floated over to Maaya, giving her a look that was equal parts stern and hurt. "I refuse to let you do such a thing. Maaya, I'm *already dead.* We did not travel across the world so that you could sacrifice yourself to save the not-even-life of your friend most people can't see."

"But this… Saber, I… I can't imagine a world without you in it," Maaya pleaded. "I don't know what else to do, and this is the closest thing we have to—"

"No, the closest thing we have to a solution is doing what Isak suggests. And if you can't imagine a world without me, you'd be creating the same problem in reverse by sending yourself to a world I couldn't reach without being sealed *anyway.* I… appreciate your intent. It means a lot to me that you would consider doing something like that for me. But I can't let you do it. You have plenty to live for here. You deserve to live in the world you've saved. There are a lot of people who can't wait to see you again."

Maaya shut her eyes tight. Saber was right, and she hated it. If there was any chance she and Saber could ever be in the same world again someday, it was Saber who had to leave this one.

Unable to speak, Maaya simply nodded. Everything was happening so fast she wasn't sure she knew what she was agreeing to anymore, but she was too tired to process any more. She had reached her limits and passed them, and now she felt like she was already starting to mourn, though she didn't know what yet.

Saber rested her hand on Maaya's shoulder, then turned to Isak. "So how exactly would I get sealed? Is there anything special we need to do for me given the situation, or…?"

"Not at all. A simple blood card would do. At the least, it would be quick," Isak answered remorsefully.

"Neat. I've always wanted to go out with a bang," Saber replied darkly, but at Maaya's quiet gasp and look of horror, she floated back, raising her hands. "Oh, *that's* inappropriate. Right. Sorry. Listen, Maaya, you uh… you might want to leave the room for this one when we're all ready. I wouldn't ask you to see this."

At these words, Isak looked as though he just might be sick with guilt.

"Oh, stars, help me… well, there's a caveat to this. As you know, blood cards can only be used by the living. And Freja, you and I are both dead. So…"

Maaya saw this coming a split second before he spoke, but she still wasn't prepared for how hard it hit her.

"N-no. No, I can't. I will not, I refuse," she cried, choking on a sob.

"Maaya, please—" Saber started, but Maaya shook her head determinedly and stepped backward.

"No! Think about what you're asking me to do! You want me to say goodbye to you, but not only that, you want me to be the one to end your life! I will *not.* I have to draw the line somewhere, and I haven't even accepted that you being sealed away is something I can accept yet."

"Maaya, listen," Saber said forcefully, taking Maaya's hands in hers. "This has to be done. You do this one thing, this one single thing, and you save the entire world. It's all over after this. It might be hard—I can't even imagine being in your shoes—but it has to be done."

"I can't," Maaya answered weakly, hardly able to speak as she sobbed. "I've done everything I've had to so far! Even when I was tired and hurt and hungry and miserable, I still did *everything* I had to. But I'm not strong enough to do this! It's too much. How can I make you disappear? We still have so much to do! You have to find out more about who you are, you have to be there for me and Adelaide, and you have to come back and see our friends, and..."

"And I want to be there for all of that, I do, but the one thing I want more than that is to ensure this world is still a safe place for you. We came all this way to do just that. I'm already dead, Maaya. And as much as I joke about wanting you in the afterlife with me, I want you to live. I want you to be happy, to find love, to grow old, and to look back and say with certainty that you did everything you wanted. Travel the world, marry the girl of your dreams, and make life better for everyone you meet, but most importantly, *be happy*. You have fought so hard all these years just to stay alive and to help your friends, and now you need to focus on you. I want this to be your world, and if this is how we can do that, so be it."

"But I... Saber... what good is the world if it doesn't have you in it?"

"Plenty. If I'm the only good you see in the world you've been looking in all the wrong places." Saber leaned closer and hugged Maaya tightly. "The good in the world is your friends who love you and the ones who have risked their lives to keep you safe and keep a smile on your face. It's the strangers who treat others with kindness even though they have no reason to, but do it just because it feels good to make others happy. It's the people who decide to give one person a compliment each day because they've decided it's the best way to become more confident. It's falling in love and being brave enough to say so, knowing you're at your most vulnerable, and it's when the person accepts you for all that you are and says they love you too. There is so, so much good in the world, Maaya, and that's what you deserve. That's why I have to do this, because I can make sure it's all still there for you to seek out. And as a friend—as your best friend—I feel like I owe you that."

Maaya couldn't speak. She stepped back, her face in her hands, as she tried with all her might to avoid breaking down completely. For all her pain, she knew Saber was right: they didn't have much time.

"How... how will I do this?" Maaya asked finally, her voice breaking pitifully. "I have no cards left."

"I, uhm... I'll go get what you need," Isak suggested, then practically dashed away over to his desk.

"Are you angry with me?" Saber asked softly as Isak rummaged in his desk.

"No, of course not. I love you," Maaya whispered, her lip trembling.

"Well, I expect the anger will come eventually. I would be surprised if it didn't. I know I deserve it at least a little," Saber continued, staring at the floor. "Maaya… I've thought about this before, and I want you to know… if this had to happen at all, I wanted it to be this way. You aren't killing me, you know? I've been dead for a hundred years. All you're doing is sending me off to where I should be. I wouldn't want to go in a battle or from some hotheaded *libris* newcomer who thinks it's their duty to get rid of me. I wouldn't want to go in some accident before I had a chance to give you a proper goodbye. No, I would prefer to move on by the hand of a friend. I know it's a terrible thing to ask, and I would never ask you to forgive me, but it's how I've always wanted this to end. This is just… a little sooner than I'd imagined."

"There's nothing to forgive. Even now you're saving my life, just like you've always done," Maaya replied with a watery chuckle. "You've always looked out for me. I just… I always pictured you there, you know? At my side, in my life. I'm not angry at you for this… if anything I just admire you even more than I always have. There was just so much more for us to see and to do. We wanted to get that big house together, remember? We wanted to get out of Sark, to move on, all of that."

"And look at us. We've done almost all of that. We've left Sark, we've found new friends, and hey, we're literally *saving the entire world.* I know not everything has gone according to plan, but we've done a pretty damn good job so far. As for a big house, well… your girlfriend is rich, so let's consider that done, too. Oh, and you have a girlfriend. That's definitely worth living for."

Before Maaya could reply, Isak walked quietly over and set a strip of paper and a small knife down on the table next to her.

"It's, uh, pretty self-explanatory, I think," he said, clearing his throat nervously. "One for each of us, if you would."

Maaya took the knife wordlessly and slid it lightly across one of her fingers. She caught some of her blood on the edge of her knife and began to write. It was crude and difficult, but after she drew the final strokes, the paper felt suddenly warm under her palms. She tore the strip neatly in two, then held one in each hand.

They were ready.

"Maaya, I… I want you to know, despite how difficult this must be, I have nothing but gratitude for you. So much that I cannot ever hope to properly express how I feel," Isak said quietly. "You brought my daughter back to me and will now give both of us peace. For all I know and all I've done, that was something I could not do. You've reunited me with my family, and I cannot possibly thank you enough for that."

"Hey. Promise me something, okay, Maaya?" Saber said, and Maaya looked up at her, tears falling freely down her cheeks. "Promise me you'll be happy. That you'll get out there in the world, find your friends, and do everything you ever dreamed of. I know you'll feel miserable after this, but that won't last. Do that for me, okay? I want to always know you'll be out there in the other world having a grand old time."

Maaya wasn't sure if she could. She knew it would be selfish not to, but this was all happening so fast. She couldn't imagine a world without Saber.

But then she remembered Kim, Sovaan, and Kalil. She had lost them, too. And she had somehow found the strength to carry on despite how much her heart hurt. She had fought on and persisted against everything that came against her, and she had come out victoriously. What's more, she had even found happiness again. She had smiled again. It had taken a long time, but she had done it. She knew this couldn't be easy for Saber, either. Maaya owed her this promise.

"I will," Maaya said with all the strength she could muster. "I will."

"You'll do me proud, Maaya. I know you will," Saber continued, looking as though she too were about to break any moment. "And hey, feel free to talk about me in your stories too, all right? If you're going to tell the world about all the cool people you knew, I should come first."

"Nah, you'll go last. That's where the best goes, right?" Maaya chuckled tearfully, and Saber nodded.

"Good point. You need to finish on a high note, after all. Now, I… I suppose we'd best get this thing done, huh?"

Maaya hesitated.

"I… I don't know… will it hurt?"

"Not at all," Isak answered kindly. "Do you know the feeling just when you're just about to drift off to sleep? When all the world seems at peace and you're lost in the taste of your dreams to come? That's what it is to pass, but all at once."

"And for what it's worth… I feel like I'm complete," Saber added. "I helped you get where you needed to go, I found out who I am, I found my family… I feel like I can go to rest with no regrets."

"I'm glad," Maaya sniffed. "I really am."

"Now, I'll just explain what you have to do so this works correctly," Isak explained. "When you, ah, use the blood cards, the gem will become tangible again. It's likely the sudden change may affect the machine, so you very quickly need to take the gem and set it inside Freja's capsule. That should be all you need to do; just make sure you do it quickly. Best do this part quickly too if you're uncertain."

Maaya nodded.

"Are you ready?" she asked, her voice hollow.

"As ready as I'll ever be, my dear," Saber answered with as much confidence as she could muster.

"I am," Isak followed. "And again… I thank you so very, very much. You're freeing us all."

"Hey… so about this other world. What's it like? Is it like coming back to life again?" Saber asked Isak as Maaya approached.

"In a manner of speaking. I'll tell you all about it once we're there," Isak smiled. "Don't be afraid. It'll be like closing your eyes and then waking up again."

"That sounds nice," Saber said calmly, then turned to Maaya. "You and Adelaide take your time. When you eventually make it there, we'll save room at our table for you, okay?"

"You got it," Maaya said, giving her last at a smile as she raised her blood cards in her hands.

She stared at Saber one last time, willing her mind with everything she had to remember this moment, her face, her voice, and everything about her. This was it.

Then, before she could second guess herself any longer, she pressed the cards against Saber and Isak's bodies.

The effect was instantaneous. Saber and Isak disappeared in a shower of red sparks, and a moment later Maaya heard a light clatter as the circlet from Saber's forehead hit the floor. As she stooped down to pick it up, the entire house rumbled dangerously.

Maaya picked it up quickly, then ran over to the capsule. Rather than slowing down, the rumbling increased, and dust began to fall from the beams above her. Maaya frantically searched for a way to open the capsule, then found two small latches on the side. She undid them, then pushed open the lid.

At first she couldn't bear to look at what lay inside, but then she opened her eyes. Freja's body was there, peaceful and still, as though she were only sleeping. Maaya had half a mind to simply throw the circlet inside and slam the lid closed again, but even as the entire house shook around her, she realized Saber deserved better than that.

With both hands she gently placed the circlet back on the girl's forehead, and then softly closed the lid again, locking it in place.

As soon as the lid shut, the machine emitted a horrifying shrieking sound. And then, slowly, the noises stopped. Before Maaya could even breathe, however, the noises began again—this time, however, in a way that sounded almost like they were echoing in reverse.

The basement was full of light, and she heard rumbling from all around her as though the very earth itself was collapsing in upon itself. She shrieked as a number of glass vials fell from a table nearby and shattered, and then she glanced up in horror as she heard one of the wooden support beams begin to splinter.

Suddenly, she realized she needed to escape. But as she made to dash for the stairs, a bright light emitted from the center wall across the room. When Maaya looked over, she gasped in shock.

As she watched, what looked like the silhouettes of hundreds and hundreds of ghosts burst forth from the heart of the machine, disappearing almost instantly. Men, women, and children alike, all fleeing the machine—or being set free from it. There were far too many to get a good look at any one of them, and they disappeared almost immediately after they erupted from the machine, but amidst their cries and what she could see of their faces, Maaya detected one feeling for certain: relief.

Just then, Maaya realized who these people must be. Every single time one of the machine's ghosts killed someone, that person's ghost was sucked away into the void. Maaya now knew that the machine had continued taking lives to fulfill its purpose, but with nowhere for the energy from those stolen lives to go, she guessed they must have remained trapped in the machine—some of them for nearly a century. And now, now that the machine thought it had completed its ultimate task, they were all finally being set free.

Maaya felt something on her shoulder, and when she looked over, she saw that parts of the roof were starting to collapse. She realized with horror that whatever power had kept the house in perfect condition, frozen oddly in time, had disappeared with the machine—and that time was catching up with the old, decrepit house.

As soon as she started for the stairs again, however, she heard a voice behind her.

"Maaya? Is that you?"

She whirled around. Then her breath caught in her throat.

Kim, Sovaan, and Kalil stood across from her, staring at her with wonder and admiration.

"It is you!" Kim cried. "You did it, didn't you? You stopped the ghosts!"

"How?" Maaya breathed, feeling her legs weaken beneath her. "H-how are you…?"

"We haven't got long; it's hard enough holding ourselves here as it is. But we just had to see you," Sovaan explained quickly.

"It's setting us all free. Good thing, too. It was pretty awful in there," Kalil added.

"I've missed you so much," Kim exclaimed. "I'm so happy for you, too. You fixed everything!"

"I… I'm so sorry, all of you," Maaya whimpered. "I couldn't save you even though I promised."

"Oh Maaya, don't, please," Kim pleaded. "We don't blame you for that. You did the best you could just like you always did for us."

"Yeah. You made it all the way to Krethus, didn't you?" Kalil continued. "I get to brag about that for eternity. 'Hey, you know that girl that saved the world? She's my friend.'"

"You made our lives worth living," Sovaan finished. "You always took care of us. Without you we would have died, but you brought us all together and made us a family!"

"Thank you. I mean it. I love you all so, so much, and I'm never going to forget you," Maaya sniffed. "Oh! Kim, I… we saved your diary. I read a little, is… is that okay?"

"Definitely!" Kim said without hesitation. "I don't need it anymore where I'm going. Besides, I feel like there's a lot of me in there I never got to share with you, and I'd feel better knowing you got to see the rest of me since I can't show you myself anymore."

"Well, damn. Now I wish I'd kept a diary," Kalil grumbled, and Sovaan snorted.

"Like you would have ever put in the effort to learn to write."

"It's still a thought! Now what's Maaya going to read about me?"

"I'm sure she knows all about how annoying you both were without having to read it in a diary," Kim continued, then quickly held up her hand for silence. "We're almost out of time. Maaya, this place won't hold up long, either. You should get out of here."

"I will. I'll keep going, okay? And I'll tell the whole world about you. Everyone's going to know who you were and what you did. I won't let *anyone* forget you," Maaya promised, fighting through every word.

"If anyone can do it, you can," Kalil grinned. "Make us look good, yeah?"

"And hey, now that you've saved the world, go back home and kick Rahu's butt for us!" Sovaan exclaimed.

"Do your best, okay, Maaya?" Kim said with a smile. "Thank you. For everything. You're the best. I'll miss you still, but… I'll see you again someday, right?"

"Definitely," Maaya finished.

She took a step back as a large beam crashed to the floor, followed by an assortment of dishes falling through the ceiling from the kitchen above.

"Go, Maaya!" Kim said urgently. "We have to go, too."

"We'll say hi to Saber for you!" Sovaan winked.

"A fitting end for the Ghost Hunters, don't you think?" Kalil chuckled. "Have a good life, Maaya."

With that, all three ghostly figures flickered, then disappeared. A few seconds later the machine fell silent and still, its lights shutting off, the humming and pulsing fading into nothing.

But Maaya was too preoccupied to enjoy the fact that the machine was finally down. The house was slowly collapsing in upon itself, and she was out of time. She dashed up the crumbling stairs, a segment of falling stone striking her painfully in the shoulder as she went.

She made it halfway down the hall when the ceiling itself collapsed upon her. She hit the floor hard, expecting to be crushed under the weight of the roof, but then the floor collapsed as well. Maaya was deafened by the sound of shattering glass, splintering wood, and crumbling stucco. How far she fell she did not know; she was only vaguely aware of being battered from all sides by the collapsing house, feeling as though she were being swept up in a furious ocean storm.

By the time everything settled, Maaya didn't know where she was. She was vaguely aware that she lay on a concrete floor, pinned down and surrounded by the broken building. She was too injured, too dizzy, and too weak to move even if she had wanted to escape.

In that moment, overcome with grief and exhaustion, she finally succumbed to the limits of her broken body, and she drifted into unconsciousness.

Maaya woke to the sound of someone calling her name in the distance. For a few moments she had no idea where she was. All she knew was that she couldn't move and that she was in intense pain.

Then she remembered what had happened, and a fresh swell of grief pierced her heart. Saber was gone. They had destroyed the machine, but Saber, her best friend in the world, was gone. The last of her family. Once, she had lived in a small house with four other people she loved and adored, and now, weeks later, every single one of them was gone, never to return.

She heard her name again, but didn't answer. She wasn't sure she could even if she wanted to, and right now, she did not. All the pain in her body meant nothing. She hadn't eaten in far too long, she knew she was badly wounded, and she had gotten far too little sleep over the past few days. This was of no concern to her. If anything, that meant she was close to death, and maybe that wasn't such a bad thing.

Suddenly, there came a crashing sound from nearby, and she heard someone scream. Before Maaya could react she felt a sudden weight lift from her body. With all her strength she turned her head slightly, and there she saw Adelaide, her purple strength augments burning on her arms, picking up large pieces of wood and concrete and throwing them effortlessly aside.

"Maaya! Maaya, are you alive? Please, say something!" Adelaide pleaded after she had freed Maaya completely, kneeling down next to her.

"I… here," Maaya replied in a voice barely above a whisper, and Adelaide let out a tearful sigh of relief. Before Maaya knew it, Adelaide gently picked her up and cradled her softly in her lap, her red hair falling lightly into Maaya's face. From what Maaya could see Adelaide had sustained yet more injuries, and she looked paler than usual.

"Thank the stars you made it. I was so scared for you. I saw the pulse and then everything went strange and I couldn't find you, and… oh, but you made it, and you're here! I'm never letting you out of my sight again, never," Adelaide cried, brushing the hair from Maaya's face and hugging her gingerly. "Here, let me get you healed up…"

"N-no," protested Maaya weakly, but if Adelaide heard her, she didn't acknowledge her. After only a moment Maaya felt warmth flood her body, and much of her pain faded away instantly.

Adelaide placed her palm to her forehead and moaned, but after a few moments of deep breathing she opened her eyes again, looking beyond exhausted but relieved.

"Better?" she asked, and Maaya nodded. "Thank goodness. Well, whatever you did, it worked. The barrier is gone, the ghosts are gone… stars, Maaya, you did it! It's over! The machine is down! It is, isn't it?" she continued quickly, and when Maaya nodded again, she squealed with glee.

Maaya wanted to be happy. She really did. And she had every reason to be. Adelaide was alive, she was alive, and they had succeeded in their ultimate task. Despite so many things going wrong, they had won.

But Maaya couldn't be happy. She had fought so hard to try to prevent any more loss of life, and she had tried with everything she had to keep her friends safe, and one last time, she had failed. Saber was gone.

"Maaya? Where's Saber?" Adelaide asked, her voice softening. Maaya said nothing, but it didn't take long for Adelaide to understand.

"Oh, no… oh, not her, too," she said despondently, her shoulders sagging. "I'm so sorry, Maaya. I can't believe she… well, never mind that now. One thing at a time. I'm so glad you're safe, though. Let's get you out of here."

Adelaide helped Maaya sit up, but before Adelaide got to her feet, she knelt on one knee in the center of a pile of wreckage, then placed two fingers to her forehead and closed her eyes. She didn't say a word, but when she opened her eyes a minute later, she stared back at Maaya with new resolve.

"She will be remembered. Now let's get back to civilization. The danger has passed, but we need to start moving now if we hope to make it back; our supplies are almost out."

She helped Maaya to her feet and then they trudged through the wreckage of Isak and Saber's home. Maaya couldn't look. She knew what she would see, and she wasn't in the mood for reminders. It was perhaps fitting that the old house had finally succumbed to the effects of time. There was no longer anything artificial about it, and it, along with its occupants and the dread machine that had terrorized the country for a century, were now dead. Everything was as it should be.

"Adelaide… you're hurt," Maaya finally managed to say as they reached level ground. "Let me heal you now."

"If you use any energy on healing me I'll be carrying you the rest of the way," Adelaide refused. "I'll be fine! Let's find some shade and get something to eat and drink before we go too far. Oh, it's so nice not to have to worry about the pulses or random ghost attacks anymore…"

"Where were you? What happened?" Maaya asked with effort.

"Well, after you disappeared inside and the pulse hit, I thought I was dead. I was so afraid until I slowly started to realize what was going on. I didn't have any blood cards left, but I tried to stand watch at the door anyway just in case. I saw a few of the ghosts in the distance, but luckily they didn't come after me. I don't remember how long I waited, but eventually something… happened, I don't know what. The ground started shaking, and then the ghosts, all of them, just disappeared in an instant! Then the house just collapsed and I was terrified you had… well, you're all right, that's what matters. Let's find somewhere to rest."

They walked on in silence, Maaya following slightly behind Adelaide. At first Maaya didn't care to look at anything but the ground in front of her, but even in her current state of grief she had to admit it quickly got boring.

It was like she had stepped out into another world. Almost everything looked the same, but the air seemed clearer, and the gloom that seemed to hang over everything inside what had once been the barrier was now gone. Maaya breathed deeply, taking in what fresh air she could. When movement caught her attention from above and she glanced upward, she noticed a small flock of birds making their way slowly overhead—likely the first life apart from Maaya and Adelaide this part of the world had seen in a century. The morning sun felt pleasantly warm and a comfortable breeze gently pushed her hair from her face as they walked.

And she could enjoy none of it. It took all the willpower she had to walk and breathe when all she felt like doing was collapsing and giving up. She didn't know where they were going—back to Adelaide's home, she assumed—but there was no place in this world that had what she wanted. She felt as though she had been left behind, forced to watch as all her loved ones moved on.

Maaya wasn't sure how long they walked or how far they traveled, but Adelaide finally guided her over to the mostly intact remains of a large wall that provided a comfortable area of shade, as well as a place to rest their legs. When they sat down and leaned against the wall Maaya realized Adelaide had been carrying both of their packs, but her heart was too full of remorse to have any room for more guilt.

"There we are. Here, have some water and I'll fish out the last of our food supplies. It isn't much, but it should last us the journey back."

"That's okay; I'm not hungry," Maaya replied monotonously.

"You need to eat. It's been too long," Adelaide pressed, but Maaya shook her head.

"You go ahead. You need it more than I do."

"Maaya..."

"I don't want to eat. Please drop it."

Even as she said these words she knew what Adelaide's reaction would be. Sure enough, before she could even register what was happening, Adelaide positioned herself in front of Maaya, her hands on her shoulders, staring intently into Maaya's brown eyes.

"Maaya, I know something terrible happened in there, but right now we need to focus on getting out of here, okay? We can deal with the rest when we're home safe, but we're still in danger, so please, get something to eat and drink so we can start heading back."

"I don't even want to *live* anymore, how can I think about eating?" Maaya replied sharply.

Adelaide opened her mouth to reply, but no words came out. Instead, after a moment's pause, she let Maaya go and sat back in the dirt, her gaze falling to the ground.

Maaya regretted saying it. As much as she felt it was the truth, she wished she could have taken it back. But this was too soon, and too much had happened. It just wasn't fair. She never got any time to process anything that happened; she was always on the move. After Kim, Kalil, and Sovaan had died she'd been forced to move on to deal with Rahu, and when Svante was killed she'd been forced to flee the city. And now that Saber was gone she still had to work up the nerve to keep moving even more. It was too much.

"Adelaide, I... I'm just tired," Maaya said softly, hoping Adelaide would hear her out and understand. "For weeks I've been doing nothing but running and fighting, and when my friends died I just had to keep going. I've had no escape from any of this; there was always something bigger looming over me. I just... I'm so tired. I can't keep doing this. I can't keep losing people and then just moving on like nothing happened. Now that this part is over I don't even know what to keep moving *for*."

Adelaide sighed and sat next to Maaya, leaning her head against Maaya's as they stared out at the endless dead landscape before them.

"I've had my own experiences with loss. When you're raised in this kind of profession you see a lot of it," Adelaide said, the lifetime of hurt in her voice belying her calm tone. "I want to tell you that it gets better—and it does—but that would be too simple. I've changed from all this. Permanently. Just like I'm sure you have. We'll live with these scars on our hearts for the rest of our lives."

"How do you do it? How are you always so cheerful and positive after all that?"

"It's a combination of things. I think that's just who I am at my core, but I've also had a lot of time to think and grieve and grow. I also wanted happiness so badly I was willing to run from my family to get it, but it didn't come immediately. Now that you finally have time to grieve it will take time for you, too," Adelaide explained, and then she turned to face Maaya directly. "But lately there has been one other thing, one thing that kept me going through certain death and danger and injury that would have killed me if I were on my own, and that was you. It *is* you. After I met you and realized what we could do together, it wasn't about making my family proud of me anymore. Part of it was doing it for my country, as I've always tried to do, but the rest was about wanting a world that was safe for the both of us. One that we could enjoy together. And wanting it so badly that I was willing to do anything for it."

Maaya gazed up at her, eyes wide in surprise.

"I'm sorry, I… I didn't—"

Adelaide shook her head, a small smile on her face.

"I know. I won't pretend to know the hurt you feel. But please, stay with me. Come with me. Everything we fought for, we achieved. We won. *You* won. There's nothing looming over you anymore. All you have to do is make it back to civilization and then we can go home and never have to worry about anything ever again. And I won't ask you to tell me what happened or even to see me until you feel like it, but I will ask you to push on just this one last time. Can you do that?"

Of course she could, Maaya thought. As she stared up into Adelaide's green eyes, everything she felt for her came flooding back as though she was feeling it for the first time. Her heart ached for Saber, as she was sure it would for years to come, but she had been wrong to think for even a moment that she had lost everything. She had spent so long desperately hoping that Adelaide would love Maaya like Maaya loved her, and after much effort and embarrassment and bravery, that wish came true.

Life in the immediate future was going to be painful, but she knew that these wounds, just like all her others, would heal. Maybe they wouldn't heal quickly or even completely, but Adelaide was still there to fill every hole in her heart. And Maaya knew she would try her best to do the same for her.

"I will," Maaya said firmly, and a wide grin broke over Adelaide's face.

"I'm so glad! I can't bear to see you so down, even though I know... what?" Adelaide said quizzically as Maaya tugged on her sleeve, pulling her closer.

"I love you."

She pulled Adelaide in for a kiss, and Adelaide seemed only too happy to accept. Adelaide knelt over Maaya's lap and leaned into her, her fingers ever so gently brushing against Maaya's cheeks and up to her forehead, pushing her hair from her face. Maaya pulled her closer until they were pressed so tightly against each other it was almost difficult to breathe, and Maaya felt every bruise and strain and cut on her body radiate in painful protest, but she ignored it. She had survived the end of the world and she was going to enjoy it with the love of her life. For the first time since discovering the source of the strange ghosts so long ago and so far away, she had nowhere to be.

Still, in their state of injury and exhaustion, they tired quickly and reluctantly released each other to catch their breath. Adelaide leaned back against the wall, gripping Maaya's hand tightly in hers. When she finally answered Maaya, her voice held all the certainty Maaya had always been hoping for when she said the words Maaya had been so desperately hoping to hear.

"I love you, too."

Maaya knew the hurt in her heart would not go away for a long time, but hearing this from the woman she loved—and truly, she did—was a start. What she feared most was losing everyone to the perceived cruelty of the world, and when even the dead were no exception she had been terrified she might someday find herself alone. But this one affirmation, this one gesture, was proof that there were still things worth pushing on for.

"Hey. Everything is going to be all right. I promise," Adelaide said warmly, handing Maaya a small grain bar and a pouch of water. "We're going to make it through this together. And don't forget everyone else back home who can't wait to see us."

"I can't wait to see them, either," Maaya said through a mouthful of food, thinking of Halvar and Inga. They had surely noticed that the barrier had fallen by now. She wondered how quickly word was spreading in the outside world. "Oh, and your parents are going to be so proud of you, you know that. Should I tell them you were the better one again?"

Maaya laughed as the taller girl shoved her sideways and rolled her eyes.

"Not this time. This one is all on you."

"It is not! You must have saved my life two or three times back there," Maaya protested.

"If you still want to keep track of who has saved who more often, you still win in that department," Adelaide said pointedly. "So I'm afraid I have no choice but to take you to dinner."

"Oh, dinner… that's a word I haven't heard in too long," Maaya replied reminiscently. "But you know what, I feel like the world should treat us. Just this once. After all we've done for it, I think it owes us one."

"That would just be the tip of the iceberg," Adelaide agreed. "How are you feeling? The sooner we get started the sooner we can get all dressed up and go have a lovely night on the town, just the two of us."

Maaya grumbled in playful protest. She wasn't surprised Adelaide had managed to find a way to cheer her up, but she still considered it quite a feat. She also knew her misery would return, as it always did, but for now it had met its match.

Onward they went, mile after hot and dusty mile. With no danger left around them Maaya was able to focus only on putting one foot in front of the other. This turned out to be quite fortuitous, as her exhaustion and injuries were quickly catching up with her. Adelaide seemed to fare little better, and though the girl was in high spirits and put forth her best effort to appear strong, Maaya could see her slowly weakening as her paces became shorter and her breathing more ragged.

By midafternoon they finally exhausted the remainder of their meager supplies, and Maaya began to feel concerned. When they started their journey she imagined that the way back would be as simple as taking a walk due to the lack of ghosts, but she hadn't accounted for the possibility of injury, lack of sleep, and lack of supplies. In fact, she hadn't counted on their journey there being so chaotic in the first place. For now they had food and water in their stomachs and enough energy to keep going, but for how long, Maaya wasn't sure. She didn't want to rest, fearing that if she sat down to rest her weary limbs she might find herself too weak to get up against.

As they walked in silence, and as Maaya's thoughts began to drift back to her friends, she started to realize she didn't want to see anybody. She knew they would be glad to see her, and that she would be overjoyed to see them alive and safe, but she knew there would be questions and discussions and perhaps even celebrations, and she didn't want to deal with any of it. All she wanted was to be somewhere quiet, somewhere she and Adelaide could simply rest in silence with each other away from the chaos that was sure to be. She still had much to process, and it would be that much harder if people bombarded her for details on what had happened.

As evening came and the sun began to fall, Maaya paused, unable to continue any further. Her legs felt like they were on fire and her vision was starting to blur, a sure sign that if she didn't rest soon she would collapse.

"Let's rest a while," Adelaide said calmly, helping Maaya sit so she didn't lose her balance. "We haven't anything left to eat or drink, but a nap might do us well."

"It almost feels strange not to ask who will be taking first watch," Maaya chuckled weakly.

"Right? We can actually fall asleep without being afraid we'll wake up to a bright light signaling our impending doom," Adelaide snorted, but then she paused, squinting out across the open fields. "Hold on. Maybe I spoke too soon…"

"What is it?" Maaya asked nervously, trying to follow her gaze.

In the distance, miles away still, a multitude of bright white lights had appeared on the horizon. There were dozens of them, coming from the direction of where the edge of the barrier used to be—and they were headed almost toward where Maaya and Adelaide sat.

"That's… not possible," Maaya breathed, fighting her way to her feet and grasping at her card pouch, remembering with a sickening feeling that she was all out of blood cards.

"Wait," Adelaide directed. There was silence for a few moments, and Maaya looked frantically between Adelaide and the oncoming lights—and then Adelaide smiled. "I was wondering when they'd show up. Hey! Over here!"

Before Maaya could ask, she heard a humming noise in the distance. As the lights got closer she realized that the lights were not those of faceless ghosts, but of vehicles. A small caravan of motorized military vehicles was making their way quickly in their direction, their headlights bouncing slightly as they crossed the bumpy terrain. After a few moments they evidently spotted Adelaide, because they turned slightly to drive straight for them.

Maaya stepped back unconsciously, suddenly afraid. She hadn't expected the military to come seeking them out, much less in such numbers. But Adelaide put a steady hand on Maaya's shoulder and smiled down at her.

"It's okay. We're safe."

No sooner had she said this than the first of the trucks came to a grinding halt several yards away, and several figures jumped out, making their way swiftly over to them. Maaya felt another stab of fear, but then she heard a familiar voice.

"Cap'n! Maaya! You all right?"

Halvar and Inga rushed over to them, staring them up and down concernedly even as relief washed over their faces.

"You're both badly injured. We need to get you treated immediately," Inga said briefly, but then she took Adelaide into a tight hug, so powerful that she lifted her captain right off the ground. "I'm so relieved you two are safe. It's good to see you."

"How did you know where to find us?" Maaya asked in astonishment as more trucks parked nearby and other military personnel began to head toward them.

"We didn't. Not exactly. The military's been combing the area since they were able to verify the barrier fell," Halvar explained.

"It's good you found us when you did," Adelaide said gratefully now that both her feet were planted firmly on solid ground again. "We're out of supplies and we can't continue much longer."

"Oh, you're not walking another step, don't you worry," Halvar reassured her. "Here, let the medics see to you. I'm sure our boys and girls have got some questions for you as well, but Inga already made it clear that this would be brief. She told off a praetor to his face. It was great."

"I only assumed you would want to focus on getting home and recovering before any extensive interviews," Inga added with a knowing look.

"Inga, you perfect, beautiful human being," Adelaide laughed. "What would I do without you?"

"Hey, where's Saber?" Halvar asked, and Maaya felt a sharp pain in her chest at the mention of her name.

"Not here, but we'll talk about that later," Adelaide said meaningfully, and Halvar seemed to catch on immediately. To Maaya's relief, he nodded and didn't say another word.

Two men and two women dressed in white smocks came next, laden with small containers of medical supplies. Without so much as a hello they immediately began studying their patients, poking and prodding and asking questions about the extent and severity of their injuries. Maaya yelped at the sting of disinfectants on her wounds, which was followed quickly by the comforting cushion of bandages. Full pouches of cool water were pushed into her hands, as well as small boxes of military rations. Whether it was Maaya's hunger or the quality of military cooks, Maaya ate with gusto, surprised at how flavorful the food was—whatever it was.

When the medics seemed satisfied with their cursory examination, they stepped back as a tall man with a severe haircut and square jaw walked briskly over to them. Rather than wearing the brown and green uniforms of most military personnel, he wore a slick dark suit with multiple colorful patches and pins on his coat. He knelt down before Maaya and Adelaide, and Maaya noticed Adelaide suddenly snap to attention.

"I'm Praetor Forsberg. Pleasure to meet you both. I'm sure you're eager to get out of here and rest, but first, I have some questions. Are you two responsible for the barrier falling?"

"Yes, sir," Adelaide said, her tone suddenly all business. "We were there to see it shut down and verify the ghosts are all completely gone."

"Good, good. I'll have some of my officers double and triple check just to be sure. Is the area safe to investigate? Are there any threats we should know about?"

"Only that the machine is in the basement of a collapsed house. It might be unsteady, but that's the only environmental risk I'm aware of. Maaya?"

Maaya stared blankly for a moment, taken off guard at being asked to offer information to what looked like a very high-ranking official. She quickly cleared her head as he watched her expectantly.

"There's nothing else. The machine filled the entire basement, but it powered down as soon as we finished our mission."

"Was there anyone else in the area? Do we need to be on the lookout for anyone?" Praetor Forsberg continued.

"It was only us," Maaya answered. The man seemed friendly enough, but he still made her nervous. Despite becoming so close to Adelaide, authority still frightened her—and while she wasn't sure exactly what a praetor was, she guessed by Adelaide's reaction that he was *very* important.

"Good. Now, how did you do it? Is there any chance it will start up again?"

"We used the gem. It got us there safely, and once we were there we used the gem to disable the machine. So long as the gem is there it won't turn back on, and now that it's off, maybe the machine can be safely taken apart," Maaya continued.

"And where is the gem?" Forsberg pressed.

"There are two capsules in the center of the basement; the gem is in one of them, in a circlet. Taking the gem out was what started the whole thing in the first place, so please be careful," she said, and almost immediately felt extremely foolish. He was a seasoned military man. Of *course* he would be careful.

"Understood. And your names?"

Maaya gulped. Giving her name to an authority figure was about the silliest thing she could ever do.

"Adelaide Sol," Adelaide said briskly, holding out her hand to Forsberg. He shook her hand confidently and nodded.

"Well met. I was informed you might be attempting something like this again. I'm happy to hear it was successful this time. And you?" he asked, turning to Maaya.

"M-Maaya. Maaya Sahni," she answered nervously, afraid he would recognize her name and become angry, but his expression did not change, and he shook her hand as well.

"Pleasure. I'll make a note of your names in my report and make sure everyone is aware of what you've accomplished here. You've both done a great service for Krethus. I do apologize for not sounding more excited, but I need to make sure the site of the machine is secured and that we begin our investigations immediately. Is there anything else I should know before we proceed?"

Adelaide shook her head, but Maaya cleared her throat.

"Just… please take care while you're there. There are two bodies in the capsules I told you about, and one of them is— was, my friend. She's the one wearing the circlet. Please be respectful of them."

Forsberg nodded and got to his feet, brushing off his already impeccably clean slacks.

"I will make certain they are treated with the utmost respect and that we can arrange a proper burial. You don't have to tell me everything, but if I could have their names for my report as well, that would help immensely."

Maaya took a breath.

"Isak and Freja Astrom," Maaya said, and a look of recognition immediately flashed over Forsberg's face.

"I… see. That explains much. Thank you for your assistance, both of you. If you need anything at all, please let any of these men and women know. Otherwise, they will see you back home as expeditiously as possible. Again, thank you for your incredible service to our nation. We are in your debt. Maaya. Adelaide."

Adelaide bowed her head respectfully as Forsberg swept off, already snapping orders at the men and women in uniform around him. Most of the trucks immediately started moving again, heading quickly in the direction of the now-inoperative machine.

As other military personnel bustled around them, Maaya felt relief wash over her. For the first time, she felt as though it was truly over. Humans were making the first footprints on these lands in a century, the investigations were beginning, and it was now out of Maaya and Adelaide's hands. While the military did their work, it was time for them to return home.

"Let's get you two in a truck and back to the train station. If it's not already there waiting for us, it'll be there shortly," Halvar informed them. "Can you stand?"

"I would appreciate some help, just in case," Adelaide replied, and Inga helped her effortlessly to her feet. In similar fashion, Halvar held out his hand to help Maaya up and then put a steadying hand at her back as they walked.

They walked over to one of the trucks where the back end opened to reveal two long benches, one along either side. It was covered with canvas, providing decent shelter from the elements, but it was clear this was designed to transport as many people as possible, and assuredly not to provide any comfort.

Still, when Maaya and Adelaide sat far inside, it might as well have been a luxury cruiser. Maaya sighed and let herself relax as Inga and Halvar sat next to them and as six soldiers filed inside after them.

Maaya didn't pay them any mind even as the door was closed behind them and the truck began to move. From the plastic windows cut into the canvas she could see two other trucks joining them as they turned and started in the opposite direction from where the caravan is going.

"Looks like we're getting an escort," Adelaide commented, and one of the soldiers nodded.

"News spreads fast, ma'am. You're going to be the center of attention whether you like it or not. We're to ensure you make it safely home through the crowds and all. It was mostly at your commander's request there."

"It was not a request," Inga said shortly, and the soldier appeared to understand it wasn't in his best interest to disagree.

After a few minutes, the cabin was filled with whispered conversation, but for Maaya and Adelaide, there was nothing to say. It was over. The machine was down. Everything they had fought so hard for had finally come to fruition, and now it was time to go home. Exhausted, injured, and worn out in every sense of the word, the girls were content simply to be in each other's company—especially given how close they had come to losing even that.

The quiet rumbling of the truck and the whispers of those sitting nearby was almost hypnotic, and Maaya soon found herself nodding off. Adelaide had already leaned against the back wall of the truck, looking as though she might fall asleep at any moment. But then she reached over and gently pulled Maaya to her, and Maaya rested her head on her shoulder with Adelaide's arm around her. Just before she fell asleep, her mind drifted back to those quiet and cool nights in the middle of the ocean where they had done the same so many times before, and she was comforted by this familiarity. As much as the world had changed, and as much as she had lost, she still had this.

37

THOUGHTS OF HOME

Four days later, Asmund's carriage rolled up to the front gate of Adelaide's estate in the early hours of the afternoon. Maaya was relieved to see that there were no government officials, military personnel, or reporters here; from the moment they had left the relative safety of the truck at the train station days ago they had been surrounded by people asking questions, making assertions, and demonstrating their total lack of respect for personal space. Maaya had been grateful for the presence of the soldiers, who had struggled to keep the steadily mounting presence of curious onlookers at bay until Maaya and Adelaide were safely aboard.

Even then, every time they made a stop there was a crowd outside. More officers asked questions. More well-wishers tried to get their attention. It was loud and chaotic, nothing like how it had been traveling in the opposite direction. Maaya felt trapped and anxious, but there was nowhere to go until they arrived home.

But here it was quiet, looking as though nothing at all had changed. She knew it had been little more than a week, but after traveling so far and doing so much, she felt like she had been gone much longer. It was almost unfathomable to her that the rest of the world was going on as though she hadn't just thrown herself into the midst of death to save the world from destruction. As though Saber wasn't here anymore.

As they stepped out, Adelaide reached into her coat pocket for some coins, but Asmund adamantly refused.

"As far as I'm concerned you're never paying for another ride again. Not after what you've both done," he said, but then sat back in surprise as

Adelaide climbed to the top of the carriage and forced the coins into his hands.

"We might have saved the world but *you* still have to make a living," Adelaide replied sternly, but then she winked. "Thanks for the ride. I expect we'll be seeing you again soon."

"After a long, long rest I hope," Asmund returned, and Maaya and Adelaide both nodded.

"I think I could sleep for a week," Maaya groaned.

"I'm going to muster up the energy for a bath first. Not being able to clean myself for a week has me feeling a little disgusting," Adelaide nodded. "Have a good evening, Asmund!"

"And to you!" Asmund called as his carriage started down the road.

The girls stood side by side at the gate, staring silently down the path toward the front door.

"Home sweet home," Adelaide said, though there was an air of uncertainty in her voice.

"Your family is going to be overjoyed," Maaya smiled.

"I'm sure. I guess I just feel like I don't want to deal with it right now." When Maaya glanced up at her in surprise, she continued, "Remember after our battle at sea how I didn't feel like doing anything at all? It's like that. I guess we've just been through so much that I want to be by myself. Or to be more accurate… only with you."

"Believe me, I know the feeling," Maaya answered. "I don't suppose everyone could just leave us alone for a while."

"I doubt it. People need answers, and at some point we'll have to give them. I can't imagine that would take too long, though. I don't intend for it to take any more than a few days. Remember, I need to get back to sea eventually. Duty calls and all that."

Maaya's heart sank. She had forgotten about that. At this point, repairs to her ship would likely be complete—or close to it—and she would soon be assembling her crew to make her journey back across the world. All of Maaya's visions had placed the two of them firmly in Krethus, but Adelaide still had work to do, and that meant taking her back toward Selenthia.

Distracted by everything else, Maaya had pushed the thought from her mind, thinking she would have plenty of time to think about what to do about that particular problem later. Now, however, it had snuck up on her, and she was still no closer to an answer than she had been over a week before.

Maaya's discomfort must have shown on her face, because Adelaide smiled down at her and put an arm comfortingly around her waist.

"Don't think I've forgotten about you. We'll talk about that later. For now, let's get cleaned up and get some rest! The offer of staying in my bed is still open," Adelaide said cheerily.

Maaya paused, then laughed.

"You know, I can't even pretend to be embarrassed anymore. You've got a deal."

Looking positively delighted, Adelaide took Maaya by the hand and led the way down the path. The gravel crunched under their feet as they walked, and Maaya felt a silly smile on her face the whole way.

Before they reached the porch, the front door was flung wide open, and Maaya was barely able to recognize Marit before she took her older sister into a tight hug.

"Adelaide, oh stars, you're home! I can't believe it!" Marit cried, and Maaya saw tears sparkling in her eyes. Adelaide winced in pain, but said nothing as she wrapped her arms around the younger girl. "I was so worried. I heard the news that the outposts had been taken over and that you and Maaya went in alone. And then we didn't hear a word for days, and I... I thought..."

"Hey, come on now, you know I'm better than that," Adelaide answered soothingly.

"I know. But you're still all beat up, and... I'm just glad you're safe. I didn't care if you succeeded or not, I just wanted you back," Marit sniffed.

"Well, now you've got me back, and we're all safe now, too."

A moment later Felix and Cajsa rushed forward, sweeping their daughters in a tight hug as well. Maaya almost giggled at the pained expression on Adelaide's face, though she felt slightly put out. This was Adelaide's family, after all. There was no one left, dead or alive, for Maaya to celebrate with.

But then Felix walked over and pulled her into a hug as well, and Maaya gasped from surprise. Cajsa and Marit soon followed, and within moments all five of them stood together in one comfortable warm embrace.

"And you, Maaya, you made it as well! I'm so pleased. The Sol house is that much brighter and happier that you've returned," Felix said deeply.

"And you're all beat up too, poor thing," Marit said, staring Maaya up and down as they broke apart. "You two both need some rest! Should I call a doctor?"

"We're fine; the military medics already saw to us on the field," Adelaide explained hastily. "I'm just looking forward to a bath to wash off a week's worth of muck, and then to sleep for a very long time."

"And after that there will be a grand party!" Felix boomed. "I'll contact all of our friends and family, but we'll leave it at that; no pesky reporters around here, no sir. But we must celebrate! Our country has been saved, and my daughter was responsible for it."

"We always knew you could, darling," Cajsa said placidly from his side.

"Did you really? Does this mean no more teasing over my first try?" Adelaide asked pointedly as she crossed her arms.

The Sol family stared between each other for a moment, and then grinned in unison.

"You get a few months, at the very least," Marit teased.

"Just remember I'll be giving a speech at your wedding," Adelaide shot back with a wink. "How nice it is depends on how nice you are to me."

"Yes, well, I want to talk to you about that at some point," Marit replied.

"We'll do that. But first, we're really exhausted, and—"

"Oh, Adelaide, sweetheart, do give us at least some details before you go!" Cajsa protested. "You don't have to tell us everything, of course, but we're ever so curious what happened."

Adelaide stared longingly at the stairs that were visible through the front door no one had thought to close, and then back at her family.

"Fine. Ten minutes. Then I am going to wash up and sleep, and heaven's mercy upon anyone who tries to wake me."

This seemed enough for the others—at least temporarily—and they led the way happily inside. As Adelaide and Maaya trailed behind, Adelaide leaned in close and whispered, "If you want to get away from all this, I can take care of my family."

"I wouldn't do that to you," Maaya smiled, though part of her wanted nothing more than to take Adelaide up on her offer. She didn't want to talk. She didn't want to celebrate. She wanted to sleep and be by herself and be miserable, and that was it.

And think about how Adelaide will be leaving you to go back to Selenthia, the annoying voice brought up helpfully.

They sat on comfortable sofas around a table in a wide room looking out over the sweeping back lawns, with Felix, Cajsa, and Marit on one side and Maaya and Adelaide on the other. Adelaide did most of the talking, somehow keeping track of the multitude of questions that tripped over each other as they fell from her family's mouths in unison. Maaya had a feeling they were the same questions she would be answering over and over again in the coming days. She did like the feeling of not being chased by law enforcement anymore, but she almost would have preferred that if it meant she could escape. Maaya missed being invisible.

A flash of light suddenly pierced her peripheral vision, and she glanced up quickly, hoping to find Saber appearing through a nearby wall, but it was only a reflection off the shiny exterior of a passing carriage outside. Maaya let out a silent breath as a fresh wave of grief swept over her. It was going to take her a long, long time to get over the fact that Saber was never coming back.

"...and after that I don't know what happened. To be honest, while I helped get us there, Maaya was the one who eventually took down the machine," Adelaide finished, drawing fresh awestruck stares from her family.

"Hey, wait a minute, I only made it inside because you distracted all the ghosts at once—and with only four blood cards, may I remind you," Maaya protested.

"That's my girl! Brave to the last," Felix rumbled approvingly.

"How did you do it, then?" Marit asked Maaya intently.

Maaya shifted uncomfortably.

"Well, Adelaide took care of the hard part, really. Once I found the machine it was just a matter of turning it off. It only took a few minutes, but it was the scariest few minutes of my life. But then I disabled it and the military came right in to take care of the rest," she finished, hoping no one would call out her lack of actual details.

"What was it like, this machine?" Cajsa continued. It seemed everyone had forgotten about Adelaide already.

"It was huge. It took up the whole room. But I didn't understand how it was supposed to work. I didn't really have time to figure it out," she added evasively. "Anyway, once it was shut down the whole house collapsed in on itself. Someone else might be able to study it but it's way beyond what I know."

As she finished, she passed what she hoped was a subtle glance at Adelaide. She already didn't want to do this anymore, especially if they were just going to keep asking for more and more specifics about the machine. She understood how important it was to them and how they might have a lot of questions for the first person in a hundred years to succeed at this task… but it was too much. Any meager mental defense she had managed to build up over the past few days was already falling to shambles.

Mercifully, Adelaide seemed to understand.

"Maaya, love, go upstairs and get your bath first, okay? I'll finish things down here and join you soon."

"Oh, but we still have so many question—!" Marit started, but she fell silent instantly under a piercing glare from Adelaide.

Maaya stood up gratefully as Adelaide's family started firing rapid questions at her instead. Maaya felt for her, but she knew it would be easier for her. This was her family, after all. And she hadn't been through what Maaya had. Not in the end.

Maaya trudged up the stairs then walked down the long hall. She had never actually seen Adelaide's room, but after spending enough time in her home she had figured out it was the door at the end of the hall. It hung slightly ajar, and as though giving a hint as to what manifestations of Adelaide's personality lay beyond, one of her shirts hung haphazardly on the door handle.

The room was everything Maaya expected. It was a strange mix of elegance and maturity with the total lack of organization she might expect from an easily distracted child's bedroom. The furniture was all made of dark and intricately carved wood and the countertops were lined with model ships, sundials, sextants, compasses, puzzles, and globes. She also noticed a few brass contraptions, but didn't know what they might be for.

An old violin case sat propped up in one corner, but the violin and bow were nowhere to be seen. A huge four-poster bed sat against the wall opposite the wide window, and it appeared as though any attempt at making it had been quickly abandoned in favor of more entertaining activities. Still, its plush comforters and collection of far more pillows than anyone would ever find necessary was enticing, and Maaya had to remind herself she was here to bathe first.

She stepped carefully over a pile of clothes and shoes, smiling softly as she thought of what Inga's reaction would be if she stepped inside, and how even though Adelaide outranked her she would still likely scold the captain severely until she cleaned her room.

Realizing she had forgotten to pick out a change of clothes, Maaya hesitated, then took one of Adelaide's clean shirts with her to the bath. Walking all the way back down the hall would have to be done another time.

Hot water quickly filled the bath, and Maaya sighed contentedly as it rose up above her shoulders. She had missed every part of this. She could almost feel the dust and dirt of over a week's worth of travel being washed from her. She took a deep breath and submerged herself completely in the water. The heat stung her open wounds, but she could already feel her sore and aching muscles start to relax.

However, the emotional weight of the past few weeks was not so easily discarded as dirt and grime, and in the underwater silence, every mistake and horror she had experienced came rushing up to meet her. She had done what she came to do, but she didn't feel satisfied. Still, somehow, it felt like there was something that needed to be resolved.

She poked her head up from under the water and began to wash her hair, but then paused as she realized what it was. When she had been fighting to destroy the machine, she had been too busy to even think about her future. Now that it was over, however, all that worry came flooding back—especially with Adelaide's casual statement about returning to Selenthia, the place Maaya had said she would never return.

A dull throbbing fear fell upon her as she pulled her fingers through her hair. They had talked so many times of their dreams for the future and how they would like to spend it together, but that had been before they had actually succeeded. Back when it was safe to dream because the future hadn't arrived yet. But now it was here, and already reality was tightening its grip on everything Maaya had hoped would happen after the machine was taken care of. Now it was time to see how things would actually go, and Maaya suspected it would result in being left behind.

Before this fear could take hold, however, she shrugged it off. While she knew a month ago she would be far too frightened and overwhelmed to try to deal with it, she had changed since then. While the prospect of confronting Adelaide over their future plans made her nervous, it didn't frighten her.

Maaya stepped out of the bath and dried herself off, then pulled on Adelaide's shirt. It was baggy on her, falling to a few inches below her hips, the sleeves reaching down to her elbows. If everything did work out between her and Adelaide, she thought, at least she would never be left wanting for sleepwear.

As she walked out and sat upon Adelaide's *incredibly* comfortable bed and started dragging a comb through her hair, her mind drifted back to something Saber had said when they had started making their way inside the barrier. There definitely was something about going through a dangerous situation that brought people closer together in some respect. It almost seemed silly, but now Maaya thought about it, it was true. When she thought of Adelaide, the stunning young woman who had swept her off her feet back in Levien, her heart no longer pounded with innocent newfound infatuation. Instead, it was something even greater. Rather than a fleeting crush where she had thought of no future beyond confessing her feelings in the moment, she now felt a comfortable but still powerful longing and love. Adelaide was the one she wanted to see every day, to fall asleep with, and to wake up beside. She was more certain of that than anything else.

Just then, she heard voices in the hall, joined with slow footsteps as whoever was outside approached Adelaide's room. Maaya glanced down at herself, suddenly feeling very exposed, and wished she had thought to close the bedroom door.

However, it appeared whoever was outside had no intention of coming in. As they spoke, she recognized Adelaide's voice, followed by the low murmurings of who she assumed were Inga and Halvar. She thought to get up and see them, but quickly decided against it. There would always be time for that later.

After only a brief moment she heard two people's footsteps walking slowly and quietly down the hall. Before they faded completely, Adelaide herself stepped into the room—then did a double take when she saw Maaya.

"Well, *that* is a sight I could get used to seeing more often."

"When I got here I realized I forgot my—" Maaya attempted, but Adelaide quickly waved her off.

"Please, forget whenever you like. I've always wanted a small girlfriend who will wear my clothes. Now then: how are you feeling?" Adelaide asked, plopping down on the bed beside her. Her hair was wrapped in a soft towel above her head and she wore a pair of thin pajamas that looked like they had been her favorite for years. Tired as she clearly was, there was a smile in her eyes that had not been there for days, and the color within seemed brighter than before.

"So much better after cleaning up," Maaya sighed contentedly. "And I'm relieved this is all over. I know I have a lot to process, but at least I have time to do that now."

"Absolutely!" Adelaide replied encouragingly. "Time to sleep, time to think, all that. I mean, even once I get back on the ship I won't have to think about work until I get back to Selenthia."

Maaya hesitated.

"Actually, I was wondering if we could talk about that. About our future."

Adelaide's eyes widened slightly in surprise, and then she smiled.

"Of course. I was hoping we'd get a chance to do that soon. What's on your mind?"

"It's just… you said you're going back to Selenthia soon, and I guess I'm a little afraid of where that will leave me, considering I'm not sure I ever want to go back there. Not after what happened."

Adelaide lay back against her multitude of pillows and invited Maaya to join her. She pulled Maaya to her side and ran her fingers softly through Maaya's hair.

"I do need to get back. I mean, I suppose I could just up and quit, but that would leave everyone else in a hard place. But I was hoping you'd join me. You don't have to, of course, but the offer is there. Wherever I go in this world, you're welcome… no, I *want* you to join me. My life is so much better with you at my side."

Maaya only felt slightly comforted.

"I would love that if going back didn't mean putting you all in danger. Whatever happened here, I'm still a criminal over there, remember?"

"Mm, that's true," Adelaide replied, though there was a tone to her voice Maaya couldn't quite decipher. "But there's time for all of this, okay? We don't need to decide right now. Actually, I would prefer we don't—not until we have more information. But above all, please know this: while my work is important to me, you factor into every decision I could ever make. I'm not leaving you behind. In fact, I'll do anything I can to keep you in my life however I can."

"That's… better than I thought," Maaya admitted, and she felt as though some of the weight had been lifted from her chest. "I'll do anything I can to stay with you, I just… feel like there's not a whole lot I *can* do."

"I understand. It feels like so much of the world is still up against you, right? Well, listen. There's one philosophy I think is important for any relationship, and that is to take on each issue as though it's the two of us against the problem, not each other. Whatever tough decisions we face, we'll face them together just like we've always done. Okay?"

She kissed Maaya on the forehead, and Maaya smiled.

"Okay. You're the best."

"I try!" Adelaide teased. "Speaking of which, I'm more than happy to talk about this at any time—especially now that we have a whole lot of it—but for now, can you give me until tomorrow night before we bring this up again?"

"What's tomorrow night?" Maaya asked, narrowing her eyes suspiciously.

"Nothing for certain, but that's when dad wants to throw his party. Don't worry; I made him promise to keep it small for your sake," Adelaide added quickly, and Maaya grinned thankfully. "It's just a lot to prepare for mentally and physically, and we'll be too busy to really have a good talk, you know?"

"Fair enough," Maaya relented. "Though... there was one other thing."

"Yes?" Adelaide said quietly, her calm tone helping to calm Maaya's anxieties.

"It's... it's about what I told you when we were out there. About how I thought the ghosts were following me."

"Oh, yes. We figured that out, didn't we? They were after Saber, not you."

"Yes, but it's more than that. You were right about what you said. Even though it turned out they weren't after me, I still didn't tell you when I thought they might be. It was dishonest of me, and... I'm sorry. You were right, and I'm so sorry. I should have done better."

Adelaide pulled her closer and softly ran her fingers through Maaya's hair, which was not the reaction Maaya had been expecting.

"I remember. I've been thinking about it since then. I know it was complicated. All of this has been. It was easier said than done to just bring up something like that when you were practically alone and new to the country, had no money, no place to stay, you weren't even sure it was true to begin with, you and I hadn't been close for all that long..."

"Does that mean... are you not angry with me?" Maaya asked, her voice nearly a whisper.

"I'm not. Not at all," Adelaide said reassuringly. "Admittedly, I was at first. But then I thought about it. I think it's safe to factor in your intent in all this. You were never malicious. No one was hurt because of it. You've been trying to do the right thing this whole time, and with everything going on all at once it's natural you might slip up here and there. So yes, it was a mistake on your part, but it's something you learned from, so with that being the case I think we can safely put it behind us, don't you think?"

Maaya glanced up at her in mild surprise.

"Are you sure? I mean, if you were upset I wouldn't blame—"

"*Yes*, I'm sure, my dear," Adelaide chuckled. "I don't think holding grudges is all that productive. Besides, it's been days and days since, and we've talked about it and put our feelings on the table so it's not like there's anything left to say on the matter. At least from me. But it's all right now, I promise."

Maaya shifted, pulling herself up closer until her head rested on Adelaide's chest. She was warm and comfortable, and though her body still protested from pain and exhaustion, she felt safe once again. This too had gone better than expected now they'd had time to think. Saber had been right about that, too.

Her heart still stung from the loss of her best friend, but even now the pain of loss was not as sharp as she had expected it to be. She supposed it was because losing Saber had been one of the few losses she had any control over. They had gotten to say goodbye and comfort each other, and it was a decision—horrible as it was—that they had both made together. She hurt from the loss of her friend, but not from the circumstances surrounding it as she had with so many others. There had been no horror and no pain, and thus she had gotten the closure she really needed. The rest was simply healing.

Adelaide pulled the blankets up, then reached over and pulled the small chain on the lamp by her bed. Darkness fell, save for what little light penetrated the dark curtains of Adelaide's bedroom. A sudden overwhelming wave of exhaustion washed over Maaya, but with it came contentment. It was really over. The world was safe—at least from this particular danger—and she and Adelaide had both made it out alive. That they were spending their first night home falling asleep in each other's arms was all she could have ever hoped for.

She breathed deeply as Adelaide put a protective arm around her shoulder, and she closed her eyes. She knew not all her dreams would be sweet, but that she would wake up next to the one person who could make all the fear and hurt go away in an instant.

"Hey, Adelaide?" she murmured, struggling with every syllable.

"Yeah?"

"We're okay, right?"

"Oh, my love, we are so much more than okay."

With this last concern put at least temporarily to rest, Maaya succumbed to her body's increasingly desperate demands for sleep and drifted off with a smile on her face.

. . .

As the sun set the following night, the Sol house was full of activity. At least thirty guests passed in and out of the house, chatting with each other or gathering around Felix as he told the story of his daughter and her friend's accomplishments for the sixth time. Maaya couldn't blame them for being so interested. When a disaster plagued a nation for a century, the story of its resolution was unlikely to get old quickly.

Unfortunately, for all his excitement and marvelous storytelling, Felix Sol was not the center of attention that night. Maaya wasn't particularly surprised by this either, but it was a source of quick frustration. Everyone at the party wanted to see Adelaide, of course, but also the girl she was dating: the mysterious and powerful girl from Selenthia who had traveled so far to save their country. She had tried to politely answer their questions and entertain their excitement for a time despite their obvious lack of knowledge of her own country, but when she heard the word "exotic" start passing around the crowd in excited whispers, she quickly decided it was time to give up.

"Fancy some food?" Adelaide said cheerily as she met Maaya on the grass just off the back porch.

"I'd fancy some silence, but food will have to do," Maaya answered darkly as her stomach growled. "Didn't your dad promise to keep this party small?"

"Oh, trust me. This is small," Adelaide chortled. "Don't worry; it'll be over soon."

Maaya almost felt like saying she wished it wouldn't be. Had she not been bothered with so much attention and so many questions she would quite like to enjoy it longer, something she herself was surprised over. Halvar and one of the other guests stood in front of a large barbecue grilling all sorts of delicious foods, and there were dozens of platters of vegetables, sandwiches, baked treats, drinks, and more. Strings of lights were draped over the eaves of the house and most of the shrubbery in the back and front yard alike, and there was a joyful air to it all. This was fun with no strings attached, and despite it all, Maaya felt peaceful.

"Good evening to you both!" came a familiar voice from nearby, and the girls turned to see Asmund coming away from the food-stuffed tables, a neatly organized plate in hand.

"Ah, Asmund! I'm so glad you could make it," Adelaide exclaimed.

"Likewise. It was torture waiting for the both of you to get home, you know. News of what you did reached home long before you did, and I was worried you'd be so tired from all the interviews and interrogations I wouldn't get to talk to you for a month."

"Believe me, we've had more than enough of those already," Maaya replied with an expression of exaggerated disgust.

At least three different government officials had come by the house during the morning and early afternoon, and a small crowd of reporters had tried various tactics to get closer to the girls to request interviews. Maaya had agreed to one, hoping it would sate their appetite, but that seemed only to make it worse.

Adelaide, thinking quickly, had sent Halvar off to deliver a message. What it was about or who it was for Maaya had no clue, but shortly before the party started, half a dozen burly men dressed in black stood posted at the edges of Adelaide's property, ensuring that only guests could come in.

"Who are they?" Marit had asked nervously of Adelaide as she watched one of the men effortlessly intimidate one of the reporters who had attempted to sneak by.

"Associates," Adelaide answered simply, and Marit appeared unwilling to ask any more.

Beyond the endless questions from reporters, government officials, and party guests, it had actually been a pleasant day. Maaya and Adelaide had spent every moment of their free time together doing as little as they could. This was partially because they were so happy in each other's company, but also because their battered and worn bodies still had much healing to do.

The only thing that had truly unnerved Maaya was the fact that apparently she and Adelaide had been requested to speak at an important government meeting the next day regarding the destruction of the machine. The courier had explained that they were both to deliver a total report as to their experiences and actions, and while he stressed they were in no trouble, Maaya couldn't help but feel nervous. She wasn't sure she'd ever get over the radical shift from spending her life in the shadows to working directly with powerful government officials.

Mercifully, however, the meeting would be held nearby which pleased Maaya greatly. She never wanted to step foot on a train for the rest of her life.

When it had come time for the party, they got ready together, helping each other choose what to wear and speaking only of trivial things. At times Maaya could almost forget that anything had happened, and she could think that they were just two girls living their lives and getting ready for a pleasant party in the evening, as she guessed girls her age did. Adelaide had lamented that her augmented arm wasn't completely repaired yet, and Chronis, who had taken to wandering the house, seemed equally displeased.

But there was no adventure, no planning, and no talk of responsibility or danger. It was something that made Maaya almost uncomfortable in its unfamiliarity, but something she was equally eager to get used to.

Halvar himself walked over to them, wiping his brow with his sleeve and giving a polite nod to Asmund as he approached.

"What a night, huh? I'm glad you didn't send me off for yet another errand, cap'n; these fine people would have been deprived of my cooking."

"You were the one who rushed home so quickly. Had it been Inga who returned first she would have gotten messenger duty," Adelaide replied, amused. "Speaking of, how is she?"

"She said she'd be home no later than an hour after sunset; she just wanted to finish up some things first," Halvar answered.

Adelaide raised her eyebrow.

"Oh? Does that mean you were successful?"

"To my knowledge, but best wait until she can give the final confirmation. It seemed pretty serious in there. Come to think of it that's probably why she sent me home."

"Successful doing what? Why are you so busy?" Maaya asked. "Shouldn't you be resting too?"

"Unfortunately, there is no rest for the poor and overworked lackeys of Captain Adelaide the Cruel. No, I jest," Halvar laughed as Adelaide swatted at him with a napkin. "The world's been saved, which means it keeps on going, which means the same for our responsibilities. You two literally saved the planet, however, so you're entitled to some time off. Besides, this is kind of a special sort of—"

"Halvar, you're doing it again," Adelaide interrupted gently, and Halvar grinned sheepishly.

"Right. We'd better hurry and finish this as soon as possible; I'm not sure how long I can keep everything under wraps."

"Eat some of your delectable cuisine. That ought to help keep you silent for the moment."

"An order I am only too happy to obey, cap'n," Halvar finished jovially, then walked off to fetch himself some food. With a polite bow, Asmund departed as well, heading over to where Felix and Cajsa stood in front of a small crowd of guests.

"Adelaide, what's going on?" Maaya pressed.

Adelaide glanced down at her guiltily.

"Remember last night when I said to leave talking about the future for later? I'm just hoping for some good news on that front. Just give me a little more time, okay?"

Just then, Inga stepped out onto the back porch, scanning the yard. When her eyes fell on Adelaide, she beckoned subtly to her.

"I'm sorry, love, I'll be right back. I just need to talk to Inga for a moment."

With a quick apologetic kiss, Adelaide hurried over to meet Inga.

Maaya sighed quietly, then headed over to the tables. If she was going to deal with Adelaide's infuriatingly vague explanations, she wasn't going to do so on an empty stomach.

By the time she'd finished putting a small plate together—and fending off two guests who offered their congratulations and then invasive questions about her personal life—Adelaide returned to join her. Maaya searched her face for any sign that the conversation had been good or bad, but she detected nothing. For a moment she thought about going to ask Inga herself, but then decided against it. If she wasn't getting anything out of Adelaide herself, she definitely wouldn't be getting anything from the commander.

Adelaide plucked a grilled vegetable off Maaya's plate and popped it into her mouth, then closed her eyes with joy.

"Never tell him I said this, but Halvar actually is an excellent cook."

"Uh huh," Maaya said pointedly. "What happened with Inga?"

"She just gave me a status update on what she and Halvar were working on. Good news, luckily. It's all boring political things; I very much don't look forward to getting back to that part of work," Adelaide replied, taking a bite of half an entire grilled zucchini in one go.

"What were they working on?" Maaya pressed.

"So many questions, my dear! It's politics, like I said—lots and lots of politics. And there's still more to come. But I'll try to explain when we're settling in tonight, okay?"

Maaya wanted to argue, but she thought better of it. A party was hardly the place to discuss politics anyway, whether or not it had anything to do with her, and especially not when a new group of people was already making its way over to the girls, eager, Maaya was sure, to shower them in well wishes and an insufferable deluge of questions.

Halfway through explaining their journey through the barrier for the eleventh time at least, Maaya was interrupted by a massive bang and flash of light. She shrieked before she could stop herself, and she whirled about to see what could have possibly caused such a noise just in time to witness another spectacular explosion of color followed by a deafening bang.

"Are those fireworks?!" Maaya gasped above the noise. Every boom seemed to come from everywhere, assaulting her senses and her very orientation of the world. And yet, for all this new sight and sound terrified and unnerved her, she found beauty in it, and she couldn't look away.

"Yeah! Have you never seen them before?" Adelaide asked, then laughed when Maaya shook her head quickly. "Great! I keep forgetting just how much of this might be new for you. All the more reason to start with a small party; my dad likes to pull out all the stops."

The shock quickly wore off, though she still winced slightly whenever one of the massive fireworks exploded in the sky, bracing herself for the tremendous bang that would soon follow. Adelaide seemed only too amused by this and held her close as they sat on the lawn and simply watched in silence.

As midnight approached, however, even Adelaide's energy appeared spent. Maaya helped her to her feet, hoping her tired expression meant they would call it a night soon enough, and she couldn't hide her smile as Adelaide yawned.

"Come with me. I'm going to tell dad we're turning in for the night."

Maaya happily followed. Despite her complaints and weariness, she had thoroughly enjoyed herself. The Sol family's friends were mostly good and kind people, and she could mostly forgive them their relentless curiosity. What happened marked a monumental change in their country's history, and she realized with some astonishment that it was likely that every single person alive in Krethus today had been born knowing only the horror of the machine. Its attacks had been going on for so long that all anyone had ever known was that constant fear, which meant this was a new page in history for every person alive on this side of the planet.

As they approached, Felix caught their eye and immediately waved his arms to clear a path for them. As soon as they reached his side he bent down and pulled both of them into a powerful hug.

"Turning to bed soon, I take it?" he asked.

"That's the idea. We're both still easily exhausted, I'm afraid," Adelaide answered apologetically.

"Completely understandable! You've kept busier than I thought you would, though I suppose some of that is inevitable with the government continuously knocking on our door," Felix chuckled. "But never mind that. I'll wrap this up so you can have some peace and quiet tonight."

"Thanks, dad. You're amazing," Adelaide said, giving him a quick kiss on the cheek.

"Anything for you, my dear," Felix replied, and then raised his voice over the noise of several conversations in the yard. "Everyone, attention please! I'm going to have to call an end to the party now our heroes are off to bed."

"Really, dad?" Marit muttered from beside him, and she, Maaya, and Adelaide shared an exasperated look.

But nothing could have prepared Maaya for what came next.

Before she knew it, every single person standing in the yard had bent down on one knee and lowered their heads, holding their right arms across their chests. The yard had fallen completely silent, and Maaya felt a sudden air of emotion from this gesture she did not understand, but that she knew was as meaningful as it was possible to be. She had expected some attention, perhaps even some last-second shouted congratulations, but not anything like this.

"Whoah, I... Adelaide, what...?" she murmured, and Adelaide clapped a hand on her shoulder.

"Consider it a thank you," Adelaide answered quietly, and her voice wavered ever so slightly.

A few moments later everyone stood up again, and for a moment Maaya feared they would all converge on them with yet more well wishes and questions, but instead they all started making their way to nearby tables and trash cans to clean up the yard, some of them smiling happily and appreciatively at the young women.

"I'm sure I'll have many more opportunities to say this in the near future, but I am so very, very proud of you, my dear Adelaide," Felix said, placing his hands on her shoulders. "I know we haven't always seen eye to eye, but it's clear that the path you chose in life was the right one for you, and for all of us in the end."

"I agree. I have had my reservations with some of your more... eccentric decisions, but I hope you understand that my faith in your ability to do good never wavered," Cajsa added.

Before the sting of jealousy could push its way into Maaya's heart, Felix then turned to Maaya and hugged her tightly again.

"And you, Maaya, for what you have done for our homeland and your assistance and bravery fighting alongside my daughter, I hope you always consider yourself at home in the Sol house, because here, you are always welcome."

"Also because we're dating, right?" Adelaide asked bluntly, and Felix laughed.

"And that, yes. But if anything that only justifies my past attempts at bringing you together with potential lovers; it was clearly your disgust with my preferences that drove you off to find someone as wonderful as Maaya here."

Adelaide snorted as Cajsa smacked her husband lightly on the shoulder. Maaya could tell this serious discussion, like every other, was all too quickly devolving into ridiculousness, and there was one thing she had to say before it went too far.

"I just want to thank all of you for letting me stay here and being so accepting of me, even when I was a stranger and even after you found out where I came from. I was terrified coming here, and at first I only came because I thought it would save my friends, but then I saw everything Adelaide loves about this place and about you. You treated me like family, and that's so much more than I ever expected or could have asked for. So... thank you, so much."

"There is plenty of good in the world, Maaya," Felix replied warmly. "You're a shining example of that yourself, and I hope you have the fortune of meeting the others like you. However you may have grown up and whatever you may have experienced, kindness is not a gift—it's what you deserve. Wherever you go and whoever you meet, believe that."

"Make sure you visit often, okay? And bring my sister, too," Marit said meaningfully.

"Of course! No more long delays between family visits, right?" Maaya smiled.

"Absolutely not! And hey, even if the rules on traveling between countries stay the same after all this, what's Selenthia going to do? Send their navy after me?" She and Maaya both laughed, but then quickly coughed and averted their eyes when Felix and the others passed them quizzical glances. "Er, anyway, we're going to get some rest. We've got that big important meeting tomorrow morning."

"Right you do!" Felix exclaimed. "Go on then, get to bed. With luck, I'll see you tomorrow evening."

The family said their goodbyes and shared their last hugs of the night, and then Adelaide led the way inside. They climbed slowly up the stairs, Maaya already dreaming of the comfortable bed where she was to lay her head again—and of who she was to sleep with again. The previous night had been wonderful, and she hoped for more of the same this evening… especially if their future together was in any way in jeopardy.

As they stepped into Adelaide's room, Adelaide suddenly snapped her fingers.

"Oh, drat. Hold on. I need to run down and make sure Inga and Halvar are all up to date. Inga needs to get me a report on my ship's readiness tomorrow, and they both need to start gathering the crew together. I'll be back up soon, promise!"

Adelaide gave a guilty wave and then trotted down the hall and quickly out of sight.

Maaya smiled slightly as she undressed and prepared for bed. As much as she hated the idea of Adelaide going back to Selenthia, it was clear that the thought of getting back out on the sea was doing her well. She didn't want to think about what that could mean, but she reassured herself by thinking that they would soon have a chance to talk about it. One way or another, she guessed Adelaide had news—and that whatever she had sent Inga and Halvar off to do earlier that day had something to do with her.

When ten minutes passed and Adelaide still had not returned, Maaya leaned over to reach her coat she had left lying on the floor. She hadn't touched it since they had arrived home; in fact, she hadn't worn it the entire way home. It wasn't so much the garb itself as it was what she kept inside it.

From one of the coat's large inner pockets, she pulled out Kim's diary. Ever since she had seen Kim and the others only a few days ago she had fought to keep herself from even thinking about it. She thought she might never feel like looking at it again. But now she felt oddly at peace even as she stared at the worn notebook in her hands. She didn't know if it was because her mind was preoccupied by yet another tumultuous and inevitable change to her life in the days ahead or whether it was due to nerves over the meeting the following morning. It could, she reasoned, even be because she was simply not the person she used to be; no longer as easily frightened or emotionally scarred, perhaps she had gotten better at taking things in stride and dealing with the blows life sent her way.

Whatever it was, Maaya opened the notebook resolutely, eager to pick up where she had last left off back in the abandoned building in the dead landscape surrounding the machine.

We went out again tonight. I was hoping we would see Anrik again, but instead we went out to the docks by the river. I'm okay with that. I miss seeing Styx. But the strangest thing happened. A ghost attacked us, but I've never seen one like it before. Maaya fainted. I'm really worried about her. We managed to get rid of the ghost, but Styx and Sylvia and Milo made it sound like there were more. I'm not afraid. Maaya and Saber are the best. And they won't have to handle it themselves.

I think I'll talk to the others and see what we can do. Maaya has only had a little time to teach us anything new recently, but we need to keep getting better. If we do good enough, we won't have to work ourselves so hard anymore. And maybe we can even find a way to leave Sark. I know we all want to. I want to get that house we keep talking about. I'll do whatever I can to make it happen.

Maaya flipped the page, quickly realizing that she was reading about the night that had started it all weeks and weeks before. As she read, the entries got longer, and Kim's handwriting progressively neater.

Every time I see Roshan I feel a little guilty. I haven't done anything wrong. It's just that Maaya has all these friends she made herself. I'm friends with them too, but I'm too shy to make friends of my own. Not that I get much of a chance. But I feel like I should. Her friends are always helping, always getting information and checking on us, and what am I doing? I wish I had people that I knew or some trick up my sleeve I could use to help. But all I have is myself, and I don't think that's enough.

Then again, Maaya did have Saber. It had to have made things a little easier having someone who's invisible to help her get food and find safe places to sleep. Not to mention that was how she found us. It was hard not to pay attention to her. Meanwhile I have no idea how to figure out if other people in Sark can see ghosts or not. Maybe I'll try to figure something out. The more of us there are, the better, right?

But I wonder about that sometimes. I was the first one here, and then came Kalil and Sovaan. Will we have another person with us someday? Maybe more? I can't decide if I'd like that or not. I want to make more friends, but I also think that it's nice to be at home when it's just the five of us. Besides, I'm not sure I could handle another Sovaan. He keeps bothering me about what I'm writing. I'm so thankful he can't read.

Maaya snorted. Sovaan had been a little cleverer than Kim had suspected, much to her chagrin.

She made to turn the page again, but paused. She never had any idea Kim felt this way about herself, that Kim felt she didn't do enough or that she constantly needed to improve. Kim hadn't exactly worn her heart on her sleeve, but she hadn't been extremely difficult to read, either. Or at least that's what Maaya thought at the time. She had guessed there were aspects to all their lives they hadn't felt the need to share with her, but she wished it wasn't the feeling of being inadequate.

Maaya turned the page again, and to her surprise saw that the ink on this page had been smudged multiple times by what looked to be droplets of water.

Tears?

I feel so used. I thought I was starting to understand why Maaya hated Rahu, but it turns out I wasn't anywhere near the whole truth. He's an evil, vile person. We've been seeing him a lot more lately, and I guess I know why. We figured out who the Krethan was. He's not our enemy at all. He's trying to help. It's Rahu that's making things harder, and it's wearing on all of us. We didn't even know it was his fault. Maaya must have known. Saber, too. Why didn't they tell us?

I can't be angry at them, though. Only Rahu. I can't believe he would do this to us. He was so kind to us and always spoke nicely to us. Now I can tell he's just been using us this whole time. Well, not for long. We're going to set things right, and we're going to get out of here. I talked to the others. We're going to find a way to bring him down eventually, somehow. He can't keep using and hurting people like this! So we'll try our best. Not now, maybe not soon, but eventually. I can imagine the look on Maaya's face when she realizes he's in jail. That thought makes me smile.

I'll hate to say goodbye to Styx and Sylvia and the others. And don't even get me started on Anrik. I'll have to find a way to tell him something. Anything. It's strange to think that someone like me could find love in this world. People like me are killed, and I've always known that. That's why I'm here with my friends instead of growing up and having a normal life. So it's strange to have even this little bit of normal. It just makes me want to try even harder. I know we can do it, though.

Maaya jumped as the bed suddenly moved. She hadn't noticed Adelaide walk in, and now the red-haired girl was slipping into bed beside her, looking almost ready to fall asleep on the spot.

"Didn't mean to startle you! You can keep reading if you'd like," Adelaide apologized quietly.

"Oh, no, that's okay. I was just waiting for you," Maaya said as she set the notebook aside, grateful for the distraction. Her heart felt heavy from what she had read. There had been far more going on behind the scenes than Maaya had guessed. Kim hadn't just been eager to get away from Sark; she had wanted to get better, to help the others get better, and wanted to plan to bring justice to Rahu. And she had started everything on her own. How very much a leader she could have been if she'd had a little more time.

"I'm glad to see you pick that up again. I was worried that after… after what happened, you might want to put it behind you completely," Adelaide said. She stacked a few pillows on top of each other and lay on her side to face Maaya.

"I thought so, too. At least at first. But I feel okay about it. It's comforting in a way."

"I'm glad. So… kind of on that note, have you give much thought to returning home? Back to Selenthia?"

Maaya sighed.

"You know my problems with that. I would love to sail with you, but if we go back to a country where I'm wanted a a traitor, I couldn't stay hidden forever and I'd put everyone in danger in the meantime."

"What about all your friends? You told me about Roshan and Styx and…"

"I'm not even sure any of them are alive anymore. Even if there was a way to find out for sure I'd rather just find another way… maybe I could somehow bring them here, I don't know. But Roshan was in Sark the night the worst ghost walks hit, and Styx… well, he's not getting any younger. And there's no steamsmith in Sark, so his systems are starting to break down. I just don't feel like there's anything left for me there. Not with how risky it would be to go back. I promised to go back for them, and I hate to break that promise, but what I'm up against is just so much."

Just then, Maaya thought she detected a hopeful glimmer in Adelaide's eyes.

"That's fair. But indulge me here. Just for the sake of this discussion, if the military and the police weren't after you anymore and you could walk around freely as you pleased—at least anywhere outside Sark—would you?"

Maaya lay back and closed her eyes thoughtfully.

"I guess that would change things a little. It might be weird, but if someone could magically make that all go away, I might like it. Levien was nice. So was Anorath. But I still couldn't go back to Sark. Even if the police weren't after me, the angry mob led by Rahu would be."

"Great! Progress," Adelaide said happily. "It was just a thought, you know. I have to go back to Selenthia and you know how much I want you to come with me. And of course, you know I would do anything for you…"

It took a few moments for her words to sink in, but when they did, Maaya's eyes snapped open, and she sat up to stare intently at Adelaide.

"What did you do?"

"Me? I don't know what you're talking about—"

"Adelaide, *what did you do?*"

Adelaide gave her best attempt at a guilty smile, but ended up only looking pleased with herself.

"Okay, okay. I wanted to keep the surprise a little longer, but as you can tell I'm a little excited to get this one out. I *may* have gotten Inga and Halvar to work with some of our connections in government to get your criminal record wiped in Selenthia."

Maaya gaped, and several seconds passed before she could reply—and when she did, she could only stammer.

"Y-you what? How… how did… what?!"

Adelaide giggled.

"It wasn't so hard! It's a long story, but the short version is that ever since the machine went down, Krethus and Selenthia have been talking about it. Krethus had held off explaining the situation in the past, but since Selenthia was now experiencing attacks and were completely unprepared, they were only too happy to hear from someone who knew what to do. And it just so happened that our government had information about a girl from Selenthia who came to Krethus to shut down the machine—one whose actions, previously thought criminal, could all be completely explained by the attacks. And when those claims to your innocence were verified by eyewitness accounts in every location you visited, it was only a matter of time before the Selenthians put two and two together and realized you were innocent."

"Wait, that's… hang on, but Krethus would still have no reason to talk to Selenthia about that! That would just be exposing their weakness to Selenthia. The only other explanation is that Selenthia reached out to Krethus, and they wouldn't do that for the same reason," Maaya protested. "I mean… the two countries are at war, they would never talk to each other—"

"Well, that's not entirely true. The war's been stagnant for a long time now so communication between the two countries isn't complete unheard of. But I will grant you that Krethus contacting Selenthia was a risk, albeit a calculated one."

"So it was Krethus… who in their right mind would do that? Why not keep silent about it, make Selenthia think they're at a disadvantage, and play it safe by just keeping me here?" Maaya asked distractedly, trying to form coherent thoughts from the mess of questions in her mind.

"Well, whoever decided that was an appropriate risk probably thought keeping you here was a part of playing it safe they didn't want to accept," Adelaide replied, staring meaningfully at Maaya.

Maaya exhaled sharply.

"I… gods, Adelaide, are you telling me…?"

"I am. I mean, I didn't send the message personally, but I tried my hardest to influence it, and it looks like it worked. And from what I hear, now that both sides are communicating officially, there's even talk of putting an end to this war. It's been effectively over for ages already, but—"

"You convinced the Krethan government to contact *my* government and expose your country's weakness... just so I could go back with you?" Maaya asked, completely dumbstruck.

Adelaide didn't falter for an instant.

"I did."

"Why? That's such a huge risk to take! Why would you do that just for me?"

"Part of it is because I was confident it would work. I didn't do this on a whim. A lot of thought and discussion with a lot of people went into this decision. Besides, if there was ever a time to discuss the end of hostilities, this was it. I merely took advantage. But the rest of it is because you're cute, and I love you."

Adelaide leaned forward and kissed her, giggling as Maaya's face burned red.

For Maaya's part, even had Adelaide's lips not been firmly attached to her own, she would have found herself speechless. She knew Adelaide had connections and some influence, both from her family and her position as a captain and ranking member of the Blackfins, but getting two warring nations to communicate with each other—and for the explicit purpose of wiping Maaya's criminal record—was a new display of power from her. Maaya knew she had a part to play in that herself given how she was the one who had traveled from Selenthia to destroy the machine, but she was still awestruck—and even a little intimidated—by what she was hearing.

A flurry of possibilities flickered through her mind, too quickly for Maaya to grasp any one in particular, but before she could go too far she remembered something that halted her cautious optimism dead in its tracks.

"Okay. So let's say this worked. What about the fact that we destroyed a bunch of their ships and killed their entire fleet's worth of sailors? Do they know about that?" she asked.

"Believe it or not, we covered that, too," Adelaide explained. "For one, now you've been proven innocent, they aren't going to punish us for defending ourselves, especially not when they fired first. We also weren't technically in Selenthian waters by that point, which makes any claim to jurisdiction a lot more difficult. Further, they're now aware that it was the ghosts who killed most of their sailors, not us. The peaceful surrender was noted in my ship's logs and vouched for by every one of my officers on pain of death. That was enough for them."

It was almost too much for Maaya to believe. She trusted Adelaide that she had managed to accomplish this, but after spending so much time on the run she couldn't fathom how it could be over just like that. Or even in progress, for that matter. Her hometown's hatred for her had been too powerful and Rahu's words had been too convincing. What's more, he'd had years to build up his reputation and poison the minds of the people of Sark against her. It only made sense that he would have similar luck with the military. What hope did one Krethan have, even if she was one of the bravest and strongest people Maaya knew?

And yet, there was an odd allure to the concept of returning to Selenthia as a free woman. The mere act of stepping foot on Selenthian soil would feel like an act of defiance, of revenge. She could walk freely in town in full view of the ones who had been hunting her, all of them knowing that she had gotten away and that no one could touch her now. Would they be angry? Would they care?

"I can tell by the look in your eye you're thinking about it," Adelaide said playfully.

"I'm thinking about a lot of things! This is… I never thought… you're not joking, right?"

"I would never joke about something like that. I know how serious the subject of home is for you. I'm just… excited? Optimistic?"

"I can go home now," Maaya breathed slowly. *Home.* However chaotic it was, however much it desperately needed to change, it was still her home. She remembered what she told Skarin about how she had no love for country, and in retrospect, maybe that was still right—but it was still the land that held all her history and which still had so many people she loved. She thought of Roshan, and if he were still alive, how he would feel if he knew Maaya had passed up a chance to come back.

"What do you say? Are you coming back with me?" Adelaide asked, her eyes wide with hope.

Maaya paused for what felt like forever, and then, finally, she nodded.

"I think I am."

Adelaide squealed with delight and pulled Maaya into a tight hug that squeezed all the air from her lungs.

"I'm so glad! You've made my night all over again. I know you don't have to do this and that it's a big deal, but I'm so glad you'll be with me. The Windfire just wouldn't be the same without you, either."

"Well, after all the work you put into this it wouldn't be right not to go," Maaya gasped as she struggled to breathe.

Adelaide released her and grinned down at her.

"I'm glad you liked that, because this is only the start."

"What? Don't tell me you have more surprises coming," Maaya said, narrowing her eyes.

Adelaide only smiled.

38

WHAT THE WORLD SHOULD KNOW

Maaya woke up slowly the following morning. She was surrounded by the warmth of the bed and heard the calm slow breathing of Adelaide sleeping still next to her. They lay as close together as it was possible for them to be, and Maaya smiled slightly as she felt Adelaide's steady breath on her neck. If every morning could be just like this one, she could ask for nothing else.

Just then there came a soft tapping from Maaya's right. She opened her eyes sleepily and glanced over to look for the source of the noise—and found herself less than a foot away from a massive spider.

Maaya gasped and jerked backward even as her brain faintly registered that she was looking at Chronis. She covered her mouth, but the damage was done, and Adelaide sat up with a yawn.

"You okay?" she asked, then followed Maaya's gaze to the giant mechanical spider sitting on the bedside dresser. Chronis waved happily at Adelaide, who glared at it. "A simple alarm would have sufficed. If I didn't know better I'd say you keep scaring her on purpose."

Though Chronis was devoid of any facial features, Maaya could have sworn it gazed back at Adelaide with amusement. However, mechanical though it was, even the spider couldn't win a staring contest with Adelaide, and it finally relented, turning away and making its way slowly down the dresser and toward the door.

"Give us some time to get dressed and then you can come back in," Adelaide called sternly after it. "And we'll be going to pick up my arm before we go to the meeting so you can stop moping already."

The spider made a gleeful clicking noise, then walked out of the room with a joyful bounce in its step.

Maaya let out a breath and shook her head.

"I couldn't have found a girl with a pet cat or something."

Adelaide leaned over and planted a kiss on her cheek.

"Please. After all you know about me, my giant pet spider clock is surely one of the more normal things about me."

"I can't argue with that," Maaya shrugged with a grin as she got out of bed.

As they started getting ready for the day, a fresh wave of nerves washed over her. She was going to be questioned by the Krethan government. Adelaide was going as well, but that only offered so much solace. She imagined anyone would be nervous in her shoes, but she was trying to fight off years of psychological conditioning that taught her that being invisible was the only way to be safe. The more recent knowledge that Adelaide had been campaigning on her behalf and causing Krethus to contact their centuries-old enemy only added to her anxiety.

As Maaya sat on the bed struggling with her hair, she watched Adelaide put the finishing touches on her outfit. The woman was immaculately dressed in a white button-down shirt with rolled up sleeves and a collared black vest to which she had attached her captain's pins. She wore a pair of dark slacks that fell just above her pointed flats, and around her waist was a fine gold chain belt. After only a moment fiddling with her hair tie, she left it done up in a simple half ponytail, letting her long wavy hair flow mostly freely behind her.

Despite the fact that this was a simple formal outfit, albeit worn in a more casual way, Maaya thought she looked absolutely radiant. Their few days of rest had done her well, and what wounds remained had already begun to fade.

Maaya stared self-consciously into the mirror as she finished wrapping her hair in a bun. Adelaide somehow made her injuries look good, but Maaya looked as though she had just gotten out of a scuffle in the yard. What's more, as she stared at herself wearing the nice clothes Adelaide had bought for her, her fear of drawing too much attention to herself only increased.

She dressed as unobtrusively as possible in a dark green sleeveless top and black knee-length skirt, hoping to let Adelaide capture most of the attention. Unfortunately, however, as Adelaide had already explained, Maaya was the one who had come so far and was the one who had the protective power of the gem at her disposal.

Adelaide walked over and stood next to Maaya, and they gazed at their reflections in the mirror for a moment before Adelaide spoke.

"What a pair we make, huh? We might just be too dazzling for them to handle."

Maaya snorted.

"The sooner this is over the better. I just hope this is the last time I'll have to do something like this."

"I completely understand. On that note, don't forget this."

Adelaide held out her hand, and in it was Maaya's card pouch with what cards remained after their final battle. Maaya hadn't touched it since they had been rescued back near Nalmar, but Adelaide had since slipped a few of her own blood cards into it just to ensure it remained complete.

"Why? Are we expecting ghosts?" Maaya asked in confusion.

"No, but I think it's important. How can I explain… like I told you, Krethus used to be like Selenthia in its view of *libris* before the machine came along. That changed a lot of minds pretty quickly, but now that these ghosts are gone, I don't want our society to slowly make its way back to prejudice. So it's important that we have some presence and keep *libris* at least somewhat in the spotlight. If people can see its good side it will be that much harder for the old problems to return."

"That makes sense," Maaya mused. "Do you really think that would happen after all this time?"

"I should hope not. There's a century of history written about how *libris* has helped us. Still, I think it's worth trying. Besides, if people start traveling between our two countries again, that positive image can only have a good impact."

"The Selenthians will probably just think you're all really weird," Maaya giggled.

"And they'd be correct, but still. They'll know what *libris* did for them. What you did for them. I mean, let's not mince words here: you didn't just save Krethus when you shut down that machine."

"I really think you underestimate how thick a lot of Selenthians are. But I hope you're right. Maybe Selenthia can see the kind of change Krethus had without having to suffer as much."

"That's the dream. Besides, you're a free woman now, and you'll be with me. We can give the people of Selenthia a show, just the two of us," Adelaide said brightly.

"Let's take this one step at a time, okay?" Maaya replied exasperatedly, and Adelaide grinned.

The house was empty as they walked down the stairs. Chronis, who had been hanging on the banister, leapt onto Adelaide's shoulder as they passed. Maaya shuddered, but the sight almost made her laugh aloud. When she had been teaching herself to read, Saber had brought her children's books with stories about pirates, and in every story was a captain with a parrot on his shoulder. At the time she had thought the concept outlandish. No sailor at sea would ever actually bring a trained bird with them. Now, however, she understood that the fiction she knew couldn't hold a candle to reality.

They stepped out the front door and walked toward the gate leading to the street where they saw Asmund's carriage waiting for them. The man leaned casually against the carriage, smoking a pipe as he waited. When he saw them he waved happily to them, then jogged to the back of the carriage to fetch a parcel wrapped in brown paper.

"Special delivery for the one and only Captain Sol," Asmund said grandiloquently as he held the package out to her. Adelaide took it wordlessly, unwrapping it uncertainly, but then her face lit up with delight.

"Oh, my augment! You went and got it for me? Thank you so much, Asmund."

"My pleasure. I figured after last night's party you might be a little slow to wake. I know I was. Do you want a minute?"

"That's fine, Maaya can help me once we're inside. I'm pretty anxious to get moving," Adelaide replied, and Maaya nodded meaningfully.

"Right-o then. Hop in and I'll get us under way. This won't take long."

"How far away is… wherever we're going?" Maaya asked curiously.

"The provincial capitol is in the next city over," Asmund grunted as he climbed back on top of the carriage. "Half an hour's trip at most, which I must say I'm glad for. Running back and forth from the military train station has me all sorts of exhausted."

Maaya had barely closed the carriage door behind them when they started moving. By now Maaya had gotten used to the movement, and so she moved over to sit next to Adelaide, who was already in the process of trying to hook the augment's support band beneath her shirt.

"This is really a lot more difficult to do in a moving carriage than I thought it would be," Adelaide laughed.

"You couldn't have asked for just a minute inside the house," Maaya tutted. "Let me."

A minute later, Adelaide tucked in her shirt again and smoothed her vest, then held out her augmented arm, admiring it as though she were seeing it for the first time. To Maaya's amazement it looked brand new, with no sign at all of any of the severe damage it had taken during their battle in the abandoned town.

"Beautiful, absolutely beautiful," Adelaide murmured. "I'm going to have to send a very nice tip their way before we leave town. Oh, yes, all right, get over here."

Chronis, who had been creeping hopefully closer and closer, bounced up with delight and wrapped its legs around the metal arm. A content whirring sound emanated from the clock face, and Adelaide patted the glass with her finger.

"Nice to have you back, too."

"Hey… did you notice there weren't any people hanging around the gate this morning? I would have thought they'd love to try to catch us on our way out," Maaya said suddenly.

"You might think so, but I assume they thought it would be better to wait for us at the capitol. Everyone's going to want to get the shot of us delivering our explanations—which is why it's so important to have that *libris* visibility. All eyes on us, so a good impression is important! But, ah, no pressure or anything."

"Yeah, not at all," Maaya replied nervously.

Maaya would have liked to spend the rest of the trip distracted in conversations of menial things, but now that the moment was almost upon her she found herself far too nervous to even speak. All she could do was run over the events of their time in the barrier to make sure she knew exactly what she was going to say, but this came with the unfortunate side effect of making her remember every horrible detail she had spent the past few days trying very hard to avoid.

If anything calmed her, it was the fact that Adelalide didn't seem nearly as anxious. The only sign that she was thinking about it at all was the way her right leg bounced up and down as she stared pensively out the window.

They rode parallel to the ocean for some time, passing out of Unshala and through lands where the only sign of humanity was the road they traveled upon and a few small beach houses and shops along the way. Through the window on the carriage door Maaya saw children playing on the white sands of the beach. Some laughed as they threw a large colored ball between them, while another ran as fast as he could, holding a long kite string behind him.

"Beautiful, isn't it?" Adelaide said quietly. When Maaya glanced over at her, she nodded to the children. "People out enjoying themselves without a care in the world. Krethans are a hardy sort. The ghosts didn't stop anyone from going out and having fun. But now I feel like I don't need to watch over them anymore, you know?"

"That must feel like a weight off your shoulders," Maaya smiled.

"Definitely. A bit too much weight off, honestly. This is what my life was all about. I guess I didn't really think about what I would do if I ever succeeded."

"You've got one of the coolest jobs in the world still!" Maaya exclaimed. "And you know there will always be a place for people like us. We've got something very few others do. All the normal ghosts will still be around.

"That's true," Adelaide said thoughtfully.

"Besides," continued Maaya, "now we can do so much more good for the world. We were so busy cleaning up after the machine's ghosts that we couldn't do anything else. Now think of everything we'll have time to do."

"You've got such a good heart. I love it," Adelaide grinned. "It's definitely something worth thinking about—after we clear up the last of our unfinished business, anyway. And speaking of…"

Maaya followed Adelaide's gaze out the carriage window, and her stomach dropped. The carriage was pulling up to a massive white marble building around which at least a thousand people were congregated. A wide set of stairs led up to a giant wooden door beset on either side by large intricately carved pillars. It was the kind of building Maaya associated with the law and men of politics. In other words, a building she wanted nothing to do with.

As the carriage approached, some of the people milling about at the bottom of the steps seemed to realize who was arriving, and there suddenly came shouts of excitement and glee as they rushed toward the carriage. Almost as quickly, a line of guards positioned themselves between the carriage and the oncoming crowd. Maaya sat back in her seat instinctively with a thrill of fear.

"Hey. We'll be all right, okay?" Adelaide said soothingly, placing a steady hand on Maaya's leg. "Ignore them. Just stay with me. We'll go inside and answer their questions and then it will be over."

"What do I say? What if I say something wrong?" Maaya exhaled nervously.

"You won't. There's nothing you can say that would get you in trouble unless you outright lied. Speak from the heart and tell the truth and you'll be fine. And I'll be right there to back you up."

"They won't even be mad that I had the gem they were looking for and didn't tell them?"

"The way I see it, they had their chance. They sent their agents and scientists all over the world and failed. If they get angry about that, I'll have to remind them that a seventeen-year-old girl and her ghost friend by themselves did what all their might and intellect could not."

Maaya's eyes widened in horror.

"You wouldn't."

Adelaide shrugged nonchalantly.

"It's the truth, and we have the results to show for it. I'm not afraid to tell them if that's what they need to hear. But I assume they won't even try. Besides, if they want to claim they'd have the right to take a *person* from you, that would get ugly for them very quickly."

The carriage pulled up slowly to the bottom of the steps and then, finally, came to a stop. Maaya was overwhelmed by the sheer number of people outside, but it seemed the guards had anticipated this crowd. No sooner had they stopped then one of the guards pulled the door open quickly, gesturing to the girls inside.

"Best get in quickly now; this crowd is only growing as time goes on. You'll get an escort to the top. Hurry now."

Adelaide gave Maaya another comforting pat on the leg, then stepped confidently out of the carriage. Maaya took a deep breath, taking a brief moment to reflect on what in the world had happened to her life to put her in this position, and then she followed.

Immediately her senses were overwhelmed by hundreds of people calling in her direction, flashes and puffs of smoke from cameras, calls to answer questions for this newspaper or that pamphlet, and the guard at her side who placed his hand protectively behind her and guided her swiftly up the steps. She didn't need any convincing. Eager to reach the relative safety of whatever lay behind the large wooden door—for it was sure to be preferable to a raucous crowd—she quickly caught up to Adelaide, and would have passed her had Adelaide not also quickened her pace.

They soon passed through the door, and only a moment later it closed behind them with a loud *thud* that echoed around the room she now stood in. When the echo faded, Maaya noticed that the din from outside had been almost entirely cut off. This comforted her only for a moment until she turned slowly to see just where she was.

She stood in a wide-open chamber with rows upon rows of benches all organized in an arc to face a grand wooden podium in the center back wall. The walls and floor were all immaculately clean, and the ceiling was so high that Maaya almost felt dizzy when she stared upward.

A split second later she realized that the benches were filled with men and women of importance, a fact she could glean only by their countenances, serious and disciplined from years and years in this intimidating hall. They wore dark robes and various decorative pins and sashes; it seemed like the more someone had the closer they were to the front. Behind the wood bench, which was raised to attract even more attention to whoever sat behind it, a woman with steely gray hair and sharp green eyes stared down at them.

Kneeling in front of the wood bench and interspersed throughout the crowd of robed men and women were about twenty people with cameras, notepads, and pencils. Unlike the reporters outside, however, they remained still and silent, staring at the newcomers with eager and hopeful expressions.

Before Maaya could move or say a word, every person in the chamber got to their feet, their eyes all on the two young women before them, but they did not speak.

"State your names for the assembly," the woman behind the podium said, and though her voice was calm, every syllable rang with unquestioned authority.

"Adelaide Sol," Adelaide answered immediately.

"Maaya Sahni," Maaya added, hoping no one could detect the tremor in her voice.

"A pleasure. I am Imperatrix Sara Torell, presiding over this executive assembly and representing the Krethan government. Now that you're here, this assembly is now in session. Please make your way to the bench."

The men and women around them took their seats again, and a low murmur filled the room as Maaya and Adelaide walked down the center aisle toward the bench. Adelaide took advantage of the noise to whisper as quietly as she could.

"I didn't think the imperatrix herself would be here. This is huge. I knew they were taking this seriously, but this is something else."

"Is she that important?" Maaya murmured back.

"That's an understatement."

"How? What's her position in your government?"

"She leads it."

As they reached the bench and climbed the narrow stairs behind it, Maaya thought she might be sick. She had little idea as to how Krethus' government was structured, but it wasn't hard to understand what being at the very top meant. If she hadn't been afraid to speak before, she definitely was now.

However, when Maaya and Adelaide took their seats next to Imperatrix Torell, the woman got to her feet and gave them a smile.

"The podium belongs to you for the duration of the session. I must emphasize that while this is an official hearing, it is only for the purpose of gathering information and having something for the record. What's more, please don't let my presence here intimidate you. My attendance is simply necessary. Are we ready?"

"Yes, ma'am," Adelaide answered. Maaya could only nod.

"I am assuming this is your first encounter with any form of our government, so I do hope it is a positive one for you, Miss Sahni," Torell said, a hint of warmth in her tone. "I will endeavor not to keep you two long, but these sessions are typically lengthy, and the nature of this particular session, well… let's just say I have no frame of reference."

Torell stepped down from the bench and walked over to one of the front-row benches, sitting down in one of the free spots that had quickly opened for her as she approached. Maaya noticed with some trepidation how even the otherwise straight-faced politicians in her immediate vicinity seemed nervous.

A flash went off and then another, and two puffs of smoke filled the room. Maaya started, then quickly regained her composure. If she was getting her picture taken, she was going to at least try to look confident.

With that, the session was under way. Maaya and Adelaide were first asked to recollect in great detail everything that they had planned and accomplished from the moment Maaya had arrived on Krethan soil until the moment they arrived back home days after the machine had been destroyed. Maaya knew, however, that there would surely be questions about her beginnings in Sark and what drove her to travel, so she decided to start her story from the very start when she and her friends spotted the first strange ghost up on the hill by the river.

Maaya recounted her version mechanically, fearing desperately that she might get caught up in the emotion of it all, but Adelaide's presence at her side helped calm her. When she noticed the imperatrix looking on with rapt attention and nodding along softly, Maaya felt even more emboldened.

Gradually she got accustomed to the flashes and smoke of the cameras, and her voice grew steady as she spoke. She recounted how she and her friends had fought off the ghosts as best they could until all but Maaya and Svante were killed, and how Rahu then foiled their escape attempt and killed Svante in the process. She continued with how she had been pursued by the military even as she did her best to protect every town she came across, and how she had only just barely escaped Selenthia on Adelaide's ship. At first Maaya wasn't sure how the assembly would take the news of her arguably illegal behavior, but when she explained how they had managed to fool the Selenthian soldiers even as Maaya stood directly in front of them, she heard snickering and saw subtle approving nods.

She detailed the battle at sea, their arrival in Krethus, how she and Adelaide had trained and planned together, and how everything had started going wrong from the moment they departed the train. She told them of the fierce battles within the barrier, how the ghosts had become more numerous and aggressive, and how they had only just made it to the house in time.

Finally, she reached the part of her story she had been dreading the most. So far she had been able to explain that the gem had been in her possession, and she made a vague mention of the friend who had been traveling with her, but she hadn't yet explained who she was or how she was related to the gem. But now there was nothing else for it. She would have to tell them everything.

"We didn't start out on this journey thinking we'd have to say goodbye at the end, but she knew what she had to do. She chose this end for the good of Krethus, as did her father. Without her we never would have made it and never would have been able to shut it down," she finished, then leaned back slightly into her seat. She felt like she had just run a marathon, so difficult was this act of sharing all of this with others.

The assembly sat quiet and still in what Maaya could only describe as utter shock. She knew the Krethans were far more accepting of the existence of ghosts than her own countrymen, but she had to admit that the story of how an unknown girl from a small town in Selenthia traveled across the world with the long-dead daughter of the machine's inventor was hard to swallow.

Adelaide told her story next, and though it was almost completely the same, everyone paid attention to her with similar interest. Maaya watched her in admiration as she spoke. With all eyes in the room on her, even as she was surrounded by important politicians and the imperatrix of her nation, she looked right at home in front of the crowd. She spoke clearly, the force behind her words an imperative demand for understanding and respect.

When she finished her retelling, it was time for questions. Maaya, who had been hoping for a quick end to the session, whimpered quietly in dismay as almost every single person in the room raised their hands when the call for questions came. This semblance of decorum faded quickly, however, as many of the assembly members began calling out to the front bench, evidently hoping that if they spoke first or loudest they would be given the answers they wanted.

The questions were, if anything, predictable. The assembly wanted more details about this and that, more names, more dates, more… everything. They probed into Maaya's history in Selenthia, eventually digging so deep and so personal that she was soon forced to explain she would provide no intimate details about her life. She and Adelaide took turns answering questions, and all the while, the cameras flashed.

An hour passed, and then another. At one point, a praetor accompanied by numerous soldiers stepped into the assembly to ask questions of his own. A nervous-looking man next to him quickly jotted down notes as Maaya and Adelaide spoke, though Adelaide soon took over as Maaya's exhaustion—or perhaps frustration—became evident. Maaya noticed the distinct lack of any sort of timepiece in the room, and the seats on the bench didn't provide her with a subtle method of glancing in Chronis' direction.

Then, after the questions seeking details came the questions ringing with doubt and suspicion. How did Maaya know the ghost she saw was really Isak Astrom? What proof was there of the great scars opening in the sky being related to the machine? Was it not awfully convenient that Freja had lost her memory? Was Rahu not correct about the ghosts being drawn to Maaya if only for her use of *libris*?

This last question incensed Maaya, and had Adelaide not quickly risen to address the question in her stead, Maaya surely would have snapped.

"The assemblyman should be ashamed at his question," Adelaide said in her calm but dangerous voice. "The ghosts were attracted to the gem, not

Maaya. You would know this had you been paying attention. The gem had been in Sark for years, which explained their presence there. Perhaps the assemblyman should instead ask what incompetence led to this gem being lost for so long, putting potentially millions of innocent lives at risk."

"That it was lost was hardly any fault of my own! We provided what funding and operatives we could. Besides, seeking it was not my job," the assemblyman scoffed.

"It wasn't Maaya's, either," Adelaide replied coldly. "But I digress. If you absolutely must exercise your pedantry in a search for unnecessary technicalities, I implore you to use even a *modicum* of common sense before trying to give the benefit of the doubt to a serial murderer—to the face of the girl whose family he killed, no less. Let's not also forget that he killed one of our own and attempted to blackmail our government over this gem. With this all in mind, is the fact that he may have been accidentally close to correct on one issue of any importance in this hearing?"

As every head and camera in the room turned to face the unfortunate assemblyman, he muttered a halfhearted inaudible response, then sank very low in his seat, his face burning.

"You know, for a while I thought he was right," Maaya added quietly after Adelaide finally sat down. Adelaide glanced at her warily, but Maaya gave her a reassuring nod, then continued speaking. "I saw evidence for it everywhere I went. He didn't know what he was talking about, and he said it to get me killed, but if he was right at all that meant I was the one putting people at risk. But he was wrong. He always is. He's not smart about the way these things work, he's just manipulative. He makes people afraid and uses that fear as a weapon. You must know that people like me can still be killed in Selenthia for being able to see ghosts or use *libris*, and he is the kind of person keeping those horrible ideas alive. Please, I beg you not to consider his ideas. Krethus is a beautiful place and I've felt so accepted here, and that's because people like Rahu don't have power. Don't let them get any back."

Finally, mercifully, it appeared as though the members of the assembly were beginning to run out of questions. When there passed a full ten seconds without a single raised hand, Imperatrix Torell got to her feet and the room fell instantly silent.

"The executive assembly and Krethan Empire hereby recognizes Adelaide Sol and Maaya Sahni of Selenthia for their actions and their service to our nation. Both of these young women demonstrated incredible skill, mental fortitude, and bravery in the face of what in all other attempts has been failure, defeat, and death. They risked their lives for Krethus, and in so doing, put an end to a century-long terror. It is the privilege of my position to honor them for their accomplishments."

Torell reached down into the bag she carried with her and pulled out what appeared to be two small pins. At Maaya's side, Adelaide gasped and clapped a hand to her mouth.

"What is it?" Maaya asked, but Adelaide only shook her head.

Torell approached the bench, and a flicker of a grin passed across her face when she noticed Adelaide's expression. She then held out the pins to them, and the girls took them wordlessly as the cameras flashed furiously in the background. When the pins were safely in hand, Torell placed a purse in front of each of them. Maaya tried desperately to keep her composure as she looked inside her own see a *very* large amount of rial.

"I give to each of you the golden seal of the Krethan Empire, the highest possible commendation and the greatest honor I can give for your actions. Though if I may be honest, I feel there is no honor great enough for what you have accomplished. And to you, Maaya," she continued, turning to face the girl, "know that you always have a home in Krethus. What you did for us despite holding no allegiance to us, and despite how much you lost, cannot be overstated."

"Th-thank you, ma'am," Maaya answered, staring down at the pin in awe. She had never seen the seal of Krethus before, and even this pin seemed but a mere trinket in her hands. But at the same time she was overcome with an almost otherworldly sense of how great an honor she had just received, and how meaningful it was for Torell herself to give her something like this. So great was the weight of this gratitude manifest in gold that she almost gave it back, thinking for a moment that she in no way deserved something this important. She had only been trying to save her home.

But instead she smiled and did her best to affix the pin to the front of her coat. Adelaide, who was now openly crying, had already done the same.

"Thank you so much for this honor, ma'am," she managed to choke out. "It was my pleasure to do this service for my country."

"Consider your service ultimately and wholly fulfilled," Torell said with a smile, and then turned back to face the wide room before her. "With this honor given, I formally call an end to this executive assembly, and I ask that you all—"

"Wait," Maaya said suddenly, and all eyes were immediately upon her. "I, er, sorry, ma'am. I just realized I… I have one last thing I want to add."

"By all means," Torell nodded.

Adelaide threw Maaya a quizzical look, but Maaya was too focused to see it. She took a deep breath. She would likely not get another opportunity like this. It was time to speak from her heart and to officially begin the process she had desperately wanted for so long.

"For all of you, I'm sure that the whole purpose of our actions was the destruction of the machine and the safety of Krethus. The safety of your home. Tonight you'll go home, maybe to your families and friends. My motivation was the same, and while I'm glad I could do something about it, I want to tell you about my friends and family as well, because they're the reason I started this journey and also why I succeeded.

"I only had a few years with my family before they were taken from me. I wasn't able to save them. But while they lived, they gave my life meaning and helped me see that there was still hope for the world. They were the good that existed in it and they made me dream of better things. They didn't make it to see us win, and the cruelty of one man almost completely wiped everything about them from this world. I want you to remember their names: Kim, Kalil, and Sovaan. They were my family, and they are responsible for me being who I am today. They're why I fought so hard. The world needs to remember them, and if I could I would make sure they were honored just like me. That they didn't survive this with me doesn't mean the intent and bravery in their hearts was any less than mine.

"Finally, my friend who traveled this whole way with me. To you all, her name was Freja Astrom, but to me her name was Saber, and she was my best friend in the entire world. She helped me not only to survive, but to live, too. She picked me up when I fell, she never backed down from a challenge, and she taught me to fight rather than run. She was so very brave, and I would not have made it without her. I want to ask you all to do something for me. Remember their names. Remember their stories and share them. Write them in your papers and tell them to your loved ones. This was my family. The world deserves to hear of them and they deserve to be remembered."

With these last words, she sat down again. Even if she had anything more to say, she wouldn't have been able to. She fought desperately to keep herself from crying, her jaw clenched tight with the effort. Out of the corner of her eye she noticed the reporters scribbling hastily into their notebooks. She had done it. She had taken the first step of what she was sure would be many, and as she watched them write, she felt a glimmer of validation and assurance. She had long been afraid that she would never be able to fulfill her wish of keeping the memory of her friends alive, but now, suddenly, it seemed like something she just might be able to do.

"Duly noted. Their memories are safe in Krethus. I hope someday the same can be said for your country. Have either of you anything left you wish to say?" Torell asked after a short silence. When Maaya and Adelaide shook their heads in unison, Torell nodded. "Then let us end this appropriately. Members of the executive assembly, you would join me."

Every person in the hall stood again, and then, like Maaya had seen before, they fell to one knee, bowed their heads, and placed their right forearms across their chests. Even through the flashes of camera lights and puffs of smoke that filled the room, it was a sight to behold. Beside her, Adelaide gripped her hand tightly in her own.

Maaya didn't ever know if it would be possible to explain how such a sight made her feel. There was gratitude, certainly, as well as the quiet but persistent thought that this should all be ignored, because something so powerful and positive couldn't possibly be for her. Then there was awe, for there was no other word to describe seeing politicians and the woman who led the country kneeling for anyone.

But there, above all, was validation. She grasped it tightly. This was a rare and fleeting feeling. For her entire life, nearly everyone she met and seemingly the world itself had told her she was worth nothing. It had manipulated and gaslit her into believing every story about how she was just a waste of space, someone who could offer nothing to anyone, and she had eventually started to sink into that pit of despair and cynicism from which the state of the world allowed no escape.

Yet here she was, and she forced herself to stare so that her mind could not force in even a moment of doubt. She was here. This was real. And she deserved it.

Only moments later it was over, though to Maaya it felt like it had lasted the whole day. The men and women of the assembly began to disperse, tiredly opening the doors that led out into the halls on the side, clearly unwilling to deal with whatever crowd may have remained—or even grown—outside.

Imperatrix Torell remained as the room emptied, though she glanced down at her own timepiece with some impatience.

"I do wish I could stay longer, but I wasn't expecting the assembly to run this long and I have much work to do on my return," Torell apologized. Adelaide looked almost offended that Torell would dare apologize for anything.

"Please, don't worry about it. It was an honor to see you here, ma'am," Adelaide said, so enthusiastically that Maaya had to turn away to hide her grin.

"The honor was mine. I will make efforts to see you again, both of you," Torell continued. "You know, I grew up under the terror of the machine, and by then it had already been going for decades. My extended family was once massive, with dozens in every province, but over half of them were lost. When I was in school I thought it was only a short matter of time before the government devised some miracle fix or before some hero rose. By the time I got into government, I realized that day would not come. It was hard going to work every day knowing that the end was inevitable. For that, I think you both are better people than I. However disheartened you may have felt, you never gave up like I did. So again, from the bottom of my heart, I thank you. You've ended a lifelong horror for all of us."

As she spoke, Maaya thought of Saber. How she would have loved to be in this room for it all, hovering behind Maaya to offer her advice on how to answer questions and making rude comments at the people who couldn't see or hear her. Most of all, Maaya thought, she would love to be in a room full of people celebrating what she had done and calling her a hero. If there was any possibility, Maaya hoped Saber was watching and grinning with pride as she had always done.

"I regret that I spend most of my time in Selenthian waters, but I would absolutely change my entire schedule if you ever wanted to, ah, get together," Adelaide said excitedly.

"My staff will make sure I know how to contact you. We'll make it work," Torell smiled, then held out her hand. Adelaide and Maaya took it in turn, and Maaya nearly winced at the woman's powerful handshake. "I'll be off, then. I expect I'll be hearing much more about the both of you."

She gave a polite nod, then swept off to one of the side doors. It closed behind her, the quiet *click* echoing and fading in the otherwise empty room.

"So, that was… something," Adelaide breathed, looking quite overcome.

"Yeah. Wow. That was not what I was expecting at all… I think I may need to go right back to sleep when we get back," Maaya said, rubbing her eyes. The assembly had definitely taxed her more than she thought it would, if only because of the sheer length of it.

"Let's get back to Asmund. I don't much feel like going through the crowd, so maybe we can figure out another way—"

She was interrupted by the sound of one of the doors quickly opening, followed by the rapid clacking of shoes on the marble floors. A young woman with dirty blonde hair and dressed in clerk's robes entered the room, scanning it almost desperately, and then, upon seeing Maaya and Adelaide, rushed toward them.

"Adelaide Sol? Maaya Sahni?" she asked hopefully, and when they nodded, a wave of relief washed over her face. "Thank goodness I managed to find you before you left. I have something for you."

She passed a small slip of paper to Maaya, who stared at it in confusion. There was writing on it, but even though Maaya could make out the letters and numbers upon it, she saw no sense to the order of them.

"What is this?" she asked as Adelaide took the slip from her.

"It's an address… but to where?" Adelaide added.

"Ah, well, the praetor asked me to fetch this with the utmost urgency. It relates to something you spoke of during the hearing. I don't personally know what it means, but I was asked to tell you that this is where you can find the home of one Svante Nordin."

Maaya's breath caught in her throat.

"S-Svante? You knew him?"

"Not personally, miss. The praetor wanted his home address found because the military traditionally visits the homes of the deceased to inform their families of their passing during their service. However, he thought you might appreciate it if this duty fell to you. What should I tell him?"

"I… I don't…"

"You don't have to do this, Maaya," Adelaide broke in gently. "You've seen a lot of pain already. There's no obligation to subject yourself to more."

Maaya didn't answer. She had almost blurted out her agreement the instant she heard his name, but she hesitated. This was a heavy task, and of all the things she had done, she felt nowhere near prepared to do this. She had experiencing fighting ghosts, and of telling them they were dead—but she had no experience telling the living that their loved ones were gone. She couldn't help but imagine how his family must feel. The machine was down and the danger had passed, so surely they must be expecting his safe return at this very moment.

But Maaya had already decided. This wasn't something she could shy away from because she was ill prepared. She may not have known him for long, but his life and hers had become inevitably linked. He had come searching for something that only Maaya and Saber had, and it was he who had thrust the plan of escaping Sark into motion. Though he hadn't made it, she had been given the chance to see what kind of person he really was, and it had been an impression worthy of making her throw caution to the winds and start her journey across the world.

Besides, she thought, on some level she had been preparing for this all along. That's what she had told Adelaide she was traveling to Krethus to do before the captain knew her true purpose, and it hadn't been a lie.

"I'll do it," Maaya answered. "I'll go there now."

"That's great news! I'll pass it along. Oh, if you please… don't mention this to the reporters. Something like this should be done away from their prying eyes," the clerk said.

"Of course! But… how do we get out without them seeing?" Maaya asked.

"There are plenty of exits! I'll show you the best one. I'll make sure your driver knows where to meet you."

39

IN MEMORY

Forty-five minutes later, Asmund's carriage pulled up in front of a quiet house on a grassy hill. Unlike many of the cities and towns Maaya had seen where even the houses with large yards were pressed close together, the houses on this street were set widely apart, each with so much space that there were no fences to be seen. There were few people out and about here, but those who walked nearby greeted the newcomers with waves and smiles even though they didn't seem to know who they were looking at.

It was quiet, but peacefully so, the silence broken only by the occasional breeze whispering through willow trees and the chirping of birds. There were just few enough trees to still provide a beautiful view of the sparkling ocean in the distance, and Maaya took a deep breath of the fresh air. It was a calm and tranquil place, and she knew with absolutely certainty that this had to be the home of the man she had gotten to know so far away.

"Are you still sure about this?" Adelaide asked quietly as Maaya sat in the still carriage.

"Yes. I'm not ready, but… I'm sure," Maaya replied slowly. "Will you be okay here without me?"

"Absolutely, I'll be fine!" Adelaide answered reassuringly. "It's you I'm worried about, love. But please, don't rush. Do whatever you need to do and I'll be right here when you're done."

They shared a quick kiss, and then Maaya stepped slowly out of the carriage. After a moment of hesitation and a deep breath, she started for the door.

All manner of thoughts and questions passed through her mind as she walked up the long path to the front door. What was his family like? How would they react? Would they be angry? Would they blame her? What could she possibly say?

When she reached the door, she paused, her arm raised halfway in the air. The feeling of doubt instilled within her was so powerful that it was almost a physical force holding her back. She stood still in the quiet and empty doorway, fighting with everything she had to push her arm just a foot farther, but with no success.

Suddenly, however, the door opened. Maaya gasped and quickly dropped her arm to her side.

On the other side of the doorway stood a tall and slender woman with light brown hair and hazel eyes. She wore a beautiful floral-patterned cardigan loosely over her dark lounge pants. Her hair was thrown back into a messy bun, the kind women often preferred when it was time to leave the bedroom but when there were no obligations to leave the house. A few droplets of water fell near her bare feet from a tea strainer in her right hand, but she paid it no mind.

"Can I help you?" the woman asked politely.

Maaya suddenly realized she had been staring at the woman with eyes wide with shock, and she blinked quickly, clearing her throat.

"Yes, I, uhm… that is, I… how did you know I was here?" she asked, her curiosity quickly getting the better of her.

"Oh! Don't be concerned, dear, I wasn't watching you. It's one of my husband's inventions; it rings a bell inside when someone comes up close to the door. You seemed nervous so I thought I might greet you."

"I… I was. Thank you," Maaya responded foolishly. "Actually, I was wondering… are you Mrs. Nordin?"

"I am! You found the right house," the woman replied warmly. "My name is Signe. Are you seeking after me?"

"Ah, yes, I am," Maaya replied shakily. The woman was so friendly. How could Maaya give her the news of her husband's death like this?

"Are you well? Do you need help?" Signe asked concernedly.

Yes! Maaya thought frantically even as she shook her head.

"Sorry, I just… I need to talk to you about something very important."

"What is it? Would you like to come inside? I'm just finishing up some tea," Signe said, and Maaya felt another jolt as she realized it was Wednesday. Svante's tea day.

In her mind, Maaya heard Saber's voice telling her flatly, *Get to the point before the sun sets, will you?*

"Oh, no, thank you. I shouldn't. It's actually… I just… I need to tell you about your husband," Maaya said helplessly.

Signe paused, and then her face fell.

"Ah. I see."

Maaya took a deep breath, averting her eyes. Signe wasn't yelling at her. That was a good sign. So far.

"I hate that I have to bring you this news, but… Svante passed away some weeks ago," Maaya explained slowly, struggling with every syllable. Gods, this was hard. "He was on an assignment in Selenthia, and he… he didn't make it back."

Signe took a slow, shuddering breath and put her free hand on the door frame for support. But while Maaya had been expecting a shocked and tearful reaction, Signe only nodded sadly.

"I was afraid of this. I knew going to Selenthia would prove dangerous. Even after the good news about the machine which meant my husband could come home, I had a feeling he was already gone. That's the world we live in, unfortunately. My heart would break at this news had I not already felt it some time ago. To hear this for certain brings me grief, but closure as well. Did you know him well?"

"Not exactly… I only knew him for a few days. But I wish I had been able to know him better. He was a wonderful person, and so, so brave. I kind of looked up to him for that. He's part of the reason the machine got stopped, actually."

Signe started, her eyes wide.

"Really? My Svante? He told me he was on assignment in an out-of-the-way town called Sark of all places, far off and away from all the bustle and danger. What did he do?"

"He was. That's where I met him," Maaya replied, and the look of shock on Signe's face only grew. "I lived there. He was new in town and searching for the gem that was supposed to be able to shut down the machine. And… I happened to have it. I had no idea it was anything special at the time. We talked and he told me everything about Krethus and the machine, and he offered to take me with him so we could destroy it together."

"You had it! Then that means… you must be… Maaya Sahni, right?" Signe continued in awe.

"That's me, yes," Maaya admitted. That was definitely going to take some getting used to. "Really, this was all his doing. I wouldn't have had any idea what to do without him."

"How about that… my darling silly husband working with the women who saved the world. What an honor to his memory," Signe said softly, putting her hand to her chest. "May I… may I ask how he died?"

Maaya, who had spent the entire ride there dreading the possibility of this question coming up, was nevertheless prepared.

"He was killed by a man in my town, someone who tried to use the gem to blackmail the Krethan government. We managed to trick him, but he caught us while we were escaping, and… Svante defended me. He tried to get the people of Sark to see what was really happening. He died trying to save Krethus, and me. I'm so sorry that he didn't make it, but… he started all this. He was a hero."

Signe covered her mouth with her hand as tears welled in her eyes, and Maaya's heart sank as she relived Svante's last moments in her mind. If only he knew how far she had come and how his actions had not been in vain. If only he could see his family again. At the very least he had helped ensure they would be safe.

After a minute of silence, Signe took another breath.

"Maaya… thank you for coming. This is no positive news, but I'm glad it was you who came to tell me. I'm sure I'll get a more detailed boring report from the military in the near future, but I appreciate hearing the news from someone who knew him, not just someone who thought of him as another name and number on a list."

"Of course. I'm glad I could find you. Will you… will you be okay?"

"In time," Signe answered, staring out at the wide lawn and the ocean far behind it. "I have a lot of thinking to do, but I will be all right eventually. Tell me… did he ever speak of me?"

"He did. He told me about how he loved his job but how he couldn't wait to get home and see you. He told me about how he loved having tea on Wednesdays to celebrate the middle of the week and having a good book to read in the evening. I could tell he loved you a lot. His home and his family were the things he loved talking about most."

Signe smiled.

"I'm so glad. He really was a genuine and lovely man. My love and faith in him was unshakeable, and I will miss him so much. But hearing this makes me feel like I was all the more lucky to have been married to him. And for what it's worth, I'm sorry that just as I lost a husband, you lost a friend. Now… I'm sorry, I wish I could take more time to talk, but I need to be alone."

"Oh, of course! I won't take any more of your time. But… if there's ever anything I can do for you, anything at all, please let me know."

"Thank you, dear. That means a lot. In the event I never see you again, I want to thank you for everything you've done and for bringing this news to me. I wish you the very best in life."

"And to you," Maaya finished quietly.

With nothing left to be said, the women smiled at each other, and then Signe closed the door.

Maaya sighed, hanging her head. It hadn't gone poorly, but she still felt a great weight on her heart. Even when done properly, there was still something about goodbyes that always hurt.

Deciding not to remain too long in case Signe opened the door to find her still there, she turned and started resolutely down the street. She didn't immediately see the carriage, and for a moment wondered if she had taken too long, but then she noticed it parked a few houses down out of view from Signe's house; no doubt they had thought it appropriate to stay out of sight while Maaya talked to her.

She reached the sidewalk and turned toward the carriage, but stopped when she heard a voice call her name.

"Maaya! Please wait, just a moment."

Maaya started, then whirled around with a gasp. She knew that voice.

The ghost of Svante Nordin stood several paces away, a friendly smile on his face as he approached. He looked exactly how she remembered him, and for a moment she felt she must be dreaming. Her lip trembled as she looked at him, and he laughed awkwardly.

"I suppose this is a bit of a surprise, isn't it?" he chuckled. "I am so very glad to see you, let me just say that. I, ah… you know, I was hoping I'd find you, but I'm afraid I don't quite know what to say. Or rather, I feel there's so very much to say that I don't know where to start."

"How… how are you here?" Maaya asked in astonishment, her voice nearly at a whisper.

"Evidently I came back. I'm still very much getting used to the feeling—most unnerving, you might imagine. It was all very confusing at first. I remember dying, but then I remember coming back, only then no one could see or hear me. It took me a little while to remember where I was, and by then you had gone! I was terrified you'd be killed just after me. I remained in Sark for a few days until I gathered from your friend Roshan that you had fled for Krethus. I had—"

"Roshan! He's alive?" Maaya cried.

"At least when I left, yes! That was days and days after my death, at which point the ghost attacks had started fading away. At that point I knew I should try to catch up with you, but you travel swiftly, Miss Sahni," Svante laughed. "I made it to Levien and found my contact still there and waiting, but by my luck, he can't see ghosts. I spent a whole day trying to communicate with him only to discover Levien had closed down the port! Anyway, one long mess after another I finally made it here just in time to hear the news that the machine had been destroyed. By then I was so far behind you I feared I would never see you again, so I… I decided to come home."

There was so much Maaya wanted to say, so much she wanted to impress upon him now that she was finally processing she had the chance. But for now, words would have to wait. Maaya stepped forward and flung her arms around him, hugging him as tightly as she could.

"I'm so sorry for all of this," she whimpered into his coat. "I'm sorry you got caught up in my stupid town's politics and that I couldn't stop this. This never should have happened; you should have come home to your family and seen them happy and known the world was safe for them—"

"And I *did*," Svante interrupted gently. "I came back seeing exactly what I wanted to see. My family is alive and well, the machine was taken care of, and those horrible ghosts are gone. I am sad, of course, but apart from my own death everything went even better than I could have ever hoped for. I can't even say that my family will never know what happened to me because you just took care of that."

"I... I suppose," Maaya sniffed, and then she managed a smile. "I'm so glad to see you again. I feel like we didn't get a proper goodbye last time."

"That's a bit of an understatement," Svante grinned. "I'm glad to see you too. How has life been since we last saw each other?"

"It's hard to say. It's either been very good or very bad and not much in between," Maaya said heavily.

"Ah! Well then, tell me of all the good. There's no reason to dwell on the bad," Svante said encouragingly.

"Well, we stopped the machine, so there's that. While I was doing that I got to find out Saber's identity, and she was reunited with her father. I, er... I fell in love, and I found out she loves me, too," Maaya explained, feeling her cheeks turn pink.

"Oh! Yes, Saber! Who was she?" Svante asked excitedly.

"Freja Astrom, daughter of Isak Astrom," Maaya said, and Svante's eyes widened.

"Really! Oh, now that just answers so many questions. The daughter of the creator of the machine. My, what a wild coincidence. That she would show up all the way in Sark! Incredible. Well then, I'm glad you found out, and I hope it brought some comfort to you both. May she rest easy now."

Maaya stared.

"How did you know?"

"Just a guess," Svante answered sadly. "She was always at your side, and now she is painfully absent—and that pain is evident in how you carry yourself. I'm so very sorry she is gone."

"Me too," Maaya replied, staring down at the sidewalk.

"Ah, well, what about this girl you're seeing? What's her name?" Svante asked quickly.

"Adelaide. She's amazing, really. I think you'd love her. She's a ship's captain, she's really talented with *libris*, and she... she's one of the most beautiful people I've ever seen," Maaya answered, and though she felt the sting of embarrassment, she also felt pleased to tell someone about the wonderful woman she had fallen for.

"I don't suppose you mean Adelaide Sol?" Svante asked, and Maaya stared up at him in surprise. He grinned again. "The *libris* elites have always been popular, and she was incredibly skilled, as was the tutor she studied under. They were both well loved here. She was in the area often as part of her patrol, as Unshala isn't that far from here. I never spoke to her, but I saw her around on occasion. She always carried herself so confidently. I'm not at all surprised to hear she's now in command of a vessel. Forgive me, but I must say congratulations. I'm pleased you've found your heart's match, and in someone of such noble spirit as well."

"She makes me so happy. I think I'm starting to understand what you meant about going home to tea and a good book with the family; the more I think about that kind of life with her, the more I want it."

"Have you asked her for that life?" Svante asked, and Maaya shook her head.

"I don't know if I'm ready. We haven't been together that long, all things considered. Besides, there's still some important things left for us to do."

"Like what?"

"She… wants to go back to Selenthia. Apparently I'm allowed to go back too, but… well, you know I have a lot of history there and not a lot of it is pleasant. My friends are there, but so is Rahu. I have a lot of thinking to do."

"I see," Svante said thoughtfully, putting his hand to his chin. "Would you like my advice?"

"Always."

"Go back with her. Go back and face your problems there, and then defeat them. You have someone at your side now who has accepted you for all of your strengths and all your faults, so just as you share in joy, you share in trials. Go back with her, and be brave. There are evils in the world, but none too great for the bravery of Adelaide Sol and the heart of Maaya Sahni combined. Of that I am absolutely certain."

Maaya smiled. Somehow she knew that would be his response.

"I think I will," she said, and Svante nodded approvingly. "Hey… will I see you around? I can come back to visit, or—"

"Ah, well, actually, I was wondering if you might be able to help me there," Svante said awkwardly. "I've had a lot of time to think about this, and while I'm ever so glad I was able to see all of these problems resolve themselves—and as absolutely wonderful as it is to fly—I just don't think this is the existence I want for myself. The in-between just doesn't seem like me."

Maaya froze as she started to understand where he was going.

"You… you want me to seal you," she uttered, more a statement than a question.

Svante nodded apologetically.

"I apologize; I'm not sure if that's a taboo request to make! But I thought if I could ask anyone free of judgment, well… it'd be you."

Maaya hesitated, fighting the urge to instantly refuse. She had done this a few times, and it broke her heart each time.

But as the seconds passed, she realized the wave of hurt and dread she had been expecting wasn't going to come. This was what she had spent years of her life doing. It wasn't just the mischievous spirits who were sealed away. Some couldn't stand the in-between and just wanted peace. Of all the people in the world to desire such a thing, Svante had to be near the top of the list. What's more, Maaya thought, he deserved it.

"I… I would be glad to do that for you," Maaya answered finally. And she meant every word.

Relief passed over Svante's face, followed by an awkward chuckle.

"Thank you. I was afraid I'd said something entirely out of line. I hope you understand."

"I understand completely." Maaya slowly reached to the card pouch on her arm and pulled out one of the blood cards Adelaide had made for her, then stared back at Svante. "Thank you for being my friend. And for everything else. I wish I could have known you for longer, but it was great having you around."

"Ah, I imagine there will be plenty of time for that eventually," Svante replied warmly. "And thank you for everything you've done, both for Krethus and for my family. We will see each other again, Maaya Sahni. Until then?"

"Until then," Maaya said, and then, with one slow motion, she pressed the blood card against him. Only a moment later both the card and Svante had vanished, with no trace that either had ever been.

Maaya remained there for a moment, taking in every sense of the world she possibly could to embed every sight and sound and smell of this instant into her memory. And then she turned and started back toward the carriage, leaving the Nordin house behind forever.

"How did it go?" Adelaide asked as Maaya stepped back into the carriage, but Maaya passed her a comforting smile.

"It went well. I'm glad I did this."

"Oh, that's good!" Adelaide exhaled. "You were starting to take a bit so I was getting worried. How'd they take it?"

"Only his wife was home that I could tell, and she took it better than I thought. But she wasn't the only person I ran into…"

THE CARRIAGE HADN'T EVEN COME to a full stop in front of Adelaide's house before her entire family rushed out to greet them, though this greeting came in the form of a bombardment of questions so loud and intense that Maaya imagined it to be the verbal equivalent of a full broadside from the Nocte Cadenza.

It was so intense that even Adelaide quickly lost her patience, and after a sharp demand for silence she directed her family back toward the house where they dutifully waited inside.

"Stars, and I thought our return from the machine was bad," Adelaide griped. "I've about had my fill of answering nagging questions for the week."

"Do you want me to take care of them this time?" Maaya asked, amused, and Adelaide shook her head quickly.

"I'm not leaving you alone with them! They'd eat you alive. It's fine. I'll answer a few of their questions and then tell them to read the papers for the rest."

"They're your family, though! It's not so strange they'd want to know all about your big day. Besides, you're leaving them again soon," Maaya protested.

Adelaide stared at her in exasperation, struggled to speak for a moment, and then relented.

"Fine. But you owe me later for this guilt trip."

"How about a kiss?" Maaya teased.

"Oh, we'll need to go a little further than that. But I'll take that as an offer, and I accept."

"Should I be worried abou—?"

"No time for questions! Well, not from you, anyway," Adelaide interrupted cheerfully. "Let's get inside."

What followed was a mercifully short session during which Adelaide and Maaya attempted to answer one question at a time. Adelaide's family seemed less concerned with what was discussed and more about the accolades and special attention they received. Her family gasped in unison when Adelaide mentioned the presence of the imperatrix at the hearing, and Marit nearly screamed when Adelaide and Maaya pulled out their golden seals.

"Imperatrix Torell gave you *these?*" she cried in utter astonishment as Felix let out a roaring cheer in the background. "You're such a showoff. There's no way I'll ever be able to top this!"

"What kind of sister would I be if I didn't constantly steal your spotlight?" Adelaide teased. "But I did this for you, kiddo. Now you don't have to worry about any tall spooky strangers showing up to wear white at your wedding."

Marit laughed, but her laughter faded quickly, and her smile didn't reach her eyes. Adelaide seemed to notice as well, because she immediately turned back to her parents, who were both trying to steal Adelaide's seal without her noticing.

Less than half an hour later, Felix finally stood up, declaring an end to the questions.

"I apologize for the additional interrogation, but there was no way you could go off to something like that without us bothering you for details, you know," he said proudly. "But to think! My daughter, the savior of Krethus, an acquaintance of the imperatrix, and holder of the golden seal of our country. I don't know why I ever doubted you."

"I have a list of reasons up in my room. It's a few notebooks long by now," Marit said, snickering.

"Perhaps young Maaya here was a positive influence on our daughter," Cajsa suggested wryly as Adelaide smacked her sister with a sofa pillow.

"It'll take me a while to get used to the idea that anyone could influence her," Felix chuckled. "But! Well done, both of you. Very well done indeed. You have done us so proud."

"Oh, before I forget, Maaya dear: a package was left for you early this afternoon. Let me get it for you," Cajsa said, getting up and walking silently from the room. Only a moment later she brought back a thick brown parcel tied tightly with brown string and bearing the mark of the Krethan seal.

"Ooh, that looks important. Open it for us?" Marit requested, only to earn another smack with a pillow from Adelaide.

"She's not opening birthday presents, you egg," Adelaide scolded. "Come on, Maaya. Let's open this somewhere private."

"Hey, how come you get to see?" Marit pouted.

"Girlfriend privileges," Adelaide answered with a straight face, then stuck her tongue out at Marit as she and Maaya left the room.

They went up to Adelaide's room where, after Adelaide securely closed and locked the door, they sat on her bed, the parcel in between them.

"Whatever this is, they sure made sure no one could get into it," Maaya grunted as she struggled with the string.

"Here, let me," Adelaide said eagerly. Setting the package down in front of her, she pulled a purple *libris* card from her pouch, burned it on her arm, and then tore the string apart effortlessly, leaving only the brown wrapping paper. She handed the parcel back to Maaya, looking quite pleased with herself.

"Was that really necessary?" Maaya asked, raising an eyebrow as the purple *libris* lines faded from Adelaide's arms.

"I don't know. Did you think it was cool?"

"...yes," Maaya admitted.

"Then yes, it was. Go on, let's have a look!" Adelaide encouraged.

Maaya delicately unwrapped the brown paper to find a brown folder stuffed with papers inside, upon which sat another wrapped package—though this one was lopsided and taped haphazardly shut. A small roll of parchment was attached to it, and Maaya could just make out what looked like handwriting inside.

"Don't tell me the government sent you a bunch of paperwork," Adelaide groaned.

Maaya gingerly set the second package aside, then opened the folder. Her eyes widened in shock, and she nearly gasped as she stared down at the stack of papers within.

On top of the stack of papers was a copy of the painting Demryn had started of Saber, but this one was complete, albeit slightly smaller than the large canvas he had used. Now in full color, the painting was so detailed and so masterfully done that Maaya felt like she was staring at a photograph of her best friend.

"Stars, look at this!" Adelaide uttered in incredulity as she reached down to flip through the papers and clippings inside. "Photos, all sorts of records, letters, government documents… her whole life is in here! This is incredible…"

Maaya said nothing, unable to look away from the painting. As she gazed down at it, looking over every detail from Saber's bright blue eyes to the way her long hair fell ever so delicately over her shoulders, Maaya felt a deep and desperate longing in her heart. She remembered the day this painting had been started and how eager Saber had been to finally discover who she had been, as well as how much she looked forward to learning all about her past after they had destroyed the machine.

"You okay?" Adelaide asked, her tone immediately softening as she paused and glanced over at Maaya.

"I miss her," was all Maaya could manage to say, her voice cracking with the effort of holding back yet more tears.

All at once, Adelaide was at her side, pulling her into a tight hug.

"I know, love. I know. I do too."

They sat in silence for a few minutes as Maaya desperately fought the sobs threatening to escape. She wasn't going to cry. Not again. There had been enough of that in the last few days.

"I think I'll see what this is all about," Maaya finally said, taking a deep breath and grabbing the second parcel, eager for a distraction.

She unwrapped it slowly as Adelaide peered over her shoulder. Whatever was inside was wrapped in so much paper that Maaya could only assume it was very delicate, and the sheer amount of paper quickly became frustrating.

When she finally tore away the last bits of paper, however, she started to cry, and she knew there was no point trying to fight it this time.

In her hands rested Saber's circlet, complete with the red gem that had started and ended a century of history.

"They didn't!" Adelaide gasped quietly.

"They did," Maaya whimpered. "This is it."

She stared down at the circlet with blurred vision, running her fingers over the smooth metal. It felt exactly as it had years and years ago when she first found it thousands of miles away in Sark. It was surreal to hold it again after seeing Saber wear it for so many years. She closed her eyes, letting the feel of it bring back every memory she hadn't recalled for years, and she suddenly felt the urge to open her eyes again, feeling certain that, just like before, the ghost would suddenly be there, freed from the grasp of the gem.

But when she looked again, Saber was nowhere to be seen.

Adelaide gingerly reached around her and picked up the small scroll of paper that had come attached with the package and unrolled it in her hands. She read over it, her brow furrowed, but then she nodded in understanding and handed it to Maaya.

Maaya set the circlet gently down upon the bed, then read the short message that looked like it had been written at the last minute.

Miss Maaya Sahni,

This circlet belonged to Freja Astrom, who we were informed was a good friend of yours in the afterlife. The gem within it was necessary for the purpose of shutting down the machine, but as this has now been done, the Krethan government no longer needs this piece. One of our libris experts has verified the gem's power has been rendered null; as it is only now a piece of jewelry, and because the Astrom family has no living relatives, we decided it would be appropriate to return it to you. We hope this, as well as the files included with this package, will serve to help you remember and honor her.

Be well, and thank you for your service.

Maaya set the note down with a heavy heart. She hadn't expected anything like this. She had assumed that this situation would be just like her escape from Sark and that all she would have left of Saber were her memories of her. There was no way she could put this feeling to words—at least not in her current state—but she would have taken this stack of paper and a piece of old jewelry over a thousand golden seals.

She sat back and leaned her head on Adelaide's shoulder. Neither of them said a word for a long while. Looking over all the material before them could come later. Just knowing it was here was something to appreciate.

Eventually, Adelaide broke the silence.

"So… it's back to Selenthia tomorrow. How do you feel?"

"I'm ready," answered Maaya without hesitation.

"Really?" Adelaide asked hopefully.

"Really. I love it here, I do, but… I think you and Svante were right. There's still more for me to do. I don't know exactly what that is yet, but I know I want to try. Besides, I know everything will be okay as long as you're there with me," Maaya answered, nuzzling her head against Adelaide's arm.

"You bet! I'm so relieved; I was worried you'd be really unsure. But it'll be great! I miss my crew, I really do. We'll be back on the water in no time, and it will feel oh so sweet—"

She was interrupted by a knock at the door. Looking slightly puzzled, Adelaide got up to unlock it. When she opened it, Maaya saw Marit standing there by herself, looking distinctly uncomfortable.

"Can I, uh… can I come in?" she asked, not meeting Adelaide's eye.

"Of course. What's up?" Adelaide asked, but Marit didn't reply. Nor did she appear at all surprised to see Maaya there; if anything, she looked almost pleased.

"Could you close the door again? Just so no one hears," Marit asked quietly, and Adelaide obliged.

"Seriously, you okay?" Adelaide pressed.

"Not really. I need your advice. Both of you, if you don't mind," she said, and Maaya stared up at her in surprise.

"Of course. What do you need?" Adelaide said, taking a seat back on the bed and inviting Marit to join her. Marit remained standing.

"Promise you won't make fun of me?"

"You have my word."

Marit hesitated, her eyes darting back and forth as she appeared to struggle with what to say next. Then she stared up at her older sister.

"How do you do it all?"

"Huh? Do what?"

"You didn't do what our parents wanted you to. I mean, you played nice with them, but when it came down to it you always did what you wanted. It didn't matter how much they shouted or scolded or guilt tripped you. Meanwhile I can't imagine saying no to them. How have you always been like this?"

Adelaide took a deep slow breath.

"The answer probably isn't one you'll want to hear. It's simply that I came to know what I wanted and wasn't going to let anyone stop me from getting it. What was right for me was too different from what was expected of me here, and you know our parents: they never listened and never offered any flexibility. I tried to make it work and I tried to make them understand, but the harder I tried the worse it got. By the end, I'd had enough experience with the things I loved to know that our respective ideas about my future were incompatible. I learned, and I still firmly believe, that my life is my own. I didn't want to waste my youth because my parents wanted to live vicariously through me and take credit for my accomplishments."

"But you wanted to do this, didn't you? Be a *libris* elite, I mean," Marit continued intently. "Setting aside all the family business nonsense, don't you love working as an elite?"

"I do. I don't know that I would have chosen it for myself, but after I—"

"Then why did you *leave*?" Marit interrupted, and now she sounded hurt.

Adelaide faltered.

"I… I left because I had to. If I didn't leave our parents would just keep stifling me. I would have been miserable. It's not like I didn't care about my work; I still came back. But our parents and I needed some time apart if there was any hope of salvaging our relationship. What is this about, Marit? This seems an odd thing to bring up out of the blue."

"It wouldn't be out of the blue if you paid any attention to me," Marit muttered. "Look, I get it. You left because they made you miserable. I would have left too if I'd been brave enough. I'm just bitter because I couldn't do the same, and when you left I was the only one left for them to focus on."

"I see… I honestly had no idea it was so bad. They always seemed to be so much more proud of you. They always compared me to you when they wanted to tell me off."

"Addy, please. You're supposed to be so smart. They changed after you left, but in a lot of ways they stayed the same. I think they thought you were a unique case and that they could treat me the same as they always had. They still did to me all the things you hated them doing to you. So what makes you think I want any part of this marriage I'm supposed to take part in? Did you really think this was something I chose myself?"

Adelaide fell silent, and suddenly Maaya understood all of Marit's reactions whenever someone broached the subject of her upcoming wedding.

"So it's true then," Adelaide said slowly. "You got pushed into this wedding and I wasn't around to help you."

"It is. Like I said, I know exactly why you left. *This* is why you left. But knowing why doesn't make me any less bitter. So now I just… I need your help. Both of you. You make this look so easy. Honestly, Addy. One day you leave after turning down the seventh person our parents brought home for you and the next you come home with this pretty girl on your arm. *And* our parents still accept it."

Maaya tried her best to keep a straight face.

"Hey. Come here," Adelaide said, patting the bed next to her. This time, Marit joined her. "I won't say this is easy, exactly, but the reason it probably comes off like that is exactly *because* I turned down all those people. This is working out so well because I chose this for myself. I didn't want my parents choosing *any* aspect of my future."

"And you just… you just went out there and asked her out, did you?" Marit continued hesitantly.

"Oh, no! In fact, we both quite fancied each other but it took us a full week or two to confess. It was a mess, really," Adelaide snorted. "Anyway, Maaya, what do you think? Any advice?"

Maaya thought hard. She'd never been in any sort of marriage situation before, much less an arranged one. Her parents had never tried to force their way of life and their choices on her, and that was mostly due to not having parents. But still, she thought, she knew love, and that was enough.

"Well, I never had parents telling me what to do. The most I had was Saber making fun of me for falling for Adelaide," Maaya smiled. "But I suppose I did have Rahu. And I know that having someone else control my life made me feel miserable. I can't imagine falling in love with Adelaide and having someone tell me I wasn't allowed to. Your family is important, but so are you. You should all work off each other and support each other, not tell each other how to live your lives."

"They'd be really upset if I went and called this marriage off, though," Marit sighed. "They wanted Adelaide to do this for the good of the business, they say, and now that failed it's fallen to me. Even if they hadn't already done all this planning they'd still be upset."

"I think eventually they would understand," Maaya continued encouragingly. "I mean, they seem to have gotten better about Adelaide, right?"

"Yeah, well, she's the savior of the world," Marit grumbled.

"I wasn't when I left," Adelaide argued gently. "When I left I was hurt and desperate. I was mostly just focused on getting out of here before it killed me. But I also knew what I wanted by then, and I took it all. The only exception was Maaya, where I asked politely."

Maaya snorted.

"Maybe not, but why do you think they're so fond of you now? It's because of everything you accomplished," Marit continued.

"First of all, no it's not. We're on good terms because they eventually realized they wouldn't win me over. They had to adapt or they'd lose me. Second, even if it was, that's more motivation for you! Where are you going to get more done? Out in the world living as you like or following mommy and daddy's rulebook?"

"I'll still never come anywhere close to you," Marit said dully.

"So? None of this is a competition. I was deprived of choice and so I made my own. I will not sacrifice my happiness for *anyone.* Now these years have passed I'm even more certain of that than ever. All I'm saying is that you should do the same. Forget this guy. You have your entire life ahead of you. Further, if you need me, I'll be there. I did this routine once with them, and I will do it again for you."

"And for what it's worth, Adelaide is one of the people I admire most because of all this," Maaya added before Marit could reply. "Not because of anything she's done—even though that's all really great—but because of what she's shown me I can do if I'm brave enough to try. I spent my whole life afraid of almost everything, so it was amazing to meet someone who just *did* things even when they were scary. I already knew that I wanted to be in charge of my own happiness, but she taught me how to fight for it, and I promise you that it was completely worth it. It was terrifying, but… well, look at us now."

"Look at us now indeed," Adelaide grinned.

"I… suppose," Marit said heavily. "I just don't know how to tell them."

"Is this really what you want?" Adelaide asked.

"Yes."

"Then that's all they need to know. Not any justifications, not any excuses, just that this is what you want. They can guide you and they can teach you, but in the end, what you want is what's important. They will either accept it or they won't, but if they want to keep you around, they will. You aren't so different from me that they wouldn't be scared you'd leave just like me if they gave you enough trouble."

Marit sighed, rubbing her eyes.

"I guess I have a lot to think about. I'm not the brave one, you know that. And I haven't had years of traveling the world with pirates to help me get any better. But maybe I—"

She broke off as the timepiece on her wrist beeped. She pressed a small button on the side of the dial to turn it off.

"An alarm at this hour? Were you planning on a nap?" Adelaide asked, amused.

Marit glared.

"Not exactly. You guys should come with me; you won't want to miss this."

Marit stood up, but instead of heading for the bedroom door, she walked over to the door leading to the balcony. Adelaide and Maaya followed in some confusion, and this confusion only grew when they followed Marit around to where the balcony overlooked the front yard and they spotted Felix and Cajsa standing not far away. Felix had his arm around his wife's waist and they stood still in a somber silence. Beside them were what looked to be five lightweight paper lanterns, though they were currently dark.

"What's going on?" Maaya asked curiously as they approached.

"Ah! Good, you're here. Just in time," Felix said, turning to greet them. He reached down and handed one lantern each to Maaya and Adelaide, and then to Marit and Cajsa.

Maaya had never held such a delicate object before. It weighed almost nothing in her hands, and she was afraid that if she tightened her grip even a little it might tear.

"Your alarm went off, right, Marit?" Cajsa asked, then stared out over the yard. "Odd. I thought they would have started by now."

"What's starting?" Adelaide asked in bewilderment.

"Just watch. And keep an eye on your lantern; you'll need it soon," Felix answered.

They fell silent. Maaya looked hard, though she didn't know what exactly she was looking for. From here she had an excellent view of their side of the hill, which stretched down toward the lower town and the ocean below. All she could see for miles and miles were the soft flickering lights of Unshala and the coast beyond. It was a beautiful sight to be sure—Maaya had never been on the balcony on this side of the house, and indeed had no idea there was such a view—but the rest she couldn't piece together.

Just then, she saw another light appear from far down near the shoreline. This one flickered just like the others, but it rose slowly into the air like a glowing balloon. Maaya squinted, trying to make out what it could be.

Then came another. And another. And another.

Maaya drew in a soft breath of surprise as the sky slowly filled with lights. Dozens, then hundreds, then thousands came from Unshala below, and then more came from the houses nearby on the hill closer to them. As she stared on in fascination, she realized that each and every light was a paper lantern like the one she held, each burning brightly and moving slowly skyward.

"Oh, stars…" Adelaide gasped quietly.

"In memory of those we lost," Felix explained, not breaking his eyes from the spectacle before them. "One light from every person who still lives."

Within minutes, Maaya could hardly see the black sky behind the lanterns that now surely numbered in the hundreds of thousands. As she looked on she saw streams of lanterns coming slowly from farther down the shore and inland, places too far away to see individual towns.

Maaya almost couldn't breathe. She had occasionally passed funerals when she dared to step foot outside town, and she had always marveled at the beautiful speeches people had come up with to honor their dead. But she had never felt so overcome, so overwhelmed by a moment as she did now, all from a unanimous honor given without saying a word. Every light was its own star, each sent skyward from someone with the name of a loved one on their lips or in their hearts. The sky glowed so bright that Maaya imagined this was not just a symbol for one world alone to celebrate; it was a message from one world to the next, where millions of flickering lights from every corner of this side of the earth all joined together in one powerful and silent voice to say: *We have not forgotten you.*

She heard a scratching sound beside her and then saw Felix light a match. He held it to his own lantern, and then, as the small candle inside caught fire, he gently pushed the lantern away into the air, and it floated ever so slowly skyward toward the others.

Cajsa took the match from him and lit her own, and then the match passed to Marit, and then to Adelaide. Finally, with four lanterns now sent off, Maaya carefully took the match from Adelaide.

She hesitated for only a moment, then gingerly lit the candle inside. The lantern immediately seemed to take on a mind of its own, pulling gently upward. She held on for only a moment as the match burned out in her hand.

"For my family. This is for you guys," Maaya murmured, and then let it go.

Maaya watched her lantern fly slowly away and stared until she could no longer distinguish it amongst the millions of others that moved slowly like a gentle wave. They moved out over the ocean and toward the mountains, so bright and so brilliant that she was sure they could be seen from even Selenthia. It was the most beautiful thing she had ever seen, and the most fitting honor she could think of for those she loved.

An hour passed, and then another. The others slowly went inside, eventually leaving only Maaya and Adelaide on the balcony. The hour was late and they were starting to yawn, but Maaya didn't want to leave just yet. Some of the emotion from the moment had worn away, and the sky began to turn black again as many of the lanterns high above either drifted out of sight or lost their light, but Maaya was comfortable here. She was in the first place she felt she could call home since her departure from Sark, and she was with the woman she loved. Tomorrow they would be heading back to Selenthia, but for now she wanted to stay awake to enjoy every moment of this.

Adelaide, however, seemed ready to at least return to the bedroom; she took Maaya's hand in hers and started walking, and Maaya had no choice but to tag along. All things considered, moving to somewhere a little more private and warm was probably a good thing, she thought.

Maaya closed the door and locked it behind her as they entered, making sure the shades on the door properly covered every inch of the window. Meanwhile, after checking the bedroom door, Adelaide got undressed and flung herself tiredly onto the bed. Maaya nearly became concerned that she had fallen asleep already when she instead rolled onto her side to face Maaya.

"Join me, darling," Adelaide said, sweeping her arm before her on the bed.

Maaya rolled her eyes as she put on Adelaide's oversized shirt.

"How can I resist something so romantic?"

As soon as Maaya slipped into bed, Adelaide put her arms around her and pulled her close, plastering quick kisses all over her cheeks and forehead. Maaya cried out with laughter and tried to escape, but Adelaide's grip was strong. It was only when Maaya tilted her head upward to kiss her firmly on the lips that Adelaide finally relented.

"You know, you seem a lot less shy than you were when we first started this; I like that," Adelaide commented.

"I need to have some of the fun," Maaya replied coyly, delicately trailing her finger down the length of Adelaide's arm. She smiled inwardly as she felt Adelaide tremble slightly beneath her touch.

"Mm, very true. I like that, too," Adelaide said softly, her voice smooth as honey. "You know… this is going to sound silly, but I'm proud of us."

"Proud? How?"

Adelaide propped herself up on her elbow and stared down at Maaya, reaching over and brushing some of her dark hair behind her ear.

"We've just been through a lot, and I'm glad we came out of it like this. What we did… stuff like that changes people. It can make them bitter and unforgiving and callous. I've seen it firsthand. And I know we're both hurting in more ways than one and that we have a lot to think about, but… I like that we're both here together like this. And I guess I… I was afraid that I would lose you, and I'm so glad I didn't."

"I'd say don't be silly, but I was afraid of the same thing. It was nice to have you by my side, but that also meant you were in the same danger I was. But I was fighting to make the world a safe place for us. The whole point of doing that was so we could come back to have moments like this."

Maaya reached over and pulled Adelaide suddenly over to her, wrapping her arms around Adelaide's back. It was Adelaide's turn to squirm in surprise, her protest muffled by Maaya's kiss. Maaya didn't let go for a moment, content to stay locked in this embrace until she was forced to let go only by lack of breath.

When she finally let the older girl go, Adelaide remained still, her eyes still closed as the moment lingered between them.

"What do you think? Am I forgiven?" Maaya asked playfully.

"It's a start. Though you remember I told you I get more than just a kiss tonight if you're okay with that," Adelaide murmured in a quiet and meaningful tone as she slowly opened her eyes. Her face was mere inches from Maaya's, and her fingers toyed playfully with the hem of Maaya's shirt and caressed her back, causing Maaya to bite her lip.

"W-we have to be up early tomorrow," Maaya protested weakly, even as she pulled herself closer until there was hardly a hair's breadth between them.

"Well, we'd best not wait any longer, then," Adelaide hummed.

The lights went out, and tired though Maaya may have been, there would be not a thought of sleep in her mind for hours to come.

40

THE FLEET

The next morning was a bustle of activity. Inga and Halvar returned from their duties at least temporarily to pack up the last of their things from Adelaide's estate and to make sure every last affair was in order before they left. In addition, Felix, Cajsa, and Marit had joined the fray, eager both to help and to get as much time with Adelaide and Maaya as they could.

"I'll be coming back more often now! You don't have to act like I'm leaving for a decade or something," Adelaide complained as Marit burst into tears for the third time that morning.

As Halvar strode off to send a bird to Asmund that they were about ready to go, Inga paused in front of Adelaide, who had managed to free herself of her younger sister's grasp.

"Report?" Adelaide said, straightening her coat.

"The Windfire has been inspected and repairs are complete to your satisfaction. Our stores are full, rigging and sails have been tested, our oar system has been cleaned and is ready for use, and all crew and their possessions are accounted for."

"Fantastic!" Adelaide exclaimed. "Did you manage to fit sleep somewhere in that schedule?"

"I decided to save that for after we left the harbor, Captain," Inga replied with the slightest hint of a smirk, "given that Halvar left more than ample time in his own schedule for such a task."

"Yes, well, he'll be working extra hard once we're out at sea," Adelaide sighed. "Once we get back to the ship your work will be done until tomorrow, so please rest as much as you need."

"Thank you, Captain." Inga then turned to Maaya. "How do you feel? About returning to Selenthia, that is."

"I think I'm okay. I had a lot of time to think about it, and I'm ready," Maaya replied confidently. Inga smiled.

"I'm glad to hear it. I'm sure some nerves will return once we get closer, but you are safe with us. Your return will be ever so different from your departure."

"I just hope it's peaceful. I don't want anything but for people to leave me alone," Maaya said.

"I hope for the same. I assume that will be the case since your record is cleared, but in the event any of them decide they don't quite agree with this change, the crew and I will be more than happy to correct them."

"Th-thanks," Maaya replied nervously. Though Inga's tone was pleasant as ever, the threat behind it was unmistakable, and Maaya again took a moment to be grateful that Inga was on her side.

They spent the next half hour double and triple checking that they had everything together. Finally, however, Felix would have no more distractions, and he put his foot down as he noticed his daughter checking her collar pins in the mirror for the fourth time.

As they sat and talked together, she noticed Felix and Cajsa passing sideways glances at Inga and Halvar, who waited attentively near the door. Though the family had been nothing but cordial to them for the extent of the visit, she detected a tense undertone to all their interactions. Maaya wasn't sure if it was because they were Blackfins or whether it was because they were part of Adelaide's crew. She felt the latter was more likely; though her family had dealings with the Blackfins in the past, she imagined it was a different thing entirely to acknowledge their daughter was involved with them.

Their conversation mostly excluded Maaya, and for once she didn't mind. She no longer felt at all insecure about her place here. They weren't quite her family, but she was feeling more at home by the minute.

Of course, with this contentment and understanding came the realization that she would soon be leaving. She wasn't sure what she was getting into, but she did wish she could stay even just a few days longer. Much of her motivation came from the idea that after bringing down the machine there would be time to rest—and while there technically had been, she had been hoping for more than just a few days before she threw herself into any danger again.

Half an hour later, Inga quietly cleared her throat. Adelaide glanced over at her, and though Inga said nothing, Adelaide nodded.

"Well, our ride's here. I guess it's time to get moving."

Everyone in the room stood up at once, and Adelaide's family converged on her with hugs, tears, and well wishes. Only a moment later Maaya found herself pulled into the middle of it as well, and her desire to stay only grew. Part of her wondered if there was still time to change her mind, to convince Adelaide to leave Selenthia behind.

But then, she thought, that wouldn't be right. Not when Adelaide had gone through so much trouble to make her safe passage possible. What's more, her friends were still there. Alive or dead, she owed it to them to return to them. Rahu and Sark didn't have to be in the picture even if Adelaide was set on going with her. As entertaining as the idea of Adelaide pummeling Rahu into a mere puddle on the dirty ground was, she knew his influence was still stronger than her and her crew.

"Well, it's been a pleasure. I love you guys, okay? I'll visit and write often—though you can come visit me too, you know," Adelaide finished as they finally let go of each other.

"Maybe we'll wait for the political turmoil to settle just a little before we make the trip, but… your father and I have discussed the possibility," Cajsa offered.

"Fair enough. I'll keep you up to date. Oh, I want to thank you as well. I know this isn't exactly what you had in mind for my future, but I appreciate you accepting my choices. I hope I can count on you to do the same in the future as well," Adelaide continued.

"Of course!" Felix replied happily. "Why do you say so? Are you planning something even more… extraordinary?"

"Not necessarily. I'm just saying I appreciate your open-mindedness. I'm glad to know my parents still accept me even after I made choices they disagreed with, is all," Adelaide said pointedly. Behind her parents, Marit smiled slightly.

"Oh, my dear. You're our daughter. I suppose parents are always hardest on the oldest—your brother would certainly tell you that—but we just did what we thought was best for you. In the end, what was most important was that we stayed together as a family," Cajsa answered warmly.

"I'm so glad. Keep in touch! I won't be hard to find. But for now we'll be off before we set a bad example by running late. Commander, Lieutenant, let's move. Oh, drat. Chronis! Where are you?"

Maaya heard a whirring noise from above, and looked up just in time to see the spider leap from the overhanging chandelier onto Adelaide's arm, wrapping tightly around it. She shuddered, remembering what Adelaide had said about its affinity for jumping onto people's faces from above.

And then they were gone, out the door and into the carriage, and Maaya felt a weight in her heart as she watched Adelaide's home disappear behind the trees. Not knowing when she would see it again was the worst part. Even when things were stable, it was still a big world out there. She took some small comfort in knowing that it would always be there for her when she returned.

The ride seemed much longer than Maaya remembered, but finally the carriage slowed and then stopped. Maaya glanced out the window and smiled when she saw the docks and the familiar sight of the Windfire.

"My baby!" Adelaide exclaimed, flinging open the carriage door and stepping out into the sun. She waited for Maaya to follow, but Maaya could tell it was taking all her energy to hold herself there.

As they approached the ship, a chorus of greetings came from the deck and surrounding docks. Maaya saw mostly familiar faces in the crowd, but there were also dozens of others who had gathered, she assumed, to pay their respects before Adelaide left Krethus. To her slight consternation, she realized most of them were staring at her, too.

Just then a figure hurried up to them, and after a moment, Maaya recognized the elderly man who had watched Maaya and Adelaide training on the field. He had been the one who bowed to her and thanked her for her service. She had never expected to see him again, but here he was.

"Ah, I'm glad to have seen you before you left! I want to pass on my sincere congratulations and my thanks. I knew we were right to put our faith in you. Thank you for making our beautiful home a safe place to live once more," he exclaimed happily, bowing slightly before them again.

"I'm glad we could help," Maaya answered with a smile.

"Really, most of your thanks should go to Maaya. I did what I was trained to do, but she was the one who found the way past the barrier," Adelaide added.

"So I heard! What a marvelous but mournful tale, I must say," the man continued. "I am sorry to hear of your friend, and I wish you all the luck in the world. If you're truly going back to Selenthia, I hope you give that man —Rahu, was it?—a good walloping from all of us here."

Maaya laughed.

"I definitely haven't ruled that out yet. If I find a way to do that I'll tell you that story, too."

Looking positively delighted, the man bowed his head again, and then stepped away to give them room.

"The crew is all accounted for, Captain, but I believe it would be prudent to give a last call before we depart, if only so we don't lose anyone like we lost our previous commander," Inga suggested. "It's nearly eleven, so we must get moving."

Adelaide grinned, then stepped up onto a nearby shipping crate and turned to face those mingling on the docks.

"May I have your attention please?" she called, her loud voice ringing through the square. Everyone quieted and watched her immediately. "To those of you who came to see us off, thank you so much for your support. It calms my heart to know my beloved hometown will be safe in my absence. For better or worse, though, you haven't seen the last of me; I'll be returning yet. And to those of you who belong on the Windfire, but for whatever reason are not already aboard, get to your stations!"

Everyone within earshot burst into uproarious applause, even those who headed swiftly for the ship so as not to be chastised again.

As the last of the crew boarded, leaving only Maaya, Adelaide, Inga, and Halvar on the docks, Adelaide put her arm around Maaya's waist and stared back across the square.

"I'm really going to miss this place. It seems to get more beautiful every time I see it."

"I'm going to miss it, too," Maaya said wistfully. "I loved it here. The town, the people, your family… everything was wonderful here."

"I'm so glad. Everything went so much better than I thought it would. And it's a shame to leave with that in mind, but that's exactly why we're doing this, you know? It's not just me getting back to work. It's also so one day you can think of your home the same way you think of mine."

"Home is where I want it to be, isn't it?" Maaya said meaningfully.

"I suppose it is," Adelaide smiled. "Still, we'll do our best. Come on; let's get aboard."

"What exactly are we going to do while we're there, anyway?" Maaya asked as they crossed the boarding platform onto the ship. Despite her time away from the Windfire, she had no trouble keeping her balance this time. "When you told me how you managed to clear my record in Selenthia, you said something about this was only the start. What did you mean?"

"We'll get to that," Adelaide answered airily, then turned around to place her hand on Maaya's shoulders and briefly kiss her forehead. "I'm sorry, but I need to get us under way; it's very important that we leave on time. Just give me a few minutes, okay?"

Maaya agreed, and Adelaide beamed, then stepped away, already calling out orders. The lines holding the ship to the dock were loosened and the ship started to move ever so slowly out to sea. A few moments later she heard the familiar sound of the steam-driven oar machine hiss behind the ship, followed by splashing water as the oars themselves got to work.

As the ship ever so slowly began to drift away from the docks and as the last of the lines were cast off, another resounding cheer came from land as everyone who had gathered to see them off pushed closer to the water's edge to watch the ship for as long as they were able. Maaya heard her own name called numerous times, and so she waved awkwardly, worrying it would be impolite to simply walk to a more private area of the ship. Now that people actually seemed to appreciate her, she thought it would do her well to at least attempt to hold up her end of that odd relationship.

With Adelaide still busying herself with the duties of the ship, Maaya took to wandering about the deck as soon as the crowds were nearly out of earshot when she was no longer obligated by custom to remain in sight. She imagined the captain would be more than just a few minutes despite her promise; she was back on her newly repaired ship and would easily want to make sure every tiny detail was in order, and likely to take on half the crew's work herself to make sure it was all done correctly. For her to do anything else would be almost concerningly out of the ordinary.

Maaya watched her, a small smile on her face, as she swept across the deck carrying the full weight of her position on her shoulders with joy. Her augmented arm glittered in the late morning sun as she took to moving and securing cargo, pulling lines, and helping her crew stay on top of things. They hadn't lost their skill, but they had lost a little discipline, which Adelaide was only too happy to restore. For anyone else a ship might have seemed a small and limiting place, but Adelaide hadn't looked so free in a long time.

With everyone too busy for idle chatter, Maaya walked over to the port railing near the bridge and leaned up against it, staring out across the ocean as the occasional mist brushed her face. She watched the gently rolling waves, the puffy white clouds above, and another ship in the distance that looked to be leaving port as well. The last time she had gazed out on the ocean, Saber had been with her, and if Maaya closed her eyes she could almost feel her presence there, floating right beside her as she prepared to offer advice or offer some snarky comment.

She sighed quietly and opened her eyes again. Even though her relationship with Adelaide had clearly changed from the last time she had been aboard the Windfire, there was still going to be a hole in her heart.

For their part, the crew seemed mildly subdued. Though they laughed and joked as they usually did, there was the faintest of somber overtones to everyone's conversation regardless of subject. None of them looked at Maaya or spoke to her save for polite waves and passing glances as they attended to their work, and so Maaya did not want to assume it had anything to do with Saber's absence, but it gave her some comfort to imagine it so.

Maaya paced the deck and then stared out off the starboard side this time. More waves, more clouds, another ship. The ocean wasn't particularly diverse in terms of things to look at above the waves. She watched the ship, trying to imagine where it might be headed, who was on board, and what their business was in the world. Unshala's port may as well have been abandoned compared to Levien, so it was nice to see they weren't as alone as she felt on the water. She hoped they remained nearby for a while, at the very least so she could take some constant reassurance from their distant presence.

A few minutes later Adelaide sprung out from below deck, quickly locating Gunnar, who was busy overseeing some last minute-rearrangements before the sails dropped. She appeared to ask him something, and he stared hard off both port and starboard before turning to give the captain an affirming nod. Whatever news he had given her must have been good, because she smiled all over again and then moved on. Locating Maaya above, she trotted up the stairs to meet her, looking positively exhilarated. Gunnar followed close behind, and he smiled in greeting as he approached.

"Pleasure to see you again, Maaya. I'm sorry we weren't able to meet at all before getting to work," he said.

"That's okay! I suppose we arrived at the last minute," Maaya answered. "How was your vacation? You saw your family, right?"

"My wife, that I did. It was relaxing, and just what I needed. Unfortunately, the Windfire will be without me for some time next year; I promised to take a few months off to spend with her as I've been otherwise so attached to duties that keep me away from her."

"That's sweet of you! I'll miss you here, but I'm sure she loved to hear that," Maaya smiled.

"She did. The captain not so much, but we're all allotted our time away for family reasons," Gunnar said, winking at Adelaide. "Am I to take this to mean you'll be joining the Windfire, Maaya?"

"Oh, I don't know. I haven't really thought that far ahead. For now I'm just focused on getting back to Selenthia, but I have a feeling I'll find myself wherever Adelaide is," Maaya said wryly, and Adelaide grinned widely.

"So I've heard. Congratulations to the both of you; I'm glad you both finally worked out how to tell each other," Gunnar returned, clearly amused.

"Was it really that obvious?" Maaya asked, her face flushing.

"To the entire ship, just about. Speaking of, Halvar owes me twenty rial. He never thought you'd manage."

Adelaide snorted and raised her eyebrows incredulously.

"He didn't, did he? Oho, he and I are going to have a conversation very soon."

"Just name the time and place, ma'am; I'd like to be in the audience."

They both laughed, and then Gunnar departed quickly to return to his work.

It soon came time to drop the sails, and as soon as they fell and caught wind, the Windfire surged forward as the crew let out a raucous cheer. Adelaide pumped her fist, and then leaned back against the outer wall of her cabin, a smile still on her face.

"It feels so good to be back out on the water again. This is where I really feel at my best."

"I have missed it," Maaya admitted. "I really could see myself doing this more often if you'll have me."

"Of course!" Adelaide answered instantly. "I don't envy Gunnar his situation; if my girlfriend wants to travel the world with me I would only be too happy to accept."

"Do you think Inga would be okay with me using her quarters that often?" Maaya asked, and Adelaide shook her head.

"No, but that's because you wouldn't be using them. You get to stay in my quarters now. The bed's more than large enough for two, but still just small enough that you might be forced to lie in my arms every night."

"Oh, stop," Maaya replied, blushing furiously as she lightly smacked Adelaide's shoulder. Adelaide laughed gleefully and kissed the top of Maaya's head.

As Maaya returned to watching the water off the port beam, her eyes fell again on the ship she had seen before. She had initially been concerned that it might sail out of sight quickly, but if anything it now seemed closer than before. Far behind it was a second ship, whose course also seemed similar.

She turned to search for the ship off the starboard beam, and noticed that it too remained steady in course and speed. Curiously, behind that ship was also a second, which also held the same course. She could only guess that the end of the war meant that travel between the two countries was allowed again, which meant much more deep-sea travel. Still, she thought, she had not seen any other Krethan vessels on her way in—or perhaps she simply hadn't noticed them, preoccupied as she had been with her anxiety over stepping foot on land deemed the enemy's.

Adelaide squinted out at the ships, and her lips moved ever so slightly, but she said nothing. Before Maaya could inquire, Adelaide smiled down at her and gestured toward the door to her cabin.

"What say we get some lunch? I didn't eat nearly enough with all the chaos this morning."

Maaya agreed, her mild curiosity no match for the rumbling in her stomach. Adelaide sent for vegetables and sandwiches, and they ate with gusto. Maaya's concerns had all but left her; beyond her grief, her surroundings and company were too familiar for her to be afraid.

Every so often there would be a knock at the door which Adelaide had left ajar, and a sailor or officer would enter the room to greet the two of them during a temporary lull in work. They greeted Maaya with the same familiarity as Adelaide, which lifted her spirits some. Most who came also offered their condolences, however brief they were, and Maaya soon guessed that the entire ship was aware of what had happened, and this too gave her heart. Here too she felt like family, and she was glad to be back.

Just when Maaya thought she might start to feel overwhelmed at the number of people entering the cabin to pay their respects, Adelaide got up and gave an order to Gunnar that she was not to be disturbed unless it was a matter of utmost importance. Then she closed the door and locked it behind her.

When she returned, rather than sitting in her chair, she pushed herself up onto her desk and sat there instead, swinging her legs back and forth. By now Maaya knew this to mean that there was something bothering her or something she wanted to discuss.

"What's up?"

"Just thinking, that's all. We have this one last task ahead of us, but after that, we're finished. No more ghosts, no more evil murderers, nothing. Apart from the usual grind there's nothing else for us to worry about."

"Finally," Maaya said with a smile. "I was starting to think I'd never see the end of it or that something else would come up like always."

"Likewise. And as much as I appreciate a good adventure, I'd rather my adventures be of my choosing rather than some outside obligation. After this I'll have just that freedom. But it has got me to thinking…"

"About what?" Maaya pressed gently.

"About my future. About *our* future, I mean. When we both have the freedom to go and do what we choose, what will that mean for us?"

Maaya felt a shiver of anticipation run down her spine. She knew this conversation would inevitably come, and she hoped it would come soon. The truth was, one reason she dreaded returning to Sark was because once she fulfilled her promise to her friends to return—however that would be done—Maaya and Adelaide would no longer be linked by any sort of outside obligation. She wanted to stay with Adelaide, but such togetherness would then come entirely of their volition, and she was afraid something about that wouldn't work out.

Still, she had to try. She knew she wanted to be with Adelaide for as long as she could be, and there was only one way to find out if Adelaide felt the same way.

"To tell the truth, I don't know. But I know what I want to happen. I want to stay with you, whatever that means and wherever you go," Maaya answered assuredly. She had run over this kind of answer many, many times in her mind over the past few days.

"Me too!" Adelaide answered enthusiastically. "I mean, I don't know exactly how that would work, but I feel like we could figure it out, right? If we can beat that machine, something like our personal situation should be a piece of cake."

"I'd like to think so. How hard could it be?" Maaya said.

"I've just been thinking about Marit, too," Adelaide continued distractedly, as though Maaya hadn't spoken. "Feeling compelled to marry someone she doesn't like at all… I know the feeling, and it's not a good one. I can't imagine being in that kind of relationship for the rest of my life. It makes me all the happier we connect on the level we do, you know? That you appreciate my strange life and are willing to come with me on my travels."

"Of course! We talked about this, remember? I'd thought mostly about settling, but realized I'd be okay with a life like this as well."

"I remember. And I'd thought mostly about living like this, but realized I'd be happy to settle in the right place with the right person. It's a strange thought, settling. My family would get such a kick out of it. But I do want to in some respect. You told me about your dreams and they seemed so wonderful."

"They really are. I would love a life like that," Maaya answered.

Neither of them looked at each other as silence fell over them. Maaya felt like they were both dancing around something they both wanted to say but that neither of them were brave enough to utter. Maaya wasn't even entirely sure what that was, but there was a feeling in her heart pushing itself closer to the surface with each passing day, and the more they talked about their future, the more this feeling took shape.

"Well! We'll figure it out," Adelaide said suddenly, hopping down from the desk and clearing her throat nervously. "Anyway, help me out, would you? I need to get this cabin at least some sort of organized now all my things are here, and I'm afraid the repair crews left something of a mess behind."

Two hours later, Adelaide confessed that their work and chatter was not enough to distract her urge to command her ship, and so they walked back out onto the deck where Gunnar and Inga now stood at the bridge. Here, Maaya did a double take.

The ships that had been traveling parallel courses on both sides of them were now definitely closer. The first ships were now less than a mile away on both sides, and the ships behind them were coming much closer as well. Now she had a better glimpse of them she could tell that they were somewhat smaller than the Windfire, but that they were still armed with guns and traveling swiftly. Maaya's curiosity quickly turned to concern as she realized the ships were on a certain intercept course for the Windfire.

"Who are they? Do you know?" Maaya asked nervously. Her only consolation for the moment was that the crew seemed entirely unconcerned by the ships' imminent arrival.

In response, Adelaide leaned slightly toward Gunnar without taking her eyes off the oncoming ships.

"Could you verify these are the guests we're expecting?"

Gunnar nodded, and his ocular implant whirred quietly as it zoomed in to provide him a better look. After only a moment, he spoke.

"Confirmed, ma'am. They're flying our flag—quite brazenly for this close to shore, too."

Maaya stared back and forth between them in confusion, then squinted at the nearest ship. She saw a black flag hanging from the mainmast, though with the wind it was hard to tell exactly what was upon it. But then, during a brief gust that pushed the flag momentarily upright, Maaya gasped quietly. The black cloth with white markings was shaped like a very familiar-looking fin.

"Ah, looks like you know who they are now," Adelaide grinned as Maaya stared back at her.

"Wh-what's going on?" Maaya asked tremulously. If they were Blackfins and Adelaide knew they were coming, they must be friendly—but for what purpose they were arriving, Maaya could only guess.

"Don't worry; they're friends," Adelaide explained. "I had to call in a few favors, but with some effort I was able to muster this group of Blackfins together. They'll be sailing with us to Selenthia."

"Why? You don't think we'll be attacked at sea again, do you?" Maaya continued, feeling her stomach drop at the thought.

"Not at all! No, this is something quite different. Some time ago I asked if you'd ever consider going back to Sark, and you said no even when I offered to go with you. You said Rahu was simply too strong and that we wouldn't stand a chance against him and all the people he's brainwashed. I realized you were right: the Windfire's crew simply isn't enough to face down a town full of people even if we're only looking for one man. So I thought I'd make things a little more equal."

Maaya stared at her, dumbfounded.

"You… they're… to Sark?!"

"Yes. If one ship and its sailors can't stand against Rahu, then maybe six can. And this isn't *entirely* because you're cute and because I love you. Here." Adelaide reached deep into her coat pocket, and to Maaya's utter surprise, she pulled out the goldpin Maaya had used when she first boarded the Windfire, and handed it to her. "In saving my life repeatedly and working with me to save my home and my country, you've more than earned this. Now it's my turn to pay you back. I give you my word upon the symbol we unite under that you will not return to Sark alone."

Maaya was too overwhelmed to speak, and she took the pin wordlessly, staring between it, Adelaide, and the oncoming ships. This couldn't be real. If everything else hadn't already been evidence she was just dreaming, this definitely was. She stuttered a few times, then fell silent, unsure of how to pronounce anything even if she did know what she wanted to say.

"Cap'n, you really should tell the poor kid at least some of your plans in advance. The big reveals are great but you've gone and done away with her voice," Halvar commented as he walked slowly up the stairs to join them.

"You know I like to wait in case something doesn't pan out! Especially here; I'd have looked very foolish if I promised something like this and then failed to deliver."

"I'm not sure failing to deliver is something you're capable of. And believe me if I had even one example of failure in mind I would annoy you about it every day for the rest of my life, which I understand would be short."

"So… so what, are you telling me that all these people are just going to come into Sark with us and… I don't know, beat up Rahu?" Maaya asked, finally regaining at least a fundamental grasp of language.

"I don't know. That's up to you," Adelaide said, and as she continued, the smile on her face grew at Maaya's increasingly flabbergasted expression. "You know Sark, its layout, and its people like none of the rest of us do. So you're in charge, if you like! Give us the battle plan and we'll carry it out. Though if you want my advice, let's go for something a little more severe than 'beating up' Rahu; I didn't call together this force to travel across the world and kick a man in the shins, you understand."

At the stricken look on Maaya's face, Inga quickly added, "I believe what the captain means to say is that this is an *offer* of service, and that you would have the privilege of leading this expedition only if you desire it."

"Well, that's just… I mean, that…" Maaya stammered helplessly. Fully aware she wouldn't be forming a complete sentence within the next few minutes, she closed her mouth determinedly and leaned her back against the outside wall of the cabin. She wished Saber were there to help her, though she could already guess what the ghost would have told her.

Are you kidding? Your record has been cleared and you're sailing home with an army at your back! I would have to disown you if you didn't take advantage of this.

The truth was, she wanted to. She very much wanted to. She had often daydreamed of returning heroically to Sark and punishing Rahu herself, whether that meant sending him to jail, or, in the case of some of her more adventurous imaginings, defeating him in a one-on-one battle while a cheering crowd of the people she liberated looked on in admiration.

But whenever she applied even a modicum of reality to these scenarios, she always came up short. Rahu's influence ran deep throughout the city like tendrils grasping every home and every person. By now he had surely turned every last person against her and cast out or killed any dissenters. Her absence meant that there was no one to challenge his version of events—not that Maaya had been at all successful in doing so even when she had the chance.

Then, as it so frequently did, the image of Adelaide dying before her just like Svante did came unbidden to her mind. She knew this could come true if she agreed, and that it would put a final, miserable, and horrific end to all her hopes and dreams.

And yet…

Maaya glanced around her, across the deck of the Windfire and off both sides of the ship. The five ships sailing together painted a formidable image, and she had seen all of the men and women aboard the Windfire in battle before. They were not simple townspeople whose greatest weapon was the fear and ignorance they wielded in spades. While these sailors' purpose was not battle, they were more than capable of engaging in it, even against impossible odds. She imagined the average sailor on board the Windfire would be almost insultingly more capable in combat than even the hardiest citizen of Sark—and, from her experience, most law-enforcement officers.

Even amidst the fear that tried to creep its way into her heart, she couldn't deny the opportunity she was being presented. Upon some reflection she realized she had never really taken any plan to return to Sark seriously because she never thought it would be possible to begin with. Going back alone or with Adelaide—even if her crew joined her—would still put them up against insurmountable odds. But if this really was happening then they actually stood a fighting chance. If she chose to do this, for the first time in her life, she might be facing a situation at an advantage.

"Hey, uh, you okay?" Adelaide asked, her smile fading slightly. "I didn't put too much on you at once, did I?"

"No, I… well, yes, you did," Maaya admitted with a short laugh. "I just never expected anything like this to happen! I've been afraid of going back to Sark ever since I left, even if you came with me, and now… now this."

"You don't have to do this if you don't want to," Adelaide continued gently. "I have more than enough reasons to pursue him on my own. He openly blackmailed my government and killed one of my country's people. Thus far he's seen no repercussions for any of his actions, am I wrong?"

"Well, no, but shouldn't that be up to the Selenthians? If Krethans come in to Selenthia to attack Selenthian people that could look terrible!"

"It could, I acknowledge that. And if I had any faith in Selenthian authorities I would put them to this task instead. But I don't. They were told of one of their citizens' actions in our communication and their response was *lacking*. The rest gets… tricky."

"The rest of what? Tricky how?" Maaya pressed.

"During peace talks between the two countries, Rahu and what he did came up a few times. Krethus wants to see him punished, and Selenthia acknowledges he was wrong, but feels that them letting you off the hook was all they needed to do. Nothing came of the blackmailing since it failed and you're still alive, so they feel they can't pursue a man for the crime of making an incorrect accusation."

"I'm not sure I understand. You already said Selenthia didn't want to do anything about him."

"Yes and no," Adelaide continued slowly. "See, in order to make peace happen, the two countries still had to agree on this issue since Krethus obviously takes it very seriously. So eventually they made something of an agreement. They said that Krethus was forbidden from acting directly on the matter, but that if the matter were in some other way resolved, Selenthia would… well, not sanction it exactly, but effectively look the other way. It's the same sort of grey area that let us off the hook after our battle even though we destroyed some of their ships. See what I meant about complicated politics?"

"Wait, so they're letting us in to do something about Rahu?" Maaya asked, aghast.

"Not exactly. No one from the Krethan government or military is allowed to take any action against Rahu as that would be an act of war from another country on their own soil, a place Krethus has no jurisdiction. But the Blackfins… now that's another thing. And that's why this works. This isn't something ordered by Krethus even if they know it's happening."

"But Selenthia knows about it too. How could they not have a problem with it even if it's not Krethus itself?" Maaya continued. Her head was spinning, and that was at least partially because Adelaide's explanations actually made some sense.

"They don't know exactly what might happen, if anything will happen at all, and they want to keep it that way. Please understand: to them, Rahu is just one man from a small town most people haven't heard of. The tradeoff is immense. If they try to protect one unimportant man for his foolishness, peace talks will be off and the war might even be spurred onward if Krethus thinks Selenthia is keeping safe a person who directly attacked their government and countrymen. But if justice somehow meets him, they get to call an end to the entire war, open up trade negotiations, encourage an economic boost the likes of which we haven't seen in decades, all sorts of things. It ends up being the best option even if it's not the most legal of solutions."

"What he did wasn't very legal, either," Maaya argued pointedly.

"And I disagree with conflating the two issues because of that. He is a manipulator, a blackmailer, an abuser, and a murderer. Responding to that using less-than-legal means does not put my actions on the same level as his."

"No, that's… I didn't mean… it's just that Sark is very far into Selenthian territory and I don't want there to be trouble, that's all," Maaya said weakly.

"I wouldn't have gone through all this trouble if I didn't think we could succeed," Adelaide said encouragingly. "We have no quarrel with Sark or its people—just one man. If we engage anyone else it will be in self-defense. Further, we're no killers. Not even of someone like Rahu."

"So… what do you hope to do?" Maaya continued. Though she argued, she hoped she would lose. She wanted nothing more than for Adelaide to convince her that this would all work out okay.

"To remove this dangerous man from power. For all I care Sark can remain exactly the same apart from his sudden disappearance, but he's proved himself a danger to the world and his influence extends far beyond Sark. He's the reason you were pursued in every place you visited in Selenthia. He's the reason the Selenthian fleet attacked us on the water. He's the reason my countryman was killed, your friends were killed, and you had to run. He is objectively a criminal, and one way or another he needs to be stopped. Even if you weren't involved, this would be done somehow."

"I suppose I understand… but what about all the people on his side? He won't be alone. How would we avoid involving them?"

"So far they've had no influence but Rahu's. I hope they'll be more inclined to reason once there's a competing power. If they aren't they can stay in Sark, and anyone who wants to leave safely will be free to do so. Listen… I'm under no delusion that we will march in there and fix all of Sark's problems. That's a far greater challenge than I'm prepared for and it's not my place. But bringing justice to Rahu would be a start."

Maaya hesitated. The more Adelaide spoke, the fairer her proposition seemed. Maaya wasn't sure if it was possible to fix Sark at all, but a smaller goal like getting rid of Rahu and helping others escape safely was much more manageable.

With that in mind, she had only two concerns remaining.

"Well… what about the crew and everyone else who's joining us? There could be fighting and people could get hurt."

"Everyone with us here today is fully aware of what to expect. They had every option to sit this one out, but none did," Adelaide explained proudly. "Obviously we'll try our hardest for diplomatic solutions. Our numbers just ensure we have a backup plan."

"That makes sense... I guess I just… it's hard to believe so many people would do something like this when they don't get anything from it. Most of them probably don't even know who I am or that Sark existed before this."

"Maybe that was true at one point, but news spreads fast. Most of Krethus knows your name now, Maaya. What's more, most of these Blackfins are here because I called in a big favor and they're happy to honor it. But that aside, who needs to personally gain something to help someone else? I explained the situation and asked for help, and these are the people who showed up to provide it."

Maaya nodded distractedly. Eventually, she thought, this was a lesson she might learn.

"Okay. Then I guess there's only one thing left. What of me? You just went through all the trouble of trying to get my record cleared, but if Selenthia decides they have a problem with me being there…"

At this, Adelaide stepped over and put a comforting hand on Maaya's shoulder.

"For this I offer you only one promise," Adelaide said hesitantly. "I promise that whatever happens, you will be safe with me. I can't promise that we'll be successful or that Selenthia might not take issue with your involvement if you choose it, but I can promise that, to whatever end, I will make sure you are safe. Even if that means having to run back to Krethus together. I don't think that will happen—in fact, I mean for it not to—but I have not forsaken thoughts of your safety in this endeavor."

Maaya let out a slow breath. This was really happening. All the politics of the situation aside—which it seemed Adelaide had gone to great lengths to account for—she was going back to Selenthia with several ships full of Blackfins at Adelaide's command, prepared to face down the one man who had made Maaya's life beyond miserable for years. Her left hand drifted over her coat pocket in which Kim's diary was tucked away safely. Kim would likely be here today if not for him. They all would.

What's more, she thought, she had proven herself to be free of Sark's influence and free of the need to return. If she was forced to leave again, so long as Adelaide was at her side… would it really be so bad?

Maaya bit her lip nervously, then stared up at the captain.

"I think I want to do this."

Adelaide beamed delightedly and hugged Maaya tightly, causing Maaya to gasp as the breath left her lungs.

"I knew you would! I'm so glad. It'll be worth it, you'll see. We'll take care of that evil man and make sure your friends are safe, and that'll be the end of it. No more fighting, no more stress. Just the rest of our peaceful lives ahead of us."

Maaya smiled happily. Adelaide's positivity was contagious, and her words comforted her.

"So how long have you been thinking of this, anyway?" Maaya asked. "I know this wasn't a last-minute decision; you've had it out for Rahu for a long time, haven't you?"

"Ever since you told me about him. Remember when you first told me your story after coming aboard and I said if I was ever out that way I might have to meet him? It's been ever since then. That's what Inga and Halvar were working on, the thing Halvar almost accidentally revealed about six times."

"In my defense, I knew you'd always be there to interrupt me," Halvar retorted.

"You really are determined," Maaya said incredulously, shaking her head.

"I just like to make sure all loose ends are tied up. Besides, I love you, and the fact that there was someone out there who'd hurt you who hadn't yet been on the receiving end of my ire was very distressing."

"My hero," Maaya teased, standing on tiptoe to plant a kiss on Adelaide's cheek. "I used to daydream all the time about a girl who loved me coming to my rescue and taking me away from Sark. But I was never able to imagine anything quite like this."

"So I'm *better* than the girls of your dreams," Adelaide returned instantly.

"My old dreams, maybe. But now you're the only girl I dream about," Maaya replied with a wink, and they both burst into laughter.

"Oh, stop it," Halvar pleaded from nearby. "I've never thrown up on a ship before, but now I just might."

"By the way, ma'am, since you mentioned our fleet of six, I just want to point out that our sixth is here," Gunnar reported, staring keenly out off the starboard side.

All eyes turned to follow his gaze, and after a moment, Maaya did a double take. She wasn't sure how she had missed *that* ship approaching.

"No," Maaya said, her mouth falling open in surprise.

"Oh, yes," Adelaide replied happily.

Even with the still significant distance between them, there was no mistaking the massive shape of the Nocte Cadenza. It was making all sail directly for them, and from what Maaya could tell it had been repaired extensively since she last saw it. She wondered if its captain would pay them a visit ahead of its arrival like last time, and sure enough she soon saw three shimmering shapes flickering over the water toward them.

Captain Skarin and his two flanking guards appeared on deck only minutes later, stopping before Adelaide and Maaya in greeting.

"It's a privilege to see the both of you again so soon, and for such a pleasurable excursion as this," he rumbled in his gravelly voice.

"And you!" Adelaide replied delightedly. "I'm glad you could make it."

"The alternative would be missing an opportunity to cause trouble for some Selenthians, and that just isn't realistic," Skarin answered, though when he caught Maaya's expression, he continued, "Of course, I would always come to the assistance of a friend in need. I was a little worried there would be no excitement left after you saved the world. It's a little hard to top that, you know."

"Maybe, but skies forbid I even think of retiring. No, I'll be sharing the sea with you until I'm old and gray, I promise you that," Adelaide said.

"Consider my fears assuaged," Skarin replied with a slight bow, and then he turned to Maaya. "I heard many stories about you. To keep up with Adelaide is a feat in itself, but to be the reason she's still alive is far beyond that. You've surprised me multiple times over, and I sincerely hope you will continue to do so."

"She saved my life about as many times as I saved hers," Maaya mumbled uncomfortably.

"Perhaps, but I expect greatness from her. I never thought I'd see her meet her match. And from what I understand, that match has been found in more ways than one."

"Absolutely!" Adelaide exclaimed before Maaya could react. "So, what do you think? Good choice?"

"If you're the one who made it, it must be. You could certainly do far worse," Skarin replied with amusement.

"A ringing endorsement coming from you. I'm glad you approve; she'll be with me for the foreseeable future, so expect many visits!"

"I'm counting on it," Skarin said, and then glanced at Maaya again. "I did also hear of your dead friend's heroics. I'm sorry she couldn't make it. My heart to you."

"Thank you," Maaya said, forcing a smile. "I'm sure she would have loved to see you again."

"I do hope so. I lost favor in her eyes when I insulted you, and I was looking forward to the opportunity to earn it back. Perhaps I may yet redeem myself once we arrive in Selenthia."

"And I expect you're doing this just because Adelaide asked you to?" Maaya continued, crossing her arms.

"Mostly. She is a very dear friend, you know. The rest is for you." He laughed when Maaya stared at him in surprise. "What, didn't think you were worthy? Please. We fought side by side in battle and you earned at least some respect and loyalty. Your enemies are mine. Would I be right in assuming you feel the same about me?"

"Y-yes," Maaya grumbled reluctantly, and Skarin chuckled again.

"There you have it. Our allegiance doesn't need to be pretty, but it exists. I'm here to prove it. The fact that it's a Selenthian we're after is only a bonus, not my motivation. Believe me, if my wrath were so uncontrolled as to put down every Selenthian who came my way I would have taken advantage of my invisibility long ago."

"Are you really patient enough to sail with us the whole way there?" Adelaide broke in.

"Indeed. Besides, your ships are fast; my expeditious nature will be thus sated."

Adelaide snorted.

"You, expeditious. Right. Anyway, it truly is a pleasure to have you, and I'm glad we have a few days outside of battle to catch up. Your ship all right?"

"Quite well, thank you. It took a full week to get even make sure she'd still be able to float, but she's in excellent shape now. I regret this man we seek is not within range of my guns."

"Yes, well, if we take him alive we can always send him off the plank and your sailors can do some target practice, what do you say?" Adelaide suggested seriously, then broke off into laughter at Maaya's horrified expression. "Anyway, my friend, I'm sorry, but I have my own ship's business to attend to, as well as some more personal matters. Would you like to catch up sometime before dinner?"

"It would be my pleasure," Skarin answered with a slight nod, and then he and his guards turned and started their return toward the Nocte Cadenza.

"I'm glad you two are getting along now. Sort of," Adelaide said, clearly amused.

"Sort of, yes," Maaya replied flatly. "If he's going to be around constantly over the next few days that might change."

"For better, I hope. He's really not so bad. I do admit his deep-seated anger at Selenthians makes me uncomfortable, but he's learning."

"Good," Maaya said simply, and left it at that.

"Hey. I'm going to take a tour of the ship and make sure everything's in order. Walk with me?" Adelaide suggested almost apologetically, and Maaya quickly agreed. As they started off down the stairs, she made an unenthusiastic promise to herself to give Skarin a chance. She had no intention of proving any of his misconceptions correct, and she supposed another friend in the world couldn't hurt—even if that friendship would come very slowly.

A WEEK AND A HALF LATER, Maaya stepped confidently onto Selenthian soil for the first time since she and Saber had taken a chance and fled what seemed like so long ago. The Windfire and her allied ships had pulled swiftly into harbor, with the exception of the Nocte Cadenza, which had traveled farther down the coast.

As Maaya walked onto the docks at the captain's side, they were stopped by a pair of guards.

"Crew manifest?" one requested in a dull voice that said he had likely said these same words hundreds of times that week alone.

Adelaide handed it over without a word.

"And your names?" the other said as the first guard looked over the sheet of paper before him.

"Captain Adelaide Sol."

"Maaya Sahni," Maaya replied, purposefully pronouncing every syllable with great care so he wouldn't mishear. She stared calmly at the guard, almost daring him to give her trouble.

The man's eyes widened slightly, and the two guards shared a quick look, but if they had anything to say about her they intelligently kept it to themselves.

"Ah, right, well, everything appears to be in order," the first guard said, checking off the two girls' names from the manifest. "Please proceed, and, ah, welcome home."

"Thank you!" Adelaide replied brightly, and without another word they stepped past the guards and into Levien.

The city was just as Maaya remembered it, and this familiarity nearly brought back a wave of fear. If nothing had changed, surely that must mean she was still in as much danger now as she was then.

But she forced this thought from her mind as quickly as it had come. Whether she was in trouble or not was irrelevant now. If anyone brought her trouble she had hundreds of people behind her to give that trouble right back.

No more running.

It was just after midday and the lunch rush was in full swing as people on break from work rushed to their favorite beach-side shops and met with friends who worked nearby. Mechanical birds of all shapes and sizes fluttered here and there, delivering messages all over the city and beyond. Some people waved to Adelaide as they usually did, and she waved back. It was like nothing had changed.

"You know, this is actually a gorgeous city. I've loved it ever since I first came here," Adelaide commented airily. "I thought about getting a place here if ever it came to it. There are some lovely flats that look out over the harbor and downtown, and it's just a quick minute to get here."

"Why haven't you done that? That sounds perfect for you," Maaya said.

"I'd have no one to enjoy it with. It'd get old fast," Adelaide answered morosely. "The vast majority of my time is spent around other people, and that's how I prefer it. Settling down would be great for a day until I remembered I'd come home to an empty flat every time I was here."

"That's fair. I don't think I could live alone either, but I really wouldn't mind a place like this," Maaya said, letting her last few words hang in the air between them. She hoped Adelaide would say something, but she only nodded.

While waiting for the crews of the other ships to finish filing in, they took a short stroll around town. Along the way, Adelaide picked up some delicious baked snacks from a street vendor.

They chatted animatedly as they went, and for a time, Maaya almost forgot where she was. But every so often they would pass a landmark she was familiar with and she would be pulled back to reality. She had no fear of Levien anymore—she had seen a number of guards patrolling the streets, and had even made direct eye contact with them on purpose, but apart from their signs of obvious recognition they had done nothing. Adelaide's plan had worked as perfectly as she could have hoped.

What truly bothered Maaya was the future, and the thought that though she and Adelaide seemed to want the same things that Adelaide would change her mind or wouldn't feel like settling anywhere. Maaya was perfectly happy to stay with her wherever she went, but living on the Windfire for the rest of her life, even if she had access to the captain's quarters, simply wasn't feasible. And it was a little too far from her dreams for her to believe she could ever make it work. She, like Adelaide, didn't want to be forced to accept something that truly didn't work for her.

The fact that Adelaide seemed too nervous to talk about it as well didn't make her feel any better. There was a chance it was because Adelaide was naturally afraid of a huge commitment like that, but equally plausible that she was simply trying to think of a kind way to let Maaya down. Maaya couldn't bear the thought.

"Maaya? Maaya Sahni?"

Maaya stopped walking and turned to see a teenage boy approaching her, panting slightly as though he had just been running.

"Yes?"

The boy sighed heavily with relief.

"Thank goodness. I've been looking everywhere for you. I heard word you were back in town but I couldn't find you! Anyway, you have an urgent message."

"A message? Me?" Maaya asked doubtfully, but the boy nodded and reached into the small bag he had slung over his shoulder. From it, he pulled a small metal bird—one that looked very familiar. A shiver ran down Maaya's spine.

"Th-that's Rahu's bird," she stammered, taking an unconscious step back, but Adelaide was at her side immediately.

"Let's hear it," she told the boy, gripping Maaya's hand comfortingly in hers.

The boy nodded, then instructed the bird to play its message. Maaya held her breath.

Hey! Maaya, it's Roshan.

Maaya nearly cried out with joy upon hearing his voice, but forced herself to remain quiet so she could hear the rest of this message.

I stole Rahu's bird. How about that? Anyway, I don't have a lot of time. I pray you get this. Sark is a disaster and we need your help. We started something big, Maaya. There's a resistance here fighting against him. But he's not alone. He's got the town guard and others on his side. And the ghosts have stopped, so more people are falling back in line with him. He made it clear what he's going to do to us once he takes control of the town back. Please, Maaya. I know you must hate it here, but if you get this, please come back. We need you. I know we can stop him together. I miss you. I hope you're okay.

The bird closed its metal beak and its eyes went dull again.

"When… when did this message arrive?" Maaya asked shakily.

"Five days ago, miss. It was marked as urgent but we couldn't find you anywhere."

"For good reason," Maaya muttered, then glanced up at Adelaide, her eyes filled with concern. She didn't need to say a word.

"All right. We'll do a head count and make sure we've got everyone, make sure everyone's got something to eat, then be on our way. Straight to Sark, right?"

"Actually, I was thinking we could stop in Anorath on our way. There's someone there I think might help us, too," Maaya said.

"Oh, yes! The infamous Emil!" Adelaide exclaimed. "That sounds good. Skarin and his crew will meet us on the way there regardless. By the time we get to Sark we'll have more than enough to help your friend's resistance."

"I hope so. This sounds serious. And if this was sent five days ago…"

"Hey. It'll be okay. If your friend is anything like you he's smart enough to have found a way to hold out. Still, we should get moving."

Adelaide reached into her pocket and pulled out a generous tip for the courier, whose eyes widened in delight as he took the rial in his hands. By the time he looked up to thank the girls, they had already turned and were now making their way quickly toward the docks.

"Have you thought about taking charge?" Adelaide asked as they walked.

"I don't know if I can. The most people I ever directed at once was four," Maaya said halfheartedly.

"That's all right. You can do the same thing here, just with divisions. You wouldn't need to micromanage every single person. Once we know the ins and outs of Sark, where to go, and what to do, the crew can take care of the rest."

"Do you… think I should?"

Adelaide smiled.

"I do. Not just that, but I think you *can.* This is your town and your fight. You're one of the smartest and bravest people I know. Besides… wouldn't it just kill Rahu inside if he saw you leading the charge?"

Maaya paused. That was the most convincing argument she had heard yet.

"All right. I'll lead."

"Aye aye, cap'n!" Adelaide cheered delightedly. "In that case, what are your orders?"

"Don't make this weird."

"Aye, cap'n."

Maaya rolled her eyes, and Adelaide beamed.

"I know the road we can take to Anorath. I also know someone who travels it, so he may be able to send news ahead of our arrival straight to Emil. After that I can go over the layout of Sark, but I'll need to find out where everyone is situated before I send anyone anywhere. To do that I'll need a small group to get me into Sark so I can meet Roshan. Until we know more I want Skarin and his crew to hang back just to be safe."

"Why? Are there others who can see ghosts in Sark?" Adelaide inquired.

"If there are, I bet anything Rahu recruited them as soon as I left. Either way, until we find out for sure, we can't risk anyone from his ship."

"I'll make sure you have the people you need," Adelaide affirmed.

They continued toward the docks, a determined look in Maaya's eyes. There was absolutely no fear anymore. She wasn't running anymore. She was going home—and she had her sights set on her oldest and most dangerous enemy.

41

THE RESISTANCE

In the early evening of the next day, Maaya caught her first glimpse of Anorath in the distance just as the sun began to set. They had taken a brief rest the evening prior, taking advantage of the vast empty fields to set up a massive encampment. Dozens of fires burned between dozens of tents where the crews of Adelaide's fleet settled to rest.

Maaya, who had very much been hoping to avoid a repeat of the sleeping situation she had experienced inside the machine's barrier in Krethus, was relieved to see tents, pillows, and blankets—even if they weren't quite of the luxury she came to expect from the beds in Adelaide's home. Their sleep had been much more restful than she had expected, but at least some of that came from the fact that Maaya had been far too self-conscious to spend any romantic time with Adelaide when they were surrounded closely by hundreds of other people, their only privacy being the thin canvas of the tent. Adelaide had been disappointed, but eventually and reluctantly agreed to sleep.

When Adelaide spotted the first of the far-off buildings, she gasped excitedly.

"Anorath! Oh, how I've missed this place. I hope it's as lovely as I remember from childhood."

"So how exactly did you and Emil meet?" Maaya asked with a small smirk.

"Well, my parents taught me to hide the fact that I could see ghosts when I was in Selenthia. I didn't really understand why, so I didn't do a very good job. Emil was… very perceptive. He talked to me as I was walking through a store with my parents; they didn't want me to talk to him, but it wasn't like they could see him to keep him away, was it? He was just very happy to see a new living person in Levien who could see ghosts; I guess that doesn't happen often."

"No, it doesn't," Maaya affirmed, already feeling exasperated as she remembered her first few minutes in Anorath. "I hope he wasn't quite as interested in you as he was in me."

"Not exactly. I was just a kid who stayed with my parents doing boring stuff most of the time, so I didn't have much to offer. He was a casual friend until I left, but I thought *he* was pretty interesting himself. I can't wait to see him again if he's still around!"

"I'm sure he is," Maaya said shortly.

Maaya had to admit she wasn't as apprehensive or annoyed as her tone suggested. She had only just considered the possibility of liking Emil when it had came time for her to leave, and while she was sure he would be his annoying self again when she returned, he was bound to be eager to help. What's more, her experiences made her more confident that she would be able to tell him off if he annoyed her, whereas that task had previously fallen to Saber.

What irked her this time was hearing Adelaide speak about someone who interested and intrigued her so much. Maaya would never ever admit to feeling even a twinge of jealousy, but as much as she tried to fend it off, trying to explain to her mind that Adelaide would likely not abandon her to skip off into the sunset with Emil, it remained anyway.

She hadn't yet seen Apostol, which disappointed her. She had been hoping to give at least some advanced notice of her arrival—and she also wanted to see him again, at least—but she guessed Emil would know somehow anyway. Knowing was his job, after all.

Sure enough, just as Maaya was about to suggest that she go in alone to look for him, she spotted movement near one of the buildings on the outskirts of town. She stared hard as she saw two figures approach. When they came into full view, she recognized both Emil and Nadya, and she smiled as she trotted over to meet them.

"Well! My goodness gracious, what have we here?" Emil said happily as they met.

"A sight for sore eyes, I assume," Maaya replied, shaking his outstretched hand. Emil beamed.

"I hope you aren't trying to sneak anywheres with that large company with you. No subtlety to them at all, no ma'am."

"We're not doing things subtly this time," Maaya replied, and Emil, if possible, looked even happier than before.

"Wonderful! And speaking of lack of subtlety, where is your friend Saber, now?"

"She's... gone," Maaya said with difficulty. She could explain without crying, but beyond that it had not gotten any easier. "We were able to destroy the machine, but it took her with it. She's the reason we're all safe."

For the second time Maaya could ever remember, Emil's smile vanished.

"I... see. I'm am very sorry to hear that. I know she was special to you. I'm glad you succeeded, but I wish it could have come at a different price."

"So do I. But we got to say goodbye, and that's more than I can say for many of my other friends. But now that's done I can take care of this last bit of unfinished business. It's... it's good to see you."

"And you. Levien has been a little too quiet without you even if traffic did pick up a little after your show."

"Well, unfortunately I'm not back for long. I did bring a few friends, though."

Before he could reply, however, Adelaide stepped up next to Maaya, hopeful anticipation in her eyes.

"Ah, and you've a pretty lady friend with you, too," Emil continued jovially. "Somehow you always manage to bring a beautiful—oh, hold on a moment, what's this? I recognize you! Don't tell me, don't tell me... it's Adelaide Sol, isn't it?"

"It is!" Adelaide exclaimed, then put a hand to her chin. "You're a little shorter than I remember."

"And you're taller. I should have seen that coming given the size of your parents. How have you *been* my dear? Tell me, how is the world so delightfully small that all my favorite people have returned in each other's company?"

They stepped away to speak, though Adelaide took a moment to glance back over her shoulder to mouth *He remembers me!* excitedly to Maaya.

Maaya rolled her eyes, but her mock irritation didn't last long. Nadya, who stood placidly at Emil's side during their reunion, now stepped forward to give Maaya a tight hug. Maaya embraced her happily.

"I have to admit I'm surprised to see you here. I didn't think you'd actually try to come back to this old place," Nadya said warmly.

"I really did want to! If nothing else it would be to see you again."

Nadya blushed ever so slightly.

"I'm so glad. I had hoped you would. I have to admit I was worried the task you had assigned yourself would prove too much and that I'd never see you again. But it appears I've underestimated you," she said, her eyes sweeping the hundreds of men and women behind her. "You're not quite as alone as you were once before."

"No, I'm not. And I don't think I ever will be again," Maaya said, and then her voice softened. "I think I have you to thank for that at least a little. It was something you said just before I left. You told me to believe there never had to be a reason for kindness. I think I wasn't sure I believed that even after I left, but… I guess I hoped. I found the kind ones. They're all here with me and there are more still coming, too."

"I didn't expect it to be a lesson that sunk in quickly; not with the past you've come from. But so long as it did, I'm glad of it. And now you can set one more thing right in the world."

"Yeah. I… how did you know? Did someone tell Emil already?"

"Not at all. He simply guessed your purpose once he saw you approaching. He told me he was confident you'd be coming back one way or another and that he wanted to be ready for you," Nadya laughed lightly. "I'm sure he would be delighted to know he was correct."

"I'm sure," Maaya said darkly. She wasn't going to be the one to tell him. Then she paused as she felt some of her uncertainty return. "So… what do you think? Is this the right thing to do?"

"I do. I understand your trepidation; the idea of personally-enforced justice seems to go against the order that keeps peace in the world, no? But we must all do what we can. Had you left the task of saving the world in another's hands—perhaps the hands of someone whose duty it was to do such a thing—the world would remain unsaved. If you see an opportunity to do good, you shouldn't worry about whether or not you were the one assigned to do it. If you are capable, then the task is yours."

"But this isn't some evil machine, this is a human being," Maaya sighed agitatedly. "I'm not doubting my ability or my desire, but I am a little worried this will take me closer to his level."

"Humans can be evil, too. I think each of us desires to see good in others, because if evil exists in them, it follows it could exist in us as well. But evil and those who fight it are not the same simply because they employ many of the same tools. It is your response that matters. You could easily go and kill him and be done with it—which would still not put you on his level, mind you—but I have a feeling that's not what you're after."

"It's not. I… I just want him to stop. I want my friends to be safe and my town to be free. That's all I want," Maaya said slowly, and Nadya smiled.

"Then there you are."

"Will you be coming with us?" Maaya asked hopefully, but Nadya shook her head.

"I'm no fighter. Besides, now that the strange ghosts have stopped coming around there are more people here both living and dead to look after. I need to make sure everything is attended… oh. Oh my."

Maaya whirled around to see what had so suddenly caught Nadya's attention and saw a dull wave of light approaching them. She immediately recognized the crew of the Nocte Cadenza heading straight for them, with Captain Skarin leading the way.

Maaya and Nadya walked over to meet them, and Adelaide and Emil did the same.

"Remarkable. Absolutely remarkable," Emil whispered, clearly impressed.

"It took us less time to find you than we thought. This empty Selenthian terrain makes it easy to find a small army. Good for us, but our enemies will have the same advantage as we approach," Skarin said, paying no attention to him.

"Glad to have you here. Emil, this is Captain Skarin of the Nocte Cadenza. Skarin, this is Emil. He's one of the first Blackfin contacts I ever made, though I didn't know it at the time."

Skarin stared Emil up and down.

"They have strange fashion sense, these Selenthian Blackfins."

"He's the one who gave me my goldpin," Maaya added hastily.

At this, Skarin seemed slightly more impressed.

"I see. Garb aside, at least you were competent. Am I to assume you're the reason we've stopped here?"

"You are indeed, my good captain!" Emil said brightly. "As wonderful as it would be to assume this whole party just dropped by to pay their respects and receive my well wishes, I wouldn't be a good friend if I didn't offer some assistance of my own."

He raised his arm as he spoke, and from behind the buildings nearby, a small crowd began to emerge. Ghosts and the living alike filed through the gates until at least thirty people stood silently behind Emil, waiting for orders.

"How did you find so many people so quickly? You can't have seen us coming from that far away," Maaya asked, astounded.

"No, but I assumed you would someday return to bring justice to your town that so badly needs it, so I was simply prepared. Besides, I do so look forward to visiting Rahu; I love when a man who views himself untouchable is so painfully and humiliatingly proven wrong."

Adelaide whistled.

"So we have roughly sixty from my ship, nearly a hundred fifty from the others, Skarin and his crew number near four hundred if I remember right, and now you, Emil, and your group… well. I'd say we could just about give Rahu a run for his money, don't you think?"

"Absolutely. I cannot wait to employ a little justice on Maaya's behalf," Emil said delightedly.

"Oh? What makes you think you'll be the one to do it?" Adelaide asked in amusement as she raised an eyebrow.

"Wait," Maaya interrupted, and all eyes turned to her. "Let's not forget what we're doing here. We're going to take care of Rahu however we need to, but that's our only goal. We're not on a mission of vengeance."

"If ever such a mission were to be undertaken, this would be it," Skarin said curtly.

"But it's not. That doesn't mean he won't be punished. I want to see that more than any of you—yes, *any* of you," Maaya continued pointedly as Adelaide opened her mouth to reply. "I frankly wouldn't mind seeing him imprisoned for the rest of his life, because he's got a while left to live yet. And I want to look him straight in the eye as the key gets thrown away."

"Delightfully dull, but manageable," Skarin commented. "I maintain that my crew and I alone would be capable of handling one man."

"It's not just him. He's had the entire town under his thumb since before I was born. Also, if he was able to find me and make me work for him, he might have found someone else who knows *libris* as well, which puts all of you in danger. *Also*, we're going to be helping whoever we can, which means we should also have people who aren't invisible there."

"Ah, this reframe works a little better. We're not just chasing down one man; we're liberating an entire town."

"Yes."

Skarin gave a rattling laugh.

"Perfect. The man whose entire death has been spent despising Selenthians will free a Selenthian town under the command of a Selenthian girl. Times have changed indeed."

"And you with them," Adelaide said, clapping Skarin on the back.

"Do we have everyone?" Maaya asked, and Skarin and Adelaide nodded. "All right. Let's keep moving. We'll take the—"

"Hold on just a quick moment," Emil interrupted. "We don't quite have everyone yet. I'm hoping he'll get here quickly."

"What? Who's missing? Emil, I don't have all—"

"Maaya? Is that really you?"

Maaya started, then turned to face the gate, her eyes wide.

Styx stood uncertainly at the gate, watching the crowd before him with some anticipation. But as soon as Maaya faced him and their eyes met, a wide smile broke out on his face.

"Styx!"

Maaya ran over to him and wrapped her arms around as much of the enormous man as she could, then gasped as he pulled her effortlessly off her feet. She made to say his name, but was already speechless from tears.

"Maaya, ye did it!" Styx exclaimed. "I knew when those ghosts stopped comin' around you'd had somethin' to do with it. Still, I was afraid you'd never come back what with this side of the world being after you an' all."

"I was afraid to, but I couldn't stay away, not ever," Maaya cried. "How have you been? Have you been okay?"

"Aye, mostly," Styx answered, putting one of his massive hands on her back. "No danger to myself, at any rate. Sark's in a lot of trouble, but I've mostly been here. S'been nice to have steady food and people to talk to. Even got some of my instruments fixed up a little. I heard whisperings of going to Sark, but never thought… well, never thought *this* would happen."

He waved his free arm toward the hundreds of living and dead before him and then set Maaya gently to the ground.

"I never did either. Not until I was just starting back home," Maaya said, wiping her eyes on her sleeve. "Speaking of which… I want you to meet Adelaide."

"So this is the Styx I've heard so much about," Adelaide said, stepping up to meet him with her hand outstretched. Styx took it gently and smiled down at her; Maaya almost laughed at the sheer difference in height between them. She had gotten so used to Inga being the only one Adelaide had to look up at.

"Adelaide, huh? Always a pleasure to meet one of Maaya's friends. I hope she's said nothin' too much about me that I can't still make a good first impression."

"I think perhaps she did, but she spoke so highly of you I wouldn't worry," Adelaide answered warmly. "I have been waiting for weeks to finally get the chance to see you, so the pleasure is mine."

"You've got a bit of an accent on ye; am I to guess you're a friend she made in a far-off place?" Styx asked.

"Actually, we became friends just nearby in Levien. It's in the far-off place that we started dating," Adelaide replied bluntly.

Styx stared down at her in surprise, and then his gaze flicked back and forth between Adelaide and Maaya even as Maaya's cheeks burned red.

"Well now, catching up is definitely necessary," Styx chuckled gruffly.

"Have you been to Sark recently? How's Sylvia?" Maaya asked.

"I, er…" Styx faltered. "Sylvia… she's gone. Few weeks ago. We were talking together, and then she said she felt a bit odd, then she jus' disappeared. Took me a few to figure out what might've happened, but I think if Sovaan's theory was anything to go by, she's really gone. I'm sorry."

Maaya's heart sank. Though they had always guessed such a day might come, she never thought it would happen while she was away. Sylvia was yet another friend she hadn't gotten to say goodbye to.

"Right," Maaya said, steeling herself before turning to the others. "We'll head around the fields behind Sark; the other main way in comes from the river so we'd be at a disadvantage there. We'll pause a mile or so outside town so I can get inside and figure out the situation. After that I'll know better what to do. Skarin, can any of yours watch the roads ahead so we aren't taken by surprise?"

Skarin gave a barely perceptible nod to one of his officers, who immediately set off with six sailors behind her.

"This is the last stretch before we reach Sark. You ready?" Adelaide asked quietly so none of the others could hear. Maaya nodded, setting her sights on the path that would lead them around Levien, and then, finally, to Sark.

"I'm ready."

THE FIRST THING Maaya noticed as Sark came into view the following evening was the smell of smoke. This was no odor of a comfortable campfire. Against the darkening sky she was barely able to make out the slight shimmering of pale smoke as it bellowed out of the town from multiple areas. She took a deep breath as they continued. The familiar shape of the town she had so long dreaded returning to, combined with the smell of smoke that reminded her of her own home going up in flames, caused her heart to pound in her chest.

"Hold us here," Maaya directed Adelaide, and she made a gesture to the officers at her side. Within moments, the entire company of just over six hundred came to a silent halt behind her.

"There are no outer city patrols or guards of any kind," Skarin drawled. "For the moment we have an advantage."

"Good. That means I can get in easily," Maaya replied.

"I have three LCs who can join us," Adelaide informed her. "Where will we be entering?"

"It seems like most of the conflict is coming from the northwest. I would recommend anywhere but there," Skarin continued.

Maaya nodded.

"I know where to go. Did you see anything else?"

"As I'm not yet permitted to get a closer vantage point, no," Skarin answered flatly. "However, I'm reasonably certain the conflict is isolated, not all over town; if you avoid the fires and screaming you should be safe. What's more, if necessary, we'll all be here to assist you should something come up."

"Thank you. I… really do appreciate your help. It means a lot," Maaya offered, and Skarin nodded.

"It's what friends do. However, while I've mastered self-restraint, that is not the case for sentimentality. You should get moving before the sunlight has abated completely."

"R-right."

She beckoned to Adelaide, and then they set off for Sark with three cloaked Blackfins following silently behind them. The rest of the company was already setting up places to sleep, preparing, if necessary, to stay the night while Maaya and the others figured out what they needed to know. If it took more than an hour, Maaya thought she would let them stay. She doubted there was anything that needed taking care of that couldn't wait the night for everyone to sleep.

"You okay?" Adelaide murmured as they approached the entrance.

"Nervous, but fine," Maaya answered. The LCs stepped up to the gates without a sound, peered inside, and then with a quick nod in Maaya's direction, slipped inside to scout the area.

"All right, looks like we're good to go," Adelaide said, and then, as Maaya straightened up to move on, held her gently by the hand. "Hey. I'm right here with you, okay?"

Maaya paused, then smiled.

"I know."

Maaya took a deep breath, and then took her first cautious step back into Sark.

Almost immediately she fought the urge to run away as the horrifying familiarity of the town washed over her. She recognized every building, every window, and every cobblestone in the road, and all she could think of was how lucky she had been last time to escape. Every shadow and every small detail was a fragment of a memory, and each one forced its way almost painfully into her mind.

This side of the town was dark, as it so often was, but there was an unnatural silence to it. If there was anyone here they were either lying in wait or too afraid to make their presence known. Maaya guessed it was the latter. The people of Sark had never been particularly brave or strategic in their thinking—at least, not the common townspeople.

The LCs were already out of sight, which comforted her. With their help she would get advanced notice of any danger, and they would also be able to give her some idea as to what was going on inside town; before she knew any more, she wasn't immediately sure where to go.

She led the way slowly, making absolutely certain she knew where she was in relation to the exit at each block. Adelaide paced quietly behind her, studying the layout of each street as they went, and she held her hand close to her pouch of *libris* cards on her arm.

They crossed a dozen streets, taking them closer and closer to the section of town Maaya knew the best. From there, she would be able to orient herself best. She tried to avoid thinking about what she might see when she got there. This was no time for sentimentality—something Skarin could have easily told her—but there was a part of her that would not rest until she knew.

And then she stopped. Adelaide nearly ran into her, then took a step back, staring around in slight confusion.

"What's up? Do you hear something?" she asked quietly.

"No. I just… I had to see this."

It took Adelaide a moment, but then she seemed to understand, and she bowed her head slightly.

They stood in front of the broken and charred remains of what used to be Maaya's home. There was hardly anything left, even though it seemed the fire had been put out before it was able to completely consume the old building. Even though most of the debris had long since been cleared away, she could see the old house in her memory, lining it up perfectly against what little remained. The base of the stairway still remained, as did the blackened remains of the sofa she used to sleep on in front of the fire.

As she stared, she could almost see the front door Roshan so often knocked on during his late-night visits, the kitchen where they had shared so many meals, and the two tiny rooms upstairs where her friends had slept.

Maaya took a deep shuddering breath. This was what Rahu and his ideas did to people. This was the only thing left to remind people she and her friends had existed at all.

"He did this, didn't he?" Adelaide whispered. "That cruel, horrible man. We'll see the end of this on our terms, not his."

Before Maaya could reply, she heard voices from down the street. She froze as she immediately prepared to run, but the voices were casual, as though whoever they belonged to were engaged in idle conversation.

"We should keep looking for your friend; the fewer people who know we're here, the better," Adelaide suggested, taking Maaya by the arm, but Maaya didn't budge.

"Wait. If they're on Roshan's side maybe they can tell us where he is."

"And if they aren't, we lose our advantage," Adelaide said hurriedly.

It was too late—two figures rounded the corner and immediately spotted them. They wore dark cloaks that partially obscured their faces, and they advanced quickly. Maaya was certain she could take just two people in a fight, and she thought with some embarrassment that Adelaide had been right. If there was to be any hope of secrecy yet, these people would have to be dealt with one way or another.

"Who are you? What are you doing there?" one asked as they stepped forward. Adelaide put her hand to her card pouch, but the figures stopped several feet away. From what Maaya was able to tell, they were unarmed.

"Well, now we're in for it," Adelaide muttered, and then turned to defiantly face the newcomers. "My name is Adelaide Sol of Krethus."

"And I'm Maaya Sahni," Maaya added, taking strength from Adelaide's bold demeanor.

The two figures froze, then seemed to relax. They glanced at each other, then reached up to uncover their faces. The first man Maaya didn't recognize, but the second…

"Roshan?!"

She barely had time to register Roshan Kulkarni lowering the hood of his cloak and rushing over to her. He placed his hands on her shoulders as his eyes quickly searched her face as though desperately hoping to dispel any remaining doubt, and then he hugged her so tightly she almost couldn't breathe. She clung to him as though letting go would mean she would have to leave all over again, and she fought the urge to cry. She had missed this so much.

"I can't believe it's you! I haven't seen you for so long… people were saying you'd been killed like the others, and then I got your message but I couldn't reach you… oh, Maaya. I'm so glad to see you again," Roshan said when he finally released her, and he seemed as close to tears as she felt.

"I'm so glad you're okay!" Maaya exclaimed. "I didn't even get to see you before I had to run and I had no idea if you were alive and no way to find out, and I had no idea if you'd even get my message… what's happened here?"

"You remember I told you my dad and I were going to try to get dirt on Rahu to get him in some trouble? Well, it worked… sort of. We found all the dirt we needed, but turns out the police didn't care. They had my dad arrested instead. Rahu's just got too much of a reputation. So I went to the people instead, and it was tough, but gradually they started to see reason. Ever since then it's been Rahu and his loyalists against the rest of us. But lately… well, that's for later. You must be tired. Do you need somewhere to sleep?"

"We do," Maaya affirmed. "And there are three more who came in with us."

"We have room for everyone," Roshan replied encouragingly. "And this is… Adelaide, right?"

"I am. And you're Roshan. I've heard much about you. It's a pleasure to finally meet you," Adelaide answered, her tone significantly friendlier than before.

"And you're from Krethus, are you? I suppose you must be the person Svante was talking about before."

"Actually, no, she… well, it's a long story," Maaya broke off. "We should hurry. I don't want to be seen by anyone if I don't have to; if I can take Rahu by surprise, all the better."

"I hope you've brought more than four people with you; he's got the police and most of the wealthy people on his side, plus everyone else he's been able to keep brainwashed."

"How about six hundred people? Is that enough?"

Roshan did a double take at her, his jaw falling slightly open, but he recovered surprisingly quickly. Then he chuckled.

"I shouldn't even be surprised anymore. You've always been incredible. Anyway, follow us. We'll take you back to where there's shelter. Where's the rest of your, ah, group?"

"Hiding out in the fields. They didn't want to be seen and give away our surprise," Maaya explained as they started moving. "They're prepared to stay the night there. I don't suppose there's anything we can do right now?"

"Not in the dark, no. Even if you were only after Rahu, he's heavily guarded—and since he's got law enforcement on his side he's well protected."

"What of the news from Krethus that the machine has been destroyed and that Maaya was innocent all along? Did it not reach Sark?" Adelaide asked, befuddled.

"It did, but Rahu's grip on Sark is that tight. He convinced everyone it was just a trick. Most people here never even heard of the machine in the first place so it was easy to convince them this was just an attempt to muddle their heads and distract from the real issue."

Adelaide muttered something irritably under her breath, though Maaya couldn't make out what it was.

They proceeded down the street, and Maaya noticed that the buildings here were still empty. It felt more and more like the ghost town of Nalmar they had walked through to reach the barrier. Maaya tried not to let her nerves show; if Roshan wasn't afraid, she had no reason to be either. Not yet.

Maaya stared around her, looking for any sign of life or light, but saw none. She jumped as she saw movement behind her, but then she noticed it was only the three LCs who had accompanied them inside. She hadn't heard them arrive, and their silence was both impressive and unnerving.

She couldn't believe this was happening. Roshan was mere feet from her, just as he had so often been before, and she was in Sark. She was *here.* She wasn't sure if she was shaking from excitement or nerves. This wasn't a dream.

Beside her, Adelaide walked quietly, obviously curious but polite enough not to ask any questions just yet. Still, she kept her hand near her *libris* card pouch the whole way, wary and ready. Maaya hoped there would be no fighting tonight.

Finally, Roshan and his companion stopped near one of the inns on that side of town. Maaya saw thin strips of light at the windows where the curtains fell loosely away, and she heard the sound of many voices inside.

Roshan made to open the door, but Maaya held him back.

"Wait. Won't the others get angry that I've come back?"

"No. They know the truth about what you did. You'll be with friends here."

Maaya hesitated, then nodded. Roshan opened the door.

The inside of the inn was filled with warm light and the smell of food. The discussions of those gathered around the small tables pushed against the walls was hushed, but not urgent or fearful. The mood was wary but calm, and this helped set Maaya's mind at ease.

Behind her, Adelaide nodded to the three LCs, who vanished instantly into the night to do more scouting now they knew where Maaya and Adelaide were staying.

They walked inside, and apart from a few people who glanced up briefly to greet Roshan, there was no change in the atmosphere.

And then someone noticed Maaya.

"Look! It's her! It's Ghost!"

The room quickly fell silent and all eyes turned to her. Adelaide took a protective step in front of her, but then it was as though the room breathed a collective sigh of relief and excitement. Many of the patrons got to their feet, but at first appeared too nervous to approach.

"She's here!"

"She got the message."

"She's going to help us!"

"What happened? How did you return?"

Roshan waved them off.

"She and her friend are tired. I'm sure we'll all get to hear the story later, but it's growing late and we need to prepare for tomorrow."

"What's happening tomorrow?" one voice cried.

"Maaya hasn't returned alone. She's brought friends, and lots of them," Roshan informed them, and excitable murmurs emanated from the room. "With her help we'll finally be able to put an end to this. I need time with her to strategize, and we all need to rest."

"But when will we know?" another asked impatiently.

"Tomorrow before sunrise. I'll make sure everyone is awake in time to get ready—unless of course you want to take part in our deliberations and get no sleep at all."

A few of the men and women glanced uncertainly at each other, then reluctantly returned to their seats. Still, after Roshan's companion departed for one of the tables and Roshan led Maaya and Adelaide upstairs, their eyes followed them the whole way until they passed out of sight. Even after they reached the second floor, she could hear almost total silence from below; no doubt at least some people were hoping they would overhear something valuable.

It was significantly darker here than below. Maaya passed Roshan an inquisitive look, but he shook his head and put his finger to his lips as they walked down the hall. Maaya quickly guessed that every room in the inn must be full of people; there was safety in numbers, after all. This would explain why so many of the buildings she had passed in her way in were empty.

Finally, they entered a room near the middle of the hall. Roshan quietly opened the unlocked door and stepped inside. She heard a scratching sound and then saw a small flame as Roshan began lighting multiple candles around the room. Apart from the three of them it was completely empty, though the single bed inside had been added to by multiple mattresses hastily covered with blankets in preparation for many more occupants.

Roshan sat on the side of the bed and invited the others to join him. Maaya did so immediately while Adelaide opted to stand across from them, her back against the wall as she stared warily at the window which had been boarded up with scraps of wood. She still appeared uncomfortable, though not as tense as she had previously been. Maaya wondered if it was the thought of being alone and without backup in such a dangerous place.

"So… wow. Where do we even start?" Roshan said with an awkward laugh. "So much has happened I don't know how we can possibly catch up."

"I need to know where Rahu is and what's happened here," Maaya pressed gently. "I need to know how I can help."

Roshan dragged his fingers through his hair and sighed.

"Right. I'll try to keep it short. Just after you left, Rahu gathered together as many people as he could to declare you an enemy of Sark. It was easy since most of them were there to see you use your magic and run in the first place. He said such vile things about you; don't ask me to repeat them. He convinced the police to start a curfew and everything. He said it was for our protection, of course. I thought that might be it for the resistance, but it actually got some people to doubting. Guess they were a little brighter than I thought. From there it was just a matter of reaching people one by one to tell them what was going on."

"You said you found dirt on him? How?"

"Oh, that was fun. That was our first big move. A few of us created a diversion while others broke into his home and took everything they could. We found so much, Maaya. His letters to Svante, his bird with all its recordings, his messages to the Krethan government… we took it all. It still took some convincing, but there was so much evidence it was hard for a lot of people to ignore—which was good, because after he discovered his secrets were out he took every measure he could to try to regain control.

"But that wasn't the only thing. After you left I had some people follow him; apparently he was hunting like mad for someone else who could see ghosts and take care of them like you did, and he wasn't having much luck.

People were still dying and disappearing, and he only had so many excuses. It started to erode people's faith in him."

Maaya grimaced.

"I wish I could see the look on his face. He said he didn't need me, that I was replaceable. His pride would never let him admit he was wrong, though…"

Roshan shook his head.

"In fact, when the attacks continued, he started blaming them on you. He said you were still finding a way to bring the ghosts upon us. But that didn't work," he added hastily at Maaya's furious expression. "People had seen enough by then. They didn't know you were innocent, but their idea was it didn't matter if it was you or not—Rahu should still be able to stop the ghosts if he was who he said he was."

"Did he ever manage to find anyone? I mean… he must have found something if he was able to keep so many people on his side."

"I'm not sure. Some people said he found some young kid, but I've never been able to verify it. It could be he found someone else who can see ghosts but not get rid of them. Either way, it was when the ghosts suddenly stopped coming that he started to regain his power. He said he'd finally managed to defeat them and that they wouldn't trouble us again."

"And people believed him? How could they?!"

"You have to understand, Maaya, this has been a living nightmare for most people here. Everything that's been happening was caused by things no one could see. When your enemy is completely invisible, can travel through even the thickest walls, fly, and make no sound and need no food or sleep, it's a horrifying experience to live under. Even the more rational people just wanted safety in the end. They were sleep deprived, exhausted, and living in constant fear. They might not have liked Rahu, but he said he could save them, and the attacks *did* stop."

"But that was *us!*" Maaya fumed, gesturing between herself and Adelaide. "*We* stopped them!"

"We all know that. Hell, Rahu knows that. I think that's why he's stepped up his game recently. When you succeeded and he got the news that your record had been cleared, I bet anything it made him afraid. Before that, the whole world was after you so he didn't ever need to worry about you coming back. But when all that happened, he realized you could."

"I'm surprised he thought I would. I'm even surprised I did," Maaya said softly. "I never even thought of coming back until a few weeks ago. Before then I was just too afraid."

"I don't blame you. Not at all. But I'm glad you came back. We really could use your help."

"Right. So, where is he? How can we get to him?"

"He's holed up in the city center surrounded by police and his loyalists. We can't get to him, so we're stuck. He can still afford to send his guys on raids, but we don't have enough people to take him down, and we're losing people every day."

Roshan sighed again, rubbing his eyes. He looked tired, Maaya noticed—more so than she had ever seen him. It wasn't the tired a person felt after coming home after a long day of work, satisfied and prepared to relax; it was the exhaustion of someone who was being worn down day after day with no end in sight.

"Hey. We'll get him, okay?" Maaya said comfortingly, edging slightly closer to him on the bed. "It's only a matter of time now. We've got the numbers, and a lot of them are dead."

"I hope so. I really do. Just… please don't underestimate him. He's got a psychological hold on anyone who agrees with him and a physical hold on anyone who doesn't."

"Can your people safely flee? He hasn't blocked off the town gates from what I could tell," Adelaide posited.

"There's nowhere for them to go and no way for them to bring their possessions. Not before the police would stop them. This is our home. I just don't know how to save it. It would be hard to take down Rahu and all the police as well; even if we won, what's to stop the government from sending troops to put all this down?"

"That's why we need to make a show of it rather than just taking them by force," Maaya said determinedly. "We can prove beyond a doubt that he's wrong."

"We already have the evidence; people just aren't listening," Roshan protested.

"That's because his hold is so strong that no one has been able to stand against him. He can downplay anything as just the work of the resistance, as propaganda. But when we overpower him and everyone is forced to listen, and when we can show them just how much of fraud he really is, we'll start to win people over. And the police are only on his side because he has money, you know that. As soon as their source of funding is taken away they'll have to turn elsewhere."

"To the people who take control," Roshan said thoughtfully, and Maaya nodded. "I suppose. That's more positive than the way I've been thinking. But it sounds like you've accomplished so much that a little optimism is expected."

"I've been through too much to let a little thing like this get me down."

Roshan raised his eyebrows, then laughed.

"A *little thing* like this? You really have changed."

"Well, I had a lot of help on the way. And a lot else has changed, too. For example, I, er… Adelaide and I…"

"We're romantically involved," Adelaide added, smiling for the first time that night. "Honestly Maaya, you should be used to telling people this by now."

Maaya glared, but could say nothing. Roshan, to his credit, took this in stride as he had everything else.

"That's great! How did you meet?" he asked eagerly.

"Well, the long and short of it is that she took me to lunch and then saved my life," Maaya grinned. "I was also stuck on her ship for the better part of two weeks so I had no choice but to get to know her. Oh, and then she fought off the Selenthian navy for me."

Roshan stared.

"Right. We're definitely catching up tonight; I'm not going to sleep until I've heard everything."

"Fine with me," Maaya giggled.

"If that's the case, then I must respectfully ask to be shown where I'll be sleeping. One of us is going to have to be awake for tomorrow," Adelaide interjected politely.

"Oh, er, sure. The room right across the hall should be free, too. I'll make sure no one else tries to use it tonight," Roshan said, hurriedly getting to his feet.

Maaya got up to join him but only made it as far as the door before Adelaide gently held her back.

"Don't stay up too late, okay my love?" she said quietly, very obviously planting a kiss on Maaya's forehead. Maaya swore she saw the slightest hint of a smile on her face at Roshan's attempt to appear unsurprised. "You can join me when you're ready; don't worry about waking me."

"I'll try not to be long," Maaya murmured, hugging her tightly.

With a final wink, Adelaide departed, heading into the room across the hall and shutting the door quietly behind her.

Maaya returned to the bed with a spring in her step, unable to hide the silly grin plastered on her face. Roshan, after making sure the door was tightly closed behind him, joined her.

"So how long has that been going on?" he asked, nodding back over his shoulder.

"A little over a month now. It might've been longer except we were both too afraid to tell each other we liked each other. Really, I was taken the moment I saw her in Levien," Maaya answered happily.

"I don't blame you. She is… definitely something," Roshan chuckled. "So you went off to Krethus to save the world and you succeeded, and found her in the process. You've done a lot better for yourself than I thought you would."

"It wasn't without its obstacles, this whole trip, but… I'm happy with the way things turned out. Mostly."

"What happened? Tell me everything," Roshan continued, turning and folding his knees under him to face her directly.

Maaya took a breath and let her memory take her all the way back to the night of the attacks. She told him how they had fought all over the city, how Kim, Kalil, and Sovaan had been killed, and then how Svante had been killed after that. She soon lost herself in her story as she explained her flight to Anorath, then to Levien, and then to Krethus, and everything that had happened there. She was thankful for Roshan's silence even as he looked like he wanted to do nothing more than break in with some comment or reaction. His eyes said it all. The hurt she saw within them when she mentioned how Saber had sacrificed herself was almost enough to cause her to start crying again.

She spoke of the hearing, of meeting Svante's wife and then Svante himself, and then her preparation for her return home. Through it all she spoke of her growing love for Adelaide, how she had finally mustered the courage to tell her how she felt, and how she was afraid they might drift apart somehow after this was all over. Even as she related her fears, she felt the stubbornness and defiance so well honed by her journey rise within her. There was only one thing left for her to do as it pertained to Adelaide, and that, if anything, she anticipated even more than her standoff with Rahu the following day.

When she finally finished, she took a deep breath and let it out slowly. She felt like a tremendous weight had lifted from her shoulders, and she suddenly felt exhaustion trying to creep its way in now she had said all she needed to say.

Roshan sat in silence for nearly a minute, his eyes darting back and forth as he processed everything he had just heard. Maaya almost smiled despite herself. Her life experiences had always been a challenge to his relentless optimism, and she wondered if she had finally caused him to reach his breaking point.

But then he leaned over and hugged her, and she thought she felt him trembling ever so slightly.

"I don't know what to say, except… I'm sorry. And I'm so proud of you. And happy for you. You've been through so much, I'm not even sure how you're sitting here explaining all this so calmly."

"If I were me from a month ago I'd probably be breaking down and feeling completely helpless. I guess I found a little more courage while I was out there. I don't really *feel* different—at least, not while I'm just sitting here like this—but I know I am. I have to be, right? Otherwise I wouldn't even be here."

"Right. Otherwise you might've just stayed safely where you were, and honestly I wouldn't have blamed you at all," Roshan agreed. "But you came back. And you might not feel any different, but I could tell from the moment I saw you. You're different, but… in a good way. I've never seen you so brave or so determined. I mean, I'm sad for all the awful things that happened, but look at you. You're marching into Sark—with an army, apparently—to take down the man the rest of us couldn't! I know how you always talked of getting out of here someday, and you've really done so much more than that. I'm really, really happy for you."

"Thank you, Roshan. I guess… I guess I am, too. We're still in the thick of it, but I never thought it would end like this. With me actually being happy, I mean."

"I know. Sark just sort of sucks the happiness right out of you, and that's when you're not being chased all over the world by ghosts and the navy," Roshan chuckled. "I'm still impressed; you're taking on Rahu tomorrow and you don't seem nervous at all. Are you?"

Maaya shifted slightly, leaning backward and placing her palms down on the bed behind her.

"I suppose. Nervous, but not afraid. I wonder if I'm finally free of the spell he had over me. Mostly though, I think it's because I'm not alone this time. This time he won't be able to hurt me."

"Damn right," Roshan agreed. "So what's the plan? What do I tell the others?"

Maaya furrowed her brow. For now it seemed they had the advantage they wanted; if Adelaide's company remained unseen until morning, that would be the best-case scenario. At that point, it would be time to play her cards.

"My friends will stay out there until tomorrow morning. Once we're all ready here I can send for them. Even if Rahu and his followers see them coming, they shouldn't have enough time to mount much of a defense."

"Sounds simple enough to me," Roshan mused. "The government square is huge; he chose that so no one could sneak up on him. If we're equal in numbers, though, that might work against him."

"Agreed. I want to trap him in his hideout if I can. Then Adelaide and I can pay him a personal visit before bringing him out."

"That sounds great. She looks like she'd be happy to smash his face in herself."

"She's first in a long line, trust me. Not that there'd be much left when she was finished; she grew up training as one of Krethus' *libris* elites, and I've seen her fight. She's incredible."

Roshan grinned.

"I want to tease you—and I'll figure out a way to do that eventually—but you've done good. She seems like a great person from what you've told me. I hope we can actually have a conversation soon. But based on what you've told me, you don't need to worry about you two drifting apart. Not after you've literally saved the world together."

"I hope so," Maaya answered quietly. "Actually… there's something else I want to do, at least when it comes to her."

"What is it?"

In response, Maaya glanced around the room as though worried Adelaide might be hiding in the corner, and then leaned closer to whisper in Roshan's ear.

When she pulled back, Roshan looked deep in thought for a moment, then nodded encouragingly.

"Absolutely. That'd be perfect for you both. At least that's what I think after everything you've told me."

"Really?" Maaya said, her expression brightening instantly.

"Definitely. This is what you want, isn't it?"

"More than anything."

"Then go for it. Tomorrow after we've won our battle against Rahu, you take care of your business with her—and I'm sure she'll agree."

Maaya thought hard. It was really happening. Tomorrow would see her showdown with Rahu, and then it would be over. The last unhappy loose end in her life would be tied up, and then she would have only her future to think about.

There was only one thing for it, she decided, and the thought brought a smile to her face. Adelaide wasn't the only one who could deliver a surprise.

42

GHOST RETURNS TO SARK

Before dawn, Maaya and Adelaide were roused from their sleep by a knock at the door. Maaya quickly pulled on a robe from the closet and opened the door to reveal one of the LCs from the night before, who greeted her with a polite nod.

"Everyone's planning to move out within the hour. There's word of a possible early morning raid, so we should move quickly," the cloaked figure informed her quietly.

"Understood. We'll be ready soon. In the meantime, signal everyone to start moving in. Oh, and find Roshan on your way out and tell him it's time."

The LC nodded again, then disappeared.

Maaya closed the door and turned back to find Adelaide already getting dressed. Chronis, who had been lying in the middle of a large pillow nearby, stood up and stretched before sauntering over expectantly to Adelaide's augment.

"At least let me put it on first, you impatient arachnid," Adelaide scolded him lightly, then glanced up at Maaya. "So, today's the day. You ready?"

"Definitely. I can't wait for this all to be over," Maaya said, pulling off her robe. She took out her old outfit she used to wear during her nightly hunts in Sark; she wanted to make absolutely sure Rahu knew who she was.

It was true: she was as ready as she would ever be. Even as her heart thudded dully in her chest with anticipation, she realized she wasn't actually afraid. Despite the eerie familiarity of the town and all the anxieties it held, despite the danger, and despite the fact that she would soon lay eyes on the man who had attempted to have her murdered, she felt so much more confident than she had before. She knew that even now her friends and all the others were on their way toward her and that the resistance was preparing to make its final move.

"With any luck, this won't be long. Besides, we've got your back," Adelaide said.

"I know. That's going to eat him alive."

"Oh, I don't doubt it. They say success is the best revenge."

"That's true for him. He tried to take everything from me. I was just a little girl who meant nothing and had nothing, and he took advantage of that. I couldn't fight back. Now… I'm going to take everything from him," Maaya said fiercely.

"Do you know what you want to do with him when we find him?" Adelaide asked.

Maaya, who had hardly slept the previous night due to just this thought, had in fact played over countless possible scenarios in her mind. It had taken a few hours, but then she had settled on what she believed to be the perfect end for the man she hated so much.

"I do. I need to talk to Roshan first, but I want Rahu alive and even mostly unharmed. If nothing else I need that to happen."

"Your word shall be done," Adelaide grinned. "I understand. Do I at least get to take a jab at him?"

"Oh, of course!" Maaya affirmed quickly as she pulled on her cloak, and then, finally, strapped her card pouch to her arm. "Honestly, I don't want to hurt him myself. I just want him to see who I've become and be responsible for what happens to him."

"You're a better person than I, but I suppose this is me taking the position of angry defensive girlfriend," Adelaide commented idly. "Oh, the joy of not being burdened with such responsibility. I promise I won't hit him too hard. I'll just break a rib. Or six."

Maaya snorted, then finished tying back her hair. She stared at herself in the mirror. She was dressed in all the same clothes she used to wear, with her hair styled the same way, and her old card pouch in its usual place on her arm. But she was still not the person she had once been. This was now a costume, something she was wearing for the purpose of demonstration and nothing more.

Adelaide, meanwhile, had dressed herself in her captain's uniform, immaculate and polished to the last detail. With this uniform came all the power and influence Maaya was used to seeing from her, and if her goal was to make an impression on everyone who saw her, she would definitely accomplish that goal.

"Ready?" Adelaide asked, finishing the last of her half ponytail.

"Ready."

They stepped out of the room and into the hall. Maaya immediately noticed it was brighter than the night before, and that there was much more activity. People walked up and down the halls and in and out of rooms, many pulling on clothes and fastening weapons to their belts. She glanced up and down the halls as they walked, but saw no sign of Roshan. She wasn't particularly worried; he was likely busy preparing everyone for their next move. He had explained to her the previous night that helping lead the resistance was exhausting, but that he had been proud to do it. Maaya was proud of him, too. For the distance that had existed between them for so long, their lives had taken similar courses all the same.

As they walked, murmurings of *Ghost!* reached Maaya's ears, but this time they were spoken in tones of awe and admiration, not suspicion. It was a sound she could get used to hearing.

When they walked outside into the chilly morning air, an LC appeared nearby so quickly that he might as well have materialized out of thin air.

"Our forces are moving inward toward the city square as requested. Their presence is now known, but they have met no resistance. Reports indicate law enforcement is retreating back to secure the square. Shall we proceed?"

Adelaide peered down at Maaya, who nodded.

"Take them in. Have Skarin and his crew hold back a little until we can verify Rahu doesn't have any *libris* users on his side. The rest should close in on the square on every side they have a safe vantage point. Don't fight or push the boundary yet, but make it absolutely clear how many are with us. Once it's safe, have Skarin and his group set up flanks on the surrounding roofs and behind the square just in case anyone thinks to escape. I don't want Rahu going anywhere."

"Understood. We will see you there shortly," the LC replied smoothly, then vanished.

"Honestly, you're pretty good at this giving orders stuff. Have you ever considered running a ship?" Adelaide commented wryly.

"No way. This was just one person; I don't know how you run a ship full of people all at once."

"Delegation and a chain of command, my dear. Anyway, I'm glad you still have it. We'll need your confidence moving forward. Shall we?"

They started forward, heading slowly but surely toward the city square.

Giving orders, Maaya thought. She wouldn't exactly call what she did with her friends giving orders, but she had been in charge and they always looked to her for instruction and guidance. She supposed that counted for something. For all Maaya said she was more comfortable being a follower than a leader—mostly due to her desire to avoid responsibility over other people's lives—she had to admit there was a certain allure to being in charge and making sure everything was done properly. Perhaps she was a little more like Adelaide than she thought.

As they went, Maaya could only think that she wanted this to be over. She wanted to be away from Sark again, away from Rahu, and away from the history this town held. No matter how this ended, she knew she wouldn't be able to stay.

Maaya caught the first glimpses of her allies in the adjoining streets walking parallel to herself and Adelaide. Then came more and more, some from the resistance, some from the Blackfins, and some from Skarin's crew. She noticed a few of them glancing up at her nearly every time they were visible to each other between alleys and buildings, and suddenly she realized they were all following her lead. Even as dozens and then hundreds of people filtered out into the narrow streets, they progressed with her. Maaya suppressed a shiver. This was an altogether new feeling, and though she felt the weight of her task upon her, it only served to boost her confidence.

She was not alone this time.

As they got within half a mile of the square, Maaya gave the order for the company to split up and begin their flanks. Three groups, each led by one of the LCs, peeled away from the main mass of people walking down the center streets, and Skarin's ghosts moved away to start surrounding the square from behind.

Just then she felt a light tap on her shoulder and turned quickly just in time to see Roshan fall into step beside her, a handful of his own resistance members behind him.

"How's everything?" she asked.

"Looking good so far. All of Rahu's people have pulled back to defend the square, so we'll be able to travel freely until we get there. We have the advantage in numbers when it comes to soldiers and police, but he's also got all his loyalists; they outnumber us about three to one."

"That many people are interested in a fight, hm?" Adelaide said.

"Unfortunately. Sark is too small for people to avoid taking sides, and that's when Rahu isn't practically mandating their support under threat of imprisonment or death. Most folks who aren't fighting are children, and I'm honestly afraid Rahu will try to recruit them too if we don't act fast enough."

"Nothing he hasn't done before," Maaya growled.

"Everyone's setting up as you've directed, though. What will we do after that?" Roshan asked nervously.

"We'll call first for Rahu to step down. If he doesn't, we'll then ask to be allowed to present our evidence. If that doesn't work… we take him by force and do it anyway," Maaya answered, her voice hard.

"Got it. I'll make sure we're ready to fight. Though… I hope it doesn't come to that."

"Me too."

"Could we not infiltrate his hiding place and take him out personally? A few guards would be all too easy to beat when we're burning cards," Adelaide suggested, but Roshan shook his head.

"Like I said, so long as his message stands, so will his support. If you get rid of him privately you might only make him a martyr. And if he were imprisoned here there'd be enough people to just break him out again once you left. We have to show everyone he's a fraud. The only other way would be to beat the whole town into submission and that's just asking for trouble in so many ways."

Adelaide sighed.

"There really ought to be more problems that can be solved with a simple punch to the face."

"Oh, you can still do that if you'd like," Roshan returned, and they both laughed.

Maaya might have joined in but for the sudden feeling of dread that had washed over her. The street they were walking down was none other than the one where her friends had been killed by the machine's ghosts; as they passed, she couldn't help but stare directly at the wall they had been pinned against when they died. Where she had seen their ghosts beg her for help before being stolen away.

This was the first real sense of horror Maaya felt since returning to Sark. She had been here before. She had watched her friends die here, then stumbled to the relative safety of the square only for her last semblance of hope to be extinguished as Rahu turned the town on her and ordered the public execution of Svante.

Still, she kept walking, strengthened by the presence of her friends and allies beside her, determined to see this through to the end. Each and every one of them was prepared to fight here for her, and it wouldn't do for her to be too frightened to face the one man they were all here to take down.

She entered the square, flanked by Roshan and Adelaide and followed by hundreds of armed Blackfins, resistance fighters, and ghosts. She saw the wide stairs she had sat upon to rest after the attacks and where Rahu had delivered his address to the town. A solid line of police officers stood in front of the stairs now, surrounded by a much larger angry mass of townspeople with a variety of crude weaponry. There were over a thousand of them easily, and as Maaya and her allies approached, they were met with jeers and shouts of anger.

Maaya gulped, but pressed onward. The others were lining up in every major entryway to the square, and Skarin's sailors were positioning themselves so that no one would be able to escape without their knowledge.

But then, in the center of the square, her courage almost failed her.

Rahu stood at the top of the stairs, surveying the oncoming company with mild apprehensive interest. The mere sight of him was enough to make Maaya's breath catch in her throat, and she fought the urge to flee or to hide lest he spot her. She held her breath for fear that he might hear her. She knew if he saw her, he would kill her.

I never should have come. I never should have agreed to this. I need to get out.

As though in slow motion, Rahu's head turned to survey the rest of the crowd gathering before him… and his eyes locked unmistakably with hers.

If Rahu was surprised, he didn't show it. Instead, he looked content, as though he had just solved a minor mystery that had been troubling him throughout the day. He held up his hands, and the jeering and shouting from those before him went quiet immediately.

"I see. This all makes sense now. Invaders in our lovely town of Sark, allying with the feeble-minded and failing protesters among you who would put innocent lives at risk… it was silly of me to think this could be the work of anyone other than our infamous and beloved *Ghost.*"

He put a special nasty emphasis on the last word, and at this, she heard gasps and murmurs from across the square, and then all eyes were on her.

Maaya trembled with terror. It was all she could do to remain standing, much less meet his eyes or challenge him. She wasn't sure what she had been thinking. She had been so stupid to think that she was free of his influence, that he had no power over her anymore.

But then Adelaide gripped her hand tightly at her side, and Maaya glanced up to see the captain staring at Rahu with no trace of fear in her eyes, and from this she felt a flicker of hope… and anger.

"We've got you," Adelaide said quietly, though her voice was firm and sharp. "It's okay if he scares you. But when this is over, he'll be scared of you."

"What is it you've come for? Let me guess," Rahu drawled. "You want revenge. You want to take out your baseless anger on the innocent townspeople—to finish the job you started while you were here. The world was cruel to you, so Sark needs to suffer for it. Is that right?"

More jeers and cries of fury came from the crowd amassed on the opposite side of the square. She remembered how easily they had called for her death under Rahu's persuasion before, how quickly they had believed the rumors about her and wanted her gone because of his fear-mongering and their own petty insecurities. And though they were no soldiers, they were armed and driven nearly to madness by fear. They would fight hard and desperately.

Maaya tightened her own grip on Adelaide's hand and steeled herself. She wasn't here for them. She was here for Rahu.

"*You* were cruel to me," she called. She was painfully aware of the sound of her own voice, but with every word, her conviction grew. "You used my friends and I, and you tried to kill us all when we wouldn't work for you anymore."

"That tired lie? Please, Maaya. You've had so long to think of something even remotely plausible. But then I suppose you must have spent all your time convincing these people—whoever they are—to drag themselves along with your hopeless cause. Oh, if only they knew the truth…"

"That is the truth, whether you want to admit it or not!" Maaya shouted back angrily. The fury she had held within her for so many years had found its way to the surface, and with this small opening, it all surged forward. "I'm not here to debate you, Rahu, and I'm not here for revenge. You're a murderer and a liar, and one way or another I'm going to make sure your hold on my town ends."

"Well, I would ask you and *what* army, but it seems you were somehow competent enough to accomplish at least that. You are the manipulator, after all. If you think they stand a chance, then please do endanger their lives to get back at me. That's what you're good at, right? Risking your friends' lives for your own gain?"

These words cut her deeply, and she fell silent. They weren't true, she knew that. But the confidence with which he delivered them, and the way he had so subtly worked himself into her mind over the years made her almost want to believe him. That's what she had been taught to believe.

But then Adelaide spoke, and her own voice, much louder and more confident, brought silence across the square.

"We come to you with demands, Rahu. Our first is that you immediately and willfully abdicate your position of power until there has been a trial to determine your guilt of the many, many crimes for which you have been accused."

"Abdicate? Crimes?" Rahu laughed. "I've done nothing wrong. I don't hold this position due to some silly ambition; it fell to me because I was capable of protecting this town like no others could—protecting it from people like *her*."

He jabbed his finger at Maaya, and the angry jeers rose again.

"As expected," Adelaide continued calmly. "In that case, our second demand is that you allow us to present our evidence to the people of your fraudulent claims and criminal actions. That should be reasonable, no?"

"What, and let you spread more of the propaganda that has already attempted to break down our town's unity? Hardly. You think a master manipulator like Maaya isn't salivating at the opportunity to bring forth well-constructed lies? She's ever so good at it; that's how she convinced all of you to fight for her."

"Spare me," Maaya growled. "That won't work now. Will you meet our demands or not?"

Rahu put his finger to his chin thoughtfully, then drew it away almost as quickly.

"You know, I don't think I will. I have no reason to abandon the position I selflessly worked so hard to reach, and I have no reason to give a criminal and a killer a free platform to spread her lies. No, there is no diplomacy or discussion to be had here; you've come pretending you have a reasonable position, but we won't be so easily fooled. You failed before, Ghost, and you will fail again—and this time it will mean your life, and the life of any person who remains to fight for you."

"Is that your final answer?" Adelaide called.

"It is," Rahu replied simply, and then raised his voice. "To those of you who ally yourselves with this girl, understand you are risking your lives for a traitor. Know that Sark and its people have defeated much more potent allies than this pitiful gathering of unkempt mercenaries. Those of you who wish to live, leave now. This is my final warning."

A tense and horrible silence fell over the square. Never before had so much doubt and panic filled her mind. Everything he said about her putting others' lives at risk, all her doubts about their success, all her fears about watching her friends die in front of her all swam through her mind relentlessly, and her feeble attempts to drown them out were lost to the flurry of defeatism and despair.

Slowly, ever so slowly, she gained ground against her fear. She knew what Adelaide would say, what Roshan would say, what Saber would say if she were here. These were lies, manipulations, and projections. Sark *hadn't* defeated anything. She had. Maaya had pushed forward against all odds, against real enemies, while Rahu had sat back and employed his manipulative tactics to create fake ones. His power came from his manner of speech that made people think he already had it and from his ability to bring others to succumb to his will through doubt and fear.

She had once wondered how the machine's ghosts had killed so freely and without any thought, entirely apathetic to the world around them. But it had turned out that they were simply trying to fulfill their purpose. Rahu, however… this was his purpose. And if she had managed to bring down a doomsday device capable of wiping out the population of the entire planet, then she knew she could handle one mortal man whose greatest weapon was his words.

Maaya took a short breath. The square was still dead silent, and all eyes were upon her. All the thousands of people in the square were waiting on her word.

She stared up at Rahu, meeting his stare unflinchingly. Though she spoke quietly, her simple order carried with it all the hurt and hatred of the years, so vicious she almost didn't recognize herself.

"*Get him.*"

The chaos began instantly. Roshan and Adelaide called out their orders, and the mass of resistance fighters and Blackfins surged forward. Only a moment later, those holding ground in the other entrances to the square pushed ahead as well, moving swiftly to converge on the citizens and soldiers standing before the stairs. The sound of ringing metal came from all sides as fighters drew their swords, and cries of the charge echoed over everything.

Up in front, those standing defensively before the stairs took a step back to solidify their footing and hunkered down to meet the oncoming wave. Behind them, police and still more townspeople on Rahu's side drew weapons of their own, brandishing them hopelessly as though hoping to dissuade their attackers like Rahu could not—but it was useless.

And then all sides met in battle.

For Maaya, who stood frozen in the crowd, it was almost like being back in the midst of battle aboard the Windfire. The only thing missing was the sound of gunfire and Skarin's gleeful laugh as he cried out his orders—though the latter came only a few moments later as she saw the first ranks of ghosts descend from the sky to enter the fray.

Far off on the other side of the square she saw the massive form of Styx wade his way through the crowd. The town police immediately before him wavered and fell back hastily as he came charging at them like a bear. It was a frightening sight to behold, especially for Maaya, who had never before seen the man even swear in his anger.

Maaya stood helplessly, surrounded by her allies as they rushed forward. Foolishly, she realized she hadn't considered this possibility. She had imagined dealing with Rahu somehow, but she thought there might be a possibility of resolving this without having to resort to this kind of violence—a violence she very much did not want to take part in. She had been hoping their numbers would work to intimidate, not to actually fight.

But then Adelaide took her hand again and pointed up toward the top of the massive marble stairway. Now that the battle was in full swing, Rahu was making a slow retreat to one of the buildings with a complement of five or six guards.

"We should follow him," Adelaide suggested.

"What about the rest? Shouldn't we help them first?" Maaya asked quickly, staring around at the fighting in all corners of the square.

"They'll be fine. This mix of townsfolk and ill-trained guards won't last long against our force," Adelaide replied confidently.

Maaya hoped she was right. She noticed with some relief that the resistance fighters and Blackfins were doing their best to disable and injure, not to kill, but that also put them at a significant disadvantage. She also remembered belatedly that at least some of the officers had guns at their disposal, and she wasn't sure if anyone on her side carried the same type of weaponry.

However, at Adelaide's urging, Maaya agreed to pursue Rahu. She took a deep breath as the realization that this was happening *right now* washed over her.

"Stay with me?" Maaya asked anxiously as they started their way toward the stairs.

"Always," Adelaide replied. "Come on; let's take a side route so we don't meet too much interference."

"Agreed. Skarin!" Maaya called, and the captain glanced down at her from his vantage point high above them. "We're going in! Can you help give us an opening?"

Skarin nodded curtly, and then roared above the din, "Get ten of your sorry hides to the captain and see them in safely or it'll be your heads!"

Almost immediately, ten of his crew dashed over to their side as they leapt up a narrow stairway on the side of the square. It was a roundabout path, and indeed Maaya had never been here herself, but the area was mostly free of defense. A few guards, as well as a few townspeople who preferred this position to the middle of battle, made to bar their way, but Skarin's ghosts pushed them aside. The guards and citizens crashed into the walls or down the stairs, looking ultimately more confused than injured.

Up and up they went across multiple halls, disabling any semblance of defense they came across. Skarin's guard proved much more effective than Maaya thought; had she and Adelaide gone in alone she knew they likely would have won, but at the cost of much of their energy. As it was, they needed only show the ghosts the way, and their path was cleared for them.

In the distance, Maaya only barely caught a glimpse of Rahu and his own guard enter a heavily fortified building with sturdy wooden doors that looked like they might require a battering ram to take down. If Rahu saw them, he gave no indication of it as he passed through, and the door closed behind him. Two of his guards remained outside, glancing about warily.

"That's all we need; get back to your captain and assist however you can," Adelaide ordered, and the ghosts nodded and flew off, disappearing through a nearby wall. "Ready, Maaya? We're taking this at full speed."

"I'm ready," Maaya panted.

They simultaneously pulled *libris* cards from their pouches, and, even as they ran toward the guards who had definitely noticed their presence by now, burned the cards on their arms and legs. Purple and green lines flickered over their limbs, and before the guards even knew what was happening, they had both been struck to the ground, too dazed to move.

Maaya grabbed the handle and pulled as hard as she could, but even with her strength augments, her efforts were not enough.

"Let me," Adelaide said, sounding almost excited.

Maaya stepped back, and not a moment too soon—Adelaide gave the door a tremendous kick, and it burst apart on the first go as though it were made of kindling. Even as Maaya squinted against the airborne fragments of wood and rushed in, eager to make use of this advantage, she let herself enjoy the sheer awe of the moment. A chill of excitement ran down her spine at the recognition of this force, and Maaya rushed on confidently.

They were in what seemed to be a large courthouse entrance, with wide shiny marble floors, high windows, and almost no furniture to speak of. What existed of the morning light filtered through the windows, aided by the dull light of lanterns and candles. A wide wooden stairway at the end of the room curved graciously upward, leading to a long hall with several identical doors. All in all, Maaya thought even in the midst of battle, it was one of the dullest places she'd ever seen.

Four guards remained in the room, but the girls were upon them even as they turned with their weapons raised. Adelaide sent one man skidding halfway across the hall with one strike, and Maaya, moving almost too quickly to see, stole another's weapons and dropped him to the floor with a powerful kick.

The other two guards were disabled with similar ease, the last one surrendering in terror as Adelaide's fist flew toward her face. Adelaide abated at the last moment, and with a whimper, the guard hastily retreated, leaving her companions moaning and dazed on the floor.

With this done, Maaya scanned the room hurriedly for Rahu, fearful of a surprise attack or additional guards, but there was nothing. Instead, Rahu himself, alone and seemingly unarmed, stood in the center of the wide room, his hands clasped calmly in front of him.

"Oh, well done. That almost looked like it took some effort. I wasn't aware your friend could use your magic, too, though. You've managed to surprise me a few times this morning," he said, his smooth voice echoing through the now-quiet hall.

"I'm a lot stronger than you think," Maaya snarled. "You couldn't even kill me when you had me at every disadvantage. I don't even need this *magic* to beat you."

At these words, her *libris* lines flickered and then died. Adelaide glanced at her warily, but said nothing.

"Ah, yes. Terrible mistake on my part, giving you that opportunity," Rahu sighed, sounding almost bored. "But it doesn't really matter either way. That you've returned, even with an army, means absolutely nothing."

"Oh? And why not? You're here at our mercy, aren't you?" Maaya snapped.

"It seems that way. And if you just wanted to kill me, then I suppose I could say mission accomplished. But that's not what you want, is it?"

"How do you know what I want?" Maaya asked defensively.

"Because I *know* you. I might have underestimated you in that I never thought a sniveling weak girl with no friends left alive could survive in this world, but I know how you operate. You see the good in everyone and you want to save everyone you can. That's why you battled the ghosts the night before you fled instead of simply surveying them, and it's why your friends died. You just couldn't resist."

"What? No... you *told* me to keep the people safe and to get rid of the ghosts," she returned scathingly.

"Please. It wasn't just my orders. You've always been smart enough to fool me over a little thing like that if you *really* wanted to. No, it was the screams, the fear, the helplessness... wasn't it? You just couldn't resist. Anything you could do to save people, even the people who hated you so much. If you had any instinct of self-preservation you consciously ignored it so you could fight, and *that's* why I know what you want. And it's why you'll fail as you always do."

"How can I? I have you right here. Once you're gone, Sark won't be under your control anymore."

"Your power is fleeting and shallow. Mine has lasted longer than you've been alive and it runs deeper than you know. You're fighting an idea, do you understand that? This town will *always* think of you as a liar, as a danger... as a poison. A force a million strong couldn't change that, and your only other option is to take the lives of those in which the idea lives on. Either they die, or they go on living and hating you. You cannot change that."

"Why? Why do you hate me *so* much?" Maaya said angrily, frustratingly aware of the tears that fought to well in her eyes. "I did whatever you wanted and never asked anything of you other than just what we needed to live. How can you so easily talk about how you've made this town hate me?"

"It wasn't personal, you must believe that," Rahu answered lightly. "It could have been you, it could have been a Krethan scientist, it could have been anybody. I never went out of my way to punish any stranger out of the blue. I'm not so callous or foolish as to expend my energy on such a thing. I only ever sought to punish the people who tried to cross me. And really, isn't that true for all of us? You can't tell me you would willingly remain in the company of those actively trying to harm you."

"We didn't try to harm you! Svante didn't break the law, I didn't break the law, you had no reason to—"

"None of you were innocent. You got it into your heads to plot against me, to spy on me, and to turn the tables against me. Is that not true? You may not have liked what I was doing, but you did objectively bite the hand that fed you. Tell me now with a straight face that you believe this would have ended the same way had you just continued to listen to me."

"I… that's not…"

"You may have believed you were fighting for good, and I applaud your morality, but all of this is entirely your fault. You know that. You chose to ally with him, to try to sneak away from me. All you had to do was *listen*, Maaya. Even as you went behind my back I was trying to pursue a better life for you. A better home, more to eat, a better reputation in town. This could have all ended peacefully; I was not your enemy until you made me your enemy."

"That's not true. My friends still died, and—"

"Which was *also* your fault. You were their leader, weren't you? And did you not also *choose* to fight that night? You brought them with you and sent them into a battle none of you were prepared for. Had you told me of the situation, that you were completely overwhelmed, I would have understood. I'm not unreasonable, nor did I particularly care to lose the people who worked so hard for me."

"But… you even gave me your bird to make sure I was out there—"

"Yes, to make sure you were out there. Whose decision was it to fight? Remind me?"

Maaya faltered. She couldn't do this. Even as they spoke the power of his words worked their way under her skin and into her mind as it always had before. She stood here now, afraid and speechless, as she always had. Part of her knew their victory was assured anyway, that Rahu couldn't possibly touch her without Adelaide coming to her aid, but that was no longer the issue.

She couldn't help but think that maybe Rahu was right. She knew that was exactly what he wanted her to think, but the thought was still there. He had spent decades in this town building his reputation, and to the uninformed, all facts seemed to align in his favor and his story. She was mildly infuriated that someone who couldn't even see ghosts managed to get the better of her on an issue surrounding them. But what infuriated her most was that, to some effect, he *was* right: she had him entirely at her mercy, but no matter what she said or did, it wouldn't change anything. Even with the strength of Adelaide's small army at her back, even with all the power she had gained from training with *libris*, even after defeating the power of the world-ending machine… before this man, she felt completely helpless.

Adelaide looked on, staring imploringly at Maaya and waiting for some cue to intervene, but Maaya would not give it. She couldn't. Stopping him wouldn't mean anything.

Rahu began to pace, taking care to stay a comfortable distance from Adelaide as he continued. His tone was steady and contemptuous, the tone of a man who knew he was getting exactly what he wanted.

"It's true, you could do anything to me right now. I welcome it. Show the people how you've come to town to hurt the man who saved them all from you. That will surely get them on your side. You can tell them about the ghosts, too. Tell them it was actually you who saved them and not I. See if you can combat the fact that the ghosts only stopped attacking once you left. I *implore* you to try your best at reasoning with them; you have no ground to stand on, but I would find it very amusing."

"You're awfully chipper for a man who's going to be punished either way," Adelaide retorted. "Whether or not your precious *idea* lives on, this is most certainly the end of the line for you."

"That's a comforting thought, isn't it? But you are oh so wrong in multiple ways. First, I know Maaya wants to save this town. She won't be able to no matter how hard she tries, and it will eat at her for the rest of her life, but she will try. Second, you still haven't found me guilty of anything. Either you shut down the whole town or eventually someone will realize a Krethan has taken over a Selenthian town and imprisoned an innocent man. I don't know how your system of justice works, but that wouldn't go over well here."

As Adelaide and Rahu went back and forth, Maaya's mind raced. This couldn't be how it ended. It just couldn't. It wouldn't be right. There was no way Maaya could bring an army to Sark and end up with the only option being to Rahu go peacefully. Everything he said sounded so rational, but there had to be *something*…

Maaya grimaced in frustration. It was those ghosts. He had used her to make everyone think he was their hero, and all because of the ghosts. They all thought she called the ghosts upon them and that Rahu was the only one powerful enough to stop them. If it hadn't been for that she might have a better leg to stand on, but as it was, she had helped build her own reputation against herself without even knowing it. Everyone thought Rahu was the one who could get rid of ghosts, and they would certainly be counting on him to do it again. Or, at least, to get rid of *Ghost.*

Maaya stopped, frowning. Rahu's reputation of getting rid of ghosts was well known, which was the primary reason he was so popular in town. In fact, Maaya would go so far as to say it was the *only* reason he was so popular anymore. He created the problem and came with a solution, and people ate it up. And it wasn't like Maaya could prove him wrong anyway; now that the machine was down, the ghosts no longer existed—and even if they had, no one would be able to see them.

Unless…

Maaya thought hard. The reason people called Rahu for help was precisely *because* they couldn't see ghosts, and because those invisible spirits were wreaking havoc on their lives. Ghosts were able to cause plenty of damage and trouble without being seen; if anything, they used it to their advantage and quite enjoyed it. With that in mind—

"Maaya!" Adelaide screamed suddenly.

Maaya whirled about just in time to see Rahu rushing toward her with a knife in his hand. Adelaide was already mid-sprint toward him, but he was so close to Maaya that it was unlikely she'd make it in time. Maaya leapt backward with all her strength, but realized a second too late that she had let her *libris* dissipate, and so she only managed to push herself backward a few feet before stumbling and falling to the ground.

The knife came plunging toward her, and Maaya could only stare upward in shock. Even as it glinted in the morning light, Maaya thought of how much of a shame it was that things could end here back in Sark when she still had so much left to do, so much life left to live. She wanted nothing more than to continue on with Adelaide at her side, and she thought it an awful thing that Rahu was finding a way to ruin even that.

But then, even as the knife just touched her skin, Adelaide collided with him and brought him to the ground. Maaya gasped and stood hastily, stepping backward several paces, her hand instinctively at her chest where the knife had almost pierced her. A light trickle of blood dripped from her shallow wound, but she was otherwise unhurt.

The fight between Adelaide and Rahu—if it could even be called a fight—was over in an instant. Adelaide was far too strong for Rahu, and she quickly disarmed him and pinned him to the ground, his own knife at his throat.

"Don't hold back on my account," he rasped. "It'd make you feel better, wouldn't it? But you know as well as I that it will do nothing but make things worse for all of you. If you thought you were wanted before, oh, that would be nothing compared to this. If you want to reignite the war between our countries, kill me now."

"Adelaide, don't," Maaya cried hurriedly, rushing back over to her. "He's… he's right. We can't do this."

"He's *evil*, Maaya," Adelaide protested. "He's evil manifest. We can't just leave him here and let him get away with all of this. Not after what he did to this town—to you! He just tried to kill you!"

"I'm hardly evil. You could call me greedy, perhaps, but again I remind you I only went after those who interfered with me."

Maaya ignored him.

"He won't get away with this. I have an idea."

"What is it? As much as I hate to say it, he has a point; how do we change everyone's minds? Better we just deal with him and then the rest as it comes."

"I can't do this anymore, Adelaide! I can't keep fighting, I can't keep running. Everything I've done is for the hope that tomorrow would be better. I want that life, and I want it with *you*. Rahu isn't worth sacrificing that."

"I… suppose," Adelaide sighed, and as she pulled the knife away from Rahu's throat, Maaya saw the slightest hint of relief in his eyes. "What's your idea then?"

"Well, he said it himself. He's the one who saved the people of Sark. He's the one who got rid of the ghosts. He did all that himself, without me. So… let's see him prove it."

For the first time Maaya could remember, she saw a flicker of doubt in Rahu's eyes.

"Prove what? Your ghosts are gone, and *you* did that, remember? If you had any leverage, you destroyed it yourself when you went off to save the world."

Meanwhile, Adelaide's face lit up as she caught on to what Maaya was saying.

"Oh! Oh, yes, I like it! He'll be ever so happy to oblige, too."

"He who? Me? I'm not obliging anything for you."

"You'll see," Maaya said coldly. "Come walk with us. We'll take it slow for you; you'll want to save your strength for the show."

"What in the world—?" Rahu protested, breaking off into a fit of coughs as Adelaide struck him in the stomach as she had promised.

They led him out of the hall, through the broken door, and across the marble path toward the sound of battle. It seemed to be diminishing even as they approached, and Maaya fought a swell of nervousness. She hoped that didn't mean her side had lost.

As they approached the top of the stairs, however, she saw the last of the town police slowly putting their weapons on the ground and stepping back with their hands raised as the resistance and Blackfins looked on. The square had been taken. Maaya's side had won.

"Look! Up there!" someone shouted, and cries of surprise and despair echoed across the square as everyone spotted Maaya and Adelaide standing at the top of the stairs, holding Rahu at the arms between them. One or two guards looked as though they wanted to rush up the stairs, but they were quickly held back.

Roshan, Styx, Skarin, Emil, and the others were at the very foot of the stairs, and they stared up from the men and women they were guarding to watch.

"Don't kill him, you witch!" a woman shouted desperately from below, and her protest was joined by many more shouts of defiance, anger, and fear.

Maaya shared a glance with Adelaide and then a brief nod. At the same time they released Rahu, who stumbled forward, barely catching his balance in time.

"I'm not going to hurt him!" Maaya called loudly, and those clamoring in protest quieted. "I've let him go in good faith because I want to prove something to you. This man is not, and has never been, who he says he is."

"You won't turn us against Rahu; don't even try your manipulation on us," someone called scathingly, and this was followed by murmurs of assent.

"We should kill you right this time!" came another.

"Yes, well, obviously that's not an option right now," Maaya replied flatly. "This is simple, and I ask only for a minute. Rahu has told you that he can stop the evils that haunt you and that I'm the one who brings them, right? What if I told you he can't do any of that at all—and what if I told you I could prove it?"

"In your dreams, witch!" came a shout.

"Just you wait; he'll get rid of you again soon enough!" said another.

Rahu chuckled, still holding his injured side as he spoke.

"You'll never make any headway. You can't prove it, and they wouldn't listen if you could."

Maaya raised an eyebrow.

"We'll see about that." Then she turned again to the crowd and raised her voice again. "Listen! I promise you this. I will prove right here and now that Rahu was never the one saving you, and I will prove that it was me instead. If it doesn't work, I promise to leave of my own accord right away and never come back. Is that fair?"

"If you think you can," one guard snarled sarcastically, earning him a smack on the back of the head courtesy of Styx.

"I think I'm owed at least that. I know most of you don't like me, even if we never met and you have no idea who I am. I won't ask any of you to like me. I just want you to know what's going on so you can make your own decisions. If I didn't care about this town where I was born and grew up, I never would have come back."

"Get to it then," the guard growled.

"How noble of you," Rahu said sardonically. "A shame you didn't come with an actual plan. We couldn't stop your pointless march into the city, but you can't do anything now you're here. We stopped you before and we'll do it again."

Maaya didn't so much as glance his way. Instead, she stared directly at Skarin, and gave him a barely perceptible nod.

"Stop this, then."

That was all she needed. Skarin, getting the hint immediately, gave a deep gravely laugh and then rose above the crowd, raising his arms wide and calling to his crew.

"There's your word, ladies and gents! Let the world of the living know just who graces their presence by the discord you bring!"

There was instantaneous uproar as Skarin's crew, only too happy to oblige, leapt into motion. They swarmed the square, smashing windows, tearing the furniture off balconies, and swiping the hats off the terrified men and women below. They ripped curtains from balconies, flung doors open and shut, and did their best to make a horrifying din.

The square erupted in a panic as guards and citizens of Sark alike attempted to flee, though they had no idea which direction to go. Further, the resistance fighters and Blackfins were only too keen to keep them at bay, and so, with nowhere to go and the unseen chaos coming from all sides, the people quickly turned to the only other source of help they could think of.

"Rahu! Stop them!"

"End this madness!"

"Save us, please!"

Rahu's eyes darted back and forth, calculating as always, but with the unnerved jerking motions of a man watching his empire fall before him. Fear had now joined the anger in his eyes, and Maaya almost enjoyed seeing it.

"Rahu! Stop the ghosts!" Maaya called above the din. "You can, can't you?"

"You evil, deceptive witch," Rahu snapped savagely. "You've called the ghosts on us like you've always done. How will that earn you Sark's favor?!"

"That I can call ghosts was never in question, Rahu," Maaya answered calmly. "Only your ability to deal with them. I suggest you do it quickly; I think the spirits are getting a little impatient."

The ghosts below were now coming closer to the terrified people below. A few of them pushed the living people back and forth between them like a game of catch while others tripped them and pulled their clothes. The screams were almost too much for Maaya to bear, and for a moment she almost considered calling an end to it. But she couldn't. Not yet.

Just then, something caught Maaya's eye. In the far corner of the square Maaya noticed a teenage boy, perhaps only a few years younger than she, huddled alone against the wall. But it was not his isolation that made Maaya curious—it was the fact that, as the ghosts swarmed about the square, his eyes darted about skyward, clearly following their movements.

He could see them.

Her attention was distracted by more cries, and she turned her focus back on the panicking masses below her.

"Rahu! What are you waiting for?"

"They're trying to kill us! Stop them!"

Rahu, for once, was speechless. Maaya was sure that, given some time to prepare, he could have come up with some kind of excuse as he always had. But now, with so many things going wrong at once, he lost his ability to speak. He locked eyes with Maaya, and she saw pure hatred burning within.

"How long will we wait? I have all day," Maaya said casually, wishing ever so much that she had a timepiece to glance at for effect.

"You stop this. Put an end to this or I swear I will kill you slowly," Rahu demanded venomously. Adelaide helpfully reminded him of her presence by delivering another swift strike to his ribs.

The screams below grew still more desperate, and Maaya began to hear cries of doubt among them.

"Can't you do something? Rahu, please!"

"Why aren't you stopping them?!"

Maaya turned to face him, willing every bit of her own hurt and anger to drip from her voice as she spoke quietly to him.

"Your reputation is eroding with every second. Do you want to live as a man with some chance of saving his character? Or do you want to die in disgrace?"

Adelaide's eyebrows rose slightly at these words. Maaya hadn't really meant it; she knew the ghosts would never kill him. But he didn't.

Rahu scowled, turning his head this way and that, and all the while the din from below only worsened. The people cried Rahu's name and stared pleadingly up at him, and Maaya saw that with every moment that passed, a new sliver of doubt was instilled with them.

And then the ghosts descended upon Rahu himself, pulling at his hair and clothes and knocking him this way and that, all while laughing gleefully at his furious and helpless protests.

"Any time will do, Rahu," Maaya said, casually examining her fingernails.

Then, finally, Rahu made to shake off his attackers, and he faced the crowd below.

"All right! I admit it then, do you hear? I can't save you! I have no more control over these spirits than any of you," Rahu shouted, staring at Maaya with loathing in his eyes with every word.

"You can't mean that! Just stop them! You always have!" someone begged.

Another person screamed as they were pulled to the ground and dragged several feet by the hood of their own cloak.

"I can't! I… I can't stop this, I never could," Rahu said, every syllable sounding as though it hurt him deeply.

"What?! How did you do it before? Just do that again!" a woman cried.

"*She* did it! It was her every time!" Rahu answered loudly, pointing a shaking finger in Maaya's direction. "She was the one to remove the spirits from your homes; I was the one you hired while she did the work."

Doubt, disbelief, and confusion shone brightly in everyone's eyes, but it wasn't the time for questions. Not yet. Skarin's ghosts still sowed panic and disorder below, and the people were still more concerned with coming out of all this alive rather than contemplating the depths of Rahu's deceit.

"Maaya? You can stop this?" a man called up to her.

"I can. Do you believe what I've said?" she answered.

"Yes! Yes, just make it stop!"

Maaya took a breath, and then called above the din, "Spirits! Stop this at once and leave these innocent people be!"

All at once, Skarin's crew stopped. They released their hostages and set down the rocks and furniture they were about to throw, and then all of them rose to hover slightly above the crowd. Within seconds, the square was completely at peace.

Rahu, shaken and angry, fell to the ground before Adelaide, not daring to look up. Adelaide said nothing and did not move, but kept a wary eye on him all the same.

"You see?" Maaya called calmly. "This is what I was trying to tell you the whole time. Rahu knows ghosts exist, but he can't see them or do anything about them. He never could. But I could, and he knew it. Every time you hired him to help you he would force me to do the work for him. He admitted that just now, and you've seen that he has no power. Not even when you were in great danger did he manage to do anything about it."

"But… if he can't see them, how does he know they're there?" someone cried dubiously.

"Some people are just a little more perceptive than others," Maaya explained, a hint of bitterness in her tone. "It's just that he found a way to profit from it rather than get burned alive."

"I don't understand… if you were gone, how then did the ghosts stop coming if you weren't here and he was?" came another perplexed voice. Maaya was relieved to hear they seemed mostly curious, not angry.

"I stopped them at the source. I was planning to do that anyway, but Rahu made that much harder by killing the man who was supposed to help me. After he got all of you calling for his death first, of course."

At this, Adelaide stepped forward.

"There was a tool in Sark that we needed to stop the ghosts. I know this because I was searching for it myself. The ghosts that troubled you destroyed my home, and so we sought their destruction in turn. However, this man tried to turn your fear into profit by holding this tool ransom. He had the ability to use it to save you, but instead he kept it to himself so he could get paid for it. He didn't care how many of you died in the meantime."

"Is… is this true?" a guard asked, staring up at Rahu in disbelief.

"It is!" Roshan called, hurrying up the steps to join them. "We have all the papers and recordings to prove it. A lot of you already saw them. He secretly communicated with the Krethan government to seek payment, and we have recordings of him asking Maaya to steal it for him. He knew exactly what he was doing the entire time, and he was willing to put your lives at risk for it!"

"Where is this proof, if you have it?" an officer asked skeptically.

"Somewhere safe. I'll make sure the lot of it is delivered to you shortly. Maybe you'll actually look at it this time?" Roshan suggested, smiling.

"This is all… a lot to take in," the officer replied raggedly, leaning up against the banister.

"It is. But don't you see? This is all I wanted you to know the whole time," Maaya said, hoping and praying that she was getting through to them. "Rahu is not a good man. He used my friends and I as tools for his gain, and he used your fear for the same purpose. You would call me Ghost without ever seeing me do the things you accuse me of, but you would call this man a hero with just as much evidence!"

The people below shifted uncomfortably. Maaya could see their skepticism of her words in their eyes. She wasn't sure it would ever truly leave. But she had succeeded in planting the first real seeds of doubt about Rahu. The people were no longer rushing to defend their beloved hero, even if some of them thought he still might be innocent.

"This man has endangered your lives, saw to the murder of at least one innocent person, willingly and purposefully interacted with an enemy government for his own gain, and manipulated and abused those powerless few who got in his way," Adelaide continued slowly. "You've just now seen him to be proven a liar and a fraud, both by his inaction and his own admission. The proof of these later claims will be delivered in due time. I implore you all to recognize that this man is a liar and undeserving of your respect and admiration. You all deserve better."

"And this isn't a slight on you," Roshan added. "This is what he's good at. He took advantage of you. It's not your fault that he did. But he *should* be punished for it."

"I won't ask you to like me," Maaya repeated, though in her voice was the smallest hint of a plea. "I can see ghosts, and I know for many of you that's too strange and too different. But I only see what's already there; I never called any evil on anyone. You just saw that yourself. I might be different, but I'm not a liar. Rahu is the one who lied to you, and I just proved that."

"Rahu… Rahu, my good fellow, do say something. This can't be true, can it?" said a man dressed in the coat and hat of the chief of police. When Rahu said nothing and turned his head away, the chief gasped quietly.

"What, ah… what do we do?" asked an officer.

"Are you joking? You can start by arresting this man," Adelaide said, all her authority of command in her tone.

"I… er…"

The officer and his men looked reluctant to approach Rahu, much less lay hands on him, and Maaya guessed this problem would definitely need to be addressed in the near future. Adelaide seemed incensed by the hesitation, and she sighed exasperatedly.

"Fine. You tell me where the nearest jail is, and I'll throw him in myself if I have to. I understand your difficulty so I won't begrudge you that right now, but if you let him escape I will deal with *you* after I'm through with him. Understood?"

"Y-yes, ma'am," the officer replied hastily. "Two blocks east. You'll see the sign; you can't miss it."

"Understood," Adelaide replied curtly, but just as she made to start hauling Rahu away, Maaya stopped her. "What is it?"

"I don't want him going to the same prison as everyone else. I want something special just for him." Maaya turned to face Roshan. "How long would it take to build a single-cell prison?"

Roshan stared back, puzzled.

"A few days at most depending where it's going, I think. Apart from the foundation the only thing that takes much time is letting the concrete dry. What do you have in mind?"

"I realize it's probably not on my authority to ask this, but if I can ask for one thing and one thing at all, it would be that I choose where he stays. It wouldn't be cruel or inhumane. It would be a cell like any other. I just want to choose where it goes."

"Where are you thinking that requires a whole new cell to be built?"

In response, Maaya stepped closer to Roshan and whispered in his ear so that Rahu would not hear. Roshan listened intently, and then a wide smile spread across his face.

"You are just full of good ideas. I'll see to it immediately."

"Thank you, Roshan. Seriously, thank you. It's… nice to start feeling like I can put this all behind me."

"Definitely. Maybe Sark will start getting back to normal slowly but surely. After we clean up this enormous mess, of course," Roshan said, gesturing to the square. Indeed, it looked like a tornado had just passed through it, and Maaya felt guilty for adding to the already heavy workload of the exhausted and frightened town.

"Never you worry," Skarin commented from nearby, his tone suggesting the matter was all a very silly thing for them to be concerned with. "We fix what we break. My crew will assist in the town's repairs—at least until we're ready to set off."

"Thank you," Maaya answered gratefully. When Roshan stared at her in confusion, she added, "Er, that was Skarin talking. The captain? He says he and his crew will help clean up."

"Oh, right. Uh, thanks, sir," Roshan said, staring awkwardly in front of him. "And thanks for your help just earlier. It was… very effective."

"Not fazed by much, this one, is he?" Skarin asked with amusement. "Pass along my well wishes. His town is in good hands."

Skarin started off, calling orders to his crew just as two police officers clumsily pulled Rahu to his feet.

"All right, come on now. We'll get to the bottom of this, I'm sure," one of the officers said, looking downright frightened to be touching the man who had essentially been in control of the town, but to his credit, he did not vocalize his fears.

"Oh, right. On that note, Maaya… I'll be happy to get everything set up for you, but first I need to make sure my parents are okay," Roshan said. "I'll see you soon, all right?"

"Of course!" Maaya replied. They shared a quick, tight hug, and then Roshan dashed off as well.

Below them, it seemed like the terror of minutes before was wearing off, and the people had begun picking themselves up, staring amongst each other nervously. Some dispersed quickly, appearing only too eager to leave.

"Blackfins! Do a headcount and then meet with your LCs!" Adelaide commanded. "Officers and LCs, once you've made sure we've got everyone, see to the wounded and start cleaning this place up. Commander Strand, take a small complement and see to it that our special prisoner doesn't escape; I don't quite trust the police in their current state. For the rest of you, if anyone from the town wants to leave, let them. Our primary business is done here."

With everyone busy, Adelaide sat on the steps and placed her face in her palms. Maaya eased down next to her, leaning gently against her.

"You all right?" Maaya asked.

"I think so. That was… a lot heavier than I expected. I know you told me how horrible it was to grow up here, but I never expected this. This was damn near cult status. I just… it bothers me to see human beings like this. It makes me uncomfortable and afraid."

"Well, that's what we came here for, right?" Maaya said encouragingly.

"Look what we managed. Rahu was taken care of and I think we might just have made enough of an impact to get people to rethink what they thought they knew."

"I suppose. And it was a brilliant plan of yours, by the way," Adelaide smiled, and then her expression turned dark. "But if there ever was evil, it was that man. He just got under my skin and I don't know how he did it. These people have spent a lifetime listening to that… did what we accomplish really do that much?"

"I don't know. But I think so. I hope so," Maaya sighed, staring out across the square. "It won't happen overnight, that's for sure. But these people were held by fear, and now that fear will start going away. Maybe… maybe this was the thing Sark needed to realize it had to change."

"You're a lot more optimistic than I am. Something about this town and what I just saw… it gives me chills, frankly. I look forward to getting out of here. We'll be able to do that soon, right?"

"Of course! I'm sorry you had to see this—I'm not proud of my hometown—but this means the world to me, I hope you know that. I never thought I would see what just happened here outside of my craziest daydreams."

Adelaide chuckled softly and draped an arm around Maaya's shoulder.

"Well, I'd say all our debts are repaid and we're about even. Not that it ever mattered; I would have done this for you anyway. But now all's said and done, what say we go get something to eat to celebrate? Assuming anyone's left cooking in town."

To Adelaide's visible surprise, Maaya shook her head.

"I'd love to," she said, scanning the square as she spoke. "But there's still one more thing I have to do first."

43

ONE LAST PROPOSAL

Maaya slowly made her way down the stairs, searching the dispersing crowds as she went. From the corner of her eye she noticed many people passing her wary glances—a few of them even something close to thankful or appreciative—but most were still too focused on gathering their wits about them to say anything.

It took a few minutes, during which Maaya became concerned that the person she was looking for had already disappeared, but then she spotted him from a distance. He hadn't moved far from where he stood previously in the corner of the square. If anything, it appeared like he was searching for her, too.

Adelaide trailed behind as Maaya approached the boy. He stood a few inches taller than her, and his dark brown eyes watched her with anticipation as she approached. He had a mess of short black hair, and his clothes were in a similar state of dishevelment; he looked even more exhausted than any of the others Maaya had seen so far, even the members of the resistance.

"Excuse me… is your name Anrik, by chance?" Maaya asked slowly. She knew she was operating mostly under a hunch, but after everything she read and everything she'd been told, she was willing to trust her gut this time.

The boy raised his eyebrows in surprise.

"Yes. And you're Maaya. Maaya Sahni. Right?"

Maaya smiled.

"I am. I was hoping to find you here. Are you all right?"

"Tired," Anrik said, leaning his back against the wall and relaxing slightly. "I've hardly slept since… I don't even remember. Hard to sleep when ghosts are everywhere."

"Well, they're gone now," Maaya replied comfortingly. "Er, the dangerous ones, I mean."

"I'm so glad. I might just sleep here," Anrik answered, closing his eyes.

"Do you have somewhere to go? If not, I can see to it that you get a safe room somewhere," Maaya suggested, and Anrik nodded.

"I can go home. If it's still there. I don't actually know. I haven't been there in weeks."

"Why?"

Anrik opened his eyes again and glanced back and forth warily, making sure no one else was nearby to overhear them.

"I've been trying to keep people safe. I know who you are, so I trust you with this. I can see them, the ghosts. I've always seen them. I'd try to take the people away from them so they wouldn't be hurt. It was… hard."

"I know. It always has been. Do you remember my friend Kim?"

Anrik stared.

"I haven't heard that name in a while. Not since I stopped seeing you or her other friends around town. Did she go with you? Is she here?"

There was a hopeful note in his voice that escaped past the exhausted monotone, and Maaya felt a sickening sensation at the thought of the news she now had to deliver.

"She's… not here anymore," Maaya finally answered with difficulty. "She was taken by the ghosts."

"Oh…" Anrik's face fell, and he pushed his hands into his pockets. "I was hoping to tell her when she came back."

"That you could see them too?"

"Well, yes. But I…" He paused and then he snapped his head up to look at her. "Did you say 'too'?"

"Yes. That's one reason she and I were friends. All four of us could see them; that's why I sought them out. She talked about you sometimes. She mentioned that someday she wished she could be brave enough to tell you that part about herself."

Anrik sighed, a mix of agitation and relief on his face.

"I can't believe it. All that time I knew her we both could see the same thing and we never told each other."

"It's okay! We don't live in a friendly place for people like us… we have to look out for ourselves."

"I guess. She made me feel safe with her, you know? Like it was okay to be myself with her. I guess now I know why. I should have guessed since she lived with you and all. She always got so angry about the way people treated you."

"For what it's worth, you made her feel safe, too," Maaya answered softly. "What else was it you wanted to tell her?"

At this, Anrik chuckled awkwardly.

"It was hard enough to think of telling her; it seems even harder to tell someone else. But I suppose I can't tell her anymore, can I? Truth is, I… I had a bit of a thing for her. I used to walk all the way to the water pump near her place, and it wasn't because the one near mine was broken the whole time. I did anything I could do to see her. I was going to tell her, I really was. I never thought I would meet a person like her in a town like this, but then there she was. And now… well. I missed my chance. Maybe if I'd said something earlier I could have helped her, maybe she wouldn't have…"

"Hey, don't think like that. I wish I could say there was something that would have saved her, but even with all four of us together we couldn't fight all the ghosts off. The only thing that would have saved her life was if we hadn't gone out at all, and she never would have accepted that. She refused to let me go on my own. Believe me, I tried."

"Yeah… that sounds like her," Anrik sighed. "It's a hard life for any good person here, especially someone who can do things like that. No good deed goes unpunished, I think that's what they say. And now… I wonder if there's even anyone left in Sark who can see ghosts like I can. I don't want to be alone here, not like that."

Maaya's gaze fell to the ground. She couldn't argue with that. It was a lonely life; even when she had found the others, there was something about being the only four people in town with that secret between them. No matter how they tried to blend in, they would always be different somehow.

But then she realized the biggest reason that difference had existed was because of the environment they lived in. Had they grown up in Krethus, no doubt they would have had a much easier time making friends and being accepted. This town had made them feel like there was something wrong with them when in fact the town had just been engaged in some pretty serious projection. And with what she had just seen and done, not all hope was lost. She now believed Sark could get better. Maybe it would be slow, and maybe it wouldn't come without more friction, but now she knew it was possible—and that was already more than she ever thought possible.

Besides, there was also something special about having friends no one else was able to see.

"Well… you know, you don't have to stay here," Maaya said. "I've seen parts of the world that are much kinder to people like us. And there are a lot more of us than you might think. But if you want to stay I think you could help Sark become one of those nicer places. There are a lot of ghosts who need friends, too. I can tell you about some of mine."

"Maybe…"

Anrik looked like he wanted to say more, but he fell silent, appearing instead to be deep in thought.

She knew her words only meant so much. Sark, at least for her, had always had the power to suck the happiness right out of her no matter how hard she fought it. She had to guess it could only be the same for someone like Anrik, especially after finding out that Kim, one of the only people who shared his secret with him, had died.

Just then, she had an idea.

She pulled one of her blood cards from her pouch, and held it out to Anrik. He looked up in confusion and took it hesitantly, staring at the strange markings upon it.

"Sometimes there's more to ghosts than just being able to see them. That's how we were able to get rid of the troublesome ones, and that's why Rahu made us do his work for him. Do you notice anything about that card?" she asked hopefully.

"I'm not sure. It's… red?" he said indecisively.

Maaya's heart sank just a little. She knew it was a long shot.

"That it is. I just wondered… well, never mind. It's not terribly important. And anyway, you—"

"And it feels weird," Anrik continued, staring down at the card as though he wanted to drop it. "It feels warm suddenly. It wasn't warm before, but now it is."

Maaya started. And then she grinned.

"That's great! That means you can use it!"

"Use it? What do I do with it?" Anrik asked cluelessly.

"Well, it's… complicated. But with a card like that you could make a ghost disappear if you needed to. You could send it to the afterlife. I've used those to protect people from ghosts who wanted to cause harm, and also to end a ghost's connection to this world if they didn't want to be here anymore. It's a very powerful card, and there are more like it that let you do different things. Not everyone who can see ghosts can do this; it's really rare. But I can, and Kim could."

"How do I learn? Can you teach me? And… do you think I should? You know how Sark treats people it thinks can do magic…"

"I know. But I think times are changing. Now that Rahu is gone and the people saw that things like this can be used for good, I think now is the perfect time. You and people like you can take the space he left and use it for good. Show people there isn't anything to be afraid of. Some people might not like it much at first, but I think there's hope now where there wasn't before. As for teaching you, I suppose I can give you the basics! But I can't stay long…"

She spent the next half an hour explaining the basics of *libris*, where its power came from, the different types of cards, and how they were used. More than anything, she tried to impress upon him that how the power of *libris* was used was infinitely more important than the power itself. It was, after all, simply a power that they were lucky enough to tap into—not control or master.

"I… think I understand," Anrik said finally. He looked even more exhausted than before, and Maaya thought she would have let him sleep first if she didn't have to leave so soon.

"Just practice. And don't worry about memorizing anything; just think about the feeling you got when you touched that card and seek that feeling when writing everything else. It'll come to you eventually. And it'll take some practice, but I think you'll be great at it."

"Was life so bad with all this? I mean, what should I expect?" Anrik asked as he handed her card back to her.

"It wasn't bad. It was hard sometimes, but it was worth it. I got to meet some wonderful people and go on some wild adventures. And I was able to do good for people. There's been good and bad, but if I had the power to change this part of me… I never would. A different world is coming, and it's going to be a lot better for people like you and me. You'll see."

Anrik smiled.

"Thank you. I'll try to do my part. Maybe I can find other people like me just like you did. And I can definitely do some good for the world. I know that's what Kim would have done, too."

"She really would. And you know, for what it's worth… she liked you too."

Maaya turned to leave, and Adelaide followed. From the corner of her eye she noticed Anrik raise his hand like he wanted to say something, but he hesitated. Then, after a moment, he put his hand over his heart and smiled.

"That was good of you. I think people like us need all the positive representation we can get here. He'll help change the world in his own little way, you know," Adelaide commented as they walked.

"That's what I hope. It's never just one person, is it? It's a lot of them put together. They just need to realize what they can do."

"Right. I think it's a lot easier for a man to do evil than it is to do good, but good always ends up winning in the end," Adelaide added thoughtfully. "Really, I'm not sure why people choose to be evil anymore. History tells them they're at a significant disadvantage."

"If someone's stupid enough to be evil, they're not smart enough to read a history book," Maaya snorted.

"Speaking of stupidity and evil, what was this I heard about a prison for Rahu?" Adelaide inquired.

"Well… mostly I wanted him to feel how I felt all those years he forced me to work for him. So I'm going to see that he's put in a cell all by himself where he'll hopefully spend the rest of his days and where he'll have to rely on others for his source of food. And I know there are more secure prisons in bigger towns, but I want him here; I want him to look out the windows and stare at the town he tried to rule. I want him to feel as powerless as I felt, knowing it's all out there but that all he can do is watch."

"Ooh, I like it. But why not one of the prisons Sark's already got? There's the one just nearby, right? He'd get to see a lot of free people that way."

"True, but I don't want that, either. I want him to be someplace where nobody knows his name, some insignificant corner of town where every time he looks at his surroundings he'll realize just how poor a life he's been forced to live."

"Yeah? And where's that?"

"Right on top of the ashes of my old house."

Adelaide whistled.

"Oh, Maaya, that is *beautiful.* I do believe that qualifies as poetic justice."

"Doesn't it? He always walked right in like he owned the place and he always insulted it. And when he forced me out of town he had the house burned down to get rid of any last memory of me. I want him to sit in that same spot for the rest of his life and remember that it was me who put him there. It was my home, but it will be his cage."

Adelaide patted Maaya on the shoulder.

"You did good, Maaya. I'm sure the police will be a little hesitant to let you dictate the terms, but I have a feeling they'll acquiesce. If not now, then after they see the proof of his actions… or after Inga and I persuade them to—"

"Adelaide, behave," Maaya interrupted, unable to keep a straight face. Adelaide grinned happily.

Just as they made to leave the square to find Roshan, he and Styx walked up to them. Roshan seemed to be in high spirits, and Styx, though there was ample evidence that he had just been in a fight, greeted Maaya with a cheerful wave. Before she could say anything, the massive man scooped her into another tight hug.

"You actually did it! Absolutely incredible," he exclaimed proudly as he let her go. "Never thought I'd see an end to that man. An' I thought I'd see Sark put an end to you if ye didn't get out eventually, but looks like it ended up the other way around, din'it?"

"I'd like to think so. He'll still be here, but hopefully with enough time he'll just be an afterthought," Maaya replied wearily. "I already can't wait to never think about him again."

"You know that'd drive him crazy, what with him basically livin' off other people's attention. And their money, that too."

"What a shame he won't have any of that, either."

"Oh, I don't know. I think I might throw a rial or two in his window every few years out of pity, just so he remembers what money looks like and how he can't have any," Roshan said airily, and they all laughed. A few moments later, his expression turned slightly more serious. "So… Rahu's been taken care of, you're no longer wanted by the police… does this mean you're staying?"

Styx stared down at her hopefully at this question, and her face fell.

"I… I can't. I'm sorry. If it helps at all, I made that decision a long time ago. No matter how this all turned out, I couldn't stay. This place holds too many awful memories for me. Too much has happened and there's too much history, I just… I can't. Besides, I've changed a lot too, and I need to go somewhere that's better for me. I'm really glad it ended like this and that Sark can eventually get better, but this can't be my home. Not anymore."

Styx nodded sadly, and Roshan did his best to give her an understanding smile.

"I thought you might say that. I don't blame you. Truth be told… I can't wait to get out of here myself."

"What? Really?" Maaya asked in surprise, and Roshan grinned.

"Yeah. Dad says I'm just about ready to get a real apprenticeship somewhere, and I was thinking about going somewhere bigger and better than this old place. I'm not sure where yet, considering my knowledge of geography is… well, nonexistent, but the idea is there."

"Levien might appreciate your talents," Adelaide suggested. "It's a busy port that'll only get busier now trade can start picking up, and they'll need skilled hands there for just about everything."

"And it's beautiful, Roshan," Maaya added excitedly. "It's right next to the ocean and there are so many friendly people, and… well, I think you should do it."

"I'll think about it! I've also thought about something in Krethus, but mostly that's just because you talked it up so much," Roshan chuckled.

"I would absolutely not complain about that," Adelaide affirmed happily.

"Where will ye go?" Styx asked, looking close to heartbroken.

Maaya glanced away. This decision was hard enough without thinking of leaving her friends all over again.

"I'm not sure yet. There are still some other things I need to figure out first. But I feel like I have a lot of options now that my only limit is where I want to go, I suppose."

"Maybe you should take some time to figure those things out before you go," Roshan said, passing her a very meaningful look.

Maaya bit her lip, hoping Adelaide wouldn't notice.

"Maybe I should. Actually, if you don't need me for anything—"

Roshan waved her away before she could even finish.

"We're fine here, especially with the help of all your friends. You two can go get something to eat and then… do what you have to do."

"Thank you," Maaya said gratefully, and the weight of her words carried more than gratitude for simply being allowed to eat. "Oh, and Styx… wherever I go, you know I'll always make time for you. Maybe we'll even end up in the same place."

"Ah, I don't know…" Styx said uncertainly, scratching the back of his head. "The world migh' be gettin' to be a better place, but I don't know if it'd want me in it. Anorath was one thing, but I'm still a little too odd to be strollin' about a big city."

"You never know. The world is changing fast, and most of it is better than what we've been led to believe," Maaya smiled, and then couldn't resist adding, "Besides, now you know what we'd do to anyone who gave you trouble."

Styx gave a watery chuckle.

"Aye, that I do. Somethin' to think about, anyhow. I did always know someday you'd grow up an' I wouldn't be able to keep you around forever. My girl Maaya, off savin' the world, and now she's off to better things."

Maaya smiled.

"Think about it. Now there's something else I need to do. Adelaide, can you come with me?"

"Sure!" Adelaide said, giving her quick goodbyes to Roshan and Styx. "I hope you're showing me somewhere we can get lunch."

An hour later, Maaya and Adelaide stood alone on one of the paths outside Sark. She hadn't taken this path often, but it was better to look at than the one which led to the river. She wasn't sure she had it in her to walk that way again anyway.

The mid-morning sun shone brightly as it rose higher and higher into the sky, and Maaya welcomed its warmth. There was hardly a cloud in the sky, and the only wind was a gentle breeze that gently rustled the overgrown grass nearby. They were far enough away from everyone else to enjoy total peace and quiet, which was all Maaya wanted.

They had stopped at a street cart to get some food, and when the large man inside turned to take their order, Maaya immediately recognized him as the man who had defended her the last time she had bought a meal from him. He welcomed her gladly and tried to make her meal on the house, but she paid him anyway.

After that, she and Maaya sat on a nearby bench to eat, but Maaya could barely pay attention to what they were talking about. Her heart pounded so quickly and she was so nervous that she couldn't even taste the food in her mouth, much less remember what casual conversation they engaged in. She felt bad, but she hoped in this one case she could be let off the hook. She had never done this before.

Before anything else, however, she had decided to pay her last respects. This would likely be her last day in Sark for the rest of her life, and so she knelt and closed her eyes. She thought of Kim, Kalil, Sovaan, Svante, and Sylvia, and all the others she had known before them, all of whom she had considered good friends, and all of whom had lost their lives one way or another here on this soil. Though Adelaide knew none of them, she knelt at Maaya's side in silence, and Maaya took comfort from it.

With that weight now off her chest, she stood again and turned to face the sun, letting it warm her face. Adelaide stood before her, staring down the distant road at the empty fields. It was the same sight she saw whenever she left town, but there was something different about it now. It wasn't as dark or frightening as it had been before. Now it was just another part of the world, one she could look at in a new light even if she expected never to see this part of it again.

The sound of wings and the rustling of leaves suddenly came from above her, and Maaya glanced up. It took her a moment to see the bird sitting on one of the long branches, and at first she hardly paid it any mind—until it tilted its head at her. It was a crow, and it had only one eye.

They stared at each other for a full minute, and the bird watched her keenly, almost as though it was making certain of who it was looking at. And then it dipped its head in what almost looked like a bow.

Before Maaya could react, the bird flew off, away from Sark. She watched it until it disappeared into the mess of distant trees. She knew she would not see it again. But something about its visit, however silent and fleeting, comforted her. It was one more goodbye she had managed to give. What's more, she felt as though they now had something in common: with nothing left for them in Sark, they were both on to better things, each going their separate ways now that the friend who had for so long tethered them together was gone.

After several minutes enjoying the quiet and warmth, Maaya decided it was time to speak.

"So… now you've seen Sark. What do you think?"

"Well, I understand why you wanted to leave. There are a few really nice people here—I can see why you liked Roshan and Styx so much—but it's not enough. I'm glad you decided to try to move somewhere better for you."

"Yeah… better for me," Maaya repeated quietly. "Now that this is all over I guess I'm not sure how to feel. I'm glad it's done, but I don't know where to go or how to start a life for myself."

"That is definitely a tough thing to consider," Adelaide agreed. "But now you've got all sorts of time!"

"Have you thought about what you want to do?" Maaya continued hopefully.

"I have, but I'm not certain yet. I guess I thought about returning to my old life. But only if you'd be okay with that," she added hastily. "I mean… well, that's tough too, isn't it? I guess we'll need to figure out how this will work. I really want you in my life, Maaya. Whatever that life entails."

"Me too," Maaya said.

A painful silence fell between them. Adelaide fidgeted slightly and stared at her boots, and Maaya thrice opened her mouth to try to speak, but found she didn't know how to say what she was thinking about. Again it seemed like they both had something to say but were dancing awkwardly around it rather than simply diving in. For all Maaya had been through and how brave she felt she had become, this kind of talk still seemed to frighten her into silence.

But Maaya had resolved to see this done, and she wasn't going to back down now.

She closed her eyes tight, building up the nerve to speak, and then opened them again to glance at Adelaide.

"Do you remember when we talked about our dreams? How we talked about how those dreams might change a little if we met the right person?"

"Of course! And for what it's worth, I think I have," Adelaide said quickly, looking grateful for the opportunity. "I think we could make something work, somehow. I don't have to be at sea all the time, you know. And I could help you look for a place. Or whatever it takes! I guess the problem is just figuring out where we want our boundaries to be and how far we want to go with each other."

Maaya smiled slightly, and she thought back to when she had met Adelaide for the first time, and her memories took her through every moment they had spent together since then leading up to now. Maaya hadn't even known what she wanted to do the next day at first, so consumed was she by stress and fear. Gradually, however, she had gotten to thinking about what her future might hold now that she realized there was a possibility she might have one. And ever since she and Adelaide had talked about their dreams, Maaya realized what her real dream was.

"You know… I still think about that dream I told you about. I would still love to come home in the evening and watch the sky turn dark as the city lights up below me. I'd love to wake up in the morning to buy some fresh bread for breakfast, to be right by the ocean, and to go sailing sometimes. I'd like to have a home, but to live the life that pulls me away from it for adventure. Most importantly, I wouldn't be alone."

"Oh, I remember. That sounds like a wonderful dream all right," Adelaide sighed contentedly.

Maaya's heart pounded faster still as she thought of what she was about to do. As she did her best to calm her pounding heart, she remembered what Svante had asked her when she had seen him for the last time, when she had confided in him that the life she wanted was any that had Adelaide in it.

Have you asked her for that life?

At the time, she hadn't. She wasn't sure then if she ever could. But things had changed even since then.

"It does. So, Adelaide…" She took a deep breath. This was it. "Would you help me make that dream come true?"

"How do you mean?" Adelaide asked, and her expectant expression held all the hope Maaya felt in herself.

Maaya stepped over and took both of Adelaide's hands in hers, staring up into her eyes.

"Stay with me. Let's find a place to live, together. A place to call home just for the two of us. We can still go on our adventures together or whatever we like, but we'll always have a place to come home to where we know we'll find each other. I love you, and I can't imagine after all we've been through that we'd just go our separate ways somehow. So… stay with me. Let's live that dream we both want."

The moment that followed seemed an eternity, and every bit of confidence, doubt, terror, and joy she had within her flashed through her mind, all of it lost in a tumultuous jumble of emotion. Despite her inexperience, the weight of the request she was making was not lost on her. She was vaguely aware that she had stopped breathing, and thought that if this were to go on for even a moment longer she would lose all sense of herself and the world around her.

And then Adelaide reached forward, pulling Maaya into her trembling arms and holding her close, and before she knew it Maaya was holding her back with all the strength she could muster, their answers to Maaya's hopes spoken aloud given in that act of physical connection long before any word even needed to be said. But Maaya wanted to hear it anyway.

"Yes! Yes, I think we should," Adelaide agreed ecstatically. "I would love so much to do that with you."

Maaya felt like the weight of the world had just been lifted from her shoulders. This was the last obstacle she had needed to overcome as an individual. The rest, whatever lay before them, would be taken on together.

"I'm so glad you asked," Adelaide continued. "I've been thinking the same thing, and I wanted to suggest it, but… I was afraid it would be too much. I thought you might be put off by it."

"No, not too much. Not at all," Maaya murmured. "It feels… right. We spent so much time together doing terrifying and exhausting things; I think it's only right we should stay together for the good things, too."

"Definitely. It's been nice saving the world with you and everything, but I can't wait to come home and do a whole lot of nothing, providing I'm doing it with you. We can finally enjoy the world we worked so hard for."

"Where do you think we should go?" Maaya asked.

"I have a few ideas, but the beautiful thing now is that we have all the time in the world to figure that out—and every place in it to choose from."

Maaya had never felt happier in her life, and she wanted this moment to last forever. Then again, she thought distractedly, maybe that's what this all meant. She wasn't sure where they were to go or what they were to do, but it did mean that they were now inextricably bound together through whatever was to come. No matter what they did or where they went, they would be doing it together. And as far as dreams went, Maaya no longer had to sleep to see hers.

44

HOW A NEW WORLD BEGINS

THREE WEEKS LATER, Maaya and Adelaide stood together aboard the Nocte Cadenza off the coast of Levien. Skarin had positioned the ship so that it was about as close to shore as it was possible for a ship of that size to be, which meant greater ease of access for guests. For all his griping about guests, he had easily agreed to this.

Maaya and Adelaide had begun and ended their search for a home in Levien. To Maaya's surprise, Adelaide hadn't felt like finding a place to live in Krethus. Her explanation had been that after living and fighting there her entire life, she was ready for something new, and that Levien had everything she was looking for. To some extent, Maaya could understand. That was, after all, why she had decided to leave Sark behind.

After a week and a half of searching they found a beautiful flat overlooking the port on one side and the downtown area on the other. It was no mansion, but it was cozy, and everything that Maaya could have wanted. The glass doors in the living room opened out to a small balcony that offered the perfect view of the port far below and let in a wonderfully cool sea breeze.

They had decided instantly that this was the place for them, and after some paperwork Adelaide had been only too happy to fill out, it became theirs. Neither of them had yet spent much time in it given that there was still much moving and last-minute renovations to be done, but Maaya didn't mind. She was still very busy, but in a good way.

It had been Adelaide's idea to have a housewarming party of sorts, but in place of their flat she decided to host their party somewhere with a little more space, and to celebrate much more than just the purchase of a home. After their efforts in both Krethus and Selenthia, it was time for a proper celebration now they all had time to breathe.

Skarin, to his credit, had ordered his ship cleaned as much as it could be, and the old warship looked better than Maaya had ever seen it before. She could sense the ghostly captain's mild displeasure, but even he was not immune to good company and festivities—providing, she assumed, that they didn't last too long.

Rows and rows of tables and chairs had been set up on the main deck, and at least a dozen carts carrying all sorts of delicious food were lined up on both sides. The ship smelled wonderful, and the crew of the Nocte Cadenza was visibly envious of the ability of the living guests to partake in the feast.

Not a single chair was left empty. Roshan and his parents, Emil, Nadya, Apostol, Asmund, Inga, Halvar, and Gunnar were among those near the aft deck where Maaya and Adelaide stood together, joined nearby by Felix, Cajsa, and Marit Sol. Imperatrix Torell had even shown up, much to Adelaide's delight; she had almost been too afraid to send the invitation, and Maaya had needed to step in to hand the letter off to the courier herself. This had nearly led to some tension, as the imperatrix's attendance involved the presence of several Krethan battleships as an escort; it also led to some excitement on deck from those—mainly Adelaide's family—who tried every which way to subtly get the woman's attention.

Styx, too large for any seat, stood slightly to the side, looking as proud as could be. Even David, the previous commander of the Windfire, had finally made it, much to the immense glee and amusement of the crew.

The rest of the seats were filled with acquaintances, admirers, and anyone who had managed to get aboard first. Space was limited even on the massive ship, and Skarin's patience was even more so.

When faced with the issue of who was to attend, they had run into a small issue when Adelaide pointed out that if *all* their friends were to show up, many of them would not be able to see each other. After a few minutes of brainstorming, Maaya had come up with the idea of giving the guests optical implants—the original, helpfully donated by Styx, to be duplicated by Adelaide's favorite steamsmith in Levien. They worked to perfection, which resulted in some confusion and discomfort as many living guests suddenly began seeing ghosts for the first time—much to the dead's amusement.

By now, many of the communications between the Krethan and Selenthian governments had been picked up by the Selenthian media, who had started sharing stories of the mysterious Krethan machine, the ghosts it created, and the people responsible for shutting it down. Outside of Sark, no one in the world had before heard of Maaya Sahni, but now they did. Many of those people were now gathered on the docks before the ship, some out of admiration and some out of sheer curiosity.

The reaction hadn't all been positive, of course. There were some who called it all a conspiracy, adamantly refusing to believe that there was any such thing as ghosts. Others demanded that Krethus be forced to pay for their crimes against Selenthia. But though these voices were loud, they were few, and they were summarily either shut down or simply ignored.

And so, to Maaya's consternation, she found herself in the spotlight in Selenthia as well—which included, she discovered, their celebration. A day before the party was to be held, she had gotten a message that several representatives from the Selenthian government wished to "drop by," which had sent Maaya into a fit of nerves. This would be the first time she would meet anyone from her own government, and her first semi-public gathering after the news about what had happened broke to the world, and so she spend the next several hours fretting over what to say, what to wear, and how to act. Adelaide had finally suggested she do and wear whatever she pleased, and that, as the girl who helped saved the world, no one was in any position to judge.

With that in mind, Maaya had chosen a sleek cream-colored dovetail dress with lace at the hems and long sheer sleeves. Earlier that morning she had gone to see someone about her hair, and the woman who took care of her somehow managed to take her long hair and wrap it in a symmetrical braid around her head complete with floral adornments. Maaya could hardly tear herself away from the mirror when it was complete, moving on only when the woman politely reminded her that it would probably be best if she showed up at her own party.

Adelaide, meanwhile, was dressed to the nines in a black vest, white button-down shirt, and burgundy tie, finished off with black dress pants, a matching blazer, and polished black dress shoes. She hadn't gone through nearly as much trouble with her beautiful red hair, letting it flow freely but for a single decorative clip she placed over one ear. Still, Maaya wasn't sure if it was the effort they had gone through to get ready or simply the excitement of the day, but she thought she had never seen Adelaide look so beautiful before.

After most of the attendees had gotten their first helpings of food and settled at their tables, Skarin raised his hands, and the deck fell silent. The living especially looked on with eager interest, still so very fascinated with now being able to see and hear ghosts; for the moment, all the discomfort of seeing those who had walked among them for so long was gone, though it was certain to return. In their fascination, not even the visage of the dead whose deaths had been particularly gruesome was enough to deter them.

"Ladies and gentlemen, I'd like to offer a little speech. This comes partially from my position as captain, and from the fact that I have never had the pleasure of giving one under such pleasant circumstances before. That this is my first is frankly a shock, given that I am widely known for my charming and loving nature."

Adelaide snorted, then covered her mouth as she started to cough, which inevitably caused the rest of those on board to start laughing as well. Skarin merely rolled his eyes.

"If you're that easily amused, this will take all afternoon. Now then… ah, yes. I have the pleasure of speaking to you all: Krethan and Selenthian, living and dead. I never thought I would find myself in this position, but here I stand, and that is due in very large part to the actions of two of my friends: Maaya Sahni and Adelaide Sol. These young women are responsible not just for the destruction of a device that would have seen the end of us all, but for the advent of peace between two nations that have been warring longer than you have all been alive. No matter where you're from or what you do, you have reason to give them thanks."

Heavy applause came at these words, and Maaya stared fixedly at the deck. Once this was over she hoped to enjoy the relative obscurity she had taken advantage of for so long—or at the very least to never be mentioned in another speech again.

"But there are others who are responsible for this, and I'd like to call attention to them now," Skarin rumbled. "Remember those both living and dead who did their part in whatever way they could. The friends and family we lost, whether they put their lives in danger to fight it or those who fled from it. And remember a girl named Freja Astrom, for she was the third heroine to brave the wastelands of the Krethan machine. She is equally responsible for this success, and though she is no longer here to see the fruits of her efforts, she must still be remembered for them."

Total silence fell over the ship as everyone bowed their heads in respect. Maaya was glad Skarin had thought to say such a thing; it was exactly the sentiment she wanted to share, but didn't have the energy or heart to. Not yet.

Still, she knew Saber would have been pleased, especially when it came to the news about Rahu and Sark. She thought with some satisfaction that Saber would have definitely approved of what Maaya had decided to do with him even if that came second to Saber's desire to see the man ultimately deceased.

As for Maaya herself, she was happy, too. Of all the things she had ever imagined happening in her life, this was one of those things she thought was least likely. She thought of how her childhood and adolescence had been marred by fears that she would never find anyone who could possibly love her. Not as she had been, anyway. She had been stuck in a town that hated her with no chance of escape, and she spent her time merely trying to survive. The thought of even looking for love had hardly entered her mind, though while some of that came from lack of time to explore such things, the rest came from the idea which had been forced upon her that she was undeserving of it.

And now here she was.

For Adelaide's part, she herself had confessed to Maaya that she never thought she was going to find anyone to settle down with, either. It wasn't for lack of people interested in her, but for lack of any shared interest. There simply hadn't been anyone who had managed to get her to even entertain the idea of settling in the first place; as it was, Adelaide had loved her life far more than she loved any individual—at least to the point where such a heavy compromise would make her worse off in the grand scheme of things. It wasn't until she met Maaya that she even second guessed herself.

But then, as she explained, it wasn't so much that Maaya was so much more remarkable than all the others, though Adelaide hastily argued that this was also certainly true. Nor was it that Maaya was so much like Adelaide that Adelaide herself wouldn't have to change anything about herself. It was more that Maaya was the first person to ever get her to consider that this change would actually be acceptable.

"I just couldn't see myself changing for any of the others," she had said. "But with you it's different. I love what I do, but… I love you more. And I guess when I figured that out, that's when I knew it had to be you."

Even here and now as they stood together, Maaya wasn't sure she could believe it. Surely this had all been a dream and she would soon be waking up on the sofa in her old house in Sark, ready to do whatever work needed to be done that night under Rahu's orders.

But the mist of the sea was cool on her face, and every inward breath brought with it the slightest hint of Adelaide's perfume, and it was all too real to deny anymore. Besides… she deserved this. She was finally ready to admit that much. The possibilities, as intimidating as they may have been, were also exciting. Now that she was free to focus on her life and her relationship, there was no telling just what the future would hold—but she knew it would be wonderful.

"Now then, I didn't stand to mar your pleasant afternoon with memories and reminiscence. We're here also to celebrate a new world and a new life for those who gave it to us. Congratulations to the both of you." Skarin bowed his head ever so slightly to end his monologue. Then, just as the guests began to stand or return to their meals and conversations, he roared, "Open fire!"

Adelaide tilted her head slightly.

"Wait, what do—?"

THOOM. THOOM. THOOM.

The cheers and applause from below turned to shrieks and cries of terror as the Nocte Cadenza unleashed a single massive broadside round from the starboard side. The noise was deafening, and it echoed throughout the harbor as an immense cloud of smoke rose from the side of the ship. Many of those mingling on the docks began to run for cover, but it was already over.

As the echoes of gunfire faded away and the massive cloud of gun smoke began to dissipate in the wind, Skarin cackled.

"In your honor," he explained simply to Maaya and Adelaide, looking very pleased with himself.

A smattering of applause broke out, followed by uproarious cheers from the visibly shaken guests, even as many of them sat down to regain their bearings.

Maaya, who was just now remembering to breathe, turned to face Skarin as the color returned to her face.

"Thanks for the warning," she said shakily.

"I assumed you'd asked me to host because of my creative personal touch," Skarin grinned. "Is it not custom to celebrate with fireworks? I only made do with what I had. But, though this type of ordeal isn't much my cup of tea, I am truly honored to have been asked, both for Adelaide and for you. My sincere congratulations to you both."

"Thanks, old pal," Adelaide said happily, giving the ghostly captain a tight hug. After a moment of hesitation, Maaya reluctantly gave him one as well.

"Now then, I've said more words here outside the purpose of duty than I typically say in a month, so I'm going to recuperate. If you need anything, please ask anyone but me," Skarin said with the slightest hint of a smirk, and then floated off to meet with some of his officers, leaving Maaya and Adelaide alone.

Maaya watched him go, then turned her eyes back to Adelaide. There was a long day of celebrating and socializing to come, she was certain, but for now she was happy to be alone with the woman she loved so much.

"So… we did it," she giggled happily, holding Adelaide's hands tightly before her.

"We did! I'm so, so happy. This is perfect; I couldn't have asked for a better life. I love you so much, Maaya."

"And I love you. I've never been surer of anything," Maaya returned, burying her face in Adelaide's chest. "Hey… do you think it'll ever stop feeling so new and exciting, being together like this?"

"I hope not. At least every time think about it I'll be reminded of how lucky I am," Adelaide hummed.

They shared another kiss, and then Maaya let go, gesturing toward the stairs.

"I think we have some guests who want to see us."

Adelaide hesitated thoughtfully, then sighed in mock exasperation.

"Oh, if we must!"

The hours passed, and Maaya spent each with a smile on her face. She had worried the joy might fade with exhaustion and exposure, but each hour only seemed better than the last. It did still seem a little strange and unfamiliar to be a part of such a big event focused solely on something about her—and something positive, too—but by now she had started growing accustomed to it. It had been a hard lesson to learn, but Nadya and Felix and all the others had been right. There was good in the world, and it wasn't too much to ask that she be a part of it.

It took a while for Maaya to be free of the large groups of people clamoring for her attention, but after she patiently sated them one by one, she eventually found time to talk to her friends. Of those who had made it, she was happiest that Roshan and Styx were there. It was a long way from Sark, after all, but they had told her they wouldn't miss it for the world, and indeed they hadn't.

Not too long after Skarin's demonstration, two tall nervous-looking men in suits walked up to her. They, evidently, were the representatives from the Selenthian government Maaya had been so nervous about meeting, but whom she had completely forgotten about during the excitement of the day. They were clearly still shaken from the gunfire—and had also clearly never been aboard a ship in their life—and it amused Maaya greatly. Whether it was their demeanor or the combination of all her experiences thus far, the men did not intimidate her in the slightest.

She had expected a multitude of questions much like those she had been subjected to in Krethus, but instead they simply informed her that the Selenthian government was interested in her assistance in the near future. When pressed for details, they said only that the details were still being finalized and that Maaya could expect communication within the coming weeks. From what Maaya could glean, parts of the government had long acknowledged that ghosts existed, but found themselves woefully unprepared and lacking in expertise, something the recent crisis had only further demonstrated. Maaya and Adelaide were being sought to provide this expertise, and the men had been careful to state that they would not be expected to work for free.

Despite the sheer number of people present, Maaya couldn't help but miss those who hadn't made it. As her life had progressed she'd always made room in her dreams for those she met along the way, and she had always hoped that they would all be there to see her for her happiest moments. She felt the ceremony wasn't complete without Saber, Kim, Sovaan, Kalil,

Svante, Sylvia, and all the others. She would have loved to see their reactions and hear their words of support—and their inevitable jokes.

Still, she comforted herself with the thought that they might be seeing this even now despite the worlds between them. And if not, she knew she would have a wonderful story to tell them all when they finally met again.

Eventually, most of the guests on board and on the docks began dispersing after eating their fill and paying their respects. As the sun started to set, Maaya met up again with Roshan and Styx, who looked like they had no intention of going anywhere.

"Are you going all the way back tonight or staying here?" she asked.

"Staying for sure; I'm not sure I could get all the way home tonight even if I was taking that ghost's carriage again," Roshan chuckled. "Besides, have you seen this place? It's great!"

"I'm the one who told you about it, Roshan."

"Yeah, well, you shouldn't have to ask then," he added with a grin.

"I'm definitely stayin' as well. In fact, I've quite taken a likin' to this place already," Styx answered in turn. "S'definitely better than sittin' on a dock outside a town nobody likes anyhow."

"This is perfect for you! There are ships everywhere. Maybe you could even think about joining a crew," Maaya suggested, but Styx frowned.

"Never been sure that life's for me. I'm content to be by the water so long as I've still got my freedom of it. And I'll be damned if I ever give up my boat."

Maaya laughed, then gave her best attempt at a hug.

"I'm glad you'll be around. We'll see you all the time!"

"And I think we're both glad you're staying here. I have to admit, I think we were both afraid you'd decide to go all the way over to Krethus," Roshan said.

"Oh, my home country is lovely, but there's just something about Selenthia that appeals to me," Adelaide answered.

"I'm from here," Maaya suggested, and Adelaide laughed.

"Yes, we'll go with that."

Adelaide's family came over next to say their goodbyes, promising to meet them for breakfast the next day since they were staying in Selenthia for several days. After many tearful hugs and congratulations, Felix and Cajsa started off, but Marit hung back, looking almost embarrassed but equally full of excitement.

"I'm going to tell them," she whispered excitedly. "I'm going to tell them tonight."

"You're officially calling it off then?" Adelaide asked in a tone of pleasant surprise.

"I am! I feel like they'll be okay with it. I know they can be thick sometimes, but even they had to notice how I was feeling about it lately."

"It's cute you still think of their awareness so highly," Adelaide grinned, then hugged her sister. "I'm proud of you, girl. I know they'll be all right."

"I hope so, because I also have to tell them about the man I *actually* want to marry."

Adelaide stared.

"What's this? You need to tell *me?*"

"One thing at a time, Addy. This is your day; I'll have mine soon enough." She winked, then started off to follow her parents. Adelaide smiled proudly after her.

"Get 'em, sis."

As evening began to fall, the deck of the Nocte Cadenza was almost completely empty. Styx and Roshan had gone off to find temporary lodgings for the night, and those who remained were mostly comprised of the crew of the Windfire; they stood attentively and waited patiently for their captain.

Skarin came over to Maaya and Adelaide, giving them a nod as he approached.

"So it's done. I suppose I'll be taking us out within the hour; it's not like me to stay so close to land this long, and Selenthian land at that."

"I appreciate the sacrifice," Adelaide returned warmly. "There's no one I'd rather have done this than you."

"A pleasure, as always. I am satisfied to hear you won't be changing your habits too heavily. I look forward to more adventures with you. Perhaps the world won't adapt so quickly that we would be deprived of a few good battles at sea as well."

"We can only hope," Adelaide chuckled.

"Now, Ms. Sahni," Skarin added slowly, turning to face the girl. "Even if I am alone in this sentiment, it has been my pleasure working with you. I do hope we'll see each other again."

Maaya hesitated. She hadn't had much of a chance to think about how she felt about the man, but she couldn't deny that her opinion of him had changed since they first met. Originally she felt a mixture of admiration and disgust, and thought it a shame that someone who was otherwise so loyal and authoritative held the views he did. But the more she saw of him, the more she saw his attempts at bettering himself. There was still a long way for him to go, she was certain of that. She hoped that if and when they did meet in the future he would be someone she would be more comfortable allying herself with again.

She suspected this was a mutual understanding between them, and so when she simply extended her hand without a word, he did not press her for an answer. He shook her hand and nodded politely, then stepped away.

"I can't promise I'll always be in local waters, but I won't be a stranger. I'll keep the seas familiar for you, Captain," Skarin rumbled.

"I'll see you out there, old friend," Adelaide answered.

They shared a glance that only those who had been through the trials of friendship and war could share, and then Skarin turned to leave, calling orders to his crew to prepare the ship to depart.

"I guess that means it's time for us to get going, too," Adelaide yawned, stretching widely. The day had done a number on them both. "We'll be seeing even more people tomorrow, and I want some energy left to finish moving all our things."

"Mm, I can't wait," Maaya purred, standing on tiptoe to kiss her. "I hope you're not too tired for our own private celebrations tonight."

"You should know me better than that," Adelaide returned with mock offense. "I also have plenty of energy to think about where we should travel for vacation once we've decided we're ready to think about that."

"Oh? What do you think?"

"I'm not sure yet. That's the thing about having the whole world open to you: it gets a little harder to choose."

"I guess it's good we've got so much time to think about it," Maaya said contentedly.

"I never thought I'd see the day. Now, my love, let's go home."

THE NEXT WEEK was spent hurriedly finishing up work on the flat, meeting with other friends and family members, and settling in to their new life. It had been a month since the battle in Sark, though it felt like so much longer than that. Already Maaya's thoughts of the place that had once been her home dwindled to almost nothing, and the only time she thought of the man who had once nearly ended her life was when she occasionally remembered that he was now a prisoner in the same place he had held her, and that with any luck he would remain that way for the rest of his life. She knew the emotional ramifications of her experiences would take a long time to get over, but now she could do so completely on her own time and terms, surrounded by people who loved her.

She spent most of her time thinking about her life in Levien and the people she still had with her. She and Adelaide had finally finished fixing the place to their liking; the hardest part had been the process of moving Adelaide's belongings across the globe. Maaya had only what she could carry, though Adelaide promised that this would soon change.

Roshan, true to his desires, had applied for an apprenticeship under a blacksmith in Levien who, with the recommendation of Roshan's father and examples of his work, had been accepted immediately. Roshan had already started to gain a reputation due to his ever-cheerful demeanor and quality craftsmanship, and when his work was done at the end of each day, he usually found himself busy socializing with his new friends—and romantic interests.

Styx opted to take up residence in a small and lightly populated corner of the city in a small house that opened right out to the beach where his boat lay tied whenever he wasn't using it. He had been uncertain about living around others at first, though it was hard for his neighbors not to notice his kindhearted and generous spirit. He also found that some new clothes, a haircut, and a shave did wonders for his confidence, and only a few weeks after moving in, he delighted in taking many of the locals just off shore in his boat as he himself learned the new waters.

Before Maaya could think too much about what kind of work she would settle into, she had been met by another representative of the Selenthian government who requested that both she and Adelaide assist them in guiding the efforts between their two countries to resume communication and travel, as well as to work at slowly healing Selenthia's prejudices. Magic and the dead existed in their world whether some people wanted to acknowledge it or not, and it was high time they began the process of learning about it all. Between a *libris*-trained elite from a country with plenty of experience in that regard and a Selenthian girl who had honed her formidable skills on the soil of the country she now sought to teach, the Selenthians couldn't have asked for better. Adelaide offered her extensive knowledge on sailing routes and the methods her country used to educate its populace about ghosts, and Maaya gave occasional talks and demonstrations of *libris* in Levien, which hundreds and often thousands of people came to see.

Prejudice was difficult to fight. It was like an invisible battle, one that many people had no idea even existed in their midst. But then, that was exactly the kind of battle Maaya was used to. And while she knew it would be a while yet before the world could even begin to say serious progress was on its way, she knew it was a battle that had to be fought. She had seen the good the world was capable of, and she now sought to try her best to show everyone else as well. While previously such a fight would have exhausted her, she took on each new task with a light heart, full of optimism. The difference now was that she knew it was possible. With that in mind, there was no reason not to try.

In her downtime, Maaya had taken to organizing their home as best she could. Adelaide delighted in Maaya's ideas for the placement of furniture and the change of color schemes and eventually gave full control of the planning over to her. Maaya had been almost overwhelmed with joy at the prospect—she had never been furniture shopping before, and though it was a task some apparently dreaded or thought horribly dull, she took it on with gusto, the excitement of being able to make her home her own only growing as time went on.

Late one night Maaya found herself alone at home while waiting for Adelaide to return from her evening errands. They would be heading out to sea again in a few days, and Adelaide had much preparation to do. But for now, all their other work was wrapping up and they finally had several days all to themselves.

The sun hung low in the deep red sky, and Maaya sat in a comfortable chair at a desk by the open glass doors that looked out over the city and the sea. A light breeze blew in, bringing with it the sounds and smells of the city below, and Maaya nearly couldn't focus for how happy it made her.

On the desk before her lay Kim's diary, open to the very last page. She had finally arrived at the end, and she felt a sense of trepidation as she realized that, after this, there was no more.

We're going out one last time tonight. We're going to put a stop to the ghosts, and then we're going to travel across the world to stop them for good. I'm scared, but I'm excited. I've never been outside Sark before, especially not for anything like this.

We're all afraid, I can see that too, but it's moments like these that I remember why I love being here. I love my friends. They're all willing to get out there and do whatever it takes to help others, and I love that about them. It's made me think a lot more recently about how dangerous things have gotten. At first, I thought I would run away if things got too tough, but now I feel like no matter what happens I'll be happy if we can keep doing this. It's dangerous, but so many people risk their lives for the good of the world; why should I not be one of them?

Whatever happens, I hope they all know I love them and really admire them. These have been some of the best years of my life. I don't like to live in the past, but if it's a good past, there isn't so much harm in that. And as much as I complain about the others, I still love them. I can't imagine my life any other way.

We'll be leaving soon. I'm going to make sure I'm ready, and then we'll be off. Wish me luck.

Maaya read the last entry three times, then let out a sigh. It was done. The last of the mysteries of her old life were behind her. She couldn't deny she felt sad at the feeling that there were no words left to read, but her sense of relief and love overpowered that easily.

Besides, there was still more for Maaya to do.

As if on cue there came a knock at the door, and then Maaya heard a key turning in the lock. Adelaide came in a moment later, holding a parcel in her arm.

"Sorry I'm late!" she exclaimed, carrying the parcel over the Maaya and setting it on the desk. "This was at the front, and it's a lot heavier than it looks. Are you ready to eat?"

"Ready and waiting," Maaya said, tugging gently on Adelaide's arm and kissing her as she leaned over.

"Great. I'll go get ready, and I won't be long," Adelaide said, but before she could rush off to change, Maaya pulled her back.

"Wait. This is our first actual free night since we moved in; let's take advantage of this view."

"Ooh, right."

Maaya stood up and led the way through the glass doors and out onto the balcony. She placed her hands on the railing and leaned over slightly, taking in the gorgeous view below.

The city was settling down for the night, whatever that meant for those who lived there. Some laborers started home while others, dressed in fine clothes, left their own flats and homes as they prepared for a night on the town. Dozens of ships on their way in and out of port rocked slightly in the waves, the last of the sun reflecting dully off their sails. Maaya was even able to spot the Windfire half a mile away, and she smiled at the thought of being back aboard soon. The smell of delicious food wafted up to them, and Maaya's stomach growled.

As they watched, the city began to light up beneath them. Those on their ships lit their lanterns, and the lights ashore burned brightly in the calm night. Strings of lights were draped around trees and over top the signs of restaurants and along the shore, Maaya watched as campfires sprung up out of the dark, illuminating the silhouettes of those enjoying the water and company.

Maaya sighed happily as Adelaide put an arm around her waist and pulled her close. It was just like the dream she had wanted for so long. It was real now, and she and Adelaide got to enjoy it together.

They spent the next ten minutes in silence, taking in everything their senses allowed. Though they would soon be down below with the crowds, for now Maaya was content to enjoy this moment alone with the girl she loved so much.

"Hey. I think I'll go get ready so we can find some place to eat before they all fill up, okay?" Adelaide murmured, nuzzling her cheek against the top of Maaya's head.

"Sounds perfect. I think I'll get started on this project while I wait."

"Oh? Are you sure you won't get so sucked into it you won't want to leave?"

"Not with how hungry I am, no."

They laughed playfully, and then headed back inside. As Adelaide strode off to the bedroom to change, Maaya turned her attention to the parcel before her, opening it carefully.

Inside was a large stack of blank paper, two quills, and at least six full inkwells. She took them all out carefully and set them on the desk. Then she gently closed Kim's diary and opened one of the drawers. Inside the drawer lay the completed portrait of Saber, as well as her circlet and the folder containing all the information the Krethan government had been able to find about her. Maaya gazed at them fondly for a moment. She would get to start on those next. For now, however, she placed the diary delicately beside them and closed the drawer again.

It could be argued that Maaya was doing this for the sake of the world, that what she planned to write was for the sake of progress and some bigger and greater good. Maaya probably wouldn't argue the point, but for her, that was not her purpose.

This was for them. For Kim, Kalil, Sovaan, and Saber. She remembered how hard Rahu had tried to erase them from the world, and how though he had failed, there was still nothing left to their memory but the diary Maaya had just finished reading. It wasn't fair, she thought. She'd spent years of her life with them, making all kinds of beautiful memories with them, and watched as they trained under her to help her make the world a better place. Beyond them, there were still others from her life before, people who deserved to be remembered. People who might otherwise not be. It was only right that the world knew who they were and what they had accomplished.

She placed the first blank paper in front of her, opened the lid of an inkwell, and gingerly picked up one of the quills. She had grown confident enough in her letters that she felt ready to begin straightaway. It was finding the right words that was the challenge.

Maaya thought for a few moments, and then smiled. Even as she heard Adelaide call from the bedroom that she would only be a few minutes more, Maaya set the quill to the paper, and she began to write.

www.ingramcontent.com/pod-product-compliance
Lightning Source LLC
Chambersburg PA
CBHW020920310726
48980CB00011B/967/J